Shadows of Memories Past

Book Two of the Dracus Saga

By J.M. Williamson

Dracus Saga

Wardens of Light and Shadow

Shadows of Memories Past

Acknowledgments

My heartfelt thanks goes out to everyone who supported me through this journey. It was a wild ride filled with such a grab bag of heartache and joy that it's amazing that I made it through it intact. So again, thank you for your support. This wouldn't have been possible without it.

Prelude

Year 2147 of the Age of Power

One year before the Exodus

Darkness — all-consuming and bastion of evil.

Darkness — insubstantial and frightening.

Darkness — mysterious and keeper of secrets.

Darkness — the beginning and the end.

*W*hen darkness fell upon the mountains — one of the few strongholds of relative peace left on Kylir — its dominance was near absolute. From the north, a frigid wind swept down the peaks, driving a torrent of snow and biting sleet before it as if the darkness were breathing forth icy daggers. There were few living creatures left in the mountains to endure the wind's harsh bite, but for those that did remain, the macabre irony of the wintery blast wasn't lost on them. It was currently the heart of summer and — if all were as it should be — it ought to have been a balmy night attempting to play nursemaid to a land and people beaten down by a sun-scorched day. Nothing, however, was normal anymore. The war had seen to that.

Once peaceful and fruitful, Kylir had been ravaged by countless battles between forces wielding titanic powers. Mountains had been flattened, enormous swaths of terrain had been obliterated or cratered beyond recognition, and the dead had long since surpassed counting. It was as if the Hells had decreed an end to all things . . . yet that was not the worst to have befallen Kylir. No, what was genuinely harrowing were the clouds of ash that almost constantly covered the sky. They were a symptom of the land's weeping scars . . . the wounds that would not heal. Ever-burning, these wounds — these infernos — littered the land like towering cataclysmic heralds. Drawing sustenance from the lifeblood of Kylir — its fir'gan — these pillars of bluish flame were unquenchable and undeniable.

Standing just inside an artfully concealed tunnel in the mountainside, Alyxaria sighed heavily as she looked upon the gloomy night. Try as she might, she could not ignore the ever-burning blazes that illuminated small portions of the sky like distant, ice-blue stars. Her large, and normally vibrant, almond-shaped green eyes were burdened with sadness as she watched the distant towering flames. Something needed to be done about them before the land was burnt dry, but to her chagrin, those with the ability to extinguish the mind-numbingly massive fires were too few and the pillars of flames too many. Moreover, the events of the last few months had practically made the blazes trivial. So they burned on, pouring more ash into the heavens and further charring a world already decimated by one man's folly.

On this night, much to her surprise, a few slivers of heavenly light managed to slip through the brooding clouds, their gentle caress ever so softly illuminating the snow-covered and ash-dusted peaks. Some of the soft, blueish-silver moonlight even managed to reach her in the tunnel. Shimmering tenderly on her mass of shoulder-length deep-red hair, it also graced her warm-ivory skin and played faintly on the golden *kasleu* earrings that adorned her long ears. Consisting of a filigree band midway along the bottom of each ear that was connected by a thin chain to a matching stud that concealed each earlobe, her *kasleu* flowed well with her ears as they pierced her hair like elegant blades before narrowing to a point just shy of her athletic shoulders.

A sudden, frigid wind cut up from the yawning darkness below. Whistling mournfully as it pierced the tunnel, the wind set both the flowing skirt and the overly long, loose sleeves of her form-fitting, high-neck red silk dress a flutter, laying bare her long-fingered hands, and her black-sandals. As the tresses of her dress and hair danced about her like tendrils of blood, and the moonlight glinted off the simple gold rings adorning each of her slim fingers, she closed her eyes and let a sad sigh slip from her gracefully slender lips.

"The land resists valiantly, yet 'tis a pitiable struggle as hope seems to spill from it as an oozing wound seeps life from one's body," she said aloud, the usual musical lilt of her voice dampened by naked sorrow.

Opening her eyes, she gazed upon the tendrils of moonlight reaching down from the clouds. "Moreover, we strive to retain hope with the same voracity as yon fair moonlight exhibits in its attempts to pierce the consuming darkness that blankets the land. Yet, I dareth not embrace it, nor shalt I let it take firm root in the bosom of mine heart, for I fear 'tis as ephemeral as the moonlight and . . ." she smirked sadly as the dark clouds swept across the slivers of moonlight, blotting them out, "just as easily vanquished."

"Such dour words, Sister. I did not believe thine spirits had waned so," a rich voice from behind commented.

Alyxaria shook her head gently as she folded her arms beneath her modest breasts. "If thine purpose is to succor mine spirits, I beg thee to expend thine efforts elsewhere, Sister. 'Tis little room for joy left in the world," she replied without turning away from the vista.

"Tch! What would Father say if he heard such woeful words from thee?"

"I suspect 'twould chastise me," Alyxaria responded with a hint of a smile as the newcomer came to a halt beside her.

2

"Aye, that he would," the woman responded, mirth dancing upon her voice. *"I would dare say he would proceed to remind thee of the power that doth reside with hope—"*

Peering slightly down at the dark-violet-haired woman, whose smiling full lips and vibrant violet eyes were awash with sympathy against normally alabaster skin that was currently a few shades paler with exertion, Alyxaria finished, *" 'And that to stray from the path the Light illuminates is to invite Darkness into one's heart.' "* She sighed. *"'Tis not due to the absence of effort, dear Sister. Yet, with all that was for not, after all that hast been done here, and with what is yet to be, 'tis impossible for mine heart not to feel the clawing weight of despair. Surely, thou cannot deny thine own heart dost not weep for all we hath lost and will lose?"*

"Nay, I cannot," Alyxaria's sister responded, pushing a wisp of hair that had slipped from her silver-netted bun behind her slender, shoulder-length ear as her fragile-looking silver kasleu gently chimed with her shaking head, *"but we art made of sterner stuff. Through trial and tribulation, victory and defeat, we hath survived all the Darkness hast pitted against us. Therefore, I dost retain hope that, ere long, we shalt prevail, and the Light shalt once more bathe this world with its grace. Moreover, should failure be our fate, and our time on Kylir reach its end, I know we shalt find succor in the Light's embrace."*

Alyxaria glanced curiously at her sister. Her sibling's figure and features were nearly identical to hers, save for sharper cheekbones, fuller lips, and a bit more of a lithe frame, but that was where the family resemblance ended. Alyxaria took after their late mother; passionate, fiery, and a master with a blade, though somehow, when she was master of her passions, that all gave way to a penchant for overthinking. Her sister, on the other hand, while she did embody some of those traits, was blessed with their father's forethought and objectivity. It was little wonder that her sister had followed in his footsteps and devoted herself to studying the wonders of fir'gan. Seeing her in the gilded white robe of a Master Alchemist, Alyxaria had to wonder what heights her sister would have ascended to had this war never engulfed Kylir. Unfortunately, the war had done so, and in ravaging the land, it had forced swords into the hands of scholars instead of books, and twisted their knowledge to horrible ends.

"What troubles thou so, Sister?" Rynthalia asked, her tone puzzled.

Alyxaria smiled weakly. *"'Twas curious how thee manages to stand firm with the Darkness all around? 'Tis the fate of the old to worry, and the young to face life with exuberance and hope, I suppose. That, or 'tis far more likely thou hath spent far too much time amongst humans."*

Her sister laughed. *"Dear Sister, 'tis only a century betwixt us! 'Tis but a blink of an eye for our people. If thou art as old as thou doth protest, then 'tis likely I shalt sprout wings anon, and soar upon the skies as the Guardians once did."*

Alyxaria smiled at the imagery, though it could not completely dispel the gloom coating her mood. "Pray, doeth inform me should such come to pass. I would very much like to bear witness to such a spectacle!"

Her sister laughed, reached out with a white-gloved hand, and squeezed Alyxaria's shoulder reassuringly. "Thou shalt be the first I call upon," she promised with a bright smile.

Reaching up, Alyxaria squeezed her sister's hand in thanks. "All jests aside, pray tell what brings thou here?" The smile on her sister's face melted away at the question, and her hand slipped from her shoulder. "What, pray tell, is wrong, Rynthalia?" she asked, suddenly apprehensive. "Is ought amiss with the siblings?"

"Nay, be at ease on that, Sister," Rynthalia replied with a gentle shake of her head. "For weal or for woe, the siblings doth rest peacefully, fully unaware of what hast transpired. We hath but to await their awakening to take full measure of the Bonding."

Alyxaria breathed a sigh of relief. So much time, pain, and sacrifice had gone into the risky venture that failure would have been catastrophic beyond measure. "Fully relieved am I to hear such tidings. Yet, if all 'tis well with the siblings, then for what dost thine face bear such solemnity?"

"Our guests hath arrived," Rynthalia stated gravely.

Alyxaria's eyes widened slightly at the announcement. "Light be good. . . . The time hast come, then, no?"

"Aye, Sister, 'tis so."

Alyxaria turned to the night sky, a tear slipping down her cheek. "Soon, the die shalt be cast, and there will be no return. A last gambit, to be sure."

"Last gambit, Sister? Perhaps," Rynthalia responded doubtfully. "'Tis true, we hath erred much throughout this war. One might say, though 'twas one man that unleashed the chaos we fight, 'twas by our hand the Darkness was bequeathed many of the weapons that hath rent us asunder. 'Tis mine belief that this moment is our chance to maketh amends. Should tonight's ventures bear fruit anon, then we will hath bought precious time for the Wardens to find a true end to this nightmare."

Alyxaria nodded. Wiping tears away, she replied, "By the grace of the Light, I dearly hope thine words prove true."

"As doeth I, Sister."

Turning to Rynthalia, Alyxaria declared, "Very well, then. I presume Father sent thee with a message?"

"Aye, that he did. The procedure rendt far more aether from him than anticipated. He doth rest and watch over the siblings as we speak."

"Light be good, Sister!" Alyxaria thought. *"It looks as if it rendt far more from all of thee than expected! Thine pallor is that of a wailing spirit! I thank the Light that the others survived such a trial!"* Aloud, she prodded, *"His orders?"*

"I am to relieve thee of duty, and oversee what remains of the evacuation."

Surprised, Alyxaria offered, *"Dear Sister, I am sorry in earnest! I should hath remained within the warehouse! I shalt speak with father anon and untangle this web! Thou should be taking succor instead of making amends for mine wanderings!"*

Rynthalia smiled and chuckled. *"Be at ease. Thou hath done nothing wrong, and thine absence hast gone unnoticed. I did volunteer for it. Though, if thou feels guilt and seeketh atonement for abandoning one's task, then what Father wishes of thee shalt suffice."*

Suddenly wary, Alyxaria felt she knew what her father was asking of her, and it tied her stomach in knots. *"He wishes me to greet him, doest he not?"* she asked with near certainty.

"Aye, Sister, thou art correct."

Closing her eyes, she let out a sigh as she thought, *"'Twould fall upon someone to assume this dubious duty. 'Tis only fitting that 'tis one of us."* Opening her eyes, Alyxaria tried to smile brightly. *"'Tis only fitting,"* she responded, echoing her thoughts aloud. *"Very well. Let us be about this night's final task. Light willing, this last night in our home shalt be peaceful unto the end."*

The sisters exchanged idle chatter as they made their way through the mountain sanctuary's winding and hauntingly empty stone corridors. Aside from some doors left open and the discoloration on the smooth stone walls and floors where decor had once resided, there was no evidence that life had once graced the halls. Such emptiness where people once thrived left the halls suffused with a morose atmosphere, which was made worse by the way they were currently illuminated. Encased in silver filigree, glass orbs of soft, bluish light lit the way from their positions high on the walls, lighting up at the sisters' approach and fading to dark soon after they passed by. Such behavior lent a unique, ghostly aura to their trek, but there was a grim symbolism to it as well that Alyxaria couldn't ignore. Like the war, the orbs' light stood bravely before the darkness, only to be pushed back and eventually extinguished. While she knew their fight was far from over so long as this night's activities proceeded without interference, it was nigh impossible to refrain from such ominous musings. As such, she found herself partially distracted from her conversation with her sister by the flow of fir'gan.

In nearly every part of Kylir — under normal circumstances — the ethereal blue currents moved in harmony with the land and the creatures that inhabited it. Even beneath the ground, the currents would typically follow such a natural pattern. Few things could disrupt that fundamental law, much less divert large quantities of fir'gan. At one time, the list of things that could accomplish such a feat were mainly of a benign nature. Now, of those that remained, most were destructive — like the weeping, calamitous wounds in the land.

Thankfully, a handful still existed that could affect the currents in a benevolent fashion. And of that handful, only one resided within the sanctuary. That majestic and immeasurably precious creature rested at the heart of the complex, its presence drawing the currents toward it with the indomitable strength of a raging river. As such, even in something as vast as the sanctuary, it was impossible for a Gifted to get lost. One simply needed to follow the currents and they would eventually find themselves in a chamber with which all the sanctuary's residents were familiar.

Eventually, the path through the complex, as well as the currents, delivered them to a circular chamber from which three other corridors branched off. At the center of the now empty and nearly unremarkable room was a spiral staircase wound about a marble pillar that vanished into dark openings in both the floor and ceiling. Exchanging smiles of comfort, the sisters parted ways, Rynthalia descending the stairs while Alyxaria, accompanied by a vast flow of fir'gan, climbed upward. Six floors and a few minutes later, Alyxaria exited the stairs and found herself greeted by architecture that was as bleakly abandoned as her starting point. Taking a deep, steadying breath, she took the corridor to the left, her stride silent and graceful despite the anxiety welling up in her stomach.

Although it was impossible to sense a particular Gifted in this part of the sanctuary due to the influence on the currents by the precious and powerful creature residing at the heart of the sanctuary, Alyxaria was certain she could still feel their guest's presence. Of course, she knew that was impossible, but there was a gravitas about the man that seemed to transcend what was normal. For Alyxaria, it was as if the mere thought of him was enough to make her believe she could feel his mark on the currents.

"Silly girl," she thought admonishingly. "Thou knoweth quiet well such is not true. . . . Still. . . ."

A few minutes later, and what seemed like an endless parade of desolate corridors bathed in the reactionary bluish light of the light orbs, Alyxaria turned a corner and came to an abrupt halt. Standing with his back to her within the glow of a singular light orb just paces down the hall, his head of horsetail-styled white hair floating above his black-cloaked figure like an apparition, was their guest. The man whose siblings were recuperating from their ordeal far below. The man who inspired both respect and daunting fear in so many. A man known by many names, but none more foreboding or damning than the one he had earned one dark, fateful day.

Death Bringer.

Doing her best to calm her nerves, she held her head high, brandished a welcoming smile, and approached. As she drew near, he suddenly turned, and she *felt her stomach twist with unwarranted anxiety as his slightly upturned coal-black eyes bore into her from astride his hawkish nose, nearly bringing her to a halt. She hid her slight misstep smoothly and continued on, eventually coming to a halt a couple of feet from him. For the briefest moment, the only sound in the hall was her soft breathing and the gentle rustle of silk as she met his gaze. Even though he was roughly as tall as her sister, the intensity of his gaze made her feel a bit like a child looking up at an angry adult. Before the moment could turn awkward, Alyxaria calmed her nerves and bowed low, the chains of her earrings mute despite swaying with her every movement.*

Straightening, she offered a gentle smile. "Light illuminate thine path, Preceptor," she said, her voice possessed of a musical lilt despite the nervous tension she felt. "I hath been sent to deliver thee unto thine siblings."

"Light illuminate thine path, Knight Alyxaria," Damionatsu returned the blessing with a nod of his own. "I am most grateful for thine presence as I am unfamiliar with this particular sanctuary," he stated, his deep voice as impassive as the chiseled features of his face.

Alyxaria nodded her understanding before turning and starting back the way she came. "Mine father believed such would be thine plight," she replied as Damionatsu fell in beside her, his cloak swaying gently above his closed-toe black sandals. "I must confess, however, that mine surprise at such a revelation 'tis remarkable. I believed one such as thee would possess knowledge of all such places in these dark times."

Damionatsu smirked a bit at the comment. "Nay, not all is known to me . . . or to any of us."

Glancing at him out of the corner of her eye, she noticed him peering into the rooms along their path as the light orbs permitted. "Quite so," she agreed with a somber softness. Turning the corner, she added, "Pray, let us maketh due haste, for I am well aware of the swiftness needed this night. Father and Lord Dracus art expecting us, and I would imagine they would be quite vexed should we dally."

Gesturing forward with a black-clad arm and gloved hand as their pace quickened, Damionatsu stated, "Lead on, Knight."

They made the trek back to the stairs at a quick pace, and once there, Alyxaria led the way down the winding staircase in silence. As they descended, the strong upward pull on the currents weakened some, making it much easier for Alyxaria to sense not only Damionatsu on the currents but also the numerous Gifted below. The growing sensation should have bolstered her spirits. Instead, she felt her anxiety grow a bit. There was so much riding on this night, and Damionatsu's presence — though not unexpected — added a layer of tension to it that made her feel as if it could all go wrong in an instant.

"Let not such musing rule thine mind," she thought, reprimanding herself. "Twould be unfair and unwise to deny him visitation. Though his motives shan't excuse his actions, one cannot deny his love for his family. Do try to find

succor in such knowledge."

Alyxaria battled with both those thoughts and her rising disquiet as they made their descent. Eleven hauntingly empty floors later, they finally exited the spiral stairs on the only permanently lit landing they'd encountered, and she felt her stomach twist a bit more. This was the only fully occupied floor left in the sanctuary, and it was home to an assortment of laboratories, manufacturing facilities, and her people's treasured warehouse and library. Given the importance of this level, its design was specialized, and it had received a more elegant aesthetic when it was built. The landing itself was significantly more extensive and featured a perimeter ring of fluted columns, every inch of which was marble-sheathed. Even the light orbs, which hung high in the air before alternating columns, were more prominent. However, it still shared some similarities with levels above, foremost of which were the stark reminders that furnishings once occupied the area, and the glow of the light orbs seemed just as dour.

Looking around briefly as she ignored the dark corridor before her and led Damionatsu left around the landing, Alyxaria couldn't help but think the richer aesthetics made this floor seem more depressing. "Nay," she thought. "Tis something more that haunts this level. . . . Our final preparations to depart art well underway here; alas, it hath lent an air of finality to this place," she mused darkly as they reached the only other passage connected to the landing.

Just as brightly lit as the landing, the passage was wide enough for two wagons to pass through with relative ease, and featured an arched ceiling twenty feet above their heads that was supported by a marble colonnade. While it was undoubtedly brighter, and the Gifted she could sense in the distance made it feel a bit more alive, the aura of finality couldn't be overcome, and that made Alyxaria's heart weep for the ordained loss to come.

Keeping strictly to the lit corridors as if they were the only path through the labyrinthian level, Alyxaria found herself occasionally glancing at the flowing elvannue glyphs that decorated the corridor. Like graceful calligraphy, the glyphs graced every column and ran along the center of the walls where they met with the glyphs that lined the arched doorframes of numerous sealed ironwood double doors. Even with the corridor as brightly lit as it was, the glyphs' blue glow was quite intense, which came as no surprise to Alyxaria. Their two primary purposes were to help channel fir'gan for use in the experiments and research conducted within many of the sealed chambers, and to power the wards that protected the rooms. However, the intensity with which they currently glowed meant they were overcharged . . . and that meant they'd been primed for more sinister purposes.

Fearing such contemplations might darken her mood further, Alyxaria glanced at Damionatsu as they kept their quick pace. The man's face was cold and unreadable as he took in their bleak surroundings; however, she believed wholeheartedly that it was just a mask. Given the stakes of this night and what she knew about him, it was more likely that he was a swirling mass of apprehension and even some anger.

"Corith," she thought sympathetically, "bless thine servant this eve, and provide succor unto his troubled mind. Let this somber night herald unto Kylir and thine children a brighter future."

After what felt like an eternity despite their pace, they reached a short staircase and descended it to another equally bleak and lit hallway. As they started along it, the presence of the Gifted on the currents quickly grew stronger, and a cacophony of noise began to echo about the empty corridor. Soon after, they started to see a mix of elvannue, humans and darlions hustling about with carts and arms loaded with a variety of items. Most of the people were dressed in simple, sturdy garments that suited their laborious tasks, which contrasted starkly with the white-robed elvannue alchemists who aided with and supervised the work.

Without slowing their pace, Alyxaria and Damionatsu easily weaved through the growing number of resolute workers. As they moved, Alyxaria was pleased to see that Damionatsu's presence did little to disrupt the preparations. Of those that noted his passage, a few nodded respectfully, and occasionally some would offer a slight bow or salute, but that was the extent of their veneration. Everyone was keenly aware that their tasks this night far outweighed even a visit by a Warden, and any disruption of significance put them at risk of failure – which was unacceptable. As such, the Knight and Warden soon reached the end of the hall where it bent right, and they turned the corner to find themselves approaching the largest arched opening on the level. Only slightly smaller than the hallway, the archway was lined with glowing glyphs, and only a hint of its twin door panels could be seen from their recessed housing in the arch. Even outside the brightly lit room, it was obvious it was vast; what's more, they could see what seemed like an endless sea of workers moving to and fro between rows of towering shelves as they carefully packed and moved a variety of crates and chests.

Leading the way into the large chamber, Alyxaria was pleased that their arrival was no more impactful to the workers here than those in the corridor. Glancing at Damionatsu as they made their way around people and shelves alike, she caught him taking in the space with a hint of awe on his face, and she cracked a slight smile. "Vast, is it not?" she asked with a hint of pride.

"Indeed," he responded as he looked around.

Nearly six-hundred feet in length, over half that in width, and close to ninety feet in height, the painstakingly built stone warehouse was the second largest space in the complex. Twenty-foot tall ironwood shelving units, which were mostly empty, lined the walls and were also arranged in orderly rows over every available inch of the ground floor. Directly over head, and evenly spaced down every row about a foot above the shelves, were light orbs that were double the size of the ones in the corridors, their light reflecting dully off the shelves' natural sheen. Beyond that, forty-foot wide walkways, their floorspace occupied by more storage shelves and workers, encircled the warehouse every thirty feet all the way up to the vaulted roof and its array of supporting beams and buttresses. Back on the ground floor, ladders could be seen everywhere, some of them occupied, and several strategically placed lifts to the upper levels were also visible along the walls.

Upon reaching the wide central isle, Alyxaria turned left against the flow of large, and heavily ladened, sleds and carts. Made of bluesteel and engraved with glowing blue glyphs, the hovering transports were being pushed or hauled toward the other end of the warehouse by a small force of workers. Glancing in that direction, she noticed Damionatsu had come to a halt and was looking that way with a slight frown tugging at his lips. Turning to face him, she gave him a moment.

At the far end of the warehouse, there was another chamber from which emanated both a bright green glow and a strong pull on the currents. While that and the line of cargo-filled transports filing into the room were note worthy, she knew what truly had his attention. A dozen crates large enough to hold two men rested atop sleds along the right side of the adjoining chamber's entrance. A group of workers, at least two per sled, were meticulously inspecting the crates both visually and with the currents. Moreover, she knew the unorthodox way the currents moved around the crates was likely troubling Damionatsu.

"Art thou well, Preceptor?" Alyxaria asked after a respectful moment had passed.

Spinning on his heel, he faced Alyxaria and nodded. "Quite. Lead on, Knight," he declared formally, nearly causing her to wince.

"Poor soul," she thought as she turned and started up the central isle again.

As they walked, Alyxaria couldn't help but peer at some of the few remaining items on the shelves. There were several weapon prototypes, a couple of pieces of civil machinery, as well as some lab tools and relics. It was a paltry sampling of the wonders that once filled the warehouse, and it wouldn't be long before even those remaining items would be boxed, cataloged and shipped out. Then, there would be only the residents to evacuate. After that. . . .

She turned right and proceeded between two sets of empty shelves.

"Nay. I shan't dwell upon the unknown," she thought admonishingly. "What will be, shalt be."

Turning left once more upon exiting the aisle, she picked up the pace a bit as she led them past three more rows before turning right again. Directly in front of them, at the end of the row, was another spacious corridor. Alyxaria made straight for it, and upon passing through its arched opening, they found themselves in a short, glyph-adorned hallway with a trio of sealed, traditional-sized doors on both walls. As they moved down the hall toward its end, where closed, bronze-banded ironwood double doors stood, Alyxaria fought the urge to look at Damionatsu. There was an enormous amount of power radiating from the room, which would have been impressive if not for the circumstances that necessitated it. Instead, it felt ominous to her, and she could only imagine how he felt upon sensing it. Then, there was the issue of how he would react to their machinations. While she hoped he would respond with understanding, there was always the chance he wouldn't . . . and that scared her.

Pausing before the door, Alyxaria took a deep breath and turned to face him, her vibrant-green eyes locking with his dark gaze. She could sense the room's occupants as well as he, and noted the brooding concern in his eyes. Offering a small, disarming smile, she declared, "Pray, fear not. All is well within. The toll paid for our efforts 'twas high, but thine siblings art stable. . . . Though 'tis mine understanding they art fragile and require the succor of time to fully recover."

A muscle flinched in Damionatsu's jaw, but he said nothing.

Resisting the urge to sigh, Alyxaria smiled once more before turning and placing her palm on the slim gap between the panels. Channeling a sliver of her fir'gan into the door, the gap flared with a soft white light before the panels swung inward on silent hinges. Gentle light spilt forth as Alyxaria stepped aside, allowing Damionatsu to proceed within, where he immediately came to a halt.

Bathed in the glow of the giant light orb hanging close to fifty feet in the air at its center, the generously large square room felt warmer and more alive than the rest of the complex. It's flanks were home to more of the glowing elvannue glyphs and a trio of alcoves each, their arched openings covered by rich-red curtains, while at the room's center stood a pair of men engaged in a hushed conversation before four curved oak tables that were snuggly arranged around a central bluesteel dais. The gentle blue light emanating from the concentric rings embedded in the top of the dais washed over the tables' polished surfaces and the men like water, setting them aglow. As Alyxaria joined Damionatsu, and the doors closed behind her, she wasn't surprised to see what had grabbed his attention.

Atop the tables, which were decorated with carved forest mosaics, were a quartet of what appeared to be polished stone seeds. Each seed was half as large as a wagon wheel, and they were laced with a web of crystal veins that originated from an oblong blue crystal set in the heart of each one. The curious objects radiated a surprising amount of fir'gan, which became somewhat concerning with each gentle pulse of the blue crystals.

Stepping past Damionatsu, Alyxaria noted a hint of alarm in his eyes as he examined the seeds. The moment was brief, however. Once he realized she had advanced, he started forward and his gaze shifted to the enormous tank resting atop the elegant, and seemingly delicate, bluesteel platform hovering about five feet above the dais. Home to glyphs along its edge, and dais-matching concentric rings on its underside, it didn't seem possible for the platform to stay aloft given the burden it was under, but somehow it did. As for the tank, it was framed in glyph-etched bluesteel with a series of glossy, flexible tubes sprouting from its sides. The twenty-foot by thirty-foot container was also paneled with seemingly thin glass, and was filled to capacity with a cloudy blue liquid that radiated a dangerous amount of power.

At the sound of their approach, the two men — one elvannue and one human — standing before the tables turned to face them, cutting short their discussion. The human stood nearly six-and-a-half-feet tall, which placed him between Damionatsu and the elvannue in height. A white silk tunic and green pants hung loosely about his muscular frame beneath layered black leather armor and mid-calf, close-toed sandals, while a robust braided sword belt was home to a pair of dragon-collar katanas in black lacquered scabbards. Set astride his broad nose, compassionate, keen green eyes settled on Damionatsu, and his young, serene features broke into a welcoming smile.

With unabashed relief, he declared in a deep voice that reverberated in his chest, "Well met and be welcome, Warden Damionatsu. Mine heart 'tis pleased to see thee hale and whole."

Alyxaria moved alongside the elvannue man and gave his arm a compassionate squeeze as Damionatsu came to a halt just short of the two men, his concern now clearly displayed on his face.

"Well met, Lord Dracus Luthur and Warden Taylexion," he intoned, his voice a bit tight and his gaze fixated on the tank. "Pray tell, is this what I believe it to be?"

"Aye," Luthur answered softly. Taking a deep breath, he ran a hand bound in black lien over his shaved head, causing the wooden prayer beads wrapped around his wrist to rattle softly, then affirmed, "Pray, set thine fears aside. Thine brother is well."

"Karalisa?" Damionatsu asked, his voice strained.

"Thine sister is hale as well," a voice soft with exhaustion replied.

Alyxaria watched as Damionatsu pried his eyes from the tank and shifted his gaze to the gaunt man standing next to her. To her surprise, she saw the same shock she felt at the elvannue's appearance play across his face.

Clad in what would typically be tightly wrapped red silk from beneath his chin to his ankles and wrists, his usually slender and deceptively strong figure seemed dreadfully gaunt. Burnished gold bracers, molded to resemble intertwined dragons, weaved their way from his wrist to his elbows, while supple leather sandals protected his feet, and a green belt of layered silk encircled his narrow hips. The strain of what must have been days of preparation, not to mention the actual procedure, was painted plainly on his long face, where his skin was drawn tight over his sharp features. His normally golden skin was unnervingly pale, and his eyes — which were similar in shape and tilt to Alyxaria's — were dull in their now sunken sockets instead of their typically bright golden-amber hue. Furthermore, his blood-red hair hung limply about his shoulders and his drooping, gold kasleu-adorned ears.

"Pray tell me — how art thee, Taylexion?" Damionatsu asked respectfully. "'Tis clear a heavy toll hath been exacted."

Taylexion's pale, thin lips pressed together firmly in a small grimace, pulling his skin even tighter over cheekbones that were the masculine counterpart to Alyxaria's. Waving a dismissive hand weakly, he replied, "'Tis nothing to concern thyself with. I will recuperate as I always hath done." Before Damionatsu could respond, Taylexion spun on his heel and began walking around the dais. "Pray, come hither. Thine sister rests in yon alcove, and the situation must be explained to thee should mine presence be unavailable."

Damionatsu looked to Luthur, who motioned for him to proceed, before everyone hustled to catch up with Taylexion.

Making their way around the tank, they saw that the tubes connected to it ran along the ground toward a lone alcove in the center of the rear wall. Trailing behind Damionatsu, Alyxaria was forced to slow down to match his pace as the tank within the alcove came into view. Built in the same vein as its larger brethren, this one was closer to human size and was eerily reminiscent of a coffin. Like its sibling, the tank floated on a platform above a dais, this time only about three feet in the air. Furthermore, it was also filled with the same blue liquid, albeit a fraction more transparent.

Gathering before the tank, they peered within and could just make out the naked form of the woman interned within. Though it was still difficult to make out details, they could see the woman had long sky-blue tresses that floated freely in the liquid, which further obscured her features. For a moment, Damionatsu simply stood there watching. Then, with deliberate movements, he gently placed a hand on the tank's lid.

Standing behind the others, Alyxaria's heart clenched at the sight. She knew he was probing the tank's occupant with the currents, and she could only imagine what was going through his mind. "To sacrifice so much . . ." she thought as her throat tightened with sympathy.

Luthur placed a consoling on Damionatsu's shoulder, and he offered in an appreciative tone, "Thine siblings proceeded with clarity of mind. The deep bond with the currents within thine family's blood hath permitted Taylexion's task to bloom where failure had once flourished. Be proud of that, mine friend."

Damionatsu nodded in response.

"The bond betwixt them 'tis strong, indeed," Taylexion added weakly. "It shalt be both their strength and their curse," he continued with a grimace. "For the closer thine siblings art to one another, the stronger they shalt be. In opposition to this boon, they will also be more vulnerable. Should one fall prey to malady or suffer severe enough injury — as is inevitable given the task they art destined for — so shalt the other suffer."

Without taking his eyes off the tank, Damionatsu asked softly, dreading the answer, "Will the death of one doom the other?"

While she didn't know all the details of the experiment, or its implica-

tions, Alyxaria felt her heart break for him as he asked the question.

Taylexion nodded. "If their trauma be great enough — 'tis possible. If thine query refers to blackheart poisoning. . . ." He took a deep breath before he stated, "Aye, it would." As Damionatsu's hand balled into a fist on the tank, he hastened to add, "I must maketh clear that for such a horror to come to pass, 'twould require an egregious amount of such miasma. Thine brother and sister's blood shalt burn far hotter than that of the Bestynes, bestowing upon them a resistance to their poison unlike any other." He took a deep breath and let it out slowly as Damionatsu's fist relaxed. "Should such a scenario ever come to pass, know that as 'twas for the dragons from which this gift bloomed, so shalt their blood be overwhelmed, thusly corrupting the flow of fir'gan."

Damionatsu's fist tightened back up, and Alyxaria cringed a bit.

"As the precious link that anchors Kiroshin's essence to this world through thine sister would transfer the effects," Taylexion continued, "'tis likely 'twould consume Karalisa at a slower pace. Alas, the end result is without question." He hesitated a moment before adding, "I shan't presume to know the depth of thine internal conflict . . . yet I understand well the want to protect one's blood. If 'twere one of mine blood—"

"'Tis not so, is it?" Damionatsu interrupted, his tone soft, but his anger apparent to everyone.

Alyxaria glanced at Luthur and her father. Both appeared somewhat chastised and chose not to respond. While she could only imagine what was going through everyone's minds at that moment, she had a decent idea as to what it might be — they were struggling to fully grasp what Damionatsu was currently feeling. Everyone was quite aware of his siblings' sacrifice this day, but she wasn't so sure any of them could completely comprehend his emotional plight. None of them carried the burdens that Damionatsu did, and without that knowledge and experience, they never would.

"Aye, Damionatsu. . . . 'Tis not mine family," Taylexion conceded gently. "Mine hope is thou mayhap find succor in the knowledge that I doth not wish an ill fate to embrace thine brother and sister. Thine family hast sacrificed much to bring an end to the blackheart plague and this accursed war. To this end, pray hear my words true and clear."

Damionatsu relaxed his fist and removed it from the tank as he turned to face Taylexion, his face a grim mask of determination.

The men's eyes locked as Taylexion declared, "Thine siblings' bond 'tis forged of coldfire the likes of which few could dream of summoning and even fewer could hope to control. Should the ill fate of which I hath spoken befall them, unlike the Bestynes', there exists options for their survival . . . limited as those may be. Mineself and mine daughters, when hale and with proper tools, could accomplish such a feat. Should circumstances not permit this, then thou art the only one in possession of the gift needed to cleanse their blood."

Damionatsu appeared to digest the news while studying Taylexion's face. Suddenly, he asked darkly, "Pray — what art thou concealing?"

Taylexion hesitated and licked his lips. "Coldfire 'tis dangerous and unpredictable, as thou well knows. While it could save them, 'tis possible 'twould merely hasten their death, or. . . ."

"Or what?" Damionatsu growled.

The weary elvannue sighed and shrugged his shoulders. "I doth wish I could say with certainty. What hast been accomplished here 'tis as much an unknown as when the Guardians blessed us. Could any of us hath foreseen the consequences of that day? A cleansing mayhap hath lasting effects — both auspicious and maleficent — or it mayhap give birth to the unknown." He shook his head weakly. "I profess a deep and profound understanding of fir'gan, yet much of what we hath done ventures unto Corith's realm. Long hath we elvannue treaded upon sacrosanct ground, Damionatsu . . . and I can only pray that with this, we can begin to atone for the horrors birthed of our arrogance."

The remorse and guilt Alyxaria heard in her father's voice nearly ripped tears from her eyes. Deep musings and wise words were a common event for Taylexion, and for many elvannue for that matter, but to hear such sorrow entrenched in his words was shocking.

After a moment of silence, Damionatsu slowly nodded and offered a small, contrite smile. "Pray, accept mine apologies, Taylexion. Thou hath done nothing to deserve such wrath."

Taylexion waved a dismissive hand. "Do not burden thineself with such worry. 'Twould be of more concern were you not angered or worried by what thine siblings hath undergone."

Amused but approving smiles cracked everyone's faces.

"Now, if all will excuse me, I must ensure mine . . ." he hesitated and his eyes briefly met Luthur's before sliding away, ". . . other works art safely transported ere we move thine siblings."

Without waiting for permission to leave, Taylexion began gingerly making his way toward the exit.

Alyxaria followed him for a moment to make sure he could proceed without assistance. Once she was sure of that, she returned to the others to see if they needed anything. To her chagrin, she found Damionatsu staring daggers at Luthur. Remaining at a respectful distance, she stayed silent as the doors closed behind her father. For a moment, she thought the two Wardens were communicating telepathically; after all, they had to be aware of her presence, and might not want their discussion overheard. Then, the silent damn broke.

"Pray — what art thou not telling me?" Damionatsu demanded, his voice thick with blame, causing Alyxaria to flinch. "'Tis an immense amount of fir'gan flowing throughout this laboratory, and I saw crates awaiting transport

awash with power as a foci 'twould be. What's more," he gestured to the seeds on the tables surrounding the large dais, "'tis the matter of those seeds! What art thou not telling me, Luthur?" he demanded again, his anger growing. "Hath I not proven myself true?" He pointed firmly at the tank containing his sister. "Is their sacrifice not sufficient to placate thine fears?"

Luthur appeared to absorb the verbal blows without flinching. "Mine trust in thee hath never been in question, nor thine loyalty," Luthur declared gently but adamantly. "I grant thine queries hath merit, but thou knoweth well and true some secrets must remain with the few. Should I divulge all to thee at this time, 'twould birth one more chance that failure could claim us."

Alyxaria's stomach twisted in knots, and she glanced back at the seeds. Much of what Damionatsu stated was important, and she suddenly found herself wishing she'd been more involved with her family's works, as she had no idea what they were for.

"Corith be good!" Damionatsu breathed. "Knight Alyxaria," he stated forcefully, drawing her attention. "What hath transpired here?" he asked as he met her gaze.

"I am afraid such knowledge is unknown to me, Warden," she replied formally with a shake of her head. "Of mine family's experiments, only the Bonding of thine siblings is known in any detail to me."

Damionatsu continued to glare at her as if plumbing the depths of her soul for the truth. Just as she felt like she was about to wilt under his gaze, Luthur came to her rescue.

"Do not cast blame upon her. What she hath stated 'tis true."

Damionatsu's focus swung back to Luthur. "Very well. Then will thou reveal the truth unto me? What hath transpired here?"

Alyxaria saw Luthur's eyes twitch a bit, prompting her to state, "I will go. I fear what thou hast to say is not for mine ears, Lord Dragon."

Without looking at her, Luthur stated, "Nay. Remain, Knight Alyxaria. Thou shalt be privy to this knowledge ere long; as such, thine dismissal is mute."

"As thou wishes, Lord Dragon," she replied meekly.

Suddenly, as if his words were a battering ram, Damionatsu asked, "Pray, tell me — Hast Mes'ilafira been complicit in thine machinations?"

Alyxaria fought the urge to gasp in shock at the accusation. The only one of the elvannue's projects that had ever been remotely condoned by the Guardians was the modification of the Bestynes, and even then, their approval was grudging. For one of them to sanction what had been done to Karalisa and Kiroshin was nearly unfathomable.

Before she or Luthur could say anything, Damionatsu took the accusa-

tion a step further.

"Nay. . . . 'Tis not the case, is it? This . . ." he waved at the tanks, "all of this 'twas the Guardian's idea, was it not?"

Alyxaria choked on the shock that welled up in her. She wanted to vehemently deny such an event, but one look at Luthur quelled that thought. There was a sadness in his gaze that couldn't be missed.

"Dear Corith," she thought. "Could it be true?"

Taking a deep breath, Luthur started to say, "Damion—" when the room shook with disconcerting violence.

Looking at one another with dread-filled eyes, Damionatsu offered in opposition to what Alyxaria knew the currents were telling them, "Earthquake?"

No one responded as it wasn't needed, and they all immediately bolted for the exit as dust and small pebbles rained from the ceiling. However, before they could reach it, the panels burst open with fir'gan-fueled violence, nearly ripping them from their hinges. In the wake of the blast, Rynthalia and a host of works carrying crates and tools bolted into the room. Barely controlled panic was painted clearly across their faces as the workers hustled to ready everything for transport while Rynthalia advanced on the Wardens and Alyxaria, her gilded robe flowing about her like an angry storm.

"What hast happened?!" Luthur demanded of Rynthalia as she approached, barking orders to the workers.

Reaching them, she responded, not bothering to hide her fear, "An attack, Lord Dragon — violent and sudden!"

"How?" Damionatsu asked, as stunned by the declaration as Luthur and Alyxaria.

"'Tis unknown to us," Rynthalia said with a shake of her head. "The Guardian's presence maketh it most difficult to discern what hast occurred. Alas, we art aware that the upper gate hast been razed, and most of the defensive wards hath been triggered." Glancing past them, she ordered two elvannue who seemed to be at a loss to start detaching the hoses from the enormous tank.

Turning her attention back to the Wardens as another explosion rocked the chamber, she practically pleaded with them, her violet eyes filled with apprehension, "Pray, return unto the Guardian with all speed! I fear this sanctuary will be lost anon! Father hast gone to prepare the Guardian's way to safety, but he needeth time! I beg of thee — defend the Guardian and bless Father with the time he doth require!"

Both men nodded, but as they started around Rynthalia, Damionatsu looked back at the tanks, a mask of naked concern on his face.

With time of the essence, Alyxaria stepped up behind him and squeezed his should with a mix of comfort and urgency. "Pray, Warden, thou must depart!

Thine family will be removed from danger anon! Mine sister and I will see it done!"

The muscles in his jaw flexed, and for a moment, Alyxaria thought he might choose to remain. Thankfully, he turned and nodded to her. "I want thine oath, Knight!" he demanded, the violent undertones in his words making it clear what would befall her if anything happened to his siblings.

Another explosion ripped through the complex, and this time, they did not need the currents to know where it originated. Whoever was attacking the sanctuary was drawing very close to the Guardian's chamber.

Pulling herself up to her full height, Alyxaria met his gaze with un-flinching resolve. "Death Bringer," she declared with all her heart, "by blood, by honor, and by deed, this I swear — thine family will arrive unscathed!"

"Thine mind hath wandered yet again, Sister," Rynthalia stated, a hint of mirth in her rich voice.

"*Hummm?*" Alyxaria offered in response, her green-eyed gaze focused acutely on both the obsidian dragon clenched between her slender fingers and the play of the hanging lamps' light on the piece.

"Thou cannot simply admire the piece, Sister. I believe I hath granted thee more than enough time to maketh thine move."

"*Humm?*" Alyxaria replied once again.

Rynthalia chuckled, and a small, indulgent smile split her full lips. "Thine mind is beset by wanderlust of late. What moves thee to such depths of contemplation that thou cannot even offer me a prop-er match?"

Seated on opposite sides of an elegant but small table of flowing white wood, the sisters were clothed in loose-fitting dresses of similar cut; Alyxaria in the red she had long favored, and Rynthalia in white trimmed with gold filigree. Both women occupied high-backed, red velvet-cushioned chairs that were a match for the table, which was topped with a chessboard and an hourglass. The frames of both board and hourglass were made of a mix of dark steel and white wood that had been artfully woven together to create a balance of light and dark that captured the eye. The twin lamps hanging from the deck-supporting lattice of sturdy, yet graceful, white beams graced the immediate area around the siblings and the table with warm illu-mination, but little else. As such, shadows swallowed the rest of the cabin and its other furnishings, which included a desk for each sister on opposite sides of the room, and two trunks at the feet of a pair of small beds flanking a wardrobe at the back of the cabin.

Glancing around the room while she awaited a response, the

furniture once again reminded Rynthalia of ghostly figures that were too afraid to step into the light, and she had to suppress a shudder. Even after all the years at sea, and all the time spent in their quarters, she still yearned for the light orbs, which rested in their wall-mounted cradles around the room, to once again hum to life. It had been five years since they could no longer spare the fir'gan to power them, but the absence of their soothing light was felt just as strongly – if not more so – than their yearning to feel the sun upon their skin. Shaking her head to banish the morose thoughts, she looked at the hourglass. Like the lamps, the sweeping tangle of steel and wood surrounding the sand-filled glass was intended to serve more as art than as a functioning device. Archaic as it was, it was a needed tool that had become invaluable over the years.

"Only four hours and this match will be over ere long. 'Tis unlike her to be distracted so. Alas, 'tis not as if we hath somewhere to be ere long. 'Tis only the sea and the raging aether to greet us in all directions with no end in sight," Rynthalia mused internally.

With her thoughts threatening to drift into melancholy realms, she wrenched them back from the looming pit of despair by returning her attention to the game. "Well, mine Sister?" she asked, cocking her head of long dark-violet hair. "Shalt we continue anon, or doest thou yield?"

Still rolling the piece between her fingers, Alyxaria appeared to ignore her sister's inquiry. However, before Rynthalia could prod her again, she asked, the melodic lilt of her voice muted, "Pray tell, Sister – doest thine mind not wonder what awaits us upon reaching shore?" Prying her eyes from the chess piece, she met her sister's violet gaze from beneath her cowl of shoulder-length, deep-red hair. "Doest it not cast thine stomach adrift upon angry waves of worry that, mayhap, we art unwittingly sailing into a trap? Mayhap, even unto our demise?"

Rynthalia shook her head and sat back in her chair. *"Striking uncomfortably close to the mark, Sister,"* she thought.

After a brief pause heavy with consideration, Rynthalia stated with conviction that belayed her own concerns, "'Twould be foolish if I did not worry, but nor will I allow it to burden me with hesitation. Our mission 'tis too important to let such musing give us more than a moment's pause." She suddenly smirked. Leaning forward, she folded her arms behind the numerous ebony chess pieces arrayed before the checkered board of black and white marble, and teased playfully, "What truly gives me pause – nay, besets mine heart with all-consuming terror – is to see thine countenance buried beneath such deep reflection! If this continues, I will hath no choice but to see if the world hast already met an inauspicious end!"

The jab drew a reproachful glare from Alyxaria, but it quickly gave way to a small smile. Returning the piece to its defensive position near the rear of the game board, she placed her elbow on the padded arm of her chair. Resting her cheek on her fist, she said, "Thine point 'tis received with only minor bruises upon mine ego, Sister. Yet, given the nature of the task before us, I would hope one and all would refrain from using such dreadful hyperbole. Father would not approve, and I certainly doeth not."

Nodding, her expression reflecting a respectful amount of chastisement, Rynthalia replied, "Aye, he would not. And I doth apologize. Mine intent 'twas only to succor thine spirits, not cast them further into darkness."

Alyxaria waved a dismissive hand. "Think of it no more. Betwixt the confines of this vessel and the time we hath spent within, 'tis a blessing madness did not collect us long ago. What's more, 'tis little wonder that our thoughts doth not ride on morose tides more often."

Rynthalia grinned. "Madness collect us, Sister? Thine continued efforts to best me in chess, despite thine ever-mounting losses, mayhap serve as evidence to the contrary." Her grin grew, and playfulness glimmered in her violet eyes. "Mayhap thine mind hath already slipped the bonds of sanity, and I should confine thee to thine quarters so that thou might find succor and yet be saved?"

Alyxaria rolled her eyes, and the sisters broke out in musical laughter. After that, their conversation turned to more jovial matters and fond memories of the home they'd left behind so long ago. Soon, their chess match was long forgotten as their conversation whiled the hours away.

Then, it happened.

In an instant, their conversation ceased. Wide-eyed, the sisters' gazes met, each seeking confirmation of what they felt. It wasn't a change in course, nor did it involve their immediate surroundings. Instead, it was a sensation; a tingling at the heart of their being that spread through their body, bringing with it a heavenly warmth that had been absent for far too long.

Joyful tears welled up in their eyes as hesitant smiles split their lips. Neither sister wanted to give voice to the giddy excitement building in them for fear of jinxing the moment. Then, as if Corithsent, an emphatic knock at their door broke the joyous tension.

"Enter!" Alyxaria beckoned after gathering herself.

The door immediately swung open on silent hinges, and their hearts nearly wept. For the first time in years, it wasn't the dreary dark gray light they'd grown used to during the trip that spilled in around the silhouette of one of the ship's crew members. Instead, the light was bright and now held a hint of true, unblemished sunlight.

"Knight Alyxaria! Seeker Rynthalia!" the crewman stated, his gentle voice ecstatic. "The Captain doth beseech thee to join him on deck and bear witness to Corith's blessing this day!"

Looking at each other with unabashed joy, Alyxaria did her best to control her excitement as she told the crewman, "Pray, tell the Captain we will join him anon, Destalan."

Bowing low, his braided blonde hair spilling over his shoulder-length ears, Destalan replied, "Aye, mine Ladies! Corith's blessing be upon thee!" Standing, Destalan hurried out of sight, leaving the door open and the ever-brightening light to bathe the room.

"Corith be praised!" Rynthalia breathed. "'Tis difficult to believe what mine eyes and senses tell me!"

Smiling wider and brighter than she had in years, Alyxaria said, "Aye. 'Tis so! Shalt we venture forth and assure ourselves 'tis more than a dream?"

Matching her sister's smile, they both stood and, with exuberance befitting children ready to partake of the winter festivities, they made for the door. Almost immediately upon exiting the cabin, they were forced to stop and shield their eyes. Exceptional visual acuity and sensitivity aside, years spent in the Storm Sea with only the iridescent flare of lightning to break the gray squalor had rendered their eyes ill-prepared for natural sunlight. However, so powerful was the joy in their hearts and their yearning to see the sun and sky again that they quickly lowered their hands and opened their eyes.

Like glittering, vibrant needles, the light stabbed at their eyes, nearly blinding them. Yet, as tears of pain and joy streamed down their faces to the sounds of high-spirited celebration around them, they kept their eyes open, drinking in every glorious moment.

"'Tis as if I am seeing the sun for the first time!" Alyxaria breathed, her bliss nearly choking her. "Its beauty is such that, though I knoweth it will blind me ere long, I cannot avert mine eyes for fear it will be lost to me once more!"

Her smile beaming despite the tears pouring from her irritated eyes, Rynthalia replied, "Aye, Sister! 'Tis a sight I thought lost to us, never to be found again!"

Alyxaria laughed. Brushing tears from her cheeks, she

chided, "Morose thoughts, Sister?"

Rynthalia shook her head, her vision focused on the gray skies that were slowly giving way to a vision of blue more beautiful than anything she'd ever seen. "Nay, Sister. An offering of thanks for where we art now, and a farewell to the barrier that hath served as home these long years."

"Mine Ladies!" boomed a deep, enthusiastic cry from above them.

Surprised by the call, the sisters spun and looked up the two-tiered aftcastle quickly, besetting them with nausea and dizziness that nearly made them tumble to the deck. Catching each other before such an indecency could come to fruition, they steadied themselves to the sound of laughter from above.

"Really now, Captain?" Alyxaria stated with a mixture of exasperation and embarrassment as she tried to make out the features of the blob leaning over the white railing against a slowly brightening sky. "Hath thine sense of decorum and discretion fled thee?"

Though she could not see his face clearly, she could sense that her chastisement had resonated with him. Yet, when he spoke again, it was impossible to miss the mirth at the edge of his words. "Mine sincerest of apologies, Knight. 'Twas not mine intent to maketh light of thine sudden . . . situation. However, we art *free* of the Storm Sea!"

For the briefest of moments, Alyxaria thought he was trying to justify his laughter with the momentous occasion – albeit, her chastisement was more to cover her embarrassment than for his mirth – then the meaning behind his words struck her.

"Corith be good," she muttered before telling the captain, "While welcome, thine apology is not needed, Captain Valmon. 'Tis I that should apologize. The moment hath overwhelmed mine senses, and 'tis our fault we did not realize it 'fore we stumbled into the light like mischievous children."

That drew a deep laugh from her sister and the captain alike.

"Mine dear Sister," Rynthalia said as she closed her eyes, "I cannot believe we hath behaved in such unseemly fashion!"

Closing her eyes as well, Alyxaria responded before taking a deep breath to clear her mind, "Aye, and human children, no less."

Rynthalia grinned even as she followed her sister's lead. In their excitement and haste to see the sun, and after years of being closed off to the chaotic and deadly currents of fir'gan that made up the Storm Sea, their training had slipped their minds. The shame they felt at such a mistake was made worse by the captain's laughter at their near inglorious tumble. However, though it took longer than either liked, they banished their emotions and quieted their minds as they centered themselves and looked inward for the source of the warmth that had initially alerted them to the change in environment.

The sisters' hearts leapt with unequivocal joy when they found the light at the center of their beings. Warm and pulsing with strength, their inner fir'gan had already grown stronger than it had been in years. The urge to take hold of that light and let it wash over them like a warm river was almost too much to resist, but resist they did. With the edge of the Storm Sea still looming over the boat, its influence over the fir'gan both within them and in the surrounding area still made it far too dangerous to embrace their power fully. At best, such an attempt would fail, leaving the wielder injured. At worst, they would be overwhelmed by wild and uncontrollable power that would either burn them out, leaving them unable to ever access fir'gan again, or simply consume them from the inside out, burning them to ash.

So, with caution foremost on their minds, the sisters reached out to that wonderful light and touched it, letting the smallest amount of power trickle into them. Immediately, their beings were filled with a euphoric warmth, washing away their dark thoughts and fears. As that warmth quickly spread through their bodies, invigorating them, the aches and pains that had been intermittent companions through-out the journey were erased, and wounds that had been tended to with mundane means at one time healed completely.

When the sisters opened their eyes once more, the light no longer stung. More importantly, they could finally see their surroundings clearly, and what they saw in the distance nearly made them weep once more.

Blue skies.

Granted, angry clouds sought to mare the welcoming sight as they were drawn to the Storm Sea, but it was still infinitely better than the drab grays and abyssal blacks that had essentially been their prison for so many years. Seeking a better view, the sisters cheerfully scram-bled past the pair of retracted masts to the foredeck of the sleek, ivory-white vessel that maintained a steady and true course despite the tumultuous waters they still traversed. The vista spread before them brought them to a sudden stop to the right of a crystalline dome set in the center of the foredeck, and tore cries of delight from them that were just as jubilant as those of the crew. In the distance was the tan-talizing sight of clear skies and calm azure seas for as far as the eye could see.

Tears of happiness once more slipped free of their eyes and streamed down their cheeks as the sisters embraced each other fiercely. "We hath made it, Sister!" Alyxaria cried softly in Rynthalia's ear.

"Aye, Sister — by Corith's good grace, that we hath done!" she responded, her words thick with elation.

With the crew celebrating all over the deck, the sisters maintained their hug for some time, basking in the warm sun and each other's joy. Finally, their personal moment came to an end when the captain approached them.

Average of height for an elvannué, Captain Valmon's long white hair hung from his head in an array of braids, and his long ears were home to simple bronze kasleu earrings. Lean of muscle with sun-darkened skin, he was clothed only in baggy red pants cinched above his bare feet and bound at his waist by a thick black belt from which hung an assortment of pouches and tools of his trade. "Mine Ladies," he interrupted respectfully.

Pulling apart, smiles on their faces, the sisters wiped their cheeks as Alyxaria replied, the reality of the moment beginning to set in, "Aye, Captain. While 'tis a momentous occasion, 'tis still work to be about."

"Aye, Knight," he responded with a nod, his green eyes shining with joy, "'tis work to be about. Yet, if thou would permit mine forwardness, 'tis leagues yet to travel; I believe 'twould be a grievous error to forgo this opportunity."

"Of what opportunity dost thou speak, Captain?" Alyxaria asked, her mind already treading the path before them and the possible threats that might lie ahead.

Smiling gently, joy still radiating from her, Rynthalia placed a gentle hand on her sister's shoulder. "Why to celebrate, dear Sister. The captain 'tis right — there art leagues still to cross. Yet, while I believe 'twould provide our souls profound succor to bask in this moment of joy and light, we knoweth not what lies before us, and 'twould be foolish to believe that we will remain free from danger. Therefore, let us take stock of our situation ere we lose ourselves in revelry."

A small, sly smile had spread across Alyxaria's face as her sister spoke, betraying her thoughts before she could give voice to them. "Aye, Sister, thou art correct. Lest we art swept away by the heady euphoria that hast already taken ahold, we must take this opportunity to assess the ship's condition ere we continue onward. 'Tis been far too long since she received proper care. Dost thou not agree, Captain?"

Valmon's smile had diminished somewhat at the mention of an inspection, but he knew what Alyxaria said was true. "Aye, Knight," he conceded. "She hath taken care of us for so long, 'tis only proper that we doeth the same for her. 'Twould be a shame to survive the Storm Sea only to be cast adrift or take on water as soon as the shield is lowered."

Seeing the disappointment in his eyes at having to attend to more work instead of further basking in the moment, Alyxaria smiled warmly. "Fear not, we needeth only assure that nothing critical is severely damaged. Once thine task is complete, all art free to enjoy this blessing of the Light."

Seeing the exuberance return to his face warmed Alyxaria's heart. Giving them time to celebrate was the least she could do for them after such a long and strenuous journey. As such, before the captain could relay her orders, she looked about and, raising her voice so all could hear, shouted with joy, "Hearken unto me, one and all!"

Almost immediately, the crew's boisterous chatter fell silent, and their gazes turned her way. Then, as a group, they moved close enough to hear her clearly.

"I knoweth thine hearts swell with the same joy as mine own at this blessing from the Light! Yet, ere we lose ourselves in celebration – and mark mine words, we shalt celebrate – we must attend to the *Sy'ladrial* She hath shepherded and protected us against impossible odds, and 'tis only right that we offer succor to her should she be in need. As our captain hast said, ' 'Twould be a shame to survive the Storm Sea only to find us adrift or taking on water soon after the shield is lowered!' "

Laughter greeted the comment, assuaging Alyxaria's concern that the crew would be disgruntled at having to put off their celebration. More importantly, it made her heart swell with pride. These men and women – her fellow elvannue – so willing to risk death on this desperate undertaking, understood that the mission took precedence over celebration no matter the situation.

"All of thee hath worked with vigor and suffered much over these years, and for that, I am unboundedly grateful! As such, once we art assured of the *Sy'ladrial* vitality, we shalt celebrate as only elvannue can! For in her grace, Corith hast seen fit that we should arrive unscathed so that her Light might yet be preserved!"

A thunderous chorus of cheers greeted her declaration, widening the smile on her face.

After giving the crew a moment to drink it all in, Captain Valmon put on as stern of a facade as he could muster before bellowing, "'Tis enough of that for now! 'Tis work to be done ere we can celebrate, and I, for one, doth not intend to procrastinate longer than necessary! All of thee knoweth what 'tis needed, so be about thine tasks!"

As the crew scrambled to attend to their duties, the captain turned to the sisters and bowed low, "If thou will excuse me, I shalt be about mine tasks as well."

"Thank thee, Captain," Alyxaria said, her words heavy with gratitude.

"Nay, mine lady. Thank thee, and thank Corith for guiding us safely through that nightmare." Bowing one more time, he hustled over to the stairs in the center of the deck and proceeded below deck.

Watching him go, Rynthalia could feel the smile on her face starting to slip, and she sensed it in her sister as well. As much as they wanted to banish thoughts of what still had to be done, not to mention what awaited them on land, they could not, and it threatened to douse the fires of their happiness. Seeking to remove themselves from the path of the bustling crew as much as possible without returning to their quarters, the sisters moved to the rail at the tip of the foredeck and gazed out over the sea. For a time, they simply enjoyed the sight, the caress of the wind, and the warmth of a sun they had missed for so very long.

Finally, and hesitantly, Rynthalia broke the silence. "How long?" she asked simply.

"If all 'tis well with the ship, a fortnight. The sails must suffice, for I dare not use the engines long. We knoweth not what – nor whom – awaits us. 'Twould behoove us to act with caution ere we know the situation on Solarson."

Rynthalia paused, unsure if she should voice her next question. There were few scenarios they had not played out on their journey, but there was one question that had come up time and again like a weed that could not be killed.

"I knoweth what thine thought is, Sister," Alyxaria stated, "and I hath only the answer that I hath given time and again. We shalt activate the compass ere long, and should we be unable to locate Luthur, or–" she choked on the word, unable to give voice to one of her overriding fears. Clearing her throat, she started again. "Should Luthur be indisposed, we can but hope the compass locates Damionatsu or his sister. Failing that, we shalt seek out whoever can be reached without drawing undue attention upon ourselves."

Rynthalia nodded, unwilling to voice her worries about such

an encounter should Luthur be gone. Then, her words hesitant, she started to ask, "'Tis true we hath done our utmost to prepare for all possible contingencies . . . however, now that we art advancing upon Solarson, I would be remiss should I not put this forth once more. If the Darkness hath–"

Turning to her sister, Alyxaria did her best to smile reassuringly. She knew what weighed on Rynthalia's heart, for the same thing burdened her heart as well. "Give not voice to it again, Sister. For I fear that should such concerns pass from either of our lips, we shalt find ourselves drowning in all-consuming fear." Smiling confidently despite her own concerns, she added, "We shalt overcome any obstacles put before us. However, should the worst greet us, then we shalt face it with our heads held high, and the Light at our backs."

Rynthalia blinked at her sister, a bit taken aback by the tenacity in her words. This wasn't the same woman who had been brooding over the subject during their chess match. No, this was the strong woman she knew Alyxaria to be. It was as if knowing they really would reach Solarson had suddenly galvanized her sister's spirit.

"It should not surprise me," she thought, gazing with pride at the fire now burning in Alyxaria's eyes. *"She hath never fancied the unknown. Yet, set before her a tangible target, and her resolve and focus art akin to steel. Father chose his Knight well. 'Tis folly that his crystal did not choose her to succeed him."*

Smiling, Rynthalia finally responded, "Dear Sister, 'twas but mere moments ago thou were the one full of concern, and I the one offering succor. 'Tis astounding how quickly we switched places."

Alyxaria's smile turned into a foreboding smirk as she turned back to the sea. "I wish that 'twas true, Sister. True, the objective now looms a bit clearer, but shadows yet play about its edges, and the fear and concern I did express earlier art still present – nay, it weighs even more." Gripping the rail, Alyxaria continued, "I doth not fancy the unknown, Sister, as thou well knows. Give unto me a tangible target, and I shalt strike truer than the most renowned of our archers. This situation, however . . ." her grip on the rail tightened, "'tis shrouded in vast darkness. There art a plethora of scenarios, few of which bode well. I fear we art sailing into a situation that we dare not turn our thoughts toward for fear 'twould destroy our resolve."

Joining her sister, Rynthalia placed a firm, comforting hand on Alyxaria's shoulder. Leaning in so that her words could only be heard by her, she said, seeking to provide a rock of confidence for them both, "Whatever mayhap come, be it joy unimaginable, or the Darkness itself, we shalt face it together, with all our resolve and might – as Father would hath wanted. Remember, we hath survived the Darkness's wrath before, and – Light willing – we shalt find a way to overcome whatever trials await us upon Solarson."

Eyes still fixed on the horizon, Alyxaria reached up and squeezed her sister's hand in thanks, but said nothing. *"I truly hope thou art right, Sister."* she thought. *"Thine words cannot mask thine fears, for they art the same as mine own. Corith, by thine grace, we hath come this far; let it not be in vain. Show us the way to redemption – a way to lift this world out of the shadow and back unto the light. For if the Darkness hath grown in strength as we dread, then I fear we mayhap be too late."*

Chapter One

Age of Twilight

5972 years since the Exodus

For each day, there is a beginning and an end. From darkness to light and from light to darkness is the pattern each day has followed since the dawn of time. It was as if these primordial elements were locked in a never-ending cycle of pacifistic warfare for dominance over each other – each having its moment of supremacy, but always unable to destroy the other and attain absolute power. For many, this unceasing battle seemed an allusion to the greater picture and power at play.

In an era known as the Age of Power, there arose a great evil that threatened to engulf all life and vanquish the Light from the world. Of all the races, only the dragons sensed the growing plight. These majestic and noble beasts opposed this evil with all their might, seeking to eliminate it before it could destroy all that was good in the world. Despite their best efforts, this entity – which came to be known as the Darkness – defeated them at every turn. In their despair, the dragons retreated against the growing corruption, escaping to lands untouched by the evil. There, they licked their wounds and asked Corith, Lord of the Light, for guidance. With Corith's guidance, along with the help of the races of the land, the dragons began to fight back.

In the end, it was not enough.

The Darkness' corruption spread through the forces arrayed against it, killing many and turning more to its cause. The dragons were slowly killed off or turned, weakening the forces of Light's ability to oppose it. Soon, the Darkness' followers threatened to consume the world.

Then, from the ashes of destruction, there arose those who had resisted the Darkness' taint. They stood against the Darkness when and where no one else could. Through their determination and sacrifice, the Darkness was pushed from the land. The people of the world – a world known as Kylir – celebrated the destruction of the Darkness. Those who had stood against the malicious entity, however, knew better.

The Darkness had not been destroyed. . . .

Dawn came as night grudgingly yielded its reign. With the patience of the infinite, the sun crept above the horizon and cast forth its tendrils of brilliance to once more claim the sky. Across the heavens, the spears of light crawled, crossing the vast, pristine waters of the Galerad Ocean to the shores of the continent of Solarson. There, the sun's children leapt the enormous continent's western barrier of rocky cliffs and towering mountains, bringing light to the dense forest homes of the humans living on the outskirts of civilization.

As the sun climbed higher, it gained in strength and expanded its reach, driving night further east. Light soon found its way into the snow-locked northern mountains, where it sought out the darkness that haunted the deep valleys and crevasses that pervaded the region. As the night peeled back, the light found a landscape ravaged by the children of Darkness. Villages were in ruin, and the dead seemed countless. As for the living, they either stood tall in victory or cowered in fear of what perverse fate awaited them that day.

At the heart of this nightmare incarnate, the sun found a darkness it could not banish. Atop the remnants of once proud, towering battlements, a crimson-armored titan reveled in his conquest. His enemies had fallen before him, and many of their heads now decorated the numerous pikes erected atop the wall's remains. Awash in the chorus of his celebratory army, the man grinned as he fingered the preserved head of the keep's former master hanging from his belt. Then, with infallible confidence, he laughed at dawn's burgeoning light.

Immune to the cares or thoughts of sentient beings, the sun and its life-giving illumination continued with their eternal task. Far to the south and east, dawn blossomed over the fertile lands of central Solarson and one of the largest lakes on the continent. Known as Lake Sol, life was already engaged in its daily dance amongst the farms and villages nestled along its shores and the two rivers that fed it. With a fervor unique to their species, the human inhabitants had begun their day well before dawn greeted them. By noon, travelers and traders alike filled the roads and barges that connected their settlements to the lakeside capital of Korval and the heart of commerce on Solarson – Solac.

Amongst the people making their daily trek to the eclectic trade city were those whose journeys had spanned days, weeks, and even months. As was common with such travelers, rumors and tales were exchanged to pass the time, to delight one's ears, and even in barter. Most prominent amongst the numerous conversations filling the air were rumors of war in the North. Such talk was relatively commonplace as the mountainous region and its reclusive inhabitants were widely viewed as inhospitable and uncivilized. Some of the travelers told outlandish tales of goblins and dark spirits, while others recounted stories they'd heard from supposed refugees of an army of demons hells-bent on conquering the North in its entirety. However, whether the tales were fables, truths or half-truths, they had remained prominent for so long that many believed war had indeed come to the North. As for its effects on the rest of Solarson, very few believed there would be any ramifications other than enormous profit for those that suckled at war's teat.

For one man, however, the tales he'd heard over the last two weeks were a constant reminder of why he was amongst the throng approaching Solac. Armed as he was with a longsword and heavy-bladed dagger sheathed at his hips, as well as a pair of knives stowed in his boots, he'd found it easy to blend in as one of the many mercenaries headed to Solac in search of work. As such, he found himself privy to an assortment of opinions on the rumors. No matter whom he spoke with or listened to, however, he managed to keep his fears from showing in his gray eyes or from tainting his strong voice. He knew the stark, horrific truth of the North's plight, and its possible implications were beyond the mortals that surrounded him.

Late that afternoon, the menagerie of travelers finally reached Solac and joined the throng seeking entrance. While his athletic frame granted him a measure of space, the cramped conditions not only cut his easy stride down to a plodding shuffle, but also brought with it an unfamiliar warmth. As such, it wasn't long before his white shirt, black breeches, bracers and knee-boots, as well as his waist-length braided black hair, were soaked with sweat. Even the menacing trio of scars that spanned the right side of his hawkish face began to itch some. Worst of all, by the time he reached the wide-open gate set in the sixty-foot tall stone wall, the nearly forgotten sensation had him fidgeting thanks to his sword belt and the straps of his hefty pack rubbing his skin raw. Mercifully, the diligent, leather-armored guards were either oblivious to his discomfort or simply chose to disregard it, as they waved him through after a brief inspection and a series of direct questions. Once through, he stepped out of the flow of traffic and into the mouth of a nearby alleyway before opening himself to his inner fir'gan. As the welcomed warmth of the currents cooled his body and soothed his raw spots, he took a moment to orient himself since it had been quite a while since he'd last set foot in the city.

As he remembered, the city was still an organized sprawl with little separation of rich from poor. From his position, he could see a number of the City Guard patrolling the well-maintained street. This close to the gate – Cresting Sun Gate, he recalled – a series of inns, taverns and stables of modest wooden construction flanked the street, seeking to grab those who were unfamiliar with, or unable to afford, the more upscale establishments deeper within the city. In the distance, he could just make out the robust spires of the palace that occupied the central portion of the city. His destination was northeast of the opulent structure, so with the spires as his guide, he set out at a steady pace.

His braid swaying gently with each stride, he weaved through the mass of humanity traversing the main thoroughfare, passing eclectically dressed pedestrians, rickety wagons, and elaborate carriages. As he progressed, he noted that the buildings, which ranged from small to generously large, now included shops and mass housing, all of which appeared relatively well-maintained. An occasional glance down one of the side streets revealed more of the same, and the few alleys he peered down appeared to be quite clean. It was impressive, to say the least, that such an extensive and populous city could sustain such a level of repair and cleanliness, but he knew better. It was all a glorious facade perpetrated by Solac's ruler, King Drugal. Granted, it benefited the ignorant populace greatly, but it was a facade nonetheless.

Shoving those troubling thoughts aside, he proceeded deeper into the city, where the cacophony of noise grew louder thanks to an increase in the number of inns and taverns, which were soon joined by a host of stalls and hawkers. He then caught sight of one of Solac's few internal walls, and it dawned on him that he was nearing the city's famed Bizarre. Separated from the rest of the city by a twenty-foot tall stone wall, the Bizarre was home to some of the city's most prominent inns, as well as nearly two-hundred shops and vendor stalls. The man figured that, despite providing a more direct route to his destination, it would be incredibly time-consuming to pass through the mass of humanity perusing the Bizarre. As such, he turned north along one of the intersecting avenues.

Making his way north and east through the city, the crowds eventually began to thin out as he neared one of the city's residential districts. Even though he'd visited the city numerous times over the decades, he still found the mix of class and architectural styles both amusing and baffling. There were brick and stone estates – albeit fenced off and guarded day and night – standing alongside modest single- and multi-family habitats, as well as homes that were little more than modest shacks. There were well-manicured grounds adorned with statuary and gardens within a stone's throw of cluttered yards and plots that were little more than cobbles and dirt.

As for the people he passed on the street, they ran the gamut from City Guard to private guard, and from rich to poor. On the surface, they appeared to tolerate one another, but he doubted it went much deeper than that. The poor always outnumbered the well-to-do, and given the hooded glances they exchanged and the air of tension he felt about some of them, he had to wonder what kind of class war might lurk beneath the surface.

An hour and three increasingly lavish residential districts later, he found himself on one of the many stone paths that ran through a park in the northeastern part of the city. Open and flowing, the park was practically empty compared to what he had encountered elsewhere in the city. There were a handful of patrons walking the paths, some were picnicking on mostly brown lawns, while others were seated on benches that were located beneath the trees or arranged around delightful flowerbeds. He also spied a few of the City Guard casually patrolling the park, and a handful of gardeners preparing sections for the winter. Such activity was a quaint reminder of Solac's southerly location. While his home was already firmly entrenched in winter's grasp, Solac was weeks away from that, and its winters were far milder than anything the North would experience.

Winding his way through the park, he came to a sudden halt at a fork in the trail. Standing there with his head slightly cocked, a few of the park patrons eyed him curiously as they proceeded along the right branch. Figuring they believed he was simply unsure which path to choose, he found their passing curiosity mildly amusing. Granted, he was unfamiliar with the park, but he certainly was not lost. As such, he soon proceeded confidently along the left branch and quickly found himself alone. However, he knew the solitude wouldn't last, for he sensed a presence ahead that prudent caution had made difficult to detect until now.

"Ah, the trials of living beneath your enemy's nose," he thought with a mix of sympathy and vexation.

A few meandering turns later, the path deposited him in a dilapidated garden. At one point, it might have been a quaint, secluded area for anyone seeking privacy. Now, however, the shrubbery was overgrown, the gravel-covered ground unkempt, and the fountain of a woman pouring water at the center of it was weatherworn and broken. Dried grass, weeds, and dead flowers crunched beneath his boots as he approached the fountain slowly. Had it been in good condition, he imagined the woman would have seemed angelic, but with the weather stains marring its surface, she appeared to be weeping dark tears – which seemed oddly apt given the circumstances of his visit.

The sudden crunch of gravel behind him snapped him from his reflections, and he spun around, his longsword half-drawn.

Clad in black leather, with a slender, athletic build, and nearly as tall as him, the new arrival had his fingerless-gloved hands extended defensively. There was an alarmed expression painted across his sun-kissed, youthful face, and his normally hooded brown eyes were wide and alert.

Cursing softly as he sheathed his sword, Caldain barked, a hint of irritation in his strong voice, "Damn it, Cid! Don't sneak up on me like that! I could have gutted you!"

The new arrival chuckled and replied with a cocky sense of confidence, "Ah, but you didn't, and that is what counts!" Shaking his head, his thin lips pulled back in a wry smile, he stepped forward and extended his hand, "Damn good to see you, Caldain! It's been far too long!"

With an equally wry smile, Caldain clasped Cid's bracer-ensconced wrist and replied, "Aye, far too long. How are you?"

Breaking the handshake, Cid shrugged nonchalantly. "Better than you, given your short, terse message. Keeping an eye on Drugal and his nest of narcissistic nobles is anything but exciting. You?"

"Could be better. This isn't exactly the way I envisioned paying you a visit."

Cid nodded his shaved head sympathetically. "A damn shame, losing Darius and Cat. Cat was a force to be reckoned with, and Darius was a good man. I wish I'd had a chance to know him better." Cringing slightly, he shook his head. "Corith be good. . . . Two dead Wardens in a matter of weeks on top of the Osterias and Uthariyan Orders long-vacant Preceptor seats. I really don't like what this could mean."

Caldain grimaced before replying, "Agreed. As for Darius — aye, he was that. As you can imagine, Greatjon didn't take his death well."

Cid laughed darkly. "Now, when has the Old Wolf taken anything of that nature well?"

Caldain flashed a dry smirk. "Did I mention Warrick was responsible?"

Wide-eyed, Cid let out a low whistle. "Damn. . . . Crossed probably doesn't even come close to how Greatjon is feeling, eh?"

"Indeed," Caldain replied with a nod.

"Well, what's done is done, and all we can do is move forward." Cid shook his head. "So, what brings you all the way from your quaint island abode? Your message was hardly enlightening."

"Your help."

Cid snorted. "That much I figured out on my own. The question is — with what?"

"I've been tasked with finding Darius' replacement," Caldain responded succinctly, to which Cid let out another low whistle. "Indeed. And while I'd normally be confident that I could complete the task with very little opposition, far too many things have gone horribly wrong to make foolish presumptions. So—"

"You want me to help you Search," Cid finished.

"Exactly."

"Light be good, Cal! I don't know whether to call you foolish, stupid, or just plain crazy! You honestly think two Seekers will be enough should we encounter a powerful Knight or — Light forbid — a Warden?"

"Honestly? No. But," Caldain grinned devilishly, "we can certainly make anyone think twice about getting in our way."

Cid barked a laugh. "Only you could make such a bleak situation sound fun."

"Will you do it then?"

Cid pondered the request for a moment, then offered, "Tell you what — come back to my house, have a drink, fill me in on the details, get a good night's sleep, and I'll give you my answer in the morn'. How does that sound?"

"Well, if that's all I'm going to get from you today, then I might as well enjoy your drink," Caldain replied, his tone rich with sarcasm.

Shaking his head, Cid quipped, "You're an ass, Cal."

Shooting him a broad grin, Caldain retorted playfully, "I know. So, why don't we get moving? I'm parched."

Night had fallen by the time they arrived at Cid's house. Situated in one of the few residential districts in the city's southern portion, the two-story brick residence was as unremarkable as the surrounding domiciles. Occupying a simple, shabby lot that was surrounded by a waist-high, rickety wooden fence, the home's structure and tiny facade appeared slightly unkempt, and all five of its front windows were shrouded with heavy drapes.

"If Cid's goal was to remain inconspicuous, he sure accomplished it with this," Caldain thought, oddly impressed, as they approached the lone gate in the fence. *"No one would think twice about whoever lived here."*

Proceeding through the gate, the hinges of which were in desperate need of oil, they made their way to the domicile's weathered front door. Surprisingly, Caldain felt a sense of relief when Cid unlocked the door and they entered the house. He hadn't been aware of the tension in his body, but upon reflection, it made perfect sense. He was effectively walking about enemy territory in the open. Granted, the members of the Torthos Order did so daily, but with the growing naked aggression of their enemies, he had to wonder if the risk was worth the vigilance.

As Cid secured the entrance, Caldain took in the house. Deeper than it was wide, the residence was bisected by a central hallway, off of which he could see four rooms and a kitchen from his position. Aside from the staircase midway down the hall on the left, and the brightly burning lamps hanging from the plank walls, there was little in the way of impediments or decor.

"It's not much to look at," Cid said as he stepped past Caldain and led him to the second door on the right, "but it is home." Opening the door, he gestured inside. "Wait here. I'll see if I can scrounge up something to drink."

Caldain nodded. "If you don't mind, have you anything to eat?"

Cid shook his head and slapped his forehead. "I must be going daft! Don't know why that didn't occur to me! It's probably been a while since you last ate."

"Indeed," Caldain responded with an amused chuckle.

"Well, no promises, but I'll see if there's something passable laying around," Cid offered before starting down the hall toward the kitchen at the back of the house.

Entering the dark room, Caldain noticed a blood-red candle sitting in a tin holder on a small stand next to the entry. With a thought, he used the currents to light the candle. Between the candlelight and the illumination spilling through the doorway, he could just make out a series of wall-mounted lamps. Picking the candle up by its holder, he started toward the pair of lamps stationed on a mantle on the far side of the room when he heard a loud crash and a string of colorful curses coming from the direction of the kitchen. Chuckling, Caldain reached the lamps and removed the first glass cover. Lighting the wick within, he replaced the cover before repeating the process with the other lamps until the room was bathed in a warm, flickering glow.

The newly illuminated room was small and cozy, but aside from the mantle and lamps, its only furnishings were the door-side stand, and a simple table flanked by two chairs at the center of the room. Unable to figure out what use Cid could possibly have for the space, Caldain blew out the candle he carried and placed it on the table before disconnecting his sheathed sword from his belt and leaning it against the table. Soon after he seated himself, Cid returned carrying a plate of food, two goblets, and a bottle of chilled Velusyian Blue.

Caldain fought down a cringe when he saw that the food was nothing more than bread that looked a bit past its prime and a small bowl of warm but questionably murky soup. Raising a quizzical eyebrow, he quipped, "What took you so long? Have a run-in with some rabid kitchen utensils?"

Cid rolled his eyes as he sat down. Removing his fingerless gloves, he replied drolly, "Har, har, har. Very funny, Cal." Tossing his gloves on the table, he opened the bottle and began pouring a generous amount into the goblets. "Just be glad I'm so magnanimous with my larder and cellar."

Grabbing the bowl of soup and its accompanying wooden spoon, Caldain scooped up a generous amount of the murky contents, lifted it to his nose, and inhaled cautiously. "Magnanimous, huh?" he questioned as he eyed the small bits of meat and vegetables floating in the spoon. "Are you sure you're not simply trying to poison me?"

"Light be good — you're a whiny bastard, aren't you?" Cid retorted playfully with a snort. "Consider it penance for drinking my wine, and just eat the damn food!"

Caldain smirked and put the spoon in his mouth. It was warm and greasy, and the bits of meat and vegetables were a bit tough, but it certainly wasn't the worst meal he'd ever had. Satisfied that it was palatable, he ate a few more spoonfuls before taking a long draw from his goblet. The cool, vibrant and refreshing blue liquid slid down his throat, and he immediately felt the tension in his muscles begin to fade away.

With a wry grin, Cid asked, "Like it, eh?"

"Aye," Caldain replied with a satisfied smile. "New Velusyia, North Fields, fifty-eight-o-two vintage, correct?

"Close. Fifty-eight-twenty-five."

"Ah. . . . Well, still a good year," Caldain offered with a mild hint of disappointment, to which Cid offered a snort of mock disgust.

"Terribly sorry I can't offer you one of those archaic bottles nestled in your keep," Cid responded sarcastically. "Some of us aren't living fossils, thank you very much."

Rolling his eyes, Caldain let the friendly exchange end there.

Taking a sip of his wine, Cid watched Caldain over the rim of his goblet and asked, "So, you want just you and me to rush headlong after the crystal's host, eh? What direction would we be headed?"

"South by southeast," Caldain replied around a mouthful of food.

"South? Into the Wildlands? You sure about that?"

"So far. I haven't checked in a while, but the signal is weak and scattered. I'm hoping for better clarity as I get closer."

Cid shook his head with disbelief. "So the best you've got is a broad, general direction that could have us potentially walking into the dragon's den? You're crazy, you know that?"

"Possibly," Caldain responded with a smirk. "But you're right – running around blindly with the Torani brothers lurking about would be suicide . . . not to mention there are fully functional blackheart nests somewhere. So, I'd prefer to go there better informed and with someone to watch my back."

"Wait. . . . You're telling me we've got to possibly worry about blackhearts as well?" Cid blurted, shocked.

Caldain nodded gravely.

Running a hand over his head, Cid answered with a snort, "Well, you're not asking much. . . ." He suddenly smiled darkly and quipped sarcastically, "Hells, I might as well add to the growing pile of good news – did I mention there are rumors that Melisia is also lurking about the Wildlands?"

Shocked by the revelation, Caldain placed his bowl on the table and sat back heavily. "I hadn't heard that. We've been kept fairly isolated by Darkon." Shaking his head, he added, "I guess I could always seek out Rivinia's help, assuming she's still in Forsaken . . . and willing to lend a hand."

"That reeks of desperation, Cal."

"Possibly. But it sounds like the wolves are circling, Cid. It's a blessing that our newly orphaned crystals are already resonating, and we can't afford for Darius' crystal to remain ownerless."

"*Humph.* I'm beginning to wish Mat was here. Sounds like you could use him way more than me," Cid declared honestly.

Caldain shrugged. "I can't say that I disagree, but it is what it is. I may not like Darkon, but he couldn't have foreseen what befell Blackstone, so I can't blame him for calling on Mat. Still," he flashed a dry smirk, "it would be nice to have Portculim travel officially available."

Cid arched a quizzical eyebrow at the odd qualifier before replying with a shake of his head, "Can't help you there." Letting out a sigh, he cracked a smile and added, "Now, why don't you finish up, and let's talk of better times, eh?"

Morning found Caldain refreshed and eager for Cid's answer. Descending the stairs while he tucked in his shirt, he reached the main level of the house and shouted, "Cid? You about?"

Receiving nothing but silence to his query, Caldain poked his head into each room as he made his way to the rear of the house and the kitchen. As he entered the aged kitchen, he noticed a small table at the center of the room, atop which sat a tin cup next to a tin plate of food. Making his way to the table, he noticed a piece of parchment pinned beneath the plate. Curious, he retrieved the paper as he eyed the biscuits and the cold, greasy bacon that occupied the plate.

"He really needs a lesson on how to host someone," he muttered as he read the note.

Cal,

Headed out to retrieve some goods. Make yourself at home. I'll be back soon.

Shaking his head, Caldain tossed the note on the table, picked up the cup, and sniffed the milk within. "Well, at least this is fresh," he quipped before returning it to the table and picking up the plate.

As he began eating the cold meal, he wandered past the diminutive, empty hearth on the left-hand wall. Reaching the small window nestled between a rickety cupboard and a sink at the rear of the kitchen, he paused and peered through its murky glass. Unsurprisingly, the minimally maintained backyard was as unremarkable as the front yard, and it was even surrounded by a fence that matched the one out front. Switching his gaze to the sky, he was pleased to see that it was clear and appeared to be a mild day.

"Should be a good day to travel," he muttered as he ate.

Once done with his meal, he deposited the plate on the table, then drained the milk. Collecting the dishes, he carried them to the sink and placed them in the stone basin. Wiping his hands on his pants, he was about to leave the kitchen when he heard the front door open.

"That you, Cid?" Caldain called out.

"Yeah! Glad to see you're awake!" Cid responded, followed by the thud of the door shutting.

As he exited the kitchen, Caldain started to retort sarcastically, "Yes, well, thank you for leaving the lov–" only to be brought up short by what he saw.

As tall as Caldain, and dressed in a white tunic, brown breeches and calf-boots, the broad-shouldered, athletic woman next to Cid was a stark contrast to his black leather attire. Hooded brown eyes peered brightly at Caldain from astride a slender nose on her defined, gently bronzed face as her full lips pulled back in a toothy smile. When Caldain made no move to speak, she shook her short-cropped, auburn-haired head and placed her black-fingerless-gloved hands on the upper curves of her broad hips.

"Well, well. . . . If it isn't the Old Hawk himself. What's the matter, Cal? Swallow your tongue?" she asked, her husky voice full of mirth.

"Didn't you get my note?" Cid quipped with a broad grin. "Told you I was going out to pick up some goods."

Blinking rapidly to clear his head, Caldain started forward and practically blurted, "I had no idea. . . . Light be good! It's good to see you, Kay!" Reaching the pair, he offered her his hand.

"*Pfft!* That's all you have for me?" she responded dismissively before stepping forward and pulling him into a fierce, warm hug. "It's been way too long," she stated tenderly.

"Aye, it has," Caldain concurred, his tone joyful, before giving her a squeeze and stepping back from the embrace.

Cid's mischievous grin widened upon noticing Caldain's flush cheeks. "I thought you might like the surprise."

"Yes, well. . . ." Caldain cleared his throat and pulled his gaze from Kay. "What's the occasion?"

Cid shrugged. "Well, I thought we could use the extra hand if we're going to charge off on some damned fool quest."

Although he never really doubted that Cid would agree to accompany him, Kay's appearance had him a bit off balance, which accounted for the shock in his voice when he blinked rapidly and asked him, seemingly oblivious to the extra hand comment, "You're coming with me?"

"That he is," replied Kay with a sly grin. "And I'm going too."

Swinging his gaze to Kay, Caldain noticed, for the first time, that she was armed. Peaking over her right shoulder was the leather-wrapped grip, and the medallion pommel of the hefty bastard sword sheathed across her back. A quick glance at her belt showed that she also had a functional long-knife sheathed on her right hip.

The sobering sight of her weapons cleared his head of any remaining surprise, and he met her brown eyes, which were alight with a hint of mirth, as he asked, "Won't this leave Torthos severely underpowered?"

Kay chuckled. "Underpowered against what? We know that Drugal is helping the Wardens of Shadow in some fashion, but in all the time we've been monitoring him, we've noticed nothing of consequence." Folding her arms beneath her modest bosom, she shrugged. "Besides, do you really think we could stand against one of the Betrayers if they struck here in force? As far as I'm concerned, this has been a fool's errand from the start, and the fewer of us here, the less likely something catastrophic could happen to us."

Caldain smirked. "I can't disagree with you. But do you really think we'll fare any differently should we run into the Toranis?"

"Maybe not," replied Cid, "but as you mentioned, we stand a mite better chance together than just you alone." A wry grin spread across his face. "Besides, there's always Rivinia," he reminded him.

Caldain hung his head. "Light help me," he said with a chuckle. Looking up, he added, "Fine. I appreciate the help. Just don't start complaining if things go sideways."

Kay grinned and patted him on the cheek as she quipped, "Same goes for you, sweetie." She then stepped around him and started down the hall, adding, "Now run along and get ready. The day's wasting away."

Watching her walk to the kitchen, Caldain said to Cid, "Well, this will be interesting."

Scoffing, Cid replied, "You're telling me. At least you didn't have to grow up with her." Shaking his head, he clapped Caldain on the shoulder and jabbed, "Now do as the lady says. Time's a-wasting."

*

Solac was silent under the moonless night, and the palace of King Drugal reflected this. All throughout the sprawling complex of ruddy stone spires, domes and bridges, the majority of the windows were dark. Most of the inhabitants had long since taken to their beds, and even a few of the night watch dozed at their posts. There were those, however, who stirred with activity while the world slumbered.

Deep beneath the palace, where darkness held sway, King Drugal Samora gazed down into the deep abyss below him. He had no idea how deep the nest was, but over the years, he had seen several unfortunate souls tumble over the wooden railings of the many walkways that circled the structure, and not once had he heard an impact. Despite the danger of suffering such a fate, the walkways were one of the few places he could tolerate in the nest. Yes, he still risked soiling his silk and satin attire. Yes, he still had to bear witness to the twisted visage of the blackhearts and their harsh, guttural language; and yes, he still had to tolerate the rank stench that permeated the air, but it was a small price to pay to avoid the slime-coated and humid incubation tunnels. The day he could be truly free of the foul nest would be a blessing, but he was no fool and understood the value of patience. If there was one thing he had learned over the last twenty years of his rule, it was that patience was more effective than loyal friends and deadlier than the fiercest of enemies.

As his contemplative black eyes stared into the dark depths from beneath his neatly trimmed, graying eyebrows, he pulled a small, filigreed silver container from his belt. Releasing the lid latch, he held the container to his nose and inhaled deeply. The florid fragrance immediately banished the odious stench that pervaded his nose, but he knew it was only a temporary reprieve. As long as he remained within the nest, the horrific odor would return.

Sealing and returning the container to his belt, Drugal then brushed his blue satin doublet and the sleeves of his white silk shirt clear of the flaky back substance that had settled there. Smoothing out his doublet over his modest belly, he sneered at the rain of flakes that flittered on the air currents like midges. Another curse of the nest that he looked forward to being rid of. The flakes were constantly there, and while he knew very well what was responsible for the incessant black snowfall, he forced himself not to dwell on such an unpleasant subject.

Running his hands over his face, which the years were slowly gracing with more wrinkles, he then ran them through his more-white-than-black, shoulder-length hair to clear himself of the black debris. Just as he finished, he felt a subtle shift in temperature behind him. Gathering himself, he set a small, welcoming smile on his full lips, turned and bowed low. "Welcome, Master."

Despite the numerous torches mounted throughout the nest, there was very little Drugal could discern about the shadow-shrouded figure before him. There was the occasional flash of yellow eyes, and a hint of pale white skin within the shadows of an unusually wide hood, but nothing that could tell him with any definitiveness who his master actually was.

"I trust thou hath kept thine eyes open to events within thine city?" questioned a cold male voice that seemed to echo in upon itself.

Easily hiding his displeasure at such a slanderous insinuation, Drugal replied smoothly in his dry, husky voice, "I have, Master. The man you warned me of left the city earlier today along with the Kaskia siblings. Quite frankly, I'm glad to be done with that farce. It was an unwanted distraction."

"I'm well aware of thine displeasure with the arrangement, but it hath served its purpose. Is the device with them?"

"Of course, Master," Drugal replied, bristling at another jab at his competency. "We will be able to track them with ease, but I see no point in this. If this Stelariuos Seeker is of such concern, why not send one of your compatriots or simply eliminate him yourself?"

"*Tsk, tsk*. Such contempt 'tis not becoming of one such as thineself. 'Tis lucky for thee I am not as volatile as mine predecessor."

Drugal inclined his head. "Your benevolence is most appreciated, Master."

"Indeed," the shadowed formed replied, his tone nakedly patronizing. "However, to answer thine question, the Seeker 'tis an itch that must be scratched, and thou art the one I wish to handle the situation."

"Me?" Drugal asked incredulously.

"Aye. I hath not the time nor the energy to spare on such an insect—"

"*And I do?*" Drugal thought.

"—and mine associates art involved with their own tasks." Seeing a hint of Drugal's dissatisfaction with the mission, he added, "Doth not fret, for I am not foolish enough to send thee or thine men after them; for one dost not kill a bear with a stick. Send two squads of blackhearts forth to trail them from a distance. Should their presence pose a threat to our activities in the South, Melisia shalt send forth reinforcements to ensure they art eliminated with judicious prejudice."

Drugal nodded. "And if their course is otherwise, Master?"

"Follow unto the end and ensure the crystal and its host art secured before eliminating the Light's minions."

"All of them?"

"Indeed."

Drugal grinned. "It will be my pleasure, Master."

Chapter Two

Nestled in the foothills of the Dragonspine Mountains, Shadowtown was the last bastion of civilization before entering the treacherous mountain range. More of a large town than a city, the wood-walled Shadowtown not only served as the gateway to the only serviceable trade route through the Dragonspine, but it was also the only significant connection to the outside world for those dwelling in the wild region.

Founded as a mining and logging community long before House Kylinis annexed the lands into Galvat, Shadowtown retained its autonomy through the years in exchange for a generous tribute. Because of the lack of House oversight and its remote location, Shadowtown and the outlying communities became a destination for those wishing to cast off society's shackles, be they criminals or those sick of civilization. With such a suspect population, it was easy for those unfamiliar with the town to perceive it as a lawless abode, which wasn't far from the truth since Shadowtown's attempts to gloss over its questionable traits were superficial. Most of the predominantly wooden structures were well maintained, the streets were kept clean, and there were regular patrols, but if one bothered to look past the facade, one could see the blatant clues to the city's true self. Its wealthy lived in considerably more opulent stone structures that were isolated behind Shadowtown's lone internal stone wall, guards were abusive and subjective in their enforcement of the law, and the poor could easily be found living in squalor all about the city.

From his position on the small, rustic restaurant's street-side patio, the powerfully-built, bald-headed Dromick struggled to ignore his displeasure with the city. Clad in brown leathers over a white shirt and black breeches, and with his naked broadsword leaning against his small table, the general sat at his small table and watched the streets while he swirled his mug of passable beer. As he had done throughout his midday meal, he watched the denizens of Shadowtown with his hard black eyes, alert for any sign of the man he was supposed to meet. The city and the behavior of its populace were anathema to his sense of honor, and while he wished he could ignore it, its presence was as intrusive and undeniable as the machinations of nobles. Too often in his already overextended stay, he had witnessed hushed conversations and dealings that reeked of maliciousness and deception. As such, be they laborer, merchant, rich or poor in appearance, he quickly found himself far warier of unfamiliar faces than usual. However, if there was one bit of solace to be found, it was in the lack of questions. As of yet, no one had inquired about his business in the city, and his reserved attitude seemed to fit Shadowtown well.

Still, such a boon did little to improve his mood. In fact, his business in Shadowtown was proving to be a further source of irritation since his contact was late. To be fair, Dromick was partly responsible for his excessive exposure to the town since he'd arrived two days early, but that was a moot point as far as he was concerned. He had a tight schedule to maintain, and the man was now a day late. Granted, his associate had a longer journey, but it was no excuse for his tardiness. There were too many unknowns to account for in this venture, so time lost on the familiar parts of the trek was time that would probably need to be made up, possibly under less-than-desirable circumstances. As such, Dromick felt it was likely to make the journey far more grueling than it needed to be.

Looking skyward, he smirked dryly. On the bright side, the weather did seem to be cooperating. While there was a chill in the air, winter had barely begun to show its face, and it rarely struck with ferocity this far south. So, there was a good chance they could make up some of the lost time crossing the mountains. Furthermore, once they were through the Dragonspine – at least as far as he understood it – winter's wrath would be nothing more than rumor and hearsay.

A sudden commotion just down the street drew his and the other restaurant patrons' attention. From what Dromick could see, a brawl had begun between two laborers, most likely loggers given their woolen attire, in front of a sundries shop. The pedestrian traffic slowed as people stopped to gawk at the two bearded, burly men, and even the shop's portly attendant appeared in the establishment's doorway, seemingly eager to watch the brawl. Punches quickly gave way to grappling, and the pair fell to the ground in an unceremonious heap. Though the crowd prevented Dromick from observing the pair on the ground, the shouts and cheers told him the brawl continued with vigor.

A dry, disgusted smirk tugged at the lips of Dromick's grizzled face as he heard authoritative shouts from down the street ordering the way cleared. If there was one thing about Shadowtown that aggravated him more than the city's questionable morals and behavior, it was the Shadow Guard. Girded in black leather armor, the right shoulder of which displayed a badge featuring a black mountain against a yellow field, the Shadow Guard was infamous for their corruption and excessively brutal tactics. While the thought of accepting such behavior soured Dromick's stomach, he could certainly understand, and even appreciate, the use of measured force to control the unruly when needed – especially in a remote labor town such as Shadowtown. However, the rumors he'd heard indicated that the Shadow Guard gleefully used disproportionate violence as their primary tool of enforcement. To his chagrin, they appeared to be living up to their reputation.

While they shouted and cursed warnings to clear the way, anyone too slow to obey found themselves on the receiving end of a fist or club. By the time they reached the brawling pair, there was a trail of bleeding and broken pedestrians in their wake. The sight was appalling to Dromick, and his sense of honor and integrity was further bruised by the Shadow Guard's actions upon reaching the brawlers. Without even attempting to pull the two apart, the guards proceeded to bludgeon the pair into unconsciousness, bringing a quick end to the melee. As the guards dragged their limp bodies away to whatever served as a prison in Shadowtown, the crowd quickly dispersed, almost as if nothing had happened.

Repressing a growl of disgust at the Shadow Guard's actions, not to mention the accepting nature of the citizenry, Dromick drained the last of his beer and set the mug down hard.

Just as he was about to stand, he heard from behind him, "Careful that you don't cause a scene yourself. I'd hate to see the carnage it would cause."

Reaching for his simple broadsword as he stood, Dromick turned and saw one of the tallest and largest Pelasians he had ever seen. Cursing, Dromick leaned his sword back against the table and declared in a throaty voice, "You're late."

"My apologies," the scarred, dark-skinned man replied with a dry smile that looked macabre on his broad, square-jawed face due to the missing portion of his upper lip, "I had an unexpected delay on the road," he rumbled in his strikingly deep voice.

Extending a hand to the man, who clasped the proffered wrist with a meaty paw of his own, Dromick arched a graying dark eyebrow and replied, "Unexpected, eh?" Withdrawing his hand, Dromick motioned to an empty chair at his table. "Why don't you have a seat and regale me with the tale? It must be something daunting to delay the terrifying Shinks."

Shinks grunted and moved to the seat, his black-booted feet thudding on the patio and his studded black leather armor creaking softly. Removing his pack, he pulled his full-moon axe from his back, the ironwood shaft of which featured a spiked pommel strung with two hawk feathers, before leaning them against the table. As he lowered himself into the chair, a middle-aged woman in a drab dress that exposed far too much olive-skinned bosom stopped at their table.

"Can I get you gents anything?" she drawled in a rough voice with a smile that exposed slowly yellowing teeth in a face marred by a hard life and topped with a mop of curly red hair.

"I'm fine," Dromick replied. Eying Shinks, he asked, "You?"

Meeting the small green eyes of the waitress with his amber gaze, Shinks asked, "Do you have any Sand Cut Ale?"

The waitress chuckled. "We'd be daft not to this close to the desert."

Shinks nodded. "A pint of that, if you please."

"One pint, coming up," she responded before making her way back inside.

"Sand Cut? Afraid I'm not familiar with that particular brew."

"It's one of the few Pelasian beverages that is affordable and isn't wine. We make very few ales, and most of those are nearly as valued by the nobility as their precious vineyards. This isn't likely to be the best — we're too far away from the breweries to get an authentic brew — but it will suffice until we're in the desert."

Dromick shook his head and chuckled. "I still find it hard to believe grapes can survive the heat."

Shinks smiled again and ran his hands over his shaved pate, which showed hints of white in the stubble. "Not all is as it seems, Dromick. The sands are a fickle mistress, but she has secrets that she will share with those patient enough to coax them from her."

The waitress returned at that moment and placed the drink before Shinks. Pulling an eight-sided gold talon from his pouch, Shinks handed it to her, which she took with a slight bow before wandering to one of the other tables in need of attention.

"You talk as if the Scorchlands is a woman to be wooed," Dromick stated as he watched Shinks sniff at the liquid before taking a long draw from the dark, frothy drink.

Placing the mug on the table with a small grimace, Shinks said, "As I said, it's not the same here; it lacks the heat of the true brew. As for the desert, she is just that — treat her with respect and love, and she will provide you with what you need to survive. Scorn her, and her wrath will flay the skin from your bones."

Dromick wanted to laugh. He'd heard similar talk from Northerners about the winters and the Highlands, and couldn't help but think they were all crazy. However, he knew better than to voice his skepticism, so instead, he said, "I'll just have to trust you. I hardly have the experience to refute your claims." Determined to return the conversation to more important matters, Dromick added, "So, you were going to tell me what kept you."

"Again, I apologize. I left the day the missive arrived and was making good progress. Along the way, I encountered an elderly Family friend who was traveling alone. I felt it would be dishonorable to ignore an elder, so I broke bread with him and escorted him to the nearest community."

Dromick silently thanked Shinks for his discretion when referencing House Suldamik, but found he had to ask, "Family friend? Who might that be?"

Shinks sipped from his mug again. "A jeweler of some renown. Apparently, he wished to spend his remaining days somewhere warm, so I pointed him in the direction of a trustworthy caravan."

"Ah, I see," Dromick replied with a knowing grin. "Well, I wish him Deo's best. His final work was quite the masterpiece."

"I would imagine so." Shinks hesitated a moment. While he and Dromick were friends, that friendship was more casual than anything else, so they tended to steer clear of touchy subjects when they were together. However, given the nature of their mission, he felt such courtesy was now ill-suited. "I must admit that I was shocked to hear the news. It made me wonder if he suffered some sort of brain injury from all our sessions."

It took Dromick a moment to figure out what Shinks was referring to, but when he did, he offered the Pelasian a slow nod. "You're not alone. I and others are concerned about his decision, thus this journey."

"I would expect nothing less from you, Dromick. Your loyalty is without question, and I know you would defend him with your life if necessary."

They fell quiet after that, each man lost in their own thoughts. Finally, after Shinks finished off his drink, he asked, "When do you wish to leave?"

"No later than noon tomorrow if possible. We are already behind schedule," Dromick stated adamantly.

Shinks nodded. "That should be possible. You will want a change of clothes, though."

Dromick smirked. "What's wrong with my attire?"

"Nothing . . . if you want to suffer, or call attention to yourself. While we trade with outsiders, their presence in the Scorchlands is reluctantly tolerated; the less attention we draw to ourselves, the better off we will be. Unfortunately, that is the least of your concerns."

Dromick scoffed. "Sounds important enough to me."

"It is, but the weather is unlike anything you have experienced. Dressed as you are now, not only will you draw unwanted eyes, but even with winter's approach, you will likely cook like a holiday pig."

"That bad, eh?"

"Words cannot describe it sufficiently."

A dry smirk crept onto Dromick's face below his broad nose. "Well then, I guess I should let you check the supplies that were arranged for us, and trust you'll see that I am properly equipped."

"Aye."

Dromick nodded. "Good. Then, if that is all settled, do you have a place to stay the night?"

"Not yet. I came straight here."

"You can bunk with me. First things first, though — let's see about the supplies we need before nightfall. The last thing I want to do is be on these Deo-forsaken streets at night."

Morning found the two men already attending to their remaining business in the city. Shinks' inspection of their prearranged supplies had seen him discard several things he deemed unfit for desert life. While they could have purchased replacements that evening, Dromick's request to be off the streets before nightfall gave them little time to peruse the vendors. So, after a hearty breakfast, they spent the rest of the morning visiting various shops for what they needed at an acceptable price. While it was an uneventful venture, it wasn't without its surprises for Dromick. Specifically, he found some of Shinks' purchases a bit . . . odd. As far as Dromick was concerned, the inordinate amount of waterskins was uncalled for, the additional blankets pointless, and the black robes absurdly silly. Shinks did his best to explain why such provisions were necessary, but Dromick had a hard time accepting that desert nights could get dangerously cold, and that dark robes would keep them cool during the day. He did, however, eventually concede that carrying as much water as possible was prudent and that a head covering would not only keep their heads from burning in the relentless sun, but would also keep the heat from addling their minds.

By the time they were done, noon was nearly upon them – much to Dromick's chagrin. Given the time of day, they decided to load their goods onto their mounts and pack mule, which were stabled near the South Gate, before partaking of a light lunch at the inn across the street. After finishing an inexpensive and altogether unsatisfying meal of day-old bread and a meaty, greasy soup, Dromick and Shinks retrieved their mounts and mule before joining the modest line of people seeking egress via the South Gate.

Even this late in the year and with the ongoing war, there was still trade, albeit exclusively with House Suldamik and its allies; as such, the line of people departing Shadowtown contained several small trade caravans. While there were some wagons small enough to handle the mountain paths, beasts of burden appeared to be the cargo transportation of choice. Dromick could see several pack mules and a few of the native, large mountain goats; one of the beasts, however, was unlike anything he had seen before.

The humpbacked beast was broad, stout, and covered in shaggy brown fur. Its mane mostly obscured its small, round head, but Dromick could see a long snout protruding from the tangle, as well as a pair of black horns curling around a pair of ears that reminded him of an alert rabbit.

"It's called a gormel," Shinks said upon noticing Dromick's curious gaze.

"I've never seen anything like it."

"Not many natives beyond Shadowtown have. The beast is desert bred and born, and Pelasians value them greatly."

Dromick eyed the beast again. "I don't see anything special about it other than that it reminds me of a stunted bramhen."

"Might be that they are related," Shinks replied with a shrug. "But you see its large humped back? The beast stores water in it."

"You're joking?" Dromick asked with a chuckle.

"I am not," Shinks answered with a shake of his head. "To survive the desert, beast and man must adapt. You will see much in the Scorchlands that is different and unusual to you."

"Oh, really?"

"Aye," Shinks replied as the line trudged forward. "There are beasts the likes of which you have never seen that call the desert home, and many Pelasians – many Ithikiains in particular – still believe magic exists in the world." He chuckled. "There are even deep-desert dwellers that still worship the ancient spirits and claim to practice the magical arts."

"Sounds like a lot of mystical nonsense to me," Dromick replied with a snort.

Shinks shrugged. "Might be that is true; I have only heard rumors. But, by Northern standards, that will not be the worst thing you will see."

Dromick looked at him quizzically, but before he could question Shinks' statement, they reached the South Gate, and one of the Shadow Guard, a particularly grizzled and stout man with a thick beard and shaved pate, stepped before them with an extended hand and barked, "Halt fer inspection, boys!"

Both Dromick and Shinks did as he asked, though each of them fought back the urge to respond angrily to the derisive way the man addressed them. Instead, Dromick flashed the man a warm smile and said, "By all means, have a look."

The man motioned to his companion on the other side of them – a shaved-headed, stout woman who had the look of a brawler about her – and replied, "Aye, we'll be doin' just that."

As the two Shadow Guards made a show of inspecting their saddlebags and the provisions secured to the mule, the man said, "Travelin' mighty light fer traders, eh? Ain't got enough 'ere ta make it much past the Spires."

"We're not traders," Dromick responded. "My friend's mother passed recently, and we're on our way to pay our respects."

"Is that so?" the guard quipped. Looking at the female guard, he asked, "Gio – how's it lookin'?"

"Nothing 'ere, Sergeant. Just appear to be a couple of damn fools, if you ask me," the woman responded gruffly.

Grunting, the sergeant returned his gaze to Dromick and said, "Right. Yer clear, but a word o' advice if ya don't mind."

"Please," Dromick stated, growing a bit exasperated with the delay.

"There's been an issue with bandits o' late, what with the number of sods fleeing tha war and tha piss-pot, hells-taken lands of House Thakian and Astica. Mind you, we patrol the pass this side o' tha Dragonspine well, and they don't go near tha waystations, but two lone souls like ye two might make fer a juicy target."

Dromick couldn't find a reason to be angry with the man for his observations of two of House Suldamik's vital supporters. After all, his own feelings on the two Houses weren't too far removed from the sergeant's, but the man's patronizing warning made him want to gnash his teeth. Fighting down his annoyance, Dromick said, "Thank you for the warning; we'll keep it in mind," before mounting up and motioning for Shinks to do the same. Once Shinks had done so, Dromick nodded to the guard and nudged his horse forward.

As the two passed through the gate, and the next group approached, Gio winked at the sergeant. Nodding to her, he fought down the urge to grin before rubbing his large nose, signaling their associate hidden in the gatehouse. Gio had a knack for spotting hidden pockets and caches, and had marked the foolish pair as much wealthier than they appeared, which, in turn, made them far too easy of a target to pass up. Whatever their reason for venturing into the Deo-forsaken desert, the two men would be dead long before they could lay eyes on it.

Scowling to cover up his building glee, the sergeant barked at the caravan that had come to a halt before him, "Alright, open them wagons and chests fer inspection! And don't be given me any lip, or I'll see yer goods confiscated and ye slapped in irons!"

"Well, those two were about as transparent as water," Shinks finally grunted once they entered the woods a few hundred yards beyond the gate.

"Agreed," Dromick said with a snort of disgust as he peered down the well-manicured path. They were alone for now, having quickly passed the traders who'd left the city before them. "I'd say we've been marked and can expect visitors eventually. Any idea where they might greet us?" he asked as he checked to make sure his sword was loose in its saddle scabbard.

"Not for a couple of days, I would guess," Shinks replied as he scratched his chin. "I don't know how much of the Shadow Guard would be involved in such a scheme, but there are too many eyes this close to Shadowtown. I'd wait till we're nearing Pinnacle Waystation; that's the longest stretch between waystations, and tends to be the most isolated."

"What about after Pinnacle?"

Shinks grinned. "That would not be wise. The Kalu'te'aure patrol the Scorchlands' side of the Dragonspine, and they do not take well to bandits."

"Well, then — we'll just have to be alert until then. I trust you're up for a fight if it comes to that?"

Shinks nodded. "Aye, I am."

Bolstered by Shinks' confidence, Dromick grinned and replied, "Good. I'd hate to think sitting snuggly behind a fort's walls has made you soft."

Shinks grunted. "While I worry about my former station, you have nothing to fear. We'll make them wish they were still babes suckling at their mother's teat if they dare to cross blades with us."

Watching from the branches of the trees flanking the path, the deceptively slim Shalusyian's dark-blue eyes followed the pair down the trail. Fir'gan or not, trailing Dromick had been a trifling task. While he enjoyed his guise as a scout for House Suldamik, it was refreshing to be free of the charade for a time, even if it meant returning to the desert.

Adjusting his position slightly, his dark, green-accented leather armor was silent, and the branch barely moved as he shifted and looked at the sky. His quarry still had plenty of daylight, and would likely make it halfway to the first way station. He was in agreement with the duo; it would be foolish for raiders to operate this close to Shadowtown. However, such interference left him concerned.

Pushing his short-cut black hair out of his slightly round, angular face, he closed his gently up-tilted eyes and reached northward along the currents. It took only a moment for him to find the familiar presence, and he soon heard a throaty, feminine voice in his head.

"Tsumasta — I didn't expect to hear from you so soon."

"My apologies, Mistress. There is a new wrinkle to my hunt, and I did not want to act without your permission."

He could almost see her patronizing, red-lipped smile as she purred, *"Poor Tsumasta . . . you are always seeking to please, aren't you?"*

"You're disappointment is the greatest shame I could suffer, Mistress."

"Ah, but you never have — no matter what I've asked of you. So, what is it that puzzled my pet so?"

"Bandits, Mistress," he replied before hastily adding, *"Nothing that cannot be handled, but I did not know if I should intervene if these bandits attack Suldamik's men."*

"You think that is a possibility?"

"It is possible."

She paused.

"Mistress?"

"Make sure Suldamik's men survive. I want them to know the fate that awaits everyone before they die."

"Very well, Mistress — I will see to it they survive."

"Good, my pet." She paused again. *"A word of warning, though — for now, do not contact me or our allies unless it is imperative."*

Tsumasta arched an eyebrow. *"Is there a problem, Mistress?"*

"Possibly," she responded with a mix of barely concealed concern and dread. *"There is a familiar presence on Triclose — and a dangerous one at that."*

Tsumasta's eyes widened at her tone. She only sounded that way when it involved one man, and that notion twisted Tsumasta's stomach. If what she believed was true, then caution had just become paramount. *"Understood, Mistress. I will be alert for his presence on the currents."*

"Good. I have matters to attend to now. Keep to the Darkness, my pet," she replied before severing the link.

Turning his attention back to his prey, Hirok Tsumasta's eyes narrowed in thought. A simple stalk had just become far more complicated than he could have anticipated. If what his mistress said was true, not only was he on his own, but he would have to remain alert for a very dangerous enemy. Granted, he saw no reason for him to come south . . . unless he somehow knew of Alestra's operation.

Still. . . .

Shrugging, he stood up, balancing nimbly on the branch, and chuckled. "A Knight's work is never done," he said to the sky before vanishing in a swirl of wind and dead leaves.

*

Finding the bandits proved to be a relatively easy task; in fact, Hirok located them that very evening. As the larger of the two Suldamik soldiers had guessed, the bandits had a camp near the empty stretch before Pinnacle Waystation. Well hidden by the mountain forest, massive boulders and stone outcroppings, they were using a series of shallow caves as their base of operations. From his position crouched in the boughs of an ancient mountain oak, Hirok noted that the group consisted of a dozen men and women who were clearly not your typical bandits. Not only did they appear well-fed and organized, but their ragtag assortment of equipment appeared to be in very good shape despite superficial efforts to make it look worn. In all likelihood, they were in league with the Shadow Guard or actually part of it. Hirok had no issue believing that the unscrupulous rulers of Shadowtown would do such a thing. Not that it mattered to him. If it wasn't for his mistress' desire that Suldamik's men make it south safely, he wouldn't even waste his time on these lowly beings.

While he could have eliminated them then and there, he decided there was no fun in that. If he was going to exert energy over such feeble prey, he figured he might as well have some fun. As such, after scouring the currents gently for a bit later that night, he found what he was looking for about an hour southwest of the bandit's camp. Leaping from his perch, he used the currents to cushion and silence his landing. Then, with fir'gan illuminating his surroundings and speeding his journey, he sprinted off. After about half an hour, he arrived at a valley that ran northeast to southwest between towering peaks. Standing on a rocky outcropping that jutted from the surrounding forest along the valley ridge, it was clear the vale was vast, with most of it enveloped by a deep darkness thanks to the moonless night. Thankfully, his fir'gan-sensitive eyes negated that handicap. Not only could he easily see the tree-filled valley walls, but also the stone-littered fields of its floor far below his perch.

He quickly realized that while there was a decent amount of wildlife in the vale, much of which was asleep, his target wasn't in the immediate area. As such, he let his gaze follow the subtle influence on the currents to the southwest end of the valley, where a modest waterfall fed a small stream that cut through a third of the vale. Smiling, Hirok took off at a fir'gan-fueled sprint along the ridge, making his way nimbly through the natural obstacle course of trees, rocks, underbrush, and the occasional nocturnal creature. Once he drew parallel to the waterfall's plunge pool, he used the currents to mask his scent and footfalls before quickly jogging down the wooded mountainside to the valley floor.

Once there, it took only a brief moment for him to reach the pool, the rippling water of which lapped gently at its banks. Jogging along the rocky shore to the accompaniment of the waterfall's soft roar, he saw that the falling liquid served as a partial curtain for a large cave in the cliffside, which doubled as his target's den. As he drew near, his instincts kicked in, and he slowed his pace. While he had nothing to fear from the creature, he not only wanted this to go smoothly, but he also found it wise to practice such precautions even when his wellbeing wasn't threatened. Therefore, he crept up to the edge of the cave on silent feet before peeking within where darkness reigned supreme. Without the soft blue light provided by the flowing fir'gan, the only hint that his prey resided within would have been the gentle rumble of its steady breathing, which was nearly masked by the waterfall's roar. However, thanks to the currents, Hirok could see his objective quite clearly and smiled.

Lying asleep at the center of the cave was arguably the fourth most dangerous member of the drakuma family. From its squared-off snout to the tip of its mace-like tail, the twelve-foot-long female was armored in rough, opalescent gray scales. Its blocky, boulder-like head with its horned snout and spiked jawline rested on massive, four-fingered, talon-tipped paws that were connected to compact and powerful arms that featured reinforced spiked joints. A mane of solid black hair framed its head like a jagged collar before running down its back, where stubby stone spikes that reminded Hirok of a pine-ferret's coat of quills protruded from the mass of hair.

"Oh yes, this will do nicely," Hirok thought as he moved to the center of the cave's maw. *"Now for the bait. . . ."*

Once more, the currents allowed him to see something no one else could have in the darkness. This time, though, it was the fir'gan's flow instead of its light that aided Hirok in finding what he sought, which was tucked tightly against its mother's flank. Only about three feet in length, with stubby horns and a back free of spikes, the drakuma cub grunted softly as it dreamed. It was much younger than Hirok expected, maybe only four months, but that was just fine by him. At this early stage in its life, a drakuma's scales had yet to fully harden and, more importantly, its connection to the currents was tentative at best, which made it very easy prey.

With a sly smirk, Hirok reached out with the currents, careful not to disturb the mother, and wrapped them tightly around the cub. The infant drakuma moaned slightly in discomfort as the strands of fir'gan tightened around it, but neither it nor its mother stirred. Readying the fir'gan within him for what was to come, Hirok then yanked on the currents binding the cub. The young drakuma awakened instantly as the strands of power clamped down on it, causing the cub to bellow forth a high-pitched roar as it was pulled airborne, waking its mother from her slumber.

The elder drakuma's mountain-gray eyes flew open at the cry, and she sprang to her feet with speed that no nearly eight-foot-tall beast should possess. With the currents already feeding her information about the situation, her enraged gaze immediately focused on Hirok and her cub, who was suspended at his side. The mother's fury erupted at the sight, bursting forth as an ear-splitting roar that rattled the cave violently before she pounced toward her child's kidnapper with lethal intent. As soon as the mother made her move, Hirok lept backward, his fir'gan-fueled legs propelling him through the waterfall, easily avoiding the bold attack. Landing near the middle of the pool on a platform of air, he watched as the crag drakuma cautiously emerged from its den.

With water pouring down her shoulders and maned head like a veil, the drakuma's gaze was keenly focused on Hirok. Her eyes and the currents told her this foolish, fleshy creature could use fir'gan, but that mattered little to her. This creature that dared to steal her child was scale-free and soft, which meant it was far weaker than a drakuma, and would die easily enough. That realization suddenly caused a violent snarl to split her maw, revealing her short but wicked, fist-sized teeth. Then, with speed that would have overwhelmed a normal human, the drakuma reared up and slammed her paws down, launching a barrage of stone spikes from the ground toward Hirok as if they were shot from a ballista.

Hirok was mildly impressed by the display, but he easily managed to leap clear of the barrage. Landing on the shore with almost casual disdain as the spikes flew off into the darkness, he watched the mother drakuma quickly follow him, propelling herself through the air with her powerful legs. Landing short of Hirok with an earth-shaking thud and a mighty roar, the crag drakuma ripped at the currents violently, causing waves of earthen spikes to erupt around her. Racing outward in all directions with horrific speed, the jagged spikes closed on Hirok far quicker than he would have liked, forcing him to quick-stepped back and leap with fir'gan-infused strength to avoid the fierce attack.

Touching down on the shattered ground just beyond the last stone wave of death, Hirok made sure the drakuma could see him clearly before he grinned and compressed a blade of air out of the currents, which he then used to slice through the vulnerable hide of the cub's leg. The beast's panicked cries flared into a roar of pain as the blade cut deep, severing muscles and tendons as if they were wet parchment. As blood poured from the wound, the dark liquid turning into a rain of pebbles that bounced off the ground before fading away, the cub valiantly tried to wriggle free of its fir'gan bindings, but nothing it did could weaken Hirok's hold.

The violence in the mother's eyes flared at the sight of her now wounded cub, and the currents around her began to writhe viciously.

"That's it, beast! I want you right on the edge of madness!" he thought as he noted the wild, enraged light burning in her eyes the moment before the currents hardened in front of her and, with a bone-chilling roar, she charged.

Stone spikes shattered before the charging mini-mountain and her ram of hardened air, launching shards of jagged rock everywhere. Quick footwork and a barrier of air kept Hirok from being hit by the shrapnel as he turned and sprinted off with enough speed to keep the mother drakuma close enough to see her frantic cub, but unable to easily strike.

Even for a Knight of his strength, the chase that late night and into the early morning was exhilarating. The crag drakuma was much stronger than he had anticipated, and her attacks were near relentless. Time and again, he was forced to dodge waves of earthen spikes and stone projectiles the mother sent his way, the yawning chasms she tore in the ground, and all the collateral debris. Every now and then, when Hirok felt the mother was losing her hunger for the chase or was slowing down a bit, he would let her close nearly within physical striking distance, or he would inflict more pain on the cub. Without fail, the prodding would reignite the mother's determination and rage, and the chase would resume at full strength once more.

By the time dawn broke in full, Hirok had led the crag drakuma nearly to the raiders' camp. Putting a bit more distance between him and the beast, Hirok eventually came to a stop and faced his pursuer. With a red sky and the woods as a backdrop, Hirok hefted the drakuma cub so that its mother could clearly see it as she approached at a run, eliciting a growl of violence from her. The infant drakuma, its throat raw from crying out for so long, could only whimper in protest as Hirok molded its bindings into strands of air wrapped around its neck and back legs, which he used to stretch the young beast taut. With malicious glee, he then forged a blade of air out of the currents before violently ripping the fir'gan weapon across the cub, splitting it in half. As bloody viscera slipped from the cub's remains, and blood showered the ground in a rain of pebbles, the mother came to a violent halt, bewildered by the death of her cub.

Hirok was momentarily stunned when the mother tossed her head back and let out a fir'gan-fueled roar filled with soul-crushing anguish. The concussive force of the cry echoed about the mountains like thunder and rattled Hirok's head violently, causing him to stumble. Shaking his head to clear it, Hirok's vision focused on the enraged drakuma just in time to see her send a massive wave of towering spikes tearing across the ground toward him. Moving quickly, he tried to jump clear and raise an air shield along his back, but this time, he wasn't fast enough. A jagged spike caught him in his right leg just as he got airborne, tearing through his knee with enough force to nearly sever it. For an instant, the pain overwhelmed Hirok, and he almost lost his fir'gan grip on the cub as he flopped over his shattered leg. Grimacing, Hirok regained his senses just as the crag began charging through the spikes. With stone shards flying about him, Hirok used the currents to slice through the spike behind his knee, freeing him to drop to the ground. Twisting so he would land on his good leg, he touched down with barely enough time to leap clear of the crag drakuma and a barrage of shrapnel as she lunged for him with an open maw.

The mother roared in defiance as Hirok sailed skyward with her slaughtered cub, where he landed on a platform of air just above the tree tops. Pulling the remains of the earthen spear from his leg, his fir'gan repaired his gruesome injury while he watched the mother futilely search for a way up to him. After what seemed to be an aggravating moment for her, she finally decided to launch a wave of stone spears his way, all of which either missed him or bounced off his platform. Furious that she'd had him and let him get away, the crag drakuma glared at him and roared with rage and frustration, which he met with a smile. Hirok then confirmed his position relative to the camp before jumping in its direction. Twisting as he sailed through the air, he was pleased to see the drakuma keeping pace below. An instant later, the camp appeared beneath him, its occupants armed and alert. Grinning broadly, he released the cub's remains, allowing them to fall to the camp, where they landed with a sickening thud.

"Show time," he thought as he landed lightly in the upper boughs of a rugged oak with a good view of the bandit camp.

Eight of the bandits, some with bows raised, the rest armed with swords and axes, had already formed a defensive line facing away from their hillside caves toward the drakuma's roar. Two of the others were standing over the remains of the drakuma cub while the remaining two bandits were watching their flanks. While he couldn't hear what was being said below without using the currents, he didn't need to hear them to know they were confused and worried; it was evident in their tense posture and the way they looked around franticly. Suddenly, the thunderous approach of the drakuma reached everyone's ears, and a moment later, Hirok heard a terrified female voice from the camp yell, "Holy Hells! It's a crag! RUN!"

The two flanking bandits, along with the two that were inspecting the cub's carcass, looked in the direction of the drakuma's approach in time to see it crash through the trees, toppling several furs and oaks as it slid to a stop in the camp. The defensive line crumbled immediately as they scrambled out of the way of the falling foliage. Unfortunately for the two bandits hovering over the cub's remains, they were too slow and were unceremoniously crushed by the trees. As for the rest of the bandits, the drakuma wasted no time unleashing her rage upon them.

With a roar, a wave of stone spikes erupted outward from beneath the drakuma's paws, tearing through wood and flesh alike as if they were little more than paper. Screams tore through the air as four of the bandits were caught in the attack fully, their impaled, broken bodies shooting skyward like grizzly trophies. The other bandits were blasted from their feet by the wave, sending two of them careening into the trees while one had his arm ripped off at the shoulder by a spike, and another was slammed head-first into a boulder. As for the final two bandits, they were laying prone on the ground, stunned, making them easy targets for the drakuma.

With what Hirok figured was joyous vindictiveness, the mother drakuma pounced on the first one, crushing the bandit under a taloned paw before, with a vicious tug of her powerful arm, she shredded the corpse like a butcher preparing meat. Even as she tore the carcass apart, her attention had already switched to the remaining bandit. With her first target dead, quick, gory steps brought the drakuma alongside the woman as she stood up. In a flash, the enraged mother's head dove toward the bandit, and its massive jaws clamped down on her upper torso. With a yank of the crag's head, the beast tore the woman in half with horrifying ease. The drakuma then, with blood and viscera sliding down her chin, dropped the woman's upper torso to the ground even as the lower half collapsed like a broken doll.

"Well, that was mildly entertaining," Hirok thought, amused, as he watched the beast look around for anyone else to vent her anger on. When she saw there were no more enemies, she slowly approached the remains of her cub, which were now stuck on a pair of stone spikes. Hirok could hear the beast whimper as she drew close and nuzzled what remained of her cub's head.

Letting out a sigh, Hirok said, "Now that that is taken care of, there's only one thing left to do. . . ."

Stepping off the branch, he used the currents to slow his descent. Landing softly, Hirok then gathered the currents to him as he approached. The drakuma was so lost in her grief that she paid him no mind as he entered the camp, nor did she seem to notice when he began wrapping her in bindings of air. She finally let out a cry of surprise when the bindings tightened, and Hirok lifted her airborne. The beast began to struggle mightily as she rose higher and higher, violently ripping at the currents with desperation-fueled strength. The attacks strained Hirok as he fought to keep his bindings intact, but he managed to hold it together long enough to lift the drakuma nearly to the tree tops and position her properly before releasing his hold.

With a roar of shock, the drakuma plunged toward the spikes

below, where she slammed into them with enough force to rattle the ground, cutting off her cry as the jagged stone spears pierced her armored hide. Sliding to a halt nearly at ground level, blood poured from the drakuma's wounds and mouth as her head rolled to the side and her eyes found Hirok. Filled with pain and confusion, the dying beast's gaze seemed to be asking him why he did this, and for a moment, as the clatter of pebbles hitting the ground filled the air like rain, Hirok felt a pang of sympathy for the beast. That moment was fleeting, however. Turning his back to her, Hirok gathered the currents and sprinted off in a swirl of leaves and wind, leaving the mother to join her child in the blissful embrace of death.

Chapter Three

The vase fell to the floor with a resounding crash, shattering into tiny pieces, drawing a frustrated sigh from the shortest of the two women in the room.

"No! No! No, child! You must stay focused!" huffed Alsa from her position in front of the small room's lone door. Using the currents of fir'gan to clear space amongst the fragments, she then proceeded to place another vase on the floor before her charge. Pressing her rosy lips together in consternation, she smoothed out the skirt of her simple, conservative green dress and fixed her intense brown eyes on her charge. "Now," she stated, struggling to contain the dissatisfaction in her lilting, but authoritative voice, "try again. And this time, do try to get it right." The delicate silver chains joining her gold wristlets to the emerald-encrusted rings on her fingers rattled gently as she motioned to the three remaining vases situated against the left-hand wall. "As you can see – we're running out of vases, and I simply don't have the time to piece them back together right now."

"Yes, Lady Alsa," replied Aseria, her musical voice heavy with frustration, as the feline features of her slender face furrowed with consternation and her ears drooped slightly.

For the better part of the morning and afternoon, Ascria had struggled with the exercise. Alsa had been relentless in her instruction and had not once allowed Aseria to move from the center of the room. Through it all, Aseria had remained determined, but the exertion had taken its toll, and it showed. Irritated exhaustion weighed heavily in her almond-shaped, blue-lavender eyes, and both her waist-length mane of blonde hair and the yellow-accent-stripped, skin-like white fur covering her body were drenched with sweat. As she struggled to gather herself, she shifted her weight to ease her aching feet in their black boots, and picked at the sleeveless white tunic and brown breeches that perspiration had plastered to her whipcord-slender body.

Even before their departure from Sentinel Keep just over two weeks ago, her instruction had begun in earnest, which saw her deeply engrossed in the ancient texts stored in the keep's library. However, the incident with Darkon and the growing plight of their situation – which she was barely beginning to grasp – had seen an aggressive acceleration to her training upon their arrival at Gray Sky. With only brief respites to eat and sleep, she had spent the bulk of the first few days in deep meditation. However, it wasn't the kind of instruction she wanted. What she wanted – no, was eager to begin – was combat training. To her dismay, Greatjon and Alsa had made it clear such tutelage was out of the question at that time. At that point, she was unable to tap her inner fir'gan or sense it in others, nor could she sense the currents flowing about her. Without access to her inner fir'gan, teaching her to fight would have been tantamount to trying to make a master swordsman out of an invalid. So, she studied and trained her mind, throwing herself fully into the basic lesson put before her.

To her chagrin, even after becoming aware of the fir'gan within and around her, her ability to grasp it and use it had remained sporadic. Because of this lack of command, deepening her control and awareness through mediation had remained a priority. They did, however, finally begin to teach her simple skills as she developed. It wasn't combat, to be sure, but whether it was lifting objects, lighting a candle, or even creating a small flame in the palm of her hand, it was something, and the minor tricks had sated her for the time being.

Taking a deep breath, Aseria let it out slowly and focused inward. Exhaustion made it difficult for her to find the speck of light at the core of her being, but to her relief, she found it and tenuously latched on to it. Turning her attention to what had become a nightmarish task, she narrowed her focus on the vase.

Alsa smiled inwardly at how quickly Aseria's purple aura flared to life for fir'gan-sensitive eyes to see. Though her darlion charge probably wasn't aware of it, her control had grown considerably – especially given her tired state. Her progress was, in fact, quite impressive in such a short amount of time. Unfortunately, the growing threat of the Betrayers made her development feel like it wasn't enough. That notion made Alsa want to cringe as it crossed her mind, but she fought off the urge. She knew that train of thought wasn't helpful, so she refocused on the current situation. For now, all she needed to do was make sure Aseria could lift and move the vase – there were more important skills to teach her, and every day spent mastering the basics was one less day they had to prepare her to face their enemies.

As Alsa looked on critically, Aseria reached out with her inner fir'gan and gently surrounded the vase. Aseria's brow furrowed with effort and her ears perked up as she forced the tendrils of fir'gan to solidify about the piece of pottery. Alsa grimaced as the vase slowly wobbled into the air. Almost immediately, the cocoon of fir'gan began to lose its cohesion, and Alsa realized it wouldn't be long before this vase met the same end as so many others.

"Concentrate, child!" Alsa chided. "It shouldn't shake like that!"

Growling her acknowledgment through clenched teeth, Aseria drew deeper on her power, and as her aura flared slightly, the vase stabilized.

Alsa clicked her tongue and tucked a loose strand of her auburn hair back into the bun holding her locks off her neck. "Bring it to eye level, child," she ordered, knowing it would both irritate and further challenge Aseria.

Sweating profusely, Aseria did as she was told. Peaking around the vase once it reached the requested height, Aseria allowed herself a tiny smirk as she quipped, "High enough, Lady Alsa?"

Well aware of what she was putting her charge through, Alsa let the sarcastic comment slide. As it was, the next part was what had been giving Aseria the most trouble. "Now, move the vase to me."

Nodding, Aseria took another deep breath and concentrated. For a moment, the vase remained stationary; then, at a very deliberate pace, it began to move. Aseria's face contorted with the strain of battling through her exhaustion to complete the task set before her. She'd made it to this point on several occasions but had yet to see it to fruition. Unfortunately, as the vase moved to within five paces of Alsa, Aseria knew she wouldn't make it when she felt her legs begin to tremble and her grip on the currents start to slip.

Seeing the inevitable, Alsa darted forward as Aseria's aura winked out and caught the vase as it started to fall. Exhausted, Aseria collapsed to her knees as Alsa placed the vase with the six remaining vessels. Alsa then approached her heavy-breathing charge and said, "Really, child – how many times do I have to tell you that focus is paramount?" Kneeling down, she put a comforting hand on Aseria's shoulder as a gentle smile spread across her middle-aged, slender-nosed face. "However, you did well today."

Sweat dripping from her, and her ears drooping noticeably, Aseria looked up at her instructor and smiled wearily as she replied, "Thank you, Lady Alsa."

Smiling, Alsa helped her student to her feet. Guiding Aseria toward the door, she declared, her gentle tone somehow brokering no quarter, "Now, let us see about some lunch before we continue. I swear that I will have you moving that vase to me before the day is out!"

With a shake of her head, Aseria groaned her objection.

Making their way through the meandering and dilapidated corridors of the keep, both women were reminded of just how depressing Gray Sky was. Alsa still found herself amazed at the decrepit state of the compound even though she felt like she shouldn't be. The Bestyne Order's ill fate was well known amongst the Orders, but that knowledge paled in comparison to seeing the results of Darkon's cleansing. From craters to shattered trees and buildings, the surrounding land bore the scars of the brief, but fierce, altercation. As for the hauntingly empty keep, only a small portion of it was still habitable, while the rest of the structure had collapsed or was in desperate need of an architect's attention.

Although the condition of the keep had certainly been a shock, Alsa found the current state of Bestyne Order's ranks greatly disturbing after all these years. The Bestynes were critically undermanned, numbering just shy of two hundred active soldiers. Granted, there was still a modest village outside the castle walls, but the number of full-blooded cyrians and their direwolf companions comprised less than half their ranks. In the best of times, this shortage of manpower would have been concerning, but with the reemergence of the blackheart threat, it left the Orders dangerously exposed. While she understood the difficulty in rebuilding the unique and Warden-less Order, it didn't excuse Greatjon from his responsibilities to the Orders. What's more, as far as Alsa was concerned, it showed just how rash and shortsighted Darkon's punishment of the Bestynes truly was.

The jaunt to the keep's dining hall further reinforced the Order's current situation. The gray stone walls were stained and relatively barren, and the rugs on the cold stone floors were faded and threadbare. Along the way, they passed an eclectic mix of lamps and candelabra, most of which were unlit. That left the weak light from the overcast sky, which seeped in through tiny and sparse, dilapidated windows, as the primary source of illumination. To say it was a miserable environment was putting it mildly. However, what was most unsettling about the trip was the lack of people. Not once did they encounter another person until they reached the gaping entry to the dining hall.

From their velvety, accent-striped skin to their four-fingered hands, swept-back ears, sharp features, and vertical pupils, the trio of cyrians they finally encountered were an intimidating sight. That daunting impression was further enforced by the red-trimmed sectional gray leather armor they wore beneath black tabards trimmed in red that were emblazoned with a howling direwolf head. As the two groups passed each other, their strides nearly a match for Aseria's toe-heel gait in grace, the cyrians eyed them suspiciously even as they nodded respectfully. Given their treatment by the other Orders, Alsa couldn't blame the Bestynes for their cordial, but cold reception. Distrust was bound to fester after such an ordeal, and Alsa wasn't sure she wouldn't feel the same way if Darkon's wrath had been leveled upon the Indigain Order. Even so, their behavior was beginning to grate on her nerves.

Unsurprisingly, they received more of the same cold stares and nods from the handful of people occupying the depressingly empty hall. The two women acknowledged the predominantly human occupants seated at the scattered collection of mismatched tables, but Alsa found her attention repeatedly drawn to her surroundings. She had never set foot in the hall until recently, but between the steepled ceiling of dark wood, the two centrally located hearths, and the trio of chandeliers, she could well imagine the grandeur that had once permeated the hall. Unfortunately, like nearly everything else about the keep, the hall seemed shrouded in a brooding, gloomy air.

Choosing a small table at the rear of the hall, Alsa made sure Aseria was situated before making for the kitchen, which was located off the right side of the dining area. After conferring with the cook, Alsa returned to find her charge slumped over the table with her head resting on her folded arms. Sitting across from her, Alsa firmly stated, "That's not proper behavior, child. You know better than that."

Sighing, Aseria sat up, her ears twitching slightly. "My apologies, Lady Alsa."

Alsa let a small smile creep onto her lips. "I understand how you feel, child, but you must not succumb to exhaustion. There's too much to teach you, and very little time to do it in. For both our sakes, you must stay strong."

Aseria gave her teacher a firm nod in response.

"Good," Alsa stated firmly. "Then, while we wait, recite the Five Masinoki."

Closing her eyes, Aseria took a deep breath and pushed her annoyance with Alsa aside as she relaxed her mind. It came as no surprise to her that Alsa presented the request since she asked it numerous times a day. In fact, Aseria was mildly irritated with herself for having to think about her answer. Thankfully, the words finally formed in her mind.

"The Five Masinoki," Aseria intoned, her musical voice muted by her exhaustion, "are the fundamental values that form the foundation of the code that both Wardens and their followers live by.

To follow these values is to walk the path Corith set before us during the Crusade.

"The first is that of Honor – keep your word to all whom you give it, and let no reason keep you from fulfilling your promises. Stay true to your heart, and never compromise your honor.

"The second value is Discipline – the root of all decisions. Discipline your mind to look upon the world from all perspectives so that you may make choices free of prejudice. Discipline your heart so that none may use your love for others against you, nor let the Darkness corrupt it. Discipline your body so that it may endure the physical hardships that life, in all forms, delivers upon it.

"The third value is Sacrifice – let neither greed nor ego influence you. Through sacrifice – whether it be material, physical, or emotional – you may show others kindness and gain allies where once you had none. Do not let scorn or hatred of your sacrifices deter you from your path, for those who react in such a way are blind to how much richer all are for your actions.

"The fourth value is Blood – protect and support those who are close to you, for family is your strength, and your friends are your support. Whether one is known to you or is a stranger, grant them respect, for in the eyes of Corith, we are all of the same blood.

"The fifth value is Deed – words carry only so much weight; therefore, let your actions overshadow your words. When you make promises, let your deeds show the strength and value of your word. Perform deeds of good and righteousness, and you shall be seen to be of noble heart. Perform deeds of questionable intent, and you shall be seen as untrustworthy and unreliable. Perform deeds of malice and wickedness, and you shall be seen as one with the Darkness.

"Follow these basic tenants and be received with open arms into Corith's bosom. Stray, and forever be prey of the Darkness. By blood, by honor, and by deed, these values we cherish in Corith's name."

As Aseria opened her eyes, Alsa graced her with a small smile and nod of her head. "Very good, child. I see that you can recite it without error even in your tired state."

"Thank you, Lady, Alsa."

Alsa waved the gratitude away. "No thanks are needed. You have committed the passage to memory and can recall it whenever asked. That is a feat of your mind, not the result of my instruction."

Though Aseria neither smiled nor responded, her blue-lavender eyes gleamed with pride at the compliment.

For a time, they sat in silence, each absorbed in their own thoughts. While Alsa pondered how quickly she could teach Aseria what she needed to survive, Aseria focused on relaxing her tired mind and body. Not once in her two-hundred-and-twenty years had she been taxed like this, and her mind felt like it was turning to mush while her body felt like she'd been in an endless battle. Thankfully, she knew a good night's sleep would go a long way to replenishing her strength.

Eventually, the middle-aged, robust cook emerged from the kitchen with a pair of food-filled plates balanced on one arm, and a jug and two cups in his other hand. Arriving at their table, the scraggly bearded, bald man spared a dark-eyed glance at the women as he deposited his cargo on the table. After procuring utensils from his stained apron's pocket and placing them on the table, he left with a mild snort.

Shaking her head, Aseria eyed the offerings. Thin cuts of roasted beef covered with onions, snow apple slices with honey, and a few pieces of day-old bread filled each plate, and the pitcher appeared to contain goat milk. Procuring one of the plates and cups, she then filled her cup. Despite the hunger gnawing at her gut, she restrained herself from attacking her food, much to her chagrin. Instead, she waited for Alsa to situate her own meal. Once Alsa nodded her permission to proceed, Aseria managed to eat slowly, but with little thought to table etiquette. Alsa, on the other hand, ate with the grace and air of royalty.

Despite their contrasting approaches, the food was soon gone. With her stomach full and a measure of alertness returned to her, Aseria sat back in her chair with a pleased expression sprawled across her face. Alsa smiled dryly to herself when she noticed Aseria's eyes alight with renewed energy. Her charge's newfound vigor would ease the evening lessons, but how quickly they progressed would depend solely on how well she handled them.

"So child, are you ready to resume your lessons?" Alsa finally asked once she was finished with her meal as well.

"No," Aseria thought before replying, "Yes, Lady Alsa."

Alsa nodded succinctly. As they stood, she said, "Good. Then let us be about our task." Making their way to the exit, she declared, "I'll have you moving that vase without error before dinner, or you'll be doing extra exercises for the next three days!"

Aseria managed a weak smile in response to the escalating promise despite the loud groan that echoed in her mind.

The rest of the afternoon and early evening was a blur for

both women, but proved fruitful in the end. It took nearly four hours for Aseria to move the vase without dropping it. While the feat was a rousing success, Alsa was more impressed by how easy the troublesome task became after Aseria had accomplished it once. In fact, Alsa found herself practically flabbergasted by her charge's progression when, by dinner, Aseria was moving three vases at a time.

Partaking of their evening meal in the privacy of the training room, Alsa expertly hid her pleasure with her charge as she continued Aseria's instruction in the mental aspects of manipulating fir'gan. She reviewed the basics of sensing the currents, control, movement of objects, separating elements from the currents, and meditation. Alsa had no real purpose in revisiting the subjects other than to help pass the time, but she knew it wouldn't hurt to reinforce the basics.

As they concluded their meal, they heard the dull ring of a church bell signaling the start of both the Night Watch and the evening services. While Alsa wasn't the most religiously devout amongst the Wardens' ranks, she was pleased to see that even amongst the carnage of Darkon's wrath, the Bestynes still maintained services for those who found succor in such acts. Aware that Aseria was one such soul, Alsa felt the reprieve it offered her charge would be a welcomed and well-earned reward; as such, she called an end to the day's lessons and led the way from the room.

Once again, Alsa took the lead through the remains of the keep. Whether by design or not, only a pair of entrances remained that granted access to the inhabitable portions of the keep. Under the assumption that the majority of those attending the service would use the remaining servant's entrance to reach the church quickly, Alsa decided to exit via the main doors. While it was a more round-about route, she felt it was worth it to minimize contact with the keep's residents. With as much as she knew they both wanted to lash out at what they viewed as their unwarranted treatment by the Bestynes, she felt limiting unnecessary interactions was the best way to reduce stress upon all parties. So far, it seemed to be the wise move, but she hoped that one day soon, such measures wouldn't be needed. After all, if the Orders couldn't trust one another, it would make it much easier for the Darkness to prevail.

It didn't take them long to reach the entry hall, and as Alsa had predicted, they encountered very few people until they reached the keep's main entrance. Relatively small compared to the grand halls of other castles and palaces, Gray Sky's entry hall was narrow and utilitarian. There was no decoration other than a colonnade of candelabra running the length of the hall, and the tabard-matching banner with its howling direwolf head hanging from the ceiling at the center of the space. As for occupants, a trio of guards manned a perimeter-spanning balcony a few feet below the vaulted roof – access to which was located elsewhere – and a pair of Bestyne soldiers flanked the sealed oak double doors of the keep's entrance.

To both women's chagrin, they could feel the guards' circumspect gazes upon them as they approached the doors. Alsa was thankful that no words were exchanged as the door guards pushed open the portal, and she even offered them a cordial, thankful nod as she and Aseria stepped into the frigid night. Whether or not the guards responded was of little consequence to Alsa; she did not expect the Bestyne's distrust to simply vanish overnight. She did, however, believe that if she showed them respect no matter how they were treated, then they would eventually warm up to them.

Outside, a thick fog hung about the grounds as it had on many of the nights since their arrival. Had there been a moon that night, it would have failed to pierce the damp veil just as dismally as the torches scattered about the grounds. For Alsa and the trained Gifted amongst the Bestyne's ranks, such an impediment was non-existent since they could see by the light of the currents. Aseria, however, had yet to manifest that talent.

With that thought in mind, Alsa ordered, "Stay close, child. I don't want to lose you in this soup."

Aseria cringed with embarrassment at the request. She was well aware of her shortcomings as a Gifted. However, given their need for her to excel, the constant reminders were as irritating as a deeply buried burr. Fighting off the urge to retort in an undignified manner, she replied simply, "Yes, Lady Alsa."

With the ethereal blue glow of the currents illuminating the way, Alsa led them toward the eastern side of the inner bailey. They quickly found themselves amongst the meager few making the trek to the church, and if any of the others glanced their way, neither woman was aware of it. Soon, a dull, ghostly glow appeared in the fog ahead of them. Alsa felt it was a bit of an eerie sight, and suppressed a mild shudder. A moment later, the mist seemed to part, revealing a modest stone church whose vaulted, dark-shingled roof gave way to a belltower before both were once more swallowed by the fog. As for the ghostly glow, it was the result of warm candlelight struggling to pierce the mist through the church's arched windows and the wide-open front doors.

Whether the congregation was oblivious to the somewhat haunting setting or simply didn't care, they reverently filed under the awning, through the front entry, and into the simple nave that occupied most of the building. Two rows of twenty pews, split by a colonnade-flanked middle aisle, were arranged from the naive entry to the sanctuary. Candelabra were positioned on the aisle side of each column, between each window, and also flanked the ironwood altar at the forefront of the sanctuary stage. From his position behind the altar, one of the many humans amongst the Bestyne Order watched as everyone found a seat.

Once everyone was settled, barely filling half the pews, and the doors were shut, the middle-aged man motioned for the dim hum of conversation to cease. Garbed in a Bestyne tabard over meticulously maintained leather armor, the moderately tall, bald man hardly resembled a priest. Seated at the back, Alsa glanced at Aseria and saw that her charge was still a bit astonished by the relaxed decorum even after attending several services. Aseria had expressed how shocked she was by it after the first service they attended, prompting Alsa to explain that such men and women regularly held the position of priest amongst the orders. The thought of her charge's reaction nearly made Alsa smile with amusement. It was easy to understand why an outsider – especially if someone was a devout follower of Corith – could easily view the Orders' approach to religion and the Light as odd or even blasphemous. Whether the views of modern-day religion on the proper way to live and worship were right or wrong was of little relevance to Alsa. The Orders had been created by Corith's appointed guardians, and they had lost countless souls defending Kylir against the Darkness; that alone gave them a unique – and as far as Alsa was concerned, proper – perspective on the Light. However, Alsa also believed that no matter which view was correct, neither group had the right to persecute or force their views on the other.

Once the congregation had quieted down, the priest ran his dark eyes over the gathering before intoning in a ragged voice, "Blessed be the children of Corith who gather here to offer praise unto the Lord of the Light."

Aseria perked up a bit at the opening words. In her already considerable years, she had experienced many forms of worship. Her own people were bereft of formal services; instead, they treated all creations of the Light with respect, for the Mother had given birth to it all. Throughout her time spent amongst humans, she had seen frenzied reverence, worship driven by fear and awe, and doctrine based on service and humility. While she didn't adhere to any one particular approach, she found a measure of comfort in the Church of the Light's services that had been lacking in her own people's practices.

As the priest droned on through his sermon, Aseria was reminded of just how unique the Orders' approach was. In other churches, there had been an adamant delineation between good and evil, but amongst the Orders, the line was blurred. Given what she had learned in her studies, she was beginning to understand why they viewed the world as they did. There was no question that the Light stood for all that was right, and the Darkness for all that was wrong and vile, but they saw the area between as ambiguous. As she understood it, both sides had done good and evil in their pursuit of victory, and the moral quandary it raised in her mind was practically mind-numbing.

As for her personal views, she believed that she did her best to follow a path of good and act with honor, but there was no escaping the fact that she had killed in defense of her friends and in the name of duty. Did this make her evil? She didn't think so, even though there were factions of the modern Church of the Light that believed otherwise. Then there was her current situation and all it entailed. It was inevitable that violence would be involved, and given what she had learned of the rise of the Orders and the Crusade that followed, she had no idea how she would react to, or feel about, the situations they'd confronted. However, she knew that the quandary wouldn't last forever. Now that she had taken the first steps on a path that could very well give her answers to that question, she often found herself terrified of the answer. Dark and terrible things had been done in the name of the Light, and she had no way to fully comprehend those actions.

By the time the service drew to a close two hours later, Aseria's mind was awash with deep contemplation. Alsa saw this clearly written on her student's face, and elected to give her the rest of the night off. Offering a small smile, Ascria thanked her teacher before Alsa stood and joined the line headed for the door.

Long after the last of the congregation had departed and the priest had excused himself, Aseria remained seated. So much had been thrust upon her in such a short amount of time, and she knew more would be asked of her in the days and weeks ahead. Long life span or not, her life had changed in such a sudden and drastic way that it was difficult to swallow. She had only a crude idea of what the future held for her, and even that was terrifying. However, she knew that she would continue to push forward – Darius' death needed avenging, Kylir needed its defenders, and she was determined to be strong enough to do both.

Alsa closed the door to her room and leaned against it with a weary sigh. The strain of the last two weeks was starting to catch up with her. Yet, despite her growing mental and physical exhaustion, she was pleased with Aseria's progress. Training a young Gifted was a trial in and of itself, but to cram everything Aseria needed to know into a short, unknown amount of time made it feel like she'd been asked to single-handedly move a mountain. Under normal circumstances, Alsa would have considered it a rousing success if Aseria had only managed to move the one vase. Unfortunately, things were far from normal, and just one vase would have been a regrettable failure. Thankfully, Aseria had inexplicably managed far more than that, providing a brief glimpse at her possible potential. This unexpected revelation, combined with the needs of their situation, led Alsa to one very reluctant conclusion – it was about time to start combat training. Smiling dryly at the thought, Alsa pushed away from the door and walked over to her desk.

Like the rest of the keep, her room had a utilitarian feel to it; the stone walls were home to a pair of unlit lamps and a narrow window, while the furniture occupying the room was sturdy and unremarkable. A modest oak desk sat in the middle of the room between a serviceable bed along the right-hand wall, and a armoire on the left-hand wall. Seating herself behind the desk in a simple wooden chair, Alsa concentrated briefly before the wicks of the wall lamps and her desk lamp ignited, bathing the room in warm light.

Gazing at the leatherbound journal before her on the desk, Alsa felt a pang of regret laced with frustration. When she initially left the Indigain compound, she had brought very few necessities with her since she had expected to return home upon retrieving Aseria. As a result of this and her refusal to further break the moratorium on Portculim travel just to return home, she'd been forced to rely on both the Bestyne and Stelariuos' generosity. Much of the clothing that filled the armoire had been provided by the Stelariuos Order, and the writing kit and journal resting on the desktop were a gift from Greatjon. While she wasn't above accepting help from others, she not only missed her own clothing and journal, but she also felt a bit ashamed that she had not at least considered Aseria's retrieval going askew. Shaking her head, she dismissed the useless thoughts and opened the journal.

Already, it was half-full of notes related to Aseria's development. While no such records were needed, it helped Alsa sort out her thoughts and monitor Aseria's progression. Flipping to the first blank page, Alsa then opened the writing kit and readied her bone-nub pen. With fluid, elegant strokes of dark ink, Alsa noted the lessons of the day, the number of breaks taken by Aseria, the number of broken vases, how long it took Aseria to move one vase, and her sudden jump in skill. As she was penning her personal thoughts about the day, there was a polite knock on her door.

Sighing, Alsa cleaned her pen and returned it and the inkwell to her writing kit before declaring with a slight hint of irritation to her soft voice, "Enter."

The door groaned open to admit the Bestyne Order's Knight. Tall and powerfully built, the man was garbed in a black shirt, boots, and brown pants. His dark-brown eyes settled on her from a solemn face topped with rust-orange hair that was pulled back in a horsetail. As he shut the door, a small, friendly smile spread across his wide mouth. "Alsa," he stated simply.

Hiding her surprise, she returned his smile and pushed her journal to the side before standing with a respectful nod. "Greatjon. I didn't expect you back till tomorrow. How are you, and how did the trip go?"

Motioning for her to sit, Greatjon seated himself on the foot of the bed. "Well enough, I suppose. The borders appear secure, and no one has seen or felt anything suspicious."

Settling back into her chair, she did her best not to stare at the jagged scar that ran from his brow to his chin over his right eye. "And your wife?" she asked. "How is she?"

Greatjon fought down the temptation to smirk. Though Alsa hid it well, he could tell she was still adjusting to his following in Valisiana's footsteps. There had been one half-hearted debate when she had discovered his breach of protocol, but that was the extent of her resistance. Greatjon understood that her words that day were not only meant to ensure he understood the possible consequences should Darkon learn of his marriage, but were also a result of her grief over Darius' death. As such, he couldn't fault her for her concerns, and he even found that his respect for her had grown.

"She's fine, though the pregnancy is taking its toll on her."

"I understand that cyrian pregnancies can be extremely difficult. Are you sure you shouldn't be there with her?"

Greatjon grimaced. "As much as I would prefer to be, there are greater things at stake right now. My place is here, and she understands that. Besides, she's got her mother to help her out, and Corith knows she knows how to handle a pregnant cyrian better than me." Shaking his head with a tired smirk, he then asked, "And you? You look exhausted."

"I am," she replied. "The pace we're moving at has been a drain on everyone – and your people's continued disdain and distrust isn't helping. Thankfully, Baris has been only a minor annoyance. If he wasn't undergoing his initiation into your Order, I'd hate to think what kind of a nuisance he'd be."

Greatjon nodded. "That's good to hear; I was, and still am, concerned about him. As for the rest of the Order, I wish I could help with that, but only time will soothe their wounds – you know that as well as I do."

"I know, but still – it would go a long way if you would speak with them again."

Shrugging, he said, "I'll try, but I don't think it will do any good."

"Thank you."

"There's nothing to thank me for," he responded with a slight grin. "So, how is Aseria progressing?"

"Considering what we're asking of her – quite well. As you know, her control of the currents is still somewhat suspect. However, I believe she is breaking through that barrier."

"Really?"

Alsa nodded confidently. "I do. Until today, I was beginning to think we would run out of pottery for her to break. Thankfully – and inexplicably – she managed to move three vases simultaneously despite her exhaustion."

Greatjon nodded slowly and thoughtfully. "That is impressive . . . and heartening. But she could just as easily regress in the morning."

Alsa sighed and rubbed her temples. "My thoughts as well. However, given our precarious timeline, I would err on the side of optimism. She has shown strength and remarkable tenacity in such a constant state of exertion – and that cannot be ignored no matter how you look at it." Studying him carefully, she added, "I was going to suggest she begin combat training, but if you feel differently, then we'll continue with the basics."

Greatjon met her gaze and held it, gauging her confidence in her statements. Finally, he stated, "While it would be prudent to give someone so raw more time, I must grudgingly agree with you. Time is not on our side, and no matter her experience, it's better than an ownerless crystal. Besides," a sudden glower flashed across his face, "just sitting here while the Darkness' agents wander unchecked sours my stomach."

Alsa couldn't hide a slight flinch at Greatjon's implied meaning. She was painfully aware of his longing for revenge, and when she let herself think about the tragic fall of Blackstone, a similar hunger threatened to swell inside her heart.

Pushing the morose thoughts aside, she asked, "Since we are in agreement, when do you want to start, and who will handle it?"

Greatjon ran a hand over his hair. "Might as well start tomorrow. We'll start off slow and keep her working on the basics. After that, we'll proceed based on her progress. As for her teacher," he sighed with a dry smirk, "might as well be me."

With a resigned shake of her head, Alsa said, "I thought that would be the case, and will not argue against it. You do have more combat experience, after all."

Standing, Greatjon offered her a friendly smile and teased, "Don't worry . . . I'll try not to kill her."

Alsa rolled her eyes and scoffed. "I would hope so."

Moving to the door with a chuckle, Greatjon said, "Good night, Alsa," before opening the door and exiting the room.

After the door closed behind him, Alsa leaned back in her chair, stared at the ceiling and muttered, "Corith be with you tomorrow, Aseria, for the Old Wolf's bite is vicious, and he won't be as forgiving as I."

Aseria's stomach was a knot of nervous excitement and trepidation. Alsa had awakened her just after dawn, as per their routine, but instead of ushering her to their training room after a quick breakfast, she'd presented Aseria with a gift from Greatjon and informed her that combat training would start today. The exciting news had washed away her aches and grogginess, but made it difficult for her to focus during her morning meditation. This was something she'd hungered for since their arrival, but she'd expected a longer wait given her tentative grasp on her power. However, ready or not, she was not about to shy away from the challenge.

Aseria's excitement was further bolstered by her attire. For the first time in what seemed like an eternity to her, she was armed and armored. While she still carried her slender longsword across her back, its leather-wrapped hilt jutting over her right shoulder, the armor she wore over her white shirt and brown pants was the gift Alsa had presented to her. Though she'd been remiss to part with her old leathers, the new suit was a substantial upgrade. Trimmed in red, the gray armor was cut in the sharp, intimidating cyrian fashion. Though the chap-styled pants and padded knee-boots were familiar to her, the upper body armor was composed of more straps and sections than she was used to. Unfamiliarity aside, she was impressed by the protective coverage and, due to both the series of slash-like vents along her ribs and the strategically placed gaps, the remarkable amount of flexibility it provided.

What she was most impressed by, however, was how well it fit her, for the armor appeared new, and not once had she been fitted for it. Then again, upon reflection, she realized it shouldn't have been so surprising. Cyrians were rumored to be distant cousins of the darlions – which Aseria was inclined to believe given their eerie resemblance – and there were a few of them amongst the Bestyne ranks that were a close match to her size and stature. In the end, it really didn't matter. She was overjoyed with the armor, and made a mental note to thank Greatjon for the remarkable gift.

Making her way through the keep, Aseria couldn't keep her anticipation from showing completely; her blue-lavender eyes were more vibrant than usual, and there was an extra bounce to her step. The usual stares she received seemed tempered by curiosity, and on more than one occasion, she thought she was the object of hushed conversations that didn't seem as spiteful. Furthermore, their scrutiny and judgmental attitude not only failed to dampen her spirits, but it was quickly banished from her mind when she arrived at the entry hall to find Baris pacing its width.

From the black breeches and red shirt he wore beneath leather armor that was akin to hers, to his red-trimmed black tabard with its howling direwolf head, Baris looked every inch the Bestyne warrior despite his eighteen summers. The attire was a visible example of his outward growth since arriving at Gray Sky, but it still broke her heart to see the horrific disfigurement that marred the young man's face. The harsh scar that ran from where his right ear used to be to the bridge of his nose was still surrounded by inflamed flesh, which stood out starkly against his haunted amber eyes and the black bandanna he wore over his shaved head. It was an outward reminder of the horrors he had survived – horrors that one so young should never have to carry. But carry it he and the other survivors did, as Blackstone's fall was a dreadful curse that would not relinquish its hold on them. What's more, it had left Baris with a hunger for retribution that was a match for Greatjon's vengeful thirst.

However, while she was slowly growing more confident that she could walk such a path and shoulder its burdens, she feared for Baris. Besides the scars he already bore, many of the Bestynes had taken to calling him T'sar, which meant 'Scarred One'. While she knew it was meant as a title of respect for surviving such a horrific injury, she often wondered if it was just another wound for him to bear. Ultimately, she knew that the best thing she could do was be the best friend she could be to him. Anything beyond that was out of her control, but she hoped time would mend his heart and soul before he followed her into something that would rend his soul beyond repair.

Noticing her approach, Baris came to a halt at the center of the hall and turned to face her. Resting his hand on the hilts of the broad-bladed shortswords sheathed at his hips instead of idly fingering them as was his habit, he offered her a weak smile.

Responding to his smile with a warmer one, Aseria quickly approached and embraced him affectionately. "It's good to see you! You look well!" she offered, her musical voice filled with delighted sincerity.

Gently disengaging himself, he cast a sidelong glance at the Bestyne guards who were eyeing them before looking up into her eyes with a sense of relief. "It's good to see you as well, Aseria," he stated, his joy at seeing her pitching his young voice a bit higher than normal. "I'm sorry that my training has kept me from visiting."

"Think nothing of it," Aseria responded with a dismissive shake of her head. "We've both been horribly busy, but I've heard you've been handling yourself admirably."

Baris shrugged. "I suppose so," he stated, his voice returning to normal. "It hasn't been too hard to assimilate. From a martial standpoint, the Bestynes do have their own way of operating, but it's not a drastic difference from what I'm used to. It's the Gifted training and the true depth of this conflict that I'm struggling with."

Aseria nodded sympathetically. "I know what you mean. Accepting that I'm Gifted was easy since there's tangible proof. But the Crusade? This war? It's astonishing and hard to believe, even with the books for evidence." She shook her head, dismissing the subject. "So, what brings you here?"

"Word has gotten around that you're to begin combat training today."

"Oh, has it now?" she quipped with a smirk.

"Aye," he glanced at the guards again. "There's likely to be few who will be there to watch."

Aseria's smirk faded as she rolled her eyes. "I'm not surprised. I guess they want to watch the wolf devour the cat," she said dryly. Shaking her head, she then asked, "And you?"

"I thought I'd go along for support. Besides that, I thought I might learn something from watching. Corith knows I need the help."

"Thank you, Baris," she stated with an appreciative smile. "But I doubt your struggles are as bad as they seem."

Shrugging, he turned on his heel and started toward the doors. As Aseria fell in beside him, he replied, "That might be true, but I've got a lot to learn if I'm going to be able to stand shoulder-to-shoulder with the others and have a chance of holding my own."

Aseria nodded sympathetically as the door guards pushed open the heavy panels at their approach. She felt the same way about her prospects, but it was likely that her instruction was far superior to what Baris was receiving.

Passing over the keep's threshold, they were greeted by a cold, overcast day. As neither of them had mastered regulating their bodies with fir'gan, they were still subject to the effects of the bitter cold. Thankfully, both of them were used to the harsh conditions of the Northlands, and their attire provided a decent barrier against the weather. As such, the cold was hardly a thought as they began to circle the keep, moving in the opposite direction of the church. While they walked, they chatted about their experiences since arriving at Gray Sky. Aseria was glad Baris was sharing with her, as she felt it might ease his troubled mind. Unfortunately, and much to her shame, she couldn't keep her gaze and thoughts from wandering to the wreckage of the keep that was allowed to remain as a macabre memorial.

The remains of the keep proper barely hinted at the square, six-story structure that she'd seen depicted in one of the few paintings hanging within the habitable areas. Only one of its towers was fully intact, and far too much of the remaining structure was marred by damage and faded scorch marks. When she looked to where the inner wall once stood, there was barely anything to impede her view. Only a few shattered sections of the barrier still stood, while the rest was nothing more than a continuous pile of rubble. The architectural carnage continued into the outer bailey where a village once stood, and beyond that, the remains of an outer wall. Serving as a backdrop to the destruction were the White Fang Mountains and its forests, along with an overcast sky, which only seemed to make the scene even dourer than it was.

Although a new village had been established, which was hidden from sight by the gentle downslope of the terrain, it was still baffling to her that the keep was left in such shape. According to what she'd been able to glean from Alsa and Greatjon, Gray Sky had remained this way for over a century. While the reasoning behind such a decision was somewhat lost on her, the depth of the Bestyne Order's anger was not. If they were willing to let such destruction stand as a memorial, then she had to wonder what lengths they might be willing to go to for revenge or absolution.

Rounding the rear corner of the keep, they saw that at least a dozen Bestyne soldiers – and a few direwolves – had gathered before the remnants of the barracks. Although Baris had informed her of this eventuality, Aseria still found herself surprised by the size of the crowd. As she and Baris approached, she felt unease take root in her stomach; every one of the Bestynes was in full armor, armed, and protectively arranged about Greatjon and Alsa, who stood at the center of the training grounds.

Baris read the unease on her face and offered, "Don't worry, they're just curious."

She nodded as her eyes alighted upon Greatjon and Alsa, who watched her and Baris approach from their position in front of a trio of sconces. "I know. But the way they look at Alsa and I. . . ." She shuddered slightly.

Baris reached up and patted her on the shoulder. "Relax and focus on the task at hand. You'll be fine."

She nodded again. "Thanks."

Returning her nod, Baris said, "I'll be watching from the crowd. Good luck," before veering off to join his new brothers-in-arms.

Gathering herself, Aseria took a deep breath and approached her teacher and Greatjon, both of whom bore practically impassive expressions. Alsa was dressed in her signature green dress, while the Bestyne Knight was garbed in durable black boots, brown breeches, and a white shirt that was secured at his wrists by a thick pair of leather bracers. Unlike Alsa, Greatjon was armed. His claymore, the steel-claw hilt of which jutted over his right shoulder, hung securely across his back from a baldric that was anchored to the sturdy belt secured around his waist by a wolf-head buckle.

The conversations amongst the gathering dwindled to silence as she halted before her mentors. Aseria immediately noted a hint of concern in Alsa's eyes that nearly made her hesitate. What's more, there was an air of formality to the gathering that further twisted the knot of anxiety in her stomach.

Doing her best to suppress her nerves and keep her musical voice from quivering with anxious energy, she saluted, fist to heart, and said, "Reporting as ordered, Knights."

Alsa and Greatjon acknowledged her with nods before Alsa stated, her soft voice solemn, "Welcome, child. Are you prepared?"

Aseria nodded. "I am," she responded confidently despite her apprehension.

"Good. For today's lessons, I will simply be an observer. Greatjon will be your instructor." Stepping forward, Alsa grasped her shoulders and said softly, "Be strong today; we are asking more of you than we have any right to at this juncture. Do not expect Greatjon to go easy, for he will push you to your limits. And keep this in mind – while there is no intent to cause you fatal harm, this is very treacherous, and you are in danger." Feeling a slight shudder run through Aseria, Alsa smiled gently and added, "You're strong, Aseria; remember that, stay focused, and you will be fine." Giving her charge's shoulders a comforting squeeze, Alsa glanced at Greatjon sternly before moving behind Aseria and taking up an isolated position well back of her student.

For a moment, not a word was spoken, and Aseria felt like squirming beneath Greatjon's scar-highlighted, critical gaze. The intensity of his focus only added to her unease, but then it occurred to her that he might be communicating with Deralina. Whatever the reason for his focus and silence, it came to an abrupt end when he finally said, "Before we begin, I need to appraise your progress." He glanced at Alsa. "Not that I don't trust your judgment, but first-hand knowledge will help me determine what we can and can't do."

"No offense taken," Alsa replied sincerely. "Proceed as you will."

Turning his attention back to Aseria, Greatjon said, "You see these torches behind me? I want you to light them." A flash of indignation crossed Aseria's face, prompting Greatjon to add, "I know it's a bit remedial, but it will give me a base to proceed upon."

"Alright then . . ." Aseria responded before taking a deep breath and focusing her mind.

As Greatjon joined Alsa behind Aseria, he felt the darlion latch on to her power and draw it forth. To his chagrin, his fir'gan-sensitive eyes saw her purple aura spring to life. It was disappointing to see such an overuse of power for such a rudimentary task, but he also understood that it was amazing that the control she now displayed was gained in such a short amount of time. Unfortunately, the Bestyne observers weren't so understanding. There were immediate snorts of disgust from a few when Aseria's aura appeared, which only grew into muted laughter and soft-spoken heckling as she proceeded to light the torches with the gross overuse of power. For a brief moment, Greatjon considered chastising his troops, but he immediately dismissed the notion. Aseria was here to train and learn, not to be coddled.

82

Once the last torch erupted in a brightly burning blaze, Aseria released her power and turned to face Greatjon. If she was aware of the derisive behavior of the onlookers, she didn't show it as she asked, "How's that?"

"Decent. But I asked you to light the torches, not to transform into a purple beacon for every Gifted for miles around to sense," he chided, drawing scattered laughter from the crowd, and an admonishing glare from Alsa.

Aseria felt indignation welling up in her at the reproach of her skill. She'd done what he asked, and far quicker than she could have a few days earlier. In her mind, while overwhelming praise wasn't warranted, neither was such criticism. However, before she could respond in any fashion, Greatjon was standing before her with a stern glare painted across his face.

"That was a very simple task, but you required enough fir'gan to make your aura visible for any Gifted to see! Add the lethargic pace with which you lit them to the ledger, and I can't see any way you'd survive in a fight!"

Like a damn suddenly breaking, Greatjon's admonishment was the final blow to the restraint she'd practiced over her fury at the Bestyne's cold treatment, and her face twisted with anger. "I'm very good with a sword . . . if you care to find out!" she snapped, her eyes alight with anger. "And as far as fir'gan is concerned – by all means, show me how it's done!"

A hush fell over the training grounds, and she could feel scornful glares leveled at her from the crowd. As for her teachers, Alsa looked ready to reprimand her, while Greatjon . . . Greatjon simply smirked.

Before she could question his expression, there was a crackling hiss from behind her. Turning around, she blinked in astonishment at the smothered torches. Just as she was about to turn and question Greatjon, the torch heads once again erupted in flames. Facing Greatjon, she examined him for any signs that he was manipulating his power. For a moment, she couldn't find the slightest trace of his actions; no aura, no trickle of fir'gan, not a single thing. Then, on the edge of her senses, she detected a faint residue of power around one of the torches. Unsure of herself, she turned and focused on that sensation to make sure she wasn't imagining it.

Once she was certain it wasn't her imagination, she turned back to Greatjon and asked with a mix of awe and disbelief, "How did you do that? I couldn't feel what you did!"

A few snickers from the crowd greeted her confession, and

even Greatjon gave a gentle, but dejected, shake of his head. Alsa, however, gave her a consoling smile before stating, "Greatjon has more experience, child. For him, such a task is quite simple. With practice, you'll be able to do the same, if not better."

Greatjon nodded in agreement. "What Alsa says is true. However, while I understand that a tremendous amount of information is being crammed down your throat, you have to realize that I am nowhere near as strong or skilled as a Warden. Once your skills develop, you'll likely be able to sense some power usage from me, but had it been a Warden performing the task, there would have been little to no indication of their actions no matter your aptitude."

Aseria nodded slowly. "I understand," she stated slowly.

Greatjon folded his arms across his chest. "Perhaps you do. But let me make it perfectly clear – I used very little power right now, and many of those here wouldn't need much more to light the torches. You, on the other hand, just used a mountain to hammer a nail. Most Gifted in the surrounding area were likely aware of your actions, and as I understand it, your training sessions have been hard to ignore, even for the Gifted in the village. So, with that in mind, you have to realize that a Warden – especially one looking for you – would likely notice you from much farther away!"

Greatjon watched as comprehension battled with frustration in her eyes for a moment before adding, his tone a bit softer, "What I need from you is better control. You must learn how to ration your fir'gan. Forgetting that there is a ban on excessive use of power for the moment, you need to use no more than you have to for a given task, and avoid using large amounts of power unless you absolutely need to. Do you understand?"

Aseria growled softly at the chastisement but accepted the scolding. "I understand. And I'll do what it takes to improve."

"Good," Greatjon stated firmly before dousing the torches once more. "Now, you're going to continue with this until I say you are ready to move on."

"But–" she started to protest.

"No buts, Aseria!" Greatjon stated forcefully. "Combat training will not start until I say so. Do you understand me?"

A hint of anger flashed in Aseria's eyes, but she repressed the urge to snap at him. Instead, she replied smartly, "Yes, sir."

As she turned her attention back to the torches, Greatjon felt a presence in his mind and heard Alsa reprimand him gently, *That wasn't nice, Greatjon. You know good and well you aren't going to withhold the training simply because her management skills are raw."*

Greatjon smirked mentally. *"True. But she doesn't know that, now does she? What better way to motivate her than the threat of losing something she wants?"*

Greatjon almost chuckled aloud as Alsa responded with exasperation, *"Wolves."*

Chapter Four

The rest of the afternoon was a blur for Aseria. Greatjon was relentless with both his instruction and criticism. It was a familiar routine, as Alsa had taken a similar approach with her, but Greatjon was far more direct than the Indigain Knight. He was also generous and sharp with his criticism, but reserved with his praise. However, unbeknownst to Aseria, his approach was having the desired effect. Though his harsh words angered her, they also spurred her to work harder.

Again and again, Aseria's attempts to light the torches were inadequate, and Greatjon would douse them, his mask of displeasure showing no signs of changing. It was frustratingly tedious for Aseria; she wanted desperately to do as he wanted, but while she did manage to trim the power she used, she couldn't reduce it to the level Greatjon demanded. As such, the tension between instructor and student grew throughout the morning until, finally, well after the noon bell tolled, it boiled over.

For what seemed like the thousandth time, Aseria did her best to skim the surface of her fir'gan. Like every other attempt, her aura flared to life, but this time, she managed to keep it much dimmer than before. Feeling a bit proud of herself for her restraint, Aseria then proceeded to pick air from her fir'gan and enveloped the torch heads before feeding fire into them until, for the first time that day, all three ignited at once. Delight swelled up in her at the accomplishment, and she turned to Greatjon with a pleased and somewhat smug look on her face.

"How was that? Better?" she asked rhetorically, her tone defiant and somewhat flippant.

Meeting her gaze with a cold glare, Greatjon scowled. Without warning, he doused the torches an instant before surrounding the brands with an excess of power and lighting them. The explosion of blinding light sent cries of shock and a rain of vehement curses through the onlookers as all but Greatjon recoiled at the sudden assault on their eyes.

Rubbing and blinking her eyes, Alsa managed to pick Greatjon out through her blurry vision and barked, "Damn it, Greatjon! That was uncalled for! She's doing the best she can with what we're asking of her!" Blinking her watery eyes again, her vision began to clear. "Besides, you know very well that darlion and cyrian eyes are much more sensitive than ours – you could have blinded them!"

Arms folded across his chest, his gaze still focused on Aseria as she struggled to clear her vision, he asked rhetorically, "Uncalled for, Alsa? Maybe. But I don't want just her best – I want her best and more! She won't see combat until she can do this without so much as a hint of her aura showing!"

"This has gone far enough, Greatjon! Push–" Alsa started to say as she stepped toward him.

"You want more?" Aseria growled, interrupting Alsa. "I am doing my best, damn it!" she snapped as her vision cleared and she was able to focus on Greatjon. "All I've heard for the last two weeks is more, more, more!"

A sudden, volatile surge in the currents in and around Aseria drew everyone's attention. Alsa's eyes widened in shock, and even Greatjon's arms fell to his sides as they noted the surge.

"Aseria–" Alsa started to plead.

"I've given it all I've got!" Aseria shouted, cutting off Alsa's plea. "But if you want more, you heartless bastard, then I'll give you more!"

A number of the Bestynes near Aseria hastily erected barriers as she drew deeply and forcefully not only on her innate power, but also on the currents. In a flash, the burgeoning power erupted, and her purple aura burst into existence, visible for all to see.

A few of the barriers crackled and flared as the excess power bleeding off of her made contact with the shields. It was an impressive display for one so new to their Gifted talents, and thankfully, it wasn't enough to pose a deadly threat to anyone on the training grounds at the moment. That, however, was hardly comforting. They could all see that the situation was deteriorating quickly. While Aseria appeared unaware of the power pouring into her as she kept her vehement glare locked on Greatjon, it was clear to everyone else that not only was she rapidly becoming a danger to herself, but she would soon pose a threat to all but the two Knights.

Thinking quickly, Alsa slowly approached Aseria with a pleading hand extended. "Calm yourself, Aseria," she managed to say gently and confidently despite the knot of anxiety twisting in her gut. "There is no need for this reaction. Greatjon may be a lummox at times, but he only wants to help. Isn't that right?" she asked, shooting a stern glare at her fellow Knight.

Well aware of the precipice that Aseria was toeing, Greatjon softened his visage and nodded. "It is," he said gently.

"See?" Alsa asked as she turned a tender smile on Aseria, only to flinch as another surge of power pulsed through her charge and the ground around Aseria began to crack. Swallowing hard, Alsa strengthened her defenses and forced herself to remain calm as she asked gently, "Please, Aseria, release your hold on your fir'gan before someone gets hurt?"

For a moment, Alsa feared that Aseria had lost herself amidst the torrent of power. To her profound relief, her words must have reached her charge on some level, for Aseria suddenly blinked and looked at her. Though her eyes appeared distant, her face relaxed slowly, and her aura began to sputter as the currents slowly began to fall away from her.

"That's it," Alsa urged. "Slowly, now – control your breathing, focus your mind, and release your hold. You can do it."

With Alsa's guiding words, Aseria gradually regained control of her emotions and focus, which, in turn, allowed her to ease her hold on the currents until the last of the power left her, and her aura winked out. As the currents returned to normal, an audible sigh of relief escaped the lips of many of the onlookers. No one would have even considered such a young Gifted capable of an outburst of that magnitude, and many of them found themselves grudgingly impressed by the display as their nerves settled down. Occupied as they were by their own mix of emotions, very few in the crowd noticed that Aseria was shaking badly from the exertion, and a moment later, she started to collapse.

Almost instantly, Alsa and Baris were at her side, catching the spent darlion before she hit the ground. Supported between the two with her head bowed, Aseria was oblivious to the concerned gaze Baris shot Alsa. Alsa answered him with a slight nod and a small smile, indicating that Aseria would be fine.

Turning her attention to her charge, Alsa said, her tone soft and soothing, "Very good, child. It's alright now. Here," she added as they lowered her to the ground, "sit and rest."

Once they had Aseria settled, Alsa examined her closely, checking her pulse, her pupils, and her temperature. She even went so far as to study the currents in and around the exhausted darlion. To her profound relief, there appeared to be no ill effects from her charge's outburst, and the flow of fir'gan within her was fine. Satisfied with Aseria's condition for the moment, she looked at Baris and ordered, "Stay with her."

"Understood," Baris answered firmly with a crisp nod of his head.

Standing, Alsa turned to Greatjon and marched over to him. Grabbing his arm, Alsa angrily demanded, "A word with you!" before guiding him away from the others.

As soon as they were out of earshot – granted, some of the Gifted amongst the Bestynes could use their power to listen in if they wanted to – Alsa brought them to a halt and turned on Greatjon with intense anger burning in her brown eyes. "What in the hells are you doing?" Alsa demanded quietly but vehemently. "Motivating her is one thing, but provoking her like that is an entirely different matter! We may have to get her ready with a sense of urgency, but we must be mindful of her emotional state! She's had to digest a massive amount of life-changing information, and we both know that's only a small amount of what she has to learn and understand! So, for the love of the Light – keep that in mind and temper your actions! We need her trained and ready, not broken and useless!"

Expecting an argument from her peer, she was surprised – and relieved – to see a hint of guilt softening his stern visage. "You're right, Alsa," Greatjon conceded quietly. "I pushed too hard, and the results could have been horrible."

Alsa relaxed a little bit at the admission and took a deep breath to calm herself. "I know," she stated as her voice regained its normal gentleness, "or I at least have a good idea of what keeps you preoccupied and drives you. We both want to see Warrick pay for his transgressions, but venting your anger by pushing Aseria will accomplish nothing." She mustered a smile for him. "Believe me when I tell you that Aseria wants to see Warrick pay as well. Don't ruin a potential weapon and ally out of ill-conceived haste; besides, that's not our way."

Nodding slowly, Greatjon glanced over at Aseria. Seated with her knees pulled to her chest and her head resting on her crossed arms, she was the picture of exhaustion. Not one of his fellow Bestynes gave any indication of approaching her, though he could see a few of them sharing hushed conversations. It was disappointing to see, and he found himself thankful for Baris who was crouched protectively beside her. To his chagrin and shame, Greatjon had given very little thought to how Aseria's situation was affecting her. He had been so focused on finding, protecting, and training her for what was to come that her feelings had never truly crossed his mind. What's more, given Alsa's chastisement and their previous conversations since arriving at Gray Sky, it suddenly dawned on him how lonely and isolated Aseria must be.

Looking back at Alsa, he asked, his tone contrite, "Very well, Alsa – what would you have me do?"

"Push, but be mindful of her current state. She is alone and still very vulnerable. Her power is still growing, but she is far from benefiting fully from her gift. The last thing we need is to make a mistake that burns her out or kills her; Corith knows she's far more fragile than you or I, let alone a Warden."

Acknowledging Alsa's advice with a thankful nod, Greatjon then made his way over to Aseria. Pausing before her, he scanned the gathered onlookers with a stern gaze. "Alright, everyone – clear out!" he barked with authority.

A few of the spectators flinched at his tone, but they all quickly saluted before dispersing.

Crouching before the fatigued darlion, Greatjon looked at Baris and ordered, "Baris – go to the kitchen and find us all something to eat."

"Yes, sir," Baris replied hesitantly. Looking back to Aseria, he asked, concern filling his voice, "Are you going to be okay?"

Aseria nodded weakly without looking up.

Noting Baris' reluctance to leave his friend, Greatjon urged gently, "Baris. . . ."

Realizing he had lingered too long, Baris stood up, snapped a sharp salute, and said, "Yes, sir. Right away, sir," before trotting toward the keep.

Turning his attention back to Aseria, Greatjon hesitated, unsure what to say. Finally, he offered, his tone deeply sincere, "I'm sorry. . . . I shouldn't have pushed you the way I did. Are you okay?"

At first, Aseria remained mute, and Greatjon found himself wondering if Alsa had missed something and she had indeed hurt herself. Thankfully, she finally looked up at him with heavy eyes and replied, her melodic voice weary, "I'll be okay. I . . . I could have really hurt someone."

It wasn't a question.

"Aye. But you didn't," Greatjon responded, his voice gentle, but encouraging. "Believe it or not, reigning in your power like that was far more impressive than anything you've done so far. That takes a disciplined mind – be proud of that."

She shrugged weakly. "Thanks. But still. . . ."

Greatjon knew there was nothing more he could say, so he

gave her shoulder a comforting squeeze and stood up. "Alsa, stay with her. I'm going to go find us something to sit on." Not waiting for a reply, Greatjon wandered off toward the shattered portion of the keep.

By the time Greatjon returned carrying a pair of structurally questionable chairs in each hand, Aseria had recovered enough to stand, and Baris had returned with a basket of food. Upon joining them, all three looked at his choice of seating with suspicion.

"They'll hold me, so you three have nothing to worry about," he said in response to their gazes as he set the chairs down.

Alas shook her head and sighed. "Corith be good – remind me why I agreed to come here?"

Greatjon smirked, but instead of replying, he said to Baris, "Don't stand there looking like a lost lamb; hand out the food and have a seat. I don't know about the rest of you, but I'm as hungry as a famished wolf."

Dubious expressions from everyone greeted his obvious attempt to lighten the mood as they sat down. Baris quickly and silently distributed the contents of the basket. Two loaves of bread and a bowl of dried fruit were shared by all, and a cup for each was used to split a bottle of watered-down wine. Greatjon allowed them to enjoy the simple repast in silence for a bit, but as the meal drew to a close, he broke the solemn atmosphere.

"Power," he stated, his abrupt words startling the others, "is a dangerous thing. It can destroy, manipulate, control, and corrupt. As Gifted, we experience its temptations on a level that mundane people can only imagine. When we train, we are tempering our minds and bodies to control our power lest it dominates us." He eyed the others intently to see if his words had found purchase. Baris was focused on him, as was Aseria – albeit with a cautious light in her eyes – and Alsa looked slightly stunned at the depth of his words.

"Aseria," he continued, "you need to understand that what we are preparing you for is above and beyond what a normal Gifted would face. The power you will be entrusted with is greater than anything Alsa or I possess. It is unfortunate that we do not have a trustworthy Warden to guide you, for their tutelage would far exceed what Alsa and I can give you. We, however, are all that you have. So if our methods appear harsh or even callous, it is because we don't want to be responsible for your death or – Corith forbid – for you falling prey to the abundant temptations that come with great power and immortality. Far too many of us have succumbed to that and ended up a thrall of the Darkness – the last thing we want is that fate for you."

Stunned silence greeted his words. Alsa still appeared taken aback by his insight, while Aseria and Baris looked like they were trying to digest it all.

Finally, Aseria blinked rapidly a few times and shook her head. "I'm sorry, Greatjon. There's so much to take in, and so much being asked of me. . . ." She sighed. "I constantly find myself wondering if this is a dream or a nightmare. I know you and Alsa mean well, but–"

Greatjon held up a hand, forestalling her words. "Don't apologize; there's no need for that. Just promise me that you will continue to work hard and stay true to yourself."

"I. . . ." She paused, then sighed again. "I promise," she said with a slight smirk.

"Good," Greatjon replied. "If it's okay with Alsa, I think you should take the rest of the afternoon off to reflect and meditate on everything. Agreed?"

With a slight, appreciative smile pulling at the corners of her mouth, Alsa replied, "Agreed."

Greatjon nodded. "Good. Meet me back here after the Night Watch Bell tolls, and we'll start your combat lessons in full. You've earned it."

The appointed time arrived far too quickly for Aseria. She'd done her best to take Greatjon's advice to heart, but her focus had been fleeting. Eventually, she went to the dining hall and spent an uncomfortable dinner as the object of her fellow diners' scornful and distrusting gazes. After the events of the afternoon, she couldn't really fault them, but the urge to lash out against their treatment of her was still tantalizing. However, she managed to check her disgust and finish her meal before making a hasty exit from the keep.

Stepping out into the cold night, Aseria took a deep breath and let it out, easing the tension in her body. Shaking out her arms and rolling her neck to remove the remaining tightness, she then made her way back to the training grounds. Coming within sight of the grounds, she grimaced when she saw that she would once again have an audience. As she drew closer, the lit torches revealed that the crowd was mercifully smaller. Not that it really mattered. A few less eyes on her wasn't going to reduce her anxiety or make this any easier.

Aseria did her best to shove the intrusive thoughts aside as she reached the gathering. She noticed Baris standing with a few others just behind the torches as she stepped into the pool of torchlight, and offered him a grateful nod as she came to a halt, which he returned. With a deep, calming breath, she turned her attention to Greatjon and Alsa, who were standing before the blazing brands. While both of her teachers' faces were stoic, their gazes fixed on her, Alsa also had her hands folded at her waist, and Greatjon's claymore stood erect in the ground before him. Neither said a word to her as she saluted, fist to heart, and for a moment, Aseria thought they might be angry with her for some inexplicable reason.

Finally, to her great relief, Greatjon asked, "Are you ready?"

Taking a deep breath, Aseria replied. "I am."

"Good," Greatjon stated before the torches abruptly went dark. "Then light the torches."

Blinking at the sudden shift to darkness, Aseria felt her ire rise at the request. She didn't like having to repeat the task that had led to her outburst, but a part of her understood Greatjon's motives, and that was the part she chose to listen to. As her eyes quickly adjusted to the darkness, she calmed herself and swiftly picked out the unlit brands. She was surprised to see that Alsa and Greatjon no longer stood before her, but instead of dwelling on their sudden disappearance, she focused inward on her wellspring of fir'gan. Cautiously, she latched on to it with as gentle a touch as she could manage and brought it forth.

Standing well behind Aseria, Greatjon grimaced as her aura flickered to life. She was still drawing on too much power and proceeding far too slowly, but to her credit, there was a marked improvement over the afternoon session. As he watched, his fir'gan-sensitive eyes saw her weave the currents about the torch heads. Once more, her technique was sloppy, but it had improved some. Looking at Alsa, their eyes met and he nodded before he readied his claymore.

With effort, Aseria finished weaving the currents and then ignited them. Even though they were expecting it, the eruption of light left Aseria and many onlookers reeling. With a feral hiss, Aseria doubled over and began rubbing and blinking her eyes to clear her vision. Before she could recover, however, her instincts started screaming at her that something was wrong.

Spinning around, she could just make out through her blurred vision someone charging at her. Throwing herself to the right, she barely avoided being skewered. Hitting the ground hard, she pushed herself to all fours and shook her head to clear it. Staggering to her feet, she found herself facing Greatjon, his claymore held shoulder-high and pointed at her.

"Defend yourself!" he barked.

Aseria barely had time to pull her longsword from her back before Greatjon charged again. With impossible ease and speed, Greatjon brought his claymore around in a vicious arc. Wide-eyed and hardly able to see his movements, Aseria barely managed to drop her sword along her left arm to intercept the attack. The crisp ring of steel-on-steel sounded as the blades connected, driving the flat of Aseria's sword into her arm, staggering her. Collecting herself quickly, Aseria assumed a defensive stance despite her throbbing appendage. To her surprise, Greatjon made no move to attack; instead, he faced her with his claymore resting casually across his shoulder and a sly grin on his face.

Nodding her direction, he suggested, "You might want to catch that."

Befuddled, Aseria dropped her guard. Then, on the edge of her senses, she felt a building power behind her. Spinning, she found a grim-faced Alsa with a hand extended toward her. In that moment of shock, Aseria's jaw nearly dropped as she watched Alsa's emerald-green aura flicker in and out of existence as a blast of air quickly expanded in front of her outstretched palm. Aseria had witnessed the end result of such fluid and expert use of fir'gan from Cat, which was amazing to watch at that time. Unfortunately, the delight she might have felt now that she could see everything that went into it was crushed by the fact that she was the target of such an attack.

Engrossed by the sight, she watched as the building air ceased, and Alsa's inner fir'gan began to pool behind the ball of air. A moment later, in the instant before Alsa launched her attack, it suddenly dawned on Aseria that she had no idea how to defend herself against this. Then, as the blast lept toward her, Greatjon's suggestion echoed in her mind, and she did the first thing that popped into her head. Dropping her sword, Aseria flung her hands before her and drew on her power. As her purple aura burst to life, she hastily gathered as much fir'gan as she could around her hands to catch the incoming attack. With a thud and a crackle of power, the blast of air slammed into her outstretched hands, sliding her back a few feet and driving her to her knees.

To her surprise and relief, her idea had worked; the blast hovered just inches from her palms, the air crackling from the clashing powers as the attack tried to bore through her defenses. Seeing this, Aseria growled and forced more fir'gan into her barrier. Immediately, the force of the attack dissipated enough for her to stand back up.

Her confidence bolstered by her success, Aseria settled her feet beneath her before looking over her shoulder with a feral grin and stating, "How's that?"

The mix of pride and cockiness in her tone nearly drew a smile from Greatjon. He knew she felt like she had accomplished something – which he almost let her enjoy – but she was far from getting it right. So, instead of replying vocally, he extended his hand and launched another blast of air at her.

Aseria was stunned by how quickly the blast formed and took flight, as there was no fluctuation in the currents that she could detect, and his aura remained hidden. Fortunately for her, her training kicked in and she snapped a hand over to intercept this new assault. To her chagrin, the reduced power repelling Alsa's attack caused her to stagger into the Greatjon's blast. Through will alone, she managed to keep her focus and catch the new assault, which stood her up sharply and began to press her back toward Alsa's attack. Trapped between the assaults, the pressure in her arms quickly built, forcing them closer to her torso. She tried desperately to increase the fir'gan around her hands, but it was all she could do just to maintain her current levels. To her horror, she quickly realized that if she didn't find a solution fast, her arms would break . . . or worse.

Greatjon watched her growing predicament with concern and pride. She was undoubtedly raw and undisciplined, but she was learning fast. Unfortunately, she had taken his advice literally, and given her vulnerable state, the weak attacks she was battling against could do catastrophic damage if her defenses failed.

Eyeing Alsa, he read the same concern on her face, prompting him to bark, "Aseria – stop trying to catch the attacks! You're not strong enough for that! Spread your barrier out and use it like a shield!"

Aseria shot Greatjon a murderous glare that was unequivocally accusing him of holding back that information – which, of course, he had. Turning her raw anger inward, she used it as fuel to overcome the challenge. Forcing herself to focus on the clashing powers just inches from her palms, she could feel the difference in skill between her and her instructors. Their assaults were as focused as a master blacksmith's blows, while her defenses reminded her of trying to catch a slippery fish with her bare hands. Growling, she forcibly began molding her sloppy attempt to catch the blasts into cohesive, deflective shields. It was an agonizing process that left her head hurting and her arms screaming in agony as the muscles threatened to tear. To her profound relief, just as her elbows were beginning to press into her sides, her fir'gan began to respond.

Slowly, the currents of air began to solidify as they curved and stretched around her hands. The barrier holding back Alsa's blast reacted first, bulging outward before shoving the attack back at its wielder. Pleased with Aseria's effort, Alsa casually used the currents to bat the blast skyward, where it quickly dissipated. That satisfaction, however, turned to dismay when she saw Aseria's other barrier falter and collapse. A sickening thud sounded, and Aseria screamed in pain as the remaining attack collided with her, sending her bouncing toward Alsa.

Cursing under her breath, Alsa latched on to the currents and used them to catch and cushion her charge. Kneeling beside Aseria's crumpled form, she checked her for any sign of severe injury. Though she appeared stunned and her face had a few minor cuts – not to mention she was likely the owner of some remarkable bruises – she appeared intact. Glancing at the onlookers, she saw a few smug looks, but there were a few who seemed to be impressed. Finding Baris, who looked deeply concerned, she gave him a reassuring nod before turning her gaze to Greatjon. His face was unreadable, but he gave her a slight nod to indicate he was pleased with what he had seen.

Fighting the urge to shake her head in disgust, Alsa returned her attention to Aseria, who, with a moan, was beginning to push herself to her feet. "Careful, child," Alsa urged.

With her blonde hair disheveled, and blood from a shallow cut on her right cheek beginning to mat her short fur, Aseria shook her head slowly and climbed unsteadily to her feet. "I'll be fine."

"*Pshaw!* You're far from it!" Alsa chided. "I think you've had enough for one night. You need to rest now."

Anger flared in Aseria's eyes, and she shook her head vehemently. "No – I'm fine. Let's continue; there's too much to learn, and I can't afford to be coddled."

Exasperated, Alsa looked at Greatjon and pleaded, "Greatjon – talk some sense into her! We over did it, and threw a bit more at her than anyone at her level should have to deal with! She should rest!"

To her chagrin, Greatjon shrugged and responded, "She's right, you know. If she feels she can continue, then who am I to argue?"

Alsa's face twisted with consternation. "Barbarians – all of you!" she snapped as she stood up. "Fine! I'll agree to it! But the next time I call for a halt, you will acquiesce!" she declared, brokering no room for argument.

Greatjon nodded. "Agreed," he stated firmly. To Aseria, he

then prodded, "Aseria — when you are ready."

Battered, bruised, and her muscles aching, Aseria retrieved her sword and faced Greatjon. "Ready."

With a grin made more vicious by the scar over his right eye, Greatjon readied his claymore and charged.

Well past the Midnight Bell, Aseria stumbled into her room and shut the door behind her. Leaning against the robust panel, she took a deep breath and closed her eyes. A few tears escaped her closed lids as the pain wracking her body flared again. Her armor was marred and tattered in places, and her longsword would need some attention, but that was nothing compared to her mental and physical fatigue. Never in her life would she have fathomed that she could hurt in so many places at once. Dried blood marred her short fur in numerous places, and the number of fist-sized or larger bruises littering her body made it difficult to move. In fact, it was all she could do not to cry out; however, she had survived — and that was something to be proud of.

Crossing the short distance to her simple bed along the right-hand wall opposite her washbasin, Aseria managed to unbuckle her baldric and lean her sword against the nightstand before collapsing on her bed. She stifled a cry of pain when she made contact with the soft mattress, which made her realize that sleep would be nearly impossible in her current state. Seeking a respite from the pain, she made a mental note to ask about using fir'gan to recover before she focused on recalling the meditative exercises she'd learned over the last few weeks. After a few deep breaths through clenched teeth, she began to pull her mind away from her injuries and focus on the lessons learned.

For a time, she struggled with the task, which nearly made her give up. Thankfully, she managed to push through the temptation and soon found the state of calm she sought, which, in turn, allowed her injuries to fade to nothing more than a distant irritant on the edge of her consciousness. With that barrier removed, and her mind distracted, exhaustion used the opening to sink its teeth into her. Slowly, her mind and body became heavy, and the deep, blissful release of sleep finally welcomed her into its waiting arms.

*

Far to the northwest, Deralina ran.

The massive black- and gray-splotched direwolf's long strides chewed up the ground, barely leaving an impression in the snow as she weaved through the trees. For the last few days, on Greatjon's orders, she had continued to patrol the outlying regions for any sign of a possible invasion. Like her master and Alsa, she felt that such a move by their enemies wasn't imminent; not only were the Bestynes weak, making them only a minor threat at the moment, it was likely the Darkness' servants were still basking in their victory at Blackstone. However, with the young and vulnerable Aseria present, caution seemed more prudent than hopeful optimism. So, like her brethren and packmates, she ran and watched, her senses alert for even the most minute change. It was that prudent behavior that had eventually alerted her to a presence on the currents.

Long missed, but not forgotten, Deralina would have wept with joy had she been able to when she sensed it. Reaching out to it, she had responded with elation. However, that elation was tempered by both troubling news and a request she could not deny. So now, a day later, she ran far from her established patrol, eager to reach her destination.

As the sun reached its zenith, Deralina slowed her run and came to a stop on a ledge overlooking a hollow. From her vantage point, there was no immediately obvious path to the bottom. However, the overlook did provide her with an excellent view of the large grove that occupied the hollow floor. Nearly two-hundred yards in diameter, the grove consisted of oaks and cherry trees that were in full bloom despite winter's firm grasp on the land. While the sight was otherworldly, and impressive in its own right, the prize at the center of the vast grove was what she sought.

Once she was sure all was well with the protective grove, Deralina backtracked along her path for a while before turning north. Familiar as she was with the terrain, it didn't take her long to find the tunnel entrance. Hidden amongst boulders beneath an overhang of stone and ice, it would have been difficult, if not impossible, to find for one unfamiliar with it. Once in the tunnel, she made her way cautiously along the steep, slick path. It took longer than she would have liked to navigate the maze of tunnels, but eventually, she emerged into the hollow barely fifty yards from the grove perimeter.

With reverence, Deralina approached and entered the grove before making her way to the glade at its heart. The clearing, like its protective trees, was out of place in the mountain winter. Lush green grass carpeted the ground along with a dash of cherry blossoms. Birdsong danced upon the warm air, adding a tranquil melody to the wondrous haven. The unique features of the area, however, were far from her mind as her yellow eyes settled on its centerpiece.

Like the other groves scattered about Kylir, this one was

home to one of the few Portculims that weren't housed within a Warden's keep. Standing almost fourteen feet wide and twenty feet tall, the white marble arch occupied the center of the clearing like a prized trophy. Reminiscent of an inverted horseshoe, its ends were embedded in the ground, and its faces were covered with ancient runes that crawled up the arch like a beautifully patterned spiderweb before terminating at an orange crystal inset at the structure's peak. Mounted on the right side of the archway, nearly chest-high on an average man, was a matching marble box that was about the size of Greatjon's hand; four rows of square gems – green, blue, red, and black – were fitted snuggly into the front of the box.

Aware that she was early, Deralina moved to the Portculim and settled herself before it to wait. Nightfall soon came, and she decided to get some sleep to pass the time. Unfortunately, the hours past slowly for the anxious direwolf as she struggled with dark dreams fueled by memories of the past and recent losses. Much to her chagrin, she eventually realized restful sleep would escape her, so she decided to take a walk to clear her mind.

For the rest of the night, she walked the grove, occasionally returning to the Portculim just in case he arrived early. Her wandering did little to alleviate her concerns or anxiousness, but she found it far more tolerable than struggling with fitful sleep, so she continued to do so until just before dawn. At that time, as her anxiety turned into anticipation, she returned to the Portculim and seated herself before it. She knew it wouldn't be long now, but her eagerness for dawn's arrival made it feel like it was lethargically slow to arrive. Finally, a hint of light broke night's hold on the land, and as dawn's glow slowly crept over the mountains, her patience was rewarded.

A gentle hum from the Portculim suddenly filled the air as orange energy began crawling up the arch from the ends embedded in the ground, igniting the runes as it touched each one. Finally, the energy reached the peak of the arch and made contact with the orange crystal, which began to throb with a dull light. The pulsing light steadily grew brighter until the crystal abruptly flared and shot a beam of orange energy toward the ground. Stopping just inches above the earth, the beam began to twist and widen until it filled the entirety of the arch with a swirling void of orange light. A few seconds later, a young man Deralina did not recognize stumbled from the swirling portal.

Standing quickly, she sidestepped the off-balance man as he fell past her and crashed to the ground, sending a shower of cherry blossoms skyward. Watching the dark-haired human with amusement as he pushed himself to all fours with a string of curses, Deralina suddenly sensed a familiar presence coming from the portal. Turning her attention back to the Portculim, she would have smiled if she could have done so as another man emerged from the orange void.

With reverence and joy, Deralina slid a paw forward and dipped her head. Reaching along the currents, she connected with the figure standing before her and stated through the link, her deep feminine voice filled with joy, *"Light bless you, and welcome back."*

Chapter Five

She firmly believed people were idiots, and she had been called such on many occasions for such a blanket statement. Those that referred to her that way were dimwits for not seeing the truth of the assertion – and she never argued with dimwits, much less idiots.

At a young age, she'd learned that one paramount truth and held it close to her heart. Abandoned when she was just a babe, her now long-dead uncle and aunt had raised her in the lowlands of Sur'datha, and served as a shining example of this reality. Eternally poor, her uncle had been an idiot for wasting his years breaking his back in a warehouse for a pittance for an obscenely wealthy merchant. Even as a child, she understood that his pay wasn't equivalent to the labor he provided, but her dimwitted uncle had always shrugged off any insinuation that he was undervalued, claiming his boss was a good and agreeable man. When he died around her tenth summer, drunk and with his wrists opened wide, she had sneered and thanked whatever gods or spirits might be listening for removing the fool from the world.

Unfortunately, in her mind, her aunt was even more of a damn fool than her uncle. While the career tavern maid had foolishly remained with her husband, she was far from loyal. Be it day or night, when her uncle was working and she wasn't at the tavern, her aunt could be found rutting with other men. She never knew if her uncle was aware of his wife's infidelity, but it wasn't long after his death that her aunt remarried and they moved to Chalin. Like her aunt and late uncle, the man was just another idiot, and within two months of settling in the city, he caught her aunt with another man. To his credit, he took issue with her aunt's promiscuity and killed both her and her lover, and was eventually arrested for their murders. To this day, she had no idea what had become of the man.

With no relatives or friends to take her in, she was left to her own devices for a time. Thankfully, she, unlike her family and the rest of humanity, was not an idiot. Chalin – the so-called City of Dreams – was a city of wealth, and one simply had to know where and how to claim it. She discovered quickly that she had a talent for acquiring what she wanted from the unsuspecting masses, and soon came to the attention of a talented thief looking to pass on his knowledge. With his tutelage, she soon found that she wanted for nothing. The disgruntled people she stole from called her a thief and a threat to decent people and society; she called them stupid for their inability to hold on to their excessive possessions. Yet, despite all their complaints, she'd never come close to being apprehended, and only a select few knew of her proficient career thanks to her cautious approach. Furthermore, she rarely stole simply to steal, and only kept what she needed. Most of her heists saw any excess either fenced or distributed amongst Chalin's destitute. She did, however, have one annoying vice – a challenging theft for pay.

More often than she would have liked, idiots approached her with foolish jobs merely to test her skills. She frequently turned such tests down as the payout wasn't worth the risk. However, on rare occasions, a challenge with pay worthy of her skills would come along that was too tantalizing to resist. Word of such a rare jewel had reached her ears through Chalin's Thieves Guild two days ago, and her curiosity was the reason she now made her way along the city's well-maintained, gently curving cobblestone streets.

Unlike many whose professions were better served by the cover of night, she walked the streets without fear of drawing attention. Her weathered clothing – a long, once rich-green tunic, supple black breeches and boots, and a red cloak – was not only inconspicuous enough to avoid suspicion when she wandered Chalin, but it concealed the array of knotwork tattoos that she wore on her toned arms and torso as a tribute to her ancestral home. Tugging at her red leather gloves, the young woman then pushed a lock of her chin-length blonde hair away from her well-defined face. Pressing her thin lips together, she scanned the street with her blue eyes, seeking her destination.

If there was one criticism she had about herself, it was her height. Where her relatives had benefited from above-average stature, she had somehow found herself bereft of the gift. Granted, her under five-and-a-half feet tall stature had its benefits when it came to her trade, but in situations like this, she found herself wishing for a few more inches or, at the very least, that she had taken to wearing heels. Frustrated with her obscured sightline, she nimbly weaved through the crowd – lifting a few unsecured coin pouches along the way – toward the buildings on her left.

Made primarily of wood and some granite blocks, the buildings that occupied the northern section of Chalin were lovely, though unremarkable, works of predominantly two-story architecture. Most of the buildings' main floors were elevated and accessed via a short set of stairs; as such, she found their landings the perfect place from which to gaze over the throng's heads. So once she cleared the crowd, she climbed the stairs of a cobbler's shop and stood upon the bottom support of the landing's railing to get a better view.

Watching the crowd for a moment as they traversed the street beneath the late-afternoon sun hanging in a nearly cloudless sky, she forced herself to suppress a scornful laugh. As they had been since the announcement of Doms Suldamik's engagement to Doma Ithikia, the fools and idiots of the city were abuzz with talk of the union and how it might improve their lives. She thought such banter was a pointless waste of time. Nothing changed, no matter who ruled or who married whom – the rich remained rich, the poor remained poor, and everyone would continue to go about their meaningless, idiotic lives. But, if such passing interests helped the foolish masses deal with their existence, then who was she to begrudge them that before death put an end to it?

Without thinking, she found her eyes drawn to the south, where the spires of Chalin Keep and the Great Cathedral of Deo loomed over the city. The black and gray stone structures seemed to be reaching skyward in an attempt to escape the looming presence of the monstrous dragon statue that stood vigil over the Utherian Valley's main gate. Given her angle, she could only see a portion of the behemoth beast's horns, neck and shoulders. However, like all citizens of Chalin, she was all too familiar with the black-and-gray-striated stone guardian. A slight smirk tugged at her lips when she pictured the giant emeralds that served as eyes below the statue's heavy, furrowed brow. Now, that would be the ultimate challenge; to steal such a prize would emblazon one's name in the tomes of history. Granted, she knew that such a heist was impossible, but it was something she liked to puzzle over when she found herself with too much time on her hands.

Clearing her mind of its childish wanderings, she peered to the north and caught sight of what she was looking for. Descending from her perch, she weaved her way through the crowded street, unfazed by the number of City Guards on patrol. Many of her fellow thieves either had been forced into early retirement or had changed their practices when Craigan increased the number of patrols, but not her. As far as she was concerned, those who had been incarcerated since then were a result of everyone trying so damn hard to hide in the shadows. In her mind, the authorities always checked the shadows. However, if one hid in plain sight, the powers that be always seemed to overlook them. That reasoning had served her well, and in line with that logic, she made no move to shy away from the Guards when they came near her. As they had numerous times before, not a single one of them spared her more than a passing glance. Chuckling smugly to herself, she reached her intended street and turned onto it.

Like the previous thoroughfare, this one was just as crowded; however, she now had her bearings. So, with a casual quickness, she followed the road for about eighty paces before turning right onto an intersecting street. Before long, the number of pedestrians had dwindled, and she found herself setting foot on one of the few gravel streets in Chalin.

The Street of Dreams, it was called, though it was anyone's guess if its title actually had anything to do with Chalin's affectionate epithet. As she casually walked the southern end of the lane, she had to admit to herself that if jewelry was one's dream, then the street was aptly named. Upon first glance, the buildings gave little indication that there was anything of significant worth to be found along the road, as the wooden structures were small and largely unpainted. However, the number of visiting well-to-do pedestrians was a clear sign that there was more to the street, and one only had to peek through the stores' windows to see why. She had no deed to do so, unlike the gawking idiots, as she was very familiar with the treasures contained within the establishments. Furthermore, acquiring any of the trinkets wasn't a matter of talons for her; she took what she wanted when she wanted from the jewelers, and had done so on several occasions when she was in need of quick coin. In fact, she liked to believe the barred windows were in response to some of her forays.

A few of the guards and pedestrians offered her passing glances, but she ignored them as she approached a small shop tucked between two larger and better-appointed establishments. A simple, hand-painted sign featuring a gold necklace about the neck of a mannequin head announced the store as Rothumb's Royal Jewels. She knew the renowned owner for which the establishment was named, and had extended him the courtesy of never stealing from him. On several occasions, she had been asked why she had shied away from his store, and the simple answer was that she liked the reclusive old man. Upon his retirement, she'd extended the same courtesy to the current owner, Rothumb's former apprentice.

Reaching the shop's door, she pushed it open and stepped into the modestly crowded showroom. For reasons she'd never fully grasped, she felt a wave of satisfaction wash over her as she looked around. In years past, business had been lethargic for the once-famed jeweler, but as word spread of the reworked wedding ring that had been presented to Doma Ithikia, Rothumb's Royal Jewels had seen a surge in patrons. She almost smiled as she watched the customers examine the delights artfully arranged in the display cases stationed about the room's perimeter. The store's current owner had laid new green rugs on the floor, replaced all the cases with stout iron-framed displays, and hired two young, outgoing women to staff the floor. There was no doubt in anyone's mind that the flood of new decor and workers was a result of House Suldamik's patronage, and she was forced to give the Suldamiks some credit for that.

Closing the door behind her, she then idly perused the displays, her keen eyes noting the new – and below Rothumb's standard quality – jewelry. The sudden drop in quality was to be expected, at least in her mind. Demand had risen, and the fools who desperately wanted to say they owned a piece crafted by the man who made Doma Ithikia's ring had eagerly bought the old pieces. She figured it was only a matter of time before items worthy of Rothumb once again graced the store, but until then, the jewelry in the displays would have to do; which didn't seem to matter, as she saw one couple purchasing a trio of the sub-par accessories.

She briefly wondered if she shouldn't relieve the apparently brainless couple of the burden of their talons before her attention was caught by the parting red curtains at the rear-right of the showroom. Short, rotund, and balding, the man's blonde-bearded face looked haggard, and his small black eyes were filled with exhaustion. Wiping his hands on the leather artisan's apron he wore over his white tunic and brown breeches, the man looked over the room, satisfaction shining in his eyes. Spotting her, he smiled and waved her over.

Making her way over to him, she gave him a friendly hug. "Good to see ye, Gathris," she stated, the deep tones of her voice filled with friendly warmth.

"You too, lass," he replied with a bit of joy in his tired, somewhat nasal voice as she pulled back.

"Ye look worn to tha bone. These snobs are askin' too much of ye."

He shrugged sheepishly. "Might be the case, but I don't mind. Honestly, it's good to be busy, and I won't take it for granted. No tellin' when it might all go away."

"Aye," she responded as she looked around at the patrons again. "So," she added as she faced him, "ye mentioned ye might be knowin' someone that has work fer me?"

Gathris' face instantly turned serious when she asked the question, and her interest in the job suddenly grew. "Aye," he responded softly but gravely. Turning to the curtain on brown-shoed feet, he pulled it back and motioned her through. "This way, lass."

Stepping through, she waited for Gathris to speak with one

of the girls tending the floor. She'd only been in the workshop on a handful of occasions, and other than being busy, it never seemed to change, that is, until recently. Though it was still organized with care, the small workshop had been rearranged. Rothumb's bench – which was now Gathris', she reminded herself – remained along the rear wall next to a small forge and crucible, but three extra workbenches had been added around the perimeter of the room. A trio of new apprentices – a young woman and a pair of teenage boys – were engrossed with their work at their respective stations. Not one spared her a glance, and she smiled at their focus.

"Rothumb would be proud of them," she thought.

A meaty hand on her shoulder drew her attention, and she turned to see Gathris motioning to the door at the rear-right corner of the room, which they quickly approached. Upon stepping outside, she took a few strides forward before turning to face Gathris. As soon as he shut the door, she asked, "Are ye gonna tell me more 'bout this job?"

"Lass, you best hear it from them – I can scarce believe it myself."

Her interest fully perked, she raised a quizzical eyebrow and said, "Lead on, then."

Gathris nodded and motioned across the small gravel yard separating the store from the small, single-story wood building that had served as Rothumb's home on the rare occasion that he chose to sleep there. Noticing her inquisitive gaze, he said, "Aye, that's where we're meeting."

"I would'a thought it abandoned," she said as they started toward the building.

Gathris scratched his head sheepishly. "Well, I couldn't just let it go unused; thought that would be an insult to the Old Man. I've been living there for a while now."

She chuckled. "Yer an odd one, ye know that? Always doin' what no one expects."

Grinning, he replied, "That's why I'm still a free man, lass. Besides, isn't it better to hide in plain sight?"

She smirked in agreement.

Reaching the small home, Gathris opened the door, and it swung inward with a groan. Stepping inside, they found themselves in a cramped, dimly lit space. Immediately before them were a serviceable kitchen and a simple table and chairs. A curtained-off room – which she presumed was a bedroom – was on the far wall, and off to their right was a den occupied by a small hearth, a lone shuttered window, a series of chairs, and a man who stood watching her with blatant suspicion.

Shutting the door, Gathris approached the man and grasped his forearm in a firm handshake. "Sorry about the wait, Logan."

Wiry and with a shaved head, Logan's tall frame was clothed in a leather vest over a threadbare tunic, and a pair of brown wool breech tucked into workman's boots. An understanding smile spread across his broad, sharp-featured face as he replied in a ragged voice that reminded her of someone who had indulged in deathweed too much, "Not to worry – caution outweighs haste." Turning his nearly yellow eyes on her, he asked, "Is this her?"

Looking at her, Gathris replied, "Aye, that's her. Logan, may I present to you, Mal."

"Mal," Logan repeated. "Not very feminine. Did your parents want a son?"

Biting back a sharp retort at the boorish comment, she said, "Might that they did; I wouldn't be knowin'. But, if ye must know, it's short fer Malia."

"Ah," Logan said. "I see, then. I suppose that would be prudent in your profession."

Mal's eyes flashed at the ignorant, chauvinistic words, but she once again held her tongue. "Gathris 'ere said there's a job to be had, so if ye don't mind gettin' to tha point. . . ."

A wry smile broke across Logan's face. "Direct. I like that." Motioning to one of the chairs, he said, "Please, have a seat."

As Gathris and Logan moved to seat themselves, Mal decided it would be best to accept the offer. Choosing a seat that put her back to a wall and gave her a clear view of the room, she turned the chair around and straddled it. Folding her arms across the top of the seat's back, she said, "Out with it, then, laddie. I don't take just any ol' job . . . so this better make domses weep, and eyes wide as saucers."

"Very well. I represent a group of respectable, wealthy citizens," Mal almost scoffed at the declaration, "that have an interest in historical relics. They have recently stumbled upon the location of a unique and very valuable object that they wish to . . . acquire."

Mal was unable to contain a half-grin. "Well, that's mighty fine, but if yer clients are what ye say they are, then why be comin' to me? Surely they have tha coin to buy what they want?" she pressed.

Logan returned the smile. "Ah, but as you've already concluded, that isn't the case. What they seek is well protected and, according to many, either doesn't exist or is impossible to acquire. In fact, should you accept and pull this off, you'll be as famous as the Lithe Spider."

Mal rolled her eyes and stood up. "Right. . . . Sorry, lad – if yer chasin' wisps, then ye've come to tha wrong lass. Sorry to have wasted yer time." Nodding to Gathris, she added, "Gathris. I'll be seein' ye 'round."

As she started to swing her leg over the chair, Logan stood up and exclaimed, "Wait! This is not some flight of fancy, I can assure you!"

Smiling to herself, Mal replied, "Then yer gonna have to give me more than gossip."

Logan shot a quick glance at Gathris and received a confident nod in response. "Very well," Logan grudgingly declared to Mal.

"That's better," she said as she seated herself.

"Based on what Gathris has told us, you have little love for House Suldamik, correct?"

"Ah, now we're gettin' somewhere," she replied. "Aye, I could be carin' less fer tha Suldamiks, and even less fer tha war. But what does this have to do with tha job? I hope ye don't have a notion to be stealin' from Chalin Keep, 'cause stealin' from them be a bit of a bore."

"You've breached the keep before?" Logan asked with a hint of disbelief in his voice.

Mal shrugged nonchalantly even as Gathris said with pride, "I told you she was good – and I wouldn't lie about my last and greatest pupil."

Mal snorted at the claim. "Ye just keep tellin' yerself that! Ye were practically out of tha game by tha time I came 'round."

"While I'm sure there's an interesting story there," Logan interrupted, "might we return to the subject at hand?"

"Aye, 'fore Gathris' pride grows anymore," Mal replied.

"Good. Where was I? Ah, yes. . . House Suldamik. What would you say if I were to tell you there was a way to bring down House Suldamik and put an end to this ghastly war with minimal bloodshed; and the means to do so reside somewhere within the city?"

Mal laughed. *"What a daft bugger this one is,"* she thought to herself before saying aloud, "Right. . . . Well, whether I believe ye or not, that's a dangerous notion, bringin' down tha Suldamiks and all. Mighty bold of ye to be tellin' me all this; I could just run to tha Guard and make a nice profit turnin' in Resistance folks." She looked at Gathris and grinned. "When did ye take up with this lot? Seems a bit forward of ye."

Blushing a bit and looking ashamed, Gathris struggled to find the words to explain, but was saved from doing so by Logan. "You're perceptive, I'll give you that."

Mal snorted to herself and thought, *"Didn't take much to figure it out; ye practically announced yer loyalties, ye lummox!"*

"Yes, I represent the Resistance, but unlike the nobles would have you believe, we are not in league with the Merandiths. In our particular case, we simply want to see the war brought to an end and Chalin's autonomy returned."

"So, ye think some item will be doin' just that, eh? Let's say yer talkin' straight with me – what's to keep tha Merandiths from ta-kin' Chalin and rulin' it?"

Logan shrugged. "Nothing. But we would fight their rule just as much as the Suldamiks. However, I do not believe it will come to that, for the object we seek may be just as damning to them as House Suldamik."

Mal arched an eyebrow. "And why is that?"

Logan leaned back in his chair. "First, I need you to agree to take the job."

Mal laughed. "I'm far from stupid, lad. I'm not 'bout to be takin' a job that I don't know tha details of, much less without bein' rightly compensated."

Logan looked at Gathris and said, "This is a waste of time! If she's not going to help, then we need to find someone else."

"Be reasonable, Logan," Gathris replied. "You're asking her to go against the Suldamiks without giving her much to go on. We have to make it worth her efforts – and believe me – she's your only shot at accomplishing this."

Logan stared at Gathris thoughtfully for a moment before asking Mal, "Alright, what's your price?"

Mal smirked, "Without knowin' tha details? Nine-hundred talons – all up front."

Logan blanched at the number. "Nine hundred? That's extortion!" he proclaimed indignantly.

Mal shrugged. "Well, this job seems important enough to ye, and yer not givin' me much to go on . . ." she trailed off with a shrug and started to stand.

Before she could leave or Logan could say something rash, Gathris said, "Wait, Mal."

Mal nodded to him and sat back down.

Looking back at Logan, Gathris offered, "What if I cover a portion of her fee?"

Logan studied him briefly before grudgingly replying, "Very well, Gathris, but she had better be all that you claim."

"Aye, she is," he responded before asking Mal, "How about Eight hundred – with half now and the other half upon completion?"

Mal smiled to herself and remained silent for a moment as if she were contemplating the deal. Finally, when she was satisfied with Logan's growing discomfort with her silence, she said, "Aye, it's a deal. So what do ye want me to steal?"

Though disgusted with Mal's behavior, her acceptance of the job brought Logan a measure of relief. "A very rare object belonging to House Suldamik."

Mal scoffed. "Ye've already hinted at that. I want details – size, weight, location, value."

Logan smirked at her irritation. Leaning forward, he responded with a question instead. "Tell me – what do you know Kylir's history, and in particular, the Second Great War?"

That night, Mal found herself standing before the behemoth dragon statue that stood guard over the city entrance to the Utherian Valley. Towering over her like a mountain, Mal could barely make out the details of the magnificent, crouching beast in the moonless night. At times, she thought she could see some of the veins of jade that ran through the black and gray stone guardian, but it was likely a trick played by a mind full of wondrous possibilities.

If what Logan told her even held a grain of truth, then the Valley contained a secret more precious than the fabled Luthur Gravit'nas. She chuckled to herself. Even if her objective was the delusional creation of a group desperately grasping for a banner to rally behind since Craigan's elder brother, Zalan, was executed, the challenge ahead of her was enough for her to take the job. Since Craigan took control of Chalin, public access to the Valley had been cut off.

Since then, those who had tried to enter received swift and violent punishment. House Suldamik's wrath, however, was the least of her worries.

Outside of Craigan himself, she knew of no one who was aware of the Valley's layout. Of more immediate concern, however, was the issue of entry into it. Though she could not see them, the giant double doors of the Valley entrance were guarded day and night, but it was only for show since they were sealed tightly and could only be opened by Doms Suldamik. There was also Craigan's private entrance, but that was also guarded; this time, by a small garrison. Of course, there was the option to try the hills surrounding the Utherian Valley, which was fraught with unknowns. Clearly, all three options had their own perils, but the thrill that the risks and challenges filled her with suddenly made her smile. Yes, this was a task worthy of her skills, and if she succeeded, not only would she never want for anything, but she would help redefine Triclose's history and set the course for its future.

With a smile on her face and a bounce to her step, Mal spared one more glance at the statue before turning and heading for home.

A moment later, swathed in a concealing pitch-black cloak and hood, a figure separated from the shadows of the stone base supporting the dragon's front-right foot. It had been an easy task for him to stalk the vermin thanks to his mistress' talents, but as he looked down the path Mal had taken, he had to give the girl some credit. From what he'd learned of this Mal, she was quite talented, but particular with the jobs she took. What's more, for a thief with her reputation, hiding in plain sight was a brazen and brave approach. Still, it sickened him that such filth poisoned this city.

His hand started to stray to the knife at his belt as his thoughts momentarily turned toward cleansing justice. It would be easy to follow the rat and end her miserable, leeching existence, but his mistress had forbidden it . . . for now. She had her reasons for picking out this particular plaything, and she was not one to cross, nor was she one to be kept waiting. So, with one last murderous glance in Mal's direction, he turned toward the keep and strode off, eager to make his report.

<h1 style="text-align:center">Chapter Six</h1>

"Hells' bloody balls! I didna think it could be gettin' this cold down 'ere!"

Gregor Netwyn, Doms Captain-Commander of Hagan's Hammer, chuckled. Shaking his head of white-speckled rusty hair, which was bound at the nape of his neck by a strip of blue and red cloth, he turned his keen green eyes on his brown-haired subordinate. Younger and slightly shorter than Gregor, Donald's attire was the same as his — a heavy black cloak made for Highland winters over chainmail, and a Sur'dathan claymore stowed across his back. A small grin split the neatly trimmed, predominantly white beard that covered Gregor's aged, sun-darkened visage and concealed a portion of the jagged cheek-to-chin scar that marred the right side of his lips. He knew that Donald's complaint was nothing more than nervous energy because both of them were used to the brutal Sur'dathan winters.

"What's tha matter, lad? Yer not goin' soft on me, ar' ye?" Gregor teased, his thick Highland accent softened by mirth, and his eyes bright from astride his crooked nose.

Donald scoffed. Running a brown-gloved hand through his short hair, he stated, irritation apparent in his normally warm voice, "It's all tha waitin', Captain!" Gesturing toward the workers, and their attentive guardians, who were digging trenches with haste around the base of a rise that was home to a robust wood-walled fort, he added, "I dunna like keepin' our enemy waitin'."

From their position deep within the tree line of a stand of evergreens, Gregor glanced back across the significant distance separating them from their target. With the sun setting, it was getting hard to see, but he could make out just enough to conclude that the laborers would continue avoiding nighttime work and the risk of losing more men to quick-strike attacks.

"Aye, I know, lad. But, ye know good 'n well that war rarely goes ta plan," Gregor reminded his subordinate.

"I know. But . . ." Donald trailed off with a shake of his head, his black eyes flashing with dissatisfaction from astride the slender nose on his long, handsome face.

Gregor couldn't fault the lad for his frustration. Like Donald, he and many others were feeling the effects of the unforeseen delay. What was supposed to be a short and violent campaign had turned into a frustrating wait. In order to advance on the Jade Talon's border fort as inconspicuously as possible, their relatively undersized army left their base camp in numerous small groups over three days. According to reports, most of the groups had arrived at the rally points amongst the thickets scattered about the rolling plains that the fort called home. This meant he had roughly two-thousand mixed infantry, one-hundred heavy cavalry, and fifty archers ready to engage. Unfortunately, that was as far as Deo seemed inclined to bless them, as hiding that many soldiers was always going to be an impossible task.

As Gregor feared, and to his chagrin, a few of his troops had been spotted or killed early on, and that was more than enough to alert the fort's occupants to a looming threat. The fort's commander had responded quickly and, to a certain degree, as expected – the gates were sealed, patrols limited, and the wall guard increased. Unfortunately, the preparations didn't end there. Be it ill or good luck, on the day that Gregor was supposed to launch the attack, reinforcements arrived at the fort that, according to estimates, more than doubled the defenders' ranks. Before Gregor and his officers could fully digest the sudden shift in the situation, a large number of soldiers had emerged from the fort and began hastily digging a series of trenches around the rise.

By the middle of the second week, several of Gregor's squads had been flushed out, with casualties on both sides. Thankfully, with as spread out as the Merandith forces were, and the nighttime strikes on the laborers, the Suldamiks seemed unable to get a handle on just what they were up against, and had yet to venture out in full. However, that couldn't keep nerves from growing thin amongst Gregor's men. While they still greatly outnumbered the defenders, their scattered numbers would be vulnerable if the Jade Talons were to attack suddenly and in force. However, if those under Gregor's command had expected him to simply abandon the mission, or for withdrawal orders to arrive from Doms Hagail, they were sadly mistaken.

Clapping Donald on the shoulder, Gregor declared, "Let's get goin', lad. Desrosa should be back by now, and we don't be havin' much time ta get ready."

Quickly and carefully, the two Sur'dathan Highlanders made their way deeper into the thicket. Along the way to their camp, they stopped at three others, all of which belonged to infantry, and made sure preparations were proceeding smoothly. While they had tried to bring as many of their fellow Sur'dathans as possible, there were still a large number of lowlanders amongst their ranks whose experience with winter warfare was limited by comparison. Granted, everyone was used to the harsh conditions of life at war, but the number of days spent hiding and the number of cold, fireless nights spent without the protection of a tent had taken a toll on both wounded and lowlanders alike. Fortunately, any fears Gregor had about the state of the lowlanders were put to rest by the fire he saw burning in their eyes and in the precise, determined manner in which they went about their preparations. This night was what they'd been waiting for, and the call to action was proving a powerful tonic for worrisome thoughts and fresh injuries.

It was already growing quite dark by the time Gregor and Donald reached their camp, and Gregor was delighted to see that his men were well along in their preparations. By necessity, Gregor had split the Hammer into ten groups. Hiding a hundred heavy cavalry together for this long would have been nigh impossible given the conditions, and even hiding ten had proven difficult. Thankfully, his men had been up to the task, and their well-trained destriders had behaved magnificently. These men had been forced to hide their armor and spend more time off their prized mounts than they preferred, but now that action was imminent, the battle-hardened Highlanders had a bounce to their step that was far more energetic than what Gregor had seen in the other camps.

Despite their apparent excitement, Gregor was pleased to see that discipline remained paramount; horses were quietly saddled and girded in steel and muffling blankets, soldiers donned their burnished-steel armor quietly and then covered themselves with heavy cloaks, and their deadly saber-lances were being unpacked with care. It was a fine display of organization and discipline to see, and Gregor knew that no matter the night's outcome, his men would make him proud.

After talking with a few of his men and dismissing Donald to finish his preparations, Gregor, as he did before every battle, took time to inspect their highly feared and notorious lances. Arranged on the ground in a tidy row, the ten meticulously maintained, ghastly weapons were made of polished northern ironwood, the upper quarter of which was fitted with a steel mount that supported a four-winged lance head. The catastrophic damage they were designed to do on impact carried over to removal thanks to the hooked ends of each wing. Because of the harm they did, the weapons were considered controversial in some circles. However, the Sur'dathans cared very little about what others thought. The weapons got results, and that's what mattered. As for their usefulness in their current situation, Gregor was unsure. Their orders were to take the fort as a base of operations, which meant they couldn't simply burn the place to the ground to force the enemy into the field where the lances could be used to full effect. If, however, they did manage to flush their foe out from behind their protective walls, then his Hammer and their lances would be ready to add to the weapon's terrifying legend.

"Your enemies will tremble with fear before the thunder of your hooves, Captain," stated a firm but soft voice.

Startled, Gregor spun around to find the human lieutenant from House Fortal and the cyrian, Solaria Desrosa, standing behind him. "Damn it, Solaria! Yer too damn quiet fer me likin'! And that goes fer ye, too, Coltan!"

Clad in black leather armor, the only color on the short, nimble, shaved-headed Coltan was a badge on his right shoulder of a grinning skull surrounded by nine balls of flame. "Wouldn't be good at my job if I wasn't, sir," Coltan quipped with a smirk, his rough voice jovial, and his small brown eyes twinkling with mirth from their sunken sockets on his long face.

"My apologies, Captain. We did not mean to startle you," Solaria added while shooting Coltan a chastising glare.

Gregor grunted. "It's fine. Just pre-battle nerves gettin' tha best o' me."

He knew what Coltan said was true, and firmly believed Solaria's apology, but he still found it difficult to believe just how silent Solaria could be. Athletic and lean, Solaria stood just over six feet, and – like all her people – her proportions were elongated. To him, she simply didn't look like she had the coordination to move in such a silent manner; recent experience, however, had shown him that wasn't the case. Beyond their unusual features – velvet-like skin and feral-shaped eyes – her people were said to be skilled stalkers and archers, which they'd proven to Gregor by serving as impeccable scouts and hunters over the last two weeks.

"So, is yer people ready?" Gregor asked.

"Aye, sir. Hells' Heralds are ready and able," the middle-aged Coltan responded confidently.

"And ye, Solaria?"

When she turned her gaze back to him, Gregor couldn't help but note the graceful tattoos surrounding her eyes. Flaring from the corners of the yellow jewels and sweeping down the outside of her broad, somewhat flat nose in a fashion that made her appear more feral than human, they reminded him somewhat of the knotwork tattoos his fellow clansmen wore. "We are. And I am pleased with the capabilities of my companion here, as well as his men. Their unit has served Doms Merandith well, and they understand what this mission requires."

Gregor nodded. Solaria's familiarity with Coltan's people wasn't a surprise. Hells' Heralds were from the realm of Ulthion, one of the small lands that now belonged to the Contested Territories. It shared a border with Caith'tol, the small cyrian realm that sat – untouched – in the heart of the Contested Territories. Some of Ulthion's people had taken sanctuary within Caith'tol's borders, while the rest found refuge within the realms allied with House Merandith. As such, Gregor surmised that Solaria and Coltan had served together in some capacity for a while. However, despite Solaria's assurances, Gregor had his concerns about their ability to function as a cohesive unit. Under Doms Hagail's new unit organization, as well as under Doms Merandith, they would typically act separately, but this mission called for the skills they had in common. Their shared talents, however, were limited, and Gregor worried the differences could hinder them.

Where Hells' Heralds wore leathers that were nearly as black as Solaria's slicked-back, short-cropped hair, and their skills were more akin to those of assassins, Solaria's people reminded Gregor more of hunters. While terrifyingly quiet, they preferred bows to knives, and their armor was reminiscent of that which a scout or hunter might wear, albeit of an unusual design. In Solaria's case, her armor was made of supple dark-brown leather that was a near match for her skin, and her upper body was protected by a padded, square-shouldered top with a high-collar neck he'd learned was called a tri'shoek. This upper torso piece was, in turn, secured to her upper arms and a padded leather bodice by buckles that had been weathered to prevent them from reflecting light. Beneath all this, she wore a black wool shirt that was secured at her wrists by a standard bracer around her left forearm and an elbow-length bracer around her right. Her hands were protected by the dark brown, fingerless leather gloves her people preferred, the left of which sported three fingers as a defense against her bowstring. As for her legs and feet, her leather pants were dyed a deep forest green along the inner thigh and crotch, which matched her supple boots as well as the piping of her bodice and the subtle highlights in her hair.

If this had been a daytime operation, Gregor would have feared the green standing out against the winter-stricken plains. Thankfully, that wasn't the case, and the moonless night would make her and her people difficult to see no matter what they were wearing. Still, that did little to alleviate his concerns. As such, he asked, giving voice to those trepidations, "Are ye sure ye should be goin', Solaria? I dunna wanna lose you."

She smiled reassuringly and folded her arms beneath her small breasts confidently. "I will be fine. We may be known for our bows, but we are just as deadly with the blade."

Gregor eyed the pair of leaf-shaped shortswords at her hips but found his eyes drifting up to the enormous, recurved heartsong bow slung across her back along with a quiver full of the largest arrows he'd ever seen. Unique to the cyrians, heartsong bows were made from white ironwoods known to grow only in Caith'tol. Cyrians were only permitted to fashion their bow when they had earned it, and the bows – from what Gregor had seen – tended to be carved into the likeness of an animal. In Solaria's case, the length of the bow resembled a feathered neck, while the ends looked like the screeching head of a mythical gryphon. Cyrians were rarely without their bows, but such a weapon would only hinder Solaria this night. Therefore, she had agreed to leave it behind. Her willingness to do so in the name of safety was commendable, but it actually added to Gregor's unease somewhat. Being without one's primary weapon was something no soldier liked; it made them less effective and left them vulnerable.

"I'll take yer word for it," he responded, keeping his concern from weighing too heavily on his words. "I trust yer bow will be well cared fer? I'd hate fer somethin' ta happen ta it."

Solaria flashed the same reassuring smile. "Be at peace, Captain, and fear not for me. My bow will be well taken care of, and the Forest Mother will see me through the night."

Gregor grunted. "Right, then. Our men at tha rear should already be movin' up, so once night falls, ye'll have half an hour ta get into position. We'll be doin' our best ta draw their attention, but ye better be quick 'bout it. If'n things go sour – get tha hells out o' there. No need ta be losin' good soldiers over nothin'."

Solaria nodded. "Quite so. We will be ready. Grove protect you," she intoned, saluting fist to heart. "And may you find shade beneath the Mother's boughs, Captain," she finished before turning and walking away.

Gregor shook his head at her retreating back. "I'll never be understandin' cyrians 'n their tree worshipin'," he muttered, which drew a bemused grin from Coltan.

"Don't discount it, Captain," Coltan replied. "Haven't you ever wondered why the war has never breached their borders?"

"Never given it much thought, lad. Figured there's just nothin' o' value there."

"That might be the case," Coltan said with a shrug, "but I've seen wonders there that would make you believe in magic, Captain."

Gregor grunted. "'N what might those be, eh?"

Coltan grinned. "Ah, but gossiping about your host's secrets wouldn't be proper, sir," he stated with a wink before snapping off a crisp, fist-to-heart salute. "I best be on my way. Deo watch over you, Captain," he declared before hustling to catch up with Solaria.

Shaking his head in befuddled amusement, Gregor muttered, "Lowlanders," before moving off to prepare for the coming battle.

*

Standing atop the battlements, tired and irritated, Doms Captain Sagan Toriv Torvan was a man in search of redemption. Nearing his fifty-fifth summer, he grew up destitute in the streets of Surandia's capital, Roland'tor. Unwilling to accept the pitiful existence fate had bestowed on him, he joined the Surandian military when he came of age in the hopes of either bettering his life or finding a meaningful and honorable end to his existence. To his surprise, during his time in the infantry, he discovered a talent for tactics and martial combat that granted him the former of his goals. Although he made many enemies amongst jealous nobles as he ascended through the ranks, Sagan also earned the respect of many for his service during the rule of Craigan's father. As such, honors and praises were heaped about his shoulders, riches were earned, and his childhood on the streets was all but forgotten.

Unfortunately, like most good things, it didn't last.

Ever since Kale Merandith took control of House Merandith and the Five Stars, Sagan was convinced fate had grown jealous of him and was determined to ruin what he had worked so hard to earn. Initially, a large portion of his wealth was lost in foolish business ventures. Soon after, his wife divorced him and took their home, children, and a large portion of what remained of their finances with her, forcing him to take up quarters in the officers' barracks. While that would be enough to dampen the spirits of many men, what caused him the most distress was the military losses. Month after month, House Merandith chipped away at Craigan's gains with what seemed like ease. Discord began to grow amongst soldiers and officers alike, but no one blamed their doms. To a man – at least publicly – they blamed themselves, and as far as Sagan was concerned during his moments of clarity, none bore the blame more than himself.

Staring out into the inky void of a moonless night with bloodshot brown eyes, this was not one of those moments. Sagan shook his sunken, long head and let a disgusted sigh escape his drawn lips. Not only did desertions seem to plague the squads under his command, but at the Second Battle of Corthas, it was his division that had collapsed, allowing the Merandiths to push the Suldamik center and eventually break them. Then, just a few months back, he lost nearly two full squads to a bandit raid when his scouts unknowingly led a patrol well into the Contested Territories. To his chagrin, those incidents weren't the worst of his men's failings.

Just a few weeks ago, it was they who had failed to protect House Suldamik's flank in the battle that was now known as the Bloody Blind. For the first time in what seemed like ages, the miserable sods had shown some backbone and had been driving House Merandith back. More importantly, according to rumors, they had even been close to killing Doms Merandith. Those gains, regrettably, had come crashing to a bloody end when a missing cavalry unit had come barreling through the forces Sagan commanded. Sagan snarled. Once again, he'd found himself on the ass-end of fate as his men's confidence crumbled as quickly as their lines, leaving him to shoulder the blame for failing to protect the Suldamik flank.

Pulling his heavy green cloak securely about him against a bitter northern wind, he leaned between two of the sharpened ends of the pylons that comprised the fort's walls and shook his head. *"No,"* his conscience whispered, *"that's not true or fair. It was your decisions and inattention that led to these failings. Accept the blame, and you will be able to overcome your shame."*

Sagan scowled and shook his head again. When a pair of the men patrolling the wall looked at him with concern, he turned his back to them in an attempt to hide his inner turmoil. The voice in his head was right, but he couldn't bring himself to accept that truth. Through the entire lumbering trek back to Chalin, he'd struggled with his guilt, and his self-loathing had led him to perceive slights and disdain from his comrades that, in most cases, simply weren't true. However, imagined or not, his faulty perception only deepened his despair. There were many times on that journey that he contemplated resigning his commission or simply committing suicide – the latter of which, given the pounding that currently assailed his temples, was tempting at that moment. In his mind, such an act would reclaim a bit of honor and even placate a number of his men and fellow officers, but for some reason he couldn't fathom, he did neither.

Instead, he withdrew from those around him and chose to drown his shame and the voice of reason in a flood of alcohol and mind-altering starlight dust. The days quickly blurred together, and he could remember nothing until the day a detachment retrieved his slovenly, drunken self from a tavern where he'd been indulging in his new vices. For two days, he found himself the target of a drill sergeant hells-bent on sobering him up. Cold baths, bitter coffee, and endless running became Sagan's personal hell until the sergeant deemed his condition passable enough to meet with Doms Suldamik.

Harsh sobriety brought with it great shame as Sagan was presented to Doms Suldamik in a disheveled state. As Craigan reprimanded him, Sagan fully expected to be discharged or even executed for both his failures and for vanishing without leave – which Craigan did present as a course of action. However, he was surprised when Craigan offered him a chance at redemption. Sagan could accept a dishonorable discharge for dereliction of duty and abandoning his post, or he could take command of the border fort standing between Chalin and the forces House Merandith had left in the South for the winter. While Sagan felt such an assignment was tantamount to exile, the voice in his head told him it was better than the disgrace of a dishonorable discharge. So, without complaint – and with as much humility as he could muster in his miserable state – Sagan had accepted. With close to three-hundred reinforcements in tow, he'd set out the next day with every intention of putting an end to the sadistic fun fate found in toying with him by redeeming himself and reclaiming his life. To his chagrin, fate seemed disinclined to accommodate him.

Not only did he find himself constantly warring with his conscience and his sudden withdrawal from drink and starlight dust, but he arrived at the fort to find House Merandith forces lurking about the surrounding area and – in his mind – the garrison ill-prepared for a possible attack. To him, the fort's roughly two-hundred defenders were lazy and lacked discipline – which, considering his current state, his conscience found ironically amusing. That introspective observation, however, didn't prevent him from doing his duty. With zeal, he threw himself into whipping the fort into shape. His enthusiasm for the task grew as he found it to be both a good outlet for his anger and a wonderful distraction from the gnawing hunger for alcohol and starlight dust that continually wracked his body.

Over the first few days, his behavior and treatment of the men earned him the nickname Hells' General. Whether it was a result of a mind twisted by withdrawal, or because he simply needed an outlet for his pent-up frustration with a life that seemed filled with constant disappointment and failure, Sagan embraced the title and drove his men with an obsessive furor to ready the fort. The east and west gates were reinforced with spare timber, cauldrons of pitch were set in their supports over the gates, buckets were filled with water from the fort's well, food was rationed, and gear was repaired and readied. However, while those tasks were important, there was one job he held paramount above the others. While the fort occupied a rise that pro-

120

vided the defenders with the superior position, it was very vulnerable to siege engines. Granted, he had no idea if a concerted attack was imminent, nor if siege engines were lurking, but he wasn't about to be caught off guard. As such, he ordered a series of trenches dug. Initially, be it night or day, he kept a large number of troops excavating the trenches with whatever tools they could find. The lurking Merandith forces responded to this with swift, late-night attacks that chipped away at his forces, which quickly forced Sagan to limit the work to the daylight hours.

Peering into the darkness, he could just make out the second of five trenches, and he scowled. The first three trenches were complete, but the fourth and fifth only protected the north and east walls. Not that it would make much difference if there were catapults present, but every obstacle the Merandiths had to overcome bought more time for the defenders and was a chance the Merandiths might make a mistake.

"Sir?" a husky female voice asked.

Startled, Sagan turned and scowled at his lieutenant. Shorter than him by a few inches, his lieutenant gazed at him with large, inquisitive blue eyes, which were perched astride a thin nose on a round face that was framed by boyishly short brown hair. "What is it, Luca? Can't you see I'm busy here?" he barked, his raspy voice raw from the cold air.

"Sorry, sir," she said calmly. The chainmail adorning her sturdy frame rattled as she adjusted the heavy green cloak that concealed most of her body. "Just wanted to inform you that the gates are sealed, and the night's watch is set."

"Good," he stated as if the news was an unexpected miracle. "I trust none of these Deo-forsaken idiots were foolish enough to seek out their bunks as if this is some damn holiday?"

Luca grimaced inwardly. She had served Sagan for nearly three years, and his downward spiral was sad and shameful. The husk of a man who stood before her was a shadow of his former self, and his behavior unbecoming of an officer. She had no intention of dying a pointless death simply because her superior was struggling with his personal demons; as such, she had confronted him during their march to the fort about his behavior. Unfortunately, the only result of her ill-timed words was the gash that now decorated her right cheek. She wanted desperately to help the man she had once looked up to, but it was clear that he wasn't ready to accept help no matter who offered it.

As for his behavior, it had become all too public. His treatment of the men had the barracks aflutter with angry muttering and dissenting chatter. Every soldier was aware that such talk, given time, could lead to open rebellion, and that was the last thing they needed with the Merandiths at the gates. As such, and without Sagan's consent, she had focused her efforts on maintaining the defenders' readiness and assuaging their concerns and complaints. Thankfully, Sagan was mute on her autonomous action. Whether he agreed with her independent measures or he simply did not care was unknown to her, nor did she care. What mattered to her was that the men seemed placated enough to obey orders. However, she knew that was only temporary if Sagan's behavior continued, and she feared what prolonged exposure to his outbursts might lead to.

"Sir, everyone is ready should the Merandiths attack. No one believes, or even infers, this is anything but what it is. I assure you — the Merandiths will not catch us off guard."

Sagan grunted sourly. "Very well. You are dismissed, Lieutenant."

Luca nodded but did not move.

Turning, Sagan fixed a scowl on her. "Did I mutter, Lieutenant? I said you are dismissed."

Holding her ground before his feverish glower, Luca stated calmly. "Sir, I think it would be wise for you to get some sleep."

"Sleep?" he asked incredulously. "That's funny, Lieutenant! What makes you think I want or need sleep? Deo be good — the Merandiths are out there, and I won't be caught napping!" Sagan barked, drawing concerned looks from the men who shared the wall with the officers.

Stepping in close, Luca placed a gentle, concerned hand on his arm and fought back the urge to grimace. Even with his chainmail, clothing and cloak between her hand and his arm, he felt sickeningly thin. "Sir," she said softly, "it is a moonless night. Nothing will happen. No one in their right mind would dare attack in such conditions. Please," she pleaded, "you need to rest."

She didn't know if it was her tone or what she said, but Sagan's face suddenly softened, and he looked around at the soldiers who were staring at them. Luca felt a shudder run through him, and when he looked back at her, she saw a hint of the Sagan that she respected in his exhausted eyes.

"You're right," he conceded softly. Then, in a louder voice, he proclaimed, "Thank you, Lieutenant. I will take your recommendations under advisement. You have the night watch. Now, if you'll excuse me."

"Sir," Luca said with a crisp fist-to-heart salute.

Stepping past Luca, Sagan quickly made his way to the battlement's stairs and descended to the overly crowded courtyard.

As Luca watched her captain beat a hasty retreat, she caught two of the wall guards snickering out of the corner of her vision. Marching over to them, their jovial mood came to a quick end upon her arrival.

"You two!" she snapped at them, drawing startled looks from the man and woman.

"Yes, Ma'm!" they both nervously replied.

"Make your way around the walls and tell the guards to douse the wall torches! No need to let anyone lurking out there have a clear view of us!" Luca barked.

With crisp salutes, the mismatched pair scrambled toward the north wall, relaying her order as they went.

Luca watched the two for a moment before, with a disappointed sigh, she made her way toward the south wall to carry out the same task.

With the arrival of Sagan and his men, the fort was once again overcrowded. From the clay-shingled, one-story command building and mess hall to the stables and forge, every inch of available space was packed with soldiers. Weaving – and sometimes pushing – his way toward the northern wall, where the command building and his quarters were located, Sagan felt claustrophobic, and his tormented mind felt like the men under his command were staring at him with judgmental eyes. At one point, he thought he heard snickering directed his way, which brought him to a sudden halt. Turning toward the group from which he believed the derisive chortles originated, Sagan shot them a murderous glare. However, none of the soldiers seemed to notice him, which only angered him further.

Just as he was about to force his way over to them and deliver a harsh verbal thrashing, the small part of his mind that still clung to rational thought said, *"Don't do it, Sagan. They weren't really laughing at you. It's not worth it."*

"Shut up! They're all laughing at me! They think I've failed Doms Suldamik too many times!" Sagan barked mentally at the unwanted logic as he returned to his original course.

"That's not true. You're projecting your shortcomings onto them," the voice of reason chided as Sagan shoved his way through the crowd,

drawing a string of angry glares and the occasional clipped curse.

"Liar! I have done my job to the best of my abilities! It's not my fault if these mewling sods can't do their jobs right! It is they who failed Doms Suldamik, not me!"

His conscience chuckled. *"Perhaps. But it was you that they followed, and it was your orders that they obeyed. Heap some of the blame on them if you must, but just remember that it was your lapses in judgment and your inattentiveness that led to failures and deaths. Nothing you say or do can absolve you of those crimes."*

"Nothing I say or do, eh?" Sagan retorted with a snort as he shouldered open the door to the command building. *"You should know better than that."*

"Ah, so the fool would take the coward's way out yet again?" his conscience chastised as he made his way through the crowded corridors.

Sagan smirked, which drew curious glances from the soldiers he passed, but smugly refused to respond to his conscience. Eventually, he reached the center of the building. Stepping through the open doors to the modest, square war room – which had been cleared out, save for the candelabra in its corners, to make room for soldiers to bed down – Sagan weaved his way around bed rolls and cots to the door on the right-hand wall that provided egress to his quarters and opened it. Closing the door behind him, he locked it before he leaned against it and grinned with relief. Once the office of the fort's previous commander, the small, candle-lit room was the only one that wasn't being shared, for which Sagan was grateful. Granted, he believed the room fell short of what he believed was befitting of an officer, but he felt certain he would have gone mad if he'd had to suffer the presence of others like the rest of the men under his command.

Pushing away from the door, he approached his bed, which was situated against the left-hand wall. Undoing the clasp on his cloak, he tossed the thick garment on the bed before removing his stout, silver-embroidered swordbelt and placing it and the heavy, gold-gilded officer's broadsword attached to it on top of the cloak. Pulling his green and white officer's tabard over his head, he added it, followed by his chainmail hauberk, to the pile. Relieved of the stifling garments, Sagan quickly made his way to the oak wardrobe on the opposite wall, his sweat-stained white shirt clinging to his torso. As he opened the doors to the unremarkable piece of furniture, a wild grin spread across his face.

"Last chance to listen to reason, Sagan. Don't shame yourself and your men any further," his conscience declared as he parted the clothing hanging within and crouched down.

*"No, "*Sagan retorted smugly as he pried open the small compartment he'd built into the bottom of the wardrobe soon after arriving at the fort, *"this is an opportunity to silence an ignorant, foolish, and annoying voice!"*

Reaching into the hidden space, Sagan retrieved a small black cloth pouch. Eyes wide with desperate anticipation, Sagan forgot all about sealing the compartment and closing the wardrobe as he returned to the bed and sat down. It took Sagan a moment to untie the knotted drawstrings with his shaking fingers, but he eventually managed the task and pulled open the pouch. With a deranged, raw chuckle, he reached into the small bag and withdrew a pinch of bright white, crystalline powder, which he settled in the palm of his hand before spitting on it. Using the fingers of his other hand, he rolled the mixture of powder and spittle around until it had congealed into a grainy, soft ball.

*"Poor, poor, Sagan. Such a waste, "*his conscience chided softly.

"To the Hells with you!" Sagan retorted before he tucked the ball between his cheek and gum line.

Immediately, he felt a wave of relaxing heat spread through his body and grinned. Pulling another pinch of the starlight dust from the pouch, he held it up to his nose and inhaled deeply. With a painfully wide grin, Sagan fell back on the bed, dropping the pouch to the coverlet, as bright, colorful stars burst across his vision.

"Yes! This is how it's meant to be!" Sagan thought. *"No voices! No damned fools ruining my life! Nothing!"* Sagan closed his eyes as the dust's mind-numbing, blissful hold sank its claws deeper into him. *"This is. . . . This. . . . Thi– . . ."* he tried to think as his thoughts trailed off beneath a wave of ecstasy.

Then, just as the drug's effects took a firm hold on him, he thought he heard the faint echo of something on the fringes of his mind. *"Damn . . . you . . ."* his conscience wailed pitifully before he slipped into oblivion's sweet embrace.

*

"Deo be good – I can barely see anything!"

Solaria grinned at the softly voiced complaint. Between the moonless night and lying on their bellies amongst the tall plains grass, she could only imagine the difficulties her human companions were having. "You and your men are doing fine," she replied just as softly. Looking at him, she added, "Though I do hope you can at least discern the fort."

Coltan snorted and met her gaze, her large pupils reminding

him eerily of a predatory cat. "Deo, I envy your people's eyes," he muttered before saying, "Aye. They may have doused the wall torches, but we're close enough to see the top of the wall with all the fires burning in there."

"That is good," Solaria responded with a playful grin. "I would hate to have to hold your hand all the way through this."

Coltan cursed and adjusted the mesh cloth hanging about his neck. Before he could respond, subtle movement from behind drew their attention.

Clad in similar attire as Solaria, one of the largest cyrians Coltan had ever seen was belly-crawling his way up next to Solaria. Halting next to her, he said to her in a low whisper with a nod of his wide, bronze-skinned head, "Kali'shir."

"Tykalir," she responded as she met his green-eyed gaze. "Is everyone ready?"

"They are, Kali'shir. We only await orders," he stated, the low timber of his voice rumbling in his chest despite whispering.

"Good. It shouldn't be long now. Return to the others and await my signal."

A wide grin spread across his bronze face, to which both the black bandanna concealing his hair and the sharp, swirling tattoos around his eyes added a horrifyingly vicious edge. "Very good, Kali'shir. May your enemies fall before you as dead leaves in winter," he offered in parting before crawling back to his position.

"You know," Coltan said with a half-grin, "I don't think we'll have to lift a sword once we're in there."

"And your reasoning for this is?" Solaria asked with a raised eyebrow.

"You cyrians," Coltan responded with a shake of his head. "You're just too damn creepy."

"Indeed," Solaria answered with a wide grin that made Coltan want to laugh. "Now, prepare yourself. It will not be long till our skills will be put to the test."

Grinning, Coltan pulled a pair of cat claws from a pouch on his belt. Sliding the fingerless gloves onto his hands, he settled the row of hooked steel spikes across the upper part of his palms. "I'm ready. I just hope these toys of yours are up to the task."

In response, Solaria pulled on a similar pair of gloves before saying as she signaled behind her for the other eight of their group to do the same, "Have faith, Coltan. Their walls will be as nothing to us.

Then our enemies will fall before us as dead leaves in winter, and they will sing our praises throughout the North."

"Well, when you put it that way. . . ." Coltan grinned at her and pulled the mesh cloth around his neck up over his nose, ready and eager for the night's work to begin.

*

"Well?" Gregor asked of the two recently arrived soldiers standing before his armored destrider.

"As we expected, not everyone from the rear has made it here with nightfall, but I'd say we've got a little less than a thousand infantry in position and ready, Captain," the female lieutenant answered with a resolved glint in her fierce blue eyes, which sat a bit close to her slightly crooked nose. "I just hope that Deo's luck is with us."

Gregor grunted, and a sly grin spread across his bearded face. "Still got yer breeches too far up yer ass about tha changes, eh, Ilvon?"

The spry lieutenant pulled herself up with indignation and tugged on the white tabard slashed with red across her chest that she wore over her chainmail hauberk. Pushing a blonde lock that had fallen free of her ponytail clear of her round face, she replied, her firm voice authoritative, "No, sir — but I wouldn't be doing my job if I didn't voice my concerns. We haven't had enough time to properly integrate the different units."

Donald, who sat astride his mount between Gregor and two Sur'dathan infantrymen, shifted in his saddle, his armor rattling dully underneath his cloak, and grinned. "I believe she just ah bit jealous o' them heavies from House Chantril, what with all tha steel makin' um look like shinin' heroes." His grin broadened. "Well, if'n that's tha case, then ye should just be lovin' us. What say ye, lassie?" he asked with a wink. "Care ta take ah ride with this stallion o' steel after we finish up with tha Suldamiks?"

The other soldier awaiting Gregor, a tall and lanky cyrian woman, eyed Donald and Ilvon curiously but held her tongue. Ilvon, on the other hand, felt her eyes bulge and her face heat up. Whether it was because she was stunned, embarrassed, or angry at Donald's advances, she didn't know. In any event, she found herself unable to muster a response.

"That's enough, Donald! Don't be antagonizin' tha lass," Gregor chided with a droll look at his lieutenant. Focusing on Ilvon, he asked, "Is there gonna be a problem fer yer men maneuverin'

127

around tha heavies?"

Still flustered, Ilvon blinked a few times at Gregor before responding, "No, sir. House Turval and the infantry – be they light or heavy – will not fail you."

"Good. Just be makin' sure ta hold tha attention of anyone that comes spillin' out o' tha rear gate."

"Yes, sir."

"Right, then. Get goin'."

Ilvon saluted crisply and gave Donald a lingering, curious glance before trotting off to the south, her hand clenched tightly about the broadsword sheathed at her left hip.

"You humans are a curious bunch," the cyrian said after Ilvon had departed, her lilting voice touched with befuddlement.

"Bah! Donald is just a fool, that's all. Tha lad has trouble keepin' 'is pants on no matter how dire tha situation be."

The giant of a man stationed next to Donald let out a laugh that sounded more like a shrill whistle as the air exited his grossly crooked nose on his well-defined, homely face. Adorned in the typical attire of a House Hagail infantryman – chainmail beneath a red and blue tabard, a half-visor helm, black gloves and boots, and a utilitarian broadsword at his right hip – the grizzled veteran smirked at Donald, his brown eyes flashing with amusement.

"Ah, shut yer trap, Whistler!" Donald barked at the large man, who only laughed a bit harder. Pointing at the visored, similarly dressed soldier next to Whistler, who held up his gloved hands defensively, he added, "And not ah word from ye, Jacob! In fact, what are ye two still doin' 'ere? Get back ta yer squad!" Turning his attention back to Gregor as his two friends beat a hasty retreat, he retorted, "As fer ye, Sir, yer just an old, jealous bugger! I just like ta remind meself why I'm fightin'. 'Sides, tha lass is pleasin' ta tha eyes, don't ye think so?"

Gregor rolled his eyes.

"I wouldn't know," the cyrian interjected. "I've always thought human males to be undesirable, and your women to be too manly. Besides, my heart and soul belong to the Kali'shir."

Donald grinned. "Ye'll be havin' ta tell me what it's like some time, Valesti. Never been with ah cyrian."

Valesti arched a red eyebrow and fixed him with an equally red-eyed, quizzical gaze that was fiercely intensified by her sharp features.

Shifting uncomfortably in his saddle, Gregor cleared his throat. "Enough o' that. Is yer archers in place, Uris'shir?"

Dressed in attire that was a match for Solaria's except for black accents instead of green, along with a quiver full of large arrows at her left hip, Valesti looked back at Gregor. The trail of swirling tattoos that ran from the corners of her eyes to the corners of her broad, full lips reminded him of a waterfall of tears as she inclined her head, allowing her long red hair to spill over her shoulders. "Indeed they are, Captain. The Suldamiks will find no escape from our rain of death."

Gregor glanced at the impressive white recurved bow that spanned her back, which resembled a roaring, large-fanged cat, and nodded. "Good ta hear. We'll do our best ta get their attention, but it's on ye ta put tha fear of Deo in their hearts. Yer people's lives ar' in yer hands."

"And we shall not fail them – be at ease on this, Captain."

Gregor grunted. "Only after this mess is over with, 'n tha Suldamiks are either dead or runnin' from us."

A feral grin split Valesti's face. "Indeed. Then we shall endeavor to achieve that end."

"Good. Then off with ye. It's on yer discretion when ta start, but just make sure tha walls are full 'n they're focused on us. I want ye ta do as much damage as possible."

"As you wish, Captain," she replied with a slight bow. "May you find shade beneath the Forest Mother's boughs."

As she vanished into the darkness, Gregor grunted and turned his destrider about. "Well, let's get ta it, lad. We got our part ta play, and I'm not about ta be shown up by some tree-lovers!"

A vicious grin spread across Donald's face. "Aye, Captain. By mornin', tha Suldamiks'll be feedin' tha mud crows, or, by Deo, I'll swear off women!"

With a groan, Gregor simply shook his head.

Chapter Seven

"**B**loody hells! How do they expect us to see anything?"

"Stop you're bellyaching, Julius! Would you rather make it easy on them?" his companion chided from her position next to him against the east wall.

"And you're a daft bugger who's too wet behind the ears, Ursa!" retorted the veteran Julius. He gestured to the numerous fires in the courtyard, and his creased features contorted into a scowl around his weary black eyes and lopsided mouth. "There's enough light down there to at least give those bastards out there a point of reference!" Leaning between two of the pointed pylons, he spit. "We'd be lucky if we could see anyone coming before they got within two-hundred paces. Hells! At the very least, we could've lit up the approaches to the fort!"

Ursa's throaty laugh drew another scowl from Julius. Leaning against the wall, she not only loomed over her fellow soldier, but she was broader and more athletic. Shaking her head of short-cropped black hair, she fixed Julius with a green-eyed, dry look as she tugged her green cloak closed with her large, brown-gloved hands and drolly asked, "Would you rather we painted a bullseye on us just so you can see a little better?"

"At least it might be a bit more of a level battlefield, then," Julius muttered, running a black-gloved hand over his shaved head before he pulled his cloak close as well. "I just don't like it, Ursa."

"Don't like what, Sergeant?" questioned a husky female voice.

Startled, both soldiers bolted to attention as the green-cloaked speaker emerged from the shadows and stepped around Julius.

"Sir!" Ursa said, her chainmail rattling against her lone steel pauldron as she snapped off a salute, revealing the House Suldamik tabard beneath her cloak and the heavy swordbelt around her waist from which a functional broadsword hung.

Embarrassed, Julius replied, "Nothing, sir," as he also saluted, his leather armor creaking beneath his House Suldamik tabard and the utilitarian belt from which his single-blade axe hung.

"Is there something we can do for you, sir?" Ursa interjected in an attempt to divert the conversation away from her Sergeant's concerns.

Lieutenant Luca Rolandson grinned wryly at the two, her inquisitive blue eyes shining with amusement. "I was wondering if there was some reason the two of you felt the wall needed extra support?" she asked rhetorically.

Julius cleared his throat uncomfortably, and Ursa blushed a bit.

Luca let the uncomfortable silence linger for a moment before finally grinning slyly with a slight shake of her head of short brown hair. "At ease, you two," she said, a hint of mirth in her voice. "I don't mind the casual posture, but you both might want to watch what you say. You seem to have a bad habit of saying the wrong thing while the wrong ears are about."

Both soldiers' eyes widened a bit as they recalled the laughter that had drawn Luca's attention earlier. "Yes, sir," Julius muttered, eager to forget the incident.

"Good," Luca replied with a nod. "Now, if you'll do me the favor of keeping your attention focused beyond the wall, I mi–" Luca's brow suddenly furrowed and she cocked her head. "Did either of you hear that?"

Puzzled looks greeted her statement.

"Hear what, sir?" Julius asked.

"That," Luca answered as she approached the wall and peered into the distance.

Flanking Luca, the two soldiers followed her example, but other than their tense posture garnering the attention of the wall guards near them, neither of them noticed anything out of the ordinary.

"I don't hear anything, sir. What about you, Seargen–" Ursa started to ask, but then she heard it. It was weak at first, but the sound soon grew in intensity. As it did so, more of the soldiers on the wall began to notice it. Then, her eyes growing wide, she recognized what it was, and so did her companions on the wall – the clank and rattle of marching steel.

"Damn!" Luca muttered before bellowing, "Sound the alarm! Archers to the east wall!"

With those words, the fort sprang to life, and the air quickly filled with barked orders and the rattle of steel as the fort's occupants scrambled to ready themselves. As Luca peered into the darkness, she felt a small hint of pride and relief as she listened to the controlled chaos within the fort. If anyone harbored ill will toward Captain Torvan, it was either buried or cast aside by the imminent danger.

"Thank you, Corith, for that boon," she thought just as she felt the battlements shake beneath her feet as soldiers thudded up the stairs. A moment later, she found herself surrounded by bleary-eyed soldiers, most of whom were archers, and a small, pleased smile tugged at her lips. Just as she was about to order their bows readied, she noticed a hint of movement in the distance. A moment later, her smile vanished.

All along the battlements, everything from curses to prayers was uttered as the darkness in the distance spit forth row after row of infantry under the five-star-emblazoned black banner of House Merandith. What little light the twinkling stars above provided glinted dully off the ranks of steel as they approached at a steady pace before coming to an orderly halt just outside of bow range.

"Deo be good! How many of them are there?" Ursa breathed.

Turning to one of the archers, Luca firmly ordered, "Flares!"

Nodding, the archer relayed the order, which spread along the eastern wall. Moments later, there were flashes along the battlements as the archers lit fuses on arrow tips wrapped in rags that were soaked with a quick-burning oil. Once the arrows were nocked and the bows raised, Luca bellowed, "Loose!"

Like a wave of shooting stars, the flaming arrows streaked skyward, where the rags burst into flames before the projectiles arched gently and streaked toward the ground short of the assembled Merandith forces. In the moments before the arrows struck the ground, the flames of which went out in a flash of thick smoke, many on the wall recoiled at what they saw. Bathed in the quick flare of fiery light, they saw not only what seemed like endless rows of patiently waiting soldiers, but also the most intimidating heavy cavalry any of them had ever seen flanking the infantry.

"Hells' bloody balls! There must be at least five hundred of them!" Julius remarked in shock.

Luca shook her head, deeply concerned. "No. . . . There's more than that. . . . But the cavalry won't do them any good," she muttered before she raised her voice and asked, "Did anyone see any archers?"

"None that I could see!" remarked one of the other soldiers.

Looking at the others around her, Luca received a similar response from each. "Good. Then we still hold a significant advantage. Deo only knows what they're up to, but they know we hold the high ground."

"Scare tactics, sir?" Julius asked.

"Possibly. I see no other reason why they would halt outside of bow range. If they were going to attack, they should have used the darkness to their advantage and rushed the wall."

"What should we d—" Julius' question was cut short by a shrill shriek just before a large arrow tore through his face, sending his body tumbling backward off the battlement to the horrified screams and curses of his comrades.

"Holy hells!" Ursa cried, aghast, as she watched her friend tumble off the wall.

Before Luca could order everyone to take cover, a hail of the terrifying arrows screamed from the moonless sky. All around her, the lethal missiles pierced armor and punched through flesh as if it were paper, pitching body after body from the wall to a symphony of pain-filled screams.

"Take cover, you bloody idiots!" Luca finally managed to bellow. It was a pointless gesture, however, as those who weren't frozen in terror or wounded had already done so.

Peaking over the walkway, Luca saw that a number of the soldiers in the courtyard were writhing on the ground, either pierced by the arrows that had missed their targets on the wall, or injured by their falling companions. Those who were unharmed were scrambling to raise their shields or find suitable cover.

Just as a soldier with his shield held high crouched over Luca, she turned to Ursa and barked, "Get down there and find Captain Torvan! And get some damn torches up here!"

"Sir?" Ursa questioned, confused by the order.

"Damn it, woman! The—" Luca jumped as an arrow punched through the shield above her, ripping a hole in the man's arm. Blinking in shock as the man fell to the side with a howl of pain, Luca forced her focus back to Ursa and barked, her blue eyes flashing with anger, "With or without the torches, they can bloody well see us! Our asses are mud crow fodder if we can't see who in the bloody hells is shooting at us!"

Nodding firmly, Ursa kept low to the ground as she scrambled to the stairs and scampered down them.

As soon as Ursa was past her, Luca looked up and down the wall, and cursed under her breath. Every living soldier she could see was huddled against the wall as low to the walkway as they could amongst pooling blood and their fallen comrades. Such violence wasn't unfamiliar to them, but this unknown assailant had planted a soul-clenching terror in them that they'd never experienced before. Someone or something was firing arrows with tremendous force not only from beyond normal bowshot, but also uphill.

Realizing she needed to project confidence at that moment, she swallowed her fear and shouted with as much poise as she could muster, "All of you – keep down! Don't give them anything to shoot at! Just pretend this is a quaint spring shower, and once it's over, we'll send those Merandith bastards to the lowest pit of the Nine Hells where they belong!"

The confidence in her husky voice appeared to bolster the spirits of some, and her words even drew a grin or two, but the fear remained, and she couldn't blame them. As she watched another handful of her men fall to the damnable arrows, their screams filling the air, she suddenly realized dread had latched firmly onto her heart, and she had no idea what to do. *'Damn it, Sagan! Don't leave my ass hanging in the wind! You better have an idea how to counter this, because if I di–* "she flinched to the side as a pair of the arrows punched through the shoulder and head of the bowman next to her, pinning him to the walkway. *'If I die because of your Deo-be-damned demons, I'll claw my way out of the Hells to make sure you burn with me!"*

*

Crouched low in the first of the trenches, Solaria grinned behind her mask as the screams erupted from within the fort. Tapping Tykalir on the shoulder, she signaled to him that she was going to have a look and to pass on the word to be ready to move. Her fellow cyrian nodded before passing on the information to Coltan through a series of simplified hand signals.

Peeking over the lip of the trench, Solaria focused on the wall. Bathed in what the cyrians described as starlight, the fort was as clear to her as if a silvery sun was hanging bright in the sky. As expected, the Suldamik forces appeared to be focused on the east wall. Most of the contingent on the north wall had vanished, most likely to reinforce the east wall or to attend to the wounded. Solaria's grin widened. Only five guards were left on the battlements, and their attention seemed fixated within the fort. Crouching below the lip of the trench, Solaria flashed up five fingers to indicate the troops she had seen before she motioned for everyone to advance.

With uncanny silence and swiftness, her masked squad scrambled from trench to trench, pausing only to double-check on the guards. Finally, they reached the wall and flattened themselves against it. Signally for the three other cyrians to ascend first, Solaria led the cautious climb. The wooden barrier, as Solaria had predicted, was no match for the cyrian-made cat claws, which were made for scaling brick or stone structures. As the cyrians swung themselves over the top of the wall with graceful agility, one of the wall guards turned around to see Solaria crouched on the battlements. She cursed silently and reached for one of her daggers even as the man's eyes widened in surprise. Before she could draw her weapon or the man could sound the alarm, a flash of steel cut through the air, and a dagger embedded itself in the back of the guard's mouth, cutting off his shout. Solaria nodded her thanks to Tykalir as he padded by to retrieve his weapon, and she silently thanked the Mother that the cacophony of screams and curses from the fort had masked the dead guard's fall. Following Tykalir's lead, the other two cyrians quietly trotted past her and silently dispatched the other wall guards just as Coltan's men made their way over the wall.

After quickly locating Coltan, Solaria moved over to him and whispered, "No heroics – simply make sure the bombs are set off amongst the masses, then return to the others."

Coltan's eyes lit up with an unseen grin, and he nodded his acknowledgment before he and his men leapt silently to the roof below.

A gentle touch on her shoulder drew her attention, and she turned to see that Tykalir and the two other cyrians had returned. Nodding to him, Solaria conveyed their orders to them through a series of hand signals. Once they acknowledged her orders, she led them a few paces along the battlements toward the west wall. Reaching the western staircase, she noted a handful of torch-bearing Suldamik soldiers making their way toward the eastern staircases as she and her men quietly descended to the courtyard, where they spread out into the shadowy chaos consuming the fort.

*

After a series of short, curse-laden questions, one of the soldiers in the courtyard finally informed Ursa that Captain Torvan had retired to the command building. Hastily shoving her way through the mass of bodies cowering beneath a ceiling of shields, she arrived at the one-story structure and entered it to find it packed with cowering soldiers. Cursing loudly, she began shouldering her way through the halls, shouting, "You stoneless bastards! Get out of my way!" When that failed to elicit any action, she added, "Fine, you gutless whoresons! You can cower in here and die by my sword," she partially drew her blade, which earned a few concerned glances, "or you can get out there and support the damn walls! Who knows, you might take a few Merandiths with you before your asses are dragged to the Nine Hells!"

At first, no one moved, and her eyes took on a deadly edge. Thankfully, some of the soldiers finally managed to muster enough bravery and dignity to scramble outside. Those that remained, she scowled at and noted their faces as she hustled through the corridors toward Torvan's quarters. Reaching the War Room, she stormed in and tore through the cots and blankets between her and the closed door to Torvan's quarters. Just as she was about to pound on the door, she thought she heard a series of thuds on the roof, but dismissed it as nothing more than a stress-induced figment of her imagination.

Slamming the side of her fist on the solid door as if she were trying to knock it down, she bellowed, "Captain Torvan! You're needed on the walls! The Merandiths are attacking!" When she received no response, her concern grew. Hammering at the door again, she barked, "Sir! Are you in there?!" When silence greeted her again, she cursed and tried the door.

It was locked.

Scowling, Ursa took a step back before kicking the door as hard as she could, causing it to crack a bit near the handle and the frame to splinter. Two more thunderous blows followed before the door finally tore open in a hail of splinters, shredding the doorframe.

"Hells' bloody balls!" she exclaimed, shocked and angered, when she saw Captain Torvan sprawled out on the bed.

Marching over to his prone form, she noted the spilt bag of starlight dust. Recognizing it for what it was, Ursa growled, "You hells-damned fool! Couldn't stay off of it, could you?" Grabbing his shirt with one hand, she pulled him into a sitting position before slapping him violently and barking, "Sir! Wake up, you bastard!" A moan was the only response she got. Growling, she slapped him again. This time, not only did he moan, but his eyes fluttered open. "Sir? Are you with me?" she asked urgently.

Blinking rapidly, Torvan looked blankly about the room. "Wha– Who. . . . Who are you?" he managed to stutter, his voice painfully raw.

Sighing with exasperation, Ursa replied as she let go of Torvan's shirt, "Private Ursa Delontis, sir."

Staring at her for a moment, Torvan could have sworn he saw horns jutting from her head. "Ursa Delontis. . . ? I–"

"Sir," Ursa interjected. "Please – I need you to focus! The Merandiths are attacking, and I don't have the bloody time to sober you up properly!"

She didn't know if it was the mix of anger and desperation in her tone or the mention of the Merandiths, but Torvan's bleary, unfocused eyes suddenly cleared up a bit. "The Merandiths? Deo be good! Why didn't someone tell me?" he croaked angrily.

Ursa gritted her teeth as he stood and began to fumble his way through donning his chainmail. "That's why I'm here, sir!" she practically yelled as the hauberk slid over his head. "Lieutenant Rolandson sent me to fetch you!"

Just as he grabbed his tabard, Torvan paused and stared at her. "Rolandson? I. . . ." He trailed off as he thought he saw a trio of demonic birds hopping about Ursa's shoulders. Shaking his head, he tugged the tabard on and began a haphazard attempt to don his swordbelt. "Rolandson?" he repeated. "Yes. . . . Yes! I left her in charge, didn't I? Well," a hint of anger entered his raspy voice, "I'll just have to see that fool whipped for her incompetence!"

Ursa couldn't contain the scowl that crossed her face at the ignorant accusation, but she did manage to hold her tongue.

"Bah!" Torvan shouted and dropped the belt before rubbing at his throat. "Feels like someone fed me sand," he rasped. Glaring at Ursa, he demanded, "Did you do such a thing, Private?"

This is taking too long! Ursa railed in her head. Crouching down, she retrieved his belt and offered as calmly as she could, "Here, let me help, sir. You are needed on the wall immediately!"

"What?" he rasped blankly, suddenly oblivious to his dry throat. "Oh, yes – the Merandiths. Right you are, Private!" When Ursa finished securing his belt, he settled it on his hips and said, "Thank you, Private. Lead on, quickly."

"Yes, sir!" she barked sharply before heading for the door, thankful to finally be on their way.

"Oh, and Private?" he asked as they exited his room.

"Sir?"

"Do something about these damn demon flies!"

Demon flies? she thought as she glanced back at him to see him swatting at the air. "Yes, sir," she replied through gritted teeth.

Making their way back to the building's main entrance as quickly as Torvan's stumbling pace and delusional mind allowed, Ursa could feel the eyes of the remaining cowering soldiers on them. Gritting her teeth hard, she kept herself from looking at them, but she could imagine what she would have seen in their eyes, for it was the same things she felt – shame, pity, and fear. The enemy was out there with weapons that defied everything they knew about bows, and to make matters worse, their commanding officer was a recovering addict who appeared to have been indulging at an inopportune time. Ursa wanted nothing more than to gut Torvan at that moment before disposing of the body and then simply inform Lieutenant Rolandson that he had died of an overdose. However, such treasonous thoughts flew from her mind as they rounded the corner into the now-empty main hallway to see a masked person in black leathers standing just inside the command building's entrance with an odd black ball in his right hand.

Coming to a sudden halt, Ursa drew her sword and shouted, "Halt in the name of Doms Suldamik! Who are you!?"

The shaved-headed man looked her way and fixed his startled brown eyes on her. "Damn!" Ursa heard him mutter.

"Who are you?" She demanded again as she took a step forward.

"Kill him!" Torvan suddenly shrieked from behind her. "Kill the demon now, Private, or I'll have your head!"

Just as she was about to turn and punch Torvan in irritation, the intruder's right hand went up and he said, "With Doms Merandith's warmest regards," before he threw the orb hard against the floor at their feet.

"What in th–" Ursa managed to utter just before the orb hit the floor and shattered, shooting a thick black cloud of dust into the air.

Immediately, her eyes began to burn and water, and her chest began to convulse as her throat tried to seize up. Coughing violently, she turned around to grab Torvan, only to find him on all fours and possessed of an equally vicious coughing fit. Fighting the urge to collapse as he did, she reached down, grabbed Torvan by his collar and dragged him toward the door.

Stumbling through the open entry with Torvan in tow, Ursa fell to her knees and – thinking they had reached fresh air – took a deep breath. To her horror, she found herself choking on more of the wretched black smoke, which was quickly followed by an overwhelming wave of nausea that twisted her stomach until she started vomiting violently. As soon as her stomach finished emptying itself, she looked up. To her dismay, she saw through her watery, hazy vision that a thick black cloud hung over the courtyard. Blinking, she managed to look around and saw that nearly everyone in sight was either coughing violently, vomiting, or had passed out. At that moment, she thought she saw figures moving through the inky fog toward the forge portion of the north wall. However, before she could even attempt to move or try to say something, a maddening scream from behind drew her attention, and she felt someone rush by.

"Damn you, Torvan!" she managed to think as she watched his hysterical sprint toward the west wall.

Mustering what strength she had, she managed to push herself to her feet. She had to stop him from doing something foolish, but breathing was extremely difficult, nausea tore at her gut, and she was beginning to feel lightheaded. Stumbling forward through the black haze, she suddenly hit something and fell to the ground, her breath knocked from her. A warmth began to spread across the back of her head, and the black cloud began to claw away at her vision. Just before her sight failed and the darkness consumed her, she thought she could just make out a tall figure with feral features looming over her, and she thought, *"Damn. He was right. There are demons here. . . ."*

"Damn it all to the Hells! They're advancing!" Luca thought as she peered over the wall.

Thanks to the recently arrived torches, she could finally see with some clarity, but she almost wished it was still dark. The Merandiths, having realized the fort's defenders couldn't retaliate effectively, were steadily advancing on the wall. Oddly enough, however, the cavalry was nowhere to be seen.

"Where in the hells did their cavalry go?" she wondered for a brief moment before she ducked behind the wall with a curse, and quickly assessed her remaining forces.

Though the hail of arrows had relented somewhat, it didn't appear that anyone felt brave enough or lucky enough to concede their somewhat-safe cover. Understandable cowardice aside, Luca was thankful that she still had a number of able-bodied archers at her disposal. "Archers!" she shouted. "Make ready! The Merandiths are demonstrating that they are truly idiots! They think they have us at a disadvantage and are advancing! Show them the error of their ways, and drive them from my sight!"

Though still clearly fearful, her speech seemed to return some of their bravery and will to them. With haste, those archers within earshot readied their bows and positioned themselves, awaiting her orders.

Peeking over the wall, she saw that the front ranks had pulled well within range. Grinning, she was just about to order the attack when an unusual sight at the Merandith's rear cut the words off in her throat. Though they were hard to see in the limited light, Luca could just discern numerous tall, lanky figures holding the largest bows she had ever seen. Cursing at herself for her hesitation, Luca pushed the curious sight aside and bellowed, "FIRE!"

With speed and precision, the Suldamik archers stood and drew back on their bows, but to Luca's horror, the Merandith's odd archers suddenly let fly with terrifying speed. Just as she ducked behind the wall, and before any of her men could fire, the oncoming flight of arrows tore into their ranks, killing nearly half of those who had followed her orders. The archers who somehow managed to survive the assault let loose before ducking for cover.

"Damn them!" Luca growled as she cautiously peeked over the wall once more. Maybe a dozen of the attackers were down, but the rest continued their advance, and the archers appeared to be readying another volley.

Crouching back down, Luca suddenly felt her eyes burning as she pondered what to do. The Merandiths had no siege engines or ladders, and their archers would surely run out of arrows. So, how did they plan on taking the fort? Looking around, she noticed that the north wall was completely empty. Coughing, she cursed and turned to the soldier next to her and ordered, "Private! Take five others and go see why in the hells no one is watching the north wall!"

The young man, his black eyes turning an ugly red, started to reply, "Yes, si–" before a violent coughing fit overtook him.

"What in the hells is the matter with you?" Luca demanded even as others along the wall began to cough.

Suddenly, the sound of coughing and retching, as well as a few howls of pain, assailed her ears. Barking a cough of her own, Luca looked around to see that nearly everyone appeared stricken with the same fit. "What in the hells?" she managed to mutter as she looked down into the courtyard. To her horror, it was covered in a black haze that was rising toward the battlements.

Aghast, she turned back to her subordinate and managed to shout, "Private!"

"Yes–" His hoarse reply was cut off as an arrow burst

through the wall in a hail of splinters, embedding itself in the man's brown-haired skull.

Wide-eyed, she scrambled back from the body as hoarse screams erupted all around her. Horrified, she watched as arrow after arrow punched through the thick wooden timbers of the wall and then through the armored flesh of her men.

Nearly paralyzed by the macabre scene, Luca racked her brain for an answer to this hellish nightmare. If the walls no longer offered protection, then they needed to get off the battlements, but the courtyard was covered in a cloud of darkness that she believed wholeheartedly was responsible for everyone's burning eyes and impaired breathing. To her chagrin, she realized evacuating the walls would just be trading one major problem for another, but she knew she had to do something. Eyes watering and her lungs burning, she was about to order the walls cleared when she caught sight of someone stumbling through the black haze toward the west gate. It took only a moment for her to realize who it was and their intent, and that infuriated her.

"STOP HIM!" she screamed, appalled. "STOP CAPTAIN TORVAN FROM OPENING THE GATE!"

Still under the influence of the starlight dust, and surrounded by carnage and chaos, reality had abandoned Captain Torvan. All around him, the fires of the Hells burned brightly, belching black smoke into the sky. With his lungs raw from breathing the hells-spawned miasma, he stumbled through the ranks of the damned, their howls ringing in his ears as they reached for him with emaciated, clawed hands.

"We have to get out of here!" he screamed madly to anyone who hadn't fallen prey to the demons.

Before he could take more than a few steps, one of the demons latched on to his tabard and brought him to a halt. Eyes wide and wild with terror, he shrieked, "Get away from me!"

With fear-born strength, he batted at the hand and lurched away violently. Almost immediately, the fabric of his tabard gave way under the force of his retreat, and he stumbled away from his assailant. Recovering quickly, he bellowed hoarsely as he sprinted away, "Run! Get free of here! Save yourselves!"

Barreling through a pair of his fellow soldiers who were engulfed in a swarm of tiny, winged demons that were gleefully stabbing at them with needle-like daggers, Torvan slammed hard into the gate and fell to the ground. Staring blankly through watering eyes at the glistening fleshy barrier that was swarming with horrific black insects, it took him a moment to realize he'd reached his goal.

"Don't do it," his long-absent conscience stated dejectedly. *"You'll doom them all if you open it."*

"Lies!" he screamed to no one as he stood up. "This is the way to safety! Remaining here dooms us!" he added as he stumbled to the gate.

"You'll doom them all," his conscience repeated weakly as he fumbled at the slick, stout timber barring the gate.

"Help me, you fools!" Torvan shouted desperately to anyone who might hear his plea.

Torvan's lungs suddenly convulsed, and he doubled over, coughing with such force that he felt like his ribs would break. When he finally recovered enough to stand upright, he found himself flanked by a number of his fellow soldiers. Swarming with demons that were trying to prevent their escape, his men struggled to lift the slippery bar. Wide-eyed, Torvan joined the line and put his shoulder underneath the timber. "Heave!" he shouted.

Faces flush with the strain, they slowly managed to lift the bar out of its iron supports. Once it was clear, they scampered back as they dropped the beam at their feet. Torvan's eyes lit up with hysterical joy. Freedom from the Hells was almost within his grasp, and he wasn't going to waste the opportunity.

Bolting forward, he slammed his hands against the heavy doors and began to shove with desperate strength. Slowly, as he watched his hands sink into the soft flesh of the gate through his drug-altered vision, the portal began to groan open. A moment later, the other damned soldiers joined him, and the doors' lethargic journey quickened. As the gate finally yielded its protective posture, a great cloud of the dark smoke filling the fort billowed forth. Torvan and the other soldiers stumbled through the dangerous cloud for a moment before finally breaking free of its influence.

With relief washing over him, Torvan fell to his knees and took in a deep breath of fresh air. *"See, you bastard!"* He mentally bellowed at his conscience. *"Freedom! The Hells cannot contain us!"*

A deep, mournful sigh greeted his declaration. *"You poor, poor fool,"* his conscience responded feebly.

Pushing himself to his feet, Torvan looked around as a flood of coughing Suldamik soldiers stumbled from the fort. To his addled mind's horror, there were still swarms of the tiny demons flittering about, and a few of the larger ones within the fort hissed and cursed at the escaping soldiers. However, he also realized that the air was clean where he was standing, and more importantly, nothing appeared to be standing in their way. Pointing down the rise, Torvan started forward, shouting, "This way! Keep moving! Be free of the Hells prison!"

A few soldiers eyed him warily as the contingent scrambled down the rise toward flat terrain, but they said nothing. In their minds, they were free of the hellish miasma and the rain of death that had turned the fort into a slaughter pin, and that was all that mattered. If their commanding officer had lost his mind, then it was a small price to pay for survival. Unfortunately, fate seemed disinclined to grant them clemency, for as they reached flat land, a thunderous cacophony reached their ears, bringing them to a foreboding halt. Turning to the south, they faced the approaching sound of marching boots and steel on steel a moment before the night parted and the front ranks of the oncoming force came into view. Addled as they were, the Suldamik troops were slow to react; many watched with wide-eyed befuddlement, and a few even dropped to their knees in defeat. As for Torvan, he saw rank-upon-rank of armored demons marching toward them, and he suddenly grinned.

Bolstered by their escape, Torvan's eyes narrowed, and he declared with almost gleeful confidence in a hoarse voice, "See, men! They send their last defense to stop us! A paltry force if I've ever seen one!" Looking around at those under his command, his eyes alight with feverish determination, he shouted, "Form ranks! We shall destroy them, in Deo's name, on our way to freedom!"

Whether they were driven by Torvan's sudden zeal, or the realization that they needed to try something if they wanted a chance to survive the night, the bulk of the haggard troops managed to pull themselves together and fall into an aggressive wedge formation.

Grinning with feverish wickedness from his position at the tip of the formation, Torvan drew his sword and brandished it in the air. "Forward to freedom and glory!"

Luca cursed loudly and vehemently from her position against the exterior of the west wall. Some three-hundred or so troops had escaped the cloudy hell within the fort so far, and though she cursed Torvan with all her heart, she had to admit – albeit grudgingly – that his mad flight had spared them from the storm of death within the walls. However, that moment of grace was cut short by the sound of an approaching force. Watching the Merandith forces advance below, she idly wondered if this was a new threat, or if it was part of the army outside the eastern wall that had broken off while the fort's defenders were overtaken by the miasma. In the end, she understood it was irrelevant. No matter their origin, she knew they had simply traded one type of death for another.

From what she could see through her red and watery eyes, around two-hundred Merandith infantry were advancing upon them – fifty wide and four deep. Most appeared to be light infantry, but the two front ranks were encased in steel and bore tower shields, which they pounded their broad-bladed swords against, marking them as heavy infantry. Under normal circumstances, the Suldamik forces that now marched forth would have stood an excellent chance, for they had greater numbers. Unfortunately, as she watched her fellow soldiers haggardly advance to meet the attack, she knew their current state negated that advantage. What's more, reinforcements could come from the Merandith forces on the other side of the fort at any moment.

Coughing, she pushed herself away from the wall and drew her sword. No matter her feelings about the situation, she was no fool. Now that they were on open ground, defeat was only a matter of time, making escape their prerogative. How to go about it was the problem. Returning to the fort was a death sentence, and fleeing would see them run down by the more able-bodied Merandiths. That left only one option – forward. To do so, they would need to punch through the Merandith ranks, and that meant they needed every able-bodied soldier they could muster.

Looking at the twenty or so soldiers around her, she pointed at the approaching Merandiths and shouted, her voice raw from the miasma, "Rally to me, men! If you want to live to see the morning, then we need to split the Merandiths like a ripe melon! Failing that, let's drag as many of those bastards as we can to the Hells with us!"

Looks of fatalistic determination greeted her rallying cry as the soldiers gathered themselves. Motioning forward, Luca led the makeshift squad down the slope to link up with the main formation.

Just as they joined the rear ranks, Luca heard a thunderous pounding from behind. Like her, a few in the back line turned to see what the cause of the commotion was, only to find themselves rooted in place by what they saw. Wide-eyed, Luca's sword slipped from her grasp as it all came together in her mind. Getting them to leave the fort had been the Merandiths' goal all along, and the foul cloud in the fort, not to mention Torvan's hysterics, had given them just that.

No one would survive this night.

Falling to her knees, she wept.

*

From her position at the center of the first row of light infantry, a grin spread below Ilvon's crooked nose on her round face as she watched the fort's western gate swing open and a small army of Suldamik soldiers spill forth. Some fell to their knees just outside the gate, retching and coughing, while others fled down the rise like a gaggle of drunken geese. Ilvon waited as long as she dared to allow as many of the enemy as possible to filter down the hill. When she finally deemed the time ripe for the attack, she settled her leather helmet on her blonde-haired head and drew her sturdy broadsword. Holding it aloft, her fierce blue eyes lit up with gleeful anticipation.

It was time to close the trap.

"Make ready!" she shouted in her commanding voice, and the air filled with the hiss of steel on leather as swords were drawn. "This is our time, men! Let's show these Suldamik bastards that we'll no longer tolerate their presence in these lands! Company – advance! And let them know we're coming!"

Grim-faced, the Merandith line advanced, and the air filled with the pounding of their boots. Ilvon felt her grin widen as the front ranks of Chantril heavies began raping their short stabbing swords against their spiked, steel tower shields. *That'll get their attention!"* she thought excitedly.

Almost as if on cue, the Suldamiks noticed the glorious anthem of impending battle, and they began to form ranks as swiftly as they could in their disoriented state. Slowly, the Suldamiks began to stumble forward, and Ilvon felt nervous anticipation flutter in her stomach. The infantry had done their job; they had their attention, and the Suldamiks knew there was no hope of flight unless they dealt the Merandiths a quick, harsh blow. Ilvon's grin turned fierce as she caught sight of the Suldamiks' leader brandishing his sword and screaming at the Merandiths like a deranged zealot.

Yes, the Suldamiks' attention was focused solely on Ilvon's advance. *The poor bastards won't know what hit them,"* she thought with macabre glee. Suddenly, she heard a growing thunderous pounding to the north, prompting her to shout, "Company, halt!"

Though a few of her men bumped into each other, they managed to come to a halt and quickly recover their lines.

"Deo be good, we've got to work on that!" she mused with mild irritation before ordering, "Heavies – set shields!"

With practiced ease, the front rank of heavies dropped to one knee and set their shields, allowing the second row to plant their shields atop the front's barrier, forming a two-tiered wall of steel.

"Alright, you bloody sods! This is it!" Ilvon barked. "Make your Houses and Doms Merandith proud!" Then, as she crouched low, she thought, *"And let's pray those Highlanders' claims are more than empty bravado."*

Eagerness filled the hearts of Hagan's Hammer as they advanced at a steady trot, their numbers four rows deep and perfectly paced. Encased in functional steel, the breastplates of which were emblazoned with a burnished-silver two-headed hammer, every rider had the visor of their half-helms down and held their saber-lance steady. Gregor, whose helm was crested with a charging kyram, rode at the center of the first line with a heart filled with pride. They had waited so long to strike a harsh blow in the war, and this was their chance.

Adjusting his grip on the reins of his heavily armored destrider, Gregor readied his wood-and-steel kite shield, which proudly displayed the badge of both his unit and rank – an angry kyram head with crossed warhammers behind it. Gregor smiled as he noted the riders to his left and right doing the same with their shields, which, except for displaying only a single two-headed hammer, were a match for his. He couldn't help but feel pride at the sight, for their methods and timing were so ingrained by relentless training that no order was needed. As he adjusted his grip on his saber-lance, he knew this night would reaffirm their legend in the minds of both enemies and allies alike.

As they closed the gap, he saw the first Suldamik to notice them drop her sword and fall to her knees. However, if she thought submission would grant her clemency, then she was sadly mistaken. Suddenly, as the rear rank turned to face the charging Sur'dathans, the alarm spread through their ranks, and a significant portion of the Suldamik forces turned and scrambled to make ready.

Gregor's grin spread and took on a malicious edge as he barked, "Hammer – CHARGE!"

Even as the last syllable left his lips, the one-hundred-strong Hagan's Hammer kicked their large, magnificent steeds into a full gallop. The thunder of their hooves and the clank of their armor filled the air as they chewed up the distance with terrifying speed. As the gap rapidly shrank, Gregor felt like he could see the fear building in his enemies' eyes. Then, as their saber-lances were lowered and set with uniform precision only paces from the defenders' hastily formed line, he saw quivering limbs and flittering glances amongst the enemy ranks that told him reality had sunk in for them.

Death was coming, and they had no way to fend it off.

In an explosion of blood-curdling screams and screeching steel, Hagan's Hammer tore into the Suldamik's ranks, their macabre saber-lances ripping through steel and flesh like ravenous monsters. Those on the infantry side of the Suldamik's ranks watched in horror as the lances ripped through torsos and out backs, sheared limbs off, or tore heads from shoulders, spraying viscera everywhere. Not one lance snapped, nor did any of Hagan's Hammer drop their lances. Instead, to the Suldamiks' dismay, the Sur'dathans' lances tore into the next line bearing the bodies of their comrades. The carnage seemed unending as each trailing rank of Hagan's Hammer seemed to pick off anyone who survived the previous assault.

As the skull of another Suldamik ripped over the vicious head of his saber-lance, and his destrider trampled the body, Gregor dropped his lance and shield and urged his mount forward, slamming her armored chest into his next foe. Drawing his Sur'dathan claymore from his saddle scabbard, he began guiding his mount through the middle of the carnage with his knees as he rained blows down upon the head and shoulders of his foes. A quick glance showed him that his fellow Highlanders were doing the same as him, and chaos now consumed the broken Suldamik ranks. While some of the enemy infantry had turned to assist against the Highlanders, the rest had surged forward to escape the slaughter only to be met by the mixed infantry of the Merandiths. Heavy and regular infantry alike were carving their way through the disorderly mess with expert ease, slowly squeezing the Suldamiks in a vice of carnage.

A sudden, burning pain shot up Gregor's leg, drawing his attention. Cursing, he lashed out with his sword, cleaving the head of his assailant in two. A quick glance told him the wound in his lower thigh was, thankfully, superficial and wouldn't impede his ability to steer the deadly beast beneath him. Turning about, he urged his mount into motion. Rearing up with a snort, the destrider lashed out with its hooves, catching one foe in the head and collapsing the chest of another. Roaring with bestial vigor, Gregor then drove his sword down through the chest of another opponent before cutting his way clear of the fray.

Once clear, he scanned the area with his keen green eyes and assessed the situation with speed born of experience. The Suldamik forces that had fled the fort were nearly dead, and those that were just now emerging from the miasma-filled stronghold found themselves quickly cut down by a squad of Merandith regulars that had taken up positions just outside the west gate. Satisfied with the situation at the fort, he turned his attention back to what remained of the melee and found that a small group of Suldamik holdouts had formed a fighting circle and were making his men's task costly. At least twenty more of his infantry were down, and many more were injured as Suldamik steel lashed out with abandon. Thankfully, the heavies were forcing their way towards the Suldamiks to intercede, and soon had their impressive tower shields between ally and foe, trapping the Suldamiks in a ring of spiked steel. That, however, did not stop the officer leading them, and many others, from hacking at the shields with a mad fury.

Suddenly, the officer's crazed eyes settled on Gregor and he pointed his sword at him. "Demonspawn!" he howled. "Show me that your foul kind has some sense of honor! Grant me a trial by combat!"

The declaration gave pause to all the combatants, and a few of Gregor's men turned to look his way inquisitively.

Grunting, Gregor nudged his destrider into motion. Once he was within a few yards of the trapped Suldamiks, he reined in his mount and leaned on the pommel of his saddle. "And what do ye want if'n I grant yer request?"

Torvan's eyes darted about as he licked his dry lips. He was surprised the demons actually had entertained his demand; after all, they were demons. Finally, he screeched, "Freedom for me and my men!"

Gregor grunted. "And if'n I win, then ye and yers are mine ta do with as I please," he declared as several of Hagan's Hammer, some mounted and some on foot, gathered behind him.

Torvan glared at Gregor suspiciously and licked his lips again. "Agreed," he replied with a raw, shaky voice.

Gregor leaned back in his saddle. "It's agreed, then! Let 'im through, lads!" Gregor ordered.

Slowly, the soldiers parted, allowing Torvan to proceed.

With his nervous eyes darting about, Torvan cautiously made his way forward, the Five Stars' ranks closing quickly behind him.

Gregor wanted to shake his head sadly as he caught the dejected expressions of the Suldamik soldiers. He recognized those looks and knew they expected defeat. The question that entered his mind then was whether or not they would accept defeat quietly, or would they decide to meet death with their swords.

Once Torvan was clear of the Merandith soldiers, he halted before Gregor and, with as much dignity as he could muster, demanded, "Get down from there, demonspawn! Face me like a man!"

148

There were a few chuckles from the Five Stars' men at Torvan's continued choice of words.

"Daft bugger," Gregor thought before saying, "Lad, I be too old ta be gettin' mixed up in such nonsense."

Torvan laughed. "I guess I shouldn't be surprised, dishonorable wretch! Fine! Name your champion!"

Fighting the urge to shake his head at the poor man's plight, Gregor barked, "Donald – front 'n center!"

"Aye, sir," Donald replied as he raised his visor and edged his mount up beside Gregor.

"Ye up fer this?"

Donald, his body spattered with blood, grinned broadly. "Gladly, sir."

"Then get ta it, lad! We dunna be havin' all night!"

Jamming his bloody claymore into the ground, Donald slid from his saddle, landing with a rattle of steel, and quickly retrieved his weapon.

"After ye, laddie," Donald said to Torvan with a mocking half-bow.

Scowling, Torvan led him away from the cavalry. Once he found a suitable spot, Torvan turned to Donald and raised his sword before his face in salute. "Prepare for death, demon!" Torvan bellowed shrilly before charging.

A gleeful howl from Donald greeted the charge as he sidestepped the thrust and kicked Torvan in the rump. As Torvan stumbled by, Donald quipped, "Have ta do better than that, lad!"

Recovering his balance, Torvan turned and scowled at Donald before once again charging. To Donald's surprise, Torvan retained control of his movements this time and leveled a series of slashes and thrusts at him. Donald quickly gave ground, intercepting the surprisingly powerful blows with ease.

"Not bad," Donald grunted as he caught an over-hand chop on the flat of his blade. With a grin, he kicked Torvan in the stomach, sending him stumbling backward. "But like I was sayin', ye'll have ta do better than that!" he taunted once more.

Torvan sneered at Donald and screamed, "Do not mock me!" before once again charging with reckless abandonment.

Gregor felt a scowl pulling at his lips as he watched his lieutenant dance away from the officer's wild attacks. This wasn't anything close to a fair fight, and he knew that Donald was well aware of this fact. "Stop playin' with him, Donald!" he finally barked.

Grinning, Donald ducked under a wild swing from his opponent. "Don't ruin me fun, Captain!" Donald retorted as he parried a wild slash and stepped to the side, allowing his wild-eyed opponent to stumble forward.

Torvan hit the ground hard but quickly shook it off before standing. Turning swiftly to face Donald, desperation and fear pitched his voice high as he screamed, "Die, you filthy demonspawn! You will not stop our escape!"

Charging forward, Torvan took a violent swing at Donald's head and came to a sudden halt. Blinking at the empty air his sword had just cut through, he started to ask, "Wha—" when he suddenly felt a warmth spreading across his belly.

Shaking his head, Donald raised up from one knee and pulled his claymore from Torvan's stomach. Looking at Torvan quizzically, he asked rhetorically, "Yer a daft bugger, aren't ye?"

Torvan coughed, and a trickle of blood escaped his lips. "You won't stop us, demonspawn. . . . The Hells . . . won't keep us. . . ." Suddenly, the strength in Torvan's legs fled him, and he collapsed to his knees.

Hefting his claymore, Donald took a two-handed grip on it and muttered, "Poor bastard," before swinging the blade with all his might. With ease and a gush of blood, the claymore cut through Torvan's neck. As the captain's head rolled off its perch, Torvan's body collapsed to the ground.

Reaching down, Donald sank his hand into the head's hair before holding it aloft with a victorious scream. "Yield, ye Suldamik bastards!" Donald bellowed. "Yer commander is dead! Victory is ours!"

Donald's declaration and the sight of the severed head caught the attention of the few remaining defenders, and to a man, they threw down their weapons and dropped to their knees.

Shaking his head, Gregor glared at Donald before nudging his mount toward the men standing guard over the surviving defenders. Once he reached them, he glared into the resigned eyes of the survivors, seeking any sign that there was fight left in them. Once he was satisfied no such fire remained, he looked to his men and punched his fist skyward. "Victory is ours!" he declared. "Huzzah!"

"HUZZAH!" roared his men in response as they raised their weapons in victory.

Gregor let the cheers wash over them for a moment before he whistled sharply for their attention. Almost immediately, the Merandith forces quieted down, though a few scatter murmurs could be heard. "Right!" Gregor finally stated, authority ringing in his voice. "Round up tha prisoners, and let's see 'bout clearin' tha rest o' tha vermin from tha nest!"

It took only minutes to eliminate the remaining opposition. Those who had remained in the fort were primarily dazed and disoriented. As for those that had escaped the brunt of the smoke's effects, they put up only minor resistance before being dispatched. By midnight, Gregor found himself standing within the fort, surrounded by as many of his victorious army that could fit comfortably within its walls. Cheers, laughter, and bright smiles were rampant amongst his men, and he felt pride swelling in his heart. Outside of Sur'datha, this was the first significant combat his countrymen had seen in the war, and its results were overwhelmingly decisive. While the war was far from won, they deserved this moment of joy, and he would let them have it.

As his contemplative gaze passed over the crowd, he caught sight of Solaria and Valesti, their foreheads pressed together and their eyes closed. While he found the cyrians baffling – and at times, bizarre – he couldn't ignore the simple fact that reuniting with a loved one after a battle was a joyous occasion . . . even if it went against his upbringing. Even as he watched, the two cyrians' lips met in a deep kiss, and he fought the urge to shake his head.

"Cyrians are certainly . . . unique, Captain, but I doubt this is the first time you've seen two women kiss," a rough voice stated.

Startled, Gregor jumped a bit and cast a scowl at the man on his right. Shaking his head of loose-hanging, and generously white, rust-colored hair, he barked, "Deo be good, Coltan – yer too damn quiet fer yer own good!"

"My apologies, Captain. Habit," Coltan replied with a sly grin, his small brown eyes alight with amusement.

Gregor grunted at the unscathed officer. "And ta be answerin' yer question – aye, I have, Commander. And while I dunna be havin' a grudge against the likes o' them, it's just ah bit damn odd ta me."

Coltan chuckled. "Love is blind, eh?" he asked rhetorically as Solaria and the read-haired Valesti, hand-in-hand, approached them.

Gregor grunted.

As the couple drew near, he asked Solaria, "All is well, I take it?"

Solaria, her yellow eyes aglow with the same profound happiness that occupied Valesti's red gaze, nodded as they came to a halt before the two men. Releasing Valesti's hand, she said, her gently firm voice rich with joyful relief, "Indeed it is, Captain. Victory is ours, and with minimal losses. As well, Lieutenant Ilvon wishes me to inform you that we have a handful of prisoners."

"Aye," Gregor nodded. "I was aware of that."

"Quite so, Captain. But she wanted you to know that there was an officer amongst them. In fact, she was found amongst the bodies felled by your charge."

Gregor's eyebrows rose a bit. "Is that so, eh?"

"Indeed. She said she appears to be a lieutenant."

"Has Ilvon gotten anything from her?"

Solaria shook her head of tousled, green-tinted black hair. "Not that she mentioned. What do you wish to do with her?"

Gregor thought about it for a moment, then said, "Find a secure place for tha lass." A slight scowl washed over his face. "Donald already went 'n killed their commander, so I dunna want ta be wastin' a possible source of information."

"Agreed," Solaria replied with a slight nod of her head. "And the other prisoners?"

Gregor didn't need to think about his answer this time. "Bring 'um 'ere," he said sternly.

Nodding, Solaria motioned to Valesti, who then made her way quickly toward the forge, which was serving as a temporary prison.

With a curious look, Solaria moved beside Gregor to await Valesti's return.

It wasn't long before the lanky cyrian returned with the prisoners in tow. The Merandith forces quickly noted the prisoners' arrival, and a hush fell over the courtyard as the guards arranged the downtrodden Suldamiks in a line before Gregor. As Valesti took up a position just behind Solaria, Gregor glared at the dozen prisoners as they were forced to their knees. Bloodied and wounded, most of their heads were hung in defeat. As for those few who looked at him, they did so with blank eyes.

"What are you going to do with them?" Solaria asked softly

from beside him.

Gregor looked at her and grunted. Solaria's actions that night had been the key to their swift victory, and she and her squad had emerged relatively unscathed. Regretfully, and most unfortunately, she'd lost two of Coltan's men to the melee. On the other hand, Solaria had escaped injury despite the blood on her leathers, while the rest of her squad had suffered only minor injuries.

"What would ye have me do, eh?" he asked, wanting her input. "We have no stockade, 'n we dunna have tha supplies ta feed extra mouths."

"Then you wish to execute all of them?" she asked with an arched eyebrow.

Gregor grunted. "Would ye have me do somethin' else?"

Before Solaria could respond, one of the prisoners said weakly, "Please, have mercy."

Walking down the line, Gregor halted before the speaker and motioned for one of the guards to haul her to her feet. Dark hair matted with blood, Ursa looked at Gregor with green eyes that were still red with irritation.

"Mercy, eh? And why should I be doin' that, lass? Yer kind be showin' no such thing when they be devistatin' my lands, nor when they be terrorizin' tha rest o' Triclose. As far as I'm concerned, killin' ye here means one less damn fool ta be bringin' harm ta me 'n mine."

"Are you and yours any different?" she responded weakly. "We kill and destroy in the name of our domses, who each lay claim to that damn, long-empty throne." Meeting Gregor's gaze, a single tear escaped her eyes as she added, "If you can tell me what makes your cause any better than ours, then I will die here, content that my death is the result of misplaced loyalty."

Though there was no hint of anger in her gaze or posture, her softly spoken words made Gregor pause. "Yer name, lass?"

"Ursa. Private Ursa Yolingarde," she replied softly.

"Well, Private, I can only be tellin' ye that tha Suldamiks be after nothin' but power 'n conquest. They dunna care who they trample before them, 'n they certainly dunna be carin' about tha sufferin' they be bringin' ta others."

"And the Merandiths?"

"Peace 'n a good life fer all. No more war. No more sufferin'. There be no reason that canna be a reality."

She tried to laugh but ended up coughing violently. When she recovered, she finally responded, her voice barely more than a whisper, "You're a fool. We're all damn fools."

Gregor grinned softly. "Maybe we ar' that, lass. But I dunna wanna see tha Suldamiks bring ruin ta us all. So," he motioned down the line of prisoners with his head to one of the guards, "I canna be lettin' ye all go free. One less soldier now is one less ta be standin' in our way down tha road."

Ursa sighed and nodded dully.

Sudden, short-lived cries sounded from the other prisoners as Merandith soldiers stepped up behind them and either quickly slit the prisoners' throats or ran their swords through the prisoner's hearts. Through the flash of violence, not one word or sound was uttered by Ursa, and not once did her eyes leave Gregor's gaze.

"I suppose you'll have the pleasure of killing me yourself?" she finally asked of him when she was the only one left.

"No, lass," Gregor replied with a shake of his head, which drew baffled looks from his fellow soldiers. "Ye, I'm gonna spare."

"Torture, then?"

Gregor grinned.

A spark of emotion flared in Ursa's eyes and she laughed. "If you think I'll tell you anything, you're a fool!" she spit defiantly.

"Might be that I am. Guess we'll just see."

Motioning to one of the guards, he ordered, "Get tha lass 'nough food 'n water ta get her ta Chalin." As the guard hustled off, Gregor said to the soldier behind Ursa, "Take our . . . guest 'n secure her in one o' tha command buildin's rooms. See tha she is attended ta, but try not ta make her too comfortable."

"Aye, sir," he responded. "Get moving, bitch!" the grizzled guard barked as he gave her a shove toward the command building.

Recovering quickly, Ursa shot Gregor a murderous glare before the guard gave her another shove.

As Ursa was led away, Gregor turned his attention back to Solaria, who had a peculiar look on her face. "What?" he asked as he stepped up to her.

"Why?"

Gregor grunted, but instead of replying, he turned and sought out Ilvon. Seeing her standing with the other officers, he pointed at her and ordered, "Lieutenant – send a messenger ta Doms Hagail.

Inform him that tha fort is ours, 'n he can be headin' our way when ready."

Puzzled, Ilvon suppressed the urge to give voice to her questions. Instead, she snapped off a crisp salute and said, "Sir!" before moving off to find someone in good enough shape for the journey.

Grunting, Gregor turned to the assembled troops. "The rest o' ye sods – clear out 'n set up camp! This place is a bloody wreck! I want all tha corpses stripped o' useable uniforms 'n gear, then dump tha bodies outside fer burnin' before ye even be thinkin' about celabratin'! Now, get movin'!"

As the soldiers scrambled to carry out his orders, Gregor turned to Solaria and Coltan.

"And the officer we found?" Coltan asked.

Gregor grunted with respect. "She's got Deo's luck, that fer damn sure. Have someone see ta her wounds, then lock her in one o' tha room in tha main buildin' fer now. We'll see what we can pry from 'er later. She's earned tha much just fer survivin'." Shaking his head, he grunted again before stating, "Now that that's all taken care o', let's be seein' if tha Suldamiks be havin' somethin' more than swill ta drink. I think we've earned a celebratory drink, eh?"

Chapter Eight

Scratching at his trimmed salt-and-pepper beard, Doms General Jerom Nolan Merandith, Sword Master and Captain of Doms Merandith's bodyguards, stared at the scene with a knot of apprehension in his stomach. As he had done many times since their small group entered the Alderian Forest, he checked to make sure the functional broadsword at his left hip was clear of the heavy black cloak draped about his stout shoulders. Crouching down, the chainmail he wore over his dark leathers and beneath his unadorned breastplate rattled gently as he adjusted his cloak. As his right brown eye took in the scene again, he cursed softly under his breath. It was obvious that there had been a battle here, but that was the only thing he could clearly glean from the baffling clues.

At this point in the Doren'thal River, the waters were relatively shallow and the banks were rocky, which, in Jerom's mind, made it an excellent place to ambush an opponent. Granted, he didn't believe they had anything to fear from House Suldamik after their last encounter, but the perplexing scene before him was another matter. It made him more nervous than the night before a battle. As such, he'd deployed the majority of the two dozen Merandith and Trivant soldiers they'd brought with them around the perimeter of the battleground. As for the rest of the group, they were busy examining the area in search of answers.

All about the roughly two-hundred-pace section of the river, black scorch marks scoured the riverbank. Every ounce of reasoning Jerom possessed told him that numerous large fires had been lit, likely to destroy the bodies of the slain. It was a logical assumption, but there was no other evidence to support that line of reasoning other than the scorch marks. In fact, they'd searched the riverbanks for hours, and very little had been found; no blood, no scraps of clothing, not even a hint of ash or charred wood. As for what they did find, only a handful of partial boot prints made any sense, and there certainly wasn't enough of those to support a large-scale struggle.

Jerom shifted his gaze to the most blatant and most perplexing clue they had discovered – an eighteen-foot-long, ten-foot-wide cut in the riverbank that was eerie to look at. He had never seen anything like it, and had no idea why someone would do such a thing.

Running his black-gloved hand through his short-cut hair, which was more gray than black, Jerom then absently scratched at the skin around his eye-patch as his gaze moved to his nephew.

Kale Jorbic Merandith, Doms of House Merandith, paced the length of the cut pensively under the watchful gaze of Jerom's fellow veteran bodyguard, Tazrim, and four of the candidates seeking to join their ranks. Kale's brother-by-marriage, Doms Trivant was also there, but his focus was on the conversation he currently shared with three of his men. As for Kale, his troubled green eyes were focused on the cut as if he could glean something more from it, which made Jerom's heart ache for his troubled nephew. The last two weeks had been taxing on Kale, and it showed. The shoulders of his six-foot frame were slightly bowed – though not from the longsword strapped across his back – his blonde hair hung below his jawline, and three days' worth of stubble covered the normally handsome features of his now drawn face. Despite all Kale had been through in his twenty-three years, this winter respite from the war was beginning to look far worse than any battle, and Jerom could not fault his nephew for his concern.

Standing with a muffled grunt, Jerom approached Kale and his retinue of bodyguards.

The last few weeks had seen Kale's bodyguards reduced to a trio of veterans, which was a troubling issue on its own. To make matters worse, soon after that horrible development, Kale's brother was assaulted in the heart of their camp by soldiers from the newly arrived House Sur'datha. Once that terrible mess was sorted out, Kale decided to send his brother, Amroth, back home with one of his remaining bodyguards as an escort.

Jerom grunted.

Sending Amroth home should have been a relief for Kale, but on the heels of the move came the violent storm responsible for drawing them near the southern reaches of the Alderian Forrest. The storm inflicted an irritating amount of damage on their supplies and wagons, and even saw a few soldiers injured. As such, they made camp for a few days while injuries were tended to and repairs were made. While their efforts proceeded smoothly, Kale's mood remained dower no matter how much Jerom tried to cheer him up. Then, as if Deo himself had a grudge against Kale, came the news that the Roselian clans had seen signs that could result in a political shift within the Five Stars' prized fighting force. That revelation was terrible enough, but when Dakan and Doms Trivant revealed that such a shift could involve Amroth's death, it was like the news eradicated all the joy from Kale.

Somehow, by the time they were ready to resume their march, Jerom and Trivant had managed to improve Kale's spirits somewhat from dark and depressed to moody and distant. That improvement, however, was short-lived. On the night before they set out once more, a bizarre light show within the forest erupted in the distance that shocked everyone in the army. This otherworldly incident set rumors swirling and spurred Kale to deploy scouts to investigate while also sending the bulk of the army ahead, under the command of Doms Grevorian of Kythir, with orders to take up defensive positions north of Haltho along their current path. Kale and a small group from House Merandith and Trivant then rode ahead of House Trivant's contingent as they cut through the Alderian Forest. Making directly for Haltho, they were eager to see if anyone in the city might know about the otherworldly display, but more importantly, they wanted to ensure the city was secure. While they were relieved to find the city intact and at peace, the relief proved to be fleeting when they learned of the news that now consumed Kale's mind.

Amroth was missing.

What's more, his bodyguard was absent as well, and a thorough search had turned up very little to the dismay of those close to Amroth. Even their belongings were nowhere to be found. It was an infuriating situation, and while Kale would have preferred to remain in Haltho to continue the search, Trivant and Jerom eventually managed to convince him that the eruption of bluish-white light seen by so many warranted investigation. Such an agonizing decision tore at Kale's heart, but as much as he didn't want to admit it, he knew they were right – at that moment, Amroth's fate was a secondary concern. If there was some new threat to the Five Stars that might impede them, then they had to know what it was.

Drawing alongside Kale, Jerom nodded to the short, burly, leather-armored man standing off to the side. Tazrim's stoic blue eyes met Jerom's gaze, and he nodded his shaved, heavily scarred, square-jawed head in return. Turning to the bodyguard candidates, the bastard sword across his back rattling gently against the studs of his armor, Tazrim motioned for the candidates, who wore purple-trimmed black Merandith tabards embroidered with five gold stars on their right breasts, to follow him before leading them a short distance away from Kale.

Assured of a small measure of privacy, Jerom then gently rumbled, "Find anything, lad?"

"Nothing," Kale replied, his voice heavy with frustration. Folding his arms across the unadorned breastplate he wore over his chainmail and dark leathers, he shook his head. "I was partly hoping there was a chance – however remote – that we might find a clue to Amroth's whereabouts here since everything happened on the same night." He caught Jerom's sympathetic look out of the corner of his eye and he grunted. "I know. I know. It was a long shot. Still. . . ." He let out a frustrated sigh. "Deo be good!" he growled as he clenched his black-gloved hands. "We've all seen far too many battle-fields, and nothing about this makes sense!"

Jerom placed a comforting hand on his nephew's shoulder. "Easy, lad," he stated gently. "You're not alone. We all are just as puzzled and concerned."

Kale closed his eyes and took a deep breath. Letting it out slowly, he then nodded. Opening his eyes, he flashed a half-hearted smile at Jerom. "You're right, Uncle. But it doesn't mean I have to like any of this damn mess."

"No one said you had to," Jerom responded with a grunt.

Looking across the gash in the ground, Jerom asked, "Any of this make sense to you or your men, Lucas?"

The muscular Doms Trivant dismissed the trio of soldiers he'd been conversing with, who wore bright orange tabards embla-zoned with a large golden sunburst, and approached the Merandiths. Taller than the six-foot Kale, Trivant wore a dark brown cloak over leather armor that was slashed with orange. Orange gloves covered his hands, and an imposing lochabre axe was slung across his broad back. Halting before the two, his bright-blue eyes looked at them with a mix of puzzlement and concern from a clean-shaven, hand-some face top with brown hair pulled back in a horsetail.

"Yes and no," Lucas stated, his deep, booming voice heavy with concern.

"What's that supposed to mean?" Kale asked in irritation.

Lucas ignored Kale's tone and responded, "It means that the majority of this is as much of a puzzle to me as it is to you. This gash," he motioned to them for emphasis, "could be an excavation of some kind, but damned if I know the who and how of it," he finished with a puzzled shake of his head. "As for the shattered stone and scorch marks – your guess is as good as mine."

Jerom snorted. "Well, you're just a bundle of help."

"And you're getting cynical and impatient in your old age," Lucas replied with a disarming smile.

Jerom rolled his eye. "Get on with it, lad."

"Right. As I was saying, there is one thing we found that is familiar."

Both Merandiths' eyes lit up, and Kale asked anxiously, "That would be?"

"Claw marks," Lucas confidently declared.

"Claw marks . . ." Kale repeated softly, disappointment clearly written across his face.

"So what?" Jerom said skeptically. "You've found some big cat or bear's markings. Likely the beastie was just passing through at some point."

Lucas shrugged. "Might be that the creature was passing through, as you say. But with Deo as my witness, no bear or cat made these – and there are a lot of them."

Kale and Jerom looked at each other suspiciously.

"Show us," Kale ordered.

As they started off, Tazrim and the other bodyguards followed at a distance.

Leading them upstream, Lucas informed them, "From what we can tell, the marks are all up and down this section of the river, but many of them are difficult to spot."

"So they're old, then," Kale stated confidently.

"Aye, they are – but not too old," Lucas replied with a nod, ignoring the interruption. "It makes me glad I didn't bring my normal bodyguards with me," he added, his tone thankful, drawing alarmed looks from Jerom and Kale. They knew all too well what Lucas was referencing, and that made their skin crawl.

A moment later, Doms Trivant pointed upstream to the last of the bodyguard candidates that had accompanied Kale and added, "There are a few of the marks that are hard to miss up here."

Crouched near the edge of the water, Dakan's intimidating visage was dark, and the leather of his dark brown pants was wet up to his knees. Despite the cold, his serpent-tattooed, powerful bronze-skinned arms were bare except for a pair of thick black leather bracers, and only a sturdy deerskin vest of clan-make beneath a Merandith tabard protected his torso from winter's bite. One look at him was enough to mark him as a dangerous man, which was further emphasized by the lochabre axe across his back. Five feet long, its polished ironwood shaft was inlaid with twin silver dragons, and its head was composed of a pair of opposing dragon heads from which sprouted an unconventional counter spike and a vicious winged axe blade etched with clan charms and wards.

160

Dakan soon noticed their approach and stood up, the spiked pommel of his axe jutting over his right shoulder. Turning to face the approaching group, he set his dark, grim eyes upon them and held up a large rock.

"What's that he's got?" Jerom asked, referring to the rock Dakan held.

"No idea," Kale replied before taking the lead from Lucas. As they drew near, Kale asked, "What do you have there, Dakan?"

Inclining his head, the dark hair of which was braided into a long horsetail, Dakan said, his deep voice heavy, "Doms Merandith. Something I wish I could find another explanation for."

Halting before the young clansman, Kale asked with an edge of impatience, "And that is?"

"Go on, Dakan – show him. I don't think he's in the mood for mysteries today," Lucas encouraged his fellow Roselian.

Nodding, Dakan presented the rock to Kale and declared with regretful confidence, "The Spirits seem to have something against us, Doms. These are drakuma markings."

Between the rock and Dakan's statement, Kale felt his breath catch in his throat. Scored down the length of the sizable piece of stone was a gash nearly two inches in width. While Kale's experience with drakumas was basically limited to hearsay and the stuffed frost drakuma he'd seen as a child in his grandfather's home, he could find no reason to doubt Dakan's conclusion. However, he still found himself asking, "Are you sure?"

"Unfortunately, yes, Doms. I found this sticking out of the water." Motioning over his shoulder, he added, "There are more up there. And from what I can see, there was more than one of the beasts here."

"Show us," Kale stated, concern flooding his voice.

Nodding, Dakan tossed the rock aside before turning and guiding them further upstream.

"Here," Dakan said when they reached their destination. Pointing at a series of larger, partially filled-in gashes in the riverbank, Dakan offered, "They're partly obscured now, but the spacing be-tween the four cuts clearly marks the creatures as drakumas. A num-ber of them overlap, and if you look around carefully, you can see two separate sets of tracks headed toward each other. As far as I can tell, two of the great beasts clashed here. What became of either beast," he shrugged, "I do not know."

Jerom scowled at the news while Kale and Lucas shared a concerned glance. None of this boded well for the potential turmoil that hung over the Roselian clans, and the question they all hesitated to ask hung in the air. Finally, Kale gave voice to it. "The scouts that discovered the area were mine, but. . . ." He paused. "Do you think the Clans know of this?"

The speed with which Dakan responded tied a cold knot in Kale's stomach. "I cannot say for sure, Doms – but it is very likely. Though mostly obscured at this point, there were some older human tracks leaving the river. There's not enough left to tell who they belonged to, but I cannot imagine someone from the Clans – especially those that might be in the area, Doms – didn't investigate this," he finished with a wave of his hand at the puzzling scene.

"So I guess it's best to assume they know of this and have come to a similar conclusion?" Kale asked rhetorically. "Damn!" Folding his arms across his chest, Kale looked up through the mostly barren canopy at the partially cloudy sky, concern etched plainly on his face.

"Don't be so quick to jump to dour conclusions, Kale," Lucas offered in an attempt to keep his already troubled brother-by-marriage from sinking into dark thoughts. "Yes, it's likely that the Clans are aware of this scene, and it's quite probable they've come to the same conclusions as Dakan. But let's be realistic – we can't know for sure how they'll respond. We are, after all, assuming a worst-case scenario."

"Aye. The lummox is right, lad. We're jumping to conclusions," Jerom offered supportively. "The Clans may be full of stubborn, tradition-bound, violent buggers, but the Clan Elders more or less have reasonable heads on their shoulders." Eying Dakan, who was looking at him with a raised eyebrow, he added, "No offense, lad."

"Indeed, Doms Captain," Dakan replied, with a forced smirk, using Jerom's rank within Kale's bodyguards.

With a subtle snort, Kale looked at Dakan and said, "You don't sound as hopeful as my optimistic family, Dakan. Tell me – what do you think?"

Dakan did not respond immediately as he met Kale's troubled green eyes. He could sympathize with his new doms' plight. Not only was Amroth Kale's adopted brother, but he was also one of Dakan's few remaining blood relatives – albeit distantly. Like Kale, he wanted to know what had happened to Amroth, but there was a part of him that also hoped Amroth had perished – hopefully, in glorious battle. He knew it was a deplorable act to wish such a fate on blood simply to avoid the alternative, but that particular alternative was likely to be far worse for everyone. If the Clans had discovered the bizarre scene along the river as he suspected, then it would be used to further validate any call for a Moot by those hungry to supplant the current High Elder. He had no reason to doubt this, for his lover and the leader of the Clan of the Wolf had made clear her intentions.

As he had thought about doing so many times since word of the ember drakuma had reached his and his doms' ears, Dakan considered divulging what he knew of Beliza's ambitions. Yet, as had happened those times before, a nagging voice in the back of his head gave him pause. "I do not know, Doms," he uttered instead. "If the Clans have discovered this, then it is possible things could go as we fear. Then again, it could be just as Doms Trivant and the Doms Captain say. Either way, I fear we will not know what they will do till the spring."

Kale looked at Dakan skeptically. He couldn't place what was nagging him about Dakan when the subjects of Amroth and the Clans came up, but something about his attitude seemed a bit off. "Very well," Kale said with a weak smile. "Then, if you do not believe we'll find anything else of use here, I'd like to be back in Haltho as soon as possible."

The urgency in Kale's voice was clear to each of them, prompting Jerom to place a comforting hand on his nephew's shoulder. "We'll find him, lad," he offered before turning to Tazrim and ordering, "Tazrim – gather everyone up. We're leaving this Deoforsaken place."

The modest, single-story inn was packed with House Merandith and Trivant personnel. Only a day north of Haltho, the quaint inn was accustomed to hosting a sizable crowd, but never had it seen so many armed soldiers. While the middle-aged innkeeper was grateful that such a significant, authoritative presence kept her more rambunctious patrons subdued or away, the soldiers had orders to stay sober, which meant drink orders had practically dried up. Granted, she had been paid a nice sum to host the pair of domses and their entourage, but as she cleaned an already spotless mug with her apron, she couldn't help but lament the possible coin crowding the inn's tavern.

The roaring fire in the hearth on the far-right wall flickered as the inn's door swung open with a slight protest, admitting a gust of cold wind that threatened to douse the numerous table and wall lamps scattered about the common room. There were some grumbled complaints from a few of her regular patrons as a small procession of soldiers into the inn kept the door open too long for their liking, but those died off quickly. As for the soldiers, those that led the way in quickly dispersed, some joining friends and companions seated at the tables and the bar, while others swiftly made their way down the hall at the back of the tavern. Eventually, the door was pulled shut behind the domses' rear guard, and Doms Merandith's second-in-command made his way over to the innkeeper.

The wiry innkeeper flashed a small smile sprinkled with crooked teeth at Jerom and fixed her green eyes, the sclera of which were tinted yellow, on him. "What can I do for you?" she asked of him with a voice that was harsh and dry from years of indulging in deathweed as he squeezed in at the end of the bar.

"Ale and dinner for nine, if you would."

She grunted and placed the mug she'd been cleaning on the bar. Wiping her hands on the stained apron she wore over her lanky figure and simple gray dress, she stated as if Jerom's request was a burden, "Don't know what's left, Shi'doms. You're all a might late for dinner."

Jerom smiled knowingly at the innkeeper. Digging around in his coin purse, he pulled out two gold talons and tossed them on the bar before her. "I'm sure you can find something that is more than adequate, lass. Take the men's meals to their rooms, and bring the domses and mine to the private dining room."

Swiping up the coins from the bar, the innkeeper dipped her head of braided brown hair respectfully. "I'll see what I can find, Shi'doms."

Jerom nodded. "Thank you, lass," he said before making his way to the open door next to the hearth.

Entering the private dining room, Jerom shut the door behind him. By no means was the small room luxurious, but it was better than the common room. A small hearth to his right, which shared a chimney with the tavern's hearth, housed a brightly burning fire that enveloped the area with cozy warmth. At the center of the room, seated beneath the somewhat low roof from which a lantern chandelier hung, was a sturdy oak table large enough to seat eight. Stripped of his breastplate and chainmail, which rested on the floor next to his chair, Kale sat across from his brother-by-marriage at the far end of the table with a pensive look on his face. Lucas' expression was just as troubled, and between the two of them, the air seemed ominously heavy.

Grunting softly, Jerom walked over and sat at the head of the table between them. "Dinner will be here in a bit," he stated, drawing a slight nod from Kale and a weak but appreciative smile from Lucas. Shaking his head at their behavior, he rumbled, "Hells' bloody balls – you two need to take a deep breath and relax just a bit!"

Rarely did Jerom use such a strong curse, and the shock of hearing it from him earned him a pair of baffled looks from his family. A smirk suddenly began to tug at the corners of Kale's mouth just as Lucas let out a laugh and shook his head.

"That's a bit better, you two! Deo knows this war has been going on far too long, and the last thing we need is for you two to start seeing every bit of bad, or possibly bad, news as the end of the world," he gently chastised.

Kale let out a deep, frustrated sigh and grimaced. "I know, Uncle, but this is Amroth and the Clans we're talking about. Deo knows the possibility of losing more of my family is bad enough, but his ties to the Clans and their," he grunted, "superstitious approach to making important decisions is a difficult situation to handle."

Jerom cast a dry glare on his nephew. "I'm touched that you're so concerned for my well-being, lad. Guess putting me between you and a sword is your way of showing how much you care about me, eh?"

"You know what I mean," Kale responded with a dry glare.

"I know you mean well, Jerom," Lucas interjected, "but Kale is right – there is a lot to be lost here. It's not that I don't believe we could suffer the loss of the Clans should an internal war for leadership arise, but we simply don't know what the consequences of such an event would be." Lucas shook his head. "We could be lucky, and nothing will come of all this . . . but I've been around the Clans far too long to hold out too much hope. If a war erupts amongst them, there's the possibility of it spilling over into the rest of Roselia. I don't want to know what the effects on the war effort would be if I have to divert manpower to contain the Clans or – Deo forbid – have to fight them. Hells, there's even these rumors of mysterious figures with poisoned weapons and a beast cloaked in shadows to deal with that Oblet mentioned! I'm not even sure where to start with that!" He scoffed, and shook his head once more.

A heavy silence descended on the trio. Kale and Jerom trusted Lucas' intuition when it came to the Clans. If he genuinely believed a struggle for leadership was imminent, then they had no choice but to believe him and attempt to plan accordingly.

"I'm sure the rumors can be addressed easily enough. The

poison that Oblet described is unlike anything I've heard of, but it isn't a stretch to say the shadowy figures are Suldamik troops," Kale stated, his words heavy with concern. "Therefore, we'll treat it as a military matter. For now, our focus should be on Amroth's situation and the Clans."

"Well, on the bright side, if no one can find him, then that reduces the chances of a leadership dispute," Lucas offered, earning an angry glare from Kale. Holding up his hands defensively, Lucas said, "Don't get me wrong, Kale. I deeply hope he's alright. Deo knows, he's got Mathis with him – that alone gives me hope. But, if we can remove him from the situation, the odds of us getting through this with minimal repercussions go up."

Shaking his head, Kale said, "I know you didn't mean ill, and rest assured, I will do my damnest to make sure Amroth doesn't get involved in Clan politics. That, however, means nothing if we can't find him." Kale's hands clenched. "If he's dead, I swear I'll. . . ."

Jerom placed a firm, comforting hand on Kale's shoulder. "He's not, lad. I'd bet my life on that. We're going to get back to Haltho and pick up his trail, and if it takes some of us staying behind to find him, then so be it."

Kale snorted at his uncle's implication. "I won't be going anywhere till he's found," he stated adamantly.

"The hells you won't!" Jerom declared with a grunt.

Kale fixed his uncle with a firm, angry glare. "And who's going to stop me?"

Jerom scratched at his salt-and-pepper beard and met Kale's glare with his lone brown eye. "No one, lad. Your duty will do it for us."

"My duty is to—" Kale started to declare.

"To Triclose and your family – in that order!" Jerom reminded his nephew adamantly. "You can't honor both if you remain here on a selfish chase." Kale started to protest again, earning a harsh glare from his uncle. "Deo be good, lad! You've got bodyguards to replace, and more importantly, a wonderful wife about to give you another child! I wouldn't be doing my duty or honoring my family if I let you remain south – and neither would you!"

Kale glared at Jerom for a moment, his mind awash with a torrential mix of emotions. Looking to Lucas for support, he instead found an apologetic look on his brother-by-marriage's face.

"Sorry, Kale, I have to agree with Jerom on this," Lucas declared firmly but apologetically. "My sister needs you right now, and

166

you need to replace your bodyguards. I won't have you upsetting her, and I sure as hells won't have you dying on her because you chose to act like a damn fool. When we get back to Haltho, I'm going to make sure you have the best and fastest ship to get you home. And if we do need to search for Amroth, then Oblet will handle it." Looking at Jerom, Lucas added, "That goes for you too. Kale needs you a hells of a lot more than anything or one else does."

Jerom grunted, and Kale simply switched between glaring at his fellow doms and his uncle.

Finally, with an exasperated sigh, Kale said, "I'm not going to be able to change your minds or order either of you to do otherwise, am I?"

"Not a chance," Lucas declared with a grin.

Jerom nodded in agreement. "It's what's best, lad. Deep down, you know it as well."

Before Kale could say anything, there was a knock at the door.

"You may enter," Jerom called out.

The door swung open a moment later, and the innkeeper walked in carrying a pitcher and three mugs. Without a word, she placed her cargo on the table between the three of them, then offered a curtsey to the trio before she withdrew. As she shut the door, Jerom filled and distributed the mugs.

While his uncle and Lucas indulged in their drinks, Kale gazed contemplatively at the dark liquid in his mug as he swirled it about. Finally, he asked, "Does Dakan's behavior of late seem odd to either of you?"

Jerom snorted as he put his mug down on the table and offered with a sarcastic smile, "That would depend on if you classify good behavior as odd for him?"

Lucas chuckled, and a slight smirk tugged at Kale's lips.

"That's not what I meant . . . though his general behavior has been a welcome change," Kale stated dryly. Taking a sip of his drink, he then added, "What I meant was his behavior when we address him about Amroth."

"I'm not sure what you mean," Lucas replied.

Kale shook his head in mild frustration. "I'm not sure I even know what I mean. He just seems. . . ." Kale shrugged.

"Lad, he has seemed a bit reserved when the subject comes

up – but wouldn't you be reluctant to discuss it, given what could be potentially asked of him?" Jerom snorted. "Hells, could you imagine if your grandfather, Deo rest his soul, had ordered your father to sacrifice me in order to claim the throne?"

Kale smirked. "I could never imagine him doing such a thing."

"You're damn right he wouldn't do such a thing!" Jerom declared before taking a long draw from his mug.

"And I guess we should be glad you didn't lead a rebellion against your brother, eh Jerom?" Lucas prodded.

Jerom eyed Lucas dryly. "The thought never crossed my mind, lad. I never had designs on the throne, and assuming leadership over this damned war is something I wouldn't wish on anyone."

"So, I guess serving as a doms general was your idea of shirking responsibility, then?" Lucas asked with a raised eyebrow.

Jerom rolled his lone eye. "You know what I mean," he said, drawing a grin from Lucas. To Kale, he offered, "Lad, I think Dakan is just trying to deal with the situation, just as you are."

"Maybe you're right. Maybe I'm just projecting my own fears and insecurities onto him." Kale took a sip from his mug, and his eyes suddenly widened. "Deo be good! I almost forgot! Jerom, see to it that a rider is sent back to the army with orders to continue on home. . . . Unless you feel there is a need for the extra men here, Lucas?"

Lucas quickly shook his head. "No. With the forces I brought home, we should be just fine."

Kale nodded. "Good. Then, just make sure the rider is on its way in the morning, Uncle."

Jerom nodded. "Aye, lad. Now stop worrying and relax!" he urged.

Smirking slightly, Kale shook his head. "Deo be good! I never thought this winter and next spring would already be presenting so many problems."

"None of us would have believed it either," Lucas offered and then smiled gently. "Be that as it may, if Amroth is really missing, then we'll find him. And if a division within the Clans does actually happen, then we'll deal with it. Then again, we could simply be fretting over nothing. Until we know for sure, do me a favor and look on the bright side – we're winning the war convincingly, and you have a new child on the way. Believe it or not, Deo is blessing us, Kale."

Kale looked at his uncle and Lucas before offering them a smile that contradicted the concern in his green eyes. "You're both right, of course." Raising his mug, he declared, "To our continued success, and the good health of our families! May Deo continue to grant us his blessing!"

"What's it gonna take, Corza? *Humm?* You can't be daft enough to keep lugging that ridiculous shield around as a bodyguard."

Corza's slim, high-cheekbone face closed up defensively as her sea-green eyes flashed with indignation. Pushing a lock of her short-cropped green hair behind her left ear, which was home to six silver rings along its edge, she said in a rich voice, "And as I've said a thousand times before – why should I? It's not my fault the sight of a woman carrying a shield like this," she patted the large steel and wood hoplon leaning against the wall next to her bed along with a heavy, leaf-shaped shortsword, "bruises your ego."

Seated on the edge of the small bed that occupied the right side of the room, and garbed in a black tunic and sturdy pants, the shaved-headed veteran snorted through his bulbous, crooked nose and rolled his large brown eyes. "And you are daft if you think that's the case! Not only could I carry that monstrosity," he declared as he gestured to his stout body, "but I've fought shoulder-to-shoulder with some damn fine women in my days! But you," he pointed a meaty finger at her as his nearly gray eyebrows furrowed in consternation, "you think you're more man than woman! Just look at you, sitting there nearly naked! It's shameful!"

Corza knew her appearance rubbed his sense of modesty raw – which she felt was oddly out of place given the close living conditions within an army – and she took great pleasure in doing so. Seated on a bed that was big enough for two along the left-hand wall, she wore only a sleeveless white undershirt, and smallclothes cut high on her broad hips. Adjusting her crossed, bronze-skinned legs, Corza smirked and cocked her head, the right side of which was shaved. Folding her strong arms beneath her modest bosom, her small, full lips parted in a coy smile as she said, "That's just nonsense, Jor. My people and Dakan's aren't bothered by the sight of bare flesh or even nudity. Isn't that right, Dakan?"

Seated in the lone chair near the door in the cramped room, his lochabre axe resting against the wall behind the chair, Dakan was lost within his troubled thoughts. As such, it took him a moment to realize he'd been addressed, and when he did, he blinked at Corza and asked, "What?"

Corza chuckled. "See, Jor? It bothers him so little that even a conversation about it is lost on him."

Jor snorted again. "And that's supposed to justify your appearance, or you two sharing a bed?"

Corza laughed. "Jealous, Jor? It could have been you if your sense of modesty wasn't such a handicap. I honestly don't mind an older man sharing my bed," she teased.

Jor's broad, aged face began to blush. "I get that we're short on beds, but that don't make it right! Dakan could show that he has some idea of what it means to be a gentleman and chose to sleep on the floor."

Dakan fought the urge to roll his dark eyes. He had been sharing quarters with the two bodyguard candidates since he'd recovered from his whipping, and this dance of verbal teasing had become all too commonplace. Quite often, he found amusement in making their Tiliean bunkmate squirm; after all, his sense of propriety made him an easy target. On this night, unfortunately, it was difficult for Dakan to find the energy to join the fun. He did, however, manage to muster a half-hearted grin as he said, "Yet, despite your gentlemanly claims, neither of us sees you offering to take the floor."

Corza barked a laugh as Jor rubbed one of his leather-encased wrists and struggled to find a retort.

"I have to wonder how one such as you survives ever being in a barracks, much less life on the march. You're as prudish as a priest," Dakan added.

"I can deal with the conditions on the march, but if asking people for a bit of decency and respectable behavior when we're not cooped up in tents makes me prudish, well . . ." Jor shrugged, "I'd rather be that than a Par'thian h–"

A flash of movement and steel cut Jor's statement short as Corza's sword came to rest on his throat. "Careful with your words," Corza purred playfully with a wry grin as she loomed over him, her free hand planted firmly on her hip. "I'd hate to have to do something about it."

Dakan didn't know why, but Corza's playful threat was enough to break the dam holding his frustration with the day's revelations at bay. Standing suddenly, he barked, his irritation spilling forth, "Spirits old and new! I sometimes wish you would make good on your threat, Corza, just so one evening could actually be peaceful and quiet!"

Startled by the outburst, both his roommates looked at him

170

curiously as he stepped to the door and opened it.

Hand on one hip, Corza casually lowered her sword to her side as she asked, "Where are you off to?"

"Outside!" Dakan practically growled before exiting the room, shutting the door emphatically behind him.

"What mud crow crawled up his arse?" Jor asked with a raised eyebrow.

"Dunno. His temperament since that Deo-awful whipping has been . . . off at times," Corza responded before leaning her sword against her shield. Grabbing her rugged, mid-thigh black breeches, she pulled them on.

"Going after him, eh?" Jor prodded.

"What of it?" Corza asked as she put on her padded chaps, which were black down the outer length and brown along the inside of her legs. "Something has been bugging him of late, that's for damn sure, and I think we'd be doing him a disservice if we didn't lend him a friendly ear."

Jor snorted. "How can you tell?" he asked as she secured the chaps' stout buckle before seating herself on her bed and quickly pulling on her sturdy black calf boots. "I mean, all clansmen seem like they've got a pine-ferret pricking their arses all the time."

Smiling at Jor, she stood and patted him on the cheek. "It's a warrior thing. Don't trouble your pretty little head over it." Securing her heavy black cloak over her shoulders, Corza left the room before Jor could muster a retort.

This far north of the Dragonspine, winter was already asserting its dominance. The evenings were swiftly falling prey to winter's bite, and this night was no exception. As such, only a handful of people walked the streets of the quaint village while the majority of the populace remained indoors, protected from the cold by the warmth of the fires burning in their hearths. With his breath escaping his lips in frost puffs, Dakan settled himself against the wall beside one of the inn's front windows and eyed the amalgam of buildings across the street, the windows of which were aglow like the stars in the cloudless night sky. The Roselian clans – which were nomadic to varying degrees – were drastically more accustomed to nature's moods than the soft people who lived in one place, surrounded by walls, and called it civilization.

A muffled snort sent another puff of white into the air.

From his vantage point on the porch, he could see a half dozen Five Stars' soldiers standing guard around the front of the red-painted inn, every one of them girded against the bitter night by thick cloaks and cowls. It wasn't that he found them weak – after all, the Five Stars had proven themselves in battle time and again – but they were soft, and that softness was a flaw that made it difficult for them to understand what it meant to be Clan. It meant devoting one's self wholly to the betterment of the clan. It meant acting with honor, and upholding that honor, no matter what, until one's death – hopefully in glorious combat. Usually, it was an easy task to accomplish since, from birth, all clansmen had those values ground into them until it was second nature. However, did that mean there were never those who strayed from that path or put personal power and glory before what was best for their clan?

Dakan scoffed softly.

His clan and their abolishment, as well as Beliza's seemingly unquenchable ambition, were proof that every culture had its flaws. Even his own quest to regain the honor of the Clan of the Fang was proof of this fact. Did it actually benefit the few scattered remnants of his clan? He wasn't sure. Was it just as selfish as Beliza's goals? There was a small part of him that believed so, but that did little to shake his faith in the duty he believed he owed to those who suffered because of his father's mistake. If life had remained the way it had been for so long, none of this would have been an issue. That, how-ever, had not been the case. Now, because of one discovery – albeit, a monumental one – everything was convoluted, which left him un-sure of his ability to overlook Beliza's lust for power no matter how much he loved her.

Adjusting his position, he folded his bare arms across his leather-vested chest and scowled. Discovering Amroth's lineage had initially done little to affect his plans. To find a surviving blood rela-tive, however distant, was something to be celebrated and relished, which he had done. Granted, Amroth's propensity for avoiding combat had been disappointing, but Dakan had felt that, given time, he could awaken Amroth's clan blood to the joys of battle. Such an accomplishment would have meshed well with Doms Merandith's wish to see his adopted brother join him on the battlefield, but when Beliza discovered Amroth's lineage, it practically shattered those hopes. She'd made it abundantly clear that the quickest and easiest way to restore his clan was to bring Amroth before the Clan Elders to answer for the dishonor his Sur'dathan clan had heaped upon the Clan of the Fang. A part of him – though he did his best to convince himself it didn't exist – was tempted by the offer, but his honor and integrity were far more important to him. Determined to restore his

172

clan through actions rather than the blood of an innocent, Dakan had ignored Beliza's proposal. His punishment at the hands of Jerom for seeking justice for the attempt on Amroth's life did tempt him – albeit briefly – to reconsider Beliza's offer, but he'd quickly banished such thoughts.

Dakan's scowl deepened.

Just as he had begun to believe he would never have to think about such a horrible path to redemption again, the unthinkable happened. An ember drakuma had appeared in the North. It was a difficult tale to digest, to say the least, and as much as he wanted to dismiss it, he simply couldn't. The clansmen that brought them the tale had no reason to lie about such a thing, and he had no reason to doubt their words. Even so, he'd desperately held out hope that his and the domses' concerns about the situation could be avoided. Unfortunately, after discovering the claw marks earlier in the day, he wasn't so sure that was possible anymore. If the evidence continued to mount like it had so far, assuming it wasn't already too late, he feared it would eventually push the clans down a path that would force him to take Amroth's life or else destroy any chance of redeeming his clan.

"There's violence burning in your eyes. I hope that's not intended for anyone we know."

Startled, Dakan took a quick step away from the wall and looked to his right to find Corza, her cloak draped about her, standing before the inn's closed door facing him.

Unclenching his fists, Dakan leaned back against the wall. "Though your banter is irritating at times," he said, referring to Corza and Jor's teasing, "it isn't enough to make me want to kill either of you . . . yet."

Corza chuckled. "I'm pleased that you have such restraint," she said, her rich voice carrying a friendly, humorous tone. Walking over to him, the steel toe and heel of her boots thudding on the wooden floor, she joined him along the wall and casually leaned her back against the wooden surface. "Something is bothering you deeply," she stated with confidence as her sea-green eyes idly searched the dark street before the inn.

"What makes you say that?" Dakan responded, doing his best to sound nonchalant.

Corza chuckled. "We may not have known each other long, Clansman, but I made about as much noise as a squad of Heavies marching in full armor, and you were oblivious to me."

Dakan gave her a half-hearted smirk. "Maybe I just chose to ignore you."

"*Humph!* That's about as likely as me growing a pair of stones and my breasts falling off."

Corza's crude humor caused the corners of Dakan's mouth to twitch. "According to Jor, that's already the case."

Corza punched Dakan firmly in the shoulder, drawing a slight grunt from him. "Don't side with that coddled ass!" Grinning devilishly, she teased, "I'm pretty sure you know I'm a woman. If I recall right, didn't I wake up with you cuddled against my back with your hand on my breast and something impressively h—"

"You know that was an accident," Dakan interrupted as the reminder of the state she'd found him in that morning caused him to blush slightly. "We were just trying to keep warm."

"*Ah-huh.* So says the man standing in the cold with bare arms." She eyed him playfully. "Not that I would really mind. I mean, could you imagine Jor's reaction if he found us rut—"

Dakan felt like his face was on fire as he turned and glared at her. "Spirits old and new, Corza!" he barked. "What do you want?"

Dakan's outburst drew the attention of a few of the guards on the street, but when they saw nothing threatening, they turned their attention back to the street.

Lowering his voice to a respectable level, Dakan continued, "If this is an attempt to get me in your blankets, then I must tell you my heart belongs to another! I will not betray her!"

Taken aback by his outburst, an apologetic look had replaced Corza's playful expression. "I didn't mean anything by it, Dakan. You've looked so troubled lately . . . I was simply trying to lighten the mood."

Dakan leaned back against the wall and folded his arms across his chest defensively. "Your concern is admirable, but it is not needed."

Pushing off the wall, she planted her fists on her hips, a pensive look on her face. "Not needed?" she repeated. "Let me tell you something, Clansman. We all have our own problems. And while it's admirable to respect each other's privacy, when personal problems affect our duty, then it becomes everyone's problem." Moving in front of him, she poked him firmly in the center of his chest. "You may not know much about where I come from, but we're not so different from the clans. You know what that taught me? *Humm?*" she questioned as she bore down with her finger. "It taught me that all this overblown rhetoric about honor and glory is nothing but bram-hen shite! When the battle starts, and the dead start piling up, the only thing that is worth a damn is the soldier next to you! They'll fight and die to protect you, and you them, but when personal shite gets in the way, you put your life and the lives of those around you at risk!"

As she watched her words sink in on Dakan's stunned face, Corza let her arm fall to her side before stating with an edge of vi-olence to her voice, "You want to have your secrets? Fine – we all have them! Just don't let them addle your pretty little clansman brain, because if I see that anyone's life is at risk because you can't sort your personal shite out, then I swear to you – you'll be lucky if I don't gut you on the spot! Understand, Clansman?"

The respectful look that greeted her chastisement wasn't what Corza expected, and it was all she could do to keep surprise from marring her intense expression.

"Am I interrupting anything?"

The firmly voiced, rumbling question startled both of them. Turning to face the speaker, they both snapped to attention when they saw Jerom standing beside the inn's open door, a concerned glower on his face.

"No, sir!" they both stated.

Jerom snorted softly. "That's good. We'll be departing early in the morning, and I want you two on guard detail. I trust this won't be a problem?"

"No, sir," Dakan stated firmly, which Corza reiterated.

"Good. I suggest you get some sleep, then," Jerom ordered sternly before entering the inn and shutting the door behind him.

As soon as he was gone, Corza cursed softly under her breath before starting for the door. Just as she pulled open the door, Dakan said, "Corza."

Pausing, she looked back at Dakan with an edge of frustra-tion in her eyes. "What?" she asked, noting that Dakan's face sported its usual impassive mask.

"Let Jor know I'll be sleeping on the floor tonight."

Corza blinked at the statement, unsure if it was in response to her teasing or their argument. A slight, almost imperceptible nod greeted her silence. Then, it struck her that, in his own bizarrely com-ical way, Dakan was apologizing. A small grin spread across her face and she nodded before stepping into the warm inn and shutting the door behind her.

*

Doms Captain Oblet de'Trivant Torwin's pensive mood was palpable. Standing before the main gate of the well-maintained and heavily manned stone wall that surrounded the Citadel, Oblet was a visibly frustrated man. Nearly sixty-five summers old, the creased features of his bald and sun-darkened, stout face were fixed with a scowl, and his heavy but muscular girth was flooded with tension. He even had his calloused hands, which jutted from sturdy leather bracers, clasped tightly behind his back simply to combat the temptation to lash in frustration.

Arranged behind him, an honor guard of House Trivant soldiers waited quietly. Adorned in an array of practical armor that was well maintained despite clear signs of heavy usage, each soldier held aloft a brightly burning torch to illuminate the moonless night. Similarly equipped soldiers also stood guard atop the walls as well as the battlements that ringed the first hundred feet of the spire jutting skyward from the heart of the courtyard. If it had been a more joyous occasion, it would have been quite an inspiring sight. Instead, it felt ominous and foreboding, almost as if they were awaiting something as dreadful as execution.

Peering into the darkness with his hard black eyes, Oblet could see the many lights beyond the dark void that occupied the open ground separating the Citadel from the Commons North. Amongst the lights that filled the windows of the opulent estates in the residential district were those of the oil street lamps that illuminated the cobblestone streets for anyone who was out at this late hour. Unfortunately, they revealed nothing that would indicate that Doms Trivant and Merandith were close to arriving.

A gentle breeze ruffled the off-white shirt and breeches with swirling gold trim that he wore beneath matching black riding boots and a blue-enameled breastplate embossed with a large golden sunburst. As if the wind was his cue, Oblet clamped his hand around the hilt of the sheathed broadsword hanging at his left hip, and hooked the thumb of his other hand behind his robust swordbelt. "Where are they?" he muttered in his throaty voice.

A few paces behind him, his sergeant, Ilisa Korgan, was just as concerned as he was as she gazed at him with gray eyes that sat above high cheekbones on her stern, but handsome face. Though she tried to hide it, her own tension could be seen in the way her sunburst orange-gloved hands were clenched about the hilts of the shortswords sheathed at her boyish hips, and how she pressed her lips together pensively. Things had been stressful since the night their guests vanished, and she couldn't shake the feeling it would get worse before it would get better.

The studded leather armor she wore over a black shirt, the puffy sleeves of which were split vertically four times by sunburst-orange fabric, creaked a bit as she tucked a lock of her short-cropped, slowly graying brown hair behind her ear. "They should be here soon, Captain," she stated in her deep voice. Dropping her hand back to the empty sword hilt, causing the weapon to gently tap her thigh, she added, "The runner said the Domses' party arrived in the northern part of the Sweeper's District to avoid creating a scene. With the late hour, and if they kept a steady pace, I would imagine they were nearly to the Commons North by the time we received the message."

Oblet grunted. "I don't like this situation one damn bit," he grumbled.

Ilisa let a deep breath out through her slightly off-center nose, and shifted her weight on her steel-greaved feet, causing the black leather of her boots and pants to creak softly. The sudden disappearance of Captain Mathis de'Merandith Sormantale and Shi'doms Amroth Merandith had shamed Oblet greatly. Granted, neither Doms Merandith nor Trivant held him responsible, but that meant little to the fiercely proud Captain of the City Guard. As far as Oblet was concerned, despite hearsay to the contrary, someone had breached their security and made off with two valuable people on his watch, and that was a stain on his honor he was intent on rectifying.

While neither she nor the men under her command had the personal connections that Oblet did with the two Merandiths, they were hardly immune to the effects of their disappearance. Not only had they been run ragged in the search for clues, but they'd also been sworn to secrecy regarding the missing Merandiths. It was a prudent move as there was no way to know for sure how such news would affect the populous. Unfortunately, such information could only be contained for so long. Eventually, someone would let it slip, or they would be forced to share the terrible news in order to seek aid with the search if they couldn't discover the Merandiths' fates.

"I'm sure all will be well, Captain," Ilisa stated in an attempt to reassure her superior. "It's still possible that they simply left without notice."

Oblet grunted. "Aye, that is still possible – Mathis is an odd one, after all . . . and there is that talk of two men riding through the streets like the Hells were after them." He grunted again. "But after talking with those two you brought in, something about this rubs me the wrong way." Scowling, he shook his head. "I've learned to trust my instincts, Sergeant."

Ilisa nodded, deferring to her captain's judgment. She did not know what the two soldiers had told Oblet, but it had left an ominous air hanging about him.

Not a word was spoken after that, allowing a silence that was as deep as the darkness between them and the Commons North to reign supreme. After a few long, tedious minutes in which Ilisa felt like the tension in her captain grew, the clatter of shod hooves on cobblestones reached their ears. In the distance, they soon saw the few pedestrians that were in the street hastily move out of the way of a sizable mounted party passing in and out of the pools of street-lamp light on their way toward the Citadel.

"Finally," Oblet muttered before barking, "Attention!"

With a rattle of armor and weapons, the soldiers arranged behind Oblet, as well as on the battlements, crisply followed his order. Not long after that, the riders reached and vanished into the dark swath separating the Citadel from the Commons North. When they finally reemerged from the night, it was clear that the two-dozen mounted and armored men were indeed the Domses' party. Eventually, the riders came to a halt in the pool of light around Oblet and his retinue of Citadel Guards, and he found himself looking up at not only the imposing destriders they rode, but also the deeply concerned visages of their riders. It was also immediately clear the riders, not to mention their mounts, were worn out from hard travel. Dressed in the same attire they'd been wearing for days, they were dirt-stained, their mounts were breathing hard, and there was a thick, dank musk about them that was begging for a bath.

Bowing, which the soldiers around him mimicked respectfully, Oblet then straightened and offered, "Welcome back, Domses. I hope your trip was safe and fruitful?"

Oblet noticed Jerom fighting off a scowl from atop his roan destrider as Doms Merandith replied, his firm voice clearly heavy with unease, "Safe enough, Captain. As for results. . . ." Kale shook his head slightly.

Oblet found Kale's tone and posture somewhat disheartening, but before he could ask any further questions, Doms Trivant nudged his black warhorse forward a bit and asked, "And what about you, Oblet? Any luck?"

Oblet grunted and hooked his thumbs behind his sword belt. "Possibly. I'll leave it to you two to decide. If you'll follow me, Domses? I think it best we discuss this in private."

Lucas nodded as Kale responded, "Very well, Captain."

Oblet inclined his head. "Very good, Doms Merandith. We've prepared some of the Cells for your men. I hope that is acceptable?"

Kale nodded as he rubbed the neck of his gray destrider. "It is." Then, to Tazrim, he added, "Tazrim – you're in charge of the men."

Tazrim dipped his head in acknowledgment as Oblet turned to Ilisa and ordered, "Sergeant Korgan, see to it that the men are shown to their rooms and their mounts are attended to."

Ilisa snapped off a fist-to-heart salute. "Aye, Captain." Then, to Tazrim, she said, "If you and your men will follow me, once we're inside the walls, we'll see to it that your mounts are attended to."

Nudging his spotted destrider out of formation, Tazrim acknowledged Ilisa as he replied in his deep, rumbling voice, "Lead on, Captain."

Nodding, Ilisa once again bowed to the domses before leading Tazrim and the Merandith soldiers through the gate.

Oblet then motioned to the gate and said to those that remained, "If you would, Domses – I have refreshments awaiting us in the Council Chamber."

Lucas nodded. "Lead on, Oblet. Oh, and before I forget, let the Watch know the rest of our contingent will arrive soon."

"Aye, Doms," Oblet replied as he turned and led the way to the gate.

Like the Merandith men before them, they found a pair of stablehands awaiting them on the other side of the gate. Dismounting, their destriders were led to one of the sizable stables flanking the main gate, where they would receive a proper rubdown and feeding. As the honor guard dispersed, Oblet quickly spoke with one of the Watch, who was soon headed back to the wall, as he led the domses across the meticulously stone-paved courtyard only a few paces behind Ilisa and her charges.

Looming before them at the center of the sparsely lit courtyard was the marbled-sheathed, buttress-supported Citadel. Though the moonless night hid most of its details, rampart-mounted torches allowed them to see a few of the gargoyles adorning every other merlon of the battlements ringing every twenty feet of the first hundred feet of the Citadel. Lamplight still glowed in several of the spire's sparse, narrow windows, and the quartet could see a ruddy glow emanating from behind the Citadel where the Academy and barracks were located. Almost immediately, the remaining House Trivant soldiers amongst their escort broke off and joined the throng headed to the rear of the bailey in search of their bunks and rest, leaving the others to continue on to the Citadel.

Passing between two of the majestic, marble-sheathed buttresses that surrounded and supported the Citadel, they set foot on the broad stone stairs leading up to the spire's main entry; a set of outward-opening, steel-banded ironwood double doors. Flanking the entryway was a pair of orange banners bearing the golden sunburst of House Trivant, and before them stood a pair of halberd-wielding guards in full plate armor. The guards seemed to pay little heed to Ilisa and her entourage as they ascended the stairs, but they immediately snapped off a fist-to-heart salute when they saw Oblet and the Domses climbing the stairs.

Acknowledging the guards' salutes just as Ilisa's group passed through the entryway, Jerom said to Lucas, "After all these years, you still haven't fixed those doors? Are you trying to give up this place, you lummox?"

"What do you mean? I think it adds character," Lucas replied with feigned innocence as they reached the landing.

Jerom snorted. "Right," he rumbled. "And that is far more important than defense," he stated sarcastically as they passed through the entry into a well-lit, tall and narrow hall, the arched ceiling of which was supported by a latticework of thick wooden beams.

As the doors were pulled closed behind them, Oblet led them down the long entry hall and replied, "I've been meaning to fix it, Jerom. There's been way too many damn things to deal with, and it just keeps slipping my mind."

Kale scowled. "That's no excuse," he declared, his irritation with the events of the last few days spilling into his words. "The war is way too close to ignore such an old and easily fixed problem. Fix it," he stated adamantly, drawing a curt nod from Oblet.

As for Lucas, any sense of amusement he felt vanished under the intensity of Kale's words. Kale was right. Such a foolish design flaw was unacceptable, even if he'd left it in place out of respect for his ancestors. "Understood, Kale," Lucas replied. "I'll see that it is fixed immediately."

"Good," Kale stated bluntly.

Chastised, they continued on, following Ilisa's group deeper into the Citadel in silence.

Free of decoration, except for the brass lanterns that were

evenly spaced along their surface, the stone walls passed by at an impressive pace. As there were very few people to hinder their trek this late at night, they soon passed the first of four intersecting hallways that circled the interior of the Citadel. Where normally the circular layout would have been bustling with activity, they saw only a few servants in the halls, and passed a lone pair of guards where the hall spilt into the level's main chamber. Round in shape and nearly two-hundred paces in diameter, the chamber was vast, with walls that soared upward to meet with its hardwood ceiling nearly fifty feet above them. A corridor like the one they had just traversed occupied each cardinal point of the compass, permitting travel to and from the central chamber from other parts of the level. There were no doors along the walls of the room; instead, they were home to three House Trivant banners along with large brass lanterns to illuminate the vast space. Elegant couches were set against the walls along with a series of tables and chairs to provide visitors and residents alike with a place to sit and talk.

Oblet led his frustrated and concerned party to the center of the room where the Citadel's centerpiece stood. Merged artfully with the massive central support column that ran the length of the structure was a sturdy spiral staircase that disappeared through an opening in both the ceiling and the floor. Unlike the marble sheathing elsewhere, the support column's cover was engraved with graceful patterns that were reminiscent of climbing vines. As for the staircase, its steel supports were forged and twisted into artful designs, and its meticulously carved, highly polished ironwood railings glowed gently beneath the light from the brass lanterns mounted on the support column.

As the last of Ilisa's group vanished down the stairs, Oblet led his group onto the staircase and began climbing. As they ascended, they passed several servants, soldiers, and courtiers, all of whom bowed their heads respectfully as the domses passed by. Focused as they were on their current situation, neither Doms Merandith nor Doms Trivant acknowledged them. Jerom knew it was unlike either man to ignore those who served them, so he offered an apologetic smile to the men and women they encountered along the way.

Upon reaching the fifth floor, they exited the stairs. Passing the pair of saluting stair guards in light armor beneath orange tabards emblazoned with a golden sunburst, they found themselves in a central chamber that bore only a passing resemblance to the ones below. Like the other floors, there were couches, banners, tables and lanterns, but their make was far richer and more extravagant, and their layout had an air of formality to it. Dark oak trim separated the walls from the rich-red carpet beneath their feet and the hardwood ceiling twenty feet above them. The most notable difference, however, was that only three corridors provided access to the outer rings.

Turning to their right, they found that a long, curved wall occupied the entire eastern section of the floor. Sturdy oak double doors, flanked by a pair of guards dressed like their stair brethren, were centered on the wall beneath a large sunburst made of gold. Seeing their approach, the door guards grabbed the elegant gold door handles and pushed the gilded doors of the Council Chamber open before saluting.

Acknowledging the guards, the domses and Jerom entered the chamber. Oblet, however, paused at the doors. "Please, have a seat," he stated, drawing their attention. Motioning to the serving table along the right-hand wall, Oblet added, "There are refreshments there if you like. I'll be only a moment." Oblet then turned his attention to the guards, speaking with them quietly.

The Council Chamber was a wide hall that gently narrowed as the curved, flanking walls journeyed to the rear edifice, which was home to three narrow windows set high on its surface. Stationed near the rear of the hall was an imposing oak desk trimmed in gold knotwork. A sturdy, high-back chair sat behind the gilded desk, its cushions covered in bright orange fabric. In the center of the chamber, a matching oak longtable and six impressive mid-back chairs sat facing the desk. Above all this, hanging from the recessed maple ceiling, were a pair of beautiful, fully lit silver chandeliers that cast their warm light throughout the chamber.

As the domses made for the longtable, Jerom walked over to the serving table. Several glass and crystal decanters, along with a pair of silver pitchers, occupied the tabletop. To his chagrin, there wasn't a drop of Velusyian Blue to be found, but he eventually settled on a rich, dark-red wine in a long-neck crystal decanter. Grabbing it and a trio of long-stem glasses, Jerom joined the domses at the longtable.

Normally, Lucas would have occupied the desk chair; however, he had chosen to seat himself next to Kale in one of the two center chairs along the longtable. Moving along the front of the longtable, Jerom briefly noted the golden sunburst set against a field of black stone on the floor between the desk and table. Setting his cargo on the tabletop, Jerom quickly filled the glasses and distributed them. Once everyone was settled, he took a sip of his drink, and his eyebrows shot up in surprise as the florid liquid hit his tongue. The mix of heady and fruity flavors that filled his mouth was something he'd never tasted before at the same time.

Swallowing, he declared, "It's not Velusyian Blue, but this is quite good! Where did a lummox like you get this?"

Lucas smiled as he put his glass down. "It's called Trivant's Rose, and it's something our family has had one of our northern wineries working on for some time now," he stated, his deep voice filled with pride. "Sadly, with the expense of the war, production has been down of late. I've only got a few bottles left, but I could send one or two with you if you want."

Jerom nodded. "Aye, I'd like that." He then looked at Kale, curious about his reaction to the wine. Unfortunately, he found his nephew idly swirling his glass, his thoughts clearly somewhere else.

Before he could say anything to his nephew, the thud of the doors closing drew his and Lucas' attention, and snapped Kale from his dour reflections. Looking past the chairs as both domses stood and turned, Jerom saw Oblet, a rolled piece of parchment in hand, leading two House Trivant soldiers toward them. Though the two soldiers were garbed in well-maintained leather armor, they appeared to be from two different worlds. From the look of the taller and significantly slimmer of the two, Jerom figured he'd seen more of war than peace; and given his gnarled hands and sun-darkened, leathery skin, he appeared to be at least Oblet's age. His companion, on the other hand, was a fairly robust, younger man with lighter skin and piggish blue eyes set in a full face that was framed by a mass of short-cut blonde hair.

"Quite the pair," he thought absently.

As Oblet led his men around the table to the center of the sunburst on the floor, Jerom proceeded around to Kale and stood next to him. "Domses, may I present to you Sergeant Leathers and Private Totts. I believe these two may have had contact with people that could be connected with our problem."

As Lucas and the Merandiths took their seats, and the two soldiers saluted, fist to heart, Kale asked, "Is what the Captain says true?"

The older of the two soldiers dipped his shaved head before offering a small smile. "Aye, Doms. Totts here," he motioned to the larger soldier, "an' me encountered an odd sort – which is ta bad. Was a generous fella, an' quite tha Pentagris player."

Lucas was familiar with the two House Guard soldiers, and knew Leathers had a propensity for embellishment and straying from the subject. With a small, apologetic smile and a flash of dry amusement in his bright-blue eyes, Lucas stated, "Please, Sergeant, let's stay focused on the relevant details."

Fixing his small, green eyes on Lucas, Leathers said, "Aye, Doms. My apologies, Doms." Rubbing the chin of his clean-shaven face, Leathers then said, "Where was I? Ah, tha Solarians."

"Solarians? Are you sure?" Kale asked, his curiosity perked.

"Aye, Doms. According ta tha lad, he and tha lovely lass he was with were from Solarson."

Seeing the skepticism on the faces of the domses and Jerom, Totts nudged leathers and uttered a wheezing grunt at him.

"Aye, Totts. Thank you for tha reminder." Then, to the domses, he added, "Their accents were hard ta miss, too. Couldn't have been anything but Solarian." Scratching his head, he said, "Though, now that I think about it, tha lass with him had to be Velusyian. I'd swear it on me mum's grave."

"Any idea what business brought them here?" Jerom asked.

"Don't know," Leathers responded with a shrug. "If I had ta venture a guess, I'd say they were searchin' for something. Tha lad asked ah lot o' questions about tha war and tha regions north and south of us."

"That fits with other reports we've gotten from various merchants throughout the Trade District," Oblet interjected. "Each one named a Velusyian or a foreign man asking similar questions." He grunted. "There's far too many of these incidents for it to be a coincidence."

Kale nodded at Oblet. "Agreed." Then, to Leathers, he asked, "Is there anything else you might tell us?"

"Aye, Doms. Though I heard it through others. As I told tha Captain here, tha word is that tha Velusyian lass paid ah visit ta tha Academy grounds a few weeks ago. If tha rumors be true, your man and tha lad with him went runnin' through the Citadel like tha Hells were after them not long after that." Leathers offered them a sheepish look. "Afraid I don't know more than that, Domses. Wish we could be of more help."

"On the contrary," Lucas stated. "You've been quite helpful. I would ask of you, however, that you keep this information to yourselves. And should you hear anything else that might be of use – report it to Oblet as quickly as possible."

Both Leathers and Totts bowed respectfully. "Aye, Doms – that we will."

After looking at Kale to make sure he was satisfied with the news, Lucas said, "Oblet, if you would see our guests out."

"Aye, Doms," Oblet replied before motioning for Leathers and Totts to lead the way.

The two hesitated for a moment before Leathers added, "If you'll pardon our forwardness, me and Totts 'ere got ta spend a meal speakin' with your men. . . . A fine pair, if'n I do say so myself. We be hopin' Deo delivers them safely home."

Kale smiled softly. "Thank you, Sergeant."

"Gentlemen," Oblet urged, once more gesturing to the door.

Saluting again, the two then turned and made for the exit.

No one said a word as Oblet escorted the two soldiers from the chamber, and when he finally returned, he positioned himself before the longtable. "We confirmed everything my men just said, and there's more," he said as he handed the rolled parchment to Lucas. "While you were gone, we received word from a handful of villages to the north that a writ in Doms Merandith's name was used to purchase various supplies just a few days after Mathis and Amroth vanished. Also – though we have no idea if it's related – there was a report of a stolen wagon around the same time."

Passing the parchment to Kale, Lucas then took a sip from his glass before asking, "Why did it take so long to discover this?"

"My apologies, Doms Trivant," Oblet said, embarrassment heavy in his dark eyes. "If Mathis and Amroth have truly been kidnapped, then their kidnappers have been cautious. All the purchases, be they in the city or outlying villages, were made in different areas and at different times; as such, it's taken us far too long to find the connection."

Passing the parchment to Jerom, who began reading it while idly sipping his wine, Kale said, "Assuming the two your men mentioned are involved, then this report seems to implicate a third person. Another Velusyian by the description. . . though one with white hair seems unusual."

Oblet grunted. "Aye, Doms. While it could be just a coincidence that the Solarians and your men appear to have vanished the same night, I'm inclined to believe it's more than that."

"I agree, Domses," Jerom said as he put down the parchment. Finishing off his drink, he then asked, "But one thing bugs the hells out of me – why would a kidnapper brazenly impersonate a member of House Merandith just to use a writ? Seems like a bloody stupid move. Furthermore, why in the hells is someone from Solarson involved, not to mention two Velusyians? Is there a daft doms over there looking to use the war as an excuse to conquer part of

Triclose? As for Velusyia, I just can't see them being involved."

"Agreed on Velusyia," Lucas stated. "Even if one of their shaogetsin's had designs on Triclose, this wouldn't be the way they'd go about it. They don't have the military might to compete in any capacity, and this would bring unwanted attention to them. As for whoever is involved, maybe it was to let us know they have them?"

Oblet grunted. "Seems like a damn vague way of doing so. A ransom letter would accomplish that a whole hells of a lot better."

"True," Lucas conceded. "As for the Solarians, I have a hard time believing one of their domses wants to get embroiled here. So," he took a deep breath, "if they were kidnapped, that would leave our enemies here. If that is the case, then I'd say they wanted an outsider to do the dirty work; someone we'd have a hard time identifying any connections to."

"Regardless of who may be responsible, intent or methods," Kale declared, "I think the evidence we have demands that we assume someone has either kidnapped them or . . ." he trailed off, refusing to finish his statement.

"They're alive, Kale. I'd bet my life on it," Jerom stated confidently.

Kale nodded. "I don't like any of this – not one damn bit. And the thought of returning home instead of hunting down Mathis and Amroth is. . ." he trailed off again. After a foreboding pause, he looked at Oblet and asked, "Did you say some of the purchases were made to the north?"

Oblet nodded. "Aye, Doms. The furthest purchases were made about two to three days' ride from here. It's reasonable to assume that they are moving north. Unfortunately, with the raids, that might also mean – as Doms Trivant speculated – there are House Suldamik sympathizers within the North that have done this to make a point."

Kale grunted in agreement. "I won't dismiss that possibility." He paused thoughtfully. "Lucas, as much as I'd prefer to remain south until Mathis and Amroth's fates are determined, I will take your offer of ship transport north. Once there, we can combat this problem from two sides."

Lucas grinned thankfully. "I like the idea."

Kale smirked weakly. "I figured you would." He then fixed Oblet with a stern gaze. "None of this is your fault, Oblet. And while I have a hard time believing that Mathis would act so rashly, if he and Amroth left the city for some damn fool reason without leaving word with you, then it is Mathis that will have to answer for such incompetence. However, we need to make sure they are found. I trust you have some raven-wing pigeons on hand, and the descriptions of these three?"

"Of course," Oblet replied, feeling a bit chastised despite Kale dismissing any blame from him.

"Good. Send word to all the major cities along their possible routes north. I want as many eyes out looking as possible. Also, send a message to Merset; Marie needs to know what's going on."

Oblet nodded. "Aye.... Though, I feel I should remind you that we're also dealing with a number of raids, which seem to be growing worse the farther north one goes. It will be difficult to take men from that task."

A brief scowl crossed Kale's face. "I'm all too aware of that, Captain. The raiders take priority – and though I'm sure Marie is already addressing the problem, I plan on putting an end to it once I'm home. However, Captain, I won't leave Mathis or Amroth to die at the hands of cowards. You're to use every spare man at your disposal until this situation is settled. Is that understood?"

"Understood," Oblet stated gravely.

"Good," Kale responded with a nod. "Lucas, how long will it take to have a ship ready?"

Lucas grinned. "Not long, Kale. There are a few military vessels resting at their berths, but they'll need to be fitted for the northern conditions. I'll have orders delivered immediately, and I'll make sure they work through the night if it takes it to ready the ship. I promise you'll be on your way no later than dawn two days from now, or there'll be hells to pay."

Kale nodded, but concern was still etched deeply into his face.

His expression growing solemn, Lucas offered, "Don't worry, Kale. We'll find Amroth and Mathis – alive. And if anything has happened to them, then Deo help the souls of those responsible."

Chapter Nine

"It's cold," he thought as consciousness slowly began to return. "No," he corrected himself as the sensation began to fully register. "It's frigid!"

Mat's black eyes flew open and he sat up with urgency. A thin layer of frost sloughed off his thickly muscled body as he looked about wildly, his ordinarily handsome face now a mask of panic. None of what he felt and saw made sense to his frantic mind. Deep darkness made it hard to see, and the air was colder than anything he had ever felt. Looking down at his body, he saw that frost still clung to his lower torso and legs, while portions of his loose-fitting blue shirt, and his black pants and boots appeared to be charred. Running a hand through his short-cut, purple-tinged black hair, he felt a few strands shatter as frost fell off his leather bracers and out of his face-framing locks.

"Alright, I'm in one piece," he thought, bringing a measure of calm to his nerves. "But where in the hells am I?"

Breathing deeply, he forced his mind to relax. Once he managed that, he then found his center of power — a tiny spec of light at the core of his being — and embraced it, allowing his inner fir'gan to flood his body. Immediately, he felt warmer, and the veil of night began to part for him as the currents illuminated his surroundings. Looking around again, he realized he was sitting on the rocky shore of a river that was littered with shattered stone. For a reason he couldn't quite grasp, he was surprised to see that, despite hearing the crisp melody of flowing water in the distance, the river appeared to be frozen over. Dropping his hand to the ground, he felt something cold and scaly beneath it. Startled, he scrambled away from the object, but came to a quick halt when it dawned on him that it was a body. A moment later, the identity of the person lying before him came rushing back to him, and with it, the knowledge of where he was and why he was there.

"Corith be good! Kara!" he breathed, his smooth voice heavy with dread as he started to scramble to his feet. Looking up the shore at Kara's last location, he saw two figures resting against one another on the frozen water in the middle of the river. Just as he was about to move toward her, a deep voice pulled him up short.

"You're finally awake. Good."

The coldly spoken words planted a feeling of icy dread firmly in the pit of Mat's stomach. Turning around slowly, Mat found a tall, athletically lean man standing before him. Slightly upturned coal-black eyes peered at him intently from beneath a heavy brow on a face that was framed by long white hair. An odd mod-

icum of relief quickly rushed through Mat upon seeing that Damion had reverted to his normal appearance. That relief was short-lived, however. Even though he was shirtless and his pants and boots were a tattered mess, there was a foreboding, almost dreadful air to the man.

Unable to muster a response, and suddenly concerned about his safety, Mat's hands darted to his hips. Finding nothing but empty air, Mat tore his eyes from Damion's gaze and looked down.

"Looking for these?" Damion asked with a hint of amusement in his authoritative voice as Mat stared at the empty sheaths hanging from his sword belt.

Looking back up, Mat saw his twin, broad-bladed shortswords tucked beneath Damion's belt along with a hilt made of bone and two katana blade fragments.

Anger and indignation swelled within Mat. "Give those back!" he stated, his cocky voice full of fury. "They're of no use to you!"

Damion arched an eyebrow. "I have no time for useless bluster, boy. But if you really think that, and you want them back, then by all means — try me."

Damion's simple, blunt tone quashed Mat's momentary boldness. As he understood it, a crusader was useless to anyone other than its master, but not only did Damion have a reputation for being a deadly swordsman — not to mention the power radiating from him — but there was also Damion's earlier statement.

'Try to stop me before then, and I'll use your own crusader to gut you.'

Mat had no idea if it was a bluff or not, but the man was an elder Warden, and he wasn't about to underestimate such a person.

"Fine," Mat conceded grudgingly. "Keep them for all I care! Darkon will eventually find out about this, and there will be hells to pay!" Mat declared, though even he doubted the veracity of his words.

Damion shrugged casually. "What will be, will be. Until then, be assured that you will get your crusader back — when I deem it proper. Understood?"

Mat scowled but finally nodded.

"Good. Now, hand over the coffer."

Mat folded his arms across his chest defensively. "I don't know what you mean."

"Don't play dumb with me, boy," Damion ordered, his tone cold. "You did well in returning the crystal to its coffer, but don't think I didn't know you were in possession of it. Do everyone a favor — hand it over, and let's see to our friends."

Mat's eyes widened at the implied violence in Damion's tone, but that shock was quickly replaced with concern for Kara, and he cursed himself for forgetting about her. Reaching into his shirt, he promptly pulled out a simple ironwoodbound, opalescent bone coffer that was large enough to hold two crystals. Tossing it to Damion with a scowl, he then spun on his heel and took a few quick steps before coming to a sudden halt before the body that had initially startled him. "Is this. . . ?"

"Amroth?" Damion finished as he tucked the coffer into what was left of his pants and stepped up beside Mat. "Indeed it is."

Mat found it difficult to believe Damion, for there was very little to identify the body as Amroth. Dark as the night that surrounded them, tiny scales had covered the greater portion of Amroth's corded body, shredding his clothing and popping the straps of his sword harness. Across his chest, as well as around his forearms, lower legs, and atop his thighs, a thicker carapace was slowly forming. As for his head, most of it was covered by a dark, bony mask that eerily reminded Mat of the dragons he'd seen in the Orders' ancient tomes. Like the growing carapace, the mask was slowly creeping across Amroth's solemn, peaceful face.

"What the hells is happening to him?" Mat breathed with a mix of awe and fear.

"His Joining is still in progress," Damion stated as if it was common knowledge. "Then again, I guess you've never seen one, have you?"

"No," Mat stated simply, enthralled by the sight of Amroth.

"Well, it happened to all of us."

Mat thought he detected a measure of concern in Damion's tone. Seeking to confirm what he heard, Mat looked up at the elder Warden, but only found a mild hint of curiosity in his gaze.

Before Mat could say anything, Damion stepped over Amroth. "Let's go," he ordered as he walked by him. "Kara and Ember need us more right now."

Sparing Amroth one last look, Mat followed Damion.

Making their way up the shore, they eventually drew even with the two figures on the ice. Stepping out onto the frozen river, their fir'gan kept their footing steady as they navigated the rocky debris littering the ice. As they neared the two exposed people, Mat finally got a clear look at them, and he came to a halt, his breath catching in his throat.

"Dear Corith!" he thought, shocked by the sight.

Bound to the frozen surface by tendrils of ice, Kara appeared to be dead. Naked as the day of her birth, her short, toned, full-bosomed figure was deathly pale beneath a thin layer of frost. Mat's growing dread gripped his heart at the sight, and he had to fight down a sense of panic. His gaze then shot to her now hairless head, which rested against the corded abdomen of the large, naked man

190

behind her. Given the temperature, he should have been able to see at least a hint of her breath escaping the full lips on her heart-shaped face, but there was nothing.

"Is she dead?" Mat asked with apprehension as Damion crouched down next to her.

Running a finger lovingly along one of her high cheekbones, Damion replied confidently, "No, but leaving them exposed like this won't do them any good." Shifting his position, Damion slid his arms beneath her shoulders and legs. The ice clinging to her cracked and shattered as he lifted her gently into his arms. Standing, Damion fixed a stern glare on Mat. "Pick up Ember."

Though he was relieved to hear Kara was alive, Mat found that amazement had replaced his apprehension when he finally looked at Ember and his appearance sank in.

No longer did the slowly dying monstrous bulk of an ember drakuma reside on the ice; instead, one of the largest humans he'd ever seen lay curled on the frozen island. Like Kara, he was hairless, and his skin was frosted and pale. Tendrils of ice adorned his thickly muscled, elongated body, and Mat could see predator-like incisors in the open mouth of his broad face.

"Corith be good — What have you done?" Mat asked as he approached and stepped around Ember's body.

"What had to be done," Damion responded matter-of-factly as Mat tried to roll Ember onto his back.

"What the hells does that mean?" Mat muttered as he was forced to use an unusual amount of strength to move Ember, shattering the tendrils of ice that clung to his naked body.

He then tried to haul Ember's limp form as upright as he could, but was shocked by just how heavy Ember actually was. Growing a bit irritated by the surprisingly difficult task, Mat amplified his strength with his inner fir'gan before trying again, and this time he succeeded. Now that he had the behemoth weight in his arms, and a good idea of what it would take to move the mountain of a man, Mat further increased his power before shoving his shoulder into Ember's midsection and lifting. As Ember's unusually broad shoulders came to rest near Mat's butt, and his full weight bore down on Mat's shoulder, it dawned on the young Warden that Ember probably still weighed nearly as much as he would have as a drakuma. The shock of that realization was fleeting as a sudden wave of anger washed through Mat. If Damion was seeking to punish him or simply keep him too busy to trouble him, then carrying Ember was a good start.

Fixing Damion with an angry glare, Mat prodded, "Well?"

"Well, what?" Damion responded as he turned his back to Mat and started for the riverbank.

"Are you going to explain any of this to me?" Mat barked angrily as he scrambled to catch up.

"Let's see about getting them warm," Damion replied, ignoring Mat's question. "After that, I'll attend to our supply needs."

"Damn it, Damion! Answer me!" Mat yelled.

Coming to a sudden halt, Damion turned to Mat and glared darkly at him. "Mind your tongue, boy! If you don't like it here, then you are free to go crying back to Darkon! But while you are here, you are mine! You will get your crusader back when I say so, and you will learn what you need to know when I deem you worthy! Is that understood?"

Mat felt dread once again settle into his stomach. Here was a man who rarely made idle threats, he realized. If he was to remain with Kara, then he had no choice but to obey — there was clearly no compromise to be found in this man at this time.

Finally, Mat nodded. "As you wish," he responded, his tone tight but respectful.

"Good," Damion stated, satisfied, as he turned and continued onward. "Let's get going. Dawn isn't far away, and I want to find a secure camp by then."

"Two bloody weeks and the bastard still doesn't trust me," Mat thought as he walked lead a respectable distance ahead of the plodding wagon.

Though the reasons were unknown to Mat, they'd been traveling steadily west for two weeks through the northern part of a small realm called Lerilia and into what Damion had informed them was the Contested Territories. During the entire journey, and even after Kara had awakened, Damion said very little to Mat, leaving him fairly isolated with his morose thoughts. Granted, Kara spoke to him often enough, but it couldn't dispel the frustration that the looming specter of Damion caused him, and it was all the fault of the dreadful night Kara almost died. After they'd found a secure camp, Damion had retrieved Amroth before he sought out supplies, leaving him alone with the unconscious trio. Once again, Damion had threatened to hold him accountable should anything happen to their incapacitated comrades, and given the events earlier that night, he took Damion at his word. That, however, did not keep him from reporting to Darkon.

The darlion had been furious, and the string of Tykani curses and disjointed thoughts Mat heard through their connection was nearly crushed by the anger he felt through the link. To his chagrin, Mat was unable to get orders from Darkon thanks to the enraged darlion abruptly cutting the connection. Since then, he hadn't heard from

Darkon, nor had an opportunity to reach out to him presented itself. So, alone with his anger and frustration, he tried to make sense of the events and how he felt about the situation over the next few days. In the end, he'd realized there was far more going on than he was aware of, and more importantly, that his faith in Darkon now showed cracks.

Looking into the woods that lined the once well-traveled road they were following, the question of who to trust once again rattled about his mind. He had no doubts about remaining wary of Damion; the man had vanished for decades, and had remained closed to Mat's inquires about what had happened to Kara. Even more disturbing was how silent he grew, and the danger in his eyes, when Mat inquired about how he knew Amroth could host Luthur's crystal. Mat's hands clenched about the hilts of the plain but adequate shortswords sheathed at his hips. Then there was the question of his crusader. The blades had remained in Damion's possession since that night, and there was no indication of when he might return them.

The leather of the black bracers he wore, which were a match for his boots and pants, creaked softly as he adjusted the dark-blue sweat rag he wore atop his head. Kara was the only person he felt he could trust, and now he wasn't sure how far that faith actually went. After all, she had a propensity for arguing with Darkon, and she'd even secretly sent Ember to Triclose for Corith only knows what task. Still, she remained friendly and communicative, and had even urged him to remain patient with Damion. If she was right, that would eventually yield the answers he sought.

Smirking dryly at the thought, he gave an almost impercept-ible shake of his head as he tugged absently on the black vest he wore over his white shirt and sighed gently. Even at ninety years of age, the patience she asked of him, and that the other Wardens possessed, still escaped him. Maybe after another century or two, he would acquire such a will, but until then. . . .

"He's still frustrated, Brother. It would be better for us all if you would trust him . . . even if it is only a little," Kara stated, her plea for understanding and compassion nakedly evident in her beautiful voice.

Seated on the wagon's bench with a cloak as dark as his pants and boots draped about his shoulders, Damion once again felt re-lieved to hear strength in Kara's soothing voice. He'd long dreaded the day he would have need of the untested technique, and in the back of his mind, he'd always wondered if it would work. After all, elvannue machinations always seemed to have unintended side effects or, on rare occasions, failed spectacularly. As such, he viewed it as a miracle that his siblings had survived the infusion of fir'gan and cold-fire while only falling prey to the former.

With the reins of the four horses pulling the wagon held loosely in his black-gloved hands, and a gentle breeze tugging at the sleeves of his white shirt, Damion glanced over at his sister. *"A miracle indeed,"* he thought with a true sense of happiness.

In her case, she had emerged relatively unscathed from the event. Her normal, healthy tan skin tone had returned, and the majority of her lush, sky-blue hair – which she had used her fir'gan to quickly grow out – was braided into a hip-length ponytail that was interwoven with a lavender ribbon he'd acquired. Kara did, however, carry two prominent souvenirs from her ordeal – there were streaks of frosted white in her sky-blue eyes, and the hair at her temples, along with a portion of her chin-length bangs along the left side of her face, had turned the same white as well. Under the assumption that the changes were merely superficial, Kara had repeatedly attempted to restore her hair and eye color, but she met with failure each time. Eventually, she accepted and embraced the changes, claiming they added flare to her appearance. That acceptance, more than anything, made Damion feel confident that she had recovered emotionally from the ordeal.

Then there was Ember, whose condition was quite alarming. The infusion of coldfire had altered Ember in shocking ways that, no matter how hard Damion racked his mind for answers, he could not explain. He did, however, find some succor for this in the knowledge that even the elvannue most likely couldn't have anticipated such a reaction. Still, Ember's current state was concerning and warranted monitoring.

"And how far do you trust him, Karalisa?" he asked plainly as he turned his attention back to the road. "He likely contacted Darkon while you were at sea, and it wouldn't surprise me if that's how Garith located you. Hells, he's probably reported what he knows of our situation to him by now – and Corith only knows if that revealed our location to our enemies."

She shot her brother an admonishing look as she stated, "You don't know that for sure. With as much as I was in contact with Darkon and Greatjon, it could just as easily been me."

Damion shrugged his indifference.

Sighing softly, a solemn look overtook her face. "As for Garith. . . ." she stated softly as she fingered the hilts of the slender katana and matching tanto in their bound sheathes at her right hip. "It's hard to believe it was him. . . . But there's no doubt, given Ember's description. And if he's really serving a new master – then who in the hells is it?" She shook her head in an attempt to banish the long, grim conversation she and her brothers had after she and Ember had awakened two days after their rescue. "As for Mat . . ." she continued. "He's young, Brother. He doesn't have our experience and patience, but I believe he has a good heart and wants to do the right thing. I believe we can trust him. . . . We just have to give him time to sort things out. Besides, he did give you the crystal coffer back."

Damion nodded slowly. Kara's points were valid, but that did little to sway his cautious nature regarding Darkon and those who followed him with near-blind loyalty. Their choices over the years since Luthur's death, given what Kara and Ember had told him, were baffling and all too often disastrous. Then there was Darius' death, not to mention the loss of Cat, and the foolish decisions that led to it. Not only did it cut Damion profoundly and deepen his distrust of Darkon and his followers, but it also reaffirmed that such caution was warranted. As such, he continued to retain Mat's crusader.

Then there was the issue of two ownerless crystals residing in one coffer. This, thankfully, had been easy to address. Soon after he had attended to his siblings, he retrieved the coffer he'd discarded after Joining Luthur's crystal to Amroth, and separated the crystals. Darkon's antics aside, having two ownerless crystals in the open was a massive risk for the Wardens. It would be a disaster if even one crystal fell into the wrong hands, let alone both of them; as such, the blue and dark-red crystals Mat and Kara had brought from Solarson now rested at the bottom of his and Kara's packs.

"Be that as it may," Damion finally responded, "I can make far better use of his crusader than he."

A small, amused smile tugged at the corners of Kara's mouth. "You know, after you vanished and Darkon took over, not only did he insist we disarm in his presence, but he almost always appeared before us with his crusader ready to be summoned." She laughed and tugged at the black leather half-vest she wore over a long-sleeve red shirt and her modest, full bosom, adjusting how it sat on her shoulders. "He was always afraid you were lurking about, or you had convinced one of us to kill him for you."

Damion grunted dismissively in response.

Shaking her head, Kara rubbed her legs with her gloved hands. Like her shirt and vest, her dark-brown pants, gloves, and black thigh boots were cut in a similar fashion to the outfit that was incinerated on that fateful night. Sadly, only her sword belt and gloves were adorned with the silver knotwork that had provided flair to her previous attire. Still, she was glad to have the clothes. After all, Damion had no legitimate reason to retrieve her and Mat's belongings when he returned to Haltho, and it simply would not do to roam about naked.

"He always suspected you had masked your presence on the currents in some extreme manner," she continued thoughtfully. "Though I wonder if he ever thought it was possible to disguise yourself the way you did."

A gentle breeze tugged at Damion's cropped horsetail of white hair as he adjusted his position on the bench. "It's possible that he did, but I doubt it." He snorted derisively. "I doubt that egomaniac could even conceive of someone sacrificing so much power to accomplish one's goals."

Kara shrugged. "Possibly. Still, he's not the same man who led the darlions for so long, nor is he the Warden we all used to respect." She shook her head. "I want to believe he really has our best interests in mind and that he truly is doing his best to combat the Darkness, but–"

"He's far more secretive than Luthur ever was, and too many of us have died due to his ego or clear underestimation of our situation," Damion declared, his disgust nakedly on display.

Kara nodded. "Something like that."

"I've seen a lot during my absence, Karalisa, and I wish I could have been more thorough like Luthur wanted of me." Damion ground his teeth together. "That didn't happen, however."

"Your other mission," Kara stated.

"Indeed. It was far more important than trying to keep track of Darkon's movements. Others helped me keep tabs on him, but we weren't able to learn much." A scowl threatened to overwhelm his face. "All I can tell you is that I don't believe he is our enemy, but neither do I feel he is our friend."

"*Humph*. . . . So what does that make him?" she asked, already aware of the answer.

"Dangerous," Damion stated simply.

Kara shook her head with a frustrated sigh. "Too many unanswered questions." Turning on the bench, Kara glanced back into the covered wagon.

Aside from the five packs and a pair of sheathed katanas secured to the sidewalls of the wagon, the wagon bed was practically empty now that she and Ember no longer shared it. However, it still

196

contained precious, though puzzling, cargo. Secured to the center of the bed with rope was Amroth, his body covered in tiny black scales. The carapace adorning his chest, forearms, thighs, and shins was thick and durable, and the sharp features of the draconic mask concealing his head were both intimidating and awe-inspiring. She had seen Joinings before, and on the surface, nothing seemed abnormal about this one. However, there was one fact about this particular Joining that gnawed at her and Damion without reprieve – how long it had lasted.

While the amount of time a new Warden spent within the shell of scales varied from person to person, not once had she seen or heard of it lasting more than a few hours. Yet here, under the protection of her brother, she found a newly awakened Warden who was still within the protective cocoon after two weeks. It was a drastic deviation from a normal Joining, and its implications were frightening.

"So, are you ever going to fill in the holes in your cryptic story?" she pointedly asked.

Damion glanced at her critically. When he'd finally chosen to reveal himself to her on the night she nearly died, it had been with many reservations. He had no desire to drag her into the situation before it was necessary, but as he'd told her that night, events were beginning to force his hand. As such, he had been contemplating just how much to share with her since she'd awakened to discover Amroth in his current state. If he genuinely wanted her to be of any significant assistance, she would need to know what was going on. The question was – just how much should he tell her? She was an intelligent woman, and it was likely she would eventually deduce any details he left out. So, with that thought in mind, he finally decided it was best to be honest with her.

"Are you ever going to tell me why – not to mention how – Ember was on Triclose?" he retorted with an arched eyebrow, unwilling to let the opportunity pass to remind her that she, too, was hiding things.

Kara smirked and shook her head in amusement. "Well met," she stated with a chuckle. "Fine. You fill me in, and I'll tell you my purpose."

Damion grunted. "Fair enough. So, as I said before, part of my mission was to watch Darkon for any signs that he was turning against us, and as you've already deduced, the other part of my mission had to do with Amroth." Kara nodded. "What you don't know is why Amroth is so special."

Kara's eyes narrowed suspiciously. "Go on."

"In the years leading up to the Exodus, Luthur, Taylexion and Mes'ilafira believed it was inevitable that the last of the Guardians would eventually fall to the Darkness' servants." Damion glanced at Kara and wasn't surprised to see shock in her wide eyes. "As such, they set in motion plans to counteract the effects of such an event."

"Corith be good!" Kara breathed. "How long have you known about this?"

"The whole of it? Only after Luthur's death," he declared solemnly. "Looking back, however," he added softly, "I believe I saw hints of this the day that Jul. . . ." A muscle flexed in his jaw. "The day you and Ember were join. . . . The day the last of the Betrayers turned on us," he finished, his tone morose.

Kara felt her heart tighten and tears threaten to well up in her eyes at the pain she heard in his voice. "I don't know what to say, Brother . . ." she stated softly, knowing all too well how devastating that day was for him.

After giving him a moment to gather himself, she said, "If not for the hints you've dropped, I would have said they failed." She paused, then asked, her tone deeply suspicious, "That isn't the case, though, is it?"

"Indeed," Damion responded as if his moment of emotional vulnerability never happened. "Though I don't believe their plans have borne fruit as quickly or as thoroughly as they had hoped. Kara, even before we finally beat back the Betrayers, shattered their crusaders, and destroyed the last of the blackheart nests, Luthur hid amongst the races living on Solarson and Triclose the key to the Light's survival and the means by which Gifted continue to be born to this day." Looking his sister directly in the eyes, he stated, "Kara – they found a way to preserve the Guardians' essence within the bloodlines of the mortal races."

Kara stared at her brother, her mouth agape. Slowly, she looked back into the wagon, and her eyes settled on Amroth. "So, are you telling me that–"

"That's right, Sister," Damion interrupted, "He is–"

"HE'S WHAT?!"

Startled by Kara's exclamation, Mat stopped and turned, curious about what would warrant such a reaction from her. The wagon had come to a halt, and as usual, Damion had an unreadable expression on his face. Kara, on the other hand, was ridged with tension as she and her brother continued to talk. It was clear Kara was upset about something, but he couldn't hear a thing from where he stood. For a moment, his curiosity almost got the better of him, and he briefly considered using his fir'gan to listen in. However, he immediately dismissed that idea. Damion had been watching him like a hawk since that dreadful night, and Mat was smart enough to realize his prying would only cause more tension between himself and the elder Warden.

Eventually, Mat shook his head, adjusted his sweat rag, and turned around, intent on scouting ahead while the siblings argued over whatever had them so demonstrative. Instead, his eyes went wide with surprise as he thought, *"Damn,"* a moment before pain erupted in his chest.

"Be calm, Sister," Damion implored as he pulled on the reins, bringing the wagon to a halt.

"Be calm?! How can you even ask that after what you just told me?!" Her back rigid with tension, Kara ran her hands through her hair. "I just. . . . I mean, this explains so much! I always thought Luthur's desire to unify Triclose was simply to make it difficult for the Betrayers to hide or join forces. But this . . . this. . . ."

"It was that, to a degree," her brother interjected. "More importantly, however, Triclose was the center of their preservation efforts, and he was determined to protect it at all costs." Damion shook his head with a half-hearted scoff. "Not that it did him much good."

"But this is good, right? You said it yourself – the number of Gifted is on the rise. More importantly, we should be better able to combat the Darkness if the strength of the currents continues to grow."

Damion shook his head. "It's not that simple. Yes, if things continue as they are, we will eventually grow in strength, but the strength of the bloodlines isn't enough to cause such a drastic surge in numbers. Corith be good, while Amroth could potentially be the strongest of us, the power within his blood is a shadow of what Luthur had hoped – it's far too diluted by mortal blood."

Kara's brow furrowed, and she folded her arms beneath her breasts thoughtfully. "But if that's the case, then why have so many potential Gifted been born in the last few years?"

Damion's face grew grim. "That's what worries me, Kara. The latent power within the blood of the Roselian Clans – and to a lesser degree, those of Sur'datha – has only been strong enough to produce two potential Gifted that could fulfill the role of a Warden. Of those two, the Gift has only manifested in Amroth fully." Damion scowled slightly. "Then there are the remains of the shadow drakuma Ember killed. This is a clear indication that the Darkness has grown strong again, and either has found a new way to breed their shadowspawn creations, or has somehow gained access to elvannue technology." He scowled. "Throw in the manner in which Luthur died, and it's clear that not only are we in the dark about so much, but someone is leading the Betrayers that isn't as shortsighted as Garith."

"Wait. . . . What do you mean, 'the manner in which Luthur died'?" Kara asked suspiciously, her tone turning hard. "What aren't you telling me, Brother?"

Damion silently cursed himself. He had not intended to bring up that terrible day and the suspicions he had about Luthur's death. He'd never voiced his concerns to anyone – though he believed Darius had harbored similar fears – and as far as he knew, the other Wardens simply assumed Luthur had been overwhelmed. Now, however, a careless slip of the tongue had breached a subject that would only lead to needless speculation at that moment.

"Kara, this is–"

"This is what, Brother? One of those things you feel I don't need to know?" she nearly yelled, aggravated. "Or is it a burden you feel I'm not ready to handle now?" She threw her hands up in frustration and sat back hard on the bench. "Corith be good, Brother!" She declared angrily as she looked up at the barren canopy. "Why can't you just accept that we can help you? It seems to me that you're the one with tru–"

A muffled cry from up ahead cut her off, and she snapped her head down to see Mat stumble backward before he collapsed to the ground, an arrow buried heart-level in his chest. Before Kara or Damion could react, a hail of arrows leapt from the shadows between the trees. Even as the projectiles tore through the canvas wagon cover, a pair of arrows caught Kara in the chest, dropping her to the bench, while three more hammered into Damion's torso, tossing him unceremoniously to the ground.

The sudden surge of violence was followed by a brief moment of heavy silence. Finally, a trio of men and women emerged from the forest on both sides of the road. Each person was dressed in an eclectic assortment of leather and chain armor that looked like it had been procured from a variety of sources. A few congratulatory gestures were shared as the ragged, though well-fed, bandits approached the wagon.

"Good job, lads!" a male voice exclaimed from Mat's direction, drawing their attention.

A stocky woman in mismatched leather armor, with a shock of unkempt brown hair atop her stout face, flashed a victorious grin at the man who was stepping over Mat's body. "Aye, Loc! That was a fine shot you made, too!"

Tall and lean, Loc was the only one whose outfit was uniform. His leather armor was decently maintained, and his chainmail-adorned right shoulder was rust-free. His long head was shaved in a manner befitting a soldier, and his shortsword and bow were of good quality. His gray eyes took in the scene quickly as he approached. As their scouts had reported, the trio appeared to hold some value. Their clothes were relatively modest, but of a fine cut, and the wagon was quite large.

What in Deo's name are people like this doing in this forsaken place? Loc thought to himself as he came to a halt before the nervous horses.

Three of his troops had already scrambled up onto the wagon, while one pilfered the dead driver on the ground, and the other two flanked the wagon as lookouts. Of the three on the wagon, the woman who had addressed him was searching the dead Velusyian on the bench while the other two searched the wagon bed. From what Loc could see, the weapons they'd claimed from the dead appeared to be of excellent craftsmanship. Whether they kept the blades or traded them for goods, it was already a fine haul.

Loc idly rubbed the nose of one of the lead horses as he awaited a report from within the wagon. When he didn't immediately hear anything, he shouted, "What's taking you louts so long? What's in the damn wagon?" When he once again received silence, Loc motioned to the woman on the bench and barked. "Kess, see what's wrong with Jox and Tavorn. The bastards better not be skimming again!"

Kess, her black eyes filled with concern, nodded and peeked into the wagon bed. Immediately, she froze, which set off alarm bells in Loc's head. "What the hells is it, Kess?"

Slowly, Kess stood up and turned around, her face a mask of shock. "Hells' bloody balls, Loc! I–" she started to say as she looked at him. Suddenly, her eyes widened and she shouted, drawing everyone's attention, "Look out!"

Reacting quickly to her cry, Loc dropped his bow and drew his shortsword as he spun around. He had fought many battles over his lifetime, but what he saw froze him in place.

Swords drawn, and shirt bloodied, the man Loc had fatally shot was approaching, the arrow no longer embedded in his chest.

"What in–" Loc started to utter just before the man seemed to vanish, only to reappear before him, his twin shortswords buried deep in Loc's chest.

"Loc!" Kess screamed in horror.

As the two men in the back scrambled out the back of the wagon, Kess started to leap from the bench when a powerful blow to the middle of her back snapped her spine and launched her forward. Her feet clipped the head of the lookout on her side of the wagon as she shot across the road and crashed into a weeping elm, killing her. As the lookout collapsed to the ground and Kess met her end, Kara stood up and leapt from the bench, ripping one of the arrows from her chest. Landing in front of the bandit referred to as Tavrom as he rounded the corner of the wagon, Kara scowled at him as she removed the second arrow and tossed it aside. Catching one glimpse of Kara's infuriated glare, and the sudden healing of her wounds beneath her bloodied shirt, the burly, unkempt Tavrom quickly dropped his sword, turned and fled.

Grinning maliciously at him as he crashed into the other bandit from the wagon, knocking both of them to the ground, Kara then approached the fallen lookout. With a snarl, she stomped violently on his neck, snapping it like a brittle twig. Kara then shouted to Damion as she watched the two fallen bandits climb to their feet and start running down the road, "You okay over there, Brother?"

"Quite," Damion responded as he stepped over the crumpled corpse of the man who had been looting him and ducked beneath the wildly swung sword of the remaining bandit. Damion's muscles coiled to launch an uppercut to the lean woman's jaw, but he hesitated as he sensed movement from behind. Ducking, the air whistled as one of Mat's shortswords shot over him and buried itself in the woman's chest. With a grunt of pain, the woman stared, dumbfound, at the embedded sword as she fell backward to the ground.

Standing, Damion glared at Mat, who simply said, "You're welcome."

Before Damion could retort, a horrified scream from the direction the two remaining bandits fled drew his attention. The burly bandit was already dead, his body split cleanly in half at the waist, while the other was held aloft by an enormous man in a blood-spattered, high-collared gray longcoat.

"This is going to be messy, isn't it?" Mat asked rhetorically as he stepped past Damion to retrieve his shortsword.

Damion simply nodded as he began removing the arrows from his torso, the lightly seeping wounds closing quickly.

Jox had never felt terror like this. The dead had risen to slaughter his compatriots, and then this giant demon had appeared to block their escape. In a flash, the demon split jovial Tavrom like a rahken with a large claymore, leaving Jox horrified by the sight. He barely managed to scream before the demon clamped a broad, tan hand with bony knuckles about the top of his head and, with ease, lifted him airborne. Jox flailed at the thick, leather-ensconced left wrist of the beast with terror-fueled strength, but was unable to faze the creature. As his horrified green eyes darted wildly about, they eventually settled on the demon's face and his struggles ceased.

Broad of face, with wild red hair and a heavy jaw that was reinforced beneath the skin, the beast's bloody face was home to cheekbones and heavy brows that were as prominent as his jaw. Nestled between his cheekbones and red eyebrows, a pair of molten, up-tilted eyes glared at the bandit with primal anger from astride a broad nose. Suddenly, its thick lips parted in an angry snarl, revealing predator-like canines.

"This is it! The Hells have sent one of its guardians to claim me!" Jox thought an instant before the beast's jaw seemed to dislocate itself and open impossibly wide. The bandit managed one last shrill shriek before the creature's head darted forward and its deadly teeth sank into his throat, turning Jox's scream into a blood-filled gurgle.

Wrenching his head back, the beast ripped the bandit's throat out. Snarling at the corpse, the beast casually tossed the body aside as he spat the remnants of the bandit's throat out. Blood dripping from his jutting chin, the beast then approached the wagon, his hobnail-booted feet thudding ominously on the dirt road.

Before he'd take more than a few steps, his mask of bestial rage was washed away and replaced by a look of shame as Kara stormed his way, shouting, "Corith be good, Kiroshin! Again with this?! You're not a damn drakuma anymore!"

Chastised, Kiroshin responded in a voice that sounded as if it had burst from the depths of the earth, "My apologies, Kara. It's hard to remember my current state. And while I may not be a drakuma anymore, I am hardly human. So, please – don't use that name anymore. Kiroshin died a long time ago."

Standing before him, Kara was forced to look up into his molten eyes, which appeared even more savage against his shock of shoulder-length hair. For all but a few, deciphering the emotions in those fiery depths would have been incredibly difficult, but Kara could read those eyes, and there was pain in them — remorseful, confused, heart-wrenching pain.

Placing a gentle hand on his forearm, she could feel the tension in the powerful muscles beneath the leather sleeve. "I'm sorry . . . Ember," she offered with an apologetic smile. "This is difficult for us all. And seeing even a hint of your old self. . . . Well, it's hard not to call you by that name."

Kara felt a little of the tension fade from Ember as he offered her a small smile — which still seemed far too macabre for her liking — and said, "I know, little 'Lisa. Forgive me. I will try to do better. . . . And . . . thank you."

Kara patted his arm. "Forget about it. However, if you don't mind, please clean the blood off your face. It's a little . . . off-putting."

Ember smirked and nodded. Turning, he made for the corpse he'd discarded. Kneeling down, he then ripped a chunk from the dead man's tunic and began cleaning his face and claymore.

Shaking her head regretfully, Kara then returned to the rear of the wagon where Mat and a rearmed Damion stood.

"We're gonna have to do something about him before we get someplace civilized. That is, assuming there is such a thing in this forsaken place," Mat commented as Kara joined them.

Handing Kara her katana and tanto, Damion stated, "The Contested Territories aren't forsaken — they're just uncivilized for the moment." Straightening his cloak, he added, "As for civilization, we're passing through the realm of Ulthion, which shares a border with the only realm in the area untouched by the war or these Corith-damned bandits."

"Right. Caith'tol — you've mentioned it before." Mat said as Kara secured her sheathed weapons to her belt. "But I mean, that's what? The fifth time we've been attacked? This is getting a little old."

"The bandits don't concern me — and we won't have to worry about them once we're within Caith'tol's borders, but I am a bit worried about the soldiers we dispatched earlier," Damion said. "We'd heard rumors that House Suldamik was sending raiders north, but I didn't expect to encounter so many in this place. It is either a bold or desperate move to venture through these lands."

Mat chuckled. "How can their war matter to you now that you've cast off your disguise and Joined the crystal to Amroth? Don't tell me you've grown attached to the mortals you've been serving?"

Damion cast a harsh glare at Mat. "You have a lot to learn, boy. There's almost always more going on than we see on the surface. Like us, the Betrayers typically operate from the shadows, and they have been at the heart of the Great Wars from the beginning." He shook his head. "How many are here, and what their objective is, I don't know. But at the very least, I believe they are after Luthur's crystal."

"Luthur's crystal?" Kara asked skeptically. "What use could it be to them other than to create a new Warden? Do they really think that would give them the advantage they need?"

Damion's face turned thoughtful. "I don't know. But let me pose this question to you – Have you encountered any new Wardens in service to the Darkness? Luthur killed two of the Betrayers for sure all those years ago, but what happened to their crystals? Admittedly, the crystals could simply be unresponsive, but we'd be foolish if we didn't consider other possibilities."

"Like?" Mat prodded.

Damion shrugged. "I don't know . . . but given everything that has happened, my instincts tell me that, despite the lack of worthy Gifted in recent centuries, we simply can't assume the crystals are just collecting dust somewhere."

The sobering implications of Damion's statement struck Mat and Kara profoundly, leaving a cold feeling of dread in their stomachs.

"You all look as if someone died," rumbled Ember as he approached.

Looking up, they saw that Ember had managed to clean most of the blood from his face, his large claymore was secured across his back in its harness, and he carried a partially empty pack in his hand.

"Where were you? Why didn't we get a warning?" Mat asked, not bothering to hide his irritation with being shot.

Ember glared at Mat. "Communication between Kara and I is still sporadic, and the currents feel clumsy to me in this form. As for where I was," he turned his gaze to Damion, "there were another dozen bandits camped about half a league northwest of here. I thought it prudent to dispose of them."

Damion arched an eyebrow. "Indeed. Did you find anything of value?"

"Not much," Ember replied. Holding up the pack, he then

tossed it to Damion and added, "Found some eatable food and a few coin purses. It's not much, but I thought it would be of more use to us." Noticing the tears in the wagon cover, Ember motioned to the wagon with his head and asked, "How's the young pup?"

Handing the pack to Mat, Damion said, "Check on him, will you?"

Mat let out a sarcastic laugh. "Really? Do you think an arrow could pierce his shell, much less harm him now?"

"Humor me," Damion stated dryly.

Scowling, Mat moved to the rear of the wagon and tossed the pack into it before climbing aboard. A moment later, he called out, "Ah . . . I think you might want to take a look at this."

There was no alarm in Mat's voice; nevertheless, Damion and Kara were quick to join him. At first, nothing appeared out of the ordinary. Granted, there were arrows embedded in the wagon bed and in one of their packs, one of the ropes restraining Amroth had been severed, and another arrow appeared to have snapped upon contact with his scaled shell, but that was to be expected. Then Kara noticed it – a series of spidery cracks across Amroth's protective cocoon and mask.

A slight smile born of nervous apprehension tugged at her lips. "I guess it won't be long now."

"Indeed. Stay with him, Kara," Damion nodded before backing out of the wagon.

Once on the ground, he started around the wagon and called out to Ember, "Find us a secure place to camp tonight. It's almost time, Brother."

Well aware of what Damion meant, Ember turned and sprinted ahead.

"What's got you all so concerned?" Mat commented as he trotted up next to Damion.

Damion ignored the question as he moved to the front of the wagon and climbed onto the bench.

Scowling, Mat hustled around to the other side and planted himself next to Damion on the bench. "Well?" he asked, his brash tone rife with annoyance at once more being ignored by Damion.

"How much training did you have before your Joining?" Kara asked as she settled herself in the wagon's opening behind the driver's bench.

Mat blinked. "I don't recall exactly. A year? Two years?"

"Right. And even then, you'd been part of the Torthos Order for a few years before Vann died."

"Yeah. So what?"

"So," Damion interjected, slightly irritated that Mat didn't understand the situation, "you were practically raised as a Gifted compared to Amroth."

"And that means?"

"It means, Mat," Kara stated, concern weighting her words down, "that an untrained, unaware Gifted is now host to a crystal."

The implications of Kara's statement hit Mat like a battering ram, and he cursed himself for not realizing it sooner. "Corith be good," he breathed.

"Indeed," Damion declared forebodingly.

*

"Where am I?"

"You are where you are."

"What am I?"

"You are what you are."

"Who am I?"

"You are who you are."

"Who is speaking?"

"You are speaking."

"Who is answering?"

"I am."

"Who are you?"

"I am you."

Again and again, the conversation echoed through the infinite void. Not once did the words change, but the voice did seem to shift positions. There was no way to be sure, but it felt like it was two different speakers engaged in some infinite, madding exchange.

"Who am I?"

"You are who you are."

"Who is speaking?"

"You are speaking."

No. . . . Somewhere in the endless tumble of words, a third voice re-peated the conversation. It was subtle, like an ephemeral wind, but it was there as the cycle continued as it seemingly always had. Had it been only seconds? Hours? Years? There was no way to tell in the empty void. Even measuring time by how often the cycle of words repeated had long since lost any meaning.

"Who are you?"

"I am you."

"Where am I?"

"You are where you are," interjected the third voice, its masculine tone louder than it had ever been.

In an instant, the void twisted and sheared apart, revealing a breathtak-ing mountain landscape of jagged and rounded peaks that were home to a generous amount of green foliage. Voluminous clouds floated lazily between the peaks as they basked in the silvery-blue light of the full moon that sat high in the star-filled night sky. There was a serenity to the landscape he'd never experienced, and a part of him desperately wanted to remain there. Unfortunately, that didn't seem to be a possibility as the scene began to flow beneath him like a fast-flowing river.

As the magnificent landscape passed by, a complex eventually came into focus. Scattered between a trio of peaks above the cloudline, the complex was con-nected by elegant, arching white stone bridges that glowed softly in the moonlight. Towering buildings of gray stone could be seen throughout the complex, their in-spiring designs adorned with sweeping roofs of green tiles, as well as arched win-dows and doorways that were framed with magnificent carvings of dragons at play. Walls topped with the same tiles protected the complex where the mountains did not, and the only access to the grounds appeared to be via an intimidating stairway that climbed from the clouds.

The vision suddenly narrowed and focused on the main building's cour-tyard. Bathed in the warm light of the torches found throughout the grounds, two groups appeared to be facing off. One group appeared to be monks, though their attire was odd. Sweeping, sleeveless robes made of layers of gold and green lien adorned them, and they all bore prayer beads and shaved heads. As for the other group, their mix of leather, plate and cloth attire was just as odd as the monks' but clearly marked them as soldiers of some sort despite their apparent lack of weapons.

Standing between the two groups, five individuals were energetically con-versing. Three of them had the look of warriors. Wearing a variety of leather armor, one was a woman with emerald-green hair, another had his sky-blue hair in a long braid, and the other man wore his dark hair cut close to the scalp. As for the two men representing the monks, both had their heads shaved, though the tallest of the two sported a long topknot of braided blonde hair.

208

Suddenly, the vision jumped and focused on the blonde man. Though the conversation appeared to be growing in intensity, the man's green eyes and serene features showed no sign of anger.

"Who is this?"

"This is me," the third voice responded.

"Where am I?"

"You are where you are," declared the third voice with more strength just before the vision twisted and shifted.

A vast basin surrounded on all sides by mountains that were eerily similar to those in the previous vision came into focus. At the center of the basin, an enormous lake reflected the heavy, gray sky above, and at the center of the lake, an island of vibrant grass played host to two dozen people. Most were human, a few were darlions, while others were unfamiliar. At their lead was the monk from the previous scene. Dressed in an assortment of leather armor and layered silks, the man was addressing something perched on the mountainside. Whatever occupied the mountaintop appeared to be obscured by fog, but whoever or whatever it was, it was huge.

Suddenly, silvery eyes began to glow high in the fog, and pair after pair appeared around the basin until there were more pairs of eyes than people on the island.

"Where am I?"

"You are where you are," came the expected response, and the vision shifted again.

This time, a rain-soaked, muddy crater in the middle of winter came into focus. Atop an island of shattered earth, three people who looked very similar to those from the first vision appeared to be the last remaining soldiers of a horrific battle. Of the three, one man looked to be on the losing end of the fight. That man, dressed in unusual armor the color of jade, was pinned to the ground by a horrific, key-notched sword that was impossibly big, and wielded by a red-armored warrior. As the vision narrowed on the dying man, it was clear that — despite a full head of deep-blue hair and red facial markings — he was the blonde monk from the previous visions.

It was unclear what had prompted such a battle, but the other two people on the island seemed to be reveling in their victory. Standing a short distance away, the green-haired woman from before grinned as she watched the warrior in red armor, whose skin was ghostly white, lean in close to the dying man. Though the pale warrior's face was littered with scars, he looked strangely like the man with short-cut dark hair from the first vision.

Suddenly, the dying man's armor faded away in a wave of midnight-purple orbs that rose toward the heavens before vanishing. A moment later, the dying man's hand shot up and latched onto the neck of his assailant. A quick, *fruitless struggle followed before the dark-haired man suddenly froze. Without warning, there was a blinding flash of light, and a new, hauntingly familiar scene came into focus when it faded.*

"I know this."

"Of course you do," came the unexpected response as the scene played out.

Laying in a pool of red light, a sickly, blue-haired woman convulsed on the ground while two men struggled off to the side.

"I know this."

The words echoed about as the shorter of the two knocked aside his opponent and approached the woman with a massive glaive in his hand. He then shouted something at a third figure. In response, the third figure, who seemed oddly familiar, leapt over the woman and threw himself into the midsection of the glaive-wielder. The forceful blow didn't budge the man, who then raised his weapon high before driving it into his assailant's back.

Sudden pain, hot and agonizing, ripped through the vision, shattering it completely. In its place, the dark void slowly returned. As the welcome darkness washed away the last vestige of the excruciating pain, the repeating conversation did not return. Instead, a single question echoed through the void, "Who am I?"

Again and again, the words raced through the darkness with growing urgency. Then, when it seemed an eternity had passed, a response finally came.

"Who are you?"

It was the third voice, strong and masculine.

"I don't know! Who am I?"

"Who are you?" the voice repeated firmly.

"I don't know!"

"Who are you?" the voice asked emphatically.

"I don't know!" came the frantic response.

"Who are you?" asked the voice again, as if the answer was simple.

"I don't k—" the response paused thoughtfully.

"Who are you?" the voice prodded gently.

"I– I–" Then, the answer struck. "I know who I am!"

"Who are you?" the voice asked triumphantly.

"I am Amroth Merandith!"

With that realization, a sense of self returned, and he could feel that he now had a body. Though it was too dark to see, he knew that he was naked; thankfully, there was a soothing warmth to the air. Suddenly, a point of blue-

white light appeared beneath his feet, bright and welcoming. Growing slowly in intensity, he saw that he seemed to be standing atop water. The near darkness was soon dissipated by the soothing light, and he could see gentle ripples moving from his position out into the dark void.

Suddenly, he noticed his reflection in the water. He appeared to be someone close to their twentieth summer with a body of strong, corded muscles. Looking at his face, he saw that it was home to a warm complexion, as well as solemn, clean-shaven features, and a pair of dark eyes that were vibrant with an inner vitality, all of which was framed by shoulder-length black hair. He knew that face and body, but his mind told him that he shouldn't be so hale. Shaking his head to banish the uncertainty, he looked up and scanned the darkness at the edge of the pool. Though he could not see anything, it felt like there was something large out there, watching and waiting.

"Where am I?" he asked, his strong, friendly voice nearly surprising himself. It seemed like it had been an eternity since he had heard himself speak, and it took a moment for him to realize the warm voice was his.

"You are here," replied the deep, masculine voice.

"What does that mean? Where is here?" Amroth responded, confusion evident in his tone.

For a moment, the darkness remained unresponsive. Then, from close behind him, he heard, "Here is you, my young friend."

Startled, Amroth turned quickly to find a man, his hands folded behind his back, watching him curiously. Standing nearly six-and-a-half feet tall, the man's golden-blonde hair was pulled back in a horsetail, leaving his serene features and green eyes free of impediments. His black-as-night leather armor was a stark contrast to his hair and eyes, and if not for the pool's illumination, it would have been difficult to see.

"You're the monk from the vision, aren't you?" Amroth asked, amazed to see the man standing there talking to him.

"I am. . . . Though it would be more accurate to say I am an impression of him," he stated, his voice reverberating in his chest.

Puzzlement crawled across Amroth's face. "A what?" He shook his head and ran his hands through his hair. "This is all too confusing."

A slight smirk pulled at the man's mouth. "Let me see if I can clarify things — though it still may not make sense to you." Motioning to their surroundings, the man said, "This place where you stand is you." When he saw Amroth's face screw up with confusion, he added, "To be more precise, this is the core of your being. Your heart, if you like."

Amroth shook his head again. "My heart? What in Deo's name do you mean?"

"I mean exactly that," the man replied as he approached Amroth, his every step sending gentle ripples across the pool. Halting before the young man, he reached out and tapped Amroth's chest. "We are here – in your heart. Everything you see here," he gestured to their surroundings again, "is a projection of your core. We all possess such a place, but most people have no idea that it exists, much less the ability to access it. However, there are those unique individuals who do gain awareness of, and access to, this core. These people are called Gifted. You, my young friend, are one of those people," he stated as if he was reminding Amroth of something he should already know and understand. As he watched bewilderment play across Amroth's face, it dawned on him that the young man had no idea what he was talking about. "You truly have no idea what I am speaking of, do you?"

Amroth shook his head emphatically.

The man let out a wry chuckle. "Ah, how things never seem to change." As he started to slowly pace around Amroth, he asked, "Tell me, Amroth – what is the last thing you remember?"

Amroth blinked, somewhat taken aback by the question. It was a simple question, yet he was finding it hard to recall anything; it was as if a thick fog clouded his memories. "I . . ." he started to say. His brow furrowed with concentration, and his vision dropped to the gentle ripples of the pool. "I. . . ." He concentrated harder, and a sudden image of the glaive-wielder pierced the fog shrouding his memory.

Sudden pain lanced through his chest, and Amroth doubled over, his arms folded protectively over where he'd been struck.

The man paused in his circle. "Yes. That's it. Let the memories flow. Don't fight it."

"I . . ." Amroth hissed through clenched teeth. "I died."

"Not quite," the man said as he placed a comforting hand on Amroth's back. "You were indeed struck down, but you did not die. The blood flowing within you kept you with the living long enough for an old friend to save you."

As the words rang in Amroth's ears, the pain vanished. Slowly, he stood upright, amazed that his chest was wound free. Looking at the man with pleading eyes, he said, "I . . . I don't understand."

The man gently patted Amroth on the shoulder. "Of course you don't." Giving Amroth a reassuring smile, he then stated, "What I'm about to tell you will likely make little sense to you, given your lack of information."

Amroth nodded cautiously.

"Young Amroth, you are what is known as a Gifted – a person with a deep connection to the lifeblood of Kylir. We call this essence fir'gan."

"Fir'gan?" Amroth echoed, the unfamiliar word rolling off his tongue *clumsily.* *"What does that mean?"*

"In the Trader's Tongue, it came to mean 'Fire of the Earth'. An appropriate connotation, but those of us with a deeper knowledge of Kylir's history know that is not its literal meaning. The word itself is draconic, the language of the dracus, Kylir's long-dead guardians. It means, 'Dragon Fire'."

The look Amroth gave him was a match for what Amroth said next. "You're crazy! Kylir has no blood, nor is there such a thing as dragons!"

The man smirked with amusement. "Is there not? You've seen a drakuma, no?"

"Yes, but they aren't dragons," Amroth stated firmly. "And it's only a myth that they descended from such beasts . . ." he finished weakly as memories of Emberscar came to mind.

"You don't sound like you fully believe that."

"I. . . . I don't know. I met this one drakuma that could talk. He . . . he called himself Emberscar."

"Ah," the man said with a wide smile. "I can see how he would shake one's beliefs. His power of speech, however, is not a result of his lineage. You have seen him breathe fire, yes?"

Amroth nodded slowly.

"And what other creature do you know of that can conjure the elements out of thin air?"

"None," Amroth stated numbly as what the man was saying sank in.

"There you have it," the man stated with a pleased smile as he watched Amroth's disbelief melt away.

"And this fir'gan you mentioned. . . . I take it that's real as well?"

The man nodded. "Indeed. It is the lifeblood of Kylir. Without it, nothing could exist. In fact, the pool we are standing on is a reflection of your inner wellspring of fir'gan."

With wide, overwhelmed eyes, Amroth glanced at the gently rippling pool beneath his feet. Looking back up at the man, he said, "I don't know what to say. I. . . ." He shook his head. "I'm so confused," he admitted softly.

The man grabbed Amroth gently by his shoulders. "Put your mind at ease, young Amroth. We have all the time in the world. I shall explain it all to you."

As the man's words began to flow in an endless stream of the fantastical and horrific, Amroth's mind swung between mystified, horrified, and amazed. What the man described seemed beyond comprehension, but as the minutes turned into hours and then into days, understanding dawned on Amroth, and he began to accept what the man said as the undeniable truth.

When it seemed that an eternity had passed, and the man's last words finally left his lips, silence descended on the pool with an overwhelming sense of finality. For a moment, the man simply watched Amroth, seeking any hint of remaining doubt. When he saw none on the young man's peaceful, accepting visage, he asked, "Well?"

"It is a lot to take in . . . but I feel it in my heart that what you've said is true. But what I still don't understand is how I can be of help? I have no idea how to make use of this power."

The man smiled gently. "I cannot tell you that, for it is up to you to discover what role you will play in the greater picture. Just know this — you have friends, trust them. You cannot carry the burdens of the world on your own, so let them help you. However, above all else — stay true to yourself. When all else fails, and the Darkness sets upon you, believe in yourself and you can overcome all challenges."

"I understand," Amroth replied solemnly.

"Good," the man declared with a smile. That smile, however, quickly vanished as the man added, "Unfortunately, you won't retain much of what you've learned. Once your mind returns fully to your body, this will be nothing more than a foggy memory at best."

"What?" Amroth blurted, shock painted on his face. "All this for nothing?! What possible good could this have done, then?!"

With an apologetic smile on his face, the man approached Amroth and placed a hand on his chest, right over his heart. "It's time to go, Amroth."

"Wait!" Amroth cried. "What's your name?"

"You know me by the name Luthur Gravit'nas," the man said simply.

Amroth's eyes widened in surprise, but before he could say anything, he felt a surge of warmth in his chest, and the world around him began to blur and fade to black.

In an instant, Amroth faded from the world, leaving Luthur alone in the light of the pool. Dropping his hand to his side, Luthur looked up into the darkness with a sad smile on his face.

Towering high in the darkness, two bestial silver eyes peered back at him.

"Some things never change, do they?" he stated wistfully before his image slowly vanished.

Chapter Ten

The climb from oblivion's peaceful embrace was slow. As the layers peeled back, his senses began to awaken, permitting what sounded like a crackling fire to pierce the comforting veil of silence. It was pleasant at first, but it was soon joined by a rushing noise that rose from a murmur to a roar that couldn't be ignored. Then, as if they were determined to be included, other sounds quickly joined the chorus – rustling in the distance that was far too harsh, a discordant mix of groaning wood and reverberating growls, and even a piercing bird cry. Every bit of it echoed about his skull, clawing away at what remained of the insulating cocoon of darkness.

A discordant jumble of voices then joined the cacophony of auditory chaos, bringing with it a greater awareness of his surroundings. A mix of unidentifiable smells assaulted his nose, and waves of cold and heat rapidly washed over his body, shattering the last vestiges of unconsciousness. With a sharp gasp, he sat upright and opened his eyes. Harsh, blinding blue light greeted him, ripping a cry of agony from his throat. Quickly, he shut his eyes as he fell backward, but it was all for not. Even with his eyes shut, it seemed as if the blue light was seared into his vision, for he could still see an echo of it. Even worse, the mass of sensory bedlam seemed to have grown in intensity with the total return of consciousness, bringing with it nightmarish pain that tore at his body and mind with morbid glee.

Thrashing about in nerve-searing agony, he could hear himself screaming, which only added to his anguish. Clutching at his skull in a futile attempt to stifle the pain, he felt blood trickling down his head as his fingernails tore into his scalp. All of a sudden, a sharp noise like wood splitting assaulted his ears, and he felt the ground shudder beneath him, followed by what sounded like stone shattering. Suddenly, urgent voices jumped to the forefront of the veil of harsh noise and pain. It was impossible to distinguish anything at first, but it was clear that there were several voices, all of which seemed franticly urgent and heavy with concern. An instant later, his thrashing ended as something forcefully pinned him to the ground. Blinded by pain, his muscles strained against the restrictive force, and for a moment, it seemed like he would break free. That moment, however, was short-lived as the force restraining him grew, hammering down on him with authority.

"Damn it! He's strong!" shouted a familiar brash voice, the clear words ringing in his ears violently, wrenching a scream from him.

"Mat – strengthen your hold!" ordered an unfamiliar, commanding voice. "Ember – sit on him just in case!"

The authoritative voice was even harsher on his ears than the previous speaker, but that observation was ripped asunder by more pain as another scream tore at his throat. Suddenly, a massive weight on his torso turned the scream into an agonizing grunt.

"Damn, this boy is a handful!" rumbled a voice that made him feel like an avalanche was crashing through his skull. "Look at the way he's still tearing at the currents! You sure know how to find trouble, Brother!"

A sudden, violent pop preceded a growing groan that ended with a crashing crescendo.

"Someone calm him down before this gets any worse, damn it! He's going to alert every last Gifted on Triclose to our location!" the second voice ordered emphatically. "Kara – you do it! He won't recognize my voice!"

He heard the thud of painfully loud feet approaching him, and then he felt a pair of hands take hold of his head. The sides of his face felt as if he'd been punched violently despite the hands' gentle touch, and another scream erupted from him.

"Calm yourself, Amroth!" a soothing female voice pleaded. "Please, we need you to do this! Focus on my voice and calm yourself!"

It took Amroth a moment to comprehend the meaning of the words through the haze of agony enveloping him, and even when it finally struck him what she was asking of him, he knew what she wanted was impossible. The pain was simply too great.

"You can do it, Amroth! I know you can!" the female voice urged as if she sensed what was going through his mind. "Focus on my voice and calm your breathing!"

Amroth struggled to do as she asked, but it was futile. His distressed state had severed any control he had over his body.

"Kara, what are you doing?" The authoritative voice asked, surprised. "That's dangerous in his state!"

"Do you have a better idea?!" she snapped in response. "We're not getting through to him!"

There was a heavy pause before the commanding voice stated

with a hint of trepidation, "Do it."

Amroth had no idea what he meant, but almost immediately, he felt something cool and firm touch his forehead. It was an excruciating sensation, but it was nothing compared to the cascade of abrasive scratches he felt running down his cheeks.

Just as he let out another agonizing roar, he felt a presence in his mind. Soothing and gentle like a mother's caress, the presence cut his scream short.

"That's it," he heard in his mind. *"Relax, Amroth. I know the shock and pain must be horrible, but we need you to calm down before you hurt someone. Don't let the pain control you. It is simply your body's response to your new state, but you are in charge of your body. Push the pain to the side and concentrate on my voice. I will help you through this, but I need you to get your breathing under control."*

Amroth didn't know why, but this time, the words carried a weight that was impossible to ignore. It was as if the presence in his mind was guiding him in a very intimate way through the chaos and agony battering his mind and body. With her guidance, and monumental effort, he managed to push aside some of the pain and slow his breathing down a bit.

"That's good," Kara said with what felt like a smile. *"Now, I want you to think of something pleasant, something that will help you relax."*

Immediately, the image of a forge jumped to the forefront of his mind. Nothing helped him relax like working a piece of steel. Despite the pain still clouding his mind, he could hear the rhythmic tapping of hammer on steel. It was hard to focus on it at first, and on several occasions, he nearly lost it. However, with that memory came the understanding of the patience and will that was needed to mold steel into objects, and the training so deeply ingrained in him began to seep forth. In his mind, the rhythmic tapping became louder and clearer, growing steadily easier to focus upon.

"Good, Amroth! Use that to your advantage. This is not a race," she gratefully encouraged him as she noticed his breathing fall into a steady, albeit strained, rhythm. *"Now, I want you to relax your mind and focus on your heart. Can you do that for me?"*

Lost in his memories of working a forge, Amroth could feel his mind focused on the task and its rhythms, pushing the majority of everything else to the edge of his senses. In his current state, the words were a muffled blur, but their meaning eventually managed to seep into his subconscious mind, and it dawned on him that his heart was still beating franticly in his chest. He understood it was far too fast for his task, and such a frantic pace would sap his strength or cause him to faint if he didn't get it under control. An image of Barniban berating him for such a lack of self-control suddenly lept to mind, and he knew he'd have to calm his heart if he were to avoid such a chastisement.

Ever so slowly, Amroth urged his heart to be at peace. It was a task far more difficult than slowing his breathing, and it threatened to slip through his fingers far too many times. In the end – to the relief of everyone around him – his heart eventually settled into a normal rhythm, followed quickly by his breathing. A moment later, the pain faded some, blessing him with a partial reprieve from its torturous confines.

"That's wonderful, Amroth!" Kara stated with joyful relief. *"I just need you to do one last thing. Stay focused on your heart. There's a light there, beautifully bright and warm. I need you to find it."*

With his mind calm, it felt like this was the easiest task she had asked of him. Effortlessly, he found it, though he felt a measure of surprise at its existence. In his mind, he saw what appeared to be a river flowing from it that filled his very being with an amazing warmth. For a reason he couldn't fathom, the urge to reach out and touch it assailed him.

"That's it. Now, I know it's tempting to embrace it – but don't. I need you to close it off. Seal it in a box, if you will. Please, Amroth – do this for me."

He didn't know why she wanted him to do such a thing, but the desperation he heard in her voice was unmistakable. So, with a bit of remorse, Amroth forced himself to ignore the light and retracted his mind from it. As soon as he did that, the river ceased to flow, and the light faded to a distant speck at the core of his being. Instantly, the warmth vanished and the last of the pain faded away, relieving his senses of their overwhelming burden. That brief respite, however, was quickly erased as frigid cold washed over him.

"Thank you, Amroth. You've done so well!" she said before Amroth felt the presence depart from his mind and the pressure on his forehead and sides of his face withdraw.

*"*Corith be good – damn fine job, Kara! That situation was getting out of hand!" Amroth heard the familiar male voice declare as he began to shiver.

"Ember, if you would?" the authoritative male voice asked as Amroth's eyes began to crack open.

Through blurry vision, he saw spots on the jaw and brow of the large person seated on top of him glow red as the man spit forth

218

what looked like a small ball of fire. With a detached mind, Amroth watched as the fireball arched through the twilight air to land on a pile of wood in a firepit. With a roar and hiss of steam, the wood ignited, washing the area in immediate warmth.

"Well, isn't that something? He can spit fire," Amroth thought absently. As the fog on his mind began to lift, the thought ran through his head again. *"Wait. . . . He can spit fire?"* he thought incredulously.

Wide-eyed, Amroth tried to sit up but found that he couldn't do so. Panicking, he began to struggle, but to no avail. He should have been able to move his appendages or head even with the enormous man sitting on him, but for some reason that he couldn't fathom, he was unable to do so. It was as if a colossal force was bearing down on his entire body, and it made no sense to his frantic mind.

"Easy now. Everything's alright," Kara urged gently.

The gently spoken words struck him like a hammer, and his struggles ceased. The voice was familiar and hale, but as harsh memories of the state she was in last he saw her flashed through his mind, he knew that couldn't be the case.

Looking up as much as he could, his eyes grew wide as Kara leaned over and her face came into view. While the familiar sky-blue hair now had frosted white in the bangs along the left side of her face and at her temples, and the matching eyes were streaked with the same color, there was no mistaking who was looking down at him with a relieved smile. Even so, he couldn't keep the surprise from his deep voice as he asked, "Kara?"

"The one and only," she replied with a small laugh.

"But how?" Amroth asked incredulously.

"A story for later." Changing the subject, she stated, "I see the gashes you tore in your head have already closed. That's good. How are you feeling?"

"I– I– don't know," Amroth responded as his mind franticly tried to make sense of Kara's hale state. "I guess I'm fine, but I can't move. What's going on?"

Looking at the large man sitting atop Amroth, Kara said, "Get off him, Ember. He should be fine." Amroth's vision jumped to the man seated on him in shock as Kara added, "Mat – let him go."

"Are you sure?" both men practically asked in unison.

Kara chuckled. "I'm sure. Everything will be fine." She looked down at Amroth. "Won't it, Amroth?"

Amroth managed to peel his eyes off Ember and looked back

at her. He had no idea what she meant, but he nodded anyway.

Smiling, Kara nodded to Ember, who then stood up and stepped around the fire. A moment later, Amroth felt the pressure lift from his body. Slowly, he sat up and looked around, and immediately saw Mat standing off to his right, looking on cautiously. Given Mat's distinctly different attire from the last time he'd seen him, it took Amroth a moment to realize it actually was him. However, once Mat's face and the hint of purple-tinted black hair sticking out from beneath his blue sweat rag registered with Amroth, apprehension gripped his heart. Just as he was about to question Mat's presence, his attention was grabbed by the surrounding area, the sight of which obliterated any anxiety he had about Mat.

Even against the fading light of day, it was clear the area had been ravaged, almost as if a natural disaster had struck. The ground looked like something massive had torn at it violently, scarring the terrain with rents and cracks approaching a foot in width. There were also chunks of stone scattered about as if they'd rained from the sky, and several freshly fallen trees – one of which was cut clean in half – surrounded the campsite. Beyond the campfire, and to the right of a series of large, sundered rocks jutting from the ground, a large wagon rested awkwardly. It appeared to have been cut nearly all the way through just behind its bench; its canvas cover was in tatters, and one of its wheels was in pieces.

Letting his gaze drift past the quartet of spooked horses still in their harnesses, Amroth began to shiver and absently rubbed his arms as his eyes shifted back to the large rocks jutting from the ground near the wagon. Most of them showed natural wear, but there were chunks taken out of them all, and the top of the largest stone appeared to have been cut clean off. There was no sign of the top's fate, but the firelight reflecting off the smooth surface of the shorn area left no doubt that something extraordinarily sharp had cut it.

"What happened here. . .? Where are we. . .? And who is that man you called Ember?" Amroth asked, bewildered, his voice thick with confusion.

Adjusting her black leather half-vest over her spare red shirt, Kara replied, "Everything is alright. We're camped near the. . . . Oh, what did he call it? The Ulthion-Caith'tol border? That's it. We're about two days away from there."

"The Ulthion-Caith'tol border?" Amroth asked, shocked to hear those words. "How's that possible? That's a good two weeks from Haltho, and we were just there the other day!" he exclaimed, unaware of how much time had passed. "That's just not possible," he added with a shake of his head.

220

Stepping around Amroth, Kara crouched down in front of him. "That's where we are, Amroth. Please believe me. You've been unconscious for quite a while."

Amroth looked into her eyes and saw no deception there. "Unconscious?" he asked as he rubbed his chest, the memory of excruciating pain flashing through his mind. "What happened, Kara?" he pleaded. "I– I– remember you being deathly ill, and I remember getting stabbed by Mat after he and Mathis. . . ." Amroth trailed off as his eyes grew wide. "Mathis!" he exclaimed as his memories of that fateful night flooded his mind. "What happened to Mathis?" he barked as he shot a glare at Mat.

Mat didn't flinch beneath Amroth's accusatory gaze; instead, he tugged on his black vest before folding his arms across his chest. "Mathis?" he said with a snort of disdain. "Right. You don't need to worry about *Mathis*."

Anger surged in Amroth at Mat's disrespectful tone. As Amroth started to stand, Kara placed a restraining gloved hand on his strong shoulder, and Mat's eyes widened a bit. The currents were beginning to stir around the young Merandith again.

"Kara!" Mat stated emphatically.

"Want me to sit on him again?" Ember rumbled as he moved next to Kara.

Shooting Ember a warning glare, Kara then looked at Amroth and stated forcefully, "Easy, Amroth! Everything is alright! There's no need to get angry!"

Amroth's head snapped to her, confusion and anger playing out on his face. "Alright?! Didn't Mat try to kill you as well?" he asked as he recalled Mat approaching her that night. "Where's Mathis? Did he kill him first?!" Amroth yelled, pointing at Mat.

With strength that seemed beyond her, Kara's grip on his shoulder tightened, drawing a wince from him as she forced him to sit back down. "Everything is fine, Amroth!" Kara declared emphatically. "I'm alive . . . as is Mathis! If you'll calm down, we'll explain everything to you."

"I – I–" Tears of frustration began to well up in his eyes as he dropped his head into his hands.

Sympathy flooded Kara, and she removed her restraining hand as he started sobbing. *"Corith, please ease his gentle soul. So much in such a short amount of time. . . . It's heartbreaking,"* she prayed as everyone looked on silently.

Eventually, his sobs grew quiet, and he looked back up with

red eyes and tear-stained cheeks. "Please," he pleaded, "tell me what's going on? Where's Mathis?"

Amroth watched as indecision danced across Kara's face, but before she could say anything, an authoritative voice declared, "I'm right here."

Looking to his left, a heavy blanket hit Amroth in the face. Pulling the blanket from his head, he watched as the speaker stepped from the shadows and added as Kara moved to stand next to Ember on the other side of the fire, "Though, that name no longer has meaning."

Tall and lean, the man standing before Amroth was dressed in a fresh white shirt that was tucked into black pants, and his long, hawkish face was capped with white hair pulled back in a horsetail. There was no weapon on him, but that did little to quell the deadliness he radiated, which almost made Mathis seem like a saint. Soaking in the man's appearance, Amroth did his best to reconcile the man's assertion with what he was seeing, but it wasn't working. Clearly, this was not Mathis. Yet, Amroth was struck by a sense of familiarity when he met the man's gaze.

Slightly upturned, and the color of coal, the man's eyes were focused on Amroth with an unnerving, but oddly familiar intensity. While such strength wasn't uncommon amongst the veterans of the Third Great War, there was an uncanny knowledge behind these eyes that he'd only seen in Mathis' gaze. Did it do anything to make him believe what the man said? No. However, he had to admit there was an eerie familiarity in the man's gaze that he could not deny.

"You're not Mathis," Amroth finally stated bluntly, breaking the tense silence that had settled on the group.

The man smirked slightly. "No, I am not," he responded as he walked toward the fire, its light dancing on his black leather boots. Positioning himself on the other side of the warm blaze just to Ember and Kara's right, he gestured to the blanket in Amroth's lap with a black-gloved hand and stated, "You might want to cover up. It's cold out here and, fire or not, you're in no shape to be as . . . exposed as you are."

Amroth blinked at the man, then cursed as he realized he was completely naked. Blushing furiously, Amroth grabbed the blanket and covered up as best he could. Embarrassed by his predicament, he couldn't bring himself to meet the eyes of any of the others as he settled the blanket on his shoulders.

"Thanks," Amroth finally muttered. Forcing himself to look at the man, he asked cautiously, "You said you are and are not Mathis.

What in the hells does that mean?"

The man smirked slightly. "The simplest answer?" Amroth nodded. "The face I once wore was nothing more than a disguise."

"A disguise?" Amroth stated with a snort of disbelief. "You're mad if you think I'll believe that. Not only are you taller and much thinner, but no one could ever make a mask that realistic! So, how about we try the truth?"

The man chuckled. "Your reaction is to be expected. However, rest assured, I am telling the truth."

Disbelief remained clearly painted on Amroth's face as he looked at Kara. "This is a sick joke, right?" he asked with a hint of rising anger. "Last I saw, you were dying and Mat was fighting with Mathis. What in the hells are you all up to with this farce?"

The look of sympathy he found on Kara's face was unexpected, but it did nothing to dissuade his anger and apprehension.

"Amroth – listen to me," Kara stated compassionately. "He's telling the truth. He did wear Mathis' face as a disguise. As for me, yes, I was dying; however, he saved me and Ember from a horrific fate."

The mention of Ember drew Amroth's gaze to the enormous man in a bloodstained gray longcoat standing next to Kara, who'd been sitting on him earlier. "I suppose you're going to tell me you're Ember, eh? You'll then say that somehow a giant red beast got changed into a human, right?" Amroth asked sarcastically, even though the man's pronounced features, wild red hair and molten eyes hinted at the truth of the matter.

Ember snorted, then rumbled, "Indeed, that is the case, boy. I may look like a human, but I'm the same beast that saved your hide from the bandits in the forest." For emphasis, ember drew on his fir'gan enough to cause the spots beneath the skin on his jaw and brow to light up.

Amroth's eyes widened in shock. There was no mistaking that trait. Between his knowledge of the events in the Alderian Forest and that distinct glow that was usually followed by viscous, fluidic flames, he had no doubt that the man was the same drakuma that had saved him.

"Crazy, isn't it?" Matt quipped.

The words cut through Amroth's shock, and he turned his head to look at Mat. "You're going to tell me it's all true, too, aren't you?"

Mat shrugged, then glared at the white-haired man for a moment before focusing on Amroth and saying, "Afraid so. It's the craziest thing I've ever seen, but with Corith as my witness, it's all true. Kara was dying, and while I could have killed Mathis, I didn't."

"And what about Kara? I clearly remember you approaching her with . . . with . . ." he ran his hand through his unkempt black hair. "Some ridiculous weapon!"

Ashamed, Mat looked away from everyone. "That I did," he answered softly. Looking back at Amroth, he declared, "And I was the one that stabbed you." Shrugging his shoulders, he added, "Sorry."

Amroth began to rub his chest absently beneath his blanket again. He recalled the shock and pain clearly, but there wasn't even the slightest hint of an injury. "I . . . I remember that clearly. I—" He looked at Kara with pleading eyes. "How is any of this possible?"

Kara's sympathetic gaze tore at Amroth's confused mind and heart. Finally, she looked at the white-haired man and asked, "Do you want to explain all this, or should I?"

"I'll do it," he replied firmly. Taking a deep breath, he stated, "Amroth, my real name is Damion Masumaite. For years, I wore the face of the man you knew as Mathis Sormantale."

"I don't believe you," Amroth retorted, his resistance to the truth wavering. "That's not possible."

"It is, and I need you to believe me; it will make the rest of this a bit easier to accept," he declared as he watched for any sign that Amroth's disbelief would budge. It was clear he was wavering, but he was still clinging to the reality he'd always known. Hiding his mild irritation with his charge, Damion stated, "Fine. Let's try this instead. The night we rushed from Haltho, I was training you in the Academy's indoor facility, and Kara came to visit me. Soon after, I retrieved you from the dining hall and gave you a pair of katanas before we left."

"You could have learned that from anyone in the Citadel who witnessed those events," Amroth countered skeptically.

"Indeed, but that's not the case. But seeing as that's not enough to convince you. . . . You are a pacifist at heart," Damion declared, turning to more intimate knowledge, "and when you were just a boy, I beat you bloody in an attempt to teach you how to fight. You also heal remarkably fast due to your clan blood."

"Fairly common knowledge amongst House Merandith – you could have come into that information with enough digging," Amroth replied, his skepticism waning even more.

Damion grunted. "Fine. I'll continue. At the age of fifteen, you had your one and only sexual experience with Barniban's niece, who eventually thought your relationship was putting a strain on her uncle's rapport with House Merandith, so she broke up with you."

The others fought off amused smiles as Amroth gawked at Damion.

"How in the hells did you–" Amroth started to ask as he blushed furiously.

"You are also the adopted brother of Kale Jorbic Merandith," Damion continued, cutting off Amroth's question, "but were born to Clan Theirigaldis, a lowland clan from Sur'datha that rebelled and was executed down to the last man for their betrayal. I was the man who found you and convinced the others that executing a babe wasn't the answer. You are the last of your bloodline . . . and a very important person to us. I have protected you for years under the guise of a House Merandith bodyguard, but when Mat stabbed you in the Alderian Forest – and with my siblings' lives in jeopardy – I had no choice but to cast off my ruse if I were to save you all."

Amroth couldn't find the words to reply. Much of what Damion said was very personal, and closely guarded, information. There was no way for someone outside the Merandith's inner circle to learn of such events, and with that realization, Amroth's resistance finally began to thoroughly crumble.

Seeing that there was no response coming, Damion fixed Amroth with a firm look and said, "You survived long enough for me to save you not only because of your blood, but also because you are what we call a Gifted – a person with a close connection to the lifeblood of Kylir. We call this essence fir–"

"Fir'gan," Amroth finished for him softly, drawing stunned looks from everyone.

"How does he know that?" Mat asked, perplexed.

Damion shook his head slowly as he examined Amroth's expression. Realization and acceptance were dawning on the young Merandith, but that did not account for his knowledge of fir'gan. "I don't know," Damion said with a hint of curiosity. "I never mentioned it, nor is it likely that he heard it from someone else. Very few people know of it on Triclose, and even then, it's spoken of as superstition." Peering at Amroth closely, he then asked, "Where did you hear that term?"

"I . . . I'm not sure," Amroth responded quietly, barely aware of the question. A jumble of thoughts and images were flashing through his mind, making it difficult to focus on just one thing. "I think. . . ." A brief image of a blonde-haired man suddenly cut through the frantic memories. "I think a man told me while I was unconscious."

The others looked at one another with a mix of concern and curiosity. "What man?" Damion prodded.

Amroth's brow furrowed. He couldn't quite recall the man's name or much about their conversation. It felt as if the knowledge he sought was there for the taking, but just out of reach. "I . . . I think his name was. . . ." A name suddenly jumped to the forefront of his mind. "Luthur?" he stated hesitantly as he looked at Damion for confirmation.

Shock hammered into the others upon hearing the name, and it was nakedly displayed on their faces. Amroth didn't know what to make of their expressions as he looked around. Where they had been brimming with confidence before, they now looked just as shaken and confused as he was. "What's wrong?" he finally asked.

Damion looked at the others briefly before stating, "Everyone, have a seat. I think we all need to have a very long talk."

For hours they talked. Amroth told them about what little he could remember while he was unconscious, and when he finally finished, Damion reciprocated. He told Amroth of the events after he'd been stabbed, and gave him a succinct summarization of who the Wardens were and their ongoing conflict with the Betrayers and the Darkness. It was a conversation filled with disbelief, shock, and amazement. Not only was Damion's explanation fantastical, but Amroth was astounded to discover that Kara and Ember were indeed Damion's siblings. In the end, however, Amroth found himself gradually accepting what Damion told him. There was nothing else he could fathom that would explain how he and Kara had survived their injuries and illness; so, while Damion's account was undoubtedly far-fetched, Amroth chose to accept his claims. His newfound acceptance was further reinforced by two things – an odd sensation in his heart, which Damion's explanation of the post-stabbing events cleared up, and a display of their power.

The demonstrations, however, were put on hold when, to everyone but Amroth's amusement, an audible rumble from the young Merandith's stomach declared his need for food. As such, a hearty stew was prepared, which Amroth consumed with a ravenous hunger that Ember declared worthy of a drakuma. Afterward, with everyone seated across the fire from Amroth, they watched as Kara, who sat next to Ember, started the exhibition. With skillful ease, she manipulated the blaze, causing it to dance and split into a dozen floating balls of flame before returning to the firepit. Mat followed that up from his spot to the siblings' left by using the currents to lift some of the rock fragments high in the air before crushing them into dust. Through it all, Amroth felt something tickling the back of his mind, but he shrugged it off as nothing more than a result of his astonishment. Their demonstrations left little room for Amroth to doubt Damion's words, but it was Damion's display that was the deathblow to any remaining doubt that he harbored.

Standing up from where he sat across from Mat, Damion stepped back from the others. "As I said before – Kara, Mat, and I are Wardens. We were chosen to protect Kylir's Guardians from the Darkness. At one time, in order to prove that we were free of the Darkness' corruption, we presented a seal made of the purest element of creation." Holding his hand out, palm upward, he added, "Some, through the years, have called it aether, and others have called it starfire, but we know it as coldfire." As the last words left his mouth, a tiny blue-white ball of flame burst into existence over his palm. Instantly, the temperature dropped around Damion and frost began to form on his palm. "This primordial element is what was used to create the bond between my brother and sister, and it is what I used to save them on that terrible night."

Astounded, Amroth watched the flame twist and turn until it formed a pair of dragons circling each other, their hands locked together as they gazed out upon the world. It was eerily reminiscent of an image he'd seen before, and how it fit with all Damion had told him was nearly overwhelming. "That reminds me somewhat of the sigil of House Gravit'nas," Amroth breathed.

"Indeed," Damion replied as he clenched his hand, extinguishing the flame. Right away, the temperature began to rise, and Damion shook his hand to clear it of the frost. "It is our seal. As I said, at one time, that seal was proof that a Warden was pure of heart and spirit. Unfortunately, that has not been the case for some time. Our enemies have long since learned to hide their taint, so on the rare occasion that the seal is presented, it is more of a formality than anything else."

Amroth shook his head. "Alright, I believe you. There's one thing that still bugs me, though. That weapon Mat was using. What was that?"

A dry smirk crept onto Damion's face. "That weapon is called a crusader. It was created to aid in our fight against the cor

rupted dragons, and it is the most effective way to kill a Warden."
Drawing the twin, broad-bladed bluesteel shortswords at his hips,
Damion held them before him. "What you see here is a crusader's
shell; a vessel, if you will. Made from pure Velusyian bluesteel, it is
nearly indestructible, and very lethal in this form. More importantly,
it contains an enormous amount of focused fir'gan that can somewhat
disrupt the link between Warden and crystal. When unleashed, however...." Damion tapped the pommels of the two swords together,
and they began to shimmer, causing Mat to slowly climb to his feet.

Amroth felt a sudden tickle in the back of his mind as the
swords began dissolving into tiny balls of blue light that rose into the
air before fading away. When the last of the spheres finally vanished,
an orb of bright blue energy coalesced in Damion's hand.

"Dear Corith! How in the hells did you do that?!" Mat exclaimed with a mix of shock and anger, drawing a curious look from
Amroth and concerned glances from Kara and Ember.

A cold, knowing grin spread across Damion's face as he
looked at Mat. "I told you I would use your crusader on you if any
harm came to them," Damion replied before clenching his hand
about the orb.

Immediately, it gave way beneath his grip and expanded outward from both ends of his hand. As the energy reached its limits,
each end of it curled gently backward before the entire mass solidified
with a flare of blue light. When the light faded, Damion was left
holding the red-leather-wrapped, two-handed grip of a ten-foot-long
bluesteel glaive. Simple, round collars separated the grip from the
two-foot wide, sweeping blades that seemed to shimmer as the blue
runes etched down the center of each wing throbbed with power.
With ease, Damion held the glaive aloft and gave it a twirl, causing the
weapon to cut through the air with a mournful cry.

Amroth immediately recognized the glaive, and his eyes widened. Before he could say anything, a sharp, angry intake of breath
drew his attention to Mat.

Hands clenched at his sides, Mat was visibly shaking as he
scowled at Damion. "That shouldn't be possible!" Mat cried. "A
crusader is keyed to its wielder's fir'gan to prevent this from happening!"

Damion gave the glaive another twirl before dropping it to
his side. "Indeed, that is the case."

"Then how are you doing that?!" Mat barked.

Damion merely grinned at Mat as the glaive suddenly began

to dissolve in the same fashion as the shortswords before it. An instant later, the twin swords reappeared in Damion's hands, and he then sheathed them. "Well?" he asked of Amroth, ignoring Mat's indignant glare.

Amroth blinked rapidly before shaking his head. "What else can I say with the proof staring me in the face? If not for the flashes I can recall from my time in the. . . . What did you call it? A Joining?" Damion nodded. "Right. If not for what I recall of my time in the Joining, and your displays, I'd say I'd gone mad." Amroth ran a hand through his hair. "Still, it's hard to comprehend. Maybe I've actually gone mad?" he finished with a sarcastic chuckle.

Ember barked a laugh, causing Amroth to jump. "How do you know you haven't? This could all just be a fit caused by a fever, or maybe you ate some bad food. . . . Say. . . some human flesh I claimed was boar," Ember teased.

"Ember!" Kara chided with a slap to his arm as Amroth began to laugh full and deep. Looking at him with a bit of a bemused expression, she asked, "What's so funny?"

Recovering, Amroth shook his head. "All of it, really! It's just so . . . ridiculous! All of you running about with these powers – by Deo, you could have conquered all of Kylir on a whim, and we couldn't do a damn thing about it!" He sighed and scratched his head. "Now that I think about it," he started to ask as he fixed Damion with an accusatory glare, "why in the hells have you not used your strength to end the war? We could crush House Suldamik in an instant!"

Damion's face turned dour.

"What you say is true," Kara interjected, seeking to head off an argument that she sensed could damage the fragile trust Damion had established with Amroth, "but what power Damion possessed as Mathis was extremely limited." Catching Amroth's gaze and holding it, she added firmly, her expression grim, "More importantly, I want you to consider this – should Damion, or I, or any other Warden for that matter, use our powers in such an overt manner, we would risk destroying the tenuous peace between us and the Betrayers. If that happened, open conflict would likely erupt between us. We've only given you a brief, paltry glimpse of who we are and what we're capable of, so can you even begin to comprehend just how destructive that would be?" She gestured to her siblings and stated, her beautiful voice overshadowed by her foreboding tone, "We've been through one war like that, and let me assure you of one thing – the consequences of such a conflict would be far beyond what you can imagine."

As she fell silent, she watched as the weight of her words settled on Amroth. With his limited understanding of who and what the Wardens were, he could only partially grasp the implications of her explanation. However, if his brief lifetime on Triclose had taught him anything, it was that when a person in a position of power preached restraint, they likely had very valid reasons to fear the temptations and consequences of such strength. The early years of Kale's rule were a prime example of the cost of giving in to such temptations . . . even if he was fueled by vengeance.

Looking around at the others, he saw their expressions were as equally grim as Kara's face. It was clear that they fully believed and supported her explanation, but as his gaze came to rest on Mat, he saw a hint of compassion in his eyes that had replaced his anger with Damion.

"I know all this is hard to accept," Mat said, "and Corith only knows you don't have a reason to trust me . . . but please believe me when I say this – I've only been a part of this for a short time, but I have seen just how dangerous the potential for destruction in us is." He nodded toward the others. "They experienced the consequences of an unchecked war between Wardens, and Corith knows I don't want to ever live through that! It's better for us all if we stay in the shadows, pick our fights carefully, and only engage the Betrayers through others if at all possible."

Mat was right – Amroth had no reason to trust him. However, he could see the conviction in Mat's eyes as he spoke. There was neither deceit nor intent to do harm in them, and that – for the moment – was good enough for Amroth.

Offering Mat a slight nod of appreciation, Amroth turned his attention back to Kara and Damion. He then asked, "Alright. So, what do you want from me?"

"To learn, and to keep an open mind," Damion declared with a hint of compassion. "Against my better judgment, you've been forced into this world long before I would have chosen. You are untrained and practically unaware of fir'gan; and while that wouldn't normally be of great concern, the power in you is no longer dormant now that a crystal resides within you. This is a dangerous mix – especially when you become overly emotional, or worse, angry."

He motioned to the destruction throughout the campsite.

"Just look around you. All this devastation is a result of your uncontrolled outburst when you awoke from your Joining. We managed to restrain you before it got completely out of hand, but imagine if these trees and rocks had been people."

Amroth's eyes widened at the implications even as he vigorously nodded his understanding.

Damion nodded. "Good. I'm glad you understand. Now, while I'm not terribly concerned about your ability to control your emotions," Damion continued, "we need to teach you – and teach you quickly – to not only sense and access the currents and your inner fir'gan, but how to control it."

"And if I can't?" Amroth asked cautiously.

"Let's not worry about that unless we have to," Kara interjected with a comforting smile.

A shudder ran through Amroth at the implications, but he managed to force a weak smile and nod in response.

"Indeed," Damion added before moving over to the ruined wagon. Hauling himself into the bed, he reemerged a moment later with one of their packs. Returning to the fire, he tossed it to Amroth and said, "In the meantime, I suggest you get dressed. A blanket isn't appropriate attire for a Warden."

"You should be sleeping."

Startled by the rumbled statement, Amroth looked up from the warm fire to find Ember standing on the opposite side of the blaze, his molten eyes peering at him inquisitively. Against the darkness of night, it was an unsettling reminder of his first encounter with Ember. Shaking off the memory, Amroth asked, "I thought you were keeping watch?"

Ember shook his head. "Damion will handle it. Now that he's back to normal, he won't need sleep."

Seated with his legs crossed before the fire, and absently dragging a stick through the dirt, Amroth now wore a thick white shirt tucked into sturdy brown breeches that ended in a pair of midcalf black boots. Shaking his head with a wry smile, he asked, "I guess that's another *wonderful gift* that comes with being a Warden?"

Ember grunted. "Not exactly. While a Warden can go long periods without sleep," he motioned to Kara and Mat, both of whom were slumbering beneath their blankets near the broken wagon, "they still need it as much as they need food. Damion, on the other hand, is . . . a special case."

"What, in Deo's name, is that supposed to mean?"

Ember stared at him, his expression guarded.

Amroth tossed the stick he'd been toying with into the fire and declared, "Never mind. I don't want to know." Dropping his hands into his lap, he chuckled with dry amusement. "You know what?" he said. "Despite all the changes, what happened to you since we parted ways is the easiest thing to believe." Adjusting his shirt, he added, "That voice that sounds like it came from the depths of Kylir, and your eyes are unmistakable."

Grunting, Ember stepped around the fire. Pushing the flaps of his longcoat clear of his legs, he crouched next to Amroth as the firelight danced over his matching leather pants, and his sturdy hobnail boots. Looking into the fire, he said, "All things considered, I'd say you're handling it well."

Amroth let out a nervous chuckle and rubbed his hands on his pants. "Not really. There's so much to take in, and it's all so . . ." he grimaced and kicked at a pebble with his booted foot, the leather of which dully reflected the firelight, "so hard to comprehend."

"Aye, it is," Ember replied with a slight nod of his head. Glancing at Amroth out of the corner of his eye, he asked, "But you know it's true, don't you?"

"Yeah. The flashes I get from my time in the Joining aren't clear, but it's enough to lend credence to what you all have told me. Still," he looked at his dark-brown-gloved hands, "it's hard to believe I'm part of this and could possess such a power. I mean, I always thought my ability to heal quickly was simply a gift from Deo." He shook his head again. "To think it's far more than that is just . . ." he trailed off with another shake of his head.

"I guess I shouldn't be surprised that you are amazed by such a revelation," Ember rumbled. "You don't even remember using it in the Alderian Forest to protect yourself from my flames."

Amroth's eyes widened in shock. "I did what?"

Ember flashed an amused grin and shifted to look squarely at Amroth. "You used the currents to deflect my flames," he stated as if it were obvious.

Amroth stared at Ember in astonishment. He remembered Ember rampaging through the camp, killing the bandits, and bathing the area in fire. He could even recall the glow of the spots on Ember's horns just before he breathed forth his fluidic flames, but he couldn't recall ever deflecting those flames. Then, with a sharp intake of breath, it hit him. The anger he felt and his desperation to live came flooding back, and with it, something else. "Blue tendrils of light," he stated softly.

Ember nodded. "Fir'gan."

"I.... I.... I used it to deflect the flames?" Amroth asked as he tried to focus on the fleeting memory.

"Indeed."

"Deo be good," Amroth breathed as he dropped his head into his hands. After taking a long moment to compose himself, Amroth looked up and said, "I don't know what to say. That I could do such a thing is . . ." he trailed off and shook his head in frustration. "It makes me wonder," he finally continued, "how many like me are a part of the Clans." Suddenly, his eyes widened as a thought occurred to him. Looking at Ember, he asked, "Deo be good. . . . Does that mean Dakan is like me?"

"I don't know who this Dakan is, but if he's related to you by blood, then it is a possibility." Turning his gaze back to the fire, he shrugged. "If you want to know more, You'd likely be better off asking Damion about that."

The mention of Damion cut through Amroth's frustration, drawing a sarcastic chuckle from him. "Right. Damion," he stated with a measure of disgust and a shake of his head. Looking at Kara, he said, "I find it hard to believe you and Kara are related to him. You two are so warm and friendly, but he's. . . . Deo be good – there's a coldness about him that is far beyond anything I felt when he called himself Mathis."

Ember grunted. "Afraid we are all Masumaites . . . though Kara took a different family name a long time ago."

Amroth smirked and glanced at Ember. "Why? Didn't like her brother?"

Ember shrugged and a hint of a knowing smirk flashed on his thick lips. "That might have been part of it, but her main reason was one of practicality; however, it's not my place to tell her story."

Amroth looked back at Kara, and a sudden, amused smirk crossed his face. "You know, it makes sense now – and it's kind of funny."

"What's that?"

"When we left you in the Alderian Forest, we took shelter in a cave on the coast. It was there that we– I mean, I first met Kara and Mat. Kara and I talked a bit the next day, and I commented on how she seemed far older than she looked." He chuckled softly. "She told me that Velusyians often look younger than they actually are. I guess – in her case – that is quite true."

Glancing at Amroth, Ember chuckled. "We're all over five thousand years old; Corith knows we have seen and done more than anyone can comprehend. It makes sense that we'd act far older than we look."

Amroth looked at Ember inquisitively. "That's so hard to comprehend! You don't look much older than thirty!"

"A good guess. I'd seen thirty-three years when I was made a Knight by Kara, and she was only twenty-three when she became a Warden."

"A Knight? That's a Solarian title, right?"

"That it is," Ember responded with a nod, "but the title goes back to the Age in which we were born. Within the Orders, Knights are strong Gifted chosen by a Warden to serve as their second in command. When chosen, every Knight receives a sliver of their Warden's crystal." Tapping his chest, Ember added, "To this day, a piece of Kara's crystal resides in me."

"Is there . . ." Amroth rubbed his chest. "Do I have a Knight?"

Ember shook his head solemnly. "As far as I know – no. He apparently died soon after Luthur's death."

"Who was he?"

Ember eyed Amroth dubiously. "Are you sure you want to know?"

Seeing Ember's reaction to his question, Amroth found himself nodding slowly.

"Mathis."

Amroth blinked at Ember, stunned by his declaration. "What?"

"Mathis was Luthur's Knight. We all thought he had decided to serve under Damion after Luthur died, but," he snorted, "we were certainly wrong about that."

Shaking his head in frustration, Amroth ran his hands through his loose-hanging black hair. "Deo be good! This is all too much!" A sudden weight fell gently on his shoulder as Ember placed his large hand comfortingly upon it. Looking up, Amroth found a consoling smile on Ember's face – though coming from Ember, the smile still felt dangerous.

"You've had far too much dumped upon your shoulders to-night," Ember stated, his rumbling voice warm and sympathetic.

"While my brother may not say it, I will – I'm sorry, Amroth. You've been thrust into this without warning or training, and that is a terrible thing. Just know that we will do our best to guide you and teach you."

Caught off guard by the apology, Amroth was stunned as he struggled to find something to say. Finally, he shook it off and gave voice to what had been chewing at the back of his mind all night. "And what if I don't want this? I never liked fighting, and your war isn't mine."

Ember's smile and the warmth in his voice quickly vanished, replaced by a cold sternness that was reminiscent of Damion. "That choice was taken from you the moment Damion put the crystal in your chest," he stated ominously. "You are a Warden now – and with that comes a responsibility that is far more important than personal desires. Should you try to discard this. . . . Well, let's not cross that chasm, shall we?"

The color drained from Amroth's face as the unvoiced threat hung in the air forebodingly. "I. . . . I understand," he said weakly as his shoulders slumped in defeat.

A sympathetic smile once more crossed Ember's face as he gently squeezed Amroth's shoulder. "Again – I'm sorry. Now, get some sleep, if you can. I'm sure we've got a long day ahead of us."

The rest of the night passed uneventfully, and with the dawn, Damion ended his watchful vigil. Entering their camp, he saw that Mat and Kara were still asleep near the wagon, Ember was seated and resting against the rock formation, and Amroth was curled up near the smoldering remains of the fire. Making his way over to the wagon, Damion climbed into the bed and leaned Mat's sheathed swords against the wagon wall before retrieving the swords he'd gifted to Amroth. He'd repaired the harness during their journey west, and it was now as good as new. Pulling it on, he secured the buckle across his chest before buckling the harness' belt about his waist, which served as an anchor for the harness' spinal scales.

Grabbing his pack, he then climbed down from the wagon. Once on the ground, he adjusted the swords on his back for comfort, the hilts of which jutted over his left shoulder, before shouldering his pack and quietly approaching Kara. Crouching down, he placed a hand gently on her shoulder. Lying on her side, her eyes immediately flew open, but she remained still. Sleeping as lightly as she did, she'd sensed Damion drawing close and that there was no hint of danger. Looking up at her brother, she saw him motion for silence before gesturing away from camp. Once she nodded her understanding, Damion stood up and started quietly picking his way across the campsite.

With practiced ease and silence, Kara extracted herself from her blankets and stood up before quickly following her brother. Smoothing out her wrinkled attire as she went, she eventually joined him on the path that cut through the woods from their camp to the road.

"What is it?" she asked softly as she came to a halt before him.

"It's time for me to leave," he stated quietly but bluntly. "First, however, I want to know why you sent Ember to Triclose."

Rubbing her face with her hands in an attempt to clear her sleep-numbed brain, she smirked slightly. "I didn't believe for a moment you'd forgotten about that."

"Indeed," he replied with a hint of amusement.

Meeting her brother's gaze, she then asked, "Are you sure about this? It may affect your decision."

Her cryptic response drew a dark glare from Damion.

Sighing, she stated, "Alright." Taking a deep breath, she explained, "With some of the troubles we'd experienced on Solarson, not to mention the rumors we heard from time to time, I was already concerned about a new blackheart presence." Seeing the look in her brother's eyes, she added, "I know. I know. Why would I even think that, given the Betrayers had no way of doing so?" She shrugged. "It was a feeling. Nothing more. So, as you can guess, when I suggested such to Darkon, he was unwilling to even entertain the idea."

Damion smirked. "I can't imagine that stopped you."

"Indeed," she responded, mimicking her brother's favorite phrase. "So, I felt it would be a dereliction of my duty to ignore the rumors." She scowled slightly. "Corith be good, it's not like it would have cost Darkon anything to investigate, but he was adamant that it was impossible." She shook her head and sighed. "I swear, for all his years, he can be so damn closed-minded at times!"

Damion grunted in agreement.

"Exactly. Anyway, as you said, I wasn't going to let his stubborn pride stop me, so I kept investigating as best I could without drawing undue attention from him. There were plenty of stories to sort through, most of which were superstitious nonsense. There were, however, tales coming from the deserts of Pelasia that were hard to ignore." Folding her arms beneath her full breasts, her countenance took on a heavy amount of irritation. "I would have preferred to investigate myself, but Corith only knows the Hells that would have stirred up, so I had Ember shipped over via barge."

An amused smile split Damion's lips. "How I would have loved to have seen his reaction to that."

Kara chuckled half-heartedly. "He wasn't happy in the least, to put it mildly."

Sensing burdensome thoughts behind her chuckle, Damion prodded, "He found something, didn't he?"

Nodding slowly, Kara met her brother's gaze. "A miasma on the land so wretched that he couldn't even come close to reaching its source," she declared, her tone somber. "It was driving creatures as mighty as the local ember drakumas away, and leaching vitality from the land in a way that could indicate only one thing."

"A nest," Damion concluded darkly.

Kara nodded. "It's the only thing it could be. His return north was as much to meet with me as it was to track a dark presence on the currents. Whether that was Garith or the shadow drakuma, neither of us knows for sure." She shook her head dejectedly. "Without seeing it first-hand, I don't know the extent of the nest, but it has to be big."

Damion nodded slowly. "Agreed. What's more, how are they breeding them?"

Kara shrugged, her consternation apparent in her posture and expression. "Corith only knows," she replied. "Darkon said he would investigate after I was attacked, but I'm not putting much faith in him at the moment." She sighed. "Anyway, unless they somehow came into possession of elvannue blood and technology, I can only guess that they found some other way, or there were eggs tucked away as a fall-back plan." She noticed how deep in thought Damion was and added, "That's not what's really bothering you though. . . . Is it?"

"Indeed. I'm much more concerned with how a shadow drakuma was birthed. Only a handful were created during the Crusade, which Taylexion said was due to the sheer difficulty of the perilous procedure. To say the implications are troubling is putting it mildly."

"Agreed. And this one was clearly more powerful. The ones we killed during the Crusade were barely more of a threat than a blackheart. However, the harm this one did to Ember and I would have taken a few dozen blackhearts damaging us at once to equal." She shuddered. "If they somehow have access to more of those crea tures . . . I have serious doubts about our ability to combat it."

Damion fought off a snarl at the unspoken part of that statement. Their chief weapon against the blackheart threat, the Bestynes, had been decimated by Darkon's purge. Granted, Kara and Ember were far more effective, but the Kydan'fir Order never had a chance to be converted. . . assuming the procedure would have worked on anyone else. As for Darkon, he couldn't have known such a threat would arise. Still. . . .

After a moment of deep thought, Damion finally said, "Thank you for telling me, Sister."

She smirked slightly, which faded as she said, "And thank you for filling me in about Amroth and . . ." her voice softened, and a lump welled up in her throat as she added, "Luthur." Pausing, she cleared her throat before asking, the strength returning to her voice, "Speaking of which, what will you do now? If all is as Ember said, you might be our best weapon against such a nest. If you wish to investigate, I'm still willing to help train Amroth. Corith knows he'll need as much help as he can get."

Damion nodded, his coal-black eyes filled with finality. "It's a dammed if you do, dammed if you don't scenario. Yes, I could investigate, possibly eliminate a nest, and draw the Betrayers' ire. To be completely honest, if it were any other Warden's training, I would do just that. However, Amroth is too important. He is my charge, and I will not betray Luthur's trust."

Kara smiled softly. She knew that would be the case. For all her brother's faults, his sense of loyalty was steadfast. "Well, don't say I didn't offer," she stated casually. "Besides, I think we both know that rushing south blind to the Betrayers' intents would be foolish at best. We know they have a nest there, and we can deal with it once our situation is stable. So, what do you want from me?"

Damion smiled at his sister, appreciative of her level-headed assessment. "You and Mat are needed here, as I'm sure you already knew. As for Amroth, a trip to Solarson will be more beneficial than anything else. Having someone in a similar situation to train with should ease both their struggles."

Kara shook her head, conceding the point. They'd had this debate soon after she'd recovered from her ordeal and informed her brother of the current state of the Wardens. While the discussion had been mostly amicable, there was one issue that still rubbed her wrong – getting to Solarson. He had refused to answer when she pointed out they were going the wrong way if a harbor was what they sought, but it really didn't matter. Their inland direction made it clear he had

Portculim travel in mind. Granted, there was a moratorium on Portculim travel – which she knew her brother didn't give a damn about – nor was she aware of a gate that existed in Caith'tol. However, it was clear that he'd thought this through thoroughly. Besides, she had to admit that he was right.

"You're right, of course. And I have to confess that handing the Searching duties over to Lan is a weight off my shoulders." She flashed a relieved smile at him. "Still, with Lan handling things, I could send Mat home and head south myself."

"No, that won't be needed," Damion responded with a glower. "Not now, in any case. The crystals' safety is paramount."

I didn't believe you'd like that idea, and I wasn't keen on it either," Kara stated with a shrug, conceding the point. "So, how long do you think it will take you to find Lan?" she added, returning to the subject at hand.

"I didn't want to risk contacting him directly from this distance – especially if the Betrayers have eyes on him. However, I do have a general location on him." Damion suddenly smirked proudly. "From what he's told me over the years, he's done a good job of keeping the Betrayers' focus on him when they weren't nosing about for ways to get into the Valley."

Kara grinned. "Indeed," she said, mimicking her brother. "It was smart to have him along. Although, now that I think about it, I have to wonder what Darkon would think if he knew you had recruited Lan into this mess. We always thought Darius had simply sent him in search of you."

Damion grunted. "It was a little of both, I suppose."

Kara chuckled. "Whatever the truth of the matter is, I would imagine it drove some of the Betrayers mad wondering what he was doing here on his own," she said with a hint of satisfied amusement. "But," she then added, her tone turning wistful, "things might have gone differently had he remained with Darius."

Damion nodded solemnly. "I know. But he was my fir'gan-sensitive eyes for me while I was . . . hampered, and he was extra protection for Amroth. Besides, he and Darius knew the risks."

"He won't be happy when you tell him about Darius," Kara stated bluntly.

"None of us were," Damion responded gravely.

Kara sighed and nodded. "Okay. Then what do you want from us while you're gone?"

"Keep moving west. You should easily be within Caith'tol territory by the time I return."

"Simple enough," Kara replied with a nod. "What should we do with Amroth?"

"Go ahead and start teaching him to meditate. He needs to be able to reach and control his fir'gan on a conscious level. As it stands now, he's a danger to everyone."

Kara nodded firmly before an amused smile crept onto her face. "Care to bet that he'll blush with embarrassment?"

Damion shook his head with an amused chuckle. "That's a loaded bet, Sister. I think I'll pass."

Kara shrugged. "Suit yourself." Eyeing the hilts jutting over Damion's shoulder, she asked seriously, "Taking those with you?"

"Indeed. I've left Mat's swords in the wagon. Make sure he gets them and hands over his current blades to Amroth."

Kara arched an eyebrow curiously. "Ready to trust Mat, are we?"

Damion grunted. "Not completely – no. However, I'm far more comfortable with him armed with his crusader while I'm gone. Besides, if he gets out of line, I'm sure you can remind him of his place."

"Understood," Kara replied with a slight smirk. "When do you plan on giving Amroth his swords back?"

"At the earliest, after I've repaired my crusader. However, he's got to be ready for them – no matter what."

Kara eyed him suspiciously. "And just how do you plan on repairing your crusader?"

Damion patted the shoulder strap of his pack. "Ember lent me one of his scales."

Kara rolled her eyes. "Well, that's reassuring. Sure, it should suffice to bond the broken bits of its shell, but just where are you going to find the tools to melt the scale and reforge the blade?"

Smiling, Damion patted her on the shoulder. "Don't concern yourself with it."

Kara rolled her eyes again, then shook her head. "Fine," she conceded. "I'll take care of Amroth while you're gone. You just make sure to get back here with Lan without incident. Okay?"

"I will," Damion assured her. Offering her a last, reassuring smile, he then turned and trotted in the direction of the road.

Kara followed him visually until he vanished from sight, then via the currents. After a moment, she felt a surge along the currents before his presence began to travel east at an impressive speed. After he turned north, Kara followed his signal for a moment longer before withdrawing her senses. Then, with a sigh and a shake of her head, she rejoined the others.

Upon entering their camp, she was pleased to see everyone was awake. A small cook fire had been lit with fresh tender, and a makeshift spit suspended a small pot over it. Mat was rummaging through a supply pack, likely in search of something to boil in the pot, while Ember was seated against the rock formation, busily maintaining his claymore. Amroth, however, was sitting before the fire with his legs crossed and his shoulders bowed.

As she started across the camp, Ember looked up at her inquisitively. Giving him a reassuring nod, Kara then positioned herself on the opposite side of the fire from Amroth and crouched down, drawing a quick glance from the young Merandith. It was clear that Amroth had not slept well. His eyes were red and bleary, his hair was tasseled, and his expression was long and empty.

"I can't blame him," she thought as he looked back down. *"Too much has changed over the millennia. Hells, it's not like it was all that easy to adapt even then."* Another more amusing thought crossed her mind, and she fought the urge to grin.

However, before she could say a word, Amroth asked without looking up, "I've been meaning to ask, why are we so far west?"

Kara blinked, caught off guard by the question, but not unprepared. "We're taking you somewhere where we can train you without putting others at risk," she stated smoothly.

Amroth let out an almost imperceptible grunt. "More mysteries. . . . Great," he muttered.

"Speaking of training," Kara stated cheerfully, ignoring Amroth's dour mood and moving the conversation back to more important issues, "let's get yours started. First, I want you to stand up, Amroth."

Amroth looked up and gave her a blank look before asking in a tiered tone, "What?"

Standing, Kara repeated, "Stand up."

With a resigned sigh, Amroth slowly did as he was asked. Curious as to what Kara had in mind, Ember stopped cleaning his sword to watch.

"What now?" Amroth asked as Mat crouched by the fire and

dropped a handful of oats into the pot of boiling water.

"One of the most important skills a Warden can master is the ability to meditate," she stated, fighting the urge to grin.

Mat looked at her knowingly. "This should be good," he muttered as he stood up and stepped away from the fire.

Amroth glanced at Mat curiously. However, before he could ask what Mat meant, Kara said, "Through mediation, we strengthen our bond with both our inner fir'gan and the currents around us. Furthermore, meditation helps us focus and find balance."

Sighing, Amroth said, "Fine. So what do you want me to do? As far as I know, I've never heard of someone standing to meditate."

Unable to fight off her smile any longer, her full lips parted in a wide, amused grin, drawing a concerned and baffled look from Amroth. She then said, "Of course not. You'll be sitting. But first — I need you to strip."

Any sign of sleepiness vanished from Amroth as his eyes widened and he began to blush furiously. "Excuse me?" he blurted.

"I need you to strip," she repeated as her sky-blue eyes twinkled with mirth. When Amroth simply gawked at her, she added, "Come now, it's not like you have anything I haven't seen before."

Embarrassed beyond the capacity to speak, the color in Amroth's cheeks grew even more pronounced as he gawked at her.

Rolling her eyes, Kara sighed before declaring, "Very well. If you won't do it, then I will."

Amroth recoiled instinctively, further widening Kara's smile. Taking hold of the currents, Kara used them to unbuckle Amroth's belt.

"Wait!" Amroth exclaimed in surprise. "What are you doing?"

Smiling, Kara said, "Undressing you, of course," as she unlaced his pants.

"I don't need to see this," Mat declared as Amroth's breeches slid to the ground.

With his cheeks redder than the reddest cherry, Amroth held his hands up, pleading for Kara to stop. "Alright!" Amroth cried as Mat moved to the wagon and pretended to inspect it. "Please stop!" he begged in embarrassment as he felt the bottom of his shirt being tugged upward.

Grinning with unabashed glee, Kara let go of the currents,

and Amroth's shirt settled into place. "Very well – but if you don't strip down, I'll do the rest," she declared playfully.

Amroth looked to Ember for support, only to receive an uninterested shrug from him. "Fine," he declared as he returned his gaze to Kara. Pulling his shirt off, Amroth tossed it to the side.

As she watched the play of Amroth's corded muscles beneath his warm skin as he fidgeted, she found herself once again admiring how handsome he was. "Boots and small clothes, too," she added as she felt her cheeks grow a bit warm.

Gawking at her, Amroth struggled to find the words to protest her order. Finding none, he sighed heavily before pulling his boots and pants off, and then, with a bit of hesitation, his small clothes. Covering his crotch with his hands, he stood upright and asked bitterly, "Are you satisfied now?"

Arching an eyebrow, Kara said, "Quite." Gesturing to the ground, she added, "Take a seat," before lowering herself to the ground and crossing her legs.

Muttering to himself, Amroth followed her example, conscious of keeping his crotch covered. "Is this really necessary?" he pleaded, his embarrassment palpable.

"That it is," Kara chimed. "Nudity is our natural state; we come into the world this way, and our flesh is as much a part of Kylir as the dirt and leaves you are seated upon. If it helps, think of it as bathing your body in the currents."

"So, I'm what? Trying to clean myself with something I can't see?" he asked cynically.

Kara laughed. "That's one way of looking at it. Being nude removes a barrier between you and the currents, and is also symbolic in that it shows a break from the material world." She smirked playfully, "If the bathing analogy doesn't work for you, think of it as making love to a beautiful girl; it's a bit of work and well worth the rewards."

Amroth somehow managed to blush even more as he dropped his eyes to the ground, drawing musical laughter from Kara. When she finally recovered, she offered, "I'm sorry, Amroth. I was trying to lighten the mood."

"Right," he muttered.

"Humor aside, this is important," Kara said, her tone turning instructional. "It will help you to strengthen your bond with fir'gan, and more importantly, it is something that will help you to deal with what you may experience as a Warden." When Amroth did not respond, she added gently, "Please, Amroth. Trust me – this is important to you and to us all. We need you to learn to reach and control your fir'gan."

After a moment, Amroth let out a deep sigh and looked up. Embarrassment was still prevalent on his face, but in his eyes, she saw a burgeoning willingness to cooperate.

"Fine," he declared. "What do I need to do?"

Smiling warmly, Kara said, "Thank you. Now, I want you to position your arms like so." Extending her arms, she rested her wrists on her knees to demonstrate.

The color began to rise in Amroth's cheeks once again as he realized such a position would leave him exposed. Taking a deep breath, he focused on Kara's eyes as he slowly mimicked her pose.

Unable to help herself, Kara's gaze briefly strayed downward, causing Amroth to turn a bright red. Feeling a sudden warmth in her own loins, Kara looked up quickly and cleared her throat, drawing an amused laugh from Ember. Ignoring her brother, Kara stated as firmly as she could, "We have a lot to teach you, and no idea how long we have to do so. By the time Damion returns, I want you to be able to find your inner fir'gan and draw it forth. Is that understood?"

Amroth nodded.

"Good. Let's get started. We've got a lot to do before breakfast."

Chapter Eleven

Old Man Gibbon was a village favorite. He'd seen more summers than most of the residents, but he still possessed good eyesight, a quick wit, and a zest for life and farming. In his younger years, he fought in the Third Great War, but he now spent most of his days helping his sons tend the farm that would one day fall to his eldest boy. At night, he could typically be found in the village tavern spinning tales of the peaceful days under Kale's grandfather, Doms Uthur Merandith, or reminding all of the tragedies and heroes of the Great Wars.

On this particular day, winter was teasing the North with its bitter teeth. A gentle but chilly wind was prevalent, and the air was just cold enough to sting the back of his throat. However, Gibbon didn't mind the conditions. Instead, it not only invigorated him, but it also made for a good day to sow his fields with the large light-green seeds that filled the burlap sack hanging over his once-strong, but now bowed, shoulders. Once planted, the seeds would spend a good portion of the early winter beneath the snow before growing up poles, which would be added later, and giving birth to tasty snow-white apples.

Standing up slowly from the trio of seeds he'd just buried in the tilled field, Gibbon ground his bony knuckles into the small of his back and stretched the aching muscles. Their work that day was relatively easy thanks to the gentle early winter snows that had been falling sporadically for days. Granted, the moisture in the ground froze overnight, but the sun would quickly turn the topsoil to a workable mush a few hours after dawn. As such, the spongy, somewhat muddy earth had worked with them throughout the morning.

Looking around with his blue eyes, which flanked a broad nose on his sun-darkened, gray-bearded face, he saw his two youngest sons – which he'd had with his third, and last, wife. Nineteen and twelve summers, respectively, they were nearly done with the small field to the west of their modest thatch-roofed farmhouse. Shifting his gaze to the east, he noted that his three oldest boys – ranging from thirty to forty-five summers in age – were nearly halfway done with the largest of their three fields. Running his hand over his baldhead, Gibbon smiled contently. While none of his fields was overly large, they would produce enough of the tasty apples to support him and his youngest through the latter part of winter and on into the spring planting season.

Wiping his dirt-stained hands on his worn, thick brown tunic, he then positioned his thumb and forefinger in his mouth and whistled sharply. The crisp noise echoed through the cold air, drawing the attention of his sons. "Lunchtime, boys! Come on in!" Gibbon shouted with a deep voice that was rough with age.

With a couple of shouts of joy, his sons finished what they were doing and began hustling toward the farmhouse. Gibbon followed suit, his thick, aged black work boots cushioned his feet as best as they could as he lumbered toward the house. As Gibbon rounded the front corner of their abode and approached the front porch steps, the oldest of his sons smiled warmly at him. Dressed in a mix of gray, brown and black wool worker's garb similar to his brothers, he looked remarkably like Gibbon did at that age.

Gibbon returned the smile as his son said, "Take a seat, Father. Crispin and I will fetch the food."

"Much appreciated, lad," Gibbon replied as he ascended the trio of steps leading up to the porch with a wince. "My bones are already aching. There's a big snow coming – mark my words."

His son smiled, his blue eyes shining against his sun-darkened skin and long locks of sweat-soaked, brown hair. "That it will, Father."

As Gibbon ambled past him and seated himself in an old chair at an equally old table that was big enough for four people, he said to his youngest son, "Crispin, obey your brother, you hear? The rest of you, wash up."

Eager to please, the boy named Crispin, a dainty youth with a head full of curly red locks, and vibrant brown eyes, nodded vigorously before scrambling to the door and opening it for the eldest sibling. As he was doing that, Crispin's other brothers left the porch and made for the stone well set between the house and the stone wall surrounding their property. Gibbon smiled affectionately at Crispin as he proceeded inside behind his oldest stepbrother. He was his mother's son, and it tore at Gibbon's heart that it was unlikely he would be around to see the boy become a man. Still, he was proud. The youngest boys were well-mannered and behaved, and the oldest always made time to help their father after attending to their own fields.

By the time Crispin and his stepbrother returned with two baskets and a pair of sealed bottles, the rest of Gibbon's sons had seated themselves around the table where they could find space. As Crispin and the oldest son went about distributing the simple meal of dried meats, bread and preserved fruit on tin plates, the rattle of tack and the clatter of shod hooves arose in the distance.

Tearing off a portion of the black bread on his plate, Gibbon began chewing on the cold morsel as he peered at the riders coming up the dirt road at a quick pace. "Looks to be the noon patrol. They're a mite early, though," Gibbon said to no one in particular. Shrugging, he asked his oldest son, "Tannis, do we have any apple brandy to spare?"

Tannis nodded. "I think we can spare a bottle."

"Fetch one for the lads. Wouldn't do not to show our appreciation."

Popping a grape in his mouth, Tannis nodded again. "Yes, Father," he stated around the morsel as he wiped his hands on his trousers and stood. Stepping around the table, he entered the house, returning a moment later with a small bottle of clear liquid.

Standing at the top of the stairs, Tannis watched as the riders came to a halt before the wall's gate and dismounted. "Welcome, lads!" Tannis declared as the three men and two women in leather armor and the five-star emblazoned, black tabards of House Merandith opened the gate and entered the grounds.

Well-armed with swords and bows, the group had a veteran presence about them. "Well met," the blonde-haired, middle-aged man in the lead declared. Gesturing to the well, he asked, "Mind if we have a drink and refill our skins?"

Gibbon peered curiously at the party of Merandith soldiers as Tannis replied, "Not at all. Help yourselves."

Nodding his thanks, the sergeant motioned to the others, who then approached the well.

As Tannis descended the steps and approached the sergeant, Gibbon pushed himself to his feet and walked over to the porch railing. "I haven't seen you all around here before," he declared with a hint of guarded suspicion as Tannis presented the bottle to the sergeant.

"Thanks," the sergeant said to Tannis before turning his stern gaze on Gibbon. "The regulars got shifted to the south yesterday," he declared as if it were common knowledge. Pulling the cork out of the bottle with his teeth, he spit it out. "We're transfers from the Ildoran Garrison; just got here today, and we're on our way to report in at Harden," he added before taking a swig from the bottle. Swallowing with a smile, the sergeant peered at the bottle and then looked at Gibbon, "Damn fine drink! Got any more of it in there?"

Ignoring the question, Gibbon asked suspiciously as Tannis ascended the stairs, "Ildoran Garrison? Seems unusual to transfer someone from so far away."

"It is," the sergeant replied as his men finished at the well and rejoined him.

Gibbon looked at his son as he stood next to him. They'd all heard the rumors of raiders in the north, and Tannis noted the concern in his dad's eyes right away. "What is it, Father?" he asked softly.

With an almost imperceptible shake of his head, Gibbon looked at the sergeant and asked, "Before you get going, mind telling me who's in charge of Fort Harden these days? Getting hard to keep track of things in my old age."

Though the sergeant smiled at him broadly, it seemed forced to Gibbon. "Captain-Commander Forthal," he stated.

By this point, most of Gibbon's sons had noticed the growing tension in the air, and many had edged toward the porch railing. "Forthal?" Gibbon asked. "I thought he'd died six months ago from a bad heart?"

The smile suddenly vanished from the sergeant's face. "Former soldier, are you?"

Gibbon nodded.

Hanging his head, the sergeant shook it. Looking up at Gibbon, he said, "Now that's a damn shame. Cloe?"

In a rush, a short, brown-haired woman stepped from behind the sergeant, and the sunlight glinted off something in her hand as her left arm went up and came down hard. With a whistle, the dagger cut through the air and buried itself in Gibbon's heart, causing him to stumble back as screams erupted from his family.

"Father!" Tannis bellowed as he caught Gibbon.

"Run," Gibbon managed to plead weakly as Tannis lowered him to the ground amidst the thud of pounding footsteps as the rest of Gibbon's sons bolted toward the ends of the porch, and the soldiers scrambled to catch them.

Eyes wide with terror, Tannis looked up to see the sergeant approaching confidently with his sword drawn.

"Run," he repeated his father's orders weakly, but his muscles refused to respond.

"A damn shame," the sergeant said as he climbed the stairs. "Not that we wouldn't have killed you, but it would have been a whole lot easier if he hadn't been so damn curious." Shrugging as he reached Tannis, he added, "Oh well."

Numb with shock and staring blankly at the sergeant, Tannis never saw the flash of steel nor felt the sword as it pierced his chest and tore through his lung.

Kicking Tannis' body clear of his blade, the sergeant watched with amusement as the body hit the porch, blood trickling from Tannis' lips as his lungs filled with the crimson liquid. Then, a thud from the sergeant's right drew his attention. Looking over quickly, he saw an overturned chair and Crispin backing away slowly with a horrified expression on his face. Grinning devilishly as he heard screams from behind the farmhouse split the air, the sergeant brandished his sword and barked, "Boo!"

Startled, Crispin flinched before turning and scrambling toward the opposite end of the porch with terror-spurred haste.

Chuckling, the sergeant let the boy squeeze between the railing's supports before giving chase. Vaulting over the railing, he landed nimbly and turned toward the back of the farmhouse. Right away, he spotted the boy, who was nearly halfway to the rear of the house, scrambling to his feet. Whether the child had tripped or fallen was irrelevant to the sergeant. All that mattered was eliminating the child. Grinning with satisfaction, the sergeant jogged toward the boy, who looked back over his shoulder at him. Horrified, Crispin took off at a sprint, prompting the sergeant to quicken his pace.

Just as it occurred to the sergeant that some of his men should have returned by now, the strangest man, wielding the strangest bow, he'd ever seen stepped out from behind the house. The sight of this man brought the sergeant to a sudden stop, and the boy stumbled and fell. In an instant, the sergeant forgot about the child as the cold grip of shock and fear latched ahold of his heart with an intensity he'd never experienced. However, it wasn't the purple-trimmed white tabard with five red stars on the right breast, or his off-white garb that caused his reaction. Nor was it the man's shoulder-length white hair, or the unbridled violence he saw in the man's ice-blue eyes. Rooted in place by fear, the sergeant barely even noted the man's skin-tight white fur, nor the white-fur-tipped long ears that flanked a cat-like face. No, what robbed him so thoroughly of his faculties was the weapon the man held at the ready.

Its ends carved in the likeness of a roaring dragon, the white bow was the largest the sergeant had ever seen. And if the size wasn't enough to inspire dread, then the bloodstained, sweeping blades affixed to its length made sure of it. It was horrifying to behold, and the sergeant knew instantly he was doomed.

With fluid movements, Allanian raised the bow in his right hand, and drew a red-fletched arrow with a barbed steel head from the leather quiver on his back. Knocking the arrow along the top of the bow-shield protecting his bow hand, he let loose. Even as the arrow cut through the air, he drew and fired a second and then a third arrow. The first slammed through the sergeant's chest, followed by the second, driving him back a bit before the third tore a ragged hole between his eyes.

As the gaping sergeant fell to the ground, a blonde-haired woman with a blood-stained sword rounded the corner just as the arrows flew by, embedding themselves in the ground a few feet short of the property wall. Surprised by the arrows' flight, she quickly turned to see her mutilated commander on the ground. Horrified by the sight, she let out a shrill scream.

Allanian's thick lips pulled back in a snarl beneath his broad, flat nose – revealing elongated canines – as he stepped past the prone and terrified redheaded boy gawking at him. With what seemed like arrogant confidence, he once more let fly repeatedly. The first two arrows tore through the woman's knees, nearly cutting her lower legs off. Screaming in raw, unbridled agony, her shattered legs collapsed beneath her, and she fell to what remained of her knees. That scream, however, came to an abrupt end as the third arrow punched through her throat, embedding itself and a chunk of her neck above the other two arrows already planted firmly in the property wall.

Ears and nostrils twitching slightly, Allanian approached the fallen woman cautiously, his toe-heel stride lending him a haunting grace. When he reached her, he spared her only a cursory glance before using his sharp senses to probe the immediate area. Once he was satisfied that there were no remaining threats, he retrieved his arrows before crouching by the woman's body. Placing his bow on the ground, he began quickly cleaning the arrows with the end of the tabard the dead woman wore while keeping an eye on the redheaded boy.

Seated on the ground with his knees drawn up to his chest, the boy was pale as he peered over his knees at Allanian with terrified eyes. Meeting the boy's distraught gaze, Allanian felt anger twist his gut. *"So senseless,"* he thought with disdain.

Retrieving his bow, he stood up and returned the last arrow to his quiver before he gave the corpse an angry kick and approached the boy. As soon as Allanian took a step, Crispin screamed and began scrambling backward. Allanian immediately froze and held up his hands in a placating manner. "Easy now," he said in an attempt to calm Crispin, his haunting voice softer than normal. "I'm not going to hurt you.”

The boy paused and his screams came to an end at Allanian’s gentle tone, but he continued to stare at the unusual man with frightful eyes.

“Good,” Allanian offered with a friendly smile. “My name is Allanian. I’m with House Merandith. We’ve been tracking these criminals for a while now. I’m so sorry for what happened to your family, but their murderers are dead now. I’m here to help you, but you’ll need to trust me. Okay?”

When Crispin didn’t respond, Allanian took another step forward and came to an immediate halt as the child once again scrambled away, maintaining the distance between them. “Okay, okay. Take it easy. I’m not going to hurt you,” Allanian said calmly. To emphasize his point, he slowly crouched down and deposited his bow and quiver on the ground. “See,” he said, gesturing to the discarded weapons, “there’s nothing to fear here.”

The boy’s eyes darted to the fearsome weapon, then back to Allanian. To Allanian’s dismay, the terror in his eyes was still as virile as before. Taking a deep, calming breath, Allanian let it out slowly. “Listen to me,” he finally said, “we can’t stay in the open. While I don’t believe we’re in any danger right now, I’d rather not take any chances.” He smiled warmly and extended a welcoming hand, “How about you?”

Once again, Crispin remained mute. Fighting down a growing sense of frustration, Allanian stood back up and stepped forward. Like before, the boy started to scramble away. Seeking to put an end to this pointless dance, Allanian took a few quick steps forward. Spurred by the darlion’s sudden advance, Crispin bolted to his feet and tried to run away.

Scowling, Allanian’s ears pinned back slightly as he darted forward with incredible speed and wrapped his arms around the child before he could go more than a few feet. Screaming and flailing about, Crispin fought against Allanian’s strong hold, but there was no budging his grasp.

“Easy, now!” Allanian said soothingly. Freeing a hand, he began to stroke the boy’s hair. “It’s alright. You’re safe. Easy, easy, easy,” he urged calmly.

Ever so slowly, Crispin’s struggles ceased, and he eventually went limp in Allanian’s arms, exhausted. Adjusting his grip on the boy, Allanian let out a remorseful sigh before making his way to the home’s front door. Climbing the stairs, he silently offered a quick prayer as he stepped over the dead bodies. Shouldering open the wooden door, he entered the home.

Modest in size, the large room he stood in featured a rustic kitchen and a living room that was separated by a large dining table and its chairs. At the back of the room, a pair of openings led to the home's other rooms. Off to his right, Allanian noticed a trio of simple chairs facing a modest hearth. Making his way over to the chairs, he gently deposited Crispin in the center one before grabbing the red and green patchwork coverlet resting on the back of the chair to his left and gently covered the boy up. Allanian then turned his attention to the hearth, where he saw a pile of freshly split logs neatly arranged within the brick opening. Suddenly, surging flames erupted from the logs, bathing the room with a rush of heat. Allanian nodded with satisfaction as the fire settled into a natural burn before he went back outside.

A moment later, he returned with his quiver and bow in hand. Depositing the items on the cedar dining table, he then secured the door before stationing himself near the front-right window. From there, he had a decent view of the surrounding area, and an unobstructed view to the north. Folding his arms across his chest, he leaned against the wall to wait.

Minutes drifted into an hour, and through it all, only the crackling fire breached the heavy silence that consumed the hauntingly empty house. Suddenly tired of maintaining his watch, Allanian checked on Crispin. It seemed like he hadn't moved at all, and he was staring blankly at the fire. With a sad shake of his head, Allanian ventured over to the kitchen and began inspecting the cabinets and containers. Eventually, he found what he was looking for and he set aside a small clay container. Moving to the porch, he retrieved the pitcher of water on the table before returning to the kitchen.

Once more, he scoured the kitchen; this time, however, he quickly found what he was looking for. Pulling the kettle from the cabinet hanging over the counter, he removed its lid before filling it to the proper level with water from the pitcher. Opening the clay container, he pulled out a generous pinch of brown leaves and deposited them in the kettle. As he placed the lid on the kettle, he glanced over at the hearth to see if there was a hook from which to suspend the kettle over the warm blaze. Once he spotted what he was looking for, he moved to the fire and positioned the hook before hanging the kettle from it.

Checking on the boy once more to ensure he was still oblivious to his surroundings, Allanian turned his focus to the fire and kettle. Gently, the flame's intensity grew, and the temperature in the room increased. With unusual speed, the kettle soon began to hiss, which quickly morphed into the telltale whistle of a beverage ready to serve. Ignoring the kettle's hot handle, Allanian retrieved it before returning to the kitchen. Finding a suitable cup, he poured the dark, steaming beverage into it before depositing the hot kettle on a towel. Grabbing the cup, he cooled the liquid to a drinkable temperature as he returned to Crispin.

Crouching down before the child, Allanian was pleased that not only did the boy meet his gaze, but he also showed no signs of panicking. Still, there was a detachment in the boy's eyes that was heart-wrenching. Presenting the cup with a warm smile, Allanian said confidently, "Here, drink this – it's tea. It will make you feel better."

Slowly, the blanket parted, and the boy hesitantly reached out to take the cup. Bringing it to his lips, he gradually sipped on it. Even as a bit of the tea dribbled down his chin, a slight smile tugged at the corners of his mouth as the tea's warmth spread throughout his body.

Smiling, Allanian said, "That's better. Take your time; I'll be over by the door if you need me."

An almost imperceptible nod greeted Allanian's statement, which he returned before standing and resuming his post at the window.

Another hour of awkward silence passed as Allanian maintained his watch. Occasionally, he would check on Crispin to assure himself that the child wasn't in danger of suffering too deeply from shock. Once he was satisfied, he would return to the window. This went on for a while longer before Allanian's sharp vision finally caught sight of what he'd been looking for all this time.

Moving to the table, he shouldered his quiver before gathering up his bow. Giving the grip a firm twist, he heard a gentle click and saw the bowstring release from the top knock of the bow. With a soft hum, the string wound itself into a recess in the bottom of the weapon. Giving the grip a firm twist, there was a click, and he pulled the bow apart at the grip, the bow-shield of which separated along its length. Allanian then gave the sword-like ends a twirl before sheathing them through a loop on his belt at each hip.

"I'll be back in just a moment," he offered to Crispin as he settled his full quiver on his back.

Unsurprised by the lack of a blatant response from the child, Allanian exited the gloomy house. Making his way to the stone fence surrounding the farm, Allanian turned his gaze to the north. Thanks to his sharp eyes, he could already see the mounted party in the distance; furthermore, his acute hearing could already discern the thunder of hooves. Within moments, could tell that the party riding hard in his direction consisted of ten well-armed soldiers in House Merandith's House Guard tabards.

Even as Allanian let out a relieved sigh, he cringed inwardly as he double-checked their numbers. Expecting only moderate resistance, he had returned to where he'd first encountered raiders just over two weeks ago, south of Gast, with eighteen of his best men. To his chagrin, they had quickly discovered that House Suldamik's presence in the North was far more extensive and deadly than they had imagined. The enemy raiders they typically encountered numbered between four and eight – and on those occasions, they managed to dispose of them with relative ease. Unfortunately, that wasn't always the case. On at least a half-dozen occasions, they found themselves tracking and confronting well-trained groups that numbered around a dozen strong.

It was in the aftermath of their first battle with one of the larger groups that they discovered the smaller parties would join up to attack villages and large farms. Overconfident from their smaller skirmishes, Allanian had sent six men to investigate reports of a burned-out village while he and the rest of his squad continued to patrol the area. When two days passed and the men did not return, Allanian led the others back to the village only to discover all six were dead, their corpses impaled on impromptu pikes and left to rot. After investigating the scene, he came to the inescapable conclusion they'd been ambushed by a force much larger than what they'd encountered up to that point.

Incensed and desperately wanting revenge, he and his remaining men tracked the offenders only to discover the tracks split up into a trio of smaller groups. Unwilling to repeat his mistake, Allanian kept his squad together as they hunted the groups down one by one. Thanks to Allanian's skills, they quickly found their targets and slaughtered them, but that did little to placate his anger with himself. Men had died under his command due to an inexcusable error in judgment – and that was unacceptable.

Since then, his unit had remained together and suffered only minor injuries. This morning, however, he'd judged it worth the risk to set out alone. There'd been word of two groups raiding the area, slaughtering farmers and unwary travelers. None of the reports indicated the attacking forces were larger than maybe six men, so Allanian had decided to track one group himself while his men hunted the other. To his chagrin, as he once again counted those riding toward him, he had to wonder if it had been a mistake to do so.

As they drew closer, Allanian's face sank a bit as he noted

that they had indeed seen battle. While a few of them were hosts to new cuts, bruises, and dressings, they all had freshly spilt blood on their clothing. Letting out a deep, calming breath, he reminded himself not to jump to conclusions. The missing men could simply be unable to ride, or they might have been given other duties to attend to. He knew it was overly optimistic to entertain those thoughts, and as he watched the lead rider spur her mount forward, he felt those hopeful, fleeting thoughts fade away.

Wry and tall, the woman riding hard toward him looked grim in her blood-spattered House Guard tabard, black shirt, and brown pants. Her gray eyes were hard astride her slightly crooked, slim nose, and the thin lips of her petite mouth were pressed together firmly. Reaching the fence, she reined in her tired buckskin and dismounted quickly. As soon as her feet in their black knee-boots touched the ground, she immediately pulled a sheathed shortsword from its place in her saddle harness and slipped it through her sturdy brown belt. Sunlight glossed over the lone star emblazoned on her elbow-length bracers as she ran calloused hands through her short, chopped auburn hair.

Dropping her hands to her sides, she then saluted, fist to heart, before saying, her normally quiet voice thick with frustration, "Captain." She then noted the mutilated corpses and smirked devilishly. "I see you sent these bastards screaming to the deepest pit of the Hells."

Allanian nodded. "Sergeant," he greeted her formally, a hard edge to his normally soft voice. "That I did. . . . Though, I was too late to save the entire family," he added remorsefully before asking, "What's the news, Camilie?"

Camilie eyed the shattered bodies once more before scowling and turning her gaze on Allanian. "Not as good as I'd like to report. We found the rest of the raiders lurking damn close to Rirdan – just like you figured." She shook her head in disgust. "There were a dozen of them, Captain, and they're all good and dead; but if we hadn't taken them by surprise, we would have fared far worse."

"Damn," he thought, chastising himself. Aloud, he asked softly, dreading the answer, "Losses?"

"We lost Illia. . . . Bastards took her head," she spit angrily. "And Lieutenant Fallain took a blade in his shoulder."

Allanian's ears twitched in irritation slightly. "Will he be alright?"

Camilie shrugged. "Should be. Riding would have hurt like the hells, but that's not why we left him behind. He thought he might be of better use to Captain-Commander Rometh given the . . . unexpected situation at the fort."

Allanian cocked an eyebrow, noting the hint of surprise and concern in her voice. "What?" he prodded.

She ran her hand through her hair again. "Dunno if it was dumb luck or sheer coincidence, but we may have avoided a disaster by taking out these Suldamik bastards when we did."

"Spit it out, Sergeant," Allanian ordered, mildly irritated by her procrastination.

Taking a deep breath, she said, "Ice Walkers, Captain. There's two dozen of them camped just outside Fort Harden."

Allanian blinked in astonishment. "This is a joke, right?"

Shaking her head adamantly, Camilie added as the rest of their party, along with an extra brown-dappled mount, came to a halt at the fence and dismounted, "Afraid not, and it gets better. It appears to be a royal party."

"Damn. . . . This is bad timing, but we should have anticipated this," he stated, somewhat annoyed, his ears twitching slightly.

"Captain?" Camilie asked curiously.

"It's likely Doms Merandith's grandfather has come to bear witness to his great-grandchild's birth. He made the trip for the shi'doma, but I never thought he'd be healthy enough to make it again." Frustrated with the unexpected news, Allanian shook his head. "That's for later," he declared before eyeing his squad. "For now, I want you all to sweep the area again and dispose of the Jade Talon bodies. There's two here in the front, and the rest are in the back. Check for anything useful, then drag the bodies into the wild. Let the animals dispose of these fools."

Camilie snorted derisively. "Better than they deserve," she muttered.

"Sergeant – you're in charge," Allanian ordered. "I want this done quickly. We have one survivor – a young boy – and I want to get him out of here. If we're not back in Rirdan by sunset, I'm sure I can find something creative to occupy your night. Is that understood?"

Camilie feigned a scowl. The squad knew he wasn't likely to mete out unnecessary punishment; this was just Allanian's way of trying to lighten the mood and emphasize the urgency of his orders. "Perfectly, sir."

"Good. When you're done with the enemy corpses, collect

the fallen farmers; we'll be delivering them to the priests for proper burial. Come find me in the house when you're done," Allanian added before turning on his heel and making for the house.

"Alright, you whoresons!" Allanian heard Camilie bark as he walked away. "You heard the Captain – let's make sure this place is as secure as a chastity belt, and deliver the Deo-damned Suldamik scum to the beasts!" As Allanian opened the front door to the house, his sharp hearing caught her muttering, "Poor beasts. . . . Deo knows they don't deserve the sour gullets they're gonna have tonight."

The sun was well into its easterly descent by the time they finished at the farm. To no one's surprise, no other raiders had been found, and nothing of merit had been discovered on the dead. As for the lone survivor of the massacre, Allanian – despite his best efforts to get the boy to talk – was only able to learn that the boy was called Crispin. Outside of that short, mumbled admission, a subtle nod or shake of the head was the best he could get from the boy in response to his gentle inquiries. It wasn't a lot, nor was it helpful, but Allanian was more than happy to be content with that. He'd seen such shock before, and the last thing he wanted to do was inflame the damage that had already been done. As such, his gently worded questions were intended more to create a warm and friendly atmosphere for the traumatized boy than anything else.

When Camilie finally informed him that they were ready to depart, Allanian did his best to collect some of what he believed to be the boy's clothing before gently gathering Crispin up in his arms. To Allanian's relief, the child was either unwilling or too tired to put up a struggle. Wrapping his arms protectively around the boy, Allanian carried him through the door, which Camilie shut with a haunting finality. As he made his way to his brown-dappled mount, he made sure to shield Crispin's vision from the sight of his dead family respectfully strapped to the back of his squads' mounts. Reaching his horse, Allanian used his eerie strength and agility to swing himself into the saddle while still carrying Crispin. Sliding back on his saddle a bit, he then settled the boy in front of him before collecting his reins.

Checking to make sure the rest of his squad was ready, he then declared as he turned his mount northward, "Let's get going. The living do not belong here right now."

Solemnly, the squad followed the main road north, each soldier keenly alert for any indication that there were more raiders about. Thankfully, only their thoughts and the occasional outlying resident of Rirdan joined them on the trek north. As they passed through the small village just north of the farm, curious glances and muffled conversation followed in their wake as the people they passed made note of the dead they carried. It was impossible to ignore the reactions; while death was all too common in this unceasing war, not once had actual combat come anywhere close to Tiliea, much less Merset. Now, however, rumors were abundant, and the growing number of dead civilians and ravaged farms was becoming impossible to hide or ignore. The bodies strapped to his squad's saddles would most likely fuel the stories and the dread of the fearful, but there was little Allanian could do to halt such paranoia other than to find and eliminate the threat. Unfortunately, the true nature of that menace was still a mystery. What he did know, however, was this latest attack was the most brazen of all. Not only had they posed as House Merandith troops, but Rirdan and the surrounding communities were also within a three-day hard ride of Merset – and that was unacceptable.

As night's grip consumed the sky, the lights of Rirdan began to twinkle in the distance as if welcoming the beleaguered soldiers home. Prying his vision from their destination, Allanian glanced down at Crispin. The exhausted and devastated child had fallen asleep at some point during their trek and remained that way.

"So damn pointless," Allanian thought as he fought back a scowl. *"Then again, this 'Great War' has been nothing but pointless for far too long."* He scoffed to himself. *"The curse of a short, mortal life, I suppose. People can't see past what's in front of them."* Even as that last thought crossed his mind, he found himself shaking his head mentally in chastisement. *'Right. . . . It's not like those of us with a long lifespan have done much better for Kylir and her people. Mother bless us – we're still fighting a war that we could have possibly ended a long time ago. What does that say about us?"*

With effort, Allanian pushed the cynical thoughts aside and turned his attention back to their destination.

Not remotely large enough to be considered a city, but not nearly small enough to be considered a village proper, Rirdan was a quaint farming and trade community built in the shadow of an impressive hillside. The small town was made up of primarily modest wood homes and businesses, their roofs shingled in earth tones, which lined its main thoroughfare and the handful of its thoughtfully placed roads. Light glowed in many of the buildings' windows like wisps in the night, and smoke rose from numerous chimneys as fires provided both warmth and light for Rirdan's residents. As for defenses, Rirdan was bereft of a protective wall, but it wasn't without defenders. Allanian's sharp eyes had already spotted several mounted patrols making their rounds about the fringe of the village. Those soldiers were residents of Rirdan's only defensive feature, Fort Harden, which overlooked the small town from its perch on the hill.

Glancing at the stone-walled fort, Allanian could see that the wall torches were lit, and the battlements were adequately manned. Home to just over two-hundred House Merandith troops and personnel, Fort Harden provided protection to the town and the outlying area; furthermore, the fort's commander acted as a local magistrate when it came to minor legal disputes. As for grievous crimes or grave issues, those were handed over to House Merandith due to Rirdan's proximity to Merset. It was a somewhat odd relationship – and some saw little or no difference between whether House Merandith proper or one of its military officers handled legal disputes – but it had worked well for as long as Allanian could recall. He just hoped the trust and relationship between the people and soldiers would remain solid and peaceful beneath the unexpected burden of the recent attacks.

As he brought the squad to a halt a few yards before the town, Allanian noted a few extra fires burning outside the fort's southeastern wall. *"Must be the Ice Walkers,"* he thought as he motioned Camilie forward.

"Yes, sir?" she asked as she pulled alongside him.

"Here," Allanian started to say as he gently lifted and shifted Crispin over to Camilie's saddle, "take him. From what I could tell, the child is related to at least some of these men, but I saw nothing to indicate they were married. I think it best to see that arrangements are made to have the child delivered to the Academy in Merset in case Commander Rometh is unable to locate any surviving, and willing, family to take him in." He grunted softly. "Which I don't believe will take long. It's not like we concealed anything when we passed by their village, so it wouldn't surprise me if someone is already on their way here to find out what happened. Still, let's cover all our bases just in case."

While Crispin offered only a slight moan of protest as Camilie settled him before her on her saddle, he remained asleep. "Can do," she responded.

"Good. Also, deliver the bodies to the priests for last rites. I'm going to pay a visit to our guests."

Camilie nodded. "Easy enough. Last I saw, the Ice Walkers were camped near the fort, and I'd bet those fires are them. They nearly had the town panicked when they showed up, so Rometh convinced them to steer clear of it."

Allanian nodded. "Doesn't look like they've moved. That's good. Report back to me when you're done, Sergeant. I get the feeling we're going to be headed back to Merset."

"Yes, sir," she replied with scornful regret.

Allanian ignored her tone as he angled his mount toward the fort while the others proceeded down the main road to the community and the chapel on the town green. Like her, he wasn't keen on returning to Merset with all the raider activity, but such an important party couldn't be allowed to arrive in Merset without a proper escort. Furthermore, no matter how rude it would be to leave them unescorted, if any harm were to befall their newly arrived guests, the stain on House Merandith's honor would be unimaginable.

Eager to assess the situation, Allanian made the trip to the fort quickly. At first, he considered approaching the modest encampment outside the southeastern wall directly. However, as he neared the fort, he noted his lieutenant awaiting him before its open gate doors. Without a second thought, Allanian adjusted his course so that he could check on his lieutenant first.

Drawing close, Allanian was soon able to assess Fallain's state despite the lack of proper lighting thanks to his keen eyes. The stout and bald lieutenant's skin was starkly pale against his short, braided black beard, and his large brown eyes appeared heavy with exhaustion as he watched Allanian approach. Dressed in a thick white wool shirt, brown breeches and black knee boots, he still had his shortsword sheathed at his left hip, which gave the impression that he was ready and willing to serve despite his injury.

"He's a stubborn one, I'll give him that," Allanian thought with a hint of amused admiration.

As Allanian reined in before him, he eyed Fallain's injured right arm, which rested in a sling, as he asked, a hint of mirth in his gentle tone, "How are you, Lieutenant? Camilie said the Suldamiks got the best of you."

Fallain's broad, lined face twisted into a scowl. "That's what she's saying, eh?" he replied with mock anger. "She's just looking to pick a fight, as usual. It's nothing but a scratch, sir. I'll be back in the saddle and strong as a bramhen in no time, sir – mark my words," he finished confidently, though the weak tone of his usually rough voice indicated that his injury wouldn't be so easily disregarded.

Dismounting with a small, knowing smile, Allanian approached Fallain and said, "Of that, I have no doubt." He then added in a more serious manner, "So, what's the situation here? Camilie said a party of Ice Walkers has paid us a visit."

Snorting, Fallain ran a thick, calloused hand down his braided beard. "Well, at least she got that right. Aye, they're Ice Walkers – there's no doubting those furs and bronze masks. They've got everyone's nerves on edge up here." He snorted again. "Guess we can't complain, though. The way I hear it, they scared a few of the townsfolk to death when they came marching in."

Allanian couldn't suppress an amused chuckle as he imagined the scene. "I wouldn't go that far, but their masks can be unnerving."

"Aye, sir. They are that," Fallain agreed with a nod.

"I'm glad we agree on that," Allanian quipped with a slight chuckle. He then asked, "So, where's Captain-Commander Rometh?"

Fallain tossed his head in the direction of the Ice Walker's camp. "Still at the camp. She's been trying all day to talk with whoever is in charge, but she's met with nothing but polite rebuffs. Guess they have something against women in positions of power," he finished with a shrug that drew a wince of pain from him.

"Careful with that arm, Lieutenant," Allanian offered as Fallain grabbed his shoulder protectively just shy of his wound.

"Aye, sir," Fallain hissed painfully. "It's such a slight wound that I keep forgetting it's there."

Flashing a knowing smile, Allanian said, "Of course. As for the Ice Walkers, gender has nothing to do with it. Out on the ice, everyone contributes or everyone could die. How the Mother endowed you probably matters even less to them than it does to us."

Fallain suppressed the urge to shrug again. "If you say so, sir. I just know she's nearly as irritated as a mad pine-ferret."

Allanian chuckled as he presented his reins to Fallain. "I see. Well, I think I'll venture over and see if I can be of assistance."

Taking the reins from him, Fallain said, "Don't know what good it will do; you both hold the same rank."

Winking at him knowingly, Allanian offered, "Trust me."

Fallain snorted as if the notion of doing otherwise was absurd. "Always, sir."

Patting his horse on the neck affectionately, Allanian then walked off in the direction of the Ice Walker camp.

Stone walls soon gave way to ground occupied by dome-shaped tents made of white-fur hide stretched between bone ribs. A quick count told Allanian that there were ten tents organized around a slightly larger, central pavilion above which flew a lone white pendant emblazoned with a black claw. There was no doubt that the tents were an exotic sight that, by themselves, would have inspired awe and fear in Rirdan's people. However, it was the camp's residents, many of whom stood guard around the perimeter of the camp, that were, as Fallain insinuated, truly responsible for evoking those emotions in many of the people they encountered.

Tall and strong, each of the Ice Walkers wore a thick, sleeveless longcoat of white fur over sealskin tunics and breeches. This far south of their frigid home, they had shed themselves of their warmer garments, leaving their dark-skinned, strong arms bare except for the bracers and bone arm cuffs that some wore, as well as the blue knotwork tattoos that adorned them all. White hoods concealed their hair, making it only mildly tricky to distinguish gender as their women tended to have ample breasts and broad hips, while the men had exceptionally wide shoulders and were usually much taller than their women. Those standing guard held a heavy spear at the ready and wore a broad-bladed shortsword sheathed at their hips. Yet, despite their primal garb and their brutal weapons, it was their masks that unnerved many who gazed upon them.

Made of bronze and molded into a haunting, wailing visage, the masks were identical and concealed the entire face. Originally worn only during the hunt or in times of war, the face coverings had only recently become a permanent part of the Ice Walkers' wardrobe when their doms had taken to wearing one to conceal the effects of his illness. As a sign of respect for him, his people took to wearing them, especially when in foreign lands or hosting visitors, which only served to further spread the mask's reputation. While there were some genuinely outlandish stories about the masks and their origins, Allanian had to agree that they were an eerie sight to behold. That sentiment was quickly reinforced by another of the mask's quirks, which he was reminded of when he drew close enough to clearly see the pair of intimidating guards who were preventing a Merandith officer from entering their camp with their crossed spears. The guards' masks did such an excellent job of concealing their features that, even up close, Allanian knew it would be difficult to tell where they were looking.

"This is an outrage!" Allanian heard the officer shout at the guards, her voice thick with frustration. "We let you set up camp, even though you arrive unannounced, yet your doms refuses to speak with me! I'm an officer of House Merandith, damn it! This goes beyond discourteous behavior, and Doms Merandith will hear of this!"

"I think you are overreacting just a bit, Captain," Allanian declared as he drew near.

Turning away from her silent blockade, her shoulder-length auburn ponytail snapped violently over her shoulder as Captain-Commander Rometh fixed her angry brown eyes on Allanian. A deep scowl tore across her large, full-lipped mouth, and the brow of her narrow face furrowed as she barked, "What in the hells are you doing in the area?" Shaking her head angrily, she smoothed out her purple-trimmed black tabard and added, "No! Forget about that for now – you can tell me later!" Grabbing tightly onto the hilt of the elegant longsword sheathed at her right hip, she stated bluntly, "These damn Ice Walkers are more of a problem right now!"

Halting before the short, incised officer, Allanian looked down at her and asked, his haunting voice calm, "And how are they a problem, Yavi?"

"Proper decorum!" Yavi Rometh huffed. "They've been here all day, and their doms has yet to speak with me or any representative of House Merandith except via messenger! It's dishonorable and an outrage!"

Allanian fought to keep both his ears from twitching in amusement and a grin from spreading across his face. Yavi's propensity for following regulations and decorum verbatim was her biggest flaw . . . if you could ignore the stout woman's Sur'dathan-like temper. As such, he wasn't surprised to find that the Ice Walkers' peculiar habits had drawn her ire.

"Be at peace, Yavi. While the Ice Walkers use our titles, their idea of proper decorum is quite different from ours. They mean no insult by denying to speak with you, and if the situation was different, I would guess that you would have already had the audience you seek. That, however, is not the case."

"What do yo—" Yavi started to say before realization dawned on her. Eyes suddenly wide, she let out a string of colorful curses before asking, "I'd heard the rumors, but it never occurred to me that it was true. Doms Volstur suffers from the Wasting, doesn't he?"

Allanian nodded grimly. "That he does. And because of this, he accepts very few visitors that are not of his blood."

Letting out an embarrassed sigh, Yavi hooked her thumbs behind her silver-embroidered swordbelt and said humbly, "Deo be good – I've been making an ass of myself for the last few hours, haven't I?"

Allanian couldn't contain his smirk any longer. As it spread across his face and his ears perked up, he offered consolingly, "Don't worry – you're not the first, nor will you be the last to do so when it comes to House Volstur."

Yavi snorted. "Well, that's just great. In the meantime, what in the hel—"

"Be you Allanian te'Hykiru Raoitae, Captain-Commander of Doms Merandith's House Guard?" A male voice, echoing from behind a bronze mask, interjected from behind Yavi.

Yavi turned, and Allanian looked up to see that a towering Ice Walker with scarred and tattooed arms now stood behind the crossed spears.

"I am," Allanian replied.

"Greetings be upon you, Ghost of the Snows. My doms would speak with you if it be to your pleasure?"

Gawking, Yavi looked at the Ice Walker, then at Allanian. "Why in the hells does he get to—"

Placing a hand gently on Yavi's shoulder, Allanian drew her attention. "Don't be offended; there is no insult intended."

Yavi bristled. "Like hells there isn't! I've been—"

"Captain!" Allanian barked authoritatively, seeking to put an end to her rising anger before she said or did something that might insult their guests.

Instinctively, Yavi snapped to attention, though she glared daggers at him for pulling rank. "Sir!" she practically snapped in response.

"This is neither the time nor place to provide succor to your misplaced indignation. They view me as part of the royal family, as such, I am accorded the same privileges that they would grant any Merandith. Do I make myself clear?" he stated, his soft voice firm and unyielding.

"Yes, sir!" she growled.

"Good," Allanian responded, his tone softening. "Now, I want you to return to the fort and make sure my men are tended to. We'll need to be on the road soon, and I want them as hale as possible. If you are needed here, I will send for you. Is that understood?"

"Perfectly," Yavi responded, her voice thick with barely contained anger.

"Good. We'll talk later," he replied before stepping past her.

Muttering to herself, Yavi stalked toward the fort as Allanian said to the towering Ice Walker, "I am ready."

The man nodded slightly in a friendly manner, though it looked odd with the wailing mask. "That is good." Stepping aside, he gestured into the camp. "Come. Doms Volstur awaits you with friendship and fire."

Pulling their spears back, the guards permitted Allanian to enter the camp. As such, with the grace of his race, Allanian walked between the guards, his sight set upon the tent at the heart of the camp. Immediately, the tall Ice Walker fell in beside him, matching his stride and pace.

The journey through the organized camp was quick, but along the way, Allanian couldn't shake the feeling that he was being watched. Granted, he was used to curious onlookers; after all, darlions were rarely seen on Triclose. However, the sensation he was feeling was different. While there was an air of inquisitiveness to those he caught looking his way, it didn't explain the underlying current of . . . animosity threatening to raise his hackles. Be they walking the camp or gathered about campfires, Allanian subtly examined those he believed were staring in his direction. Despite his best efforts, however, he could find nothing to warrant the feeling.

"Easy, Lan. You're just a bit on edge, that's all. There's no one here that would seek to harm you," he told himself in an effort to calm his nerves.

Eventually, as they neared the main tent, he managed to partially squash the dreadful feeling. Much to his chagrin, what remained of the hateful sensation crawled up his spine as the two Ice Walkers guarding the pavilion's entrance turned their attention upon him and his escort. Examining them closely, he noted both were on the short side for Ice Walkers, but nothing in their posture or presence indicated they were responsible for the feeling. Scolding himself again, he once more tried to quell the sensation as they reached the guards.

Acknowledging the sentinels with a nod, the tall Ice Walker pushed aside the heavy tent flap before stepping inside and holding it open for Allanian. Nodding his thanks, Allanian started to walk through but almost came to a halt. Out of the corner of his eye, he thought he saw the guard to his left staring directly at him. However, when he glanced that way as he continued into the tent, the guard appeared to be looking straight ahead, as he had the entire time.

"These raiders have you jumping at shadows, Lan. This isn't you, and you know it. Best that you get some sleep and relax before you do something foolish," he chided himself as his escort stepped back outside and let the tent flap drop back into place.

Coming to a halt before a blazing brazier in the center of the tent, Allanian quickly took in his surroundings. Shadows danced throughout the sparsely decorated tent, but instead of lending an ominous air to the lodging, it made the space feel oddly cozy. Glancing to his right, he could make out a sturdy chest at the foot of a spacious cot that was generously padded with warm blankets, while to his left, he could see a modest table and two chairs made of hide stretched between bone supports. As for the tent's two residents, they were on the other side of the brazier. One was a tall and proud woman whose aged, but strong figure was adorned in a sleeveless sealskin tunic along with white-fur pants and boots. The other resident, who was clearly frail despite a wailing bronze mask and a blanket of white fur, was seated next to her in an ivory sedan chair that was generously padded with white pelts.

Meeting Allanian's gaze, the woman nodded slightly, acknowledging his presence, to which he kneeled in response and said, "Doms and Doma Volstur. To what do we own this unexpected honor?"

"Rise, Ghost of the Snows, and be welcome at our fire," the woman responded in a throaty, aged voice that seemed a perfect match for her round, sun-darkened and lined face.

Standing, Allanian examined her. The sides of her head were still shaved in the popular fashion of Ice Walker warriors, but unlike last time, her braided white hair was devoid of any hint of the ice-blonde of her people. The hard life of an Ice Walker showed on her creased, tattooed skin, but her bare arms were still muscular, and she still appeared fit for battle.

Meeting her strong, blue-eyed gaze, Allanian said, "My thanks, Doma Volstur. But I must admit, we had no idea you would be making the journey this time."

A slight smile tugged at the corner of her thin lips. "To be sure, we did not know ourselves. But," she cocked her head toward the masked person sitting on the throne of furs, "my husband wished to see his great-grandchild again and hopefully bear witness to the birth of another. To deny him such a pleasure would be foolish."

Turning his attention to the frail, fur-enshrouded man, Allanian declared respectfully, "Doms Volstur. You are looking well."

A wheezing cough echoing from behind the man's bronze mask greeted Allanian's statement. Waving a bandage-wrapped hand dismissively, Doms Volstur declared, "Your pleasantries are welcome, but unneeded, Ghost. The Wasting has left me frail and torn my flesh; the cold now cuts deep, and I must cover my body in furs and bandages to conceal my weakness and remain warm. I am little more than a shadow of what an Ice Walker should be. Death breathes upon my neck, and I am ready to embrace it, Ghost – so do not seek to spare my feelings with sympathetic lies."

An amused, though somewhat sad, grin spread across Allanian's face. "You have my apologies, Doms Volstur. How long do you have?"

An almost imperceptible shrug of the shoulders greeted Allanian's inquiry. "Not long. It is unlikely that I will see another Melt. Thus, I seek to spend my remaining days in relative warmth and with the blood of my daughter."

As Allanian inclined his head respectfully, he felt something tugging at the edge of his senses. Ignoring it, he said, "House Merandith welcomes you with open arms, as always, Doms. I must offer apologies on Doms Merandith's behalf, however. Last I heard, he is far to the south, and it is unlikely that he will return for the birth of his child."

Doms Volstur began coughing violently, but managed to wave away his wife when she moved to help him.

Casting a worried glance at her husband, Doma Volstur only returned her gaze to Allanian when her husband's cough weakened. "We expected as much," she said to Allanian, though there was a tremor to her voice that spoke volumes about her concern for her husband's health. "There is no insult in his absence – be assured of that, Ghost. Our grandson has honored us – and our daughter's memory – with his actions, and we could ask for no more. It is enough that we pay our respects to his mate and our great-grandchildren."

"Indeed," Allanian responded with a grateful nod. "Moreover, if I may speak on behalf of Doms and Doma Merandith, you are welcome to stay for as long as you please. Our home is your home, and our fire is your fire."

Doma Volstur nodded her thanks respectfully. "Our thanks, Ghost."

With his cough finally subsiding, Doms Volstur spoke once more. "I have two requests to ask of you, Ghost," he croaked in a hoarse voice.

Allanian felt the sensation again. This time, it tugged at his mind insistently. Trying his best to ignore it, he asked, "What is it that you need, Doms?" The urgency of the tug grew in strength as he added, "I will do my best to meet your needs should it be within my power."

"Good. My requests are simple in nature, Ghost. Though we do not fear trouble or conflict, I would have you provide an escort so that our remaining journey remains uneventful. It would also please me greatly if you would speak with us for a time. It has been long since we heard accurate word of the events of the Southlands, and I would know what kind of life my grandson fights to create for my great-grandchildren."

When Allanian didn't immediately respond, Doms and Doma Volstur looked at him with concern and a bit of indignation. To them, he appeared to be staring at nothing, oblivious to what Doms Volstur had just asked of him.

"Ghost? Are you alright?" Doma Volstur asked with a mix of concern and rising anger. "My husband has just asked of you two minor favors. I find it rude that you would deny him a response."

Blinking, Allanian looked at her blankly for a moment before realization dawned on him. Eyes going slightly wide, Allanian shook his head. "My apologies, Doms and Doma! I did not mean to seem ignorant of your request," he replied hastily. "We have had issues with raiders in the North, and to my shame, I'm finding it difficult to keep my focus off of them for very long."

Even as Doma Volstur eyed him with an edge of skepticism, Doms Volstur asked, "Then the war has touched Tiliea?"

Allanian nodded. "Unfortunately, it has – though, only mildly. It is nothing we cannot handle, but they have done damage and cost us lives."

"Then it is good that I have asked for the extra escort," Doms Volstur declared.

"It is prudent, Doms Volstur, and that was one of the main reasons I came to your camp this night. I had planned on offering an escort, just as you have requested," Allanian declared.

"That is good," Doms Volstur said with a slight nod of his head.

"Unfortunately, Doms, I may have to excuse myself from joining you on your journey to Merset initially. Doma Merandith has charged me with combating the raiders, and I must make preparations for its containment in my absence. However, I will do my utmost to avoid lingering here."

"That is unfortunate, Ghost," Doms Volstur responded, "but understandable." Another coughing fit overtook him, but this time, it faded quickly. After catching his breath, Doms Volstur continued. "Pray tell, would this keep you from speaking with us for a time?"

Smiling, Allanian responded, "Not at all, Doms. It would be an honor and a pleasure to do so."

"That is good," Doms Volstur responded, pleased.

"Come," Doma Volstur interjected with a welcoming smile, "seat yourself and tell us of the Southlands and of how the blood of our blood fairs."

For nearly four hours, Allanian spoke with Doms and Doma Volstur. It was enjoyable to catch up with Kale's grandparents, and he found the time with the Doms and Doma to be a nice escape from the bandit problem. However, he now had more important matters to attend to that trumped even the bandits, and he eventually excused himself. When he left, he noted that the guards outside the Volsturs' residence had changed, and he felt oddly relieved. That relief held up as he made his way through camp free of the sensation he'd felt upon his arrival, which he knew was foolish.

Chiding himself for such ridiculousness as he made his way to the fort, Allanian sought out Fallain to inform him of the escort duties and briefed him on the raider situation. Allanian then went about the rest of his evening like normal. He ate a hearty meal and conversed with his men before attending to Yavi's bruised ego, which was as frustrating and exhausting as ever. Once Yavi was pacified, he then filled her in about the raiders' recent activity and their encounters. After providing some grudgingly received suggestions about patrol routes and tactics, he finally excused himself well after midnight and withdrew to the modest quarters that had been provided to him. Once he was sure the bulk of the fort's residents were asleep, he then snuck out with stealthy ease.

Making his way to the southwestern wall unseen, he ascended to the battlements between patrols, where he quickly vaulted over the wall. With a cushion of fir'gan absorbing the force of his landing, he quickly jogged into the distance until he was sure no one on the walls could possibly see him. Coming to a halt, he took a deep breath and thought, *Well, this should be interesting.*

Then, Allanian took a step forward and, in a swirl of wind, vanished.

*

At such a late hour, no one noticed that one of their party members was missing.

Standing north of the camp, a lone, unusually short Ice Walker gazed intently to the south. It had amused him to toy with Allanian. Poking and prodding at his senses like a child toying with an ant, he'd found immense pleasure in teasing him. Was it dangerous to do so? Absolutely. He knew that if he was discovered, he risked igniting open conflict before he and his allies were ready – assuming Warrick's conquering of Blackstone hadn't already set that in motion – but he'd been unable to resist the urge to do so. Thankfully, Allanian was oblivious to his prodding, and he was pleased with himself.

Now, he followed the darlion's movements with profound curiosity. Allanian was skilled at masking his presence, yet at this moment, he was trackable. Granted, he was making it difficult to follow him, but something had made him lower his guard some in favor of speed. While he had an idea as to what would make Allanian disregard caution in such a way, he couldn't be entirely sure. As such, he found himself weighing the risks of following him against postponing his mission. They were both heading in the same general direction this night, so it wasn't likely that a small detour would be a problem. Unfortunately, just as he had made up his mind to sate his curiosity, he felt a presence in his mind.

As the voice spoke, a deep scowl crept onto his face behind his bronze mask. He hated bending knee to his master, but he had learned a long time ago that disobeying the Darkness' chosen was foolish. Still, it was quite the task to keep his temper in check and listen like a dutiful soldier. As a result, when the voice finally withdrew, the Ice Walker was shaking with anger, and if not for his gloves, his hands would have been bleeding from how hard his fingers were digging into his palms. Eventually, however, he managed to calm himself. He would be meeting his master in person soon, and it would not do to be angry when he did so.

Facing west by southwest, the man took a deep breath. *"Soon, all this will be nothing but a terrible memory, and these damn fools will all bow before me,"* he thought with a malicious grin before the darkness around him seemed to swallow him and he vanished from sight.

*

Although his natural vision was quite keen, and the man had white hair and was wearing a white shirt, it would have been nearly impossible for Allanian to see the man from a distance on this moonless night. Thankfully, his fir'gan-enhanced vision negated such a hindrance, and granted him a clear view of his friend well before he reached him.

Slowing to a walk, he approached the man seated on an ancient tree stump set in a field just a few hours by horse south of Rirdan. Meeting Damion's dark gaze, Allanian declared, his happiness to see him evident in his haunting voice, "Considering that display a couple of weeks ago, I cannot say I'm shocked to see you like this." He chuckled as the man stood, then quipped, "So much for the ban

270

on excessive use of fir'gan."

Smirking slightly at Allanian's observation, Damion stated in his deep, authoritative voice, "Thank you for getting here as quickly as you did. Your expedience is appreciated, Lan."

Allanian scoffed a bit as he drew near and replied, "I'm sorry it took me as long as it did. I had to extricate myself from an Ice Walker camp before I could get here." Stopping short of Damion, Allanian found that he no longer had to look as far down to meet his friend's gaze, and a sudden, pleased grin spread across his face. Extending his hand, he stated happily, "By the Mother, it is truly good to see you whole again, Damion."

Clasping Allanian's forearm, he gave it a firm shake. "And it is good to be whole once more . . ." he smirked dryly, "though it is far earlier than I would have liked." Releasing his grip, Damion let his arm drop to his side. "So, it was Ice Walkers that held you up?" he asked as his smirk faded. "I take it Doms Volstur decided to pay a visit?"

Still drinking in Damion's appearance, Allanian's ears twitched slightly as he said, "That he has. It couldn't have come at a worse time, though."

Damion arched an inquisitive eyebrow.

"We've had Suldamik raids as far north as Rirdan."

Damion chuckled darkly. "Craigan has some large stones, I'll give him that."

Allanian laughed just as darkly. "Indeed he does. But," his grin vanished, "I am positive you are not here – wearing your actual face – to chat about Triclosian politics." His face grew serious. "Has he awaked to his powers?"

Damion shook his head slightly. "He's started, but that wasn't it."

It was Allanian's turn to raise his eyebrows curiously. "Then what warranted your change?" he asked, knowing full well it would take something dire for Damion to forsake his disguise earlier than he would have liked.

The grim look that filled Damion's dark eyes twisted Allanian's stomach even before Damion uttered a word.

"Kara and Ember are on Triclose, Lan – and they were nearly killed by blackheart poison."

The words almost didn't register with Allanian as shock tore through his mind. "What?" he finally managed to ask.

"Blackhearts, Lan. Someone has been breeding them," Damion stated bluntly.

"Mother protect us," Allanian breathed with a shake of his head as if he were trying to deny the reality of the declaration. "Are you positive?" he asked as he met Damion's dark gaze.

"Unequivocally," Damion responded with a firm nod. "Oblet had a blackheart arrowhead in his possession, which I incinerated, that was brought in from Haltho's outlying settlements. Furthermore, Kara was attacked on Solarson even before journeying here. As for the surge of power you felt all those days ago, that was me purifying them."

Allanian's eyes widened. "I thought that was just you changing! But no – that was you summoning coldfire, wasn't it?"

Damion smirked. "I did just say I was purifying them, didn't I?" he quipped, causing Allanian to gawk at him.

"By the Mother!" Allanian blurted in response. "Every potential Gift would have had a restless night, not to mention that any of our enemies would have sensed you if they were north of the Dragonspine! So much for the ban on excessive use of fir'gan, indeed!"

Damion gave an indifferent shrug as he said, "I'm afraid that is likely the case . . . and it only gets worse."

Planting his hands on his hips, Allanian gazed up at the night sky and let out a slow deep breath. Finally, he looked back at Damion and said, "Alright – what are we dealing with?"

Damion shrugged slightly. "I'm not entirely sure. When I retrieved mine and Luthur's crystals, as well as the remains of my crusader, the Valley informed me–"

"Wait," Allanian interrupted, the tone of his calm voice deeply puzzled. "You retrieved Luthur's crystal, too?"

Damion nodded.

Allanian's ears perked up and he rolled his eyes. "What in the hells is going on, Damion? It sounds like every last shred of the plan has been incinerated!"

A dry smirk pulled at Damion's lips. "I'd say that is an apt observation, Lan. You see, Mat nearly killed Amroth," he stated, his stern voice so calm that it was almost comical.

"What?!" Allanian exclaimed, drawing a dark, amused grin from Damion.

"There is a lot to tell you, Lan, and I don't have much time to do so. So, if you can refrain from interrupting, I'll tell you what I know. Afterward, I need your help with something."

Folding his arms across his chest, Allanian took a deep, settling breath before replying, "Alright. I'm all ears."

For the next hour, Damion told Allanian of the events of the last few weeks. Through it all, the darlion found his emotions pulled between shock and sadness. Yorien and Trina's crystals were finally resonating, Darius and Cat were dead, Blackstone had fallen, a shadow drakuma had assaulted Ember, there were active blackheart nests, and Amroth had nearly died. By the time Damion finally fell silent, a mix of anger and deep concern had consumed Allanian.

"What now, then? Darkon's," he practically spit the name, "actions have always been suspect. And I would call the loss of two Wardens and Blackstone a gross error to be laid solely at his feet." He scoffed. "As for Tykandrith's withdrawal. . . . Yoshali toqua!"

Damion smirked at the colorful Tykani curse before saying, "I cannot disagree on either point. However, as far as Darkon is concerned, there's not enough evidence to convince me he is guilty of anything more than poor judgment and a bloated sense of self-importance."

"Those aren't exactly the traits you want in a Warden, much less the person leading us," Allanian drawled.

"No, they are not. Those flaws, however, do not make him a traitor."

"No, just a fool that is costing us greatly," Allanian retorted with a scowl.

Damion pressed his lips together grimly. "Agreed," he stated, his deep voice ominous. "And if it looks like his leadership is truly putting Kylir in jeopardy – or if I find he is a traitor – then I will deal with him with extreme prejudice."

A feral grin slowly spread across Allanian's face. "That I would like to see. However, whether or not you have to eliminate Darkon, you might want your crusader."

"I plan on taking care of that soon enough. Until then, if a crusader is necessary," he patted his harness, "I have these."

Sadness filled Allanian's eyes as he looked at the pair of hilts jutting over Damion's left shoulder. "Luthur's crusader. . . . It's hard to believe our little Amroth will soon possess them," he mused, his haunting voice wistful.

Damion grunted. "Indeed. I had hoped to slowly bring him

along, but fate had other plans."

Allanian laughed darkly. "That's a mild understatement, wouldn't you say?"

"Probably, but this is where you come in."

Allanian eyed Damion suspiciously. "What? You want me to train him?"

Damion smirked. "No. I don't hate you that much."

Allanian laughed. "Well, that is a relief! So what then?"

"Greatjon is training another newcomer to our ranks, so I plan on taking Amroth to Grey Sky so I can oversee the training of both."

Allanian let out a low whistle. "I'm impressed. Amroth and this other Gifted should be able to help each other through the whirlwind of revelations and new information." He smirked. "And Darkon will think twice before setting foot in Grey Sky again."

"My thoughts, exactly."

"Then what do you need of me?"

"I want you to perform the Searches that Mat and Kara came here to do."

Allanian quickly nodded in agreement. "Done. It was a damn foolish plan to have Wardens perform such a task."

"In general, I agree. But while it was foolish, it was the only option Darkon had. Could you have imagined him approaching Caldain?"

Allanian laughed. "Mother, no! But it would have been entertaining to see him do so." Shaking his head in amusement, he then said, "Alright. Given that you need to get to Grey Sky, I take it you also need me to ease your way into Caith'tol?"

"It might be needed," Damion responded with a smirk.

Grinning, "It never gets old hearing you ask for help, you know that?"

Damion grunted.

"Well then, lead on," Allanian said, motioning south. "I have a feeling time is growing short faster than we'd like; no need to waste it."

Nodding his agreement, Damion turned to the south, and in a swirl of wind and grass, the two men vanished.

Chapter Twelve

"**H**umans and their penchant for violence shalt never cease to amaze me," he thought as his fir'gan-sensitive eyes took in the long-abandoned, ruined city on this moonless night.

High atop the remnants of a tower that belonged to the skeletal remains of a once proud keep, he had an unobstructed view of the city and the surrounding area. This deep into an area known as the Contested Territories, nature was doing an excellent job of reclaiming the ancient site. Large trees dotted the landscape in an attempt to reestablish a forest, vines clung to stone ruins like nature's veins, and tall grass obscured roads and foundations like a winter-touched carpet. He had no idea what the city or keep was once called, nor did he care. Humans were a pestilence, and their achievements were paltry, unworthy of more than passing indifference from him.

Standing on the vine-choked landing of a crumbling, twisting staircase, he glanced up at the star-filled sky as a gentle breeze stirred his voluminous black cloak, and a slight smile tugged at his thin lips amongst the shadows cast by his oddly wide hood. *"Ah, Darkness.... Thine presence graces this world all too briefly. Thine embrace swaddles us in gentle silence, suppressing the violence and tragedy that the Light expels en masse. How doth so many refute thine truth? The Light 'tis but fool's gold — shining bright and with a fel warmth that but gilds the violence it creates."* He closed his elongated, upturned gray eyes and he sighed gently. *"I mourn for mine people and those of the First Race, for their birth in the Light blindeth them to the curse that is humanity, and to thine truth. Should all return unto thine embrace, peace greater than thou renders each night would be eternal. Alas, they art ignorant of their folly, and 'tis mine and thine other devotees' task to remedy this and provide succor unto a scorched world. The Light's greatest mistake hast provided shelter for thine servants and machinations, and soon it shalt bear fruit. Grant unto us thine blessed favor for a while longer, Father Night, and we shalt deliver Kylir back unto thine embrace, releasing my people from the Light's traitorous servitude."*

The gentle clatter of disturbed rubble from behind him drew him from his reflections. Turning, he saw the first person to accept his leadership and goals, which he found deliciously ironic since she was half human, ascending the stairs. Short of stature, the lean muscles of her curvaceous figure were girded in molded layers of black leather armor that were trimmed with deep violet piping and strategically studded with blackened steel. Flowing, graceful elvannue tattoos spanned her toned, sun-kissed arms between the fur-trimmed, black-enameled steel bracers girding her forearms and the matching pauldron on her right shoulder, as well as the studded leather guard on her left shoulder. Meeting his gaze with her own slightly elongated eyes of vibrant green, she stepped on the landing, her steel-reinforced sabatons of black leather silent as death.

"Master," she intoned respectfully in a voice that was as haunting as it was lovely.

"Melisia," he responded with a slight nod as he watched the light of the currents play subtly on the black ear cuffs framing the slightly pointed and out-turned ears of her broad but sharp-featured face. "Hath all arrived?" he asked, the tone of his warm voice making it clear he already knew the answer.

She nodded slightly as the wind gently rustled her short and curly ruby locks. Pushing a stray strand out of her vision with a hand wrapped in violet linen, her small, but full, violet-painted lips parted in a small smile. "Quite so," she replied as she grabbed the red-leather hilt of her hefty bluesteel falchion, which hung from her sturdy swordbelt in a matching scabbard at her right hip. "They but await your presence."

"Indeed," he stated before he approached her.

Stepping aside, she allowed her master to take the lead before following him down.

As they descended the worn and vine-littered stairs, her master asked, "Is there ought I should knoweth ere we join our compatriots?"

Melisia chuckled slightly. "Nothing beyond normal, Master. Juliana . . . or should I say, Alestra, is as irritating as always, and Warrick won't shut up about his victory. The twins are typically aloof, and Horus makes a stonewall seem chatty."

She paused.

"And Garith?" he asked with a knowing half-smile.

"*Garith*," she practically spit, "is Garith," she finished with a scowl. "Sharing the same space with him even this much makes my skin crawl."

"For now, we hath need of him still," he stated, acknowledging her unspoken thoughts.

She sighed. "I know, Master, but he is chaos incarnate. I still

276

do not believe he has submitted fully to you after all these years."

He chuckled. "My dear, Melisia. . . . Of course he hath not. 'Tis his nature to crave power, and his soul shalt never find succor for his fall. Well and full do I expect him to seek my death at some point, mayhap sooner than later."

Melisia started to protest, but he cut her short.

"Pray, doth not worry nor protest, for Garith is wiser than he acts. He understands I needeth him, and he needeth me. Indeed, a reckoning shalt occur, but 'tis far afield for now. Ere our thoughts lead us astray, let us focus upon what 'tis before us and leave the future to Father Night," he declared with a confidence that brokered no argument.

Swallowing her disquiet with Garith, Melisia simply replied, "As you wish, Master. Your way is the truth, and I am but your instrument."

Nothing more was said as they finished their descent. Eventually, the stairs deposited them in the remains of a corridor that barely qualified as such given the lack of walls and a roof. Without pause, he led the way through the ruins at a quick pace. This was the first time all of the Wardens of Shadow had gathered together in over a year, and although he didn't show it, he was anxious to hear their reports in a group setting and appraise where their plans stood.

As they drew near the center of the former keep, they began to hear one excessively loud, grating voice. Although they couldn't understand what was being said, there was no doubt that it was Warrick who was speaking. Soon enough, as they drew near what the man assumed had once served as a throne room, Warrick's blustery words finally grew clear enough to understand, which elicited an almost imperceptible sigh from the man.

"Humans," he thought ruefully.

"What can I say? Darius was always a pushover! I can't believe you lot always treated him like some fearful demon even after I sacked the Vale the first time!" Warrick declared proudly as the man and Melisia closed in on what remained of the room's entryway.

"Darkness give me patience!" they heard Alestra cry, her throaty voice heavy with strained irritation. "Do you ever listen to yourself? Such endless bragging doesn't make you look grander! In fact, I'd say it makes you look like a child desperate for approval! Darkness have mercy! You proudly carry Darius' head on your belt like a well-earned trophy, but it wasn't even your blade that fell either of them!" she barked as the man and Melisia entered the room.

Leaning against a broken pillar on the far-right side of the roofless, dilapidated room that nature was desperately trying to reclaim, Alestra's perfectly sculpted, alluring face had aggravation displayed unabashedly on it. Her full red lips were pulled down in a scowl as her uptilted, amber eyes glared daggers across the room at Warrick. Moonlight played on the extravagant hinged silver and gold ring adorning the ring finger of her left hand as she pushed a lock of her long white hair out of her tanned face. She then folded her athletic arms beneath her ample breasts, which were barely concealed by the clingy, sleeveless red and green silk dress she wore, and spread her red-leather booted feet apart slightly as she added derisively, "Your blackhearts just got lucky with their shots, in all likelihood – but do keep expounding on your greatness if it helps your pathetic ego!"

The cloaked man looked around the room as the words left Alestra's lips, and he quickly assessed the situation. Standing near her, his tall, lean figure dressed in white furs and sealskins, and his bare arms decorated with swirling blue tattoos, Garith seemed to be enjoying the exchange. Wildly spiked black hair topped a long, lean, and scar-littered face that sported mirth-filled, blood-thirsty black eyes that were nearly overshadowed by the truly feral, malicious grin that he displayed. The currents caused the numerous golden earrings lining his ears to glow slightly as his gaze shifted between the two Wardens in anticipation of what might be brewing.

The man's gaze quickly switched to the back of the room where the Torani brothers were stationed nearly between the two Wardens like anxious, unwilling mediators. Tall and slender with unkempt, shoulder-length blond hair, both men were clad in matching black attire that consisted of unadorned sleeveless tunics, breeches, boots and bracers. It was clear they were concerned about the escalating argument by the way their yellow eyes swapped between the pair from the dark sockets on their broad, drawn faces, and how a slight frown pulled at their thin lips.

The man's eyes then darted to the dark expanse behind Warrick, where the short and muscular tree trunk of a man known as Horus was hard to miss. Garbed in a full suit of sectional dark leather armor, he would have blended perfectly with the shadows if not for his ghostly pallor and his equally white, tightly braided locks. The clean-shaven man's square jaw was set firmly as he watched the exchange with violet eyes shot with red that seemed almost disinterested. However, the way his thick lips and the nostrils of his wide nose kept twitching indicated otherwise.

"Alas, Warrick's self-veneration 'tis as unwelcome as always," he thought, already exasperated with his comrades' antics. Yet, despite

how close he felt the situation was to erupting into violence, he decided to let it play out for a bit longer.

Warrick, for his part, was unaware of the new arrivals as he glared at Alestra with red eyes filled with simmering violence from astride a broad nose on a stern face that sported a raven wing tattoo over its left side. It was clear to all that Warrick was fighting the urge to lash out at Alestra as his powerful hands were clenched tightly at his sides below studded red bracers, and one could see the muscles of his corded bare arms and his brown-leather-clad legs twitching. What's more, his deep, but increasingly fast breaths caused the leather of his studded black vest to creak. Suddenly, his eyes darted to his massive fullmoon axe, which sat atop a pile of weapons in the center of the room that consisted of a katana, two bastard swords, a claymore, and a slender longsword. Warrick then took a threatening step forward, and the currents began to gather around him, causing his red aura to flare into existence.

Just as his heavy, black-sabaton girded foot thudded down, Alestra's green aura flashed to life and she grinned maliciously. In an instant, the auras of the others in the room burst to life; Garith's crimson mixing with Alestra's green to cast the area around them in a brown reminiscent of vomit, and the brothers' auras washed the rear of the room in deep purple light, while Horus' violet aura banished the shadows surrounding him as its light joined with Warrick's to turn the area an angry magenta.

"Not that that stand-in would do you any good, but do please try it, Warrick," Alestra purred. "I would love to witness the skills that laid low two Wardens firsthand," she mocked gleefully.

Exasperated and unwilling to let this go further, the man tossed back his hood, allowing the light of the currents to grace his slender face with its nearly shoulder-length pointed ears and sliver-streaked black hair. Amplifying his warm voice with fir'gan, the elvannue man barked, brokering no quarter, "ENOUGH!"

The single word echoed through the chamber violently, rattling debris and kicking up a cloud of dust. Almost in unison, the six agitated Wardens looked at him, surprised by both his arrival and outburst. No one dared to move or speak as the man's storm-gray eyes glared at them from astride a slender nose behind chin-length silver-streaked black hair, the bangs of which hung at eye level like teeth. There was a frightening amount of power in both his gaze and the single word he'd spoken, and everyone there understood that crossing this man would invite dreadful repercussions.

As the silence dragged on, Melisia stole a glance at her master, and her breath almost caught in her throat. Power radiated from him even though his aura was not visible, and the way the currents' light played on his fair-skinned features and danced along his silver ear cuffs was enthralling. Polished to a mirror-like sheen, the cuffs were engraved with a sweeping pattern reminiscent of a leafy vine, and protected the tops of his ears as well as his earlobes before tapering down to two silver strips on each side of his face, one along his jawline and the other along his high cheekbones. Between their design and polish, the currents' seemed to set his face aglow in a way that made Melisia want to believe he was blessed by the Darkness.

"This display," he suddenly stated, shattering the silence and shaking Melisia from her musings, "'tis pointless! That Warden Warrick laid low two Wardens is no small feat regardless of the path! If 'tis by his own hands, or by blackheart blood, it matters not! They art dead, and we art stronger for it! Succor thine bruised egos in that knowledge!"

He took a deep breath and let it out slowly. "If, however," he continued, his tone turning low and menacing, "thine egos can only find succor at the teat of violence, then know I shalt happily lay low the instigator. Every Warden 'tis needed to bring Father Night's dream unto fruition, but knoweth this – unity of purpose 'tis paramount, and one less malcontent shan't be missed."

The elvannue's declaration seemed to resonate with the others and they each released the currents . . . save for Garith. His crimson aura remained visible for a brief moment longer than the others as he directed a vehement scowl at the man. Without hesitation, the man met Garith's gaze with unflinching confidence, making it clear he wasn't intimidated in the least.

"Darkness have mercy!" Melisia thought as she looked on. The malice between the two men was palpable, and it made her nervous. *"Is my master wrong? Has Garith chosen this moment to lash out?"*

Just as she decided this indeed was that moment, and she was about to ready herself to intervene, Garith suddenly released the currents and his aura winked out. Glaring at her master a moment longer, he then folded his arms across his chest, scoffed and looked away.

A satisfied grin played at the corners of the man's mouth before he stated, "Excellent. Now that such childishness 'tis behind us, let us address the purpose of this gathering."

"Agreed," Warrick nearly barked. "What is so bloody damn important to drag some of us across the bloody ocean?" he asked angrily as he idly touched the emaciated head hanging from the left side of his belt by its stringy black hair.

The man glanced at the head and felt a sense of revulsion run up his spine. The scar-littered, broken-nose face was frozen in a wail, its brown eyes hauntingly empty in their sunken sockets. It's not that he felt pity for Darius. Far from it. Darius was dead, which meant one less enemy to contend with. Yet, there was a part of him that felt such mutilation was barbaric. Granted, collecting such trophies was the way of Warrick's people. Still. . . .

"On this, I agree with the lout," Alestra declared with a wave of her hand toward Warrick, her venom-laced words drawing the el-vannue's attention away from the ghastly souvenir. "If this is just to inform you of our status, we certainly don't need to gather like this."

The man's gaze swung to Alestra, and for a moment, he found his attention caught by the hinged ring she wore on her left hand. Made of gold and silver that had been fashioned into fine cy-linders of swirling, gracefully interwoven knotwork, the two-piece ring enveloped her ring finger and was hinged at the second knuckle. Tiny shards of jade encrusted the front part of the ring like pinpricks of green light, while the slender oval diamond on the back of the ring shone in the currents' light like a star plucked from the sky.

The man hid his brief distracted state masterfully, and he smiled slightly before responding, "Doest thou hath plans that super-sede thine duty to the Darkness? While I am not fully aware of the customs of this land, it appears thou art bejeweled in the raiments of engagement."

Alestra scowled and absently fingered the ring. "What I do for entertainment is none of your concern, Master Raefalzyn. Just know that it serves to keep Triclose in chaos, and that chaos keeps the few of Light's servants that still bother with this land occupied and off our trail," she stated a bit patronizingly, and with no small amount of scorn in her tone.

Raefalzyn held up his black-gloved hands defensively, allow-ing a bit of the currents' light to grace his darkly armored, slender fig-ure. "Aye, thine amusements art of little concern to me so long as they doth not hinder the Darkness' plans. If, by chance, they doth elevate those plans, then all the better."

Dropping his hands to his sides, he then shifted his gaze to the others and declared, "Warden Alestra 'tis both right and wrong. 'Tis true that this serves to receive thine reports as our plans quicken with haste, and I doth not possess the time to visit each of thee sepa-rately."

He strode to the center of the room, stopping short of the weapon pile, then fixed a stern gaze upon each Warden as he contin-ued, "This gathering also serves two other purposes — to inform all of thine allies as to what each of thee hath nurtured, and to conclude the promise I did maketh unto thee nearly two centuries ago."

At the mention of the promise, Warrick, Horus and the Torani brothers perked up.

Before they could say anything, Raefalzyn's gaze swung to Garith, who met it as the elvannue added, "We shalt soon set into motion actions that shalt achieve what, in part, the Darkness hath sought – and failed, alas – to attain since the Exodus."

Garith snarled at the jab, but wisely kept his mouth shut. He was well aware that his own lust for power was partly to blame for Raefalzyn's ascension to leadership, and no words their current leader could utter would ever sting as much as the Darkness' . . . displeasure. Still, he wasn't about to let Raefalzyn's jab slide completely. So, with all the malice he could muster, he flashed a wide, feral grin at him that was made all the more bloodthirsty by his enlarged canines.

Raefalzyn's gaze remained locked with Garith's for a moment longer before he broke the enmity-filled deadlock and let his eyes wander to the others before he concluded, "We shalt bring unto an end our isolation in these lands and return home to extinguish the Light's taint on this world!" Turning to Garith and Alestra, he then said, "Since we hath already touched upon thine dealings, deliver thine reports, Wardens Alestra and Garith."

The two Wardens looked at each other as if asking the other for permission to speak. The look lasted only a brief moment before Garith smirked and gestured to the open room as he bowed mockingly. "The floor is yours," he teased.

Flashing Garith a menacing scowl, Alestra stepped closer to the center of the room and faced Raefalzyn. Fighting the urge to turn the scowl on Raefalzyn, she composed herself and stated, "As you observed, I am engaged."

A scoff from Garith drew an irate glare from Alestra.

"However," she continued and returned her gaze to Raefalzyn, "while I do find some amusement in the charade, its purpose grants a few boons. Chiefly, more direct influence over House Suldamik. That, in turn, allows us to better inspect the Utherian Valley, and continue to sow discord on Triclose." Here tone turned condescending as she folded her arms beneath her breasts and asked, "Is that satisfactory?"

Raefalzyn smirked in response. "Dear Alestra, I declare unto thee once more – thine dalliances art of no concern of mine as long as they doth not interfere. If thou believes such actions art of benefit, I shan't protest."

"I'm overjoyed that you feel that way," Alestra intoned sarcastically. "Is there anything else?"

Raefalzyn nodded. "Pray tell, art thine nests ready?"

Alestra sighed as if she was not just irritated by the proceedings, but exhausted by them. "My nests are beyond ready. In fact, I have already begun shifting blackhearts into position. Nearly two hundred are with the forces that will be joining me in Chalin very soon.

"And the drakumas?"

"Darkness – I keep forgetting how exacting elvannue are!" she uttered in aggravation. "Other than the one you had me lend Garith, they are hale and well hidden. They won't be moved until you order it."

Raefalzyn nodded once more. "Very good, Warden Alestra. I am pleased."

Alestra curtsied mockingly. "I'm so glad you are, Lord Shadow," she said, her tone condescending, before she moved to rejoin Garith.

"Speaking of drakumas – thine report, Garith," Raefalzyn stated, his tone growing hard.

"Your turn, my dear," Alestra said softly and mockingly to Garith as she rejoined him and patted him on the cheek.

Stepping away from Alestra with a threatening scowl planted firmly on his face, he glared at Raefalzyn and said, "What would you like to know?"

Raefalzyn frowned. "Spare me thine melodramatics, Garith," he ordered, his tone taking on a violent edge.

Garith shrugged and looked around the room before responding. "Let's see. . . . I'm doing as ordered – I set the shadow drakuma and a handful of blackhearts loose on that bastard, Emberscar, which he may have survived, by the way. I'm also sowing chaos from the Merandith's side, investigating the Utherian Valley with Alestra, and what was the other thing. . . ." He tapped his chin sarcastically and struck a thoughtful pose for a moment before snapping his fingers and looking at Raefalzyn with wide eyes. "That's it! Seeking hosts for two crystals that haven't resonated in damn near two centuries!" He laughed derisively. "Oh, I forgot, that total is four now, isn't it? Thank you again, by the way, for trimming the weak from our ranks," he quipped, sarcasm dripping from every word. "Unfortunately," he continued, "it continues to look like the number of potential gifted hasn't gone up despite your assurances it would." He shrugged. "Oh well, you can't win them all."

Raefalzyn frowned at the barbed jabs.

"Darkness give me strength!" Melisia suddenly barked from behind Raefalzyn, drawing his gaze to her. Gripping her falchion's hilt tightly, she stepped forward and declared angrily, "Your antics grew old a long time ago, Garith! Why the Darkness saw fit to let you live is beyond any of us!" she nearly roared. "You are a self-indulgent, egomaniacal, would-be tyrant who acts like a child whose favorite toy was stolen from him! Do us all a favor and either grow up or fall on your crusader and spare us your lunacy!"

Through the entire tirade, no one budged an inch as Melisia spent her vitriol on Garith. In fact, all but Raefalzyn and the Toranis seemed a bit amused by it. Alestra found herself smiling, Warrick was grinning widely, and Horus even grunted in amusement. As for the Toranis, they appeared bored by it all, while Raefalzyn's face was unreadable.

Garith, on the other hand, placed a hand over his heart and feigned shock. "Why, I am so deathly hurt by your assertions, half-breed! I didn't know such malice resided in your heart toward me. Please," he cried as he clenched his hands together as if begging, "show me the error of my ways and how I might redeem myself in your eyes!"

Her rich blue aura bursting to life, Melisia roared with rage and started to draw her sword. Suddenly, before she could make a move, Raefalzyn's hand was atop her sword hand. The touch was gentle, yet it restrained her as if her hand was pinned under a wall.

"Enough of this!" Raefalzyn bellowed. He then glared at Melisia and stated, "Remember thine place, Warden Melisia! Do not believe thine position by mine side curries thee such leniency that I would overlook what thou art considering!"

The words were heavy with authority, and drew Melisia's gaze to Raefalzyn's stern gray-eyes. The conviction she saw in them told her all she needed to know – he wasn't bluffing.

Flashing a scowl at Garith, she settled her falchion in its sheath before releasing her grip on it and stepping back. "My apologies, Lord Shadow," she declared, her tone humble as her aura winked out. "I have overstepped, and I will accept any punishment you see fit to employ."

"Yes, Lord Shadow . . . do punish her," Garith stated, a mix of pleasure and animosity coating every word. "I do believe you said you would 'lay low' any instigator? Seems Melisia did just that."

The surge in the currents caught everyone off guard, and before anyone could react, Raefalzyn vanished and reappeared before Garith an instant later, his skin now ghostly white and his black-tinted golden aura writhing about him as a pain-filled moan filled the air. Garith's eyes grew wide as he gazed into Raefalzyn's now black sclera and yellow irises the instant before the elvannue's fist connected with his jaw, shattering it. Spewing blood, bone and teeth, Garith shot to the right and crashed through the wall, his neck broken and his head nearly twisted backward. For what seemed like an eternity, his flight punched his broken body through the ruins with the ease of a ballista bolt through paper, filling the air with the roaring symphony of collapsing architecture.

As they waited for the noise to die down, Raefalzyn turned his yellow gaze full of chaotic energy on the remaining Wardens and, for the first time that night, he saw complete respect in their eyes. Granted, it was terror-inspired, and both Warrick and Alestra had turned nearly as pale as Horus, but it was respect nonetheless.

When all they could hear was the occasional groan of mortally injured timbers or the sporadic clatter of falling debris, Raefalzyn turned his attention fully to Alestra.

Mouth partially agape, and her amber eyes full of fearful respect, Alestra immediately dropped to one knee, her head bowed, when his gaze fell on her. "My life is yours, Lord Shadow," she intoned, terrified, her lips trembling with every word.

"Good, Alestra. That is good," Raefalzyn responded, his voice grating and echoing in on itself. "Retrieve thine weapons and collect Garith. Then return to thine duties," he ordered.

Alestra shuddered as she picked up on the unspoken threat. "Yes, Lord Shadow," she replied before she stood and hustled over to the weapon pile, her head bowed.

Quickly collecting Garith's dragon-collar katana in its black scabbard, and her own elegant, slender longsword hanging from a brown leather baldric, she then turned to the new hole in the wall and, with a surge of fir'gan, sped off to find Garith.

As soon as she was gone, Raefalzyn released his hold on the currents, and his skin and eyes returned to normal as he turned to face the others. "Now," he stated, his voice and tone calm and normal as if the outburst of violence had never happened, "let us proceed with thine reports." Facing the Torani brothers, he ordered, "Brothers, pray tell, how goes thine nest and preparations?"

*

The path of destruction Garith's flight carved was straight and unerring, roughly three-hundred yards through dilapidated stone and wood, as well as winter-stricken vegetation, making it easy for Alestra to find him.

Splayed on his belly in a trench at the foot of a pile of debris, Garith's face was a bloody, shattered mess atop his grossly twisted neck as he glared at the night sky. Standing over him, Alestra tapped her cocked hip with Garith's katana, a wry smirk on her full lips that couldn't fully offset the fear that haunted her eyes. "I'd say Raefalzyn left an impression on you with that, wouldn't you agree?" she quipped in a poor attempt to lighten the mood.

Garith's eyes darted to Alestra, and he scowled at her. Pushing himself up, his vertebrae and the muscles in his neck popped and cracked as his fir'gan realigned them and returned his head to its proper orientation. Once his head was back in place, he turned to face Alestra, one hand clenched at his side and the other extended toward her. All too familiar with Garith's temper, Alestra didn't flinch as his rage-filled eyes focused on her. Instead, she calmly placed his katana in his outstretched hand.

Snapping his hand closed about the sheathed weapon, he rammed it home beneath his belt before stating, his tone controlled but seething, "Yes. . . . Yes, he did. The bastard's arrogance does his people proud – and that will be his undoing."

The irony wasn't lost on Alestra as she thought with a mental chuckle, *"Just as it was yours."* Aloud, she stated in agreement with a slight nod as her anxiety over Raefalzyn's display of power started to fade some, "That it will."

Garith's gaze suddenly shifted back in the direction of the gathering, and for a moment, Alestra watched the currents surge around him. Then, as quickly as it happened, the currents returned to normal, and Garith spun on his heel before marching off.

Slinging her longsword over her shoulder, Alestra quickly pulled alongside Garith as he weaved his way through the overgrown ruins and asked, "What now? There is no doubt now that he is closer to launching his campaign than we thought, and we are not ready."

Garith grunted and scowled. "I am well aware of that!" he spit, his dry voice rough with rage. "But there's not a damn thing I can do about it!" Coming to a sudden stop, he screamed and kicked one of the large stone blocks lying in front of him, launching it deep into the night. Spinning, he glared daggers at a slightly startled Alestra. "We've delayed all that we can! With his actions against Darius,

Warrick can no longer siphon forces for us, leaving only your extra projects in the south and what the Toranis have managed to scavenge on the side! It is now more important than ever that I claim the knowledge and power of Luthur's crystal! If that bastard is allowed to bring his plans to fruition, there won't be anything left for the Darkness to rule over!"

Alestra smiled knowingly. "For the Darkness to rule over . . . or you?" she asked rhetorically.

Garith smirked, and his eyes lit up with a mix of power and lust. "We all know the Darkness wants this world plunged back into blissful night, but it will be by my hand, and I shall rule over it. . . . With you by my side, of course."

Alestra matched his smirk with one of her own. "Of course, my dear," she purred, all thoughts of Raefalzyn's outburst suddenly washed from her mind by what she sensed from Garith.

Moving close enough to Alestra that he loomed over her, he placed a finger under her chin and tilted her head. Immediately, she was drawn in by the chaotic mix of rage, power and lust she saw in his eyes, and she felt the surge of longing in her turn into a flood, drowning any remaining anxiety the night had inspired.

"Now, about Luthur's crystal . . ." he stated, his voice low and husky.

She nodded slightly and swallowed. She flexed her legs slightly as her loins grew warm, and she breathed, her voice quivering slightly, "We'll know how weak the Valley is soon enough, and we should be able to sow more chaos with the results. Of course, I still think it wise to acquire all the amulets. We've never been able to get a firm grasp on just how much power resides in the Valley."

"Of course," Garith practically purred.

Suddenly, his smirk grew into a wide grin and he stepped into her, grabbing her arms with enough force to bruise her before kissing her roughly and passionately on the lips.

A sense of euphoria washed over Alestra as he bit down on her lower lip hard, drawing blood. Grabbing his elbows, she sank her fingers into him and forcefully pressed her breasts into his chest as she pulled herself deeper into the embrace. A moment later, as they kissed, bit and pulled at each other's lips, he released her arms and grabbed at the front of her dress. With a yank, he tore at the silk garment, splitting it as easily as the wind cut through the sky. Stepping away from their embrace, his lips bleeding in numerous places, he drank in her curves as the currents' light caressed every luscious inch of her.

Relishing the lust she saw in his eyes, Alestra's bleeding lips parted in a knowing smile as she stepped out of the remains of her dress, wrapped her arms around his neck, and lept onto him. As soon as her legs locked around his torso, she began grinding her hips into him, and Garith flashed her a dark, hungry smile.

"Oh yes, my love," he growled, "when it's all over, you and I will be standing atop our enemies' corpses, and we will rule over Kylir as gods!"

*

"As you thought, Master, Kydan'fir and the Indigains haven't budged. With Catharina dead, and Kara possibly dead, both Orders are extremely vulnerable," Horus stated in a haunting, monotone voice. "It would be my pleasure to dispose of either Order . . . though I would suggest Kydan'fir. Should Kara have survived, then their threat is still greater than the Bestynes despite their lack of soldiers."

Raefalzyn nodded. "Thine time will arrive soon enough, Warden Horus. For now, ensure thine forces art ready and strong."

Horus nodded. "Your will be done, Master."

Turning his attention to Warrick, Raefalzyn declared with a raised eyebrow, "And thou, Warden Warrick. . . . Hast thou found time to seek that which was requested of thee? Or hath the heady fruits of victory inebriated thee beyond reason?"

Warrick snarled, insulted at the insinuation. "Much to your displeasure, I think, I have not forgotten why I took Blackstone."

A slight smirk tugged at Raefalzyn's lips. "Pray tell, what hath thou found, then," he ordered.

Warrick shrugged. "Nothing so far." He snarled and spit on the ground. "The bastard rigged the keep to collapse. Took damn near the entire mountainside with it. If the Ansei Grove was on the grounds, it was likely destroyed. If it was beneath the mountain," he shrugged, "then your guess is as good as mine as to where it is now."

Raefalzyn frowned, his eyes taking on a dark edge. "That is . . . disappointing," he stated, his voice laced with venom. "Fear not, 'twould take more than a landslide to undo that particular Ansei Grove." His eyes grew malicious, and a hint of an echo filled his voice as the currents stirred around him. "Mark mine words, Warden Warrick – thou shalt find the grove ere thou advance further. Dig, sacrifice, and do what thou must. We cannot afford to leave even one unfound. Do I maketh mineself clear?"

288

There was a blatant snarl on Warrick's face, but with Garith's thrashing still fresh in his mind, he thought better of arguing. Instead, he nodded. "Aye. . . . I'll find it."

Raefalzyn's expression quickly morphed into a broad grin, and he declared with a clap of his hands as his voice returned to normal, "Excellent! I am pleased we art of an accord. However, ere thou return to thine tasks, let me fulfill mine promise unto thee." Glancing at Melisia as the remaining Warden's eyes lit up with joyous anticipation, he ordered, "Retrieve the crate."

Standing in Raefalzyn's shadow, Melisia nodded curtly, then exited the room. As her footsteps faded into the distance, a nervous tension filled the air. Each of the Wardens moved closer to the center of the room as they shared knowing glances and smiles with each other. Seeing the anxiousness in their eyes, Raefalzyn decided a word of caution was warranted. "Pray, listen closely, Wardens."

The gravity of his tone drew their attention and dampened their excitement a bit.

"Thine vigor for this moment 'tis applauded, but doth not forget our enemies doth reside on Triclose. Therefore, doth not give in to temptation. We shan't risk drawing undue attention unto this gathering by drawing forth thine new crusaders. Is this understood?"

Disappointment was clearly written on their faces, but each Warden understood the risk and nodded their understanding. Assured of their compliance, Raefalzyn said nothing more, and the others followed suit. As a few tense minutes passed, their anticipation began to grow once more, though tempered this time. Eventually, they heard Melisia's footsteps once again, and a moment later, she reentered the room with a long, sizeable wooden crate held with ease on her shoulder. Moving to the center of the room, she used the currents to swat the pile of weapons away and to cushion their tumble so they would land quietly.

With the area clear, she placed the crate on the ground before facing Raeflzyn and bowing. "At your leisure, Master."

Raefalzyn nodded, prompting Melisia to return to his side. Smiling at the dark glee he saw in the others' eyes, Raefalzyn approached the crate. Stopping before it, he looked at the eagerly waiting Wardens and said, "With this, mine promise 'tis fulfilled. No longer shalt Father Night's Wardens stand in the shadows of the Wardens of Light. Nay, thou shalt possess thine teeth once more, and a bite the Wardens of Light shalt feel most keenly! Hearken unto me, mine fellow Wardens, and receive the Darkness' generous blessing!"

Bending down, Raefalzyn grabbed the lid of the crate and easily tore the top off. Discarding it casually, he then reached in and removed a magnificent bluesteel claymore. Hefting it easily by its black leather-wrapped hilt for all to see, he turned to face Horus and presented it to him. "Thine sword is returned to thee, Warden Horus. Wield it with pride and in honor of Father Night."

Awe-struck, Horus didn't hear a word of what Raefalzyn said as he was focused solely on the claymore. It was everything his original had been and then some. Every inch of it was made of pure Velusyian bluesteel and inlaid with silver knotwork. A massive spiked pommel anchored a sizable hilt that terminated in a crossguard molded to look like a screaming kyram skull. Oriented as it was, the mouth of the skull served as the base for the enormous blade that jutted from it like a demonic tongue. It made for a terrifying visual, and that thrilled Horus.

Eventually, the ghostly white Warden managed to tear his gaze from the claymore and approach Raefalzyn. Stopping before him, he bowed low and said, his haunting voice full of gratitude, "I am honored to receive such a gift, Lord Shadow." Righting himself, he added, "I shall wield it for the Darkness, and send Father Night's enemies screaming to the Hells."

Raefalzyn nodded as Horus reached out and grabbed it with both hands. Immediately, he felt the power within the weapon as it recognized its wielder. A joyous warmth spread through him as it keyed to him, leaving him heady with a power he hadn't felt in centuries. Enamored with the weapon, Horus backed away from Raefalzyn without waiting to be dismissed.

Well aware of the gravity of the situation, Raefalzyn disregarded the lack of formalities and instead reached into the crate once more with both hands. This time, he pulled out a pair of broad-bladed, Velusyian-bluesteel rapiers. Larger by far than a typical rapier, the long, double-edged blades were anchored into simple, elegant cuffs that topped silver-inlaid, black leather-wrapped hilts with teardrop pommels. Holding them up, he tested their weight and smiled.

"Ah, an elegant weapon rarely witnessed in this time," he declared with pride before giving them a twirl. The blades hummed as they cut through the air, causing Raefalzyn's smile to grow wider. Looking at the Toranis, he nodded slightly before tossing the blades to them, which they caught deftly by the blades' hilts. "Thine blades art returned to thee, Wardens Torani. Wield them with pride and in honor of Father Night," he once more intoned.

Matching small smiles cracked the brothers' faces as they examined the rapiers in the moonlight, during which the weapons keyed to them, spreading the warmth of their power through the twins. Eventually, the brothers looked to Raeflzyn and bowed respectfully. "Our thanks, Master," they declared in unison as they righted themselves, their malevolently deep, but soft voices filled with glee. "We eagerly await the time we can unleash these on the Light's cursed followers."

Raefalzyn nodded their way before turning to Warrick, who stood there, arms folded, with a mask of boredom on his face. It was an admirable attempt to downplay his excitement, but Raefalzyn knew better. The man was by far the most eager of all the Wardens of Shadow to once more have a crusader, and had been outspoken about it since Garith received his all those years ago. His vocalness only grew after the disastrous results of their attack on Luthur. So, for him to act disinterested now that the moment was here was almost laughable to Raefalzyn.

Warrick eventually noticed Raefalzyn looking at him, and he dropped his arms to his sides as he quipped sarcastically, "Finally! Is it my turn?"

Raefalzyn fought off the urge to grimace at the lack of decorum. While he was willing to overlook proper thanks due to the situation, Warrick's childish behavior made it difficult to continue to do so. "Aye, Warden Warrick, 'tis thine moment," he said through clenched teeth before bending down and retrieving a massive fullmoon axe from the crate.

The fearsome weapon immediately caught Warrick's eye, and his face lit up with lustful violence that was nearly a rival for Garith's derangement. Taking a step forward, Warrick hesitated and quickly looked at Raefalzyn as if seeking permission to take it. With a slight snarl, Raefalzyn tossed the axe to Warrick with a flick of his wrist. The massive Warden deftly caught the axe, and with a twirl of his wrist, he brought the weapon to rest in his other hand. As the warmth of the weapon keying to him flooded through him, he took a moment to examine his new axe.

Devoid of embellishments, the Velusyian-bluesteel monstrosity was nearly five feet in length, and its grip was sheathed in red leather between the ring surmounting its ball pommel and the ring nearly halfway up the shaft. Atop the shaft, the crescent blades of the fullmoon head were reminiscent of bat wings, with tips that stretched from just above the top grip ring to nearly half a foot beyond its spiked cap. Running his thumb along the edge of one of the wings, he felt a slight tingle as the powerful weapon easily split his skin and briefly interrupted his connection to his fir'gan.

Smiling broadly, he then hefted the axe to his shoulder before looking at Raeflzyn once more. "No flowery speeches needed, Master," he quipped. "It'll be my pleasure to wield this in the Darkness' name – you can count on it," he stated before turning and rejoining Horus without waiting for a response.

Raefalzyn watched Warrick's retreating back with naked animosity, but before he could say anything, Melisia started forward. Immediately, he placed a restraining hand on her, bringing her up short. Looking up at him with incised eyes, it was clear that Melisia desperately wanted to retaliate against the indignities that had been heaped at Raefalzyn's feet this night. Unfortunately, as much as he would have liked to indulge her at this moment, he knew it would be unwise. So, with a slight shake of his head, he conveyed both his sympathy for her and his desire not to escalate the night any further.

Although his response wasn't what she wanted, she wasn't about to cross her master. As such, she nodded her acknowledgment and returned to his side.

When Raefalzyn looked back at Warrick, he found him standing next to Horus, smirking at Melisia. *"Darkness, give me patience,"* he thought, aggravated. Aloud, he declared, "Thus armed, mine promise 'tis fulfilled, and thou art whole once more. Return to thine tasks with the knowledge that the time approaches when we shalt lay low the Light's Wardens and bring the Darkness' succor to a scorched world."

Thus dismissed, the Toranis and Horus bowed respectfully before they stepped into the shadows and vanished. Warrick, on the other hand, gave a half-hearted, somewhat mocking bow. Before he could depart, however, Raefalzyn spoke once more, bringing him up short.

"Hold, Warden Warrick," Raefalzyn declared, his tone making it clear he would not be disobeyed. "I would speak with thee a moment more."

Frozen in place by the words, Warrick let out an audible sigh before he turned to face Raefalzyn. "Yes, Master," he stated a bit more respectfully than he had all evening.

Approaching Warrick, Raefalzyn stated. "Do not mistake mine leniency with thine decorum for weakness." Coming to a halt before the massive Warden, he added, "Thine success garners thee a modicum of clout, but no more. Persist in thine childishness, and thou shalt find mine treatment of Garith to be . . . merciful. . . . Doest thou understand?"

Throughout Raefalzyn's admonishment, Warrick's jaw muscles flexed hard as he fought to control his anger. Authoritative figures rarely sat well with him, and Raefalzyn was barely tolerable. However, unlike Garith, Warrick knew when to check his rebelliousness. Mustering as much respect as he could, he responded, "Understood, Master."

Raefalzyn smiled at the response. "Good. Now, I hath one more task for thee."

"What would you have me do?" Warrick asked, his rage simmering below the surface.

"Prepare for me two squads of blackhearts. I shalt join thee anon so that I may see the state of the Bestynes for mineself."

Taken aback by the unexpected order, Warrick's mind immediately jumped to the conclusion that Raefalzyn would try to take down the Bestynes in his stead, and that set his blood boiling. *"You bloody bastard!"* Warrick thought, infuriated. *"The wolf pup is mine! How dare you even think of stealing that from me!"*

Both Raefalzyn and Melisia could see the emotions playing out on Warrick's face, and for a moment, they both thought violence might ensue. Instead, Warrick managed to choke down his anger before responding, his voice tight, "As you wish, Master. They will be awaiting your arrival. Is there anything else?"

Raefalzyn shook his head, careful to keep his satisfaction at Warrick's submissive state from showing. "Nay. Thou may return to Blackstone and thine search."

Without responding, Warrick backed into the shadows, his seething red eyes fixed squarely on Raefalzyn until the darkness swallowed him and he vanished.

Once Warrick was gone, Raefalzyn turned to Melisia, whose expression told him all he needed to know.

"Thou art disturbed and angry, Warden Melisia," he stated as he approached her. "I do apologize for restraining thee, but this is not the time for indulgences."

Meeting his gaze, she did her best to keep her tone respectful as she responded, "I understand, Master. However, Warrick is an incessant itch that needs to be scratched before he becomes a true problem! As for Garith – please grant me the privilege of ending him before his threat ascends once more!"

Offering her a consoling smile, Raefalzyn reached out and cupped her chin gently. "My dear Melisia. . . . Thine loyalty and concern art commendable. Attaining this state of the Darkness' plan is in part due to thine diligence and craftsmanship."

"Thank you, Master," she replied humbly as she looked into his gray eyes, relishing the power she saw there.

"Knoweth this – when the time comes, and it will, I shalt be overjoyed to unleash thee upon Warrick and anyone else who seeks to usurp me." His hand tightened on her chin, drawing a wince of pain from her, and his smile vanished beneath a wave of sternness as his expression hardened. "Pray, listen closely as I shan't repeat myself again – Garith is mine," he stated, his voice dripping with the promise of violence. "Should thou seek to deprive me of that, no matter thine protests, I shalt end thee. Doest thou understand?"

Unbridled fear radiated from Melisia's green eyes as the threat left Raefalzyn's lips. While she knew she was powerful enough to handle the likes of Garith and Warrick, there was no doubt in her mind that Raefalzyn could and would do as he promised. The man lording over her was the Darkness' chosen, and had taken down Garith at the height of his power thanks to the Darkness' blessing. As for how deep his power now ran, no one knew, but she wasn't about to be the first to test it.

Nodding as best as she could, Melisia stated, her tone contrite, "Yes, Lord Shadow. I understand."

Suddenly, Raefalzyn smiled and he released her chin. "I never doubted thee, Warden Melisia." Stepping back from her, he added, "Now, return to the Wildlands and see that thine duties proceeded unerringly. I shalt call upon thee next I needeth thee."

Melisia was still a bit rattled by his threat as she bowed low and declared, "As you wish, Master. My life is yours until the end."

A heavy silence greeted her declaration, causing her unease to grow. For a moment, she remained bowed, fearing she had somehow further upset her master. When nothing happened, she finally righted herself only to find she was alone in the ruins.

"Darkness," she prayed aloud as a shudder ran through her, "keep my course true and protect me from that man's wrath."

Taking hold of the currents, she then crushed the discarded weapons into dust before incinerating the crate until nothing was left. Once the task was complete, she smothered the flames before she, too, stepped into the shadows and vanished.

Chapter Thirteen

"**O**nly a week out, and something already feels wrong."

Crouched low in tall grass that was brown with winter's onset, Caldain gazed upon the village in the distance with concern-filled gray eyes, and he knew he could no longer ignore the foreboding tingle running down his spine.

The trek south from Solac had been slow going by Gifted standards. With little knowledge of their enemies' movements, and eager to avoid drawing their attention, they had refrained from using their fir'gan as much as possible. Furthermore, Caldain had insisted on sticking to well-traveled paths in the hope that they could pick up information about what might lie ahead. While Solac remained in sight, that decision seemed foolish. Nothing they heard or learned from idle chats with the traders and villagers headed for the city was new to them. However, by the time Solac and its outlying settlements were behind them, that changed.

Travelers became sparse, and those they did meet seemed beleaguered at best, or traumatized at worst. To the trio's chagrin, there was very little to glean from the distraught people. Most of those they encountered went out of their way to avoid them, and some even cursed or spit at them. It was baffling behavior, to say the least, as the denizens of Korval weren't known to be overly hostile to travelers or outsiders. Such an oddity was enough to make the trio both curious and somewhat guarded. Regrettably, their encounters continued on like this until they chanced upon a wandering merchant making his way back to Solac, and they finally got some answers.

According to the veteran merchant, he'd met with similar distrust and angst on what was a routine trek for him. He was well known by the villages and hamlets he visited, but of late, few were doing business with him, and more and more settlements were simply turning him away. From what he'd been able to gather from those still willing to trade – let alone talk – with him, there'd been an increasing number of people disappearing without a trace. When it grew beyond mere youngsters running away to seek their fortune elsewhere or the occasional banishment, the people began to suspect something more sinister. As such, sellswords and hunters were hired to track down those who had vanished and either return with information or bring back who or what was responsible for the trend.

At first, the legitimate hunting parties had returned empty-handed, while the unseelie sorts tried to pass off local predators as the offending party. Then, one day, one of the groups did not return. A second party, who was part of the same organization, went after them, and their return put an end to the practice. According to the merchant's source, the hunters brought what remained of their brothers-in-arms back in a one-horse cart. To a man, everyone was horrified to discover that the remains consisted solely of nearly unidentifiable body parts and chunks of necrotic flesh. What's more, the cart's macabre cargo, despite some of the remains featuring what appeared to be bite marks, was supposedly afflicted by some disease that even carrion feeders were avoiding with extreme prejudice.

While Caldain and the Kaskia siblings knew it was wise to believe the merchant's story held a fair amount of fear-inspired exaggeration, there were elements of the story that, when combined with the presence of blackhearts at Blackstone's fall, could not be ignored. After that, they decided to stay the night in any village that would allow travelers in. If blackhearts really were out there, then the presence of a large number of humans would provide extra cover for the trio. Still, given the rumors and their earlier encounters, they expected such a boon to be scarce. So, it came as a bit of a surprise when quite a few settlements actually allowed them in, albeit with restrictions on their movement. At one point, Caldain reflected on their good luck, and he had to admit they shouldn't have been so pessimistic. After all, even villages gripped by fear still need coin and trade to survive, and a trio of well-armed travelers staying the night seemed to assuage some people's fears.

Much to Caldain's chagrin, it wasn't long after their chat with the merchant that the tingle started. It wasn't there all the time, but it seemed to routinely creep into being toward sundown. If the sensation hadn't been so consistent, he would have brushed it aside as nothing but nerves. However, Caldain knew better, and he trusted his instincts. Something was definitely wrong, and more importantly, he couldn't shake the notion that they were being watched.

Glancing at the sun, he estimated that a little less than an hour remained before it completely vanished. Thankfully, he could sense that Kay and Cid were making their way back to him. They had repeated this process each night whether they reached a village or not — scout the surrounding area for suspicious activity and defensible campsites, then report back. If there were a village to stay in, they would then see about acquiring lodging. If not, they'd make their way to one of the campsites. Caldain would have taken similar precautions even without the fear of a blackheart attack, but given the nature of their mission, such safety measures suddenly felt inadequate. Thankfully, no one had reported anything dangerous lurking about so far, but that did nothing to lessen the tingle.

A few minutes later, the first of the siblings returned.

"Anything interesting?" Kay asked as she walked up from behind, her husky voice curious but calm, which eased Caldain's nerves a bit. Dressed in a white tunic, brown breeches, calf-boots, and black fingerless gloves, her broad-shouldered, athletic figure barely made a sound as she approached and crouched down next to Caldain. Placing her pack on the ground next to his, she looked at the village, curious.

"If it wasn't for the chimney smoke, you'd almost think the place was deserted," he replied, his apprehension about the situation clearly on display in his usually confident voice. "Light, with all the trees around here, why in the hells are they burning peat?"

Adjusting the bastard sword strapped across her back, the medallion pommel and leather-wrapped grip of which jutted over her right shoulder, Kay shook her head of short-cropped auburn hair, and wrinkled her slender nose at the smell. Even at this distance, it was intense. "Seems like the further south we go, the worse this is getting."

Caldain nodded in agreement, his waist-length braid of black hair sliding gently across the back of his white shirt. "So it seems . . . and it's damn disconcerting."

Kay glanced at him, her hooded brown eyes filled with concern. During his weeks on the road, Caldain had allowed the sun to tan his northern complexion somewhat, lending him a warmer air than normal. That, however, could do nothing to hide that he was very much on edge. What's more, with the way his white shirt, black breeches and knee boots fit him, he could do very little to mask the near-constant tension in his lean muscles. "Still can't shake the feeling something is very wrong?" she asked, her voice matching the worry in her eyes.

"Oh, very wrong is obvious to all of us. Nothing about any of these villages' behavior is close to normal," he stated dryly. Flexing his hands absently, which hung across his knees from his black bracers, he then looked at Kay and added, his tone bordering on patronizing, "Something dreadful has these people on the brink of hysteria, Kay. It's that something that has me on edge."

Kay gripped his shoulder reassuringly, and the full lips of her bold-featured, gently-bronzed face parted in a gentle smile. "We can feel it too, you know. Besides, if you've been worried this whole time that we would think you daft if you voiced your concerns, then you've really forgotten how much you mean to us," she stated firmly. *"And to me, you lummox,"* she thought remorsefully.

She couldn't read the look Caldain gave her, but his next words told her all she needed to know about where his mind was.

"I shouldn't have brought you two out here," he stated, his tone heavy with regret.

Immediately, she gave him a firm, swift smack to the back of his head.

"Ow!" he cried. "What was that for?!"

"For being an ass!" she chided. "We may be younger than you, and sure, we essentially joined toward the end of the war, but you are truly an over-concerned ass if you think we cannot handle ourselves! Your reason for having us along is sound, and if you really are this worried about what's going on, then it's doubly good we're here!"

Rubbing the spot where she'd hit him, Caldain tried to think of something to say. Before his thoughts could coalesce, a cheery voice laced with mock concern called out from behind, causing both of them to turn around.

"What'd he do now, Sis?"

Tall and slender, Cid approached them casually with a sly grin splayed across his youthful face. Dressed in black leathers that contrasted starkly with his sun-kissed complexion, his silent footfalls belayed the relaxed way he carried himself. Once he reached his companions, he removed his pack and dropped it on the ground before he adjusted the broad-bladed shortsword stowed at his right hip so he could crouch next to his sister comfortably.

"The Old Hawk here – emphasis on the old – was trying to tell me that he thinks all this might be too dangerous for us, and that we probably shouldn't have come along," Kay informed him dryly as he settled himself.

Cid ran a fingerless-gloved hand over his shaved head as he let out a low whistle just as Caldain's cheeks grew slightly red with embarrassment. Placing his hand over his heart in feigned indignation, Cid declared, his hooded brown eyes twinkling with mirth, "I'm hurt, Cal! Truly hurt! We came out all this way to lend our dear old friend a hand and watch his back, and now my sweet sister tells me you don't think we can cut it? You have sliced me to the quick!"

Caldain rolled his eyes. "Alright! You've both made your point!" he huffed. "I'm sorry I even said anything!" He shook his head before adding with a clear hint of regret, "I'm just concerned, that's all. If there really are blackhearts lurking about, then it's better that only one person is at risk than all three of us."

Kay smacked him again, harder this time, drawing a glare from Cal and a laugh from Cid. "Idiot! If blackhearts are about, then it's better to have us and not need us than the other way around! The more eyes the better!" She suddenly grinned. "Besides, you're less likely to muck it all up with us around. Corith knows someone needs to be around to pull your ass out of the fire with as often as you find trouble if memory serves. Isn't that right, Brother?" she finished with a raised eyebrow.

His brown eyes twinkling with mirth, and with an ear-to-ear grin splitting his thin lips, Cid held up his hands and replied, "Leave me out of this one. I came along to watch his back, not get involved in a lovers' spat."

Awkward silence slammed down on the group with authority, leaving Cid grinning with glee as his sister and Caldain blushed furiously with awkward embarrassment.

After the uncomfortable silence dragged on for a moment, Caldain cleared his throat. "Yes, well. . . ." He paused and glanced quickly at Kay to find her looking at him with a level of affection that hadn't graced him in years. Fighting the urge to squirm in his boots as a mix of emotions flooded his mind, he did his best to ignore her look and continued. "Did either of you find anything?"

"Other than a few old footprints and game trails? Not one bloody thing," Cid declared, still grinning at Caldain's discomfort.

"Afraid it's the same for me," Kay agreed. "I even scouted a bit to the south just to get an idea of what lay ahead, and I found nothing. No animals, no recently used trails. Nothing."

Cid's grin vanished as the implications of their findings lent more credence to their fears, causing a tense silence to enshroud the group. The ominous moment dragged on for a bit before he finally growled in anger, "How could any of this have happened right under our noses?!"

"I don't know," Caldain replied, morose. "It seems we've been blind to an awful lot . . . and for quite a while. It takes an enormous amount of fir'gan, food, and Corith-be-damned elvannue engineering to create blackhearts. I don't want to believe it, but Blackstone's fall is ample evidence that, somehow, the Darkness has managed to breed another army. The how of it is beyond me, and —

quite frankly – is a problem for another time."

"So, what do we do?" Kay asked.

"The only thing we can do – we keep moving," Caldain declared with a slight scowl. "The crystal keeps telling me south and east, but that's it."

Cid scratched his chin, then rubbed his shaved head. "Seems like it's leading us into something dangerous, Cal. I really don't like how things are developing, but don't let it be said the Kaskia siblings backed down from a challenge!" He flashed a grin that belied his concerns. "We've got your back, Cal. Besides, if things get really dicey, all we have to do is outrun you."

Caldain and Kay both laughed and grinned slightly at the quip, and the tension began to ease somewhat.

"Good to know, Cid. I'll make sure to trip you as you run by," Caldain informed him, his tone dry.

Scoffing, Cid stood up and shouldered his pack. "You're so damn tall, you're more likely to trip yourself trying that! Now, why don't we see if that village is warmer than the ghost town it appears to be? I'd rather not spend the night in the open, if you know what I mean."

The other two stood, grabbed their packs, and the trio started toward the village. As Kay fell in beside her brother, she patted him on the back and offered playfully, "Don't worry. If they turn us away, I found a nice hollow where we can camp. It did kind of smell of excrement and rotten meat, though."

Cid cringed. "Delightful," he replied, his tone droll.

Kay laughed. "Come now, I would think you would feel right at home. After all, it does kind of remind me of your house."

Rolling his eyes, Cid scowled at her and tromped ahead. "You're more trouble than you are worth, Sister! I should have strangled you when we were younger! It would have saved me from a lifelong pain in my arse!"

Caldain looked at Kay, expecting to see her fuming at the harsh retort. Instead, he heard her laugh, throaty and rich, and he couldn't help but join her.

It was soon apparent their approach had not gone unnoticed. By the time they were halfway to the village, two dozen villagers lined the chest-high wall of loose stone that encompassed the community. Even from a distance, the three friends could see that the people were apprehensive at best. Most looked haggard, their clothes were threadbare, and some even displayed clear signs of terror. Given what their emotional state was probably like, and the naked display of weapons, Caldain already knew they would be unwelcome. That, however, wasn't what bothered him the most about the situation before him.

"Corith be good!" Kay breathed. "They're mostly women!"

"Indeed," Caldain replied gravely, his nostrils flaring at the strong, acrid smell of the peat fires. "And the few men I can see can't be older than ten summers, or are far too old to be taking up arms." He glanced sideways at the siblings, and asked rhetorically, "What has been going on around here?"

Their only response was to share a concerned glance with one another.

Just as they drew within about fifty yards of the makeshift barricade blocking what served as the town entrance, one of the older women, dressed in a ragged brown dress, raised her bow and, without warning, let fly. While the arrow landed well short of them, its intent was clear. Coming to a halt, they heard the woman shout, "No further, er the next one 'll be right between tha eyes!"

Caldain held up his hands as a gesture of peace. "We're not seeking trouble!" he shouted. "We're just making our way south, and thought we might find a room for rent for the night!"

The woman's angry dark eyes, and unkempt, mostly gray hair lent her an air of unhinged, barely contained violence as she yelled, "Ye'll find no room here, mister! Now be gone! We've 'nough of yer kind already!"

Caldain looked at the siblings, confused. Thinking it was worth the risk to prolong the conversation, Caldain asked, "Forgive us, madam, but what do you mean, 'our kind'?"

She seemed to look at them oddly, unsure of whether they were mocking her or genuinely baffled by her statement. She seemed to decide on the latter, but didn't lower her bow. "Sellswords! Mercenaries! Or whatever yer lot call yerselves! Too damn many of yer lot been comin' around since tha trouble began, and it's done nothin' but make things worse!"

Deciding to push his luck further now that she had taken a slightly less combative approach, Cal said, "We've heard mention of some sort of trouble as we've moved south! Can you tell us anything about it?"

"Yer really not from around 'ere, are ye?" she asked, a bit surprised by his response.

Caldain shook his head. "We're from up north!"

She shook her head before she replied, her words growing thick with emotion as she went on, "Well, all I can tell ye, is that our hunters began slowly disappearin' a few months back. I'm guessin' other towns did tha same as us, and looked fer swords to find out what Corith-be-damned thing was makin' off with our men! Those that took our offer went south and east, coin in hand! Not a damn one returned! The few young men we had went lookin' for 'um, and even they're gone now!" She paused, unable to speak anymore as her emotions overwhelmed her.

One of the younger women standing next to her put a comforting hand on her shoulder and said something to her. The older woman nodded, lowered her bow, and walked away from the wall. The younger woman, her blue dress no less weathered than her elder's, and her short blonde hair and dark eyes no less worn, then shouted, her tone terse, "That's all ye be gettin' fern us! Now, be off with ye! Go wherever ye want! Just steer clear o' us!"

Flashing a sympathetic smile as a peace offering, Caldain replied, "We thank you for the information, and we will be on our way! Corith be with you and your village!"

Whether or not the woman heard or even cared for Caldain's platitudes, he couldn't tell, as she quickly turned her back. With the bulk of her fellow residents in tow, she made her way back into the village, leaving only a few armed women to make sure Caldain and the siblings went on their way. Caldain spared one last worried glance at the village before motioning for Kay to lead the way. Setting a steady pace, they put a respectful distance between themselves and the dower community before Kay turned them south.

By the time they reached her choice of shelter for the night, only a sliver of sunlight clung to the horizon. As she'd indicated earlier, it was a hollow. What she'd failed to mention, however, was the hollow was in an ancient colossal oak. Unlike any tree they'd seen in other parts of Kylir, it was located in one of the stands scattered about the region that were once part of the largest forest on Triclose. As they approached the enormous tree, Cid could only imagine what such a continent-spanning feature must have looked like. That musing made him glance at Caldain, whose reflective expression told him that his friend recalled that period with crystalline clarity.

"What a time it must have been," Cid thought, slightly envious of the sights the elder veterans of the war must have seen before Kylir was ravaged by the conflict.

For a moment, as they stood before the dark opening in the

tree, Cid considered asking Caldain about what the area was like back then, but he quickly thought better of it. Instead, he scratched his head and eyed the hollow skeptically as he asked his sister, "Are you sure there's nothing better in the surrounding area?"

"Why?" Kay responded with a dry smirk. "Too rustic for you?"

"Hardly," he replied dismissively. "But I would prefer something less . . . confining."

"We could always camp in the open," Kay offered, knowing full well her brother was teasing her.

Cid immediately shook his head. "That's okay. Spending the night in the open with blackhearts about does not make for a restful night. At least it doesn't stink like you said, and they can only come at us from one direction in there."

Caldain glanced at him sideways. "Expecting a fight?"

Cid shrugged uncomfortably. "With everything we've seen and heard, wouldn't you?"

Caldain nodded. "Of course," he stated sternly. "Just making sure you're focused despite your attempts at humor."

The unexpectedly gruff tone of Caldain's words took both siblings aback. Adjusting his swordbelt, Cid replied, his words sour, "I am damn well focused and aware, Cal! I just prefer a little humor to ease the tension instead of being coiled up like an angry snake all the bloody time! We're all in this together, you know!"

Kay was glad for her position between the two men. Everyone was tense as night rushed to overtake them, and the cross look Caldain shot her brother was evidence enough for her that the situation had him — as her brother aptly put it — coiled like a snake ready to strike.

"Stop this right now!" She scolded, giving each man a stern, reprimanding glare. "We're all tense right now, and badgering each other isn't helping! We've already spent a few uneasy nights on this trip, and I seriously doubt it will be the last! So unless either of you two lummoxes has an actual gripe, I suggest you drop the animosity before I'm forced to beat some sense into one or both of you!"

Kay's firm chastisement seemed to be precisely what was needed . . . at least for Cid. Releasing a stress-relieving chuckle as he shook his head, Cid then said, his cheery voice contrite, "Point taken, Sis. I don't know what possessed either of us." He looked at Caldain and added, "Didn't mean to make light of the situation, Old Hawk. It's just my way of dealing with the stress. Sorry."

Eyes closed, Caldain took a deep breath and let it out slowly. Opening his eyes, he forced a conciliatory smile. "I know, Cid. And I'm sorry as well. I shouldn't have reacted like that."

Cid nodded slightly. "Apology accepted, old pal," he stated with a friendly grin. "What do you say? Let's see about making this tree hole a passable shelter for the night?"

His jab at the chosen shelter earned him a sharp prod to his ribs from Kay's elbow. Winching in pain, Cid nearly protested the blow until he saw the grin on Caldain's face. It was clearly strained, but Cid decided his momentarily sore ribs were worth seeing something other than dour concern on his friend's face.

The smile was fleeting, however. "I think I'll leave that to you two," Caldain replied as his smile was quickly replaced by concern once again. "I want to make another pass around the area."

His statement harshly washed away the siblings' mirth. "Is something wrong you're not telling us?" Kay asked, suddenly uncomfortable standing in the open.

"No. But . . . ." Cal shook his head. "I can't shake this feeling that something is . . . off," he admitted, his frustration glaringly obvious in his normally confident tone.

"Off?" Cid asked, puzzled.

Caldain shrugged. "That's the only way I know to put it. Something just isn't right about this situation."

"Well, that's stating the obvious," Cid replied drolly.

"Cid!" Kay chided.

"What?" he asked incredulously.

"You know what," she replied, her husky voice stern as she glared at him.

Rolling his eyes, Cid held up his hands in defeat. "Fine! I'll be in the hole," he declared, his irritation apparent in every word.

A bit cross with her brother, Kay glared at him as he sulked his way over to the tree. Once he'd vanished inside, she sighed and turned her attention back to Caldain. His focus was clearly on the surrounding area, his eyes darting about like a cornered animal desperately seeking an escape route. She nearly shuddered at his blatant display of unease, but she managed to repress it.

"Care to tell me what is wrong?" She asked softly, her gaze drifting to the trio of scars running down over his right eye. "I haven't seen you like this since—"

"Honestly, Kay, I'd tell you if I knew exactly what has me on edge," he stated sincerely, his words soft despite interrupting her. "It's like a gnawing itch. . . . No – it's more like a knotted muscle in the middle of your back that you just can't reach. I knew this would be dangerous, especially given the direction we are heading . . . but . . . ." He shook his head angrily.

"What?" she prodded.

"So much has gone wrong in such a short amount of time," he stated, his grim words heavy with dread. "Yet, all we know is that blackhearts are somehow roaming free again, and that means the Darkness is stirring. Beyond that, we're blind, Kay. And I fear we've been blind for far longer than any of us dare to imagine."

Kay's stomach coiled into knots at his words. "I'd say that's Damion's paranoia talking, but I know you aren't that way," she replied, doing her best to hide the sudden rise of worry in herself. "What can we do to help? After all, that's why I– we are here," she finished, cringing in her mind at the slip of the tongue.

If Caldain noticed, he didn't show it. Instead, he shook his head in frustration. "Stay alert and watch my back."

She smiled reassuringly. "Of course."

His next words hit her like a battering ram, obliterating her smile. Meeting her gaze, he stated, his confident voice forceful, "And if I tell you to run – take the crystal and run."

The finality of his statement and the ferocity in his eyes left her stunned and her heart crushed. Unable to find the words to respond, or the will to move for that matter, she was amazed she could even meet his gaze. To her surprise, he did not press her for an answer when she didn't reply. Instead, his eyes seemed to be gazing deep into her soul as if he could divine her willingness to obey such an order. After a moment of heavy silence, he appeared to find the answer he was looking for.

Removing his pack from his back, he handed it to her. Numbly, she clenched it to her chest as she watched him check to make sure his weapons were loose in their scabbards and his boot knives were easily accessible. When he was satisfied, he spared her a brief nod and a fleeting half-smile before trotting off into the darkness.

Hugging his pack fiercely against her modest bosom as if doing so would force him to come back, she stood there staring into the night, following him with her senses until he was beyond her reach. Even after she could no longer feel him, she continued to stare, her mind awash with a chaotic mix of fear and the implications of Caldain's concerns.

"Sis?"

The gently asked, concern-filled question shattered her cocoon of isolation, startling her. Jumping slightly forward, she spun, her arm cocked to hit whoever had spoken.

Hands held up defensively, Cid took a quick step back, shocked at his sister's reaction. "Whoa! It's just me, Kay!"

Staring at her brother, her eyes wild and apprehensive, it took her a moment to gather her wits. Eventually, she lowered her fist. Taking a deep breath, she let it out slowly before offering, "Sorry, Cid. I was lost in thought."

Cid flashed her an accepting, and disarming, smile. "Clearly," he said, his ordinarily snarky tone droll. "Are you okay? You've been standing out here for a while. I thought you might have turned to stone." His attempt at humor dragged a subtle smile from his sister, and he could see some of the tension flow out of her. "Did Cal go out scouting?"

"Yes, to both," she replied with a nod. "I'm just worried about him."

Cid barked a laugh. "Worried? About Cal? Come on, Sis - it's Cal! The Old Hawk can take care of himself – even if there really are blackhearts roaming about. Besides, he's got us to watch his back."

"That's just it," she said, hugging his pack tighter. "I think he is firmly convinced blackhearts are out there, and. . . ." She trailed off.

Concerned, Cid stepped forward and rested his hands comfortingly on her shoulders. "What is it, Sis?"

Worry flooding back into her eyes, Kay met her brother's gaze. "Corith be good, Cid – he's scared!"

"I shouldn't have brought them," he thought, his gaze focused on the currents that illuminated the area with their normally soothing ethereal blue light.

Crouched atop the same rise that overlooked the village from earlier, the thought kept rattling about his head like a swarm of mud crows ravaging a fresh carcass. With his senses stretched out to observe not only the village but the surrounding land, the thought was making the task far more difficult than it needed to be. He'd tried to

306

banish the notion, but it was dug in like a stubborn, irrational tick. His mission was vital, and having the siblings – not to mention another Seeker – with him increased the chance of success, especially if they ran into trouble. Yet, at the same time, his heart railed against putting his long-time friends in such a dangerous position. Fighting Gifted was one thing. Fighting blackhearts was something drastically different.

Shifting his weight, Caldain pulled his mind back. He didn't like all the ambiguity that had sprung up around this mission, and he always found the best way to combat uncertainty was with answers. As such, after hearing the village's story, he'd decided that such answers were needed before they stumbled into a potential disaster. Returning to the village seemed like the logical starting point since they'd been more forthcoming than most about the disappearances. Knowing he'd hardly be invited to sit down for a chat, he chose to eavesdrop via the currents. At this distance, he knew it could be unreliable, but it ended up paying off somewhat. From what he could glean, the village's favorite hunting grounds were a few miles to the north and east, which made far more sense to him than the story about the mercenaries going southeast.

"Unless the sellswords had already done some scouting… or they simply were scamming these frightened people," he muttered aloud. Shaking his head to keep his mind from embracing all the possibilities, he stood up. "One step at a time," he said aloud before heading out, his path set to take him northeast of the village.

As he moved, his mind was once again besieged not only by the sensation that something was very wrong and that he was being watched, but also by his nagging concerns for the siblings. There was no doubting their skills as fighters, but they had – by Corith's good grace – never had to fight blackhearts. Granted, like all the Wardens' soldiers, they'd been taught the tactics to combat the Gifted-killing abominations. However, as the loss of countless lives had harshly proven, practice was no replacement for practical experience… and even then, it was too often not enough.

It took him only a few minutes to reach the general area that his snooping had gleaned from the villagers. Like most of the region, the trees were sparse in the immediate area, but there was plenty of scattered vegetation, and even a few dense stands of trees in the distance. More than likely, there were even herds of deer, wild bramhen, and possibly the occasional torgen that passed through the area. It wasn't the most ideal hunting spot, but it was close to the village and most likely met their needs.

Slowing to a walk, he did his best to shove his concerns aside before unsheathing his sword and focusing keenly on what the currents and his senses were telling him. Initially, he felt a surge of relief when he couldn't find any obvious signs of blackhearts on the currents, or any danger for that matter. Experience, however, prevented him from taking the news at face value. Slowing his pace, he turned his attention fully to the flow of the currents. While he saw nothing to indicate a lurking threat, there was something about their movement that seemed . . . odd.

"Why are they so calm? This should be the hunting grounds. And even if I'm mistaken, there should be more obvious signs of life. But I sense . . . nothing?" he asked the night, puzzled.

Coming to a halt, every fiber of his being was suddenly on edge. Nothing wasn't quite true as there were a few vermin lurking nearby in the tall grass that were likely trying to avoid the attention of the pair of hawks floating in the sky. What's more, there was even a faint sensation of insects going about their nightly routine.

"This isn't right at all. Even if all the life in the area was holed up for the night, it should still register more impactfully on the currents. But they are practically still . . . almost as if nothing lives here or ever has. Corith, what in the hells is going on out here? How were we not aware?"

Shoving the dreadful thought out of his mind, Caldain knelt down and scanned the immediate area. When he was positive he was safe, he took a deep breath and closed his eyes. *"This is hardly the best place to do this,"* he thought, *"but I've got to get a better picture of the situation."* He smirked as he tried to calm his mind. *"At least if there's a Gifted out there, I won't put Cid and Kay in danger."*

After crafting a few simple alarms around him from the currents in case someone approached, Cid took another deep breath and let it out, emptying his mind. A moment later, his consciousness was soaring along the ethereal blue strands of power.

It was a risky move, especially out in the open. If the enemy found him while his mind searched along the currents, his alarms would give some warning and even less time to react. Normally, he wouldn't take such a bold risk, but it was clear to him they needed answers of some sort and needed them quickly. So, he let his mind soar, his consciousness spreading far into the night. Using himself, the village, and his friends to orient himself, he searched in all directions, seeking any indicator of ordinary life as a reference. Once he found it, he then backtracked to each orientation point while comparing the flow of fir'gan along the way. Between returning to his body to ensure his safety and the meticulous nature of his search, it took nearly two hours to complete it. To his horror – and chagrin – he found within the void between areas of active life the same lifelessness that afflicted the currents around him. He had no way to know just how widespread this condition was, but it sent a chill down his spine.

Returning to his body, his consciousness looked down on it like a spirit gazing upon the corpse it once inhabited. The only relief he'd found this evening was that, besides the cold sweat that had broken out as a result of the strain of the prolonged search, his body had remained safe.

"I'm not gonna leave myself much strength to get back to camp if I don't end this soon. There has to be something out there that can provide some sort of clarity to this nightmare," he thought, irritated by the lack of answers. *"There's no immediate pattern to all this other than the voids of lifelessness between hubs of life. At best, there's been a few minuscule bumps in the currents caused by the remnants of life in the voids, like around here, but nothing that can tell me exactly wha—"*

If his eyes had been open, they would have been wide and round like a full moon as the realization struck home.

"Corith! I'm a damn fool!"

Withdrawing his senses, he returned his consciousness to his body. Anger tore at his face as he stood up and focused his senses on the surrounding area, seeking one of the bumps of life. *"How did I miss it! Corith damn it all to the deepest of the Hells — I'm a damn idiot!"*

It took him only a moment to find what he was looking for. With a growl, he took off at a run; part of his mind focused on his surroundings while the other part sought more of the minor anomalies in the currents. As he traveled, he found a myriad of the abnormalities, the bulk of which seemed to be leading northwest and southeast. Those other anomalies, however, were purged from his mind when he finally spotted his destination. Slowing to a cautious walk, and bringing his sword to bear in a defensive posture, it was immediately evident why he'd failed to recognize them for what they truly were. Slivers of fir'gan were snaking their way through the dead spots in the currents, feigning life's effect, albeit weakly, on fir'gan. To his horror, when he was finally close enough to see the anomaly without the aid of the currents, he saw that those slivers of power were the only thing that remotely resembled life amongst a dark swath of death.

With the lack of fir'gan to fully illuminate the dead area except around its edges, it was difficult to pick out details. However, between the size of the blighted terrain and the lack of grass, it was clear an ample amount of blackheart blood had been spilt here. There also appeared to be at least five corpses, but there was most likely more, given the severed limbs and chunks of flesh he could see. Whether the remains were human or blackheart, he could not tell. Every inch of the heavily decayed flesh was blackened and covered in leaking, pustulant boils. The thick, oozing liquid glistened dully in the weak light, making the sight even more nauseating than it was.

Caldain crouched down, his sword cradled in his arms and at the ready. He'd seen far worse in the war, so the macabre display factored only a small amount in the disgust writhing in his gut. There were far too many of these splotches on the currents for him to believe they were all a result of dead blackhearts. If there were only a small handful of them, the missing people could be explained away. Blackhearts were just as mortal as any mundane, and humans could easily kill one, but a mundane rarely survived such an encounter unless it was at range. So, if the humans had killed the blackhearts and had survived, stories would have been told, and those stories would have eventually reached the ears of a Warden. What's more, blackheart deaths would result in an obvious blight on the currents. Yet, here he had a spot that somewhat mimicked life's effect on the currents . . . almost as if someone or something was trying to hide their presence.

"Corith be good. . . . Could that really be the case? Could they be trying to mask their deaths, and by extension, their presence, somehow?" he thought, aghast.

Scowling in frustration, Caldain stood up. He could worry about the answer later. For now, he needed to get back to his friends, inform them of what he'd found, then get word to Quinn. Quinn could then get word to the Bestyne and Kydan'fir Orders so they could start hunting the blackhearts and their nests, assuming that wasn't already the case. Hells, even Darkon would need to be informed, the thought of which deepened his scowl. There was no lack of love or distrust between Darkon and the Stelariuos Order, but if the blackheart threat was even a portion of what Caldain was beginning to suspect, the Orders would need to work together to counter it.

His rising anger at the situation mixed with his frustration and irritation, making him feel inept and useless. The urge to do something – anything – about this growing disaster was overwhelming, and while he could have chosen to calm himself and return to his friends, the urge to do something won out. Making one last check of the surrounding area to make sure there were no lurking threats, he turned his attention to the blight. Focusing inward, he latched on to his fir'gan with a ferocity he usually reserved for battle and drew it forth. Immediately, his dark blue aura burst to life, writhing with blistering power and anger, illuminating the area. Seeing the details of the macabre blight with a bit more clarity drew a growl of rage from Caldain. Like so many others amongst the Wardens' ranks, he never wished to see such a sight again, but here it was, in all its sinister glory, splayed before him like a feast for the dead.

"I can't do anything about the blackhearts right now," he growled, "but ridding the land of this spot is a start!"

As the power within him swelled, the color drained from his right eye, turning it white, and the scars began to ache as the air around him grew colder and his aura's color bled to an icy blue. Raising his sword, he pointed it at the scarred land and focused his building power at the tip of the weapon, causing a thin sheet of ice to coat the blade as the fir'gan flowed along its length. It was then that a single thought rang out in his mind.

"A new war has begun."

It should have made his soul weep and howl with dreadful sadness. Instead, it was as if that thought had tapped the darkest depths of Caldain's soul, releasing the part of him that thrived – no, enjoyed battle. As that portion of him filled his being, carried on waves of icy fir'gan, a grin as dark and sinister as the blight before him spread across his face.

"If war is what those bastards want to bring to this world, then it's war they'll get!" he thought vehemently. *"Throw all the blackhearts you shadowspawn want at me, for I am one of the cursed! A bringer of death! No spawn of the Darkness will keep me from my mission; and once that is done, I will see to it the blackheart blight is purged once more! By blood, by honor, and by deed – this I swear!"*

"He's been gone far too long," Kay stated once again.

Standing just to the side of the hollow's entrance, Cid tore his gaze away from the darkness outside and looked back at his sister.

Seated next to their packs with her back to the wall, she still clutched Caldain's pack to her chest and her gaze was fixed beyond the hollow's entrance. Her worry had not dissipated over the last couple of hours, and Cid had given up hope that she would settle down. She'd never been good at concealing her feelings for Caldain from him, but this was something more. For whatever reason, she was genuinely concerned that she might not see him again. While he understood her feelings, it was beginning to grind his nerves thin. Fighting off a grimace of irritation, he offered his sister the same reassuring smile he'd offered numerous times since Cal took off.

"Damnit, woman! Get your act together! You're a Knight, and you damn well know that Cal has been in worse situations than this or anything we could dream up! If you were any other woman, my respect for you would be dead and buried!" he thought in disgust.

Though he was sorely tempted to speak those words – if for nothing more than the hope that the shock of it would snap his sister out of her distress – he knew better. At best, she would outright attack him in anger. At worst, she might decide to run after Cal.

"That might not be so bad," he thought as he peered at her, the cold light of the currents making her look even worse off than she was.

Instead, he did his best to reign in his irritation and said, as he had done so many times that night, "He will be fine, Kay." However, after seeing her like this for so long, he couldn't help but let some of his irritation slip through as he added, "If you'd just take a moment to calm down and reach out, you'd see he's leaving subtle marks on the currents so that we at least know he's still alive and kicking."

His exasperation wasn't lost on Kay. Even before he'd finished, Kay's fearfulness was suddenly replaced by anger as her hooded brown eyes snapped to her brother. Fueled by her sudden rage at what she perceived as insensitivity from her brother, she shot to her feet, dropping the pack, and darted forward. Before Cid knew what was happening, her hand lashed out, slapping him violently. Dazed, he rolled against the hollow's wall before unceremoniously falling to the ground. Blood trickling from his mouth and his head spinning, Cid somehow managed to push himself into a seated position. In his disoriented state, he almost laughed when he looked up at his sister and found three visages glaring down at him.

"Calm down?!" she growled. "Don't you dare tell me to calm down! With what might be out there, I'm worried sick not just for Cal, but for us!" She took a threatening step forward, and Cid knew he couldn't stop her if she wanted to hit him again. "Blackhearts, Cid! Corith-be-damned blackhearts! All the training in the world can't prepare us to face such a nightmare! I'd rather face a Warden than those creatures!"

As Cid's vision cleared, he noticed that not only was his sister trembling, but tears were streaming down her cheeks. Whether they were tears of rage or fear, he did not know. What he was sure of, however, was that his sister was truly scared to the point of panic.

Using the wall for leverage and balance, Cid pushed himself to his feet. "Alright, Kay! Alright!" he said, his tone contrite, seeking to pacify her. "I didn't mean it that way, and . . . and I don't think I've ever seen you this upset. I'm sorry, I really am! Please, Sis – for both our sakes – just take a moment to reach out, and you'll see that he's leaving us signs that he's still kicking."

For a moment, he thought she might hit him again, and he braced himself for the blow. Mercifully, she didn't. Instead, she spun and stomped out of the hollow, sobbing. Although he didn't like the idea of her standing in the open, he knew she needed a moment to compose herself and calm down. So, instead of going after her, he took some time to gather himself. When he was sure the dizziness was gone, all his teeth were still in place, and the bleeding had stopped, he gave her a moment more before finally leaving the hollow. He was aware she'd gone only a few feet from the shelter even before he'd gathered his wits, but given her state of mind, he didn't feel a full measure of relief until he saw her with his own brown eyes.

Illuminated by the currents, she looked like a beautiful statue at the center of a lake of cold, soothing light. Back straight, arms at her sides and her head bowed, it was hard to believe she just tried to slap his head off his shoulders. Where she'd been nothing but a blatant knot of anxiety that oozed anger moments earlier, she now seemed calmer, those other emotions only apparent in the rigidity of her stance.

Leaning against the hollow's entrance, Cid shook his head, and a wry smile split his lips. *"Well, if hitting me is what you needed to regain some of your composure, I guess it's a small price to pay."*

Looking back at her, he felt a sudden pang of guilt grip his heart. *"This isn't the life either of us wanted, nor is it what I promised you when our parents died, is it?"* he thought. *"I don't think we had a clue about where life would lead us when Vann found us. Hells, we were nothing but two scrawny mongrels waiting to die in the gutter. We would have done anything for a crust of bread at that point, so life as a scullion or servant seemed like paradise in return for food. I often wonder, Sis, if we would have made the same choice if we'd known what awaited us? I promised to care for you and make a better life for you, and it seems like all I've given you is war and heartbreak.*

"Do you ever think about it, Sis? I doubt you'd ever show it if you did. Still, when I see you like this, full of fear and dread, I can't help but feel like I failed you somehow. Hells, with as long as we've lived, and could live, this isn't the first time I've felt this way, and it probably won't be the last. If we make it through this – and I'm sure we will – maybe we should walk away from it all like we've talked about. After seeing you like this, I'm more sure about it than ever. We were never cut out for this world of shadows and madness. I promise, Sis – when this is over, we'll leave all this behind and I'll give you the life I promised you all those years ago."

"I'm sorry, Cid."

Her softly spoken, heart-felt words startled him from his thoughts. "What?"

"I said I'm sorry," she stated, her husky voice remorseful. "I shouldn't have been so cross with you. You were right about Cal, and I overreacted."

Cid smirked. "Overreacted?"

Though she did not move, he could picture the devilish smile on her face. "Careful, Cid . . . unless you want me to hit you again."

Although she still appeared tense, he was relieved that she had calmed down and regained her composure. "No, no. Once was enough to remind me not to get on your bad side, thank you very much," he quipped, a hint of relief in his confidently cocky voice. "Although – not to push my luck – I'd feel much better if we were back inside. Between you and Cal's behavior, being in the open suddenly makes me feel naked."

Turning, she offered her brother a small, apologetic smile. "You're right. It was foolish of me to leave the shelter."

Cid shrugged. "It's okay, Sis. It's not like we're blind in the dark."

"I know. But, still–" Her thoughts slammed into a wall, and her eyes bulged in shocked surprise as a sudden surge of power from Caldain's position rippled violently along the currents. "Cid!" she declared ominously.

Like his sister, he felt the surge and was just as astonished. Turning northward, he focused on the origin of the ripples. It took only a moment to realize he couldn't make out what had happened. Cursing under his breath, he told his sister, worried that she might bolt at any moment, "Cal's alive, Sis! I can't make heads or tails of the chaos, but he is alive . . . and at the center of it."

Turning back to Kay, to make sure she had both heard him and had not run off, he froze. The color draining from his face, he stated, his tone insistent, "Sis."

Hand gripping her sword hilt tightly, her focus on the mass of power, she barely heard her brother, nor did she notice his sudden apprehension.

Cid forced himself to move despite his sudden urge to run the other way. Stepping forward, he repeated himself more urgently. "Sis!"

"What?!" she started to shout, irritated that he'd interrupted her focus, when he suddenly plowed into her, driving her to the ground.

Stunned by the sudden assault, and her breath driven from her as she hit the ground, she barely noticed the hiss of an object cutting through the air where she'd been standing. Before she could muster her voice, Cid rolled off her and positioned himself between her and the archer, all the while forging a large shield of air. "Go!" he barked even as a half-dozen poison-coated, obsidian-tipped arrows hit his shield.

Kay's instincts kicked in almost as soon as her brother rolled off her. Scrambling into a combat crouch, she quickly scanned her surroundings. Still a bit dazed, she barely heard her brother's order, but she didn't need it. They were in the open and the currents, though the signals were hard to read, made it clear they were surrounded. Without another thought, she reached back and grabbed her brother by the collar, and with fir'gan-fueled strength, dove back into the hollow. Hitting the ground hard, she released her brother before she slid violently into the back of their shelter. This time, however, she was ready for the impact and managed to absorb most of the force with her legs. Using that to her advantage, she propelled herself to the side and clear of the entrance even as several arrows whistled home into the back of the hollow.

Scrambling into a crouch near their packs, she was relieved to see her brother crouched on the other side of the shelter. He appeared to be a bit stunned but was otherwise fine. Assured that her brother was unharmed, and with her wits quickly returning, she took stock of what the chaotic currents were telling her even as more arrows thudded into the tree. One even pierced through the wood surrounding the entrance, but she managed to ignore it and keep her focus on discerning just how many assailants were out there.

"Corith, it's like the currents have been poisoned! There are dead spots everywhere, and the currents feel like thick, sluggish honey! I can't get a clear idea of just what's out there, but it isn't good!" she thought with a horrified and frustrated scowl.

Even as the tree was peppered with more arrows, and their attackers drew closer, Kay realized they needed both better protection and a better idea of just how bad their situation was.

"Cid! Is your brain still functioning?!" she asked as she scooped up Cal's pack and secured it on her back.

"Yeah! No thanks to you!"

"Good!" she barked as she grabbed her pack and tossed him his pack. "Seal the entrance and stand clear of the walls! I want a better look out there!"

Nodding his agreement, He quickly sealed the entrance with a barrier of air as he secured his pack to his back. Arrows immediately rained against it, falling harmlessly to the ground, while others thudded into the tree trunk. To their horror, more of the arrows managed to pierce the tree. Careful to remain deep in the hollow, the siblings moved to where they could see outside, and were greeted by a nightmarish sight.

Dead spots littered the currents, disrupting their flow and casting their light about in a mad dance. That light frolicked angrily across poison-tipped arrows knocked on dark, twisted bows, as well as black leather armor, and glossy, pockmarked skin that reminded Kay of a slime-coated toad. The sight twisted her already fear-knotted stomach even further. Swallowing hard, she did her best to keep her voice calm. "I count at least a dozen."

Cid nodded, his eyes fixated on the advancing force. "At least. It's too damn hard to read the currents! I'd say there's more, but . . . ." He shook his head in frustration. "Bloody hells! I thought we were ready for something like this, but the taint on the currents . . . and the sight of them! I feel like I'm on the verge of vomiting endlessly!"

Kay tried to laugh, but the nervous chuckle she let out was more akin to a high-pitched, stressed twitter. Before she could say a word to her brother, another rain of arrows peppered the tree. Both of them flinched back at the rapid percussion. The tree's interior wall was beginning to look like a slobbering maw full of dark teeth whose poisonous drool was pooling on the ground. Thankfully, the poison wasn't immediately life-threatening; however, it was disrupting the currents around them. A quick glance at her brother's face was all she needed to confirm its effects on him.

Straining mightily to maintain his shield, perspiration coated his slowly paling face, and his eyes were pinched. The situation was clearly untenable, but she could not see a clear way out of it.

"I know that look," Cid stated through clenched teeth. "Please tell me you're dreaming up some way to get us out of here, and you're not just worried about little ol' me?"

She couldn't bring herself to lie to him, so she shook her head and offered, "No — I cannot see a realistic way in which one or both of us survive."

Cid grimaced in pain as more of the vile arrows slammed home. Whether it was her words, the arrow's taint, or both that elicited the display, she did not know, nor did it really matter. What mattered, was finding a way out. So, with her fear for their lives driving her, she grasped onto an idea that seemed somewhat plausible.

"But I have an idea. . . . It's a reach, but it's all I've got!" Kay blurted, her voice tight.

"Let's have it! I don't have all day!"

"I'm going to detonate the tree," she stated bluntly.

Cid grimaced again. "And here I thought this was hopeless."

Kay glanced at him sideways. "I could take over the shield, but you're weak as it is, and all we'd be doing is buying a little time for Cal to return. And let's be honest, we have no way to know if he's aware of our situation or even if he's alive."

"Point taken," Cid said, his voice strained thin. "I suggest you get on with it. . . ."

She nodded. "Be ready to run!" she ordered as she began to gather tendrils of power.

Like her brother, she was quickly drenched with sweat as she fought with the discordant currents. Desperate to gather as much external power to amplify her inherent fir'gan, Kay did her best to shut out the outside world with little effect. No amount of training could have prepared her for the reality of facing a blackheart. She didn't blame their instructors; none of them could have, or were capable of, creating the toxic and disruptive environment the creatures produced. Still, she'd thought herself prepared for the severity of the cold, hopeless terror gripping her heart, and the chaotic nature of the currents under the blackhearts' influence.

Hissing aloud at the discordant thoughts, she shook her head to clear her mind as best she could. However minuscule their chances of survival were, it depended on her ability to stay calm and manipulate the currents.

You can do this, Kay! she railed at herself. *Focus!*

For a moment, she broke through the chaos and latched onto enough fir'gan to begin weaving her desperation plan. *Got it!* she thought, victorious, as an orb of concentrated air began to coalesce a few feet above their heads.

Cid, his extremities shaking and his pallor that of a ghost from the strain, noticed the orb and grinned ever so slightly. "You've got it, Sis," he encouraged weakly.

Kay heard her brother and managed a small smile that belayed her alarm at her brother's appearance. "Just a bit longer, Cid," she pleaded.

Cid tried to nod, but mustered only the barest of movement. Kay then turned her focus entirely back to her work, but before she could nurture the blast any further, a double flight of arrows hammered into the tree, and her world exploded into a nightmare.

The first barrage ripped deeply through the weakened wood, with a few of the toxic arrows clearing the barrier, only to drop to the ground and slide close to the siblings. The proximity to the two and the currents they were battling with sent a massive ripple through the fir'gan. To Kay's horror, the blast she was weaving began to untangle, sloughing off as if the currents were dying. Before she could even fully register what was happening, the second wave of arrows blasted into the tree just as her brother collapsed and started vomiting as if his guts were trying to squeeze every drop of life from him.

Somehow, Kay's instincts took over her nearly paralyzed mind, and she flung herself atop her brother as another volley tore through the weakened wood and slammed into the back of the hollow, peppering her with wooden shards. It was all she could do to remain still atop her brother while the air hissed in rage as flight after flight of toxic barbs cut through the air, showering them with splintered shrapnel as they tore into the hollow. It was a nightmare incarnate, and her terror was only deepened by the symphony of retching and coughing from her brother.

"Corith, what do we do?" she prayed, even as she began to feel blood trickling over her body from where the wood shards had scraped or pierced her skin. *"I can't even shield myself now! Corith, please! My brother may be dying, and I'm helpless! Show me a way out of here, or at least make our deaths quick!"*

Kay didn't expect an answer. As far as she and many others were concerned, if Corith had ever been involved with their struggle, he had long since abandoned the Wardens to their fate. So, it came as a bit of a surprise when, after what seemed like an eternity, the arrows stopped, and an ominous silence descended on the area. After an agonizingly quiet moment, Kay finally opened her eyes cautiously, dreading what she would see. The dying glint of hope in her heart received a small boon when she noticed that her brother still lived. His skin was ghastly pale and his breathing was ragged and shallow, but he was alive.

Assured of his condition, she slowly climbed off of him and looked around. As she positioned herself in a protective crouch beside Cid, careful to avoid the arrows and the growing pools of poison on the ground, she knew the inevitable would soon befall them, and that brief infusion of hope died out. Where solid wood once protected them, gaping, jagged holes now granted prying eyes passage, while beyond their shattered sanctuary, the currents had completed their descent into violent chaos, preventing her from seeing much beyond the shelter's entrance. Disjointed as the currents were, their soothing light had followed suit, flickering in and out of existence with chilling speed. However, Kay didn't need to see to know what was cautiously approaching. The sound of numerous footsteps unhindered by a need for silence had already reached her ears, accompanied by short, guttural statements.

Defeat hammering at her soul, Kay suddenly let go of her pack and sat down hard. Pulling her knees up, she wrapped her arms around her legs as she dropped her head against her knees. "I'm sorry, brother," she sobbed softly through her tears. "I failed you and I failed Cal. I'm so very sorry." Anything else she might have said lodged in her throat as the tears became a stream, and her chest heaved with the weight of her grief.

"Damn you, Corith! I cannot even end things for us before those cursed creatures get their hands on us! What kind of god grants immortality to people, leaving only a few macabre paths to death open?" she wailed internally. *"Damn you! Damn this conflict and this world to the deepest hell!"*

By this point, fifty-strong blackhearts had surrounded the tree and drawn close before letting silence reclaim the area. Had she bothered to look up, she would have seen the assailants in detail against the frantic light of the currents. However, she had no reason to do so. What did it matter if she knew the faces of their killers? Dead was dead. The only question that remained was whether they would make it quick, or would they delight in the agony of a slow and painful death?

As the situation continued to drown her, her mind grew numb to it and she suddenly realized she didn't care how it ended. Death would end the pain of having failed her brother and the man she loved. As for a torturous death, she believed it was a fair punishment for that failure.

"Bak'to jok'ad'va!" barked a guttural voice, breaking the deathly silence, and a solitary set of footsteps began to approach.

Slow and methodical, it seemed to Kay that the advancing blackheart was trying to savor the moment. Without looking up, Kay stated, despondent, "Get on with it, Shadowspawn. . . . You'll find no resistance here, and even less satisfaction."

The footsteps paused just inside the hollow, and there was a gleeful cackle from the blackhearts that reminded Kay of a swarm of chittering rats. When it died down, Kay expected the footsteps to resume. Instead, in its rasping, guttural voice, the blackheart stated with glee, "Thine declaration 'tis born of falsehood, Light Touched. For thou art woefully ignorant of our blessing and the agony that awaits thee. Thine suffering shall nurture us, and through us, the Darkness. Be blessed, Accursed, for soon thou shalt bask in the truth that is the Darkness."

The blackheart's pompous confidence pierced the shroud of defeat numbing Kay. Sneering slightly, Kay spit, her breath coming out in a puff as her body grew cold, "Burn in the deepest of the Hells, you Shadowspawned bastard!"

Cackling, and its almond-shaped, pitch-black eyes shining with glee astride a hooked nose, the blackheart took a step forward and raised its jagged obsidian sword. Before it could take the next step, a rush of seething cold air slammed into its sharp-featured head, and bewilderment took hold. Oblivious to the commotion behind it, the blackheart was trying to figure out why some of its greasy black hair was falling free, and why blood was sliding down its veiny, boil-covered face. It then felt a snap and crunch before the world went dark.

With her mind as numb as it was, the frigid scythe of air that cut above her before slicing out the back of the tree barely registered with Kay, but the commotion that followed caught her attention. Looking up, she saw that the approaching blackheart in black leather armor stood rooted in place not three steps away, blood pouring down its face from an ice-trimmed gash that cut diagonally across its dark, molted-skinned visage. With eyes resigned to death, she watched as the upper portion of the blackheart's head slid free and fell to the ground. On the tail of the chunk of flesh, bone and brain, the body tumbled forward, spilling the remaining contents of the head toward Kay.

Her dull eyes followed the pool of dark, viscous blood as it raced toward her feet, its blighted touch scarring the surrounding terrain. Part of her knew she should move, but shock had quashed all logic and reason in her.

"Just a little further and it will be all over," she thought as if beckoning the toxic fluid would expedite the process.

"Kay!" A voice in her head suddenly yelled even as screams of agony rained about the tree and explosive bursts of hellishly fridge blue-white flames erupted amongst the blackhearts.

"Damnit, Kay! Shake it off! There's too many of them for me to hold off!"

"What?" She thought, unaware that she was responding.

"It's Cal, Kay! Pull yourself– Argh!! Bastards! Burn in hells!" A bright burst of cold flames lit up the area, immediately followed by screams and the smell of charred flesh.

The acrid smell made Kay's nose twitch as she watched the blackhearts scramble in search of their attacker. Clearly, they had forgotten about her, but she knew it wouldn't last. Even so, she found herself unwilling to move as she replied to the voice, *"It's not you. Cal is dead. The blackhearts got him before us. Just let us die in peace."*

"Corith take your soul, Kay! It is me! I tracked them back here! I'm sorry I'm late, but damnit, I need you to act like the Knight you are! Pick up your brother and be ready to move when I say so!"

More screams and guttural calls accompanied a blast of angry flames from behind the tree.

"I'm imagining this. Cal is dead. Otherwise, he would have come for us."

"No, I damn well am not! We don't have time for this! You mean the world to me, Kay! But by Corith, I will not risk the mission any further!"

Those words echoed in her head and seemed to crack her shroud of fatalistic acceptance enough for her to notice and comprehend that a pair of blackhearts, both scorched badly and littered with ice, had finally noticed her and her brother. The blackhearts suddenly screamed, whether in pain or rage, she did not know, but their cry and sudden charge with raised weapons made their intentions clear.

"Kay!" the voice screamed in her head as a swath of ice-blue flame cut between her and the blackhearts, a tendril of which engulfed the fluid slithering toward her, eliminating the threat. *"This is your last chance!"* the voice continued, its words heavy with desperation. *"Either move when I tell you or die where you sit!"*

With that final proclamation, the flames stalling the blackhearts, as well as those about the battlefield winked out, and she felt a surge of blistering heat above her. Looking up, she felt her breath catch in her throat.

A magnificent ball of dancing fire had coalesced, its angry, natural flames licking at the sides of the tree. As if the fire had returned life to her body, she regained some measure of her senses. Right away, she noticed the ball was not only contained in a barrier of air, but an explosion of said air had massed at the center of the blaze.

"We've got to move," she thought, echoing the pleading voice of Caldain.

Grabbing her pack, she stumbled to her feet and immediately saw that the blackhearts had retreated at the sight of the flaming concoction. Awkwardly, she grabbed her brother. Legs trembling from the strain, she secured him over her shoulder and, with her senses fully returning to her control, she looked about for an exit. Blackhearts, now cowered by the agonizing light emitted by the fire, still filled the area before the tree. In all likelihood, they'd be spotted despite the painful situation the shadowspawned creatures were experiencing. As such, going forward would amount to the same fate as staying put. But then, where could she go? The blackhearts, not to mention the rest of the tree, surrounded her. In her current state, she saw no option.

"Cal, if that really is you, I'm ready, but there's no way out!"

A sharp crack caused her to spin around. As a human-sized chunk of the tree fell inward, she heard Cal's voice say, *"Shield and go!"*

The words had barely entered her mind when she felt the power in the giant, floating blaze peak, causing it to bulge dangerously. With no time to think, and a death grip on her brother, she instinctively gathered what fir'gan she could, and dropped a shield of raw power on her back. At the same time, tendrils of fir'gan surged through her legs with enough strength to propel her through the opening and onto a newly blazed path through the blackheart ranks.

An instant after she cleared the tree, the blaze exploded with a deafening roar, turning the tree into a hail of burning shrapnel even as it punched Kay through the air and clear of the foul creatures. While her shield absorbed some of the blast, much of it and its accompanying flame made it through, driving the breath from her and lighting her clothes on fire. Screams from the blackhearts hit by the burning shrapnel tore through the night as she hit the ground hard, her brother ripped from her grasp by the impact. Reeling from the blow, it was all she could do to try to breathe. Before she could take more than a few ragged breaths or gather her wits about her, two hands came out of the darkness and yanked her to her feet.

"Run!" Caldain hissed as he smothered the flames on her back, took her pack and shoved her forward. "And don't stop till I tell you! I've got your brother!"

Unable to do more than keep herself upright as she stumbled forward, she did just as she was ordered. It was a hectic scramble at first, but as the currents cleared of the blackhearts' taint, she was able to gather more to her and fuel her pace. Her lungs burned, and she knew many of her bones were broken, but she didn't spare a drop for healing. She wanted out of the nightmare now, and pain would not hinder her escape.

For how long she ran, she did not know, but woods soon

gave way to endless rolling fields, and with the appearance of open terrain and clear skies, she dug deeper and ran harder. Running was the only thing that mattered; the only way she could escape the nightmare. So, she ran even as blood began to pool in her mouth and slide down her chin. She ran even as fluid rattled in her lungs. She ran even when she felt bone break skin along her right shin. She ran until, finally, her broken legs gave out and she fell to the ground, driven to unconsciousness by endless waves of agonizing pain.

Cursing, Cal placed Cid gently on the ground and shouldered Kay's pack before racing up to her prone form.

"Corith be good, you are a strong one, Kay," he said, his strong voice and gray eyes full of compassion and pride as he knelt down beside her and felt for a pulse. "A hundred steps in your condition wouldn't be possible for anyone. But you? Mat would be proud . . . as am I. Five miles, Kay. . . . Five hellish miles." Shaking his head in both amazement at the feat and relief that she was still breathing, he stood up and looked around.

There was nothing to see for miles. No trees, no rocks, and most importantly, no signs of pursuit. "Well, we're in the clear . . . for now. And it looks like we're at least headed in the right direction," he muttered. Laughing darkly, Caldain shook his head. "Guess we'll have to make do."

Returning to Cid, Caldain picked him up and placed him alongside his sister. After assuring himself that the siblings were free of blackheart blood, he examined Cid more closely. To his utmost relief, Cid was free of any blackheart corruption save for the ill effects of trying to handle the tainted currents. Caldain then proceeded to weave several explosive traps around their impromptu campsite before slumping to the ground next to Kay. He knew they all needed rest, and as such, he had aligned the traps to the three of them. This would prevent the traps from triggering if one of the siblings awoke before him and decided to wander around.

Looking down at Kay, he was relieved to see that the currents, now free of Kay's interference, were already at work healing her wounds. Her legs had set themselves, and the broken skin was now whole. Furthermore, all bleeding had stopped and her breathing had cleared up. It would likely take a while for the siblings to fully recover from such a debilitating encounter, especially from a mental standpoint, but they now had some time. Granted, Caldain didn't know how much, but he had to hope it would be enough.

Reaching down, Caldain gently caressed her cheek as a mix of love, sorrow, and apprehension played across his gray eyes. "Get some rest now," he whispered before lying down. Gazing up at the stars, he added, "You just heal up and gather your strength. This is far from over, and as much as I hate to say it, there will be far worse to come. However, you have my word – I'll keep you safe. By blood, by honor, and by deed, this I swear."

Chapter Fourteen

"**S**o, what you're telling me is — you all are basically instruments of destruction?" Amroth asked with a hint of uncertainty marring the friendly bass of his voice.

"That's a harsh way of putting it, kid," Mat responded dryly as he ran his hand over the blue sweat rag concealing most of his purple-tinted, black hair. Walking behind Kara and Amroth, he added, "What would you have us do? Fight the Darkness with harsh words, or invite its servants over for a quaint dinner to discuss a peaceful resolution to our conflict?" Mat scoffed. Pushing the opening of his black vest behind his twin, broad-bladed swords, he rested his black leather-encased wrists on their plain hilts, which hung at his hips for the first time in weeks. "I haven't been at it for very long compared to the others, but I can assure you that such an option — if it ever existed — died millennia ago," he stated, his smooth voice as cocky as ever.

Looking back at Mat in the fading light of the late afternoon, Kara frowned slightly. His attitude had improved only marginally since Damion's departure. Unfortunately, with the return of his swords, his confidence had grown, and with it, a bold — and sometimes spiteful — sarcasm.

"What?" Mat asked when he caught sight of Kara's look of dissatisfaction.

Shaking her head of sky-blue hair, she let a small, disappointed sigh escape her full lips and turned her attention back to the path before them.

They had made good progress through the day, stopping only for a brief meal and to work on Amroth's meditation. Glancing at Amroth out of the corner of her eye, he still looked embarrassed. The thought of his protests and blushed face nearly made her giggle. With as modest as the young Merandith was, his discomfort with what had been asked of him so far wasn't surprising. Still, it was amusing, and she had to admit to herself she had found a certain pleasure in teasing him. Unfortunately, that pleasure was about all that came from the brief sessions. Amroth was young, untrained, and until recently, unaware of his ability; to expect anything from him this soon was well beyond unfair. However, the sense of urgency gnawing at the back of her mind refused to listen to such rationale. It wanted immediate results, and she found she was having to remind herself — more often than she would like to admit — that such expectations were unreasonable.

Pushing a lock of the white hair along the left side of her heart-shaped face behind her ear with a brown-gloved hand, she then adjusted the black leather half-vest she wore over her red shirt as she said, "Mat is right, Amroth," she stated with a bit of a lecturing tone to her soothing, beautiful voice. "Reasoning with the Darkness is an impossibility. It is a force of chaos — unrelenting and unpredictable. Our job is to counter it and its agents wherever and whenever they strike. As for the limitations on our powers," she let out a sigh, "they vary from person to person. Unfortunately, the ability to heal another is something no Gifted or Warden can do. Call it the price we pay for the strength of our gift."

Amroth shook his head, seemingly unwilling to accept that limitation. "But your brother healed you and Ember — I'd say that's proof it's possible."

Folding her arms beneath her modest bosom, Kara shook her head adamantly. "What Damion did is unique to him; and while he did save us, it wasn't healing. It was a cleansing of the blackheart poison in our systems — and it was a risky move." She smirked darkly. "He could have just as easily finished us off."

"Still sounds like healing to me," Amroth muttered with a shrug.

"Let me put it to you this way," Kara responded as she let her arms drop to her sides. "The reason we don't get sick and can regenerate from practically any injury is that our inner fir'gan knows our bodies; it understands its rhythms and functions. For a Gifted to heal another person, they not only would have to have near unimaginably precise control over fir'gan, but they would have to perfectly understand the body of their patient. Now, while such precise control of fir'gan is, in theory, possible, no one can understand another's body on such a level. Attempt to heal someone else, and you will — at best — severely injure them. Otherwise. . . ." She let the unvoiced implications hang in the air.

Amroth grunted derisively and crossed his arms across his broad chest, causing his thick white shirt to pull a bit tight around his shoulders. "Well, that just makes my earlier observation seem more relevant," he stated confidently. "You're instruments of destruction."

Kara ground her teeth together. "We were created to protect

Kylir and its Guardians. We failed in that duty, and ended up fighting a devastating war against those that sought our destruction and the ruination of the world. But, if it helps you to see us as nothing more than mindless tools of destruction," she managed to say with restrained frustration, "then fine."

Kara's tone drew concerned looks from Amroth and Mat.

"I didn't mean to . . ." Amroth started to apologize, then let out a frustrated sigh. Running a hand through his black hair, he tugged on his horsetail of hair at the nape of his neck violently. "It's just all too much, and it's so damn frustrating!"

Reminding herself that she needed to be patient with Amroth, Kara said as calmly and as sympathetically as she could, "I know it is. But these are things that you need to understand – and understand quickly. Once our enemies know of your existence, you will be in the same danger as we all are. The faster you learn to access and control fir'gan, as well as accept your new life, the better your chances of defending yourself and surviving."

Before Amroth could find the words to respond, a deep, rumbling voice drew their attention. "You'd think none of you understands what it means to be quiet in hostile territory."

Coming to a halt, they watched as Ember approached from the woods off to their left at a casual pace. To their relief, there were no new bloodstains to join the faded ones on his longcoat, and his large claymore appeared unused. Even so, Kara still asked, ignoring his jab, "I take it you didn't encounter any more bandits?"

Stopping before Kara, Ember grunted and said with a hint of disappointment, "There's none out there, and I suspect you won't find any for miles."

"The cyrians?" she asked, even though she knew the answer.

Ember nodded. "Indeed. I doubt we'd notice them if it wasn't for the ripples in the currents. Granted, they're gentle about it, but they're out there." He grunted. "Hells, I can smell them, too." Ember suddenly smirked mischievously. "At least you noticed someone is around this time."

Kara shot her brother a reprimanding look. "We were distracted last time. Besides, we had you walking perimeter so we wouldn't have to be so focused . . . not that it did us much good."

While Mat figured the siblings' exchange was likely playful badgering, he didn't feel the need to risk an actual – and wholly unnecessary – argument. Therefore, he quickly stepped up beside Kara and asked, "You said something about cyrians?"

Offering Kara a quick, friendly smile, Ember turned to Mat and grunted. "If you want to call them that, sure. I'd almost say they're an insult to their pureblood cousins if they didn't do such justice to their old ways."

"Sounds like they're more cyrian than the purebloods," Mat responded, to which Ember merely grunted.

"Wait," a shocked and befuddled Amroth interrupted as he glanced at the trees lining the path. "You're telling me we're being watched?" Settling his gaze on Kara, he added, "Cyrians are renowned for their stealth, but – assuming you're right – you're telling me you know they're out there watching us? How, in Deo's name, could you know that?"

Grinning broadly, Kara patted Amroth on the shoulder, "They've been following and watching us from a distance since noon. As for how I know that – you'll just have to progress in your training to find out."

Frustration spilled across Amroth's visage at yet another exasperating puzzle, which almost drew an amused laugh from Kara. However, for Amroth's sake, she suppressed it and, instead, asked of Ember, "I take it they're likely to make contact soon?"

"If we're as deep into their territory as I think we are, then yes. Honestly, I'm amazed they haven't approached us already. That being said, I'd wager we'll get a visit from them sooner rather than later," Ember responded.

"Well then, we might as well keep moving forward for as long as they allow us," Kara declared before stepping past Ember and continuing down the path.

Grunting, Ember turned and followed his sister.

Stunned by their casual disregard for the danger of their situation, Amroth shouted at their backs, "Wait! Are you saying we're already in Caith'tol territory?"

Ember shouted back, "Since around noon, I believe!"

Aghast, Amroth pleaded, "This is a serious breach of their protocols! It's amazing we haven't been shot already for encroaching on their lands uninvited! I think it would be wise for us to wait here for them to approach us!"

Mat laughed at Amroth's concern. "You're forgetting, kid – they can't kill us." When Amroth looked at Mat like an ashamed child, Mat grinned. "Oh, it's not like we go about things casually, but where's the fun in always playing it safe?" When Amroth didn't respond, Mat laughed again before slapping Amroth on the shoulder in a playful but rough manner. "Come on, kid; they'll leave us behind if we don't keep up," he said before starting after Ember and Kara, leaving Amroth to catch up.

Two hours later, as night pushed the last of the daylight away, a large arrow screamed out of the darkness above them and embedded itself in the ground ten feet in front of them, startling Amroth and bringing the group to a sudden halt.

"Remain where you are!" a rough male voice shouted from the darkness. "You stand within the borders of Caith'tol without invitation! State your intent with haste, or pray that the Mother welcomes you gently into her embrace!"

"Told you this wasn't a good idea," Amroth muttered after he'd regained his composure.

"Hush," Kara said quietly, but emphatically, leaving no room for argument, as she looked into the distance. Thanks to the ethereal blue light of the currents, she had no issue finding the person responsible for the warning and arrow. "I count a dozen of them – four in the trees, and the rest fanning out around us," she stated softly.

Ember, who had donned a pair of dark, round glasses to conceal his eyes and turned up the closed collar of his coat to hide his unusual features as much as possible earlier in the day, nodded slightly even as his nostrils flared. "That's them, alright."

Before Kara could respond, the male voice barked from the darkness, "Well? My patience is not eternal! Speak, and be quick about it!"

Kara could tell there was no bluster in his tone, and as she slowly walked a few paces forward with her hands held up, the cyrians in her field of vision drew back on the bowstrings of their large, animal-inspired heartsong bows. Coming to a halt, she shouted to the man while keeping her eyes moving to avoid giving away that she could see them, "Peace be upon the children of the Forest Mother! We are travelers on a journey, and seek peaceful passage through your lands!"

Kara watched as the speaker returned the large arrow he had readied to the quiver on his back before shouldering his wolf-inspired bow of white wood and descending to the ground. Clad in green-trimmed, brown pants and a sleeveless, tri-slit longcoat beneath a uniquely cyrian tri'shoek, the man barely made a sound as his brown boots made contact with the forest floor. Dark bracers secured the ends of his shirt sleeves about his wrists, which was a match in color for the numerous braids of forest-green hair cascading from his angular face. Kara almost grinned with amusement as the man's feral yellow gaze set on her with a curiosity to match the expression on his whorling-tattooed face.

"You know our greeting," he stated even as he took his bow in hand once again and slowly approached Kara with a predatory grace that reminded her of a darlion. "'Tis not unheard of for an outsider to know such a thing, especially a Child of the Sky, but these are dark times, however, and I would be remiss if I did not exercise caution."

"A wise course of action," Kara replied, doing little to disguise that she was focused on him now. "Triclose has known little of peace for a long time, and I would imagine that makes trust a precious commodity," she stated amicably. "But our reason for being here is just as I stated. Whether you choose to believe that or not is totally up to you."

A wry smirk broke across the man's face as he came to a halt close enough to be seen clearly without the aid of the currents. "I see," he stated in an off-handed manner as he examined their group closely. Upon setting eyes on Ember, he raised a curious eyebrow. Kara fully expected him to question Ember's odd appearance, but was both surprised and relieved when he instead said, "Most of you do not appear to be from Triclose. . . . Although," he added as he stepped past Kara, who dropped her arms and turned to watch him stop before Amroth, "given who your companion is, I do not believe I should be surprised." Looking Amroth in the eye, he added, "You are Shi'doms Amroth Merandith, brother to Doms Kale Merandith, no?"

Stunned that the man recognized him, it took Amroth a moment to answer. "I. . . . Yes, I am," he stated a bit sheepishly. "But, how did you know?"

The man touched his fist to his heart and bowed respectfully before answering. "I spent some time with the Five Stars before rotating home last year. You may not have seen me, but I most assuredly saw you at Doms Merandith's side."

"Oh," Amroth stated as he quickly sought to regain his composure. "My apologies for not recognizing you. . . ."

The man smirked as he watched Amroth struggle to come up with a name. "No apologies are needed, Shi'doms. My name is Gykanli Kyrosa, Ty'roshin of the Kanragni."

"Well met, Gykanli," Amroth replied. "I find myself apologizing again, but I have to – my familiarity with the cyrian tongue is

330

admittedly lacking. The Kanragni are your rangers, correct? And your title makes you a captain?"

Gykanli smiled. "I do not believe you are as lacking in familiarity as you believe, Shi'doms. You are correct on both accounts."

Amroth let out a laugh, relieving the stress and some of the confusion warring within him. "Thank you for the compliment, Ty'roshin."

Gykanli nodded. "Pleasantries aside, I fear I must ask you if what the Child of the Sky says is true?"

"Child of the . . ." Amroth started to ask before it dawned on him that he was referring to Kara's lineage. "Oh, you mean Kara!" he declared, recovering quickly. "What she says is true – we are seeking passage through your lands." Amroth hesitated a moment before adding, "Speaking of which, I must apologize once more for crossing the border without permission. Kale did not want to risk a missive."

"I see," Gykanli replied thoughtfully. "'Tis well that I recognized you, and we exercised some restraint," he said with a slight smirk.

Amroth smiled, relief nakedly displayed on his face. "Our thanks for that, Ty'roshin."

Gykanli nodded. "Think nothing of it. However, may I inquire as to your destination? You are, after all, a long way from the army, and it is even more curious that someone as important as you would be venturing through the Contested Territories with such a minimal escort."

Amroth fought off the urge to laugh at Gykanli's astute observation. Instead, he smiled and chuckled softly. "It is unusual. And while my escort is minimal, I can say with confidence they are not to be taken lightly," he stated, recalling the small sample of power they had displayed while convincing him of the truth of their story.

Gykanli quickly examined the others once again before finally shrugging casually and saying, "Very well. You are welcome within our borders, Shi'doms, as is your escort. It would also be our pleasure to see you to your destination . . . if it lies within our power to do so."

Amroth smiled and nodded. "I would be honored if you were to do so."

"Excellent!" Gykanli replied before raising his hand and making a series of gestures. Within moments, the remaining eleven men and women of his squad emerged from the darkness, each of them dressed and armed similarly to Gykanli. "If you would, where are you headed so that we may see you upon the most expedient route?"

"We are–" Amroth started to say as he franticly searched for an answer he did not have. "We are awaiting others in our group. They are supposed to join us soon; after that, I may be able to reveal our destination. However, until then, I must ask you to understand that I cannot divulge that information at this time."

Gykanli looked at Amroth curiously for a moment before nodding slightly. "Very well. Until such time that you wish to depart or share your destination with us, might we at least offer you fire and shelter for the night? Winter's teeth are growing long and sharp, and it is not wise to spend the night in the open without either."

Amroth smiled broadly. "That is most generous of you, Ty'roshin. We humbly accept."

Smiling broadly, Gykanli declared, "Very good! My men shall provide escort. If you will, follow me and stay close; the way is complicated and meant to confuse outsiders. I would hate for you or your compatriots to get lost."

"Our thanks, Ty'roshin. Please, lead on," Amroth replied.

"Very well, Shi'doms," he responded with a nod before using a series of hand gestures to give orders to his squad.

With speed and silence, the cyrian rangers dispersed into the darkness, taking up flanking and rear guard positions even as Gykanli began leading Amroth and the others down the path.

"Way to think on your feet," Mat said in hushed tones as he stepped up next to Amroth and patted him on the shoulder. "I'm kind of surprised you didn't spill it all in an attempt to get away from us and what's been dumped on you."

"It's not like I didn't consider it," Amroth muttered. "Deo knows they wouldn't believe me . . . and besides that, I get the feeling one of you would just hunt me down if I tried to run."

"Accepting your fate, are we?" Kara said quietly with a grin as she dropped back to them.

Amroth scoffed. "Accepting my fate? I don't know about that, but I do know I'm not dumb enough to fight a losing battle. I'm outnumbered and have no chance of winning against the likes of you. So I'll wait, learn, and see if what you all are saying is true."

"And if we're lying to you?" Kara asked with a hint of amusement.

"Then I'll be done with you all, and damn the consequences," he stated quietly but firmly.

"And if we aren't?" Mat asked.

"We'll see when we cross that river," Amroth replied, even as he thought to himself, *"I won't sit back and watch Triclose tear itself apart like you. I'll learn to control this power, then use it to help Kale put an end to the Suldamiks and bring peace to all of Triclose."*

"I'd heard the rumors, but they don't do this justice," Amroth declared to no one in particular a few hours later as they came upon the first signs of civilization.

"What were you expecting?" Kara asked as he took in the torch-lit village spilling from the night around them.

Amroth shrugged. "I'm not sure. We knew the cyrians had taken in Ulthion refugees, but this looks . . . permanent."

Kara nodded in agreement. She had seen more than her fair share of refugee camps and shantytowns, and while the village they'd entered may have started out as such a place, it had clearly evolved beyond that. Practical wood buildings, the tallest of which were two stories, flanked clearly defined and skillfully planned dirt roads that weaved through the trees and were surprisingly full for the late hour. From what she could see, the greater majority of the people in the streets were human, but the cyrians amongst them were easily spotted. Whether the natives walked amongst the crowd or stood watch at intersections, it was clear from their demeanor that while the humans were welcome in their lands, the cyrians would not tolerate any breach of their hospitality or their laws.

"How long have these refugees been here?" Kara asked of Gykanli from behind him.

"Far longer than they, or us, would have liked or imagined," he responded with a hint of sadness as he led them along the street. "Ulthion bore the brunt of many battles in the early years of the war, and while there were attempts to reclaim their lands at first, no such venture has been undertaken for a while." A small, remorseful grin tugged at his lips as he glanced at the humans who looked their way in passing. "We had hoped to possibly reclaim a portion of their realm after Doms Merandith's successful push south, but many are wary of such an undertaking until there is true peace."

"I see," Kara replied as she gazed about. There were tired and worn faces amongst the human refugees, but there were also young and hopeful visages smiling and laughing in the night. This place was clearly home for the young – many of whom she figured knew little of their former lands. It was likely that any push to reclaim their former realm would be spurred by the older generations' memories of home and any of the youth that sought the glory and honor such a campaign might bring them. "It is a great thing you have done, providing refuge for so long. There are few realms or individuals that would do so," Kara added even as she pondered just how determined any effort to reclaim Ulthion would be after such a long time.

Gykanli inclined his head slightly. "The Ulthions have always been kind and generous neighbors deserving of our respect. While allowing them this close to a Heartwood proper is normally forbidden, turning away any of the Mother's children in their hour of need would bring shame and dishonor to us all." Reaching an intersection, Gykanli turned down the right-hand lane as he added, "It is unfortunate we could not do more for the Mother's children; however, for these few, we have been able to provide fire and shelter. Furthermore, many of our sisters and brothers fight alongside Doms Merandith to bring peace once more to the outside world."

Without seeing Gykanli's face, it was difficult to tell how much of what he stated he believed. However, she had known cyrians since the birth of their race, and while they were almost as reclusive as their darlion cousins, they were an honorable and kindhearted race . . . or at least the original cyrians had been at one time. Listening to Gykanli, she found no reason to doubt the veracity of his words, even if there was a hint of regret in his tone. In fact, she had to fight off a remorseful smile as Gykanli reminded her of what the pureblood cyrians had once aspired to be despite their origins.

"So far removed from their pureblood progenitors, and this offshoot has managed to embody what the cyrians have lost," Kara thought as she fought off a dour frown. *"I guess we all lose something when you're created for war. I can only hope that Corith sees fit to guide the cyrians back to what they once were, especially after the destruction Darkon brought down on them,"* she mused, even though experience told her that, generally, returning to what once was was wishful thinking. *"Thankfully, for some of us, the ages and the war haven't managed to completely obliterate what we once were. So if that's possible, and these cyrian relatives are what they appear to be, then I guess there's hope for the purebloods."*

"Ah, here we are," Gykanli declared, drawing Kara from her thoughts.

Made of dark wood, the one-story building stood out against the human architecture that dominated the village. Broad, with a flowing steepled roof made of dark shingles, the structure was built around the large ironwood reaching skyward through the roof. Kara's gaze followed the elegant staircase that spiraled up the tree's trunk, and she saw several cyrians diligently keeping watch from a series of platforms and simple bridges spread amongst the tree's barren limbs. Seeing the graceful structure and the way it flowed with the tree, Kara felt ancient memories clawing their way to the surface, and an almost imperceptible smile tugged at her lips. Glancing at Ember, she could tell he was also dealing with similar memories as he gazed upon the building.

"What is this place?" Amroth asked as the other cyrians in their escort began to disperse, some vanishing around the corner of the building and others entering the structure through its swept-conical door.

Gykanli looked at Amroth and replied, "Our outpost for this region's Heartwood. It isn't as large as most Kanragni stations, but it serves our purposes."

"Ah, I see," Amroth responded thoughtfully.

Gykanli smirked. "Is this not to your liking, Shi'doms?"

"No, it's fine," Amroth quickly replied, his tone apologetic. "I'm just not sure what I expected."

Gykanli's smirk broadened. "This settlement does not have an inn or anything resembling such. However, if it would make you and your escort more comfortable to be amongst your own kind, I'm sure we can find accommodations until such time as your friends arrive. I merely thought staying here would avoid unwanted scrutiny."

Amroth shook his head and smiled gratefully. "No, that won't be necessary, Ty'roshin. This will do just fine, and your forethought is appreciated."

Dipping his head respectfully, Gykanli said, "Thank you, Shi'doms. Now, if you will follow me, I will show you where you can rest." Without waiting for a response, Gykanli opened the door and led the group inside.

Circular in shape, the outpost's main room flowed around the trunk of the tree. What appeared to be a clerk, wearing garments similar to Gykanli's attire, sat behind an organically flowing desk off to the right, busily combing through the organized documents on the desktop. A hearth, in which a fire burned warm and bright, occupied a portion of the left-hand wall, over which hung a wood-carved elk head. A trio of cyrian rangers stationed around the room paused in their duties just long enough to shoot inquisitive looks at them before resuming their tasks.

Leading them around the tree trunk, Gykanli continued through an entryway at the rear of the room. They encountered several more Kanragni as they traversed a series of narrow corridors, and Gykanli exchanged greetings with them in passing. As for Amroth and the others, they were the subject of mild, cursory glances. Much to Amroth's surprise, he even received a few salutes from what had to be Five Stars' veterans who recognized him.

Eventually, Gykanli came to a halt before a door bearing a wooden plaque that featured a carving of a wolf's head against a crossed bow and bundle of arrows backdrop. Turning to the others, he said, "Until we can make better arrangements, please make use of my quarters. They are a bit small, but comfortable. Should you require anything, I will also station one of my men outside the door."

Before Amroth could respond, Kara stepped forward with a warm smile and said, "Thank you for your hospitality, Ty'roshin. I'm sure these will do just fine. Our friends should arrive sometime this evening, assuming they haven't already entered your lands, so I do not expect we will be staying long. If it is acceptable, would you see that our friends are brought to us as soon as they arrive?"

Gykanli glanced at Kara curiously for a moment before looking to Amroth for confirmation of her statement and request.

"It's alright, Ty'roshin. What she says is accurate."

Gykanli grunted. "Even after living in close quarters with humans for so long, I still find you to be a curious species." Chuckling, he then added, "Very well. I will spread the word and see to it that your friends are brought to you upon arrival. If I may ask, what do they look like? I would hate for a misunderstanding to result in something untowardly happening."

"There will be two of them," Kara responded. "One is a tall, white-haired Velusyian with dark eyes."

Gykanli's eyebrows rose with curious surprise. "I did not know such traits existed amongst the Children of the Sky. Does he possess the blood of those touched by Shadow?"

Kara fought off the urge to cringe at Gykanli's observation. "No," she offered without any hint in her voice of the nerve he'd touched on. "He is merely an oddity – much like an albino."

"Ah," Gykanli replied, his tone making it clear he didn't quite believe her explanation. "And the other?"

"A darlion," Kara answered simply.

Surprise clearly overwhelmed Gykanli's face. Glancing at Amroth quickly, he then looked back at Kara and said with a hint of respect that had not been there before, "My apologies for any disrespect I might have shown to any of you. I did not mean to–" Gykanli

336

paused and then smiled respectfully. "I will see to it they arrive here with all due haste and respect. If you will excuse me. . . ." Bowing with a fist-to-heart salute, Gykanli then walked past them before vanishing around the corner at the end of the hall.

Looking at Kara curiously, Amroth asked, "Mind telling me what that was all about? He looked like he suddenly realized he'd been treating a doms like a beggar."

Kara offered Amroth a wry, knowing grin before saying as she pushed open the door and entered, "All in due time. We have other things to concern ourselves with right now."

As they filed into the room, it was immediately clear – especially with Ember's size – that the room was indeed small. Windowless, only a pair of oil lamps hanging from the ceiling provided illumination. Along the right-hand wall of the square room sat a simple bed dressed in brown and white linens. A small, well-organized ironwood desk occupied the back wall, while an oak wardrobe and a small water basin stand occupied the left-hand wall. As for ornamentation, the room was free of it except for an extra standard bow and a quiver full of appropriate-sized arrows hanging on the wall behind the desk.

Planting herself comfortably on the bed, she crossed her legs and said, "Alright – let's get to it."

Amroth cringed inwardly and blushed a bit even as he and the others maneuvered to find a comfortable spot in the overly crowded room. "Really? Here? The first time was awkward enough with the tiny bit of privacy I was given. But there's nowhere for Ember and Mat to go to now."

Uncrossing her legs, her black thigh boots barely making a sound as they touched the floor, Kara leaned forward and grinned. "So what you're telling me is you don't mind being naked with me around?" she teased.

Amroth blushed furiously and struggled to find something to say, drawing a laugh from Kara and a chuckle from the others.

"Don't worry," Kara finally said when she'd recovered, putting an end to Amroth's struggle for words. "As much as being fully nude helps you build your connection to the currents – especially so early in your growth – I'll only ask that you take your shirt off."

"Well, that's a relief," Mat drawled as he leaned against the wall between the wardrobe and wash table. "Don't suppose you'd mind taking your top off as well, Kara? It'd give me something pleasant to look at instead," he joked, though there was a hint of excitement in his cocky voice.

Standing near the door, Ember growled low in his throat at Mat, but before he could say anything, Kara responded dryly, "I don't think so. I'm pretty sure you were nearly as upset as Amroth here when you got a look at me on the beach after the shipwreck."

Both Amroth and Ember stared at Kara in surprise as Mat squirmed uncomfortably against the wall.

"That was different then, and you know it!" Mat muttered, embarrassed, drawing an amusingly pleased laugh from Kara.

"Of course," Kara stated with a sly, teasing grin.

Rolling his eyes, Mat muttered something unintelligible. Catching an accusing, angry glare from Ember out of the corner of his eye, Mat held up his hand defensively and said, "Nothing happened, damn it! We wrecked, and both our clothes were shredded! It was nothing more than an embarrassing accident. Corith be good, she even laughed about it!"

"Let him be, Brother," Kara ordered with a small smile, her lovely voice full of mirth. "It was as he says. I was just teasing him."

Ember grunted. "That better be the case. You can do a whole lot better than him," he rumbled.

Mat scowled. "Thanks," he said sarcastically.

"All kidding aside," Kara said as she turned her attention back to Amroth, who appeared uncomfortable with the banter, "there are more important things to deal with. Take off your shirt, Amroth, and have a seat."

Slowly and awkwardly, Amroth first removed his swordbelt and placed it on the floor before removing his shirt. Tossing it atop his weapons, he then sat down and crossed his legs. Adjusting his black-booted feet a bit for comfort, he then rubbed his hands on his brown pants nervously as he asked, "Just like before?"

"Not quite," Kara responded as she moved to the floor before him. Holding her hand up, palm upward, she brought a small flame to life above her hand. "We made very little progress earlier, and I have a feeling it was due to your own self-doubts. I want to see if we can overcome that."

"Alright," Amroth replied skeptically. "But what is the flame for?"

"I want you to relax and focus on the flame."

Taking a deep breath, Amroth let it out slowly as he settled into the meditative pose, and nodded. Focusing on the flame, Amroth did his best to let his mind relax. After a few frustrating minutes, he scowled and let out an irritated breath while shaking his head.

"I can't do it," he declared. "The few times I can get my mind to shut up, I can't sense even a hint of what you say I should."

Kara offered Amroth a patient, reassuring smile. "It's there, Amroth. Trust me. It's unfair that we're asking you to learn at this unreasonable speed, but unfortunately, it's what is needed. However, I assure you that it is within you to do this."

Amroth scoffed.

Watching Amroth's frustrated, confused emotions playing out on his face, Kara searched for some way to help him accomplish what Damion wished of him. Suddenly, an idea occurred to her, and she cursed herself for not thinking of it sooner. "Alright, let's try a different approach. . . ." Tying off the currents so that the flame was self-sustaining for a time, Kara left the flame hovering before Amroth and stood up.

"What are you doing?" Amroth asked as she moved behind him.

"Something I should have thought of earlier," she replied as she adjusted her brown pants before kneeling behind him and placing her hands on his broad shoulders. Amroth tried to look back at her, but she ordered, "Stay focused on the flame."

He started to protest, but thought better of it and returned his gaze to the flame.

"Is this a good idea?" Ember asked suddenly.

Kara smiled dryly. "It's certainly not the option I would choose, but there's far less risk now than earlier."

"What are you talking about?" Amroth demanded, confused.

"I'm going to try to guide you to your core of fir'gan," Kara declared.

Amroth could hear the hint of concern in her voice. "What's the catch?"

"The catch is," Mat chimed in, "doing something like this with an untrained, and basically unaware, Gifted is dangerous. Kara could die if something went wrong."

"What?" Amroth asked in surprise. "I thought you guys were immortal?"

"We are, but that doesn't mean we can't be killed," Kara answered. "Sever our connection to the currents by destroying our heart or cutting off our head, and we're as dead as anyone else."

Amroth's look of surprise took on an edge of dread, prompting Kara to add, "Don't worry, it's extremely difficult to do, and impossible for a normal person to accomplish. However, what I'm going to attempt comes with a certain risk."

"And that is?" Amroth asked with trepidation.

"You could draw too deeply on your fir'gan," Ember answered bluntly. "If your untrained mind lashes out in this state, or there's a backlash of power, you could sever Kara's consciousness from her body and the currents."

Amroth's eye bulged. "What?!" he practically bellowed. "Then there's no way you should do this!"

Kara's long fingers dug into Amroth's shoulders as she gave him a reassuring squeeze. "Relax. I'll be fine. I've done this before in the past, and it's how I calmed you down when you awoke from your Joining," she assured him.

"Huh?"

Mat laughed dryly. "He wouldn't remember that, Kara."

"I know," Kara replied, giving Mat a dry look. Leaning in, she rested her forehead against the back of Amroth's head. "Just relax and trust me," she said softly with another comforting squeeze of his shoulders.

Taking a deep breath, Amroth let it out slowly, then nodded. "Alright. What are you going to do?"

"Simply put – I'm going to enter your mind."

"What?" Amroth asked, shocked, drawing an amused smile from Kara.

"We Wardens can use the currents to telepathically communicate with others whose presence we are familiar with across vast distances."

"That sounds . . . dangerous," Amroth said ominously.

"It has its . . . disadvantages," Kara replied. "But the dangers can be guarded against."

"So what's so dangerous about this situation," Amroth asked, despite Ember's answer from earlier, "and why do you need to be touching me?"

Leaning back, Kara said with a hint of agitation marring her lovely voice, "Because I'm not completely familiar with your presence, and you aren't consciously connected to the currents. I need the

340

physical contact to establish a link. As for the danger, I'll be forcing your mind to subconsciously draw upon your inner fir'gan. Should your mind violently reject me, it could cause a dangerous surge of power to flow backward through the connection, which – as Ember said – could destroy my mind, severing my connection to the currents."

"Killing you," Amroth finished with quiet remorse.

"Yes," Kara answered simply.

"I see." Taking a deep breath, Amroth added hesitantly, "I trust you. . . . Let's get this over with."

Nodding, Kara offered both Ember and Mat reassuring looks before leaning her forehead against the back of Amroth's skull once more. "Now, I want you to relax," she ordered as she closed her eyes and let her mind reach along the currents in search of Amroth's presence.

She felt the tension fade in Amroth's shoulders as he took a deep breath and let it out. To her surprise, she found Amroth's foreign presence on the currents almost as soon as he relaxed. It was the same subtle, tenuous existence that she'd felt in the woods, and she took a moment to familiarize herself with it. When she was sure she could find him like every other Warden she knew, she said aloud, "That's good. Now, I want you to clear your mind and focus on the flame."

She felt him nod slightly, then she cautiously let her mind approach his signal. As soon as she got close, she was able to make gentle, but brief contact before she felt a layer of resistance rebuff her. She'd expected this, as well as the brief wave of jumbled thoughts that washed over her during her short contact. "Relax Amroth, and empty your mind – let the flame burn away all the thoughts that are clouding your mind and preventing you from seeing inward with clarity," she stated reassuringly.

Amroth almost scoffed at her instructions, thinking it absurd. But as the minutes passed and he continued to watch the flame, he could feel himself becoming hypnotized by the dancing tendrils of fire. His breathing soon slowed to a calm and deliberate pace, and what tension that remained in his muscles melted away. Relieved of its cluttered restraints, he felt his mind float free on a sea of tranquil emptiness, and for a time, he reveled in the serenity he found. Then, at the edge of his awareness, he noticed a light. Dim, but rhythmically pulsing with strength, the light was a source of warmth in the darkness that was so profound that he couldn't fathom how he'd missed it.

At the same time, the resistance Kara felt weakened, allowing her to establish a tenuous connection with Amroth. It wasn't enough to communicate with him, but it would serve to let her guide him as if he were her puppet.

"Alright, Amroth," she thought to herself, *"let's see if we can make this work."*

With a bit of effort, Kara managed to help corral Amroth's focus and keep it on the light. With a bit more coaxing, she then got him moving toward it. As he got closer, the light steadily grew brighter, bringing with it a comforting and welcoming warmth that she felt spreading through his body. Upon reaching the light, she felt his reflexive urge to touch it, and without a second thought, she nudged him to do so. A measure of pride welled up in her as she felt him reach out with his mind to do just that. However, before he could make contact, Kara withdrew a bit to reduce the chance her presence might interfere with him making a solid connection to his fir'gan. A moment later, Amroth made contact and smiled as the light seemed to radiate with a euphoric warmth the likes of which he'd never felt.

Kara grinned at his success, and with his connection now established and strong, the remaining opposition she felt melted away. She also noticed that the resistance and trepidation within Amroth had been replaced by a calmness and joyfulness that put to rest any fears she had of this exercise resulting in disaster. Still, time had taught her to be cautious, and she kept her guard up even as she once again reached out toward the presence that was Amroth. This time, with no resistance to rebuff her, she was able to make contact and establish a solid connection.

"Well," she thought to herself, the easy part is over. *"Now for the tricky part."* To Amroth, she asked through their connection, *"Can you hear me, Amroth?"*

"Kara!?" came the loud, excited reply. *"Is that really you I'm hearing? Corith be good! How can I hear you in my head, much less talk to you?"*

Kara laughed mentally with genuine amusement. *"One of the many advantages of your new life and abilities! The currents allow us to connect and share our thoughts. Eventually, though, you'll need to be able to do this while fully conscious and without physical contact."*

"I. . . . I don't even know what to say. . . . This is amazing!"

"I'm glad you think so," she replied, happy to see him finding some joy in the role that had been thrust upon him, *"but we have other things to attend to right now. There'll be time for you to revel in this later."*

"Alright," Amroth replied, his excitement muted. *"What now?"*

"Now we see if we can get you to tap into your inner fir'gan in a controlled way."

"Right," Amroth replied, a hint of worry in his voice.

"That light that you grasped onto, that was merely the gate to your power. By opening it, you granted yourself access to your inner fir'gan. After that, it will never be fully closed off to you, even when you let go."

"Is holding onto it why I feel warm and . . . pleasant?"

"It is, but let's focus on the objective at hand."

"Okay."

"Good. Now, I want you to look around. You should see something that looks like a pool of water lit from within."

"Look around? A pool of water? That seems so odd to hear, given this setting. I mean— Wait. . . ." He laughed in surprise. *"Well, I'll be a mad pine-ferret! There it is!"* he thought. *"It's beautiful and huge!"* he added in awe.

Kara smiled inwardly. *"There's nothing quite like it."*

"So what now?"

"I want you to approach it and touch just the surface. But be warned — the temptation to plunge further in will be strong. You need to resist it and stay on the surface," Kara stated firmly.

"Okay. Just the surface, then," Amroth responded with a hint of nervous trepidation.

For what seemed like an eternity, the connection was silent, and worry began to gnaw at Kara. Then, she felt a sudden, gentle surge of fir'gan and Amroth's presence on the currents became more defined.

"This is just. . . . I mean. . . ." Amroth laughed. *"I don't have the words to describe it! I can't believe something like this exists inside me!"*

Kara's laughter rolled across their link. *"I'm glad you find it so amazing!"*

Amroth laughed again. *"I didn't know anything could feel this wonderful! Can I go a bit deeper, please? I'm pretty sure I can handle it."*

"Not this time. Our goal was to help you find your inner fir'gan so you can find it on your own."

"I don't see how anyone could forget how to find something like this!"

"That's good. Now, let's—" A surge in the currents brought her statement to an abrupt halt. *"Amroth? What are you doing?"* she asked, alarmed.

"Just a little more. I know I can handle it."

"Wait! Don't—"

"Damn. Are they still at it?" Mat asked as he shut the door.

Without taking his molten eyes off of the linked pair, Ember said, "Indeed. He finally found his inner fir'gan after a few hours. Took him long enough," he finished with a grunt from where he stood against the back wall. "Did you find us something to eat?"

Holding up a basket, Mat said, "It was a bit difficult to find something this late, but the guards were quite helpful." Placing the basket on the table, he pulled back the cloth cover. "We've got bread, some grilled rahken, and a bottle of some sort of wine . . . I think."

Ember snorted. "At least there's something resembling meat."

"Is it going to be enough for you, or do I have to worry about someone going missing to satisfy your beastly appetite?" Mat responded sarcastically.

Ember growled. "If that were the case, I would have eaten you a long time ago just to put an end to your mocking and snide behavior," he rumbled.

Mat laughed as he broke the seal on the jug of wine. Sniffing it, he declared, "Not bad." Grinning slyly at Ember, he added, "Careful, big guy. I might not share this with you if you don't behave."

Ember started to take a playfully threatening step forward but was brought up short by a surge of fir'gan from Amroth. "Shield the room," he stated ominously as he focused acutely on the linked pair and his eyes narrowed with concern.

Nodding, Mat put the bottle down and quickly latched onto the currents. "Done," he replied as he finished raising a barrier to not only prevent anyone outside the room from hearing what went on within, but also to hopefully contain the growing power within Amroth should it become a danger. Watching Ember cross the room in one long stride, Mat asked with concern, "Ah, Ember—why is your nose bleeding?"

Crouching down next to Kara, Ember absently wiped his nose. "Hells — he's too damn raw to be drawing that deep," he declared as he wiped away the blood trickling from Kara's nose with his thumb. "Kara? Can you hear me at all?" he asked of his sister. When he didn't receive a reply, he let out a concerned growl.

"What should we do?" Mat asked as the building power began to cause items in the room to shake.

Ember shook his head in frustration. "I don't know! I'm trying to sever the connection, or at least get a barrier between Kara's mind and Amroth's, but I can't get anything to hold!"

"Well, we better think of something quick!" Mat declared.

Thinking fast, Ember seated himself facing the connected pair and said, "I'm going to try to forcibly insert myself into the link."

"Isn't that dangerous? And will it even work?"

"Yes," Ember stated bluntly. Looking at Mat with grim intensity, he added, "I won't lose my sister to something as stupid as this. If it looks like this isn't working – kill Amroth."

"But, Damion–"

"To the hells with my brother!" Ember roared. "I'll deal with the–" He blinked in surprise as the furniture in the room stopped shaking.

A relieved laugh burst from Mat. "That is an amazing sister you've got!"

"Indeed," Ember replied as he watched the currents return to normal.

"Worried, were you?" Kara suddenly asked, exhausted, as she leaned back and opened her eyes.

"Are you okay? What happened?" Ember asked, his voice thick with concern.

"Oh, the usual – young Gifted finds his inner fir'gan and gives in to temptation," she said casually with a half-hearted smile.

A sudden, deep intake of breath from Amroth drew everyone's attention. Blinking rapidly in an attempt to focus his vision, Amroth looked about the room quickly before settling on Kara. Seeing the remnants of fresh blood on her upper lip and chin, his eyes grew wide. "Deo be good!" he exclaimed as he turned to face her. "Did I do that to you? I'm so very sorry, Kara! I don't know what came over me!"

Kara waved his apology away as she sat forward and offered him a weak, consoling smile. "Don't apologize. This was a dangerous exercise."

"Don't apologize?!" Mat exclaimed. "He damn well could

have killed you!"

"But he didn't," Kara said firmly, fixing Mat with an equally stern glare. "Our situation demanded this, and we had very little choice but to comply."

"More like your brother demanded this," Mat replied with a derisive sneer.

"True. But sometimes we have to take such risks, no matter the consequences," Ember stated gravely.

"Right. This coming from the . . . man that just asked me to kill Amroth if it meant saving Kara."

Silence fell on the room with a crushing, ominous weight.

Shocked, Amroth kept glancing back and forth between Ember and Mat as Kara slowly faced her brother and asked, her tone grave, "Did you actually order Mat to do that?"

Jaw firmly set, and his molten eyes unapologetic, Ember declared, "I did, and I would do it again without hesitation. Not only are you family, but your years of experience are irreplaceable. Warden or not, Amroth is young and inexperienced, which makes him expendable compared to you."

A hint of the love she felt for her brother flashed on Kara's face for a brief moment before anger washed it away. That wave of anger, which he felt through their link, was the only warning he got before the currents surged and Kara's hand lashed out, catching him full on the side of the face. The loud, sickening crack of bone echoed through the room as Ember's head jerked to the side. Even before he straightened his head, everyone could see that his heavy jaw was dislocated and broken, a portion of which had torn through his skin.

Setting his jaw, his fir'gan worked quickly to mend the ghastly wound as Amroth and Mat stared on in shocked silence.

Fuming, and her white-streaked, sky-blue eyes alight with fury, Kara struggled to find something to explain her reaction. Amroth was far more than just another Gifted chosen to become a Warden, but Damion had deemed that knowledge too valuable to be shared openly. To her immense relief, she was saved from having to say a word by a firm knock on the door.

Standing, with her eyes still locked on her brother's, she said calmly, "Mat, release the barrier and open the door."

Confused by Kara's reaction, and worried that the situation might escalate, Mat nodded slowly and released the barrier. Just as he opened the door, Ember pulled his dark glasses from the pocket of his longcoat and slipped them on.

"I'm not interrupting anything, am I?" Gykanli asked, immediately noting the tension in the air as he stepped into the room.

Kara smiled brightly at him. "Not at all," she said, her voice and visage devoid of any of the anger and frustration she currently felt.

"I see," he replied as he quickly eyed Amroth, noting his barely hidden surprise, and shirtless appearance.

"What can we do for you, Ty'roshin?" Kara asked.

Looking back at her, Gykanli smiled warmly. "I apologize for interrupting you at this late hour, but my men told me you were still awake. Your friends have arrived."

"Thank you for letting us know," Amroth said hastily as he grabbed his shirt and stood up, "but where are they?"

"I must apologize again," Gykanli responded as Amroth pulled on his shirt, "but the Quel'tokari insisted upon speaking with the Matri'terona of this Heartwood as soon as they arrived. The Quel'tokari has asked that . . ." Gykanli grimaced visibly, "I bring you all to meet with him and your other companion. If you would please follow me, I will escort you," he grimaced again, "to your friends. They await you at the Heartwood."

Amroth blinked in surprise. While he didn't know much about cyrian culture, he knew that their Heartwoods were sacred to them. Outsiders were rarely – if ever – permitted to enter or even get close to it. "I . . . We are humbled by such a gesture."

"Yes," Gykanli responded with a noticeable wince. "If you would please follow me. The Quel'tokari awaits."

Chapter Fifteen

Following Gykanli through the dark, nearly quiet streets, he eventually led them to the far side of town and deep into the woods beyond its borders. For almost half an hour, they walked in silence along a path lit by tree-mounted orbs that seemed to be filled with fireflies. Eventually, they came to a stop at an arch guarded by two hooded female cyrians that were armed with spears and girded in cyrian-style white leather armor and cloaks. The arch, which resembled woven branches, provided passage through a natural barrier composed of white ironwood trees that had merged together at some point in their growth. In the dark of night, it was hard to tell just how tall the barrier was, or how far the wall of trees extended, but it was a sight unlike anything Amroth had ever seen.

Turning to the others, Gykanli declared, his rough voice laced with a hint of frustration with the situation, "This is as far as I may go. Stay on the path, and you will find your companions awaiting you at the center of the Heartwood."

Pulling his gaze from the barrier, Amroth replied with sincere gratitude, "Thank you, Ty'roshin."

"This is an unusual honor that has been granted to you all," Gykanli stated, suddenly grave. "Very few would agree with this, but the Matri'terona has spoken, and we will honor her wishes. Be mindful, though – there is no violence permitted within the Heartwood. Should you, for any reason, violate this tenant, the consequence will be most severe. Is this understood?"

"It is," Amroth replied stoically for his group.

"Good, for the Matri'troshia will be watching. Now, you may proceed, and may the Mother grant you shade," he offered with a formal salute.

Amroth and his companions responded with their gratitude before they filed past Gykanli and into the Heartwood. When they finally vanished from sight, he shook his head in disbelief before returning to his post.

"So," Amroth finally asked nearly a quarter of an hour later, during which they'd traversed a well-manicured path between the towering white ironwoods and passed through a second guarded gate, "who or what is the Quel'tokari? I've never heard of that title."

"And you think any of us know?" Ember asked.

"Well, given that you all seem to have far more knowledge of the cyrians than anyone else – yes, I thought you might know. Besides, Kara mentioned that one of the people we're expecting is a darlion. Those are an even rarer sight on Triclose than cyrians. I just thought they might be one and the same," Amroth responded, his voice carrying an overtone of the hurt and anger he felt regarding Ember's order to kill him in order to save Kara.

"They are the same person," Kara interjected, seeking to keep the situation from turning argumentative despite her own feelings regarding the nearly disastrous evening. "These cyrians' native tongue is a bit different from the ancient dialect, but I believe it means something along the lines of 'Champion of the Mother'."

Ember snorted. "You're rusty, Sister."

"Oh?" Kara asked with a raised eyebrow as she shot her brother a cautionary glare.

"Heartseeker would be a more apt translation."

"Heartseeker?" Mat interjected. "Isn't that–"

"You're right, of course," Kara interrupted. "It has been a long time since I've had to translate their language."

Looking curiously at Ember and Kara, Mat then met Amroth's inquisitive gaze and shrugged.

Rolling his eyes, Amroth muttered, "Too many damn secrets and questions." Then, in a normal tone, he asked, "So, who is this Heartseeker?"

"That would be him," Kara replied, pointing down the path, concern filling her beautiful voice.

Standing in a small circular clearing that was centered on a towering, robust white ironwood engraved with graceful runes were two men that he recognized. Both were looking their way with concern. Damion with his dark, cold eyes, and the other. . . .

Something in Amroth snapped at that moment, and before anyone knew what was happening, the currents surged and Amroth dashed forward with inhuman speed. Neither Damion nor Allanian made a move to stop him as his fist connected with the darlion's face.

Taking a step back to absorb the thunderous blow, Allanian

righted himself, the skin-tight white fur of his face unmarred by the punch, before meeting Amroth's stunned, angry visage. "I suppose I deserve that," the darlion stated.

"You!" Amroth hissed, the currents returning to normal just [as quickly as they'd surged. "You were part of this, too?"

"Afraid so, Amroth. I'm sorry for the deception, but it was unavoidable," he stated, his haunting voice contrite.

"I . . ." Amroth started to say, his body trembling with anger and betrayal. "I . . ." he growled, before barking, "Damn you, Allanian!"

Allanian grimaced, his ice-blue eyes filled with remorse. "I'm sorry, Amroth. I really am. But we couldn't openly interfere. We needed to–"

"Yes! Yes! I know! Work from the shadows, avoid open conflict, and protect me! This bastard," Amroth pointed angrily at Damion, "already gave the same Deo-be-damned speech to me! I. . . . Argh!" Amroth bellowed before tossing his hands in the air and stalking over to the edge of the clearing where he leaning against one of the trees, his face a mask of seething frustration.

Glancing at Damion, who shrugged nonchalantly, Allanian then walked over to Amroth and stopped a respectful distance from him. "You may not want to hear this, or even care, but I am truly sorry for the deception that has been wrought upon you and the Merandiths. This is the way we have to operate to avoid a conflict that would devastate Kylir in ways you cannot imagine. I have served you and Doms Merandith faithfully, as did Damion, and we did all we could to assist the Merandiths while completing our mission."

Amroth snorted. "Right. So you're telling me that letting all those people die, as well as Kale's father and mother – when you two could have done so much more – was serving us?" He snorted derisively again. "Next, you'll be telling me you're a Warden, too."

Allanian grimaced. Calmly and patiently, he replied, "No, I am not a Warden. I'm what's called a Seeker. As for how you perceive mine and Damion's service to House Merandith. . . . I do not expect you to understand any of it right now, but I hope – in time – you will and can forgive us."

"To the Hells with you!" Amroth snapped, angry and hurt.

Sighing, Allanian turned and approached the others. "How are you fairing?" he asked upon joining them.

Smiling warmly, Kara replied as she hugged him, "Very well, thanks to Damion."

Pulling away from her, he smiled. "The white looks good on you. Adds a bit of a wild flare." Looking at Ember as Kara smiled gratefully, he quipped, "After what Damion told me, I would have thought you'd look terrible. Still a little on the draconian side, but it fits you."

Ember grunted. "Good to see you, too."

Chuckling, Allanian turned to Mat and offered, "And you must be Mat. It is unfortunate that we have not met before, but circumstances did not permit such introductions."

Mat fought off the urge to respond sarcastically, and instead said with only a hint of mockery in his cocky voice, "Indeed."

Allanian shrugged off the barb with a raised eyebrow before turning back to Kara. "It seems I find myself apologizing a lot tonight, but I must," he offered solemnly. "I am sorry that my absence put you in such a predicament. While I don't know if I could have changed Darius' fate, you never should have been asked to perform a Search."

Kara dismissed his apology with a smile and a wave of her hand. "Don't worry about it. Darkon could have easily gone to Caldain or Cid, but he didn't." She chuckled darkly. "Given what we have already encountered, I'm glad it was us."

Allanian nodded. "Right. Well then, on to business. If you will follow me." Without waiting for a response, Allanian turned and strode into the dark forest beyond the towering ironwood and its ring of guardian trees.

The other men fell in line quickly, but Kara paused at the tree line and turned to Amroth. "Come along, Amroth. There will be time enough for you to be angry with us later, and I'm pretty sure you can't see in the dark. Besides, I don't think you'll want to miss this."

Rolling his eyes, Amroth pushed away from the tree and approached Kara. "Really? Is this not the heart of the Heartwood?"

Kara nodded. "It is, but it isn't our destination."

Puzzled, Amroth asked, "Then what is our destination?"

Kara smiled. While it seemed like her usual warm smile, Amroth noted a bit of concern in her eyes. However, before he could pursue it, Kara held up a hand and ignited a ball of fire over her palm before she turned and walked into the woods, forcing him to quickly follow. Once he caught up with her, he considered asking what was bothering her, but then thought better of it. There was already enough on his mind, and if she wanted to talk about it, she would do so in her own time.

A few minutes later, after weaving between trees like it was some sort of chaotic maze, all of Amroth's concerns and anger were washed from his mind as the air grew warmer and a captivating, fluid melody filled the air along with a soothing blue glow. "What in Corith's name is tha—" he started to ask as they left the maze of trees and a sight that dwarfed everything he'd already seen that night – or ever seen for that matter – came into view, obliterating the question on his tongue.

Towering over sixty feet in the air with elegant grace, a ring of frosted-blue trees vanished into the darkness in both directions. Beautiful and long-limbed, each crystalline tree was molded into the same likeness of an elegant nude woman who seemed to exude a haunting balance of sexual allure and maternal warmth. Awe struck by the sight, Amroth couldn't decide if the evocative structures were supposed to be trees or works of art. His opinion, however, shifted heavily to the latter as they drew closer and he could observe just how detailed the structures were. Excruciatingly precise, every cut, every angle, and every curve lent an air of vitality to the trees that made the women seem alive. The muscles in their full thighs – one leg positioned slightly in front of the other – were tone and supple, flowing into the wide, curvaceous hips of a long, unmistakably feminine torsos whose arched backs thrust their full breasts forward proudly. These crystalline women also had their delicate faces titled skyward, their flowing hair tumbling past their buttocks like frozen waterfalls, while their long-fingered hands were splayed wide at the ends of graceful arms that stretched forth as if welcoming visitors to their embrace.

Then it dawned on him, bringing him to a sudden halt just before he bumped into Kara – the blue light illuminating the area was coming from the trees. Vibrant and fluid, it seemed as if tendrils of ethereal blue light flowed through the crystalline women like water dancing joyfully downstream.

A bit surprised by the sight, even though she suspected its existence, Kara extinguished the fire ball hovering over her hand as she softly said to herself, "Well, well. . . ." She then pried her gaze from the trees and looked at her brother. Letting some of her concern and frustration with him seep into her tone, "I've always wondered if there were more on Triclose, Brother. Another one of your secrets?"

Damion looked back at his sister with an arched eyebrow but said nothing.

Shaking her head, Kara let out a resigned sigh before glancing back at Amroth. Immediately, her angst was replaced with delight upon seeing his bewildered expression. Smiling broadly, she declared warmly, "May this be the first of many joyous wonders you see, young Amroth. Welcome to the Ansei Grove."

Tearing his eyes away from the trees, Amroth asked, his voice thick with awe, "Ansei Grove? What is this place? Is this what you were referring to earlier?"

"Kara had no knowledge of this particular grove," Damion interjected as the rest of their group walked back to her and Amroth, earning him a glower from his sister. "As for what this is, it's a nexus of fir'gan, to put it simply." Motioning to the trees, he added, "What you see flowing within the crystal trees is a convergence of fir'gan that is large enough, and powerful enough, to be visible to the naked eye."

"I. . . ." Amroth stopped, unsure of what to say. Shaking his head in amazement, he then asked, "And the woman the trees are shaped to look like? Who is she?"

"That is a point of some debate," Allanian chimed in. "Some believe she is the Mother. Others believe it is actually Corith – or Deo in Triclose's case. While others claim that she is indeed the Mother and that the Mother is actually Kylir." Allanian smirked, "Then, of course, there is the more outlandish and little-known theory that the Mother and Corith are one and the same." He shrugged indifferently, "No matter your viewpoint, she is indeed beautiful."

Looking at Allanian with sheer befuddlement, Amroth asked, "Wait. . . . Did you just say Deo and the Mother are one and the same? That preposterous!" Amroth finished with a dismissive laugh. "Everyone knows Deo is a man. For Deo's sake, even his name is masculine!"

"And what proof do you have, young one?" Allanian challenged. "We are ancient beyond your imagination, yet we have never seen Corith, nor do we have proof that Corith has a gender. Only the ancient Guardians ever met Corith, and they never shared such knowledge with us mortals."

"I'd like to think Corith is female," Kara interjected. "It kind of makes sense, if you think about it. After all, women give birth, and Corith gave birth to us. Even those that worship the Mother seem to lean in that direction."

Allanian nodded in agreement. "I would not argue with you on that. But, in the end, does it really matter? It seems a trifling debate in the grand scheme of things."

Kara smiled and laughed. "It does, doesn't it?"

Amroth stared at them all as if they'd gone insane. "You're

all mad," he declared with a laugh of disbelief.

Mat chuckled. "It's possible that they are, but a woman is something worth worshiping; so why not have a god be female, eh?"

"Well, there's some unusual logic for you," Ember declared with a grunt.

Damion cleared his throat, drawing everyone's attention. "As enlightening and entertaining as this discussion may be, we have other matters to attend to."

"Indeed," Allanian replied, his face growing serious. "You know the way as well as I do," he told Damion. "Please, lead on."

Following Damion's lead, they passed between two of the crystalline women, and Amroth saw that the crystal trees beyond the outer ring now resembled towering oaks. Crystal branches and leaves that were reminiscent of large snowflakes weaved a beautiful canopy of dancing blue light above them, while the harmonious melody flowed soothingly through the air.

"Where is that melody coming from? Is it the trees?" Amroth asked as he walked beside Kara in the middle of their group.

"The trees are called kastusoul," Ember rumbled from his position at the rear of the group along with Mat.

"Kastusoul?" Amroth asked, rolling the foreign word around on his tongue.

"It means 'crystalsong' in the Trader's Tongue. Right, Brother?" Kara teased Ember, who grunted in response. "The song you hear is created by the trees' resonance with the currents, and it is the source of their name."

"So beautiful," Amroth breathed as he tried to soak in the majestic, otherworldly scene.

"It is that," Allanian declared as he trailed Damion. "Ah! We are here."

Coming to a sudden halt, which forced Ember and Mat to step around him, Amroth's eyes widened at this new, otherworldly sight. "Deo be good," he breathed. "It just gets stranger and stranger!"

Spread out before him was a large clearing of pristine, soft grass that was home to the Grove's centerpiece, which Amroth was currently struggling to comprehend. In a matter of mere days, he'd been fed a large amount of fantastical information, and seen sights he never could have imagined, which would have been enough to overwhelm most people. However, it was the sight before him that once again made him wonder if this were some mad dream, or if he was actually dead, since he believed nothing this magnificent could exist without someone – anyone – speaking of its existence. In the end, he realized it didn't matter if it were real or not. This was clearly something few had ever seen, and he wasn't going to allow his flabbergasted state to stop him from trying to absorb the sight.

At the heart of the clearing was a large chunk of the fir'gan-filled crystal, which was somehow shaped like an unusual flowing ring that was close to ninety feet in diameter. Puzzled by its appearance, Amroth blinked and narrowed his focus on it as he started forward, oblivious to the others watching him. No, it wasn't a ring, he soon realized. A seemingly endless number of scales covered the crystal structure, making it appear organic . . . even bestial. As he slowly moved around the mass of crystal, his eyes soaking in every detail, it began to dawn on him that the structure looked a lot like two reptilian creatures whose limbs were locked together while the beasts circled each other. It took a moment for that realization to sink in, but when it did, his mind eagerly pulled back to absorb the entirety of the crystal structure. Instantly, his gaze was drawn to where the creatures' limbs should have met, but instead of meeting, the crystal twisted and spiraled upward into a magnificent tree whose height should have been visible for miles around.

"That's impossible," he thought as he came to a halt, unaware of the stone staircase behind him that descended below ground. *"No one has ever seen such a thing. . . . There would be rumors and tales if anyone had! Deo be good – this place would have been fought over time and again just so one could say they owned this!"*

"How . . ." Amroth started to ask aloud.

"How does no one know of this?" Damion finished as he approached the awe-struck Merandith.

Amroth nodded as he gazed up into the tree's branches.

Coming alongside his charge, Damion said, "This is an ancient sight, and most of its workings are beyond me. What I can tell you, however, is this area is a pocket of reality removed from the outside world that was created by harnessing a tremendous amount of fir'gan. No one can see this tree from the outside because, in a sense, it is not there."

"I– I–" Amroth laughed. Looking at Damion, he said, "I don't think I understand, and I'm not sure I want to!" He shook his head in bewildered amusement. "Are there others on Triclose?"

"Yes, Brother, that's something I'd like to know too," Kara declared, her arms folded in consternation beneath her breasts, as the others joined them.

Glancing at Kara, Damion replied, "Only a few, Sister – most of which you know of."

Kara hung her head and shook it in resignation before looking back up and asking, finally giving voice to the question that'd been rattling in her head since their talk about the current state of affairs, "And Portculims? How many do we not know about?"

"Counting the one beneath us? Three."

Kara's eyes bulged, the shock she displayed a match for what was painted across Mat and Ember's faces. "Three?! Corith be good! Are they active?"

"Yes."

"Corith be good!" she reiterated. "Who else knows of these? Do the cyrians know that this is here?! More importantly, the Betrayers could have been using the Portculims this whole time without our knowledge! We're blind enough as it is, but if they've been using unknown Portculims to get around, it completely negates the moratorium on Portculim travel and really does put us at a disadvantage!"

"Peace, Sister," Damion urged. "Has the moratorium really done any good? Besides that, these three were known only to myself, Luthur, and Taylexion; and only Luthur and I knew where they were installed. Furthermore, one of the Portculims is isolated off the network. Believe me when I say that if anyone had used them, we would have known. As for the cyrians, you know quite well that the same wards that govern our keeps hold sway here. The Grove would be nothing more than a hazy memory or dream to anyone that didn't have a Warden's blessing or wasn't an exceptionally strong Gifted."

Damion's declaration about the grove and memories cut through Amroth's fascination with the tree and caught his attention. Focusing on Damion, he interjected, "What does that mean? How could someone not remember seeing this?" he asked, gesturing to the tree. "For that matter, Didn't Gykanli say we were being watched? They would have to know about this if that's true!"

"How the grove affects people's memories is a complicated matter that you'll learn about eventually, Amroth. As for Gykanli's threat, it is an empty one," Damion replied, never taking his eyes off Kara. "Without permission, no one is allowed beyond the second gate save for the Matri'terona. So, whether they've seen the Grove or not, as far as anyone is concerned, the Grove doesn't exist, and the Heartwood is nothing more than a sacred site that only the Matri'terona and a select few are worthy to set foot in."

Amroth stared at Damion, a bit dumbfounded. Gykanli's reaction to them being granted passage made more sense now, but it was hard for him to believe that no one knew of this fantastical place. That doubt raised a host of questions that Amroth had no desire to find the answers to, and he did his best to repress those queries.

Kara, who'd been eyeing her brother warily through the entire exchange, nodded cautiously. "Alright," she stated before Amroth could say more. "I guess I have no choice but to take you at your word."

Suddenly, she looked pointedly at Mat and stated with a glower that brokered no debate, "And I don't want to hear a word from you about any of this! Is that clear?"

Taken aback by not only what had been divulged, but also Kara's tone, Mat merely nodded.

Fighting the urge to let out an exasperated sigh as she briefly wondered if Mat telling Darkon about all this would be an issue, she turned back to Damion and asked, "What now?"

"Now," Damion declared, "Amroth and I make for Solarson while you four attend to your duties here."

Startled by Damion's statement, Amroth blurted, "Wait? What did you say? I thought this was our destination?"

Turning to Amroth, Damion said, "Partly. Our actual destination lies on Solarson."

Amroth laughed derisively. "That's just great! And just how are we going to get there from here? Seems to me we've gone a long way in the wrong direction!"

A slight, knowing grin split Damion's face. "Even after all this, you still find room to doubt me?"

"Well, I'm still not sure this isn't some mad fever dream! I keep expecting to wake up back in camp all beat up!"

"It's all real, Amroth, and the sooner you accept it, the better," Damion said firmly. "As for how we'll get to Solarson – you did hear us talking about something called a Portculim?"

"I did," Amroth said cautiously.

"That's how we'll get there." Pointing toward the stairs behind Amroth, Damion added, "Down there, if you would."

Turning, he was surprised to see the stairs. Amroth then looked back at Damion and asked hesitantly, "Down there?"

"Indeed."

Amroth quickly looked to the others, desperately seeking confirmation that what Damion said was true. Mat still seemed stunned by Kara's outburst, but both Kara and Ember offered him nods, which eased his concerns a bit. Looking back at Damion, he said with a small measure of confidence, "Right," before moving to the stairs and descending them with determination.

Amused, Damion smiled slightly.

"Better get going, Brother; I doubt he can see," Kara stated with a small smirk.

As if to emphasize her point, there was a muffled crash followed by a string of vulgar curses.

Damion's grin grew. "Indeed," he said before adding, his deep voice heavy with concern, "Be careful. We already know the Betrayers are moving, and that things are far worse than we know. Don't take any unnecessary risks, but find those crystals' hosts and get them to safety."

"Don't worry," Allanian replied, "We'll find them and ghost them away before our enemies even get a whiff of what we're up to."

Nodding grimly, Damion made his way over to the stairs and descended them, vanishing into the darkness below.

"Now," Allanian said cheerfully, turning to the others, "Damion already gave me one crystal. I take it you have the other one on you?"

Nodding, Kara put down her pack and opened it. Digging around, she removed the opalescent coffer and handed it to Allanian. Eyes wide with exultation, Allanian took it and opened it. "Beautiful," he breathed as blue light spilled forth.

"When will you search?" Mat asked, finally over Kara's chastisement.

"Now," Allanian said as he sat down.

"Now?" Mat asked incredulously as Allanian removed a similar coffer from his pouch and opened it, allowing red light to spill forth. "Won't all this fir'gan interfere?"

"Not at all," Allanian stated confidently as he pulled the crystals forth, holding one in each hand. As large as a man's hand, each crystal pulsed dully with its respective light. "Well, well. . . . Aren't we lucky. . . ." he muttered. Aloud, he continued his previous thought, "The mass of power will, in fact, mask my Search and allow me to travel vast distances with little effort."

Mat let out an impressed whistle. "I don't think Cid could

even do that."

"Of course not," Ember declared with a snort. "Lan is the best there is. Cid is an amateur at best compared to him."

Allanian smiled his thanks for the compliment. "I would argue that Caldain is the better of the three of us, but let's not debate semantics, shall we?"

"Which one first?" Mat asked. "Do we need to defend you in any way?"

Allanian grinned. "Not at all, but your concern is appreciated. As for which one first–"

"Both," Kara answered for him with a knowing and impressed smile.

"Indeed," Allanian said with an anxious grin.

"You're kidding, right?" Mat asked as he looked at Allanian's exuberant visage with a mix of doubt and concern.

"No, he isn't," Ember replied firmly.

Mat looked to Kara for confirmation and found her looking at him with a knowing grin. "Just relax, Mat, and be quiet. Let him work."

Inclining his head thankfully to Kara as Mat fell silent, Allanian then turned his attention to the crystals. Eyes alight with excitement, he closed them and reached inward. Finding his inner fir'gan quickly, he latched onto it and funneled a gentle current into each crystal, joining his consciousness and synchronizing his heartbeat to each one. Kara smiled softly at the sight. Unlike a Warden's search, no cocoon of fir'gan was needed. The intrinsic way a Seeker was able to meld with a crystal to perform the task was a very rare, and unique skill that was nearly impossible for someone not born with it to learn. It not only made it difficult to notice a Seeker performing a search, but it also allowed them to do it far quicker than any other Gifted.

In an instant, Allanian's mind was soaring along the currents at a furious, exciting pace that made his soul soar. As he neared the ghostly anomalies on the currents that were the crystal's hosts, he could feel the pulse in the crystals quicken, and a measure of curiosity alight on his mind. Where he had expected to be torn in two directions, he instead found his mind racing inexplicably toward one location, and as that place came into focus, he laughed aloud.

"You cunning, knowing bastard. . . . We were there for more than just Amroth, weren't we?" he thought as he confirmed the location before

withdrawing his mind.

"Well?" Kara asked, even more curious about his findings after his laugh.

Opening his eyes, he cut his connection to the crystals and reverently returned them to their coffers before closing the lids. Scooping them up, he handed Kara's back to her before giving the other to Mat.

"Me?" Mat asked in surprise as he hesitantly took the coffer.

Allanian nodded. "Should the Betrayers learn of the crystals and come after us, they will think I have them and will focus on me. Depending on who would face us, it is likely that I would fall before either of you. Better that you have it than I should it come to that. Besides, I have other duties to attend to that could be affected by having them on me."

Slowly, Mat nodded his acknowledgment before carefully tucking the coffer into his shirt.

"So?" Kara asked, a hint of impatience in her voice.

Turning to her, Allanian grinned. "Your brother is either a very knowledgeable or wise man, Kara," he said, to which Kara rolled her eyes. Solemnly, though his eyes glittered with excitement, he told her, "We head north, Kara. The crystals' new hosts are in Merset."

Chapter Sixteen

Surprise was already becoming a constant on their trek south. Despite preparing themselves to deal with bandits after they left Shadowtown, no such encounter had occurred. In fact, the only unusual incident they experienced was the distant – albeit loud – roar of what they believed to be a crag drakuma on their first morning out of Shadowtown. As for the rest of their trek through the towering mountain range, it was uncomfortably smooth, and they made good time . . . that is, until they entered the Scorchlands of Pelasia.

While a brief, cordial encounter with the Kalu'te'aure was a minor inconvenience, it was the shocking way the heat assaulted them even before they could see the vast expanse of sand that made up the bulk of Pelasia that truly impacted their pace. For Dromick, it didn't seem like there was a gradual increase in temperature; instead, it was as if the heat was held back by the border, awaiting anyone foolish enough to enter the sun-scorched realm before unleashing its wrath upon them. The conditions were far beyond what he could have anticipated, and even after a week of grueling travel, he still could not believe such a hellscape existed outside the Nine Hells. Not only was it hot enough to kill a person well before thirst or starvation could do them in, but there was also a dryness that left one parched even after drinking enough water to fill a lake . . . and that was assuming you could find water, which seemed scarcer than the clouds in the sky.

As if that wasn't enough to confirm this realm was truly one of the Nine Hells, there were the illusions that Dromick fell prey to one swelter day near the end of their first week in the desert. Thanks to his skepticism of Shinks' warnings about the desert, the heat already had him battling with dehydration, and his brain felt like headfog was his new permanent state by the time they set out that inauspicious morning. According to Shinks, these illusions, or mirages as he called them, began to consume Dromick early in the day. It started with him muttering to himself, which eventually turned into him complaining about a lack of unhappy clouds and the need to make them cry. By noon, he'd reached the apex of his delusional state when he started screaming about a vast river before running headlong toward what was in actuality a ravine. If not for Shinks' quick reaction, Dromick's journey would have come to a sudden and embarrassing end that day.

After that shameful misadventure, Dromick was firmly convinced death wasn't just lurking around the corner in this land of sand and heat – it was more like it had a grip on one's throat and was just waiting to squeeze. Thankfully, he was still alive. Granted, he had to contend with horribly cracked lips and an ego-driven sunburn on his arms and head, but he figured it was a small price to pay for his foolishness. What's more, he knew that his ability to pay said price was unequivocally due to Shinks; for without the Pelasian, Dromick had no doubt he would have likely perished even before his attempted plunge into the ravine.

Remarkably, the years spent away from his native home had not dulled Shinks' knowledge of the land nor his survival skills. He found them suitable shelter each night and led them unerringly during the day, all while steering them well clear of dangerous creatures and terrain. His choice of food for their rations provided nourishment and spoiled slowly in the heat, while his foresight to bolster their water supply spared them, their mounts and pack mule from the worst of the heat's machinations. Even the clothes Shinks had insisted upon kept them cool and protected from the sun just like he promised . . . albeit after Dromick's pride folded beneath the sun's assault.

If all that wasn't enough to mark Shinks as a Deo-sent blessing, the man never once appeared phased by any of it; not by the change in environment, not by the dangers, and not even by Dromick's ignorant mistakes. This made it comical when, without a hint of mockery, he had confessed to Dromick on more than one occasion that his time in the north had made him soft. Dromick never challenged Shinks on that assertion, even though he felt the admission of weakness was more for his sake than the truth. After all, if the man thought he was helping Dromick's morale through such a thinly veiled farce, then who was he to deny him that?

As they trudged ever southward across the sun-scorched, never-ending hell on Kylir, they sought out news when and where they could. Initially, this was a fruitless venture. After their conversation with the Kalu'te'aure, the only soul they encountered came in the form of a native shepherd and his herd a day later. While he provided little more than gossip he'd heard from caravans passing through his tiny village, he did leave Dromick dumbstruck. He couldn't fathom where or what goats could graze upon amongst all the sand and rock. As such, he wasn't completely surprised when a heartfelt laugh preceded Shinks' explanation after they had moved on, but it did nothing to quell the embarrassment that accompanied the morsel of knowledge. After all, how was he supposed to know goats could survive in such an inhospitable environment?

After that, they journeyed in solitude until the end of the first week, when they came upon a northbound caravan resting at an oasis. The divine haven of green and water provided Dromick with a reprieve he desperately needed while Shinks haggled with the caravan's leader over fresh supplies. Although Dromick understood very little of the native tongue, he found it fascinating to watch as the Pelasians exchanged words. It was far more animated than anything Dromick had participated in or witnessed. Their voices swelled at times with what seemed like anger, and violent gestures often clashed with softly spoken words. Some of the exchanges seemed like threats to Dromick, and on more than one occasion it looked as if the two would come to blows. However, when they finally finished, both men slit their palms before clasping hands, sealing whatever deal had been struck. By the time they parted ways early the next morning, Dromick had managed to wash the sand out of every nook and cranny of his body, while Shinks had acquired another two weeks of supplies, a salve for Dromick's burnt skin, and exchanged their mounts and mule for two sizable, dark brown gormels. The prize of the stop, however, was the much-sought information.

As Dromick would expect from caravan gossip, there were elements that ranged from the absurd to the outright bizarre. From the former category, many of the caravan workers profusely claimed that not only were ember drakumas emerging from the deep desert in record numbers, but that they had seen such a migration themselves. Dromick had a hard time believing such a tale. From what he knew of the beasts, they were solitary creatures that very rarely left their natural habitat. What's more, drakumas were without a natural predator as their strength, durability, and ferocity were unrivaled. So, for a drakuma to leave its territory, it would take something drastic like a natural disaster. However, according to the caravan, the reason for the drakumas' flight was far more sinister. They professed that dark creatures whose mere touch brought about agonizing death were emerging from the deep desert as well, and it was they that the drakumas were fleeing.

Dromick chewed on that assertion as they traveled further south that day. Everything he knew about drakumas told him this was a ludicrous idea. Granted, they were intelligent beasts and knew to withdraw on the rare occasion that they were at a disadvantage, but the list of things that could accomplish such a feat consisted of their own kind, and perhaps exceptionally large parties of armed people. While it could be true that one or two were fleeing hunting parties, that still wouldn't be anywhere near enough to cause a mass exodus. Couple that assumption with the likelihood that the beings with a deadly touch were probably marauders using poisons, and it simply did not add up. With that conclusion, Dromick should have been able to dismiss the tales outright. However, the adamant ferocity with which the traders spoke left him convinced that they believed it to be unequivocally true. Thus, even after sleeping on it, he still found himself unable to dismiss it outright.

The following evening, after they'd made camp in the shelter of a heavily eroded butte, Dromick finally broached the subject.

A small fire, above which two moderately sized lizards cooked, crackled between the two men, casting dancing shadows against the butte. While the brawny Pelasian's attention was focused on the browning lizards, Dromick's black-eyed gaze was fixed on the endless sea of sand that awaited them in the morning. Arms resting on his bent knees, a half-full water skin hung from his hands untouched despite his parched lips and nagging thirst. This venture had started as a simple reconnaissance, but it had already become far more complex and puzzling than he could have ever contemplated.

Frustrated, and his mind weary from the day's heat, he asked, his throaty voice heavy with exhaustion, "Your thoughts, friend?"

"About?" Shinks rumbled, his amber gaze focused on the lizards as he turned them on a makeshift spit.

Dromick fought off an irritated sneer. "What the traders told us."

Shinks sat back next to his full-moon axe, its hawk feathers hanging limply from its spiked pommel, and settled his tattoo and scarred mass against his pack before he responded, "Ah. You mean the Drakumas?"

Dromick couldn't fend off his irritation this time. Rolling his eyes, he snapped, "Of course the bloody drakumas! What else would I be talking about?"

The sudden noise caused one of the gormels, both of which were bedded down against the butte, to look Dromick's way, its rabbit-like ears erect and twitching.

Shinks nodded his shaved head and motioned to the waterskin dangling from Dromick's hand. "Drink, Dromick. The water will help cool both body and temper."

"I wouldn't be angry if you'd stop playing–" his retort stopped short when he noticed Shinks' benign expression. Blinking a few times, Dromick shook his baldhead before uncorking the skin. "I'm sorry. First the heat, and now this bewildering tale." He shook his head again before taking a long draw from the skin. When he finished, he dumped a splash on his head, drawing a shudder as the tepid water hit his warm flesh.

As the water ran down Dromick's face, the gormel tucked its mane-cloaked head down between its folded legs, the black horns curled around its ears scraping gently against the stone beneath it. Shinks then responded, "Again, there is no need to apologize. For those not born to the desert's embrace, the heat brings the demon within to the surface."

Dromick, his eyes closed as he basked in the relative coolness of the water, nodded his appreciation.

"As for the tales. . . . We both know that such from the mouths of traders can be embellished." Dromick grunted in agreement even as Shinks added, "This time, however, I am tempted to take them at their word, my friend."

Stunned, Dromick opened his eyes and asked, "You can't be serious? I can believe drakumas are leaving the deep desert, however far-fetched that may be. The reason behind it, though — that is simply ridiculous! I am well aware that I am no expert on the beasts, but there are few things they fear. Plus, the whole 'creatures whose touch is deadly' is more than likely just hunters with poisoned weapons! So, unless it's an army chasing them, the drakumas have nothing to fear!"

Shinks slowly nodded, his eyes thoughtful. Running a scarred hand over the white stubble atop his head, he stated, his deep voice weighed down by uncertainty, "I would normally agree, but there is something . . . wrong with the desert."

Dromick offered a quizzical look in response. Adjusting his dark robes, he sat forward a bit and asked, "Something is wrong? What do you mean by that? And more importantly, when were you going to tell me?"

"I haven't mentioned it before because I wasn't sure. I have been away for so long that I felt it was nothing more than unfamiliarity. But to answer your first question, I don't know how to describe it other than to say the land feels . . . off."

"Off?" Dromick questioned with a cocked eyebrow. "The whole place feels off to me. Then again, I'm from greener lands. I guess I'll just have to trust you when you say it's off," he conceded. "But I need something more than that. If there is something malign going on, I do not want to stumble into it."

Leaning forward, Shinks began to turn the lizards slowly over the fire and thought about what he was sensing from the desert. It was a sensation that began to puzzle him soon after they entered the harsh environment. So far, he couldn't pinpoint exactly what was wrong, other than to say what he told Dromick – something was off. Finally, a thought occurred to him. "Do you know the feeling when you enter a familiar room and a piece of furniture has been moved? Or the difference in taste between fresh water and water that has been stored in a barrel?"

Dromick thought about it for a moment. Scratching the scraggly brown beard adorning his face, he replied, "I think I get what you mean; like the room, for instance. It's a familiar place, but with just one piece of furniture out of position, it can suddenly feel like a new room."

Shinks nodded. "That is it. This is my home, and something has been 'moved'. . . . I just cannot figure out what that something is."

Dromick sat back against his gormel, drawing an irritated grunt from it, his expression thoughtful. "I was hoping that this trip would be fruitless," he stated, the roughness of his voice softened by contemplation. "While I have my suspicions about Doma Ithikia's motives and objectives, I also know that the loss of trust between allies – or worse, the loss of an ally – would be dire at this juncture in the war. Unrest within a nation's people during war is understandable, even expected, but this is beginning to feel like more than that."

Shinks nodded, his grim visage made more so by the missing portion of his upper lip. "That it does, but let us not be too hasty. We do not know if Doma Ithikia is involved or even knows of the situation. Spirits, we do not even have a full grasp of what the situation is!"

Dromick eyed him. "I take it from your tone you have a suggestion?"

"I do."

"Let's hear it, then."

Pulling the lizards off the fire, he said as he removed the lizards from the spit, "I think we should make a slight detour."

"To where?" Dromick asked as he watched Shinks decapitate the lizards with a heavy dagger before placing them on palm leaves he'd acquired at the oasis.

"A trade city roughly three days south of here," he stated as he handed one of the crispy lizards to Dromick. The fire-roasted creature smelled divine to Dromick as he gingerly took the meat by the palm leaf. "It is popular with desert denizens who prefer to avoid the bustle of the city," Shinks added as Dromick sat back and eyed his meal.

"That's quite a detour. What makes you think it is worth it?" Dromick asked as he pulled a tender chunk of meat off the bone.

Shinks smirked at the surprise on Dromick's face as he consumed the meat. "Good, eh?"

"Better than I thought it would be," Dromick responded. "It's a lot like rahken." He took another bite, then prompted, "You were saying?"

Shinks swallowed the meat he was chewing before responding. "It is a free trade city run by the largest of the desert tribes, the Frath'mongii, which means it does not fall under The Merchant's Guild's supervision. Because of the lack of direct oversight by the Guild or the royal family, people are much more generous with their words and thoughts."

Eyebrow raised in curiosity, Dromick asked, "Why would they fear speaking their minds?"

Shinks nibbled at the meat on one of the lizard's legs. "Desert life is very different than what you are used to. To survive here, people must trust in their leaders without question and follow their guidance. My people long ago found that if too many offered dissenting opinions or railed against a leader's commands, it would often lead to disorder and chaos, which frequently ended in substantial death. So, to ensure order, a strict code of laws was created and enforced with little room for error. Minor violations are met with harsh punishment, while severe crimes usually result in death, or worse, banishment."

"That sounds extremely oppressive," Dromick stated, shocked by Shinks' words.

"It is," Shinks nodded in agreement. "While it has kept our society from collapsing into chaos, there were – and still are – tribes that refused to bow in subservience to the crown. Many times has House Ithikia tried to grind the dissenters into dust and bring the entire desert under its rule, but they have never had the manpower to effectively do so. After this was proven time and again through bloody wars, the deep desert dwellers and the crown came to an agreement. The desert clans would no longer try to usurp the crown or rebel against it, nor could they maintain a standing military, and they would be required to send one hundred able-bodied men to serve in the military for ten years. In return, House Ithikia would allow them to govern themselves with minimal oversight, and would protect them should war break out with another kingdom."

"Still sounds like a lopsided deal," Dromick replied even as he wondered if this could be the reason Shinks left home. From what

Dromick knew of the man, he talked about Pelasia occasionally, but not once had he said why he left. After hearing Shinks' explanation, Dromick made a mental note to ask Craigan about the Pelasian's past.

Shinks greeted Dromick's observation with a grunt. "Perhaps, but aside from a few skirmishes, it has worked. The desert clans have taken advantage of it by establishing a network of free trading posts that, despite heavy taxation by the crown, has made the clans wealthy in terms of coin and information."

"Given what you've said, I'm surprised House Ithikia allows them to accumulate that much wealth."

Shrugging, Shinks added around bites, "House Ithikia has its spies among them, I'm sure. It is also likely that those that run the posts work with House Ithikia in some fashion, or are even paid to turn a blind eye to House activities." He shook his head. "That doesn't matter at the moment. What is important is that we should be able to gather more uncensored information than we would in the city, and there's less likely to be those that would question an outsider's presence. I suggest strongly that we take advantage of this. Once we reach Qatal'ran, you will be marked as an outsider and watched. People will be reluctant to talk to you, and even less likely to share information."

Putting down the remains of his meal, Dromick sucked the juices off his fingers. "Now that you've painted such a lovely portrait of Qatal'ran," he stated sarcastically, "I must agree. Maybe we shouldn't or won't have to pay a visit to the city."

Shinks, his own lizard finished off, broke off a small piece of bone and began to pick at his teeth. After a brief moment of thought, he said, "No. . . . I think it would be unwise to avoid the city. At the very least, we should take the temperature of the people." Dromick smirked at the phrase. "Even with their words guarded, they will still talk to me." Glancing at Dromick, he smiled. "Besides, you have never seen a more beautiful city. The dull stone towns of the North are nothing compared to the majesty of our sandstone spires."

Dromick rolled his eyes. "Just for that, you get the first watch," he stated as he stretched out and tried to make himself comfortable against his gormel.

Shinks laughed in response. "So be it. Rest well, for the sun will bath us in purifying heat once more on the morn."

Dromick could only respond with a loud, heartfelt groan.

Three days. Three torturous days of unfathomable heat and

thirst followed by three nights of almost welcomed cold. Three days of praising Deo for the rare cloud that graced them with a modicum of relief from the unrelenting sun. Three days for Dromick to find more and more creative curses. Three days for Dromick to continue to question why Deo would place what must be one of the Hells on Kylir.

By mid-morning of the fourth day, they arrived at the Frath'mongii trade city. Worn down by the heat, Dromick was more than happy to remain with their gormels and supplies while Shinks, who appeared no worse for wear, took the lead and sought entry into the city. However, despite his exhaustion, Dromick wasn't about to forget his mission. So while Shinks talked with the dark-robed, spear-wielding guards stationed at a smaller gate to the left of the city's main entry, Dromick studied the trading hub.

To his right, a half-dozen wagons, pulled by a variety of gormels or mules, were awaiting inspection before passing into the walled city. Fifteen feet in height, the sandstone barrier protected the buzzing hub and provided an elevated station from which guards watched over the surrounding area. As for the city proper, from what he could see currently and during their approach to the trading hub, it appeared to be dominated by a plethora of sandstone buildings whose designs were both foreign and familiar. Switching his gaze to the main gate, he could see a few smaller sandstone structures through its open maw, which, if the city was anything like its northern counterparts, were most likely a combination of guard stations, bureaucratic offices and warehouses. Not too far beyond those buildings, and before the road vanished around a bend, he noticed that tents and canvas stalls began to line the road beneath a canopy of various materials suspended between the amalgam of buildings and a plethora of large support poles. Furthermore, he noted that the street narrowed significantly at that point, forcing the likes of wagons and large carts to peel off on a side road.

"That took longer than expected," Shinks declared with a hint of mild irritation in his rumbling voice, drawing Dromick's attention.

"That it did. What took so long?" Dromick asked as the large Pelasian approached, the hawk feathers hanging from the pommel of his axe swaying gently with his stride.

Shinks motioned to the roadside and they moved out of the growing line of pedestrian traffic awaiting entrance into the city.

When they were clear of prying ears, Shinks finally responded. "Aside from an assault of questions? The guard was happy to explain that the Ta'sha – that's the leader of the Frath'mongii here –

tightened security after the first sightings of the drakumas.”

Dromick appeared skeptical. Adjusting the dark wrap atop his head, he said, “I can understand a heightened alert, but the interrogation the guards are administering isn’t going to deter a beast, even if it was as long as yours was.” He scoffed.

Shinks smirked. “Quite so. No, the . . . heightened security is aimed at preventing enemies from entering the town.”

“Ah, I see. So, is it something we need to be concerned about?” Dromick asked even as he briefly fingered the pommel of the broadsword sheathed at his left hip.

Shinks nodded his dark cloth-wrapped head, “I would be. While I wouldn’t take the guard’s explanation without a little distrust, he said there had been a number of half-hearted raids against the city and numerous reports of similar actions in the surrounding area.”

Troubled Dromick’s brow furrowed. “Odd that none of the traders mentioned that.”

“I agree, but they may not have had that information. Either way, it is of no consequence at the moment.” He cringed slightly. Lowering his voice, he added, “You will not be happy about this, but given the circumstances, I felt it prudent to make it clear we are envoys of Doms Suldamik, which is partly why it took me so long to return to you.”

Dromick’s dark eyes bulged a bit. “We were to do our best to be inconspicuous, Shinks! Remember?” he declared quietly but forcefully.

Shinks nodded. “I am aware, but the situation seemed to merit that disclosure. If I hadn’t, we’d likely be in shackles now. Fortunately, that is not the case, and instead, we are to be immediately escorted to meet with the Ta’sha.” He snarled a bit, then stated with a hint of disgust, “The guard was generous enough to grant me a moment to explain the situation to you.”

Although irritated, Dromick conceded the point. “Alright. I can’t argue with that. But why shackles?”

“The guard mentioned that the raiders were said to be ‘outsiders’. So, as you are an outsider, he figured you might know something.”

“Damn,” Dromick muttered. “I would hazard a guess that this . . . Ta’sha, was it?

“Aye.”

“This Ta’sha could decide that I’m a part of it?”

Shinks nodded seriously. "I believe it is a possibility. However, the order to bring us to him came well after I stated our allegiance. So, I think it is far more likely that the Ta'sha merely wishes to speak with us." He suddenly looked over Dromick's head and nodded. "The guard is growing impatient. We should go unless we wish them to think we are considering running."

"Let's not do that, shall we? The situation is already more tenuous than I would like," Dromick responded, irritation evident in his rough voice, before turning and leading the way back to the guard station.

Once there, the guard Shinks had spoken with grunted. "Your gormels will stay, and you will follow," he declared from within the shade of his dark hood, his thick accent making the words sound heavy, and his amber eyes dour with suspicion. "Keep hands away from weapons and you will be safe," he added with a snarl, displaying crooked yellow teeth that seemed even more dastardly against his short white beard.

Dromick grudgingly nodded in agreement.

"Good." The guard grunted before turning and motioning to two other sentries. The two similarly dressed guards approached quickly before one fell in behind them while the other took the gormels' reins from Dromick. "Follow," the lead guard then stated before leading the way to the pedestrian gate.

Much to Dromick's chagrin, their escort drew the interest of those around them, and he dipped his head slightly. Sunburn aside, he wasn't the only fair-skinned visitor to the city, but that marked distinction made him stand out far more than he liked. The last thing he wanted was to draw even more undue attention to himself. Too much, and his already difficult mission could quickly become impossible if word of his inquiries somehow reached the wrong ears. With a mental scowl, he found himself – not for the first time since entering Pelasia – wishing he could have delegated the task to someone adept at infiltration, or even Shinks himself. It would do him little good to dwell on it, however. So, he squashed the thought as he had done many times before and focused on the situation at hand.

Once they passed through the gate and joined the milling throng, some of the tension Dromick felt melted away as they became just a few amongst many. Beneath the haphazard canopy, they found relief from the unrelenting sun and heat; however, the milling mass of humanity kept that respite to a minimum. Sweaty bodies pressed in close despite their escort, even as a cacophony of voices filled the air with a roar that made communication seem impossible. To Dromick's surprise, he picked up on a smattering of the Trader's Tongue amidst the rolling Pelasian dialect. It was oddly comforting to hear the familiar language amidst the foreign surroundings, and it brought him a measure of peace.

As they slogged their way through the throng of humanity, Dromick also found a bit of amusement in the vendors' behavior. No matter what realm he was in or what the people's traditions were, trade was always trade. Where ever he looked, hawkers and vendors alike professed the value of their inventory; and while he couldn't understand most of what he heard, the inflections and posturing told him all he needed to know about their tactics. Some vendors were embellishing, some were tactful, while others were clearly trying to be forceful. Many would-be patrons ignored them all; others chose to bypass the vendors that held no appeal, or they simply examined the goods for themselves before making a decision. On more than one occasion, the verbal jousting between patron and vendor appeared to be on the verge of violence, which was reminiscent of what he witnessed between Shinks and the caravan merchant. Only once did the bartering actually devolve into hostilities, and on that occasion, guards were quick to descend on it with a ferocity that nearly matched that of Shadowtown's sadistic protectors.

This hectic environment of barely controlled chaos was their home for far longer than Dromick would have thought, given their small party, and by the time the crowd began to thin, he was sure they'd been traveling more than an hour. At that point, the endless sprawl of commerce finally gave way to less crowded streets and what he could only assume served as a residential district. Most of the architecture was comprised of simplistic sandstone or mud-brick structures with either thatch or palm-leaf roofs, and featured narrow windows and doors. While the majority of the buildings were single-story, there were the occasional two-level homes, and even some with more lavish decor. All of it was an interesting study in architectural differences; however, Dromick's attention was soon caught by a sandstone wall in the distance that appeared to surround towering, lush palm trees behind which hints of a large structure could be seen above the tree tops.

As they drew closer, pedestrian traffic gave way to a number of covered sedan chairs and a heavier guard presence. Their path became more direct, and with the thinned-out crowd, it wasn't long before they drew near the ten-foot tall wall that separated what Dromick figured was the Ta'sha's estate from the rest of the city. In Dromick's mind, there was nothing overly impressive about the barrier. It wasn't very tall, and likely wasn't very thick; as such, he figured its purpose was more aesthetic than defensive. The only feature that garnered some credit from him was the lone, double-panel gate centered on the wall that they were approaching. Granted, it appeared large enough to admit a wagon, and was only manned by two spear-wielding guards in similar attire as their escort, but at least it seemed to be a lone point of egress.

One of the gate guards soon took note of them, and he said something to his partner, prompting them to move before the sealed gate and cross their spears defensively. Once Dromick's group drew close enough, the guard held up a hand and declared, "Sez'topa kor!"

The lead guard of Dromick and Shinks' escort brought them to a halt before approaching the gate guard and speaking with him quietly.

After speaking with their escort lead for a bit, the gate guards retracted their spears before the one on the right moved to the gate and pounded on it, shouting, "Mek'tor agappa!"

A moment later, they heard what Dromick decided was a heavy crossbar being removed before the robust panels were pushed inward by the gate guards. Once the entry was fully open, the guard on the left turned to them and motioned them forward as he stated, "Frith'ardwa!"

Looking back at Shinks and Dromick, their escort lead waved them forward before walking through the gate, leaving them to catch up.

Upon passing through the opening, Dromick gave the Frath'mongii a bit more credit for the manor wall as he spied a pair of guards supporting a thick timber. *"It barely qualifies as a defensive fortification,"* he mused, *"but at least the panels and crossbar are sturdy and thick."*

All thoughts of the town's defensive capabilities were suddenly pushed to the side as his gaze fell upon the lush oasis before them. Occupying the bulk of the courtyard, this shock of green amidst the desert sand was home to grass, palm trees, and a variety of well-manicured shrubs, as well as a spring whose precious waters glistened in the sunlight. A handful of people in loose, colorful garments lounged by the spring, while others casually strolled along paths made of expertly-fitted octagonal stones of an umber hue. It looked enticingly peaceful, and might have been entirely so if not for the sounds of bustling activity that seemed to be coming from the other side of the oasis' lush confines.

Leading Dromick and Shinks to the right along a path akin to the ones in the oasis, they circled the green wonderland and soon saw the start of what was responsible for the commotion. A small horde of workers and servants were dashing to and fro in a hurry to carry out their assigned tasks while the disjointed symphony of construction and loud conversations filled the air. As Dromick's group drew closer to the far side of the oasis, he noted that some of the workers were erecting stages and stalls, while others adorned the grounds with a plethora of decorations in a variety of bright colors and earthy tones. Clearly, they were preparing for a celebration. As for its purpose, Dromick had no clue, and when he looked to Shinks for an answer, he received a simple, perplexed shrug.

Once they rounded the final bend of the oasis, they finally saw the heart of the festival preparations near the oasis' edge. If Dromick had expected to see something extravagant or impressively grandiose, he would have been disappointed as there was nothing new to see, just more construction and decorating. Granted, it was on a much larger scale and carried out by significantly more workers, but a stage was a stage, and a stall was just a stall, no matter its size or embellishments. Still, Dromick was a bit impressed by the scale of it all, especially given the size of the city and its isolated location. Those musing, however, fell by the wayside when he finally got a clear look at the large sandstone manor that occupied the rear of the grounds.

Eight stories in height in many places, and built atop a foundation of stone, the sprawling complex dwarfed any other structure in the city, and featured some of the most unusual architecture Dromick had ever seen. Multi-tiered in a way that broke up the lines of the manor in a pleasing fashion, the structure was littered with arched windows and crenellated balconies. Burgundy-tiled domes thoughtfully supplanted the structure's flat roofs in a number of places and provided a notable organic flare, while peculiar human-cat hybrid sandstone sculptures could be seen perched all about the complex like desert gargoyles. Yet, despite those oddities, not to mention the brightly colored, unusual banners and bunting adorning its sunbaked walls, it was the section towering over the building that intrigued him the most.

Situated at the heart of the manor, the triangular sandstone structure was composed of five tiers, each smaller than the previous as it climbed skyward well above the manor's highest level. To Dromick's eyes, it was a curious sight made even more so by what looked like balconies on each tier that were overflowing with greenery. While such lush vegetation was a rare sight in the desert lands, the fact that it was at such an elevation was what made it so perplexing. Dromick couldn't imagine carrying water up so high just to keep greenery alive, and was about to ask Shinks about it when he noticed something flowing down the structure's corner edges. Blinking in shock, his mind struggled to accept what his eyes were telling him, and he almost came to a halt.

"This has got to be another one of those Deo-be-damned mirages," he thought in amazement. *"Is that actually water running down that . . . thing?"*

Noticing Dromick's enthralled gaze, Shinks leaned in and offered, "It's called a Sky Garden."

Dromick tore his gaze away from the structure and looked at him curiously. "Sky Garden?" he asked in awe.

Shinks nodded. "I am not familiar with how it works, but having one is a mark of substantial wealth," he noted with a hint of admiration in his deep voice as the path led them toward the manor's main steps and widened to match the stairs' breadth.

Before Dromick could say anything else, their escort lead brought them to a halt before the staircase and turned to face them, cutting their conversation off. "Wait here," he ordered gruffly before ascending to speak with the lone guard standing before the sizeable, and wide open, main entrance to the manor.

After a brief exchange, the door guard vanished inside, and their escort lead turned to watch his charges in silence. After a short wait beneath the blistering sun, the sentry finally returned with what appeared to be an attendant in tow. Their escort spoke with the new arrival for a moment before they both descended the stairs. When they reached the bottom, the guard briefly fixed a stern, admonishing glare on Dromick and Shinks before he signaled his fellow escort to follow and started back the way they came in.

Sparing a glance at the two guards as they left, Dromick then turned his attention to the new arrival.

Garbed in a clean black robe trimmed with elaborate gold stitching, as well as a silver torque around his neck, the attendant was an older, balding man of short stature. Fixing his amber gaze on Dromick and Shinks, he inclined his head of sparse white hair slightly. "Greetings," he declared in a dry voice with a small bow, the word heavy with the man's thick accent. "My lord offers humble apologies for any inconvenience caused. Northern visitors are rare, and trustworthy word of the north more so. If you will follow, my lord would have words."

Dromick eyed Shinks for a moment before nodding. "We don't know how much we can offer, but we'd be happy to do so."

The man's drawn lips parted in a smile, revealing yellowed teeth that were at odds with his somewhat rich attire. "This is good. Come, come," he gestured toward the door. "He awaits with refreshment."

Without waiting for a response, the attendant led them up the stairs. Once they were inside the manor, the sentry grabbed the stout iron ring that served as a door handle and pulled the heavy wooden panel closed, sealing it shut with a muffled thud and cutting them off from the bright desert sun. The sudden cessation of sunlight not only cooled the room noticeably, but it also made Dromick feel like he'd been dropped into total darkness. Thankfully, his eyes quickly adjusted to the lack of intense illumination, and he saw that they stood in an entry hall, which displayed a level of opulence that was both alien and familiar to him.

Broad and deep, the hall was wide open save for the colonnade that spanned the length of the chamber. Without the sun's influence, the sizable space was dimly lit, but it was still bright enough for Dromick to just make out the room's sandstone walls. Adorned with lit golden candelabras, as well as an assortment of tapestries and paintings that hung at roughly eye level, the walls vanished into the shadows as they rose to meet the recessed ceiling overhead. As the group started forward, Dromick cringed slightly as the click of his and Shinks' booted feet against the tiled mosaic floor echoed through the chamber. Glancing down, he saw that the mosaic was composed of bright shades of blue and green. While there didn't appear to be a discernable pattern or image to the layout, the way the colors flowed made Dromick think of the ocean.

Looking up as they approached the colonnade of robust, square wooden columns that supported the roof, Dromick noted they were coated in the same dark, rich lacquer as the main entry and were flanked by unlit sandstone lanterns. Passing between the first pair of columns, before which two spear-wielding guards stood stoically, they made directly for the rear of the room and the only other point of egress Dromick could see. Illuminated from within, the arched opening stood beneath a balcony that spanned the rear wall roughly halfway up it. Glancing at the shadow-shrouded balcony as they neared it, Dromick couldn't see any noticeable access to it, but he did note two vigilant archers watching them from the walkway.

"Practical and defensible," he thought. *"Only two points of entry, and a limited access battlement from which to rain death on would-be attackers. I must applaud whoever built this; they wanted to project wealth, but not at the cost of defensibility. This person is either paranoid or smart,"* he mused with respectful caution.

Beyond the archway, they found themselves in a long, somewhat narrow corridor. More of the golden candelabras adorned the walls; this time, however, they were as dark as the unlit sandstone lanterns that flanked the staircase halfway down the hall, as well as the trio of passages that intersected the corridor. Despite this, the hall-way was still well-lit thanks to the sunlight pouring in from the far end of it. The attendant led them directly toward that light, ignoring all else, including several servants. Consisting exclusively of women clad and veiled in sheer silks that accentuated their dark skin, white hair and amber eyes, they bowed their heads and either padded past them on bare feet or quickly made way for the trio of men.

Dromick had to fight off a sneer every time he glanced at one of the women. Between their see-through attire and submissive behavior, he felt more like he was walking past sex slaves whose spirits and resolve were long broken. His sense of propriety and honor was offended deeply by the display, but he knew this was neither the time nor place to judge or condemn.

"Just another mark against Doma Ithikia . . . assuming this isn't an isolated situation. The rich and powerful always have their vices, and this wouldn't be the first noble to treat women or servants like property," he thought with a contemptuous internal scoff.

Coming to a halt at the end of the hall, the attendant blocked the opening as he turned to face Dromick and Shinks. Holding a weathered hand up to signal they should wait, which they did, he then declared, "My Ta'sha awaits beyond. Be aware – you are allowed your weapons as a sign of friendship. Eyes are everywhere, and if you make any move of violence, you will be killed without warning or question."

Dromick nodded. "We understand," he responded, his rough voice calm despite the indignation he felt at such an insinuation.

The servant nodded, then moved aside, motioning them forward.

Stepping fully into the light, it took their eyes a moment to adjust. Once they could see clearly, they realized they were now standing in a large plaza that was comprised of four descending concentric, and gradually shrinking, tiled squares. Dromick noted several other corridors that emptied into the plaza along its perimeter, as well as at least six of the silk-clad servants waiting in the shadows or attending to other duties. His attention, however, was quickly grabbed by the center of the plaza. Bathed in the sunlight pouring in from above, the concentric squares featured a mosaic similar to the entry hall that was broken up by the sandstone staircases that flowed down to the bottom square.

"Must be below the sky garden," Dromick thought as he eyed the center of the room where a statuesque man in a luxurious robe of

white and red silk stood before a pavilion of opulent silks.

Casually approaching the stairs on their side of the plaza, Dromick quietly asked, "The Ta'sha, I presume?"

"Indeed," Shinks rumbled in response.

"Ah! Welcome, my honored guest!" the man declared in a rich voice as they started down the stairs, a broad, toothy grin plastered across his full face below amber eyes and a wide nose. "I do hope my guards were not rough with you? They take their jobs very seriously, and are suspicious of all . . . especially those not born of the desert."

Dromick nodded, wary of the wide grin. Smiles like that tended to hide sharp knives. Furthermore, given the way his bright, keen eyes, and short, wavy locks of white hair projected an image of carefree exuberance, Dromick was inclined to believe the smile was hiding an army of such blades.

"Not at all, Ta'sha," Dromick responded kindly as they reached the bottom. "I admire their caution and thoroughness."

"Splendid!" he replied with a clap of his hands, the rings adorning his fingers chiming. "Please," he motioned to the pavilion, inside of which awaited plump pillows that surrounded a table laden with bountiful platters of fruits and nuts along with a large, sweating silver pitcher, "join me for some refreshment. The desert's caress is not gentle on its children . . . so I cannot imagine what it is like for those of the North."

Dromick glanced at Shinks before the two approached and lowered themselves to the pillows.

"Our thanks," Dromick offered as he tried to find a position that wasn't too awkward. "The desert is far more unforgiving than I would have thought."

Seating himself opposite his guests, the Ta'sha picked out a round orange fruit from one of the plates. Leaning back, he said, "The desert is an unforgiving mistress, but if one listens carefully to her wants and desires, one can learn to find her gentle side and coax hidden riches from her." He flashed the fruit as proof just as a blue-silk-clad beauty, her long white locks framing her veiled face, emerged from the shadows and picked up the pitcher. Sinking a sharp nail into the spongy flesh of the fruit, he began to peel it away absently as he watched the servant fill their cups with a fragrant red beverage.

Once she was done, he waved her away before removing a section of the slightly pink meat of the fruit and popping it in his mouth. Chewing on it, he sat forward and lifted his cup. When he saw how guarded his guests were, he cracked a smile and laughed. "Where are my manners? I have you brought to me, present refreshment, and I have yet to tell you why I have done so. Let me assure you there is no ill intent; my invitation is to sate my curiosity. We get very little information about the war in the North, and even fewer visitors – especially ones of such standing. I would merely have what news you can provide, and in return, I shall provide aid if you need it. Let it not be said that allies of House Ithikia were treated poorly."

Dromick and Shinks exchanged cautious, puzzled glances before Dromick nodded slowly. "I'll be happy to answer what questions I can. However. . ." he added as he politely acquired his cup. Taking a sip, he was shocked to discover the liquid was quite cool and refreshing. Reflexively, he took another, longer draw and was stunned at the wave of refreshing coolness that spread through his body.

The Ta'sha chuckled at Dromick's reaction to the drink. "Refreshing, is it not?"

"It is!" Dromick replied, unable to hide his surprise and pleasure with the beverage. "What is it? I've never had anything like it!"

"T'shel – it is made from a variety of fruits and plants," the Ta'sha explained. "Our nomadic ancestors created it to combat the desert heat when water was scarce. The original wasn't quite as tasty . . . or so I've been told. Through the years, it was adjusted and made into a wonderful, light wine. Do not let its lack of headiness fool you, however. Too much, and the next morning will be quite unpleasant."

Dromick paused mid-drink and swallowed the mouthful he had. "Good to know," he said as he put down his half-empty cup. "However," he stated, continuing from where he'd left off, "I find it troubling that news of the war is as sparse down here as knowledge of the desert is in the North. While I have found Doma Ithikia to be . . . reserved with information about her ventures and realm, I did not believe that extended to her own subjects."

The Ta'sha amber gaze suddenly lost its boisterous glint, turning hard and grave, causing unease to swell within Dromick and Shinks. "As you are new to our ways and clearly unfamiliar with how Pelasia functions, I will caution you to guard your tongue in regards to House Ithikia," he stated firmly. "Slander, however slight, is considered a high offense, and is met with harsh punishment. It would be wise to choose your words carefully going forward."

The unease in Dromick's stomach turned to dread, and he glanced at Shinks, both angry that his declaration that this place was free from royal oversight suddenly appeared untrue, and in hopes that he didn't know that Pelasia was in such a state. The concern reflected in Shinks' face and eyes assured Dromick that he wasn't aware of the nation's status, and that he was just as worried about their situation as Dromick was.

The Ta'sha noted the apprehension, and he flashed a sudden smile that was meant to be reassuring. "Thankfully, you find yourself amongst people who have the luxury of being more liberal with their thoughts and words!" he declared, his rich voice once more boisterous. "House Ithikia's reach holds very little weight here in my little piece of the desert. You are safe to express yourselves here within my walls, though I would advise caution with my words in town. One can never tell where a trader's tongue may choose to wag. Therefore, while you are here, you are under my protection, and by extension, the protection of the Desert Clans."

Dromick nodded, guarded.

Chuckling, the Ta'sha continued. "I can tell this does little to assuage your fears, and that I understand. Therefore, I shall speak first in the spirit of trust. No matter what Doma Ithikia may say about our nation with her honeyed words, ours is a nation unsettled and shrouded in fear. Tales of dangers most dreadful abound on the winds, creeping into the light from the shadowy depths of tavern corners and drinks. Authorities ignore the chatter, and our Doma has moved a large portion of our military north to honor our alliance with House Suldamik . . . no offense intended, I assure you."

The blunt assessment of Pelasia's state settled some of Dromick's unease. "None taken," he offered.

"I would venture you are referring to the situation with the drakumas, Ta'sha?" Shinks interjected.

Looking at Shinks, he nodded gravely, declaring, "I am, brother."

Shinks leaned forward, any concern he had for their safety pushed aside by unease for his homeland. "How much do you know? What we heard from traders on our way south was sketchy."

"I'm afraid no one knows much," the Ta'sha stated, grim. "We know the drakumas are leaving the deep desert in alarming numbers. At first, we assumed the goron'turls' migration patterns had shifted, and the drakumas were merely chasing their food. Still, some of the clans were alarmed, so they sent trackers and hunters to discover if this was true."

"They discovered this was not true," Shinks declared confidently.

The Ta'sha nodded. "You are correct. As you know, such an exodus was alarming to begin with. The presence of such beasts in the more populated regions would be catastrophic. So, having failed to discover why such a thing was happening, the clans then decided to send scouts well into the deep desert to investigate, but few returned. Those that did, spoke of being stalked by evil spirits in a land barren of all life. None, I'm afraid, made it very deep."

Shinks' expression grew grave at such a pronouncement.

"What's wrong?" Dromick asked, the concern on the Pelasians' faces clear and undeniable.

"The tribes are respected for many things, and their bravery and combat skills are spoken of with reverence throughout Pelasia. They can take down a drakuma if necessary, and House Ithikia has long avoided trying to bring them under heel," the Ta'sha stated.

"So, for their warriors to be frightened is ominous," Shinks finished. To the Ta'sha, he asked. "Are you sure? Have you spoken to any of them?"

The Ta'sha shook his head. "Directly? No, I have not. We do, however, trade with many of the tribes, and I trust those who have brought the information to me. I hope that you can trust my word on this, but should you require further proof, there is a group of tribesmen due in two days. Should you wish it, I can arrange for you to speak with them."

Dromick looked at Shinks. "I abdicate to you on this, my friend. If you believe this would benefit our venture, then I am willing to wait."

There was no hesitation by the brawny Pelasian. "I do, indeed."

"It's settled then. We'll need to find accommodations—" Dromick started to say.

"Do not concern yourself with that," the Ta'sha interjected. "You are allies and my guests; I insist you stay under my roof."

Dromick eyed Shinks to gauge his reaction. He responded with a slight nod, echoing his own thoughts. While Dromick didn't fully trust the Ta'sha, rejecting his hospitality would be foolish. He seemed willing to part with what could prove to be valuable knowledge, and rejecting his offer risked making an enemy of someone who clearly was in a position to make their journey either fruitful or a disaster.

"Our thanks, Ta'sha. We are humbled by your generosity," Dromick responded.

"Excellent!" the Ta'sha declared with a pleased clap of his hands. "Now, while I am sure you have plenty of questions, I believe I have shown myself to be generous and trustworthy, so reciprocation would be in order. So, tell me of the North, and what glory our Doma has earned for us."

The three days spent with the Ta'sha were both enlightening and concerning. They discussed many things over that time, ranging from Pelasia's political climate to more mundane subjects such as Pelasian culture and art. The Ta'sha even offered to ease their way into Qatal'ran once he learned of their intent to visit. While this served to somewhat convince Dromick he wasn't their enemy, he wasn't so sure the Ta'sha was their friend either. What he was sure of, however, was that the Ta'sha was an opportunist and no friend of House Ithikia. In that regard, he felt he was worthy of guarded trust. Unfortunately, that was the only thing he was confident about at the moment.

Stars filled a cloudless sky that was cast partially aglow by the blue-tinged light of the crescent moon as Dromick watched the jubilant fete in the courtyard from a third-floor balcony located below the sky garden. The sense that he had waded into a swamp whose opaque, murky waters harbored a host of unknown predators gnawed at his gut. His instincts told him that there was only one way out of the predicament with his skin intact, but he had no idea where that path was. He was walking blind, with nothing but speculation to guide him, where a misstep would either see him drown in the dark abyss or deliver him into the jaws of a waiting predator.

Emerging from the brightly lit hall where a plethora of guests were enjoying the Ta'sha's generosity, Shinks approached his companion. "It is troubling, is it not?" he observed as he joined him at the railing, drink in hand.

"Which part?" Dromick responded with a snort of derision as he absently stared at the raucous guests walking and dancing across the grounds beneath a veil of fire light. "The surprise and cold reception news of Doma Ithikia's engagement was met with? The abject fear the tribesmen oozed when they spoke of the deep desert being 'consumed by death'? Or could it be that our Doms is to marry a woman that is far more vile than any of us thought?"

A stiff breeze rose up at that moment, ruffling both the loose, unadorned dark robes the two men wore, as well as the earth-tone bunting and banners suspended from the balcony.

"All of it," Shinks replied from behind his mug of t'shel before taking a long draw from it. "House Ithikia was respected when I left home despite some of its more heavy-handed ways; and the young woman I once served, while she reveled in the luxury of her birth, was not near the devil we've heard about. I am finding it hard to believe ascending the throne could change someone so much."

Dromick grunted. "The stories have it that Doms Astica was a gentle man when he was younger, but after the uprising that saw his father slaughtered, he became the man we know today," he stated, his rough voice weighed down by concern. "He put down the rebellion with extreme prejudice, and there hasn't been so much as a murmur of revolt since then." He sipped from his mug. "Then again, I'm finding a lot hard to believe at this moment. There is clearly discord in Pelasia, and instead of seeing to her people's needs, she's apparently shifted more resources north than we saw in Chalin. Though for the life of me, I cannot imagine where it's all gone. We would have seen some sign of it, given our route, or at the very least, there would have been talk in Shadowtown of such manpower moving through the area." He took another, longer draw from his mug.

"They could have taken another route?" Shinks offered, sending a chill down Dromick's spine.

"It is possible," he ultimately conceded, "but other routes are exceedingly treacherous and would likely incur unwanted losses. Besides, such a large force would eventually attract attention." Dromick scowled. "What I do know for sure is that even if I disregard some of the more outlandish stories and take the rest at face value, Doms Suldamik was right to be concerned. . . . At best, she's power hungry."

"And at worse?" Shinks prodded.

"I don't want to contemplate that right now," Dromick replied, his words fraught with dark thoughts.

Before they could continue their dour reflections, the warm voice of the Ta'sha called out from behind them. "Ah! There you are, my friends!" he declared loudly so he could be heard over the din of noise from both inside and outside the manor.

Without a hint of hesitation, Dromick and Shinks turned to face the Ta'sha, covering their concern with joyful masks.

"Ta'sha, how are you this evening? This is a fine fete you have put on," Dromick remarked, smoothly hiding the disquiet weighing on his soul.

The Ta'sha, clad in an extravagant, flowing red and gold silk robe, smiled in response. "I can only take partial credit," he stated with feigned modesty as he waved away the compliment with a hand that sported a plethora of lavish rings. "The entire city contributes, and that is why all are welcome. In that vein, you two should go and partake. Assuredly, there are foods and games you would find interesting."

"Assuredly," Dromick responded with as congenial a smile as he could muster. "However, the fewer that know of our presence, the better. As has been pointed out on a number of occasions, I stand out."

"Well, that is true," the Ta'sha agreed with a dismissive shrug. "If you do not wish to partake of the revelry, then perhaps a bit of good news is more to your liking?" he offered, smoothly changing the subject.

Sharing an anxious glance with Shinks, Dromick asked, "The caravan has agreed to take us to Qatal'ran?"

"Quite so!" the Ta'sha declared with a broad smile. "There are, of course, rules you must abide by. Should you agree to them, you will depart in two days."

"What kind of rules?" Shinks asked, skeptical.

"Nothing untoward, I assure you," the Ta'sha replied with a dismissive wave. "As your companion aptly pointed out, he stands out. So, he will have to be properly disguised. As for yourself, you will act as a guard."

"Simple enough," Dromick said.

"As I thought it would be." The Ta'sha paused, drawing concerned looks from the two northerners.

"What else?" Shinks asked, crossing his arms.

"It is nothing to be worried about, but there is a matter of discretion. You are not to inspect their cargo nor inquire about it. They deal in many goods from various tribes, and those tribes prefer to keep their methods of crafting to themselves."

"I see," Dromick responded, skeptical. "So, there's nothing . . . untoward about their dealings that could get us entangled with the authorities?"

The Ta'sha's broad smile told Dromick all he needed to know before the honeyed words left his lips. "Of course not! I dare not dabble in contraband, nor do I deal with those that do. You will arrive in Qatal'ran unharried by man or beast."

Dromick suppressed a sly chuckle. "That's good to hear," he replied, knowing very well that the first part, at least, was a bald-faced lie. Whether illicit goods or people, smugglers were smugglers no matter what part of the world you were in, and he had no doubt the

Ta'sha wouldn't trust this task to anyone but a professional. "We appreciate all you have done for us, Ta'sha."

"Think nothing of it . . . just, if you would, keep me in mind when you report back to Doms Suldamik?" he asked with contrived humility.

Dromick couldn't hide his knowing grin this time. "But of course, Ta'sha. Doms Suldamik will be pleased to know he has a dependable ally in Pelasia."

The Ta'sha gave a half bow. "I am but his humble servant."

"Laying it on thick, aren't we?" Dromick thought as the Ta'sha stood upright.

"Now that that is settled, I must see the good news delivered, and see to my other guests. If you gentlemen will excuse me. . . ."

"Thank you, Ta'sha," both men said in parting.

After the Ta'sha was inside once again, Dromick turned to Shinks and asked, "Just what have we gotten ourselves into . . . and why do I feel like I've just made a deal with the Hells?"

"I do not know. I can only hope we do not find ourselves in a nest of vipers," Shinks responded with a scowl, his tone dour.

"I couldn't agree more, my friend."

By the time the fete reached its conclusion, the Ta'sha was exhausted. Yet, it would be hours more before the last guests were ushered off the grounds, and his staff could finally dispose of the mess left behind. By then, his body and mind were begging him for sleep. However, as he made his way through corridors now void of revelry and lit only by moonlight, he knew sleep for the would-be-ruler of Pelasia would have to wait. There was still one guest to attend to. . . . One guest whose presence he tolerated only because his survival required it.

Arriving at the plaza situated below the sky garden, the Ta'sha was bathed in soft moonlight as he descended to the pavilion at the center of the room and stopped. To anyone else, the shadow-filled plaza would appear void of any other occupants. However, as he peered into the deep shadows, he knew he was far from alone.

"Don't you and your kind tire of this melodramatic farce?" he finally stated with a hint of exasperation.

An amused chuckle from the shadows greeted his query. "A farce, you say?" a deadly soft male voice responded. "What you call a farce, we call prudence," Hirok finished as he stepped from the darkness, cloaked in black, and approached the edge of the top tier to the Ta'sha's right. "Is it done?" He demanded, putting an end to any further banter.

Turning to face his guest, the Ta'sha looked up into his gently upturned dark-blue eyes, which watched him intently from astride an angular nose on his slightly round face. He then said with a curt nod, "It is. Is there any more Lady Alestra wishes done?"

"Not at this time, Ta'sha," Hirok replied with just a hint of mockery lacing the title as he shook his head of short-cropped, dark hair.

The Ta'sha pressed his teeth together at the slight, biting back a retort.

As if reading his mind, Hirok then said, "Do not worry. . . . You have never failed our mistress. See to it that you continue to serve her admirably, and the desert will be yours very soon."

Taken aback by the blunt statement, the Ta'sha couldn't help but gawk for a moment before gathering himself. "Soon?"

Hirok grinned. "Oh yes, very soon. Everything is nearly in place in the North, and her army is almost ready." His eyes grew bright with fervent resolve. "Once she marches, all of Triclose will tremble and bow before us!"

Terror took root in the Ta'sha's stomach as it always did when the zealousness of Mistress Alestra's servants was on display. While he knew he would rule the dessert once Alestra moved on, he still felt a myriad of questions cascade through his mind.

Hirok must have noticed this, for his attention turned sharply to him and he flashed a malicious grin. "*Tch!* Careful with questions and where your mind wanders, Ta'sha. Do not spoil my mood. I would hate to have to explain why one of my mistress' more capable servants was found slaughtered in his own home."

Any sense of doubt the Ta'sha had was driven from him as if a drakuma stood before him ready to bite his head off. Dropping to his knees, he prostrated himself before Hirok. "My body and soul belong to Mistress Alestra. If it serves her purpose, strike me down. I gladly give my life to her cause."

Deafening silence greeted his declaration. As it dragged on, the Ta'sha fully expected to feel cold steel separate his head from his shoulders. When that didn't happen, he cautiously looked up. To his profound relief, Hirok was nowhere to be seen, and his ominous presence no longer occupied the room. Sitting back on his heels, the

Ta'sha let out a profound sigh of relief. It was only then that he realized he was drenched in sweat.

"Spirits protect me from that man and his mistress' wrath!" he thought before climbing to his feet and making his way to his room, where he hoped slumber's embrace would rid him of the dread consuming his soul.

Chapter Seventeen

"*Light bless you, and welcome back,*" Damion heard a deep feminine voice intone in his mind as he emerged from the portal.

As his gaze fell upon the massive, familiar black and gray-splotched direwolf bowing to him, a genuine smile spread across his face. "Light bless you as well, Deralina," Damion replied aloud, his authoritative voice filled with delight.

"Deo be good!" Amroth barked angrily from behind the direwolf as he stood up and turned to face Damion. "You didn't have to shove me lik–" Seeing the massive direwolf, Amroth's words stuck in his throat as his eyes widened in fearful shock. "What in the hells is that?!" he asked as he took a few anxious steps back.

"Relax," Damion ordered calmly as the Portculim closed with a bang behind him. "Deralina is a friend."

"A what?" Amroth asked, his deep voice a thick mix of trepidation and bewilderment.

"A friend," Damion repeated patiently. "She's here to greet us and escort us to our destination."

"I don't–" Amroth started to say before hanging his head and shaking it in exasperated confusion. "Fine!" he conceded as he looked back up at Damion. "None of this should surprise me anymore, so I give up!" He let out a sarcastic laugh. "I won't be surprised if you tell me that this . . ." he waved at Deralina, "giant wolf can talk."

Damion smirked. "In a way, she can."

"I–" Amroth began to say before shaking his head and offering, "Just forget it." Looking around, he then asked, "Where are we, and why is it bright?"

"To the latter, Solarson is roughly half a day ahead of Triclose," Damion informed Amroth. "You really should pay attention to your lessons."

Amroth snorted. "I did pay attention, thank you very much. With everything I'm trying to digest, recalling such a small detail seems pointless."

"Indeed," Damion replied with a small grin.

Ignoring his amused, cynical tone, Amroth asked, "So just where are we on Solarson?"

"We're in the northwestern portion of the White Fang Mountains."

Looking at Damion curiously, Amroth asked, "Is it spring here? I would have thought it was winter here as well."

Stepping past Deralina, Damion approached Amroth and patted him on the shoulder sympathetically. "It is outside the grove; in here, however, it is eternal spring."

"Do I dare ask how that's possible?" Amroth muttered.

Smirking, Damion said, "The simple explanation is that the grove is a pocket realm, similar to the Utherian Valley and the grove we just departed."

Amroth's eyes grew wide at the mention of Triclose's most treasured location. "The Valley?" he asked incredulously. Shaking his head once again, Amroth then declared, "You know what? Forget I asked."

Nodding with barely contained amusement, Damion looked at Deralina and said, "If you would, Lina, lead on."

"As you wish," she replied through the link as she trotted past them, her deep voice taking on a grave tone. *"It would be wise for us to be cautious and travel quickly."*

"Is that so?" Damion inquired, falling in next to Amroth as they followed Deralina along the path.

"It is. We do not know if Warrick has remained at Blackstone or not, but with the reappearance of blackhearts, we're all on alert for any encroachment. My brethren and I have been patrolling long and far from Gray Sky so that we can hopefully detect any advance long before they near the keep."

"The appearance of the blackhearts troubles us all, Lina. They've even appeared on Triclose, and very nearly cost Kara her life," Damion informed her as they exited the grove.

"Corith be good!" Deralina exclaimed in shock with a quick, worried look over her shoulder at Damion. *"Is she alright?"*

"She is, thank the Light," Damion responded.

"Deo be good!" Amroth breathed in shock, with a white puff of air, as he came to a halt and craned his neck to look up at the top of the rocky incline surrounding the hollow that the grove occupied. "You don't expect us to climb this?" he asked as he looked around for a way up.

"No," Damion said, his troubled tone drawing a curious look from Amroth. "There's a hidden path leading out of here if I recall correctly. As I said, Lina knows the way, so let's keep moving; while Lina nor I are affected by the cold, we haven't had enough time to show you how to make yourself immune to such things."

Damion's words drew Amroth's attention to the frigid conditions, quickly shattering any of the questions that had formed in his head in response to Damion's tone, as well as his declaration about Lina and himself. "Deo! You're right! It's colder than anything I've felt in Merset!" he stated as he began to shiver slightly.

Motioning for Deralina to continue on, he and Amroth fell in behind her once more as Damion said, "I'm not surprised. We're farther north than Merset."

"So we're as far north as the Ice Walkers?"

"Not quite, but both places are cold enough to kill the unprepared."

"You don't say," Amroth replied sarcastically as he rubbed his arms.

Grunting, Damion took control of the currents surrounding them and began to raise the air temperature. Within moments, the surrounding area became comfortably warm, melting the snow at their feet and drawing an awe-filled expression from Amroth.

Letting his hands drop to his side, Amroth asked, "Did you do that?"

"Indeed."

"Then why in the hells didn't you do it earlier? You said it yourself, I could freeze out here! So why let me suffer?" Amroth demanded.

"To build patience and character," Damion stated simply as they neared the entrance to a tunnel.

Amroth scoffed. "Right," he said.

Smirking, Damion turned his attention back to Deralina and their conversation. *"Sorry."*

"Not at all," Deralina replied with a hint of amusement. *"It's always a shock to the new ones, and it is a lot to take in."*

"Indeed."

Amusement that felt like laughter trickled through the connection. *"So much said in such a simple word – ah, how I have missed you!"*

Deralina's tone quickly turned serious, and she said, as they entered the tunnel, *"The others should know of your contact with blackhearts on Triclose; we need to have a better idea of what we're dealing with."* Her tone grew even grimmer as she added, *"You know as well as I do that even with the power of Kydan'fir after Kara and Ember were successfully joined, we lost far too many of both Orders exterminating the blackheart pestilence. If the blackhearts' numbers are even just a small portion of what they used to be, we will be ill-equipped to deal with them."*

An ominous silence fell on their connection, and Damion let it remain as they made their way through the maze of slick tunnels. After a few minutes, and a few curse-ladened slips by Amroth, they emerged from the underground maze and were greeted by towering, snow-covered mountains set against a crisp blue sky.

"It's beautiful," Amroth declared in awe as Deralina steered them in a southeasterly direction.

"It is," Damion agreed as they followed the direwolf.

As freshly thawed ground sucked at their boots, they followed Deralina at the steady pace she set. Overhead, the sun continued its ascent, setting the mountains alight with tranquil, pleasing light. Looking about as they traveled, Amroth found himself enamored with the scenery. Mountains were a common landmark in northern Triclose, but nothing he had seen compared to the majestic landscape he now trod.

"I'm not sure even the Highlands compare to this," he declared around mid-morning as he paused atop a ridge that gave them an awe-inspiring view of rolling white hills far below them.

"There are Sur'dathans that would disagree with you," Damion countered as he stopped next to him.

Amroth grunted, "Let them. If they saw this, their protests would die in their throats."

A slight smile tugged at Damion's lips. "I can't disagree." Clapping Amroth on the shoulder, Damion added, "Come, we still have a hike ahead of us."

Offering one last longing look at the landscape as Damion resumed their trek, Amroth nodded and fell in behind him.

Reaching along the currents, Damion asked of Deralina as she trotted ahead, *"Does Greatjon know we're coming?"*

"No," she responded sternly. *"Not that it would make a difference. While he has all but broken ties with Darkon over Darius' death, he still holds you partially responsible for what happened to the Bestynes."*

"To a certain degree, I cannot disagree with him, but it's been nearly two centuries since Darkon's temper tantrum — that's a long time to hold a grudge."

Deralina laughed darkly along the connection. *"He wouldn't be the first to nurse a grudge over the centuries,"* she stated matter-of-factly.

Conceding the point, Damion changed the subject and asked, *"What of Gray Sky and the Bestyne numbers?"*

"Standing in ruins," Deralina replied to both regretfully.

"Why in Corith's name has he not rebuilt?" Damion asked incredulously.

"Part of his grudge, I suppose. However, I do know that he intends it as a reminder of what happens when an Order is 'punished'," she replied, practically spitting the last. *"Either way,"* she continued calmly, *"the keep is livable, and we built a new village a long time ago. As for our numbers, there are far, far too few of us. Gifted cyrians have grown far too rare over the years, leaving us to work with other Gifted when we can find them. It's a tedious task to find ones that possess the right qualities; and of those few, even fewer survive Blending."*

Damion's face turned grave. *"That is . . . unfortunate. And your Ansei Grove?"*

"Standing."

Damion hesitated a moment. *"And . . . Blackstone's?"*

"Unknown," Deralina replied, an edge of anger to her deep voice.

"Understood," Damion stated, his tone sympathetic. Seeking to change the subject, he then asked, *"And the future Indigain Warden? What is she like?"*

Damion felt Deralina practically smirk. *"Very much a darlion in many ways. On the other hand, she is very different from her kin, and I sense something in her that is as unusual as what I sense in the boy you brought. Speaking of which, the boy practically oozes power and smells of Luthur. Is he already Joined?"* she asked with guarded curiosity.

"Indeed," Damion informed her bluntly.

"Corith be good! That's just about one of the most idiotic things I've ever heard! You Joined what is clearly an untrained, practically unaware Gifted to a crystal? What in the hells could have possessed you to do such a dangerous thing?" she demanded, her voice a mix of shock and twisted amusement.

"Events beyond my control, sadly," he said simply before adding, *"That story, however, is for another time. Right now, just be satisfied to know that his survival gives some validation to what Luthur started all those centuries ago."*

"Corith be good," Deralina breathed in awe as she quickly looked back at Amroth, whose attention was fixated on his majestic surroundings. *"That explains what I'm sensing from the boy. How strong is he? For that matter, how complete is he?"*

Damion shook his head mentally. *"I can honestly say that I don't know. He is, however, more complete than any of the others; the mere fact that he successfully Joined with Luthur's crystal proves that. As for how strong he is. . . . Given enough time, I'm sure we will find out."*

Deralina let the conversation die off after that, her mind flooded with the implications of what Damion had just told her. For the next hour, she mulled the situation over and, as she led them into a pass barely wide enough for a sizable wagon, she found that Damion was right. They could guess and assume all they wanted, but only time would reveal to them just how successful Luthur's gambit had been, and just what that meant for them now.

About halfway through the pass, another thought bolted to the forefront of her thoughts, nearly causing her to come to a halt.

"Oomph!" Amroth exclaimed as the near halt caused him to bump into Damion hard. "Is there something wrong?" he asked, flashing Damion an apologetic smile as he looked back at the young Merandith.

"Deralina just stumbled," Damion informed Amroth. "Are you alright?" he asked with a raised eyebrow.

"Fine," Amroth replied, belying the pain he felt in his chest.

"Indeed," Damion responded with a small, knowing smile.

Though her mind was distracted, Deralina looked back to make sure everything was okay. *"Is it really possible?"* she thought absently as she continued onward.

"Is what possible?" Damion asked.

Cursing herself for not realizing the connection was still open, she thought about keeping her theory to herself before realizing it would be futile to do so. Damion would see her soon enough.

"The darlion training under us. . . . Is she like Amroth?"

A heavy, thoughtful silence greeted her inquiry, and for a moment, she thought Damion had not heard her. Then, as the pass widened and delivered them upon the top of a rise, he told her, *"We shall see."*

As his statement sank in, Deralina then heard him say aloud, "Amroth, welcome to Gray Sky."

After the breathtaking landscapes he'd witnessed during their trek, Amroth's hopes for what their destination would look like had grown to fantastical proportions. However, as his dark eyes took in the bleak scene before him, he realized that even had his expectations been conservative, Gray Sky was a monumental disappointment. In fact, he felt like the devastated and bleak scene was something right out of the Contested Territories, with the only difference being that this village and keep were occupied.

Shattered, dead trees surrounded a ruin-littered village that flowed up the rocky, cratered terrain to an equally ravaged keep that stood atop a rise like a broken king. The few signs of life Amroth saw made the scene seem even more depressing. It was as if the few standing buildings spoke of a people who had tried to rebuild before inexplicably giving up.

"What happened here?" Amroth asked as he saw a few people take note of them and begin walking toward the edge of the village.

"Corith-be-damned foolishness," Damion replied gravely as he and Deralina started down toward the village. "And proof that even we can be short-sighted and stupid," he added as Amroth scrambled to catch up.

Given Damion's tone and his dark expression, Amroth decided to let the subject drop. Instead, he focused on the growing crowd on the simple dirt road that ran alongside the crumbling remains of what Amroth suspected had once been a wall around the village. At first, between their swept-back ears and feral appearance, Amroth thought the denizens of the village were darlions. But as he drew closer, he began to note differences in their appearance – in particular, their four-fingered hands – that indicated they were something similar yet different.

"Are they cyrians?" he asked of Damion, giving voice to his curiosity.

"Indeed," Damion responded, his vision focused on the nearly fifty cyrians – all of whom were armed and appeared tense – gathered on the road. "These are what remain of the purebloods."

"Ah," Amroth responded. "I can see the relation, but there's something about them that's more . . . darlion."

Damion nodded but said nothing.

Between Damion's clear unwillingness to discuss it further, and their proximity to the cyrians, Amroth remained silent despite his gnawing curiosity. Suddenly, a soft patter of feet from behind drew his attention. Expecting to find that more cyrians had snuck up behind them, Amroth stole a quick glance. To his surprise, instead of seeing more of the dangerous-look people, he found a dozen massive direwolves trailing them.

"Ignore them," Damion ordered without looking.

Looking back around, Amroth asked, his face a shade paler and his voice thick with concern, "We're as good as dead if they decide we're a threat, aren't we?"

Damion smirked darkly. "I'll be just fine. As for you . . . well, just don't give them a reason to think you're food."

Amroth blanched, thinking that what Damion said was true. Then, it dawned on him that Damion was joking. "You're an ass," Amroth muttered.

"Possibly, but I still wouldn't do anything to provoke them. While I don't think we're in any danger, their feelings toward me might be less than cordial."

"What a surprise," Amroth muttered sarcastically.

Other than the occasional pair of twitching ears, there were no overt signs of aggression from the cyrians, but Amroth still felt a knot of anxiety take root in his gut as they drew closer to the gathering. The irrational part of his mind screamed that these creatures, most of which were armed and armored, would attack at any moment, but to his surprise, the cyrians parted, granting them passage. Still, he felt like defenseless prey as their vertical pupils followed their advance up the dirt road. Once they were clear of the gathering, Amroth found himself looking back. To his relief – though still disconcerting – the cyrians and direwolves remained where they were.

Turning his attention back to the path before him, Amroth let out a deep, relieved breath. "Deo, that was uncomfortable! Now I know what Allanian's enemies must feel like."

Grunting in amusement, Damion said, "Come on, they're awaiting us."

Raising a curious eyebrow, Amroth followed onward.

"I thought I was imagining things, but it really is him," Greatjon declared, his tone unreadable, though the scowl on his typically solemn face and his dour dark-brown eyes made his mood clear.

Claw-pommel claymore in hand, and dressed in a dirt-stained white shirt, black breeches and boots, Greatjon stood before the remnants of Grey Sky's main gate watching the new arrivals approach.

Like the Bestynes gathered behind him, and Alsa to his right, he had sensed the approaching newcomers shortly before they appeared on the far side of the village.

Watching the advancing pair with her hands folded at her waist, Alsa replied, her tone tinged with anger, "There's no mistaking that power."

Noting her tone, Greatjon glanced at her curiously. Because of Greatjon's demands that she dress in something more appropriate for combat training, she had already been in a pensive mood for most of the morning. After a short, heated debate, she had conceded and now wore a loose-fitting red shirt, and gray pants tucked into calf-length brown boots. The outfit already seemed out of place on her, but with the addition of the carefully designed, emerald-dotted hairnet holding her auburn hair in place, and the gold circlets around her wrist that were connected to an emerald-encrusted ring on each of her fingers by delicate silver chains, she simply looked absurd to Greatjon.

Standing to Greatjon's left, Aseria seemed oblivious to her injuries. Her short white fur with its blonde accent stripes hid the numerous bruises littering her body and face, but could do little to disguise the fresh cuts on her face and arms. As for her red-trimmed gray sectional leather armor, chap-style pants and knee boots, they were already marred and in need of some repairs. Leaning on her slender longsword, her blue-lavender eyes wide and her ears twitching some, she declared, her musical voice filled with awe, "Corith, even I can feel something from him! It's like. . . . It's like a thunderstorm barely held in check."

"An apt description, child," Alsa said. "He is the eldest, as well as one of the most powerful of us, and is arguably the deadliest of the Wardens," she informed Aseria before noting that Deralina was leading the new arrivals up the road. She then asked of Greatjon, an edge of concern to her soft voice, "Did you know he was coming?"

Greatjon shook his head, the scar running from brow to chin over his right eye making his scowl look more severe. "No," he responded with mild irritation, "Deralina told me nothing."

"Interesting," Alsa responded with a raised eyebrow. "How do you plan on greeting them?" she asked as the group came to a stop about sixty paces from them.

Grunting, Greatjon planted his claymore firmly in the ground before starting forth with determined strides.

"Oh dear," Alsa quipped with a hint of dark satisfaction.

"What?" Aseria asked with concerned curiosity.

"This could get ugly. I suggest we remain here."

Unnerved by Alsa's tone and the anger she sensed radiating from Greatjon, Aseria nodded and watched.

Watching the intimidating man with rust-orange hair pulled back in a horsetail approach, Amroth didn't need enhanced senses to know something was wrong. Not only was this man furious, but the same intensity in the man's eyes was something Amroth had witnessed in the gazes of many bloodthirsty soldiers.

"Ah, Damion . . . this doesn't look good," he said, alarmed.

Damion nodded, "Wait here," he ordered before he and Deralina moved to meet the man.

As the two neared each other, the large man's pace increased, and Amroth felt an ominous tingle build in the air.

"Oh Deo, this isn't going to be good," he thought with dread.

Coming to a halt, Damion saw the building power around and within Greatjon. *"I'd stand clear,"* he suggested firmly to Deralina.

Deralina spared a concerned glance for Damion before trotting swiftly past the quickly approaching Greatjon.

Turning his attention back to the Bestyne Knight and General, Damion braced himself and bowed respectfully. "General and Knight of the Bestyne Order, Corith bless your soul," he said loud and clear, using a bit of fir'gan to project his voice so everyone watching could hear. "I, Damionatsu Masumaite, Preceptor of the Stelariuos Order of the Light, request permission to—"

A loud growl of pent-up rage, followed by a thunderous blow, cut Damion short as Greatjon's fist connected squarely with Damion's face, cracking the bones with a sickening crunch. Amroth gasped in horror as a quick uppercut followed, launching Damion unceremoniously skyward, the concussive force of the blow buffeting the young Merandith, and further demolishing some of the surrounding rubble. To his surprise – though he had no idea why he should feel that way anymore when it came to Damion – Damion righted himself and landed nimbly just a few feet in front of Amroth.

With the bones in his face already mended by the time he touched down, he wiped the fresh, bloody remnants of a now-closed mouth-to-brow laceration from his chin as he righted himself. Immediately, his gaze found Greatjon already barreling toward him. Without a hint of fear, Damion stood tall and fixed an uncompromising glare on the charging Knight.

Damion's posture drew a snarl from Greatjon as he cocked his arm for another blow. As soon as he was close enough to ensure Damion couldn't dodge, the currents in and around Greatjon surged as he launched his attack with blinding speed. To his chagrin, Damion's right hand lashed out and caught the punch with ease, shredding the muscles and ligaments in Greatjon's right arm as he came to a jarring halt.

"I think one punch is enough, don't you?" Damion asked casually.

Growling with pain-filled anger, Greatjon hissed, even as his left hand clenched into a fist, "Who in the hells do you think you are, showing your face here and now?! Give me one reason that I shouldn't order you gutted and your crystal removed!"

Calmly, Damion arched an eyebrow and said, "One? I'll give you two. First, what happened here is Darkon's fault, not mine. Second–"

Greatjon's left fist came flying toward Damion's face, which he caught with similar results, drawing another growl of agony from the Bestyne Knight.

"Second," Damion repeated coldly, "My mission was more important than my presence here could have ever been. I am truly sorry for what befell your Order; and while Darius and Cat's loss is unacceptable, if my mission had failed, the results would have been disastrous beyond compare – especially given the growing Darkness. However, if holding me responsible for being unable to stop those atrocities makes you feel better, then, by all means, do so. Such accusations are a pittance compared to what Corith will hold me accountable for when I finally pass from this life."

For a tense moment, Greatjon stared hard into Damion's cold, coal-black eyes, searching for any deception in his words. When he saw that there was none, he growled, "What could be so damn important to leave us all in the cold and with Darkon guiding us?!" Glancing at the shocked, and more than a little terrified Amroth, Greatjon demanded, "Was it him?"

Damion nodded slowly. "He is very important to us – especially given our current situation."

"Why is he so damn important?"

Ever the teacher, Damion instructed, "Calm yourself and use your senses. What do you sense?"

Snarling at Damion derisively, Greatjon managed to calm his mind and do as he was asked. Immediately, it was clear the young man was a Gifted as he noted the man's flickering emerald aura, but there was something else there . . . a power lurking at the edge of the man like a flittering shadow. Narrowing his focus, Greatjon tried to discern what that power was. Then, his eyes growing wide, the power came into focus, and the knowledge of what it was hit him like a mountain had been dropped on him, draining the tension from his body.

"Corith be good!" he breathed. "That power. . . ." Looking back at Damion in shock, he declared incredulously, "He's got Luthur's crystal! He's a Warden!"

Sensing that the danger had passed, Damion released Greatjon's fists and nodded. "Indeed, he is that," he said as Greatjon's fully healed arms dropped to his sides. "The details can wait for another time, but right now, all you need to know is I am back, and the boy needs training."

"An untrained Gifted is Joined?" Greatjon asked in disbelief.

A regretful frown tugged at Damion's lips. "An unfortunate situation caused by unforeseen, and dire, circumstances. But as I said before, those details can wait. Right now, he needs training. Kara informed me that you were teaching another here, and I thought this would be an ideal situation and location to train him." Fixing Greatjon with a serious glare, he added, "These two young Gifted have had a lot dropped upon them; it could be a boon to them both to learn together. If you don't want us here, however, I will understand. Corith knows the boy could be a danger to us all with the power he now possesses if something were to go wrong, but I believe this is the best situation for them both. So please, Greatjon Durmont, General and Knight of the Bestyne Order, grant us leave to enter Gray Sky?"

His deep voice still tinted with anger, Greatjon responded, "Two hundred years you've been gone, and you still know how to get in someone's head." Shaking his head with a dark, amused chuckle, he added, "I have a bull to gut, you know? I won't have you and your charge complicating things or getting in the way of that."

Motioning to the scar over Greatjon's right eye, Damion asked, "I take it that is a reminder of that?"

Greatjon nodded.

Suddenly, a small but dark smile split Damion's lips, sending a chill up Greatjon's spine. "Then let me assure you," he stated, his authoritative voice turning vicious, "that whether it be by my hand or yours, Warrick will pay for the deaths of Darius and Cat, and the destruction of Blackstone. By blood, by honor, and by deed — this I swear."

Flashing Damion an equally malicious grin, Greatjon clapped the elder Warden on the shoulder and said, "You know, Darius said to tell you he appreciated you greatly. I have a feeling your declaration would have made his heart soar."

Damion smiled softly, regret flashing across his dark eyes.

"In any event," Greatjon continued, "I, Greatjon Durmont, General and Knight of the Bestyne Order of the Light, grant leave for the Preceptor of the Stelariuos Order of the Light, Corith bless your soul, to share shelter and bread with us until you see fit to journey onward."

Nodding, Damion said, "You have my thanks."

"Save it for when Warrick is dead," Greatjon replied.

Damion nodded. "Indeed."

Grunting in agreement, Greatjon then gruffly stated, "Well, I guess we shouldn't stand out here like a menagerie spectacle. Come in, and let's get the introductions over with. We're wasting daylight."

Nodding as Greatjon started back toward the keep, Damion turned and motioned Amroth forward.

As the cyrians at the village began to disperse, Amroth approached Damion cautiously, his face unabashedly awash with awe. Once he reached him, Amroth asked, "Are you okay? I've never seen anything like that! I'd swear that punch should have taken your head off!"

"It wasn't bad for a Knight," Damion replied with a slight shrug.

"Not bad?" Amroth said incredulously. "He nearly caved in your face!"

"Sometimes, Amroth, it's a victory to let an ally have a sense of success, lest you make him an enemy," Damion offered in a lecturing tone.

Amroth blinked. "You let him do that much damage?"

"Something like that." Damion smiled slightly. "Come, we should meet our hosts and your fellow trainee."

Still trying to process what he'd just seen, Amroth followed Damion as they joined Greatjon and approached the others standing before the shattered gate. Upon reaching the two women and direwolf, who watched them with looks ranging from cold to curious, Greatjon positioned himself between the two groups. Motioning to Alsa and Aseria, he said, "Damion, I'm sure you remember the Indigain's Knight and General?"

Bowing respectfully, "It has been a long time, Lady Alsa."

"Quite," she responded, her pensive mood plainly displayed on her face and in her tone of voice.

Looking her in the eyes, Damion added respectfully, "My belated congratulations on your promotion. I do believe the position fits you."

Suddenly, Alsa stepped forward and slapped Damion hard across the cheek, barely budging his head. Damion responded by simply meeting her dagger-like glare until she spun on her heel and stalked away.

"I suppose she also holds me accountable for Darius' death?" he asked with a grunt. "I guess it was true that she had feelings for him."

Smirking, Greatjon offered, "It wouldn't surprise me. I received similar treatment when she arrived at Sentinel Keep."

"Indeed. You'll have to fill me in on what happened; Kara wasn't able to give me too many specifics."

Greatjon nodded grimly. "I will. For now," he gestured to Aseria, "may I present to you Aseria Mitsurea, Preceptor-in-Waiting of the Indigain Order."

Turning his attention squarely to Aseria, Damion studied her carefully. Beautiful in the cat-like way of the darlions, the air about her seemed to lack the usual arrogant haughtiness of her species. More importantly, he was pleased to see that the purple aura surrounding her, while somewhat sporadic, was strong.

Offering her a respectful bow, Damion said, "A pleasure and an honor. If you don't mind me asking, were you ever aware that you were a Gifted?"

Feeling somewhat awkward being bowed to, and momentarily caught off guard by the question, Aseria blinked in surprise as her mind raced to catch up with the conversation. "I. . . ." Shaking her head, she regained her composure. "No, I wasn't. It wasn't until after Blackstone's fall that I had anything to go on besides what Darius and others told me," she replied, her voice strained when she mentioned Darius.

"Indeed," Damion replied simply before turning his gaze to Greatjon. "You've done a remarkable job with her in just a few weeks, especially given the circumstances."

Greatjon grunted. "Training a Gifted certainly isn't a specialty of mine, so the majority of the praise should go to Alsa. She may be young by our standards, but she has a knack for it."

"Indeed. Nevertheless, it is an accomplishment."

Motioning to Amroth with his head, Greatjon asked, "And the boy?"

"Ah, where are my manners," Damion responded. "May I present to you Amroth Merandith, Preceptor of the Syvantoza Order."

Greatjon suddenly bowed deeply, drawing a befuddled look from Aseria. "Welcome, Preceptor," Greatjon said as he stood upright. "I imagine this has been quite a lot to take in, and that you've been a handful for Damion."

Already baffled by the title Damion had introduced him with, a sense of embarrassment and awkwardness welled up in him at Greatjon's question and the probing gaze of Aseria. Doing his best to ignore her beautiful blue-lavender eyes, Amroth offered awkwardly, his nervousness clearly displayed in his deep voice, "That would be an understatement. Most of this still doesn't make any sense. As for Damion, what little training I've had has been at Kara's expense."

Greatjon looked at Damion inquisitively, to which Damion responded, "There were other tasks to attend to initially, so Kara is responsible for the few days of initial training he's had."

"Just a few days, and he already has a crystal in him!" Greatjon thought incredulously. *"What on Kylir could have possessed him to do such a thing? This boy is a catastrophic disaster waiting to happen!"*

"I'm sure he had his reasons," Deralina responded.

"Listening in, are we?"

"Always, Master."

Greatjon grunted mentally. *"That reminds me, are you going to tell me why you didn't inform me of their arrival, and just why you were leading them here?"*

Before Deralina could respond, Damion asked, "Shall we proceed inside?"

"That would be a good idea, wouldn't it?" Greatjon replied, mentally noting to question Deralina later. "I'll see what rooms we can find for you two, and then you have a lot to explain to me and Alsa."

Damion nodded. "Agreed."

Nodding, Greatjon barked at the gathered Bestyne troops,

"Back to work, all of you!" As the Bestyne's dispersed, Greatjon motioned for Aseria to follow before setting a solid pace toward the keep.

Falling in beside Greatjon, she asked, careful to keep her voice low so Damion and Amroth wouldn't hear, "I may be new to all this, and my control still very shaky, but there's something . . . different about him that feels more like what I sense coming from Damion. And just why did he call someone that is even more inexperienced than I a Preceptor?"

"The Syvantoza Order was disbanded soon after Luthur's death. With his crystal presumed lost, most of the members were absorbed by the other Orders, or they retired; either way, most are long dead. As for the boy," Greatjon responded, his voice solemn and thoughtful, "he has already been Joined to a crystal. More specifically, the crystal that belonged to Luthur."

Aseria's eyes grew wide. "Corith! I still don't know what I should think about Damion, but what could possess him to do such a thing?"

"I don't know," Greatjon responded, his tone laced with worry, "but I intend to find out before I let someone that dangerous train here."

Nodding, Aseria stole a glance at Amroth. She found him somewhat handsome, and he was clearly physically strong, but there was no denying that he appeared just as overwhelmed as she had been just a few short weeks ago – if not more. Turning her attention back to the keep, she found herself in agreement with Greatjon. Even though she couldn't see an aura, it was clear that he possessed tremendous power, and after her outburst two days ago, she now understood just how dangerous that kind of power was in virgin hands.

Sparing one more quick glance at Amroth, who appeared a bit awed and overwhelmed by it all, her ears twitched a bit as she found a slight smile tugging at her lips. *Well, I guess this will make things very interesting . . . and if I'm going to be training with him, at least he's a lot better looking than most of the humans I've met.*

With only a few lingering Bestynes around him, Baris stood in the shadows of the gate on the inside of the broken wall, jealousy twisting his stomach as he watched the newcomers pass by and approach the keep. He knew it was an irrational feeling, but between the power that even he could sense from the youngest of their guests and the way Aseria kept glancing at him, he found it impossible to smother the envy. From the moment he'd met Aseria in Blackstone, he found himself enamored with her, but any hope he'd had of ever courting her had been crushed by the scars he now bore. He had no illusions that it would be nearly impossible for her to find him attractive now, but he had held out hope that one day, Aseria might see past his physical flaws. But now, with the way she was looking at the new arrival, that hope felt like it was sputtering out; and while he knew that it would eventually happen, he still felt pain tear at his heart.

"T'sar!"

Startled, Baris looked around to see his lieutenant, who'd been chatting with a pair of squadmates, glaring at him with a hint of mild displeasure. "Sir?" Baris asked as his squadmates headed back toward the keep.

Dressed in a red-trimmed, black wolf-head tabard over gray leather armor similar to what all the Bestyne troops wore, Lieutenant Salina's fists were planted on her narrow hips, and the sharp features of her dark brown, red-accent striped face were furrowed with concerned displeasure. "Corith be good, I don't know where your mind goes sometimes, T'sar!" she declared in a rough voice that seemed at odds with its soft tones. "I know you've been through the Hells and back, but we've all seen fighting, and you've got to learn to get past it. You're a Gifted now, and that means you'll see more years than a mundane – that is . . . if you keep your head on your shoulders. So, pull yourself together, and let's get back to the training grounds and get to work!"

Unable to shake the jealousy in the pit of his stomach, Baris nodded his head and replied, his tone slightly morose, "Yes, sir. Sorry, sir," before trotting towards Salina.

Shaking her head as Baris trotted by, her long braid of black hair swinging gently across her back, Salina then fixed her golden gaze on T'sar's retreating back and muttered, "Corith be good, T'sar . . . . I hope you get that troubled mind straight before it dooms you."

Chapter Eighteen

How long had it been? Ursa no longer knew.

In a perfect world, and if she'd been in good health, reaching Chalin should have taken only three or four days, but that was hardly the case for Ursa. She'd spent her first night after the disaster wandering aimlessly, distraught and angry about her survival. She didn't discover just how far off course she was until the next morning, and by then, her growing depression had sapped her of her ability to care, slowing her progress to a crawl. At such a sluggish pace, the cold days and colder nights soon blurred together in her troubled mind, while hunger, thirst, and her injuries made it difficult to think with clarity. Without realizing it, she went through the majority of her supplies in a mere three days. While a part of her knew that was foolhardy at best, to her irrational thinking at the time, it made sense. Not only had it eased her guilt for surviving, but also — if she was honest with herself — a small part of her had thought of death as a far better option than reaching her destination. Still, even when it became clear that the decision was a horrible mistake, she compounded it further by continuing onward instead of seeking what nourishment she could find in the open expanse of the Chalin Sea.

When she was blessed — or cursed, she wasn't sure which — with lucid moments over the next week, she could barely understand how she'd survived for so long. Now, as she licked her wind-burnt and chapped lips, she glanced up at the late morning sun with bloodshot, fevered green eyes and once again decided that it didn't matter. Whether Deo had blessed or cursed her with survival, she had survived, and all that remained was to fulfill her duty. Doms Suldamik needed to know that the Merandith threat was far more dangerous than they could have imagined. After that, she welcomed death with open arms.

Looking ahead through her disheveled, short-cropped black hair, which stung her burnt skin as it brushed against her face, Ursa drew what strength she could from the growing silhouette of Chalin. That blessed bastion had appeared on the horizon the previous evening, granting her a tantalizing trickle of hope as it grew steadily larger.

"Hope . . ." her fevered mind abruptly scoffed at the notion. *"It's nothing but the wishful conjuring of an ignorant mind. It's a fool's errand to*

harbor such a thought; I now know that. . . . You have to make what you want out of this life — the fort's fall taught me that far better than anything else this war has thrown at me."

"Damn!" a hoarse voice croaked as the world suddenly went askew and her foot began to throb.

Stumbling over the hidden rock, Ursa fell to the ground, hitting her head hard. Eyes fixed on Chalin, she lay there, unmoving and numbly detached as her swimming vision began to fade.

"Damn," she thought again. *"So close. . . . To the Hells with hope . . ."* she managed to think before darkness claimed her.

*

"That's not proper behavior for a lady! And being of noble blood doesn't excuse her from acting in such a manner!" the older, full-figured maid with braided black hair lectured as she and her young counterparts walked down the hall. Each wore a simple, white-trimmed, green dress beneath a white apron, and carried a pile of neatly folded linens.

"*Pffft,*" the young and slender, homely brunette responded, her skirt swaying with every stride. "And what noble do you know that behaves all proper like? That woman will rut with anyone she fancies she can get between her legs."

"And that's not proper language or a proper topic of discussion from anyone working for this House!" The older woman chided. To emphasize her point, she smacked the younger woman on the back of the head with her meaty hand.

"Ow!" the young woman exclaimed, her braid swaying sharply as her head recoiled. Rubbing the back of her head, she said, "I'm sorry you're a crusty old maid who hasn't had a man in her in Deo only knows how long – if ever – but that's no reason to hit me!"

Smacking the girl harder, the older woman retorted through a thin-lipped scowl, "And what do you know of it? It's not like the boys are just dying to get beneath your skirts."

The younger woman grinned, her brown eyes twinkling mischievously. "Aren't they? I had myself a tasty roll with that new stablehand last night."

"That black-haired boy? The one that looks more muscle than brains?" the older maid asked in disbelief.

"That's the one," she responded with a big smile. "I'm surprised I can even walk straight today."

"Deo be good, Lucinda! Are you daft? Spreading your legs

for every boy in sight isn't just immoral – it's wrong! What if you end up with child?"

Lucinda shrugged. "Ain't worried about it. I know an apothecary who makes an elixir that's guaranteed to keep that from happening, before or after. No child is ruining this figure or my life, I just won't stand for it!"

Suddenly, they came to a halt, and the older maid turned to face the maid with chin-length red hair following them. Fixing a stern, dark-eyed glare on her, Silvana pointed down the hall to her own left and ordered, "Down that hall, and take a left. The door is the third on the right. And don't be mentioning a word of what's been said here, you understand, Jaylee? What's said amongst the help, stays amongst the help."

Jaylee managed to keep her irritation off her thin-lipped, well-defined face even as she ground her teeth together. She'd heard that more than once during her training beneath the old hag, and it, like the constant conversations between the elder maid and her young friend, grated on her nerves. As much as she wanted to knock their skulls together or slit their throats simply to put an end to their irritating lives, she knew better than to indulge such reckless and pointless urges. She was here for a singular reason, and nothing else mattered.

"Of course, Silvana," Jaylee replied with a small curtsied, her husky voice showing proper respect to the elder maid.

"See, Lucinda? That's proper behavior there! You should learn from her."

Lucinda, her eyes filled with jealousy, met Jaylee's blue-eyed gaze and scowled at her. "Nothing to learn from her except how to be a pretty, brainless dullard. Looks won't get you very far, Jay-Jay," she taunted patronizingly.

Silvana cuffed Lucinda again. "What am I going to do with you?" she said with a huff. Then, to Jaylee, she said, "Off with you now, and be quick! We have other chores to attend to."

Curtsying again, Jaylee swiftly made her way down the indicated hall. As soon as she was out of earshot, she let out a deep and frustrated, but relieved, breath. The entire trip from the laundry had been an exercise in self-control. Upon her placement under the tutelage of Silvana, Jaylee quickly learned two things about her and Lucinda. First, their favorite topics of conversation – despite Silvana's contradictory protests – were Doma Ithikia's bedroom habits and Lucinda's supposed conquests. Second, and most importantly, they were either too stupid to care if they were caught talking about Doma Ithikia in such a way, or just lucky that anyone who did care had

overheard them. Had she been so inclined, Jaylee could have reported such chatter to the Chamberlain. However, not only did she
believe the man wouldn't accept her word over the more established
maids, but more importantly, she simply didn't care. If they were
eventually caught, then maybe they'd learn some 'proper behavior', as
Silvana liked to order Lucinda to do. However, that was not her concern. Her reason for being there was far more important and lucra-
tive than snitching on two gossiping idiots.

Located in the keep's main spire, this section of the glorious
structure housed the residences of Doms Suldamik and his closest
advisors and administrators. Despite having set foot in numerous
parts of the palatial keep during many of her clandestine ventures, she
had never been in this area until recently. However, it was blatantly
clear that the only similarities it bore to the rest of the keep were the
high-arched ceilings, and the plush green rugs covering the stone
floor. While the chambers were obviously larger, which was clearly
indicated by the increased spacing between doors, it was the opulent
decor that bluntly declared the occupants were far richer and more
important than everyone else. Marble niches framed by graceful, florid reliefs contained elegant pottery, the occasional sculpture, or flamboyant suits of armor. Exemplary tapestries and paintings depicting
battles, mythical beasts, and even long-dead members of House Suldamik graced the white walls, while a mixture of natural light flowing
through exterior windows and lamplight from chandeliers of silver
and bronze illuminated the halls. Though she kept her face impassive
as she walked down the hall, the thought of these treasures, and what
might be hidden in the multitude of chambers, had Jaylee practically
drooling on the inside. There was a mountain of talons to be made
here, and all she would have to do is relieve the keep of its fanciful
burdens.

"Keep yer mind focused, lass. Don't let flights of fancy lead ye astray,"
she chided herself with a mental shake of her head.

As she neared the intersection where she was to turn left, a
muffled, lilting melody reached her ears from her intended direction.
With a mild hint of curiosity taking root, she turned and made her
way down the hall toward the music. As she neared the source, the
melody grew clearer and louder, and she felt her breath catch in her
throat. She'd heard many street musicians and tavern performers play
the flute before, but never like this. In fact, she couldn't recall ever
hearing a flute that compared to what was gracing her ears. Mesme-
rized by the song, her pace slowed as her heart soared on the swells of
the enchanting melody. Without realizing it, she came to a halt in the
middle of the hall, enraptured by the song.

"You look lost."

Startled, Jaylee turned around to face the speaker, and the joy she felt in her heart was suddenly washed away by fear as she recognized the man.

Short and bald, Magister Tythis stood a few feet away from her, his plump figure clad in a royal purple robe with golden embroidery down the middle of the rich fabric. A part of her wanted to chastise herself for becoming so distracted that not only had she failed to notice that she'd come to a halt, but that she'd let someone get so close to her without noticing. However, that part of her mind was quashed into silence by the dread she felt crawling up her spine as she met his gaze. Set astride a flat nose on his aged face, his beady green eyes bore into her as if he were peering into her soul and burning away the layers of lies in search of the truth of her being.

Suddenly, Tythis raised a curious eyebrow and said, "Are you alright, my dear? I did not mean to startle you, but you appeared lost."

"I. . . ." Shaking her head, she then ducked it and curtsied quickly. "My apologies, Magister. I'm new here, and was on my way to change Doms Suldamik's linens when this music distracted me. Again, I apologize." She curtsied again for emphasis.

"Your apology is accepted, but not needed," he responded, his tone flat and unemotional. "The music is indeed hypnotic, and you would not be the first to be enthralled by it."

"Yes, Magister," she replied, keeping her gaze lowered.

"You said you were on your way to change the linens for Doms Suldamik?"

"Yes, Magister."

"Curious. . . . It is highly unusual that someone new would be assigned such a task." Jaylee's heart began to race as the man peered at her intently. "Is Silvana ill, or has the Chamberlain lost all sense of protocol?"

Jaylee shook her head firmly even as she tried to keep her face clear of worry while keeping her heart and breathing under control. "No, Magister," she replied as she did her best to shake the feeling that this man knew why she was there. "Silvana ordered me to perform the task. I apologize if this is not proper. I was simply doing as ordered."

"Indeed," Tythis replied succinctly. "Very well, then. I shall have to have a word with the Chamberlain about this breach of protocol, and see that Silvana is properly punished for shucking her duties." There was an edge to his voice that made Jaylee want to shudder. Suddenly, he sighed as if the conversation had grown boring and become a burden. "However," he continued, his tone droll, "for now, follow me, and I shall show you the servant's entrance to his chambers. After all, it would be rude to interrupt Doms Suldamik's entertainment – Silvana knows that, and should have informed you."

Jaylee curtsied once again. "Thank you, Magister."

Turning around, Tythis led her back down the hall with surprising quickness, forcing her to hustle to catch up. As they crossed the intersection, Jaylee worked up the courage to ask, "Pardon my forwardness, but may I ask who was playing the flute?"

"There is nothing to forgive, child," he replied as he ran a heavily-ringed forefinger along the embroidery on his robe. "The musician is Doma Ithikia's herald and handmaiden."

"And the instrument? I've never heard a flute like it."

"No, I don't believe you would have. It is a Velusyian wind-flute; which is apt, given that the musician is from there. Ah. Here we are."

Tythis had come to a halt before a heavy oak door upon which was mounted a gold medallion depicting a scroll surmounted by a crown.

"His office?" she thought as a lump of anxiety welled in her throat. *"Deo be good! He be knowin' who I am!"*

Pushing the door open, he motioned her in. Jaylee hesitated for a brief moment before proceeding inside. As the door closed with what felt like an ominous thud to her, she fought the urge to panic. To her profound relief, instead of feeling a dagger in her back, she watched as Tythis walked past her and approached the trio of bookcases on the far wall of the small, meticulously organized office. As her fear and panic receded some, she took a moment to quickly examine her surroundings just in case she needed a distraction or needed to make a hasty exit.

There were no windows in the office, which would have been of little use given how high up the room was, but there was a door to her right, which she presumed led to the magister's sleeping quarters, making it equally useless. To her left, there was a table covered with neatly arranged decanters, which were filled with an assortment of wine and liquors, standing next to a small, cold hearth bereft of firewood. Finally, there was a scrupulously organized mahogany desk and its matching chair stationed in front of the bookcases, as well as the uncomfortable-looking chair seated between her and the desk.

Much to her chagrin, the only apparent way out was the way they came in. As for a distraction, if she could move fast enough, the lamps and the alcohol could make for a suitable fire.

"Bloody hells," she thought as Tythis beckoned her over from his position between the desk and bookshelves.

Approaching, she changed her train of thought and did her best to seek out a possible weapon. She immediately ruled out the brass lamps mounted on the walls, but as she stepped around the desk, she noted a small dagger with a gold hilt lying next to a white oak writing kit at the head of the desk. Standing this close to the magister, she didn't know if she could reach the blade in time, but she readied herself to spring for it anyway, even as she thought, *"Corith! I canna be believin' I'm even considerin' this! If I were forced to kill him, they'd hunt me to tha ends of Kylir!"*

"As you are aware, the keep has a series of hidden corridors for discreet travel when it is called for. As you may or may not have already figured out, they are not used much, but when you need to do your job without disturbing the keep's residences, or circumstances require the keep staff to be invisible, this is how you are to move about." Reaching behind the books on the middle shelf of the central bookcase, Tythis found the hidden latch and pulled.

Jaylee heard a muffled click and then watched as Tythis pushed on the bookcase, which swung inward easily. A rush of cold and mildly musty air hit her in the face as a poorly lit stairway was revealed.

Stepping aside, Tythis motioned to the open doorway. "Proceed down the stairs, then take a left. Follow the hall until it comes to an end. Seek the third stone below the right sconce, and press on it. That will release the hidden door. Climb the stairs, and find the large knot on the wood panel at the top. Pressing on that will open the door to Doms Suldamik's chambers. When you are done, leave via the passage. If you proceed to the right from here, follow the hall, then make two rights, a left, descend another staircase, then another left, that will bring you to a spiral staircase that will take you to the lower levels. You should be able to make your way from there. Do you understand?"

Jaylee nodded and curtsied. "I do, Magister. Thank you for your kindness."

"You are welcome." His voice then turned hard and took on an uncompromising edge as he added, "Just be aware that such kindnesses should not be expected beyond this. Learn your duties with haste, and the proper way to perform them, else find yourself back in whatever alley you crawled from." He suddenly shot her a glare that carried an air of violence. "More importantly, I have overstepped my bounds for the sake of expedience. As such, you would be wise to forget about this entrance. After all, accidents do happen, and servants are easily replaced. Is that understood?"

The undercurrent of venom in his voice caused the feeling of fear he inspired to come rushing back, and she fought to quell it. "I understand," she managed to reply as calmly as she could. She then curtsied once more before proceeding swiftly down the stairs.

As Jaylee vanished down the dimly lit staircase, a cruel smile split Tythis' lips. *"You have your way in, and a way out. . . . Now run and dance for my mistress, little Mal. After you have served her purpose and she cuts your strings, I'll gut you like the vermin you are, and send your soul screaming to the Hells."*

The hidden passage was not only illuminated by wall-mounted sconces, but it was nearly as clean as the rest of the keep, proving the Magister's declaration about its use was a lie. Fictitious statement aside, he was right about Mal's knowledge of the passages. She had long ago found out about the keep's maze of hidden corridors, and had made use of them before. However, she'd never realized just how extensive the system was. This discovery, unfortunately, was buried beneath the weight of her encounter.

She shuddered as she turned the corner and made her way down the indicated hall, which appeared to wind its way back toward Craigan's chambers.

Magister Tythis Udarlin. She'd heard rumors of the eunuch's cold and intimidating presence, but the stories fell short of what she'd just experienced. The way he'd looked at her, and the fine, sharp edge to his words had made her feel like he knew why she was in the keep. Even more disturbing, she felt a sense of violation . . . like he was searching her soul against her will to find both her motives and evidence of anyone else that might be involved.

"That's one man I wouldn't be wantin' as an enemy," she thought resolutely as she approached the end of the hall.

Reaching the base of the stairs, she found the stone Tythis had mentioned and gave it a firm push. She felt it slide in a bit, and heard a muffled click as it locked into place. Ascending the stairs, she shook her head to clear it of the chilling thoughts. Already, albeit faint, she could hear the beautiful flute, and its melody helped to soothe her mind. Taking a deep breath, she let it out and examined the panel. Finding the knot, she pressed on it firmly. She immediately heard a click, then she pushed on the panel. At first, it barely budged, forcing her to lean her shoulder into it. With a grunt, she put her weight behind the effort, and the panel slowly swung inward, allowing a rush of cool air to wash over her along with the now crisp notes of the wind-flute.

Once the hidden door was open far enough for her to enter the room beyond, she slipped in to find that the door served as the back of a section of a black-streaked, gray stone wall that was covered by green cloth panels. Glancing around, she quickly took stock of the spacious, square room. To her left, the wall was home to a pair of shields flanking a variety of swords above which unlit lanterns were stationed. To her right, on the opposite side of a large bed and bedside table, was a lone window, the shutters of which were open, granting passage to the warm sunlight illuminating the room. Next to the window was a carved oak wardrobe, while the wall directly in front of her was occupied by an empty hearth, flanked by dark lanterns, next to a sealed door. Turning to her right, she set her focus on the luxurious and unkempt bed awaiting her attention. With haste, she stripped it of its linens, tossing them haphazardly toward the open passage, and replaced them with clean sheets. As she made up the rich piece of furniture and organized its numerous pillows at the head of the bed, she ground her teeth together.

Every instinct she had screamed at her to examine the room and get out with all due caution and haste. If this had been any other theft, she would have given in to her instincts, but this situation was different, and such behavior would likely expose her. On top of that, there was the issue of her target. To her chagrin, not only was the description of what she was to steal vague, but she had only a rough idea of where to find it that didn't include around Doms Suldamik's neck. Lifting it from such a dangerous location was, for the most part, out of the question. Sure, she could seek to render him unconscious, but not only would that be difficult, it was practically suicide.

No. She would need to learn Craigan's habits and where he hid things, and that conclusion is what had led her to her current state – a maid in service to House Suldamik. Thanks to help from well-placed members of the Resistance, she had attained a position that would let her move, for the most part, freely about the keep and relatively close to Doms Suldamik. Typically, the maintenance and cleaning of the upper floors and royal chambers was reserved for veterans of the keep staff. As such, her appointment had drawn curious and even jealous looks from some of the elder servants. Thankfully, nothing was said to her, nor had she been confronted on the subject, and for that, she was grateful to whoever was responsible for her position. The fewer questions she had to answer, the better.

Vexingly enough, it had taken a week to get her first look at Doms Suldamik's quarters, and even then, her initial visit was supervised, which prevented her from exploring the room. As the days passed, her anxiousness grew, as did her aggravation with the delay. However, experience had taught her patience. So she quelled her exasperations and waited.

Unfortunately, her encounter with Tythis decimated any joy she might have felt at finally being alone in his bed-chamber . . . or at least as alone as one could be with people in the next room. In fact, she felt like her anxiety had grown exponentially. Therefore, when she finally finished with the bed, she quickly and quietly proceeded to investigate the room in search of other hidden panels or stashes where one might keep valuables. Normally, it would have been a simple matter to do so, but the music kept distracting her. Determined to complete her task, she did her best to ignore the song as she searched the walls, the wardrobe, and even under the bed. Predictably, she found some of the same compartments she'd seen in countless homes of the wealthy, which were filled with the typical boring items she stole and fenced as needed.

Sprawled beneath the bead, she snorted derisively and thought, as she made sure the assortment of coin purses and folded papers were arranged in the hidden chest just as they had been before her intrusion, *"Deo, do all rich people think tha bloody same way? They all might as bloody well paint red Xs in their homes."* Sealing the chest and then the compartment with expert skill, she slithered out from under the bed, thinking, *"I was expectin' a whole lot more from someone of Doms Suldamik ilk. Guess original thought ain't somethin' rich folks be carin' much about."*

Having found nothing so far, Mal smoothed her dress out and brushed away the dust as she quietly padded over to the last place she considered a decent hiding spot – the hearth.

Having already been cleaned, and with fresh logs stacked neatly in its large mouth as her only impediment, her initial examination of the hearth was quick and made it clear that its visible portions were free of clandestine compartments. Maneuvering herself so she could check the lower portion of the chimney without getting her dress dirty, she was about to reach up the shaft when the music cut through both the dull whistle of the wind in the chimney system, and her focus. Pausing, she listened thoughtfully and felt herself being carried away by the sweeping melody. Cursing her gnawing curiosity, she extracted herself from the hearth before moving to the closed door.

Crouching, she peeked through the keyhole just below the

polished door handle. Though her field of vision was limited, she could see several plush chairs, all of which she presumed were in use, arranged beneath an elegant chandelier in the center of the room. Of the two chairs she could clearly see, they appeared to be occupied by a pair of elderly men. As for the other chairs, she could only assume Doms Suldamik was seated in one of them. Those thoughts, however, were quickly brushed aside as her vision settled on the person who was responsible for the music, and it immediately occurred to Mal that this girl would enthrall most men without the help of her hypnotic melody. In fact, Mal believed that she might be what storytellers envisioned when they talked of the muses that inspired them, or when they waxed poetic about goddesses whose beauty was the envy of all.

Modest of height, and around twenty summers of age, a young woman stood before her audience dressed in a blue dress of foreign design. A white floral pattern flowed down the silk, robe-like garment, making its way onto a white silk wrap that encompassed the girl's waist above her wide hips, where the pattern turned blue. The baggy sleeves of the garment hung loosely from her upraised arms as her hands held a flute, which was painted to resemble a star-filled night sky, to her pursed, full lips. High cheekbones, which were dotted with subtle freckles, complimented her closed, upturned eyes. A lone emerald stud glinted in the lamplight from its position on the left nostril of the girl's slender nose, while her mass of hair, the color of which reminded Mal of blue-tinged snow, flowed down to just past her hips.

Seeing the girl firsthand, Mal concluded the descriptions of this woman fell far short of the mark. What's more, it was obvious why jealous undertones accompanied the words of many of those who had seen the silent herald and handmaiden of Doma Ithikia. In fact, as she watched the exotically beautiful woman, Mal felt a rising sense of jealousy within her, which made her angry. She had no reason to envy Doma Ithikia's handmaiden. After all, what good were looks if one was not only weak, but practically a slave?

Captivated as she was by the melody that the girl coaxed from the instrument, Mal's self-reflection, as well as her jealousy and anger, faded as time lost all meaning for her. Furthermore, the longer she listened, the more she felt her heart swell with a blissful euphoria that she didn't know existed. In her mind, the melody summoned visions of otherworldly fields of lush grass beneath radiant skies the color of a vibrant sea. She could picture the grass swaying to the rhythm of a soothing breeze that carried warm pink petals through the air. It was a surreal experience, and Mal could feel her body relax as if the wind's gentle caress was washing over her and the petals were alighting on her skin with snowflake-like grace.

A sudden, urgent knock at the study's main door brought an abrupt end to the music, shattering the ethereal vision and startling Mal. For a panicked moment, she thought she might have bumped into the door before her and given away her presence. This was especially true when she heard a strong, authoritative voice beckon someone to enter. Mercifully, that was not the case as she heard a door within the study open.

Standing, she stepped away from the door and closed her eyes before taking a calming breath to slow her racing heart. Suddenly, she noticed a wet sensation running down her face and she wiped her cheeks. Opening her eyes, she held her hand before her and was shocked to see that it was wet.

"Deo be good! Was I cryin'?" she thought incredulously.

Before she could ponder what had elicited the tears, the conversation on the other side of the doors caught her attention.

"My apologies, Doms. I did not mean to interrupt your entertainment," she heard a hauntingly familiar voice state.

"No need to apologize," the deep voice responded pleasantly, though there was an edge of irritation to his tone. "What is it, Magister?"

Eyes wide with shock, Mal quickly returned to the door. Crouching, she peeked through the keyhole once again. *"What's tha eunuch doin'?"* she wondered, fear twisting her gut. *"Deo, was this all a trap? If it is, I better get tha hells out of 'ere!"* she told herself sternly. However, despite her strong urge to flee, she remained where she was. *"Yer nosiness will be tha death of ye one day!"* she chided herself as she listened to the curious, and possibly dangerous, conversation in the other room.

"Doms General Corandit urgently requests your presence, Doms. A messenger from the Chalin border fort has just been brought in," Tythis replied, his tone droll despite how important the message must be for him to interrupt his doms. "And, may I say, the message she brings appears rather urgent."

The relevance of his interruption wasn't lost on Doms Suldamik. "The border fort?" he asked with an edge to his voice as the two elderly men stood up, accompanied by a rustle of silk just outside her vision.

"Yes, Doms – the border fort. General Corandit's message also indicated that the messenger looks as if she's standing in death's shadow."

"Deo curse them!" one of the older men declared in a passive voice that was rough with age, drawing Mal's attention to him and the other older man.

The speaker was tall and appeared frail, with hawkish features that were devilish in their cut. Long of limb, his bald head appeared far too big for his slender frame, which his green rich robe seemed to be trying to swallow. In contrast, the man standing next to him was short, burly, and dressed in black trousers and a black shirt that would have been more at home on a soldier if not for the rich silver filigree that generously adorned the garments.

The more rotund man scowled and folded his arms across his chest. Grunting, he declared in a rough voice, "Well, Craigan – this isn't good if it's what we're all assuming." Turning around, he said to someone beyond Mal's field of vision. "It's not looking good for your strategy of sit and wait, eh Doma?" he taunted.

"Jumping to conclusions, as usual, Astica," replied a throaty and alluring female voice that was laced with near-haughty arrogance. "Though, I will concede it is indeed not a good sign . . . if the state of the messenger is as Tythis has stated."

"There is no exaggeration to my words, Doma. Some ill fate has befallen the woman. And I mean no disrespect, Doma – but it is logical to conclude her condition is a result of something foul befalling the fort."

"Odd," Mal thought curiously at Tythis' respectful tone when addressing the doma. *"I'd say tha man either respects this woman far more than Craigan or. . . . He fears her?"*

"Childish taunts and wild speculation is pointless," Craigan interjected, seeking an end to his compatriots' ill-concealed bickering. "Where is the messenger now, Magister?"

"She is with Doms General Corandit in the North Barracks, Doms."

"Right, then," Craigan declared. "See that mounts are readied, Magister."

"They await you at the front gate, Doms."

"Excellent," Craigan replied before saying to the other nobles, "Domses and Doma – I think you should join me. We should all hear this." As the domses moved out of her sight, she heard Craigan add, his voice soft and apologetic, "My dear Flute, I must apologize for the abrupt end to your enchanting performance. Another time, perhaps?"

The girl with the snow-blue hair dipped her head. "No need to apologies, Doms," she replied in a voice that was soft and as melodic as her music. "It would be my honor to perform whenever you wish."

"Excellent," Craigan responded. Then, to the others, he said, his voice taking on its commanding edge, "Let's go."

"I will be along momentarily, my dear," said the throaty voice. "I need to speak with . . . Flute for a moment."

"Don't be long," Craigan replied sternly.

"Of course not, my dear."

A moment later, Mal heard the door shut, and silence descended on the room. To Mal's uneasy surprise, a look that reminded her of fearful subjugation came over the girl Craigan had called Flute. Eyes downturned, and her head bowed slightly, her posture became submissive, almost repentant.

"Deo, what level of tha Hells has this girl been put through?" Mal thought as a rustle of silk alighted on her ears just before the remaining occupant of the room moved into view. Though she could only see her back, Mal knew it was Doma Ithikia.

Mal had little doubt that the alluring curves, slender figure and brown skin that her layered emerald-silk dress barely concealed was the object of many men's lustful gazes and thoughts. A mass of white hair tumbled down to mid-back on her relatively tall frame as she positioned herself before Flute, the heels of her delicate, knee-high black boots barely making a sound on the stone floor.

"What to do with you, my pet?" Doma Ithikia asked with mock exasperation. "Performing in public, and even earning an absurd pet name? You are certainly not worthy of such . . . public extravagances." Ithikia let out a mock sigh. "But, Darkness forbid, I suppose it's better than letting you run free."

"Darkness?" Mal thought, her face twisting with puzzlement. *"That sounds . . . forebodin'."* She shrugged mentally. *"Well, she's a barbarian desert-dweller. It's not like they'd be havin' a proper god to worship."*

"Mark my words, my precious lalashia," Doma Ithikia continued, her voice full of an incredible amount of rancor. "Do not get used to such leniency from me. You are far from atoning for your father's sins, and if it weren't for the needs of our situation, the punishment for such luxurious frivolities would be severe. Is that understood?"

Though Mal could not see Flute's response, it was clear to her that the girl had responded in the affirmative by Doma Ithikia's posture.

"Excellent," Ithikia declared, her voice quickly taking on a pleased, haughty air. "Now, you have other far more important duties to attend to. And do change out of that ridiculous, light-cursed giku, and into something more fitting of someone in my service. That absurd thing conjures memories that are best left to the dead."

With powerful strides and graceful haste, Doma Ithikia turned and proceeded to the door. Flute waited until the door shut behind her doma to look up, and when she did, Mal's breath caught in her throat and she froze. There were tears running down the girl's cheeks that seemed to be leaving trails the color of blue ice. Mal knew that was impossible and shook her head in denial. When she looked back through the keyhole and saw the streaks were still there, a part of Mal suddenly wanted to profess that the tears falling from her cheeks were indeed ice. It was an absurd notion that was quickly drowned by shock as she noted a change in Flute.

For the first time that Mal was aware of since peeking through the keyhole, Flute's eyes were open. Sky blue and beautiful, her eyes would have been radiant against her snow-blue hair if not for the sorrow haunting their depths and the inflammation around their edges from crying. However, the state of Flute's eyes was not solely responsible for Mal's breathless state, nor was it the fault of the chill that crept up her spine. Mal's shock was, in fact, the result of the undeniable focus of Flute's gaze.

She was staring at Mal.

*

It had been only a few weeks – albeit, busy ones – since his unexpected promotion to Doms General of the Jade Talons, and already Jeinis Corandit not only looked older than his near thirty-three summers, but he was beginning to rue his decision to accept the appointment. Upon his arrival in Chalin, whatever regrets he might have had about leaving his beloved fort had been buried beneath a landslide of ceremonies and political functions, as well as the daunting task of familiarizing himself with the current state of the Jade Talons. However, the stress of his early days in Chalin was nothing compared to the anger and self-reproach that now flooded his mind.

Tall, and normally proud, Jeinis paced the center of the cobbled courtyard of the North Barracks as if he was determined to wear a trench in it. His slender face was marred with barely contained anger and concern as he tugged at the new, and significantly more elaborate, green and white officer's tabard he now wore over the heavy, dark green tunic, brown pants, and black leather knee-boots girding his moderately strong physique. Giving up his trusty tabard, which had been with him for years, was just another annoyance that had come with his promotion. An irrational part of him thought that his appointment and the loss of his prized tabard had opened him up to bad luck – which, at that moment, he found it easy to believe that part of his mind.

"You're a damn fool if you believe a change of venue and attire has any-thing to do with this horror!" Jeinis chided himself. *"If what she says is true, there's nothing you could have done to save the fort."* Sighing with regret, he ran a black-gloved hand through his short red hair and let his brown eyes scan the courtyard again.

The largest of Chalin's three barracks, the North Barracks was a small fortress unto itself. Sturdy, tower-anchored stone walls surrounded a well-maintained courtyard that was home to six long-houses that were split between the east and west walls, while a well-equipped blacksmith and a large stable resided along the south wall. Hidden from view by the centrally located, three-story command building with its black-tile roof were a practice yard, storehouse, and a secure armory. Soldiers garbed in a variety of armor beneath their tabards went about their daily routines with an edge of unease that Jeinis knew was spawned by the arrival of the messenger. It had been impossible to hide her condition from everyone, and while Jeinis knew he could have squashed such rumors, he was well aware that his agitated state would have nullified any such efforts. Even now, some soldiers cast quick, curious, and sometimes nervous, glances at their new general. While he understood that their looks were likely more inquisitive than anything, Jeinis found he was unable to meet any of their gazes, for the guilt choking his soul lent a reproaching edge to his eyes.

That same guilt had made sitting with the messenger far too difficult. As such, he had attempted to occupy himself by inspecting the barracks after he'd sent word to the keep. When it became clear to Jeinis that his mood was making those he came in contact with uncomfortable, he took to pacing before the command building. Granted, he knew it was far from proper behavior for an officer, but he couldn't bring himself to return to his quarters while he awaited Doms Suldamik's arrival.

A quick glance at a sky marred by a few wispy clouds in-formed him that he'd been pacing for the better part of an hour. Shaking his head, he once more tried to convince himself that what had befallen the border fort could not have been avoided even if he'd been there, but the thought once again fell on an unwilling mind.

"Riders approaching!" shouted one of the gate guards, snap-ping Jeinis' attention from his morose thoughts.

Coming to a halt, Jeinis peeked through the open gate to see a small party and their escort crossing the open ground between the North Barracks and the city proper. To his chagrin, he saw that some of the flanking escorts were garbed in the emerald green of House Ithikia, the gray of House Astica, and the black of House Thakian. There was no way to escape the fact that these three Houses were by far House Suldamik's chief supporters, but that did little to bolster Jeinis' opinion of them. While his experience with the domses and doma was limited, it was enough for him to find them despicable, profoundly arrogant, and generally unworthy of being in the same room as Doms Suldamik. However, he understood his personal feelings toward Craigan's most powerful supporters were practically irrelevant. Without House Astica and Thakian's seemingly endless stream of supplies, House Suldamik might have lost the war long ago. As for Doma Ithikia. . . . Jeinis had to fend off the urge to scowl as his eyes focused on the white-haired temptress riding sidesaddle alongside his doms. Rumors of the vast influx of wealth she'd brought to Craigan's cause aside, she was now betrothed to him, and that was more than enough reason for Jeinis to keep his thoughts on her to himself.

It wasn't long before Doms Suldamik's group arrived at the gate, and as they rode into the courtyard, it seemed to Jeinis that the clatter of their mounts' hooves sounded foreboding and almost angry. He knew it was just a trick of his imagination, but it still sent a cold chill up his spine.

"Get ahold of yourself, Jenis! This is not the time to be jumping at ghosts!" he reprimanded himself mentally as Craigan brought his party to a halt before him and the twelve-guard escort — three for each noble — fanned out to the sides.

Grabbing the leather-wrapped hilt of the gilded officer's broadsword sheathed at his left hip, Jeinis saluted fist to heart, and bowed respectfully. "Domses and Doma," he offered as he stood upright, his strong voice courteous despite his anxiety. Looking at Craigan, he then said, "My apologies for interrupting your day, Doms. I would not have done so if it were not important."

Like the other nobles, Craigan dismounted and handed his reins to one of the four stablehands in green and white livery who had rushed out to attend to their mounts. Nearly six-feet tall, Craigan cut an imposing figure in his richly embroidered white wool shirt, black leather bracers, boots and pants. His heavy green cloak was secured around his neck by a brooch featuring the lone talon of House Suldamik, and his piercing blue eyes bore into Jeinis from his chiseled and scarred face. "Tythis conveyed the urgency of the matter," Craigan responded gravely as a gentle breeze ruffled his short, white-flecked, brown hair. "Is the situation really as bad as he inferred?"

Jeinis grimaced inwardly, and a slight frown pulled at his thin lips. "I am afraid so, Doms," he replied as Craigan approached him. "The messenger seemed near death when she was brought in. However, before she passed out, what she was able to tell me was dreadful and unmistakable."

"How is she now?"

"Resting, Doms."

"And what did she tell you, General?" Alestra asked, clutching her white fur cloak about her as she and the elder domses joined Craigan.

"Quite right, Doma," Thakian interjected, grudgingly agreeing with her. "If the messenger is in no danger of dying, then the state of her health can wait. So if you please, General, tell us what is important enough to drag us out into this damnable cold," he stated even as he pulled his dark cloak tight about his green-robed figure.

Jeinis pressed his lips together firmly to keep from delivering a stinging retort to Thakian's blatant indifference toward the wellbeing of one who served their cause. *"No man such as he or his compatriot should ever be allowed to lead,"* Jeinis thought even as he caught Craigan shooting his fellow doms a reproachful glare. "This matter is best discussed in private," he said aloud, his tone measured and respectful. Gesturing to the command building, Jeinis added, "If you would, we can discuss this in my office, Domses and Doma?"

Craigan nodded. "Agreed. Lead on, General, and let's get out of this miserable cold."

Entering the command building with the nobles in tow, Jeinis led them through the practically arranged halls. Narrow for defensive purposes, the floors and doors were made of sturdy oak, and the walls of tightly fitted stone blocks. Soldiers – predominantly in House Suldamik colors – made way for the party as they traversed halls lit by brass lanterns that hung on the walls alongside trophy weapons and armor, as well as paintings of respected military figures. Craigan and Alestra briefly acknowledged some soldiers they crossed paths with a nod or a smile, while Astica and Thakian all but ignored the troops.

Soon enough, they reached a staircase near the center of the building, and Jeinis led them to the second floor before proceeding to his office at the front of the building. Upon reaching his office, Jeinis retrieved a simple key from a pouch on the back of his belt and unlocked the heavy door, which was surmounted by a head-high gold badge that depicted crossed broadswords behind a kite shield emblazoned with a talon. Pushing the panel open, Jeinis stepped aside and permitted the Domses and Doma to enter before he followed them in and closed the door behind them.

Unlike many other high-ranking officers and officials, Jeinis had chosen a modest square room to serve as his office. A large window on the left-hand wall allowed ample light into the room, illuminating the simple, organized pine desk and chair stationed before it. On the far side of the small oak map table at the center of the room, which sat atop a thick brown rug that covered most of the floor, were bookcases full of tombs and scrolls. The cases flowed onto the right-hand wall, where they flanked a fire-filled hearth, above which was a mantle that supported two large oil lamps. It was truly a utilitarian and functional space, which was just the way Jeinis liked it.

Stepping pasted the others as they approached the map table, which was home to a single chair at each end, Jeinis motioned to the decanter of wine and the trio of goblets resting near its far edge. "There is wine should you wish it," he said as he made for his desk. "Though I can send for something else if it is not to your liking," he finished as he reached the modest piece of furniture.

"Thank you for the offer, but we are fine," Craigan answered for them all as he and Alestra took up positions before the map table while Thakian and Astica seated themselves in the chairs at the opposite ends of the table.

"Respectfully, Doms," Astica interjected from his door-side seat as he shifted aside his gray cloak and reached for the decanter, "but some of us have to deal with the frailties of age, and wine in these kinds of conditions is an appealing way to warm those of us with thin blood." Filling one of the goblets partway, Astica took a drink. Smiling, he placed the goblet on the table. "See, I already feel warmer."

"And if only wine could cure your dull mind," Alestra quipped drolly while idly examining the map of Triclose that occupied the majority of the table.

"Now is not the time to engage in verbal jousting," Craigan interjected sternly as Astica glared darkly at Alestra. "There are more important matters to attend to right now. Afterward, if either of you feels the need to discover whose words can cut the deepest, be my guest."

"Eloquently put, my love," Alestra purred before looking up at Jeinis, whose face was a mask of barely contained irritation. "Please, General, enlighten us as to what ill fate has befallen the fort," she ordered in her throaty voice even as she rolled the green miniature that represented the fort between two of her fingers, the nails of which were painted black.

Looking to Craigan for permission to proceed, he received an approving nod. "Thank you, Doms," Jeinis said as he picked up a piece of parchment tucked beneath his writing kit. Moving in front of his desk, he leaned against it and quickly perused the document. "As I mentioned earlier, the messenger was only able to tell me a little of what had transpired." He looked up at Craigan, his eyes grim. "But what is clear is that the border fort is now in the hands of House Merandith."

"Are you sure of this?" asked Thakian, an edge to his elderly voice. "You know better than any of us the defensive capabilities of the fort. Could it have really been taken this quickly?"

Jeinis grimaced visibly. *"Aside from Chalin, any fort or castle can be taken given enough time – that is an inescapable fact,"* he thought before sighing slightly with a nod. "Yes, it could be taken. As for the terrifying speed with which it appears to have fallen. . . . I'm not sure how they managed it without a shocking and unforgivable lapse in judgment by the fort's new commander."

Thakian turned an accusatory glare on Craigan. "I believe you named Corandit's replacement, did you not?"

Craigan nodded grimly, his jaw muscles flexing as he ground his teeth together. "That I did," he practically growled in irritation. "Sagan was a sound tactician and excellent officer before his shameful decline. I thought it prudent to give the man one final chance before casting aside a potentially useful resource." Craigan's nostrils flared. "It appears I may have given him one too many chances."

"Well, if the man was truly a liability, then at least the Merandiths have taken care of him for you," Alestra quipped. Looking at Craigan, and ignoring the cold reproachful glares focused on her, she suggested, "It might be wise to recall Dromick, my love." She glanced at Jeinis and added, "No offense intended, General."

A muscle flexed in Jeinis' jaw in irritation. "None taken, Doma," he responded, his tone cold but respectful.

"I'm not averse to that – if needed," Craigan declared, drawing Alestra's attention back to him. "For now, I want his attention focused on the Resistance group that's been harassing Surandia for right now. Deo forbid they spill over into the surrounding realms and they somehow interrupt our supply lines; such a failure would be far more disastrous than the border fort falling." He then looked Jeinis squarely in the eyes and stated firmly, "As for a possible winter campaign, General Corandit is quite capable of leading our forces."

Jeinis inclined his head gratefully, but said nothing.

Alestra flashed a small, agreeable smile. "As you say, my love." Looking back at Jeinis, she then asked, "Did the messenger give you any idea what may have led to such foolish decisions by this Sagan?"

"Nothing that made any coherent sense, Doma," Jeinis replied with a frustrated shake of his head. "She mentioned something about dark clouds that rained death, and armored juggernauts. I cannot even guess what she is alluding to with the clouds, but as for the armored juggernauts. . . ."

"Hagan's Hammer," Craigan finished for him.

"Hagan's Hammer?" Astica reiterated with a scoff of disbelief. "How in the bloody hells could a heavy cavalry unit prompt any commander – even one whose wits are addled – to leave the safety of their walls? The woman's brain is twisted by her injuries, or I'm a whore's son."

Alestra smirked. "Careful with your boasts, Doms. Someone might just take you at your word."

Astica grunted. "That's rich, coming from someone whose rumored dalliances would make a whor–"

"That's enough, Astica!" Craigan barked. "As I said before – save your verbal sparring for another time, else you find yourself on the wrong side of my temper! Is that understood?"

Astica grunted but remained silent.

"Good. As for you, Alestra. . . . It would be a favor to me if you would refrain from goading our compatriots," he stated sternly.

"Smiling broadly, Alestra replied, "Of course, my love."

Craigan fought to keep doubt from his face at her overly conceding tone. Turning his attention back to Jeinis, Craigan said, "I cannot find any reason to doubt the veracity of the fort's fall. However, the circumstances of its downfall are perplexing at best. We need to know what in the hells the Merandiths possess that could bring down a fort so quickly. When do you think she'll be able to speak with me?"

Jeinis shook his head. "I don't know for sure, Doms. She was in bad shape when she was brought in. She might be well enough tonight, or it may take a day or two. In either case, it is clear that the cause of the fort's downfall left its mark on her."

"A day or two may be too long to wait, General," Craigan stated thoughtfully.

"I cannot disagree with you, Doms." Jeinis hesitated a moment before adding, "Pardon my forwardness, Doms, but if you are considering a military response, I feel it is my duty to remind you of the hazards of a winter campaign. We may be far south of the harsh northern winter, but a winter campaign still carries serious risks. Furthermore, this may be nothing more than an attempt to goad us into such a campaign."

Craigan shook his head. "Your warning is not lost on me, Cousin. However, with the Sur'dathans running the show in the south now, it is horribly clear to me that weather we consider harsh will most likely fail to discourage them. Furthermore, this close to Chalin, we cannot afford to sit idle and let this aggression go without a response." He took a deep breath. "However, for now, I simply want you to take stock of what is needed to retake the fort quickly with minimal losses before the first snows. I also want you to have Sergeant Galanti dispatch his scouts with orders to observe from afar and report any movement. Is that understood?"

Jeinis nodded grimly. "Completely. The scouts will be on their way within the hour."

"Good," Craigan responded, an edge of dark concern to his tone. "As for the messenger, I will return this evening after the Night Watch bell tolls. We need to know as much as we can, as soon as we can."

Jeinis grimaced inwardly. "I will see to it that she is as fit as possible to speak with you . . . but I cannot promise much, Doms."

Craigan tried his best to offer an understanding smile, but he knew it came off as concerned. "I'll take what I can get, General. As for the rest of you," he looked sternly at the other nobles. "I want you in my chambers in two hours with asset assessments in hand." Looking at Alestra, his voice took on an aggressive edge, "That goes double for you, my dear. I think it's time that House Ithikia started bringing more to this conflict now that it is to be wed more deeply to it, don't you think?"

Alestra grinned devilishly before leaning in and kissing Craigan full on the mouth, drawing a disgusted grunt from Astica and a roll of the eyes from Thakian. Pulling away, she smiled once again. "Of course, my love. After all, we can't let the Merandiths believe they can actually win this war, now can we?"

*

Mal was petrified.

She had no doubt the exotic young woman was looking directly at her. Her heart was aflutter with fear that threatened to overwhelm her as the girl suddenly stood and glided toward the door.

"Move, ye lummox!" Mal's mind screamed. *"She knows yer there, and knows yer purpose!"* Yet, while her mind pleaded with her to run, her muscles refused to yield to its demands.

Suddenly, Flute was standing before the door, and there was a click as she turned its polished handle. As the panel began to swing inward, Mal's body finally, and futilely, conceded to her mind's wishes, and she scrambled backward. Her frantic retreat was brought to an unexpected halt when her head banged into the footboard of the bed.

"Ow!" she exclaimed, followed by a hiss of pain.

"My apologies," Flute said with genuine concern from the open door. "I did not mean to startle you. Are you alright?"

"I . . ." Mal started to say as she rubbed the back of her head. Looking up at Flute through squinted eyes, Mal's frantic search for some excuse as to why she was spying faded as she noted the concern on her face. "I'm sorry," Mal finally replied humbly, burying her accent. "I did not mean to intrude in any fashion on your performance." Standing up, Mal added, "I was simply here to replace Doms Suldamik's linens when I heard the music. If you don't mind me saying, you have a remarkable skill, my lady." Mal punctuated the compliment with an awkward curtsy.

Flute offered Mal a slight smile that had a hint of sadness to it. "No need to apologize to me. . . . I don't think I caught your name."

"Jaylee, my lady."

Flute met Mal's gaze and replied thoughtfully, "Jaylee. . . . A pretty name, though I get the feeling that it isn't your real name, is it?"

Already dreadfully unsettled by the situation, Mal couldn't help but gawk at the girl. *"Dear Deo, there's far more goin' on 'ere than that bastard Logan let on,"* she thought as she scrambled for something to say.

Flute flashed that same small, sad smile at Mal. "Fear not, my mistress informed me that you were in the keep, Malia. I am to help you in any way that I can to expedite the completion of your mission."

Mal's blue eyes grew wide at the mention of her real name. Leaning back against the footboard heavily, she thought, *"Damn it all to bloody hells! There's no doubtin' I've landed meself in a messy situation!"* Now firmly convinced that there was no deceiving this girl, Mal let her fake accent drop as she replied, "Seems ye be knowin' who I am and why I'm 'ere."

Flute nodded. "I do. After all, it was my mistress – via the Resistance – that commissioned your job."

The blunt admission stunned Mal, leaving her mind racing. It took her a moment to recover as a flood of questions and fears stormed through her mind. Eventually, despite every instinct crying for her to run fast and far, she managed to collect her thoughts and reign in her fear. *"Ye've gone and got caught in a royal web o' shite, Mal, and there's no backin' out now,"* she thought. *"Too many dangerous people be knowin' yer name and yer face."*

Taking a deep breath, she asked, seeking more insight into the situation her job had landed her in, "And just what is tha job? It's gotta be more than just stealin' a trinket like I was told."

Flute smiled slightly. "I'd say you are astute, but you already know it is far more than that. You are also already aware that your objective is the acquisition of a relic interred within the Utherian Valley that could bring about the downfall of House Suldamik, and put an end to the war."

"Hells' bloody balls!" Mal thought. Aloud, she asked, smoothly concealing her concern, "Okay. Say what yer sayin' is true – why in Deo's name would ye be wantin' to bring down House Suldamik? Yer mistress is to be wed to Craigan, fer Deo's sake!"

Flute cocked her head thoughtfully for a moment before she stated, "Observant. To answer your question, I can only offer that my mistress always prefers to attack an objective from more than one angle."

Mal scoffed. "That's not sayin' much, lass. What's to guarantee she's not just gonna be worse than Craigan once she be takin' over? Hells, what's to stop me from runnin' to Craigan with this news?" she boldly taunted despite her anxiety.

The small, sad smile crept onto Flute's lips again, sending a chill up Mal's spine. "Nothing. . . . Although, if your actions should threaten my mistress, then I have orders to prevent such behavior."

Looking at the lithe, snow-blue-haired girl standing casually before her in an elegant garment, it was hard for Mal to imagine her acting violently. However, there was a cheerless, almost regretful edge to her sky-blue eyes that unequivocally told Mal that Flute was intimately familiar with violence. "Alright," Mal said with a nod, her husky voice guarded, "I believe ye. So, what can ye do to help?"

Looking around the room, Flute said, "I take it you were using your duties to seek the item needed to grant you entrance into the Valley?"

Mal nodded.

"Well, you won't find it in here."

"I've already discovered that, lass."

"Indeed," Flute said with a slight hitch to her voice. "Between my mistress and I, we have managed to search both rooms rather thoroughly."

"And what did ye be findin'?" Mal asked impatiently as fear of being discovered by someone less amicable to her clandestine job began to set in.

"That Craigan never had such a place in his quarters until recently." Motioning toward the study, Flute added, "Come, I will show you." Turning, Flute entered the study, leaving Mal to catch up.

Making her way into the study, Mal took in the rest of the room. Eight-sided and large, the study's gray and black stone walls were adorned with paintings of landscapes from across the breadth of Triclose, providing an air of beauty to offset the brutality conveyed by the weapons mounted high on the walls throughout the chamber. Above her, the roof was composed of a latticework of thick, polished oak beams from which an elegant, oil-fed chandelier hung at the center of the room. Off to her left was a simple ironwood desk that seemed out of place in the study, as well as a pair of leather highback chairs behind an end table ladened with partially filled crystal goblets and a crystal decanter of Velusyian Blue. Looking to her right, she noted a sealed set of balcony doors in front of which was a large table and two plush chairs that appeared to have been displaced, likely by the four matching chairs in the center of the room.

Moving to the table across the lush, red carpet, Flute stood next to it, her face unreadable. Motioning to the table, she said, "Here, take a look at this table and tell me what you see."

Approaching the beautiful and rather lewd piece of furniture cautiously, Mal examined it as requested. Large and made of oak, the legs and frame were artfully carved into the likenesses of nude women in provocative poses. *"Men,"* Mal thought with a scoff as she walked around the table inspecting it.

Crouching down, Mal made another pass around the table before crawling beneath it. After studying the underside of it for a moment, she extracted herself from under it. Standing, she straightened her skirt and said, "If there's a compartment there, it's hidden better than any I've seen."

"There's that same damn smile again," Mal thought as Flute offered her the sad smile once more.

"That is good to hear from someone as skilled as yourself. The installation was difficult, so it would be a shame if it was easily spotted," Flute declared as she moved to the left leg of the table.

Puzzled by the declaration, Mal asked, "This ain't one of Craigan's normal hidin' spots, now is it?"

"Astute," Flute replied. Motioning Mal over, Flute added, "No, it isn't. My mistress had it installed for just such an occasion while Doms Suldamik was afield."

"Damn. They've been planning this fer a while now, haven't they?" Mal thought as she joined Flute. "Well?" she asked aloud.

Motioning to one of the table legs, all of which were carved to resemble a nude woman with her back arched and the tabletop supported on her upraised arms, Flute ordered, "Please, if you would – press the right nipple and then the left."

Crouching down, Mal muttered, "This is tha kind of lock I'd expect from a man," before doing as she was told. There was a muffled click after she depressed the second nipple, and Mal stood back up. "Now what?"

"Repeat the procedure on each leg, moving to your right," Flute informed her.

With a sigh, Mal moved to each leg in the indicated order and repeated the process. Muffled clicks followed the completion of the procedure on each leg, but on the last, the click was followed by another click and a muffled scrape as if something had been released. Standing up, Mal circled the table while Flute looked on attentively. Reaching the side that faced the sealed doors, Mal noticed that a portion of the face, which served as the midsection of a sprawled woman, now jutted slightly from the table. Looking at Flute for silent approval, Mal then approached the dislocated table section and pulled it out. Placing what was a small box on the table, she used the finger-sized hole in its lid to open it.

Though she couldn't fathom why she expected the box to contain her objective, she still found herself looking at Flute and exclaiming, "There's nothin' in 'ere!"

"No, there wouldn't be," Flute responded as she joined Mal. Closing the lid on the box, she added as she returned it to its proper place, "My mistress had this installed to serve as a drop-off point for the object of interest once she has acquired it from Doms Suldamik."

Mal laughed at the absurdity of the statement. "Well then,

why in tha hells do ye need me if she can so easily acquire tha amulet? Deo knows it was gonna be difficult to find out when he took tha damn thing off!"

"Indeed," Flute responded as she looked Mal in the eye. "Doms Suldamik is rarely without the necklace. However, my mistress has ways of relieving him of it."

"Then why do ye need me?" Mal reiterated.

"Because we cannot risk being caught with it."

Mal scoffed. "So I'm yer patsy, eh?"

"That is a harsh way of looking at it, but yes. My mistress will relieve Craigan of the amulet and hide it here. You will then be informed of its deposit. Once you have retrieved the amulet, you are then to enter the Valley and procure the ultimate goal of this venture. Is this not to your liking?"

Mal ground her teeth together, furious at being used and so easily deceived by those who had approached her. "Fine," she finally said with a slight scowl pulling at her thin lips, "but this will cost ye more. I didna take this job to end up as someone's scapegoat."

"How much?"

"Five-hundred talons," Mal declared.

"Done," Flute replied too swiftly for Mal's liking. Noting the worry on Mal's face, Flute added, "Wealth is of little consequence to my mistress. Fear not. Your fee shall be paid in whole upon completion."

"Fine. So when should I be retrievin' tha amulet? Assumin', of course, yer mistress can remove it from his possession without him noticin'."

"She can and will, have no doubt. As to when you can retrieve it," Flute cocked her head thoughtfully. "That day will be soon. I believe that Doms Suldamik will have need to venture from Chalin rather quickly. That would be the perfect time to complete this venture, wouldn't you say?"

Mal nodded cautiously.

"Good. Now, I would imagine you need to return to your duties. We don't want you to draw suspicion upon yourself, now do we?"

Cursing silently, Mal cast one more wary look at Flute before hurrying back to Craigan's bedroom and collecting the dirty linens.

Flute followed her and watched from the entryway, a thoughtful, almost sad look upon her face. As Mal exited the room through the hidden door and closed it behind her, Flute thought sadly, *"I'm so very sorry, Malia."*

Chapter Nineteen

The journey northeast was tedious.

Had it just been the four of them, a trip that was closing in on two weeks would have been a matter of hours. However, as much as she itched for expedience, she understood how necessary it was for Allanian to maintain his charade. Still, had their travel time been the only thing bothering her, it would have been easy to ignore it. Unfortunately, the gnawing concern that tormented her stomach made it impossible.

From the moment they had rejoined Allanian's squad and found themselves also burdened with a sizable caravan of people, Kara had felt something was amiss. She'd immediately dismissed the guarded and curious glances she and Ember received as the source. Being Velusyian, she was used to the looks and stares that her presence prompted. As for Ember, she would have found it odd had they not gawked. Even amongst the enigmatic Ice Walkers and the unique presence that was Allanian, Ember was an oddity. Granted, his upturned collar and his dyed-glass spectacles hid his more . . . unique traits, but it was impossible to ignore his size and shock of fiery hair. Thus, she initially attributed her irritation to another delay piled atop the unforeseen revelations and incidents they'd already battled through. She even went so far as to consider the unease inspired by the caravan of masked people as the source. Such delusions were short-lived, however. The disquiet she felt was all too familiar, and she knew better than to believe such mundane occurrences could be its source.

Still, without firm evidence as to the cause, she kept her concerns to herself in the hope that she was wrong. Mat and Allanian had enough to worry about, and for the moment, there was no need to add to it. So, she did as every elder Warden had learned to do in times of unease – she waited and observed.

The terrain they slowly traversed was rugged in places, and the snow stretched for as far as she could see without aid. There were mountains to the distant north and west, and there were hints of a few sizable forests in every direction. The fact that she couldn't see anything to justify her unease did nothing to squash the feeling. So, with the hope that she might find some answers, Kara would cautiously let her consciousness ride the currents a short distance in all directions from time to time. While she found generous signs of winter wildlife, as well as a few villages and one sizable town in the outlying area, she encountered nothing of consequence. As for her immediate surroundings, there was an air of caution about the men and women of Allanian's squad that, as Allanian had explained before they rejoined his unit, was born of their conflict with raiders. As much as she would have liked to put their fears to rest, she knew that offering such assurances would have spawned a bevy of questions that she could not have honestly answered, thus giving birth to distrust and most likely marring their confidence and faith in Allanian.

Yet, as the days of trudging through fresh snow passed and the sense of bother refused to yield, she finally had to accept that something was unequivocally amiss. However, what rankled her the most was her inability to discern the source of her unease. Experience had taught her – sometimes harshly – that unexplained and unknown trouble, more often than not, came to fruition with terrifying consequences. This was something she wholeheartedly wanted to avoid. Unfortunately, for the time being, all she could do was hope to figure it out before it was too late.

"Eh, my coin is on him being her lover," the man declared, his brash voice full of confidence.

Camilie's gray eyes briefly shifted to the two strangers at the neighboring fire and she snorted. She wasn't as sure of that as her friend was; however, without a doubt, they were quite the pair. Dressed in a black half-vest over a red shirt tucked into brown pants that flowed into black knee boots, the Velusyian was quite beautiful. In contrast, the large man with wild red hair was intimidating in his gray longcoat with its upturned collar. Turning back to her fire and the two men she shared it with on the southern edge of their modest-sized encampment, she fixed the speaker with a knowing gaze and quipped in her soft voice, "Don't be daft!" Breaking off a piece of bread, she sopped up some of the murky soup in her wooden bowl. Biting off a chunk, she added as she chewed, "A man that big, she'd break something!"

The man sitting across from her, adorned in the same attire as she – a black shirt, knee boots, and brown pants beneath a white tabard trimmed in deep purple with five red stars embroidered on the right breast – grunted and wiped a meaty hand on his pants. Picking up his spoon from his bowl, he pointed the utensil at her, causing the fire to sizzle as some soup splashed on the warm blaze. "And how do you know that, Cam? I can't believe you've even got ah inkling of what it's like to be with a man . . . unless," he grinned broadly behind his manicured beard, adding deep wrinkles to his already aged and weather-worn broad face, "you drugged him."

Camilie's small mouth split into a devious grin beneath her slightly crooked, slim nose. "Because – you oaf – a woman knows. Taking a man that big to bed would be awkward as hells at best. Although," she snuck another quick glance, "with the way she moves, I'd say she's limber enough to make it work."

The man's dark eyes twinkled beneath his heavy, hairless brow. "Jealous, are we?" he teased.

Glaring at him, she barked, her normally quiet voice full of sarcasm, "Jealous, Garn? I'm about as jealous of her as I am—"

"Corith, you two could drive a man to kill himself with your senseless banter!" their other companion snapped, a layer of pain in his rough voice.

Glancing at their stout and bald companion, Camilie said, "That's just cruel, Lieutenant."

Using his good hand to rip a chunk of bread from the small loaf he had pinned between his black leather-clad legs, Fallain jabbed the morsel at her as if it were a weapon. "Cruel, Sergeant?" he asked rhetorically as a flash of pain crossed his broad, lined face. "I'll tell you what's cruel – listening to you two banter about someone's rutting habits, that's what! Corith knows we've already got a lot to deal with, but my shoulder," he gestured to his right arm, which was tightly pinned against his tabard-encased chest, "hurts like all hells, it's cold, and we've got a small host of Ice Walkers to deal with," he ended with a shudder, then flinched. "The last bloody thing I need," he added with a hiss of pain, "is your prattle giving me a headache!" Fallain bit hard into the bread, punctuating his statement.

"Sorry, Lieutenant. Didn't know a bit of chatter about a hot romp in the sheets would get your small clothes in a bunch," Camilie teased.

Fallain's large, pain-filled brown eyes flashed, but he refrained from retorting. Instead, he muttered something unintelligible as he brushed crumbs from his short, braided black beard. "Corith," he suddenly declared running his good hand over his head forcefully, "I need more wine!" Standing abruptly, he ignored his remaining bread as it fell to the sodden ground around the fire.

"Damn, Lieutenant – that's a waste!" Garn cried, bemoaning the discarded food.

Ignoring Garn's protest, Fallain said, "I'm going to find

something for the pain. Corith knows I'll need something strong after this brain-scarring conversation! Good night, you two!"

Camilie barely contained her laughter as Fallain stalked off into the camp in search of relief from his ailments.

"Poor bastard," she muttered with a slight smile tugging at her lips. "Now," she declared, turning her attention to Garn, who was contemplating the muddy bread, "Where was I? Ah, yes – I'm about as jealous of her as I am your boulder of a bald head, Garn! Corith, the way that thing shines in the firelight, you must be an oil merchant's dream customer!"

Garn sat back, his attention jumping to her, feigning shock. "I'm hurt!" he cried sarcastically. Setting his bowl aside, he ran a hand over his head, which the firelight played off just as Camilie insinuated. "Women love a bald head – that's common knowledge. Illia lov–" he started to say when he noticed Camilie's pained expression. "Corith, I didn't think!" he apologized. "I didn't mean anything by that! I know how close you two were."

Swallowing hard, Camilie nodded. "I know," she said softly as she fought off tears and thoughts of her close friend. Smiling weakly, she offered, "You know, she fancied you." She suddenly laughed, drawing a few curious glances. "Corith, she even liked your bald head!"

Garn's expression sank. "I suspected, but I never. . . ." He shook his head sadly. "She'll be missed," he stated morosely.

"Aye," Camilie said before suddenly standing up.

"Where are you going?" Garn asked softly.

"To speak with our guests," she declared around the lump in her throat. "They're friends of the Captain's, and Corith knows we didn't give them a proper reception."

Garn grimaced. "Right."

Starting toward the other fire, Camilie stopped and turned back to Garn. "And by the way, if anything, he's her bodyguard."

"How do you figure?"

"Because of the looks in everyone's eyes on the day they walked into camp." She laughed. "Corith only knows, I'm not too sure that a few of the others aren't still cleaning shite out of their breeches."

In a wave of amusement, Garn's morose thoughts suddenly vanished and he laughed.

The decision to approach the two strangers had been defensive. The loss of Illia was hard on everyone. Between her martial skills, quick wit, warm personality, and her beauty, she had endeared herself to her squadmates in numerous ways. Her death was still an open, raw wound for many of them, including Camilie, and she found discussing her was still next to impossible. So, to escape the painful talk, she took the only way out she saw at the moment. Now, only a few steps away from the fire that the targets of their taboo chatter occupied, she found herself unsure of what to say.

The Velusyian and her two companions had arrived at Fort Harden as the Ice Walkers and her squad readied for the march back to Merset. To say Allanian was surprised by the arrival of the two foreigners would be a bit of an understatement; in fact, they'd never seen Allanian quiet so exuberant. What was even more stunning was that he even went so far as to delay their departure for a bit just so he could chat with them. Eventually, after talking with them for a little while, Allanian finally introduced them to the rest of the squad. What's more, he informed the squad that not only were the foreigners friends of his from his days on Solarson, but they would also be joining them on their trip to Merset. Beyond that eye-opening display of uncharacteristic behavior, and the brief introduction, only Allanian had spent much time with them, which made the trio a bit of an enigma to the rest of their squad.

"To answer your question," the Velusyian suddenly said as she looked up at Camilie, "he is as you thought, my bodyguard."

Frozen by the unexpected statement, Camilie felt herself blush furiously beneath the intensity of the woman's white-streaked, sky-blue eyes.

"Hells, you heard all of that?" Camilie managed to say, mortified, as she forced herself to take the last few steps to their fire.

Kara's full lips suddenly parted in a disarming smile, lighting up her tan, heart-shaped face, which further surprised Camilie. Brushing aside the lock of white hair along the left side of her face with a brown-gloved hand, she added in a beautiful voice that soothed Camilie's aching heart, "My hearing is sharp, though not as keen as my friend's is."

"Sorry if we overstepped! Nothing was meant by it," Camilie offered humbly.

Kara waved a dismissive hand. "Think nothing of it." Motioning to the fire, she added, "Care to join us?"

Still feeling like her cheeks were on fire, Camilie moved to an empty spot opposite the two and crouched down. Her vision flickered between them for a moment before it landed on Ember. Without realizing it, she found herself staring at the unusually large man. To be sure, he was intimidating, but add to it the dark spectacles he wore beneath a heavy brow on his broad face, and the large claymore resting next to him, and he became absolutely terrifying.

"Is something wrong?" Ember finally rumbled when Camilie's gaze lingered.

Camilie felt her cheeks grow even hotter with embarrassment. "Sorry," she muttered, averting her eyes. "It's just. . . . Well, can you actually see with those on? I mean, with it dark and all. . . ."

Ember laughed and used a forefinger to push his spectacles up on his nose. "Quite well, actually. My eyes are sensitive to the light, and I've grown used to them," he lied smoothly.

Camilie looked at him skeptically. "Right," she uttered, not entirely convinced by Ember's excuse.

"Camilie, isn't it?" Kara interjected, drawing the conversation away from Ember's unique qualities.

Switching her attention to Kara, Camilie nodded. "Aye. Though I don't remember any of us introducing ourselves," she said, surprised by Kara's knowledge of her name.

Kara smiled. "No, none of you did, but Allanian took the time to brief us on who we would be traveling with. It is a pleasure to meet you. Allanian thinks highly of all of you. And coming from him, that says a lot."

Camilie felt her cheeks warming up again, this time with pride. "He's a good man and an even better captain. We're all proud to serve and fight alongside him." She suddenly grinned. "Besides, it's not too often you get to see the enemy turn sheet white! He scares the hells out of most people!"

Kara chuckled, and Ember grunted.

"He does, indeed," Kara agreed.

"He does indeed, what?" a haunting voice from the direction of the main camp asked.

Turning as Camilie stood to attention, they saw Allanian, adorned in his House Guard tabard and off-white attire, moving in their direction.

Reaching them, he motioned for Camilie to sit.

"Scare an enemy to the core," Kara said with a wry smile as Camilie sat back down.

Moving next to Camilie, Allanian crouched down with a humble grin that seemed much too feral with his large canines. "Well, I don't know about that, but I've seen a few that have turned tail and run." He shrugged nonchalantly. "I merely figured they'd thought of something more urgent to attend to."

Everyone at the fire chuckled.

"So, what brings you to this fire, Sergeant?" Allanian asked of his subordinate.

"Didn't feel right about the greeting we gave your friends, Captain. Thought I might make amends." She scratched her head sheepishly. "Didn't mean to get distracted."

Allanian inclined his head gratefully. "Admirable, Sergeant."

"Thank you, sir." She hesitated. "If you don't mind me asking, how do you know them?"

Allanian smiled. "Not at all. We worked together from time to time before I came to Triclose."

Camilie nodded thoughtfully, then said, her tone respectful, "Pardon my bluntness, but it seems a long way to go just to visit."

"Sergeant–" Allanian started to say, his tone taking on an authoritative edge.

"It's alright, Allanian," Kara interjected. Turning her gaze to Camilie, she then said, ignoring Allanian's concerned gaze, "We're here on business. We were told that we might find help from House Merandith, thus our journey north. Running into Allanian was a pleasant and welcome surprise."

"Ah," Camilie replied. "If you don't mind me prying further, what business brings you this far?"

"Sergeant!" Allanian declared sternly. "Their business is theirs, and I would ask that you be respectful of that!"

Looking at her commander, Camilie saw the warning in his gaze, and she nodded respectfully. "Sorry, sir. I didn't mean anything by it."

"I know," Allanian responded, smiling to soften his statement. "If you would, give us the fire, Camilie. I need to speak with my friends for a moment."

Standing, Camilie nodded. "Aye, sir." Turning to Kara and Ember, she bowed respectfully. "I apologize if I offended in any way.

Welcome to Triclose, and be welcome within House Merandith's walls."

Kara nodded. "Thank you," she replied with a warm smile.

Nodding again, she turned to Allanian. "Captain," she stated respectfully, inclining her head, before returning to Garn and their fire.

Once she was settled at her fire and talking with Garn, Allanian turned his attention back to Kara and Ember. Keeping his voice low so that only they could hear him, he said, "I'm sorry if she was bothering you. She can be a bit nosey, and even over-exuberant, but she's a fine woman and an excellent soldier."

Kara dismissed his concern with a wave of her hand. "Think nothing of it."

Allanian nodded. "So, where's Mat?"

Fighting the urge to touch her katana and tanto resting next to her, Kara's expression turned serious. "I sent him to scout a bit. Something has been bothering me, and I'm wary of extending myself too far. So I sent him to put eyes out there." Noticing that Allanian looked concerned, she prodded, "You've felt it too, haven't you?"

Allanian nodded slowly. "I have. . . . Actually, I noticed something before I left to meet you, but I dismissed it as nothing more than my nerves after the battle that afternoon." His brow furrowed in thought. Looking to Ember he asked, "What about you? I don't know how your change affected your connection to the currents, but I would think if there's a problem, you of all people would have a better grasp on it."

Ember slowly sat forward and stared into the fire. "It's hard to miss, but as to who or what is the cause," he shook his head, "I can only guess. But what I can tell you is that whatever it is, it's close . . . and it reeks of the Darkness. It . . ." he trailed off thoughtfully.

Leaning toward her brother, Kara asked, "It what?"

Ember glanced at her, concern displayed clearly on his broad face. "It reminds me too much of what led me to the shadow drakuma. I don't need to remind you that I found Garith that night," he stated gravely.

Kara nodded slowly even as Allanian let out a low growl. "I'm still having trouble accepting the implications of such a discovery," he said, his voice troubled, "but I would be a damn fool to dismiss your findings or the evidence displayed clearly on you two." He took a deep breath and let it out slowly. "So what are we to do? We will be in Merset in two days, and while I have my reservation about

440

the attention you will draw," he shot a concerned look at Ember, "the mere thought of what could happen if blackhearts, or a shadow drakuma," he shuddered slightly at the thought, "or Corith forbid, one of the Betrayers showed up in the city is horrifying!"

"And then there are the crystals' new owners," Kara added, her tone and expression deeply concerned.

Ember grunted and shook his head. "A damn mess if I've ever seen one. And one that could get ugly fast." He shook his head again. "I'm not sure how much good I'll be to any of you. I don't know if my new form is permanent, and my connection to the currents is too damn sporadic." He folded his arms across his chest. "I don't like being a liability."

Kara smiled consolingly at him, placed a loving hand on his knee and gave it a reassuring squeeze. "What will be, will be. But you are far from a liability. Even with as tenuous as your connection is right now, you're still a force to be reckoned with."

"Thanks," Ember replied with a weak smile. "Still, I don't want to put that to the test."

"Let's hope it doesn't come to that . . . but we can count on you in a fight, right?" Allanian asked.

Ember fixed him with a stare, the intensity of which he could feel even though spectacles hid Ember's eyes. "I may not have a full grasp on my powers or my current state, but you can be damn sure they won't have it easy if it comes to blows!"

Allanian grinned. "Just checking." Switching his gaze back to Kara, he asked, "So the question at hand is, what do we do now?"

Leaning over, Kara rested her elbows on her knees and balanced her chin on her interlocked hands. "What we do best – we wait."

Allanian snorted and Ember grunted. "That's hardly what I wanted to hear," Allanian replied.

Kara smirked dryly. "And hardly what I want to do. But we both know rash actions would do us no good. For now, we proceed as planned – locate and protect the crystals' owners. Should whom or whatever is responsible for the disturbance we've felt make a move, we'll respond accordingly. Until then, I suggest we all stay alert and on guard. Agreed?"

"Agreed," both men echoed.

"Well then," Allanian stated, "once we get to Merset, it won't take long for me to see that the Ice Walkers are settled. After that, I'll make sure all is well with Doma Merandith, then I'll start my Search in earnest. I can also see to it that you all have quarters in the keep if you wish."

Kara shook her head. "It's appreciated, but not needed. We'll stay in the city; more freedom that way."

Allanian nodded. "Very well, but at least let me introduce you to Doma Merandith. Triclose is a very different place from the last time you were here – it might not hurt to make some friends in high places."

Sitting up, Kara nodded. "Agreed. After all, Amroth did offer us the help of House Merandith."

Standing, Allanian nodded. "That sounds good. Until the morning, then."

Kara nodded and offered him a parting smile before Allanian made his way back toward camp.

"Things won't remain calm for long, will they?" Ember grumbled after Allanian had left.

Looking into the fire, Kara sighed regretfully. "Calm, Brother? I think that hope died with the emergence of the blackhearts." She shook her head. "No, Brother – a storm is coming, and I don't know if we can weather it this time."

*

Resting his wrists on the pommels of his sheathed broad-bladed shortswords, Mat let out a low, impressed whistle. "This is . . . impressive. I'm not too sure it doesn't exceed Solac," he stated, awe nakedly displayed in his cocky voice.

Standing off to the side, Ember grunted. *"I guess this might be one reason Brother has spent so much time here,"* he speculated through his connection to his sister.

Standing next to her brother, her eyes wide with surprise, Kara nodded as the rest of their traveling companions started down the gentle slope that led from their position outside a heavily logged forest down to a rolling, predominantly snow-covered bowl, and the community that occupied it. *"He and Luthur loved this city,"* she agreed as she inhaled a deep, refreshing breath of cold sea air. *"But my oh my, it has grown!"*

Originating at the northern edge of the distant cliffside, a towering, crenellated wall of gray stone bowed its way around the city proper before diving to the southeast along the other side of the bowl to rejoin with the coast before jutting out into the ocean. From their position and without aid, Kara noted that not only were robust towers spaced along the barrier at regular intervals, but they also flanked its imposing main gatehouse and its twin far to the southeast. Movement all along the top of the wall indicated that it was manned, though it was hard for her to tell just how many soldiers there were without aid. Numerous columns of smoke climbed skyward from both the bowl and from behind the wall; some were the gray of hearth fires, while others were the darker hue of forge and tannery fires. Countless rooftops were visible beyond the wall as the city marched, tier-by-tier, up the promontory to another wall, beyond which she could just make out a third wall and the towering spires of a keep.

"The city doesn't look like it's changed all that much, besides the growth, but the outer wall looks relatively new," Kara told her brother.

"She's beautiful, isn't she?" Allanian asked as he strode up and stopped next to her, a full quiver on his back and the halves of his dragon-inspired, bladed white bow sheathed at his hips.

"Quite," she responded softly so only those close to her could hear. She then reiterated confidently for Allanian, "The outer wall is new."

"Aye. The city has grown quite a bit since you were last here," he answered just as quietly. "The main wall was added during the reign of Kale's grandfather. Then, at the onset of the Third Great War, Doms Merandith's father started the southern extension to protect the port and the growth around it. It was finished last year, leaving us with close to seven miles of wall to defend if – Deo forbid – the war ever reached our doorstep."

"Could you defend it adequately?" Mat asked.

Allanian shrugged. "If the main army was here? Yes . . . for a time. Eventually, we'd have to pull back to Vallum Prime – but let's not speculate about such things," he finished with a dry smirk.

"So what's the new wall call?" Kara prompted.

"Vallum Superior."

Kara chuckled. "Not very imaginative, but I think Luthur would approve."

Allanian's smirk turned thoughtful. "Damion thought so."

Kara fought the urge to grimace. "Yes. Yes, he would."

Motioning to the community at the base of the slope, Allanian looked at Kara and asked, "Shall we proceed? I'd like to get everyone settled in as quickly as possible so we might attend to more important matters."

Kara pressed here full lips together and nodded. "By all means."

Taking the lead, Allanian guided them alongside the trail that the column followed. Below them, a wide, sluggish river flowed from the northwest to southeast, bisecting the sprawling mass of farms and other facilities that filled the large bowl.

"What in the hells are the people down there doing?" Mat asked, befuddled by the number of fields that were clear of snow and showed signs of tilling.

Kara laughed. "I keep forgetting that your exposure to anything beyond city life and Solarson is limited."

"Hey now!" Mat protested, shooting her a hurt look.

Smirking, Kara added, "There are several crops that take to the cold, and even frigid weather, young one," Kara teased, her soothing voice playful. "Snow apples, snow grapes, ice melons, frost cabbage, to name a few."

Matt grumbled something unintelligible before saying, "Sounds horrid to eat. Makes me think I'd be munching on food made from ice or snow."

Allanian chuckled, then said over his shoulder, "Hardly. But I am surprised you don't know of those foods. Never had any, I take it?"

"Sure he has," Kara answered for Mat.

"I have?" Mat asked incredulously.

Kara nodded. "Uh-huh. I know on at least one occasion where I've seen you enjoy snow grapes."

"Huh?" Mat responded, scratching his head.

"Plump, juicy, and the color of blue ice; sound familiar?"

Mat's brow furrowed in confusion. "Sea berries?"

Kara nodded again. "They've been called that. But trust me when I say they are indeed snow grapes. They're grown mostly in the north, as I imagine they are here."

"Huh. . . . Imagine that? I always thought they came from coastal regions," Mat replied, surprised.

Kara laughed, its lilting melody softening the blow to Mat's ego. "My dear Mat, there's always something you don't know – remember that."

"Right," Mat muttered as they reached the bottom of the bowl.

A chest-high stone wall surrounded the large community, entry to which was provided by a stone arch over a wide, cobblestone road. A surprising number of villagers were gathered along the road and wall, watching with unabashed curiosity as the column of Ice Walkers in their white furs, sealskins, and bronze masks crossed into the town, with Allanian's men in the lead, and made for the river. As Kara's small group neared the gate, the villagers' garb surprised Mat. While a few of them, which Mat assumed were merchants or warehouse owners, looked better groomed and were dressed in reasonably expensive attire, the majority of the onlookers showed clear signs of strenuous toil in the winter conditions. Most were dressed in layers of wool garb that were host to numerous patches and repairs, while their heavy boots showed ample signs of wear.

However, despite their threadbare appearance, Mat noticed that their red faces, many of which were partially shielded from the cold by hoods, played host to eyes that spoke of pride in their work. In fact, Mat found himself impressed by the lack of animosity and regret he saw. So many of the villages and towns he'd visited that rested in the shadow of a great city were home to those who envied the city dwellers, believing that city life was a better life; and with that jealousy came animosity and hate. Yet, here he saw not beleaguered acceptance, but pride. Whether that pride was born of the knowledge that they contributed to the war, or simply from the work they did, Mat found such an environment refreshing.

With the main road clear of impeding snow, their trek through the community did not take long; all the while, curious onlookers, children and adults alike, dodged snow piles, as well as stone and wood fences. as they did their best to follow alongside them. Their efforts drew a slight smile from Allanian. The Ice Walkers were most likely the most unusual and spectacular thing many of them had ever seen, and this experience would stick with them throughout their lives, especially with the children. Amidst the gloom of war and winter, he was glad such they'd been graced with such a unique experience, and a part of him wondered what tales and dreams it might inspire.

As he looked around, he noticed Mat's curious glances at their impromptu escort. "A large portion of them are refugees," Allanian informed him and the others solemnly.

"How many?" Kara asked, her white-streaked, sky-blue eyes heavy with sorrowful sympathy.

"Hard to say accurately," Allanian offered as he waved in gratitude to a few of the villagers who shouted greetings and thanks his way. "Officially, we've taken in around four thousand refugees. Unofficially," he shrugged, "there could be significantly more living in the wilds. The war displaced thousands from the Contested Territories alone."

Kara nodded thoughtfully, recalling the impressive number of refugees they'd seen in Caith'tol. "The number of impoverished and homeless must be terrible," she said softly, recalling the numerous times she'd born witness to the price of war.

Allanian nodded slowly in agreement. "There are far, far too many of them. . . . However, Tiliea has been much luckier in this than most."

"How so?" Kara asked.

"House Merandith established quite a few communities," he gestured to the surrounding area, "throughout Tiliea in hopes of not only providing a life for the displaced, but in hopes of easing the burden of trying to feed and arm a large military engaged in a never-ending war."

"Has it worked?" Ember inquired.

"Very much so. Granted, the other realms that serve in the Army of Five Stars contribute greatly in their own way, but it has been Doms Merandith and his father's efforts that are largely responsible for maintaining both supplies and manpower."

"Manpower?" Mat asked, his brow furrowing in confusion. "What does he do? Conscript those that aren't fit for farms or factories?"

Allanian chuckled. "Hardly, but your guess is close. There are no conscriptions in House Merandith's army. Everyone is a volunteer; what's more, many orphans, and even adults, find a home in the Academy, where they are trained to fight and to potentially become an officer. Upon graduating, they can either join the military or choose to use their skills in another way."

"A noble endeavor," Kara stated with a nod.

Allanian smiled. "Quite. House Merandith's actions may not solve their problems, but it has given many hope and a life they never thought they would have again," he finished as they reached what Kara assumed was the center of the town.

Several large buildings with an official air about them were centered on the circular plaza. Hints of grass peeked through the snow at the heart of the plaza, leading Kara to believe the area was the town green.

"Captain!" cried a rough, aging voice. "Might we have a word with you?"

Glancing to her right as she and her companions came to a halt, Kara saw one of the larger buildings on the plaza. Made of stone instead of wood, and roofed with clay shingles, the single-story structure struck her as an administrative building. Stone stairs, partially cleared of snow, led up to a broad door flanked by windows. As if to confirm her suspicions about the building's purpose, three elderly men enshrouded in fur-lined red cloaks stood before the bottom stair. Two of the men still had a full head of gray hair, while the third wore a cap over his bald head, and all three bore meticulously trimmed and oiled beards.

Glancing at Allanian, she noticed he was fighting the urge to scowl. Smirking, she asked, "Friends of yours?"

"Hardly," he muttered. "They are the Town Elders. Good people in their own right, but. . . ."

"Officials are officials?" Mat finished for him.

"Indeed. No matter how much time passes, it seems that most people in a position of power always think they are the center of the world." He cringed and then waved at the men as he took a step forward. Turning to his companions, he said, "If you will excuse me, I must assuage their egos and concerns. It shouldn't take long. Continue on with the column, and I should rejoin you before you enter the city."

Kara chuckled and smiled. "Do resist the urge to strangle them."

Allanian arched a confused eyebrow. "Strangle them? My dear Kara, I wouldn't dare. That would be too quick for them," he finished with a smirk. He then trotted off to retrieve his horse before advancing on the Town Elders, leaving Kara and the others laughing as they continued onward.

Reaching the far side of the Town Green, the column set foot on a wide, gray stone bridge that arched its way across the river below. Sluggish this time of the year, chunks of ice careened along the currents, occasionally bouncing off one another or creating temporary dams that the water struggled to dislodge. Once the bridge deposited the column on the other side, they quickly made their way along the road before exiting through an arch identical to the one they passed through when entering the town. Their escort of children and curious farmers accompanied them for a while longer, but once the terrain started to climb toward the looming wall, they broke off in a trickle and returned home.

With the pace their column was setting, it wasn't long before they caught up with a wagon train making for Merset from the community. Most of the wagons were covered, but a quick peek inside those with exposed cargo revealed to Mat crates containing a variety of produce, meats, as well as construction materials, weapons, armor, and a variety of other trade goods and sundries.

"Huh. . . . Seems like they have an efficient operation here," he commented off-handedly.

Kara smirked. "It is," she agreed, "but I've seen better."

Mat snorted. "Of course you have. I'd wager good coin that not much measures up to your . . . past experiences."

Kara's smirk widened.

"Tell me, though," Mat added as he examined some of the people they were quickly passing, "do you think they've seen someone as large as your brother?"

Looking about, it was immediately clear to Kara that quite a few people were casting naked stares at the column. While some of the people appeared to be jealous or angry at the favoritism being shown to outsiders, there were many others who were focused on the Ice Walkers and Ember with brazen curiosity. Glancing up at her brother, she saw the muscles in his broad jaw twitching. Smiling softly, she gently placed a hand on his arm and offered, "Don't let it bother you. You'd draw attention no matter what efforts we could make to hide your more . . . obvious features."

Grunting, Ember adjusted the weight of the large claymore on his back with his shoulders before he pushed his dark glasses up on his nose even though there was no need. "Your platitudes are so reassuring," he rumbled drolly.

Laughing, she squeezed his arm reassuringly as they entered the shadow of the wall. "I try. Look on the bright side — at least you're not bigger than the wall."

Ember grunted again and looked up at the monstrous structure.

Made of large blocks of gray stone, he quickly estimated it to be around ninety feet tall. Despite the steep angle of their approach, he could just make out several soldiers garbed in chainmail and black tabards peaking over the crenellated battlements at the organized throng of people and wagons seeking entry to the city. Following the line of the wall toward the magnificent gatehouse, from which hung a pair of gate-bordering black banners embroidered with five gold stars, he focused on the giant trebuchets flanking the gatehouse towers.

"I'm guessing the wall is some sixty feet thick," he rumbled absently.

"How can you tell?" Mat asked, following Ember's line of sight.

"Wall-mounted trebuchets," Ember stated as if that was the only explanation needed.

"Huh?" Mat asked, confused.

"It would need to be a wide, sturdy wall to support the weight of a siege weapon like that, not to mention ammunition," Ember responded as he examined the gatehouse. "Furthermore, the trebuchets are on a rotating dais, giving them a wider range of attack." He grunted, impressed. "Hells, I'd hate to imagine what it would take to break through this wall."

"How in the hells can you tell all this?" Mat responded, stunned by Ember's assessment of the fortifications.

"Intuition," Ember responded cryptically.

"Huh . . .?" Mat uttered as his brow furrowed. Suddenly, his eyes widened as realization dawned on him. "Right! I catch your meaning," he said quietly, drawing an amused smile from Kara before he, too, let his mind reach out along the currents to probe the fortifications.

Though the growing interference from the denizens of the Merset made it difficult to get a clear reading on the wall, much less what lay beyond it, Mat's penchant for city life made it a little easier for him to sort through the noise. When he finally managed to get a good read on the wall and the immediate area behind it, he forced himself to repress an impressed whistle. "Impressive," he stated softly. "It looks like they can be raised and lowered behind the wall, and even moved back on rails, depending on defensive needs . . . and there's a lot of them. Never seen anything like it."

Ember nodded. "Indeed," he agreed as the column came to a halt in the shadow of the gatehouse. "Well, that's a surprise," he said with a grunt as his attention focused on the open gate. "I haven't seen a gate like that in a long time."

Following her brother's gaze, Kara smirked dryly. "I wonder where *that* idea came from," she said drolly.

Five feet thick and banded by equally impressive strips of riveted steel, the panels that made up the main gate jutted from their recessed position in the arched opening which, with the way the steel portcullis loomed above them like a row of wicked teeth, reminded her of a gaping, deadly maw. Anchored midway up the interior of the doors, chains with links thicker than her brother's forearm vanished into the interior gatehouse walls where Kara knew a mechanical system resided to ease the closing and opening of the doors.

"I don't even need to . . . use my intuition to guess it's a triple-layer defense," she said with a knowing smirk and shake of her head. "Woe be to the fool that would dare attack that juggernaut."

"Quite," a soft male voice said from just behind her.

Startled, she spun quickly to find Allanian, a wicked grin on his face, standing behind her, his horse in tow.

"Damn it, Lan!" she said with mock irritation. "You could scare someone to death like that!"

Allanian arched an eyebrow curiously. "Isn't that the point?" he asked innocently.

Rolling her eyes, Kara turned her attention back to the gate and gestured with her head toward where Camilie was pointing their direction while talking with another soldier in a black tabard. "Don't you have someplace to be?"

Smirking, Allanian started around the others. "It appears so. Do try not to get lost," he tossed over his shoulder. "I'd hate to have to come and find you."

Kara rolled her eyes at him and folded her arms beneath her full breasts in consternation.

Seeing Kara's reaction, Ember smirked. "Admit it."

"Admit what?" she replied as she watched Allanian join his fellow soldiers.

"You missed him."

A smile tugged at her lips. "Didn't we all?" she asked, the joy in her voice belying the mock frustration she displayed, as well as the nagging concerns about their situation that weighed on her heart and mind.

Ember shrugged nonchalantly. "Perhaps. At least if we're ever in a bind, we won't want for food. Darlions do make for a good snack, after all."

Kara erupted in loud, musical laughter, drawing curious looks from those closest to them.

Shaking his head in bewilderment at the siblings, Mat said,

"Twisted humor, Ember. Just twisted. Is that a side effect?"

Smirking at Mat, Ember replied, "Of what? Old age? Don't worry, youngling, you'll get there. You've got to have a sense of humor to survive as long as we have."

Rolling his eyes, Mat responded dryly as they and the column started to move again, "Right. . . ."

By the time they reached Allanian, Camilie had moved on with his horse in tow, permitting him to lead his friends onward. Passing within the gatehouse tunnel, the Wardens and Ember quickly examined it. As Kara suspected, the large door chains vanished into steel-reinforced holes in the walls. Furthermore, they noted evenly spaced murder holes in the curved ceiling, as well as a generous number of arrow loops along the flanking walls.

As Ember's gaze returned to what was before them, he smirked and rumbled, "Good guess, Sister."

Smiling as her eyes landed on the raised portcullis and the open second set of doors that were drawing close as they neared the center of the long tunnel, she replied, "Was there ever any doubt?"

"Impressive, isn't it?" Allanian said.

"Not really, no," Kara replied sarcastically as they reached the secondary barrier. "His idea, right?"

Allanian nodded. "To mimic Vallumn Prime and Finallis? Indeed."

Their pace continued to increase as they neared the far end of the tunnel. When it finally deposited them on the far side beyond a third set of the gates, Camilie was waiting for them. Taking the reins of his horse from her, Allanian turned to face his friends and said, "My friends, welcome to Merset – Capitol of Tiliea, and home of the Army of Five Stars."

Reminiscence glowing in her eyes, Kara and the others did their best to take in the multi-tiered city spread before them. Paved with meticulously placed stones and wide enough for four large wagons to travel abreast easily, the avenue they began to traverse cut a gently ascending path through the city, leveling off at each tier before climbing again toward another gate far up the sloping terrain. Piles of snow littered the sides of the city's thoroughfares as if they were haphazard decorations. Most of the structures in their immediate vicinity were made of stone, and smoke pumped skyward from many of their chimneys. Ranging from stout, multi-story inns to broad, single-story businesses and taverns, each building seemed to be reaching eagerly skyward. A coat of snow garnished their dark-blue shingled roofs, while beautiful icicles reached toward the earth from overhangs and windowsills alike. But what impressed and surprised Kara the most as Allanian led them toward the head of their column, were the people.

Granted, she had seen similar brevity, and possibly forced ignorance of the war, in the residence of Haltho. However, here she saw genuine happiness. Yes, there were clear signs that the city was well aware of the war; there was a noticeable military presence in nearly every direction, numerous supply carts moved turtle-like through the main avenues and the narrower side streets, and there were even an unusual number of weapon shops. Yet, despite the dour atmosphere that the weather and such signs should create, she noted joyful laughter in the drum of noise and voices, brightness in the gazes that turned their way, and even open awe in the comments she heard as people stopped for a moment to gaze at their unusual procession.

"Corith continue to bless you all," she thought, happy to see such a sight, but worried that it would not last. *"I cannot imagine life is easy this far north, but while you know of the war — and have surely felt the pain of what it steals without remorse — you have been sheltered from its wrath. I pray it remains so for a very long time."*

"Well, that's an odd sight."

Mat's puzzled tone drew Kara from her thoughts. Startled to realize they were halfway up the first of the broad ramps, it took her a moment to realize Mat was now standing behind her at the ramp's sturdy, chest-high wall. "What's that?" she asked as she returned to him. Coming to a halt next to him, she followed his perplexed gaze.

"This," he said, gesturing over the side of the ramp as Ember came up behind them.

Forty feet wide, and roughly twenty deep, a man-made channel cut northwest to southeast for as far as they could see. Several ramps similar to the one they stood on could be seen in the distance, but they were surprised to see a number of makeshift wooden ramps and scaffolding within the channel. Furthermore, the channel appeared to be home to a number of shelters and piles of refuse, as well as a few fires with people huddled about them. As far as Mat was concerned, it was a clear misuse of a blatant defensive feature that already had him a bit puzzled.

"I don't get it," Mat stated, scratching his head. "Unless this city is sitting above an underground lake, which they intended to pump up to the surface, what reason could they have for making this?"

"Kill channels," Allanian stated as he joined them, startling them.

"Damn it, Lan! What did I tell you?" Kara blurted, this time genuinely irritated that he'd snuck up on her again.

Grinning, he rubbed the nose of his horse. "Sorry," he offered, to which Kara rolled her eyes. "As I was saying, we call them kill channels – though the name may not be all that accurate. We have them between each of the five tiers in this part of the city, all the way up to Vallum Prime, and three more between Prime and Vallum Finallis."

Ember suddenly grunted. "Well, this is new. They're meant to impede enemy progress, I take it? And I'm guessing you can drop the ramps?"

Allanian nodded. "Exactly. What's more, we could fill them with spikes, water, or even oil. It was some time after Doms Gravit'nas' passing," he said with a slight hitch in his voice, which caused Ember and Kara to frown slightly, "that one of the Merandiths – I can't remember which – had the idea to add them to the city. . . . Though, if you ask me, I think someone we're all familiar with had a say in it."

Kara smirked dryly and Ember grunted.

Shrugging slightly, Allanian added with grim pride, "Still, it's an impressive defensive measure. We may not have the imposing walls of Chalin, or the mountainous terrain of Sur'datha, but mark my words – anyone that dares to attempt to take Merset will pay in blood."

Suppressing a shudder, Mat looked at him and asked with an arched eyebrow, "And what about the people?"

Grimacing, Allanian stepped to the wall and looked out over the canal. "Every city, every war," he stated, his voice and eyes soft with regret, "takes its toll – Merset is not immune to this. We've done our best to educate and find work for those with no home or those for whom the war has exacted a costly price, but we can only do so much. There are some down there that find employment in the mines or as day laborers, and there are others whose reasons for such a life are their own. It's a harsh existence, and I would not wish such a life on many. Still," he forced a smile, "there are others that do their best to help. See the bald man in the white robe?"

"A monk?" Kara asked.

Allanian nodded. "Aye. One of many that provide succor to the homeless and destitute."

"Don't they worry about being attacked or robbed?" Mat

asked, surprised.

"I wouldn't doubt it, but they are servants of the Holy Church of Deo, and to assault a holy servant would not only invite House Merandith's wrath, but that of Deo," he finished with a knowing half-smile. Pointing in the distance, he added, "You can see the cathedral's spires over there."

Looking up, they could see the array of spires jutting skyward like elegant pieces of white ice. Sunlight reflected off the blue shingles that peaked through their snow-capped roofs, but without aid, they could make out very little else.

"How big is it?" Ember rumbled.

"Big enough that even you would find it large in your . . . other attire," Allanian responded with a smirk, drawing an impressed grunt from the large man. "Though you cannot see it from here, the Academy lies on the opposite side of the city, facing the cathedral and overlooking the ocean."

Kara shook her head slightly with a disappointed sigh as she turned to face Allanian. "War and religion, with the masses trapped between them; each one bleeding them in their own way. Seems . . . poetic in a morbid fashion." She chuckled sarcastically. "Luthur would have found it less than amusing, all the while debating the hidden meaning behind such an alignment with vigor."

"Really, Kara?" Allanian said, feigning shock. "I don't believe any such intent existed in their placement. The Academy exists on the only ground that was available . . . or so I was told."

Rolling her eyes, she waved him onward. "Don't we have someplace to be?"

Grinning, Allanian responded, "Quite so," before leading them on at a pace that saw them quickly catch up with the column.

Between their large group and the crowded road, their trek to Vallum Prime was slow going. Along the way, the buildings gradually shifted from commercial to residential. Initially, most of the homes they saw were reasonably modest, but between their location and the quality of stone and wood used in their construction, Kara figured their inhabitants were far from poor. Most likely, she thought, the homes of those with smaller incomes were located well off the main thoroughfares. She had never known anyone of noble blood, no matter how altruistic or philanthropic they were, who would want to present their city as anything less than a wonderful place to live, and she doubted Doms Merandith was any different.

As they drew closer to Vallum Prime, and the homes grew

more impressive and opulent, she began to wonder if the area beyond it still resembled, in any fashion, the town that had once stood there. Reaching the wall, her curiosity was briefly put on hold as they paused so that Allanian could confer with the gate's guards. It didn't take long for the sentries to wave them onward, and the column made its way quickly through the gate, which was identical to Vallum Superior's egress point. Once on the other side, any hopes Kara had of their being remnants of the old town were summarily dashed.

Where once the area was home to a modest town, now the new tiers played host to a surprising number of manors. From what she could see as they journeyed toward Vallum Finallis, not only were the ramps lavishly embellished, but even the most humble estates were larger than most people could ever afford. Every structure was made of stone and had at least two chimneys, many of which belched forth smoke. Most of the homes also featured lavish adornments ranging from marble pillars to iron decor and beautiful shutters. Furthermore, each of the manors on the main road was surrounded by either stone walls or iron fences. While some of the barriers looked to be an attempt at privacy, most seemed to be for appearances only. As Kara took it all in, she noted that whether or not the homes were occupied, their approaches were clear of impeding snow, and on more than one occasion, private guards were stationed at the estate's gates near blazing braziers.

As for the people they encountered, there were relatively few. Aside from a couple of stately carriages, the windows of which were shuttered, they passed only a small number of pedestrians. Most of the people had the look of estate servants or officials, but there were a few whose luxurious cloaks and furs were an announcement to all that they held a higher station. However, no matter who they were or their station, their reactions to the eclectic column ranged from simply ignoring them to hushed conversations, or even stares of surprise before they hustled along. Kara, for the most part, ignored them easily enough, and she imagined the opinion of strangers hardly mattered to the Ice Walkers from what she'd been able to glean about them. However, there were a couple of times when the looks cast toward the column were so haughty, so indignant, that even Kara found it difficult to resist the urge to laugh at or slap a few of them.

"Self-righteous, self-important fools," she thought with a sigh. *"No matter the Age or city, they're always there, and always far too many of them."*

"Ideas and civilizations change, but there will always be those who think themselves superior to all," Ember responded through their link, drawing a sad smile from Kara.

"Indeed," she responded plainly.

Upon reaching the last of Merset's grand walls, Vallum Finalis, they paused once more. As Allanian chatted with the guards and gave orders to his men, Kara moved beside Mat and grinned at him knowingly. Seeing this, he gave her a confused and somewhat worried look.

"What?" he finally asked when she remained silent.

"You're in for a treat," she stated coyly.

His face screwed up in puzzlement. "You mean the keep?"

Kara nodded.

"I could make out some of it from afar, and as we climbed through the city. I must admit, it certainly looked impressive."

Kara's grin widened. "Oh, it is."

Before Mat could respond, the column started moving again. When they reached Allanian, he fell in beside Mat.

"First time here, correct?" he asked as they entered the tunnel, his soft voice laced with anticipation.

"It is."

Smiling, Allanian added, "Well then, you are in for a treat. I don't imagine you'll see anything like this on Solarson, save for a few *select* places."

"So Kara stated," Mat responded, unimpressed by their cryptic statements.

Grinning, Allanian clapped him on the back, and winked knowingly at Kara.

Mat's puzzlement vanished beneath a wave of unexpected awe as he caught sight of the keep through the other end of the tunnel. As they drew closer to the exit and more of the keep came into view, his pace began to slow, and it finally began to dawn on him just what Kara and Allanian were hinting at. With anticipation now starting to build within him, it seemed like it took an eternity to exit the tunnel. However, when they finally did, he, along with a few of the Ice Walkers, came to a complete stop and openly gawked at what stood before them.

Leaning into him, Kara whispered gleefully, "I told you so."

Turning to face his friends with a wide grin on his face, Allanian announced, his ears twitching with pride, "Welcome, my friends, to Stoneheart."

Taller and wider than any keep Mat had ever laid eyes upon, Stoneheart was a towering mass of gray stone blanketed with a shimmering coat of snow and bejeweled with magnificent icicles. Sweeping buttresses seemed intent on occupying as much of the stone-paved courtyard as they could even as they gracefully supported the multitude of elevated walkways, spires and walls that comprised the keep. As for the cathedral-inspired main building, it and its four primary spires were seated atop a landing that could be reached via a staircase that grew wider as it descended the foundation some sixty feet to the courtyard. A beautiful steepled roof of blue shingles capped off the main structure at nearly two hundred feet, and primary egress was provided by an impressive set of steel-banded, ironwood double doors. Set deep within a layered recess beneath a circular stained-glass window, which featured five gold stars against a blue field, Mat felt like the towering doors were there to keep the mortal realm separate from a glorious land that resided within the confines of the keep.

Eager to get a better look at the magnificent structure, he let his senses float along the currents high into the sky, and what he saw made his breath catch in his throat. The foundation of the keep was in the shape of a five-point star, the arms of which flanked staircases similar to the one he was facing. Adding to the grandeur of the sight were the large number of balconies, patios, and gardens he could see, many of which were elevated or hidden away from prying eyes. It was spectacular to behold, and he was positive he could spend quite a bit of time studying what was before him, but he knew that wasn't possible at the moment, so he forced himself to continue his tour. As such, he soon reached the back of the structure where he found, at the top point of the star, a gold-domed rotunda off which a sweeping balcony overlooked a trio of waterfalls that spilt from the cliffside into the sea far below. Trimmed in gold, and decorated with faux arches that were home to celestial carvings and a dozen stained-glass windows, it seemed odd that such a wonderful piece of architecture was hidden from sight.

Beautiful and breathtaking as the rotunda was, Mat still found himself surprised by the artistic touches he spotted around the keep as he continued on. From the sweeping lattice and knotwork patterns that adorned buttresses and arches alike, to the marble used in the gardens, balconies and pillars, there were aesthetic choices to both please and astound the eye. Furthermore, he found the five-star sigil featured both prominently and subtly throughout both the keep and grounds. Yet, what astounded him the most were the dragons. Be it on the roof edging, atop an arch, or around spire tops, stone dragons, both intimidating and regal, looked out upon the courtyard and city like tireless sentries.

"It's . . ." he started to say when he finally found his voice.

"Like something you expect from a Warden's keep?" Kara interjected in his mind.

"Yes," he responded in awe.

"This place . . ." Kara started to inform him, her tone suddenly wistful. *"This place is old, Mat."*

"How old?" he asked, unable to pry his senses from the keep.

"Very old. It was one of the first keeps we built after the Exodus."

Mat's eyes widened with realization. *"Corith be good! Whose was it?"*

"For the sake of others, Allanian gave you the name they know it by," Kara replied, seemingly ignoring his question. *"Its true name is Dragon's Rest, and it was home to the greatest man I have ever known. . . . Welcome, Mat—"* she stated to say, her tone so sad that it prompted him to look at her for tears. Though she was not crying, the deep, haunting sorrow in her eyes was evident. *"Welcome, Mat, to Dragon's Rest — Luthur's first keep on Triclose, and the last home of the Syvantoza Order."*

Chapter Twenty

"**S**even-hundred thirty-five talons, Doma! Paid in full and in advance, no less! And not only was the delivery late, but it was barely more than half the agreed-upon amount!" the aged merchant declared indignantly, pointing at the weathered man next to him.

Clad in worn, functional brown wool attire that was as marred with dust and soot as his bald head and lined, full face, the weathered man's green eyes burned with anger, and his calloused hands clinched tightly about his leather cap. "Doma," he stated, his rough voice civil despite his obvious disquiet with the accusation leveled against him. "I won't argue that the shipment was smaller than the total amount agreed upon. But," he glared at the merchant, "the mines are overburdened as is – begging your pardon, Doma. He was told that his shipment might be split."

The mix of sun and lamplight bathing the room played over the merchant's well-manicured black hair and silver-embroidered knee boots as he turned to glare at his opponent. "Paltry excuses!" he nearly barked, his disgust plain to hear in his aged but somewhat soft voice. "A deal is a deal, and it should be honored in full!" he declared vehemently, his blue eyes flashing as he tugged on the silver-embroidered black coat he wore over a white silk shirt tucked into ruddy pants.

Doma Marie se'Trivant Merandith fought the urge to sigh and managed to keep the expression on her slightly plump face amicable as the older men argued. The number of petitioners was more extensive than usual today and seemed to be growing by the week. It was undeniable that the increase in complaints and demands for aid was the result of the growing number of attacks by raiders, but as disheartening and frustrating as it was for her, it was the news she'd received in the early morning hours that was responsible for her lack of focus. Between brief moments of illness and the business of the morning, she had yet to share the emotionally conflicting news with anyone, and she was growing more anxious to do so by the hour. Glancing out over the throne room in an attempt to ignore her churning emotions and the bickering of the two petitioners she was currently entertaining, she quelled the urge to scream in tired frustration at the number of people awaiting her.

Located at the rear of the keep, the vastness of the domed throne room made the number of petitioners seem less than they really were. Halfway between the walls and a large, raised dais at the center of the chamber, an arched colonnade of stone circled the rotunda. Silver, florid knotwork patterns inlaid in the colonnade were bathed in a mix of light from the magnificent lamp-lit chandelier hanging well above the dais, as well as the sunlight passing through the sealed glass doors at the rear of the room and the twelve stained-glass windows evenly spread around the exterior wall. Throughout the day – to varying degrees – the effect it produced immersed the central area in a soft glow that, as it did now, struck Marie as otherworldly. Even the way the light played off the banners of their allies, which hung from the colonnade's arches, seemed ethereal.

A polite cough from the House Magister, who stood to the right of the two petitioners, snapped her attention back to the situation at hand. Shifting on the plush, black-upholstered seat of her husband's throne, she tried to get comfortable and refocus on the petitioners. Made of rich ironwood, and situated at the heart of the dais, the throne's tall, broad back was made of cold steel and molded into five overlapping stars. Silver knotwork, similar to what adorned the colonnade, gracefully decorated stars and wood alike. Under normal conditions, she would have either been standing beside the large throne or occupying a smaller seat, but with Kale away, she was in charge, and that meant sitting in a chair that was clearly not meant for a heavily pregnant woman.

Running a hand over the white and blue gown of silks draped over her swollen belly, she pushed a lock of mulberry-red hair behind her ear that had fallen free from the array of pins holding her mass of tresses in a jeweled bun. She then tugged close the thick white cloak of bear fur draped about her petite frame as she struggled to stay focused on the subject at hand. Tired and growing increasingly irritated with the men, she quickly glanced at the throng of petitioners and spectators that were kept at a respectable distance by a dozen House Guards, and fought down an agitated sigh.

Forcing her attention back to the two men before her, she fixed them with a firm, blue-eyed stare and bade them with as much authority as she could currently muster in her soft voice, "Gentlemen! If you please – is there not a compromise you can reach on your own?"

"Doma," the merchant began, his tone and posture bordering on belligerent, "we have a binding contract! While I understand that the mines are controlled by House Merandith, and there is a war going on, I do not believe it would look favorably on Ho–"

"Careful, sir, lest you forget yourself," Marie interrupted, her words taking on a hard edge.

Stunned at the interruption, the merchant recoiled a bit beneath the sudden firmness of Marie's gaze and words. "My apologies, Doma Merandith," he finally offered as he struggled to regain his composure. "I did not mean to give offense or impugn House Merandith's good name. You have always been fair and just with dealings both judicial and financial. My deepest apologies," he finished with a bow, hoping to salvage his position in the case.

Nodding slowly, Marie flashed him a disarming smile. "No need for an apology, sir. Your passion for your business is commendable. I shall dismiss it as nothing more than a flare of excitability such as one might see in an exuberant child."

A few chortles greeted the thinly veiled jab, and the merchant grew flush with embarrassment as he bowed again. "Thank you, Doma."

"Now," she stated, "if you are not willing to come to a compromise, do either of you have proof of your claims?"

Almost in unison, both men brought forth folded parchments and presented them to her.

"Magister, if you would?" Marie asked sweetly of the stout, middle-aged woman in a black and silver robe standing off to the right of the petitioners. White-streaked, auburn hair flowing about her shoulders, she nodded and moved before the men. "Documents, please," she declared in a robust voice that brokered no quarter as she fixed them with a steely, gray-eyed glare.

Taking each document in her hands, the long fingers of which were adorned with silver rings, she unfolded them both, revealing them to be three pages long. Examining each quickly with her trained eyes, she then turned and approached Marie. Handing the documents to Doma Merandith, she then moved to the right side of the throne, leaned in and spoke softly with her.

Reading over the documents, Marie listened to her magister as the woman pointed to a number of the clauses in the contract. Finally, Marie nodded and said, "Thank you, Magister," as she handed the contracts back to her. As her magister returned to the petitioners and presented them with the documents, Marie stated, "There does not appear to be any discrepancies between the documents; furthermore, they are standard House Merandith supply contracts. As such," she fixed the merchant with a stern glare, "I fail to see what grounds you have for demanding nearly three-fourths of your payment back."

"As I've stated before, Doma," he responded, his tone growing agitated and indignant. "Failure to deliver, both on time and in full! This is a clear breach of contract, and the compensation I have asked for is equal to the breach!"

Sitting forward as best she could, she declared forcefully, "There is no doubt that the full amount agreed upon was not delivered, but what you did receive was on time. However, your bold – and outrageous – demands for this kind of compensation are disgraceful!"

The mine overseer fidgeted nervously as Doma Merandith stared down the merchant. Finally, as the main door to the throne room opened and shut, Marie sat back and said with a more peaceful air, "That being said, the mine is at least in partial breach of contract, and the terms of the contract will be honored in full." Turning her gaze to the mine overseer, she asked as hurried footfalls echoed about the room, "Will you be able to fulfill the order as promised?"

The man dipped his head eagerly. "Yes, Doma. His order will be ready in two days – I swear it."

Marie nodded. "Good," she stated, suddenly curious about the whispered conversations growing amongst the spectators and waiting petitioners as a few of them looked toward the main doors. Turning to the merchant, she declared in a tone that brokered no argument, "Magister Tyleana will escort you to the treasury, where you will receive the contractual late fee of seventy-five talons per day – as you agreed to."

"Yes, Doma," both men stated with a bow, the overseer relieved, and the merchant disgruntled.

"Good. You are dismissed." As Magister Tyleana stepped forward and led the two men away, Marie looked to the elderly scribe in an official black and silver robe sitting to her left in a simple chair with a portable desk on his lap, and asked, "Who is next?"

Pushing his spectacles up on his broad, flat nose, the pale man with short white hair said in a wizened voice, "Doma, if it pleases you, the next petitioner is from the Tanner's Guild. She seeks–"

"Excuse the interruption, Doma," interrupted a smooth male voice from the front of the crowd.

Turning her attention to the speaker, she said, "Yes, Commander Fulorton?"

Average in height and of medium build, Katan Fulorton cut a striking figure as he walked past the partition of guards, the impact of his black knee boots echoing dully about the room. Short-cut brown hair topped a clean-shaven, strikingly handsome face that was the adoration of many of the keep's female residents, and his loose black shirt and brown pants were well-maintained. His movements were smooth as he approached the throne, and the way he carried himself displayed the pride with which he bore the five red stars embroidered on the right breast of his purple-trimmed House Guard tabard.

Ascending the dais, his vibrant blue eyes fixed on Marie, he then leaned in and stated for her ears only, "Allanian has returned."

Stunned by the statement, she blinked rapidly as sudden apprehension gripped her throat. "He wasn't due back for at least another week. Is there something wrong?" she asked, keeping her voice low.

Katan offered her a reassuring smile. "No, Doma. In fact, we have guests."

"Guests?" she prompted as a few impatient grumbles made their way through the awaiting petitioners.

"Ice Walkers, Doma."

Eyes suddenly wide with surprise, Marie said, her voice turning joyful, "This wasn't totally unexpected, but given Doms Volstur's health, I. . . ." She shook her head. "Never mind. I'll receive them here. Please dismiss everyone, Katan."

"Yes, Doma." Turning to face the gathering, he declared loud enough to be heard by all, "That will be all for the day, ladies and gentlemen!" Groans and curses of disappointment greeted his declaration as he continued, "If your disputes or petitions cannot be handled by Magister Tyleana's office, you may return here next week!"

Slowly, the guards ushered the gathered petitioners toward the smaller doors on the right and left sides of the throne room near the front of the rotunda, both of which now stood open with two House Guards flanking each one. A small number of petitioners lingered, begging to be heard, but a few words from Katan, along with the urging of other members of the House Guard, eventually saw the throne room emptied.

Once the side doors were shut tight, Marie composed herself and then nodded to Katan. "Send them in."

Katan repeated the order, his voice echoing throughout the chamber, and the guards at the main doors pulled them open, revealing Allanian at the head of a small contingent. Behind him were four bronze-masked guards carrying a fur-lined ivory sedan chair and one frail-looking occupant. Girded in white furs, and sealskins, and adorned with blue knotwork tattoos, the Ice Walkers were normally an impressive sight to behold, but the person seated in the sedan chair sapped some of that aura away. Bundled in white furs, with his face hidden behind a wailing bronze mask that matched those of his guards, Doms Volstur looked as if the furs and chair were trying to swallow him whole. As for the last of the party, Doma Volstur was dressed similarly to the guards as she stood mask-less and proud at the chair's side.

Striding forth from the throne room's elegant, sun-lit ante-chamber, Allanian led the party toward Marie at a respectful pace. Bringing the group to a halt just before the dais, Allanian stepped upon the dais and bowed deeply as the sedan chair was carefully lowered to the ground. "Doma Merandith," he declared as he stood upright, "may I present to you Doms and Doma Volstur of House Volstur, rulers of the icelands of Tol'radir."

As Allanian stepped aside, Marie stood with Katan's assistance. Grimacing slightly, Marie steadied herself on Katan's arm before smiling warmly at the royal couple. "Be welcome at our fire, Doms and Doma Volstur," she intoned respectfully with a welcoming nod of her head. "Your visit is a surprise, to be sure, but a warm and welcome one, nonetheless," she finished with a bright smile.

Doma Volstur returned the nod with a welcoming, thin-lipped smile on her lined, sun-darkened, round face. Marie had spent very little time in the doma's presence, and in every instance, the shaved sides of her head, her now entirely white braids, and her strong blue eyes lent her smile — no matter how warm or welcoming — a somewhat vicious air.

"Our thanks, Doma Merandith — wife and mother of blood-of-our-blood," Doma Volstur responded formally. "Please seat yourself, Doma. There is no need for you to exert yourself on our behalf."

Marie smiled gratefully. "My thanks, Doma," she responded before taking her seat with Katan's aid.

"I hope our presence is not unwelcome?" she asked as Marie settled herself, her throaty, aged voice taking on a casual demeanor.

Taking a deep breath, Marie let it out slowly in an attempt to ease some of her discomfort. She then responded with a broad smile, "Not at all. I only wish we had known of your impending arrival sooner. We could have prepared a proper welcome for you."

"My apologies for not sending word; our decision to descend from the ice was made at the last moment. With my husband's health, we had to be sure it was . . . the proper time," she finished with a barely perceptible grimace.

464

Marie's heart broke for the pain she saw in her counterpart's eyes. The constant worry over Kale's wellbeing was maddening in its own right, but to watch a loved one steadily march toward the inevitable and know nothing could be done to prevent it? It was a hell she hoped to never know.

Turning her attention to the masked man in the sedan chair, Marie smiled warmly. "And how are you, Doms Volstur? I hope the journey treated you well?"

Doms Volstur made a rough attempt at a chuckle, which drew a concerned glance from his wife, before stating in a voice weakened by age and failing health, "Frail, but strong enough to visit the blood-of-my-blood, and see my great-grandchild greet the world with a cry of defiance."

Marie offered him a smile that belied her urge to grimace at the imagery his remark unjustly summoned. She wished with all her heart that her children would know a life without the horrors of war, and though she knew his remarks were not intended to summon such thoughts, they had, and it made her stomach twist with fear. "The child will be strong, I have no doubt," she responded confidently, shoving her concerns aside. Caressing her swollen belly, she added, "It won't be long now. I had long feared Kale would not be here for the birth. However," she smiled bright and wide, "much to my relief and great joy, it appears that he will be home in time!"

Looks of surprise greeted her statement.

"Are you sure of this, Doma Merandith?" Katan asked, giving voice to what he and the others were thinking.

Looking up at Katan, she nodded. "I received word this morning via raven-wing. It must have slipped my mind amidst the morning duties. My apologies, Katan."

Katan bowed respectfully. "No apologies are needed, Doma! This is joyous news!"

"If I may," Allanian interjected, "When is Doms Merandith due to arrive?"

"Weather permitting, in four days or so," she said, turning her attention to the darlion.

"That is fast . . . and concerning," Allanian said, his tone grave.

Marie forced a smile. "I believe he only wishes to be here when his child is born," she stated with confidence.

Allanian saw through her facade, but held his tongue.

"We shall have to make arrangements to celebrate his safe return, but that is for later." Looking at her guests, she said, "This is hardly the proper place to visit with family. Would you care to join me for dinner?"

Doma Volstur nodded. "It would be our pleasure."

"Excellent! Allanian, if you would, please see to our guests' accommodations."

"I took the liberty of putting them in the north wing, Doma. I thought it would offer them an excellent view of the sea, and its hearths are quite warm."

"An excellent choice," Marie agreed.

Allanian nodded. "Katan, please see our guests to their lodging – I need to speak with Doma Merandith."

Katan saluted, fist to heart. "Yes, sir," he stated before approaching Doms and Doma Volstur. "If you would, please follow me?" he asked courteously.

"Until dinner, Doma," Doma Volstur said to Marie, inclining her head respectfully as the sedan bearers carefully lifted their frail doms' chair to their shoulders.

As they followed Katan back toward the throne room's main doors, Marie fixed Allanian with a curious look. Once the Ice Walkers were gone and the doors were closed, she asked, "Why did you pass the task to Katan? Is there something wrong?"

Approaching Marie, Allanian replied, "Nothing that I am aware of, Doma. I do need to make a report on the raiders, and I am curious as to why Doms Merandith is returning home so soon; however, we can address those issues at your leisure, Doma."

Marie nodded her approval. "That still doesn't explain your decision. It's not like you to pass on such a task."

Allanian grimaced slightly, the reproach in Marie's tone clear to him. "I know, Doma, and I ask for your forgiveness in that matter. But we have other guests this day."

"More guests, Allanian?" Marie asked, surprised. "Were you out fighting off the bandits, or busy rounding up a menagerie for some party I'm not aware of?" she asked, amused.

"Fighting, Doma," Allanian responded with a chuckle. "Both the discovery of the Ice Walkers and our other guests were quite by accident. I felt it proper that I escort them here. Rest assured, my squad and I will be back out there on the morrow unless you have need of us here."

Marie smiled gently. "Relax, Allanian. I am hardly upset with you. I simply could not resist teasing you a bit."

Allanian inclined his head. "My thanks, Doma."

"Now, who are these guests of yours? Anyone Kale or I know?"

Unlikely," he responded with a shake of his head. "They are friends of mine and Mathis from Solarson."

Heartache clamped down on Marie's chest at the mention of Mathis, but she managed to flash a warm smile as she stated, "Oh really? That is indeed a surprise and a welcome one at that. It would be my pleasure to receive them."

"Excellent, Doma," Allanian replied with a respectful bow. Turning toward the main door, he bellowed, "Send them in!"

The guards once more pulled open the large doors, and a moment later, three people stepped into view. As they approached, Marie had to suppress a shudder at the sight of the large man walking behind the other two. Never had she seen someone so large and so .. . demonic. Dark spectacles concealed his eyes, and a gray longcoat swallowed his massive fame, but between angry red hair and a jaw so large that she imagined he could bite a rahken in half, she had no trouble believing the man was one to be reckoned with.

As for the other two. . . .

Her breath caught in her throat and her hands tightened on the throne's arms as they drew close enough for her to make out their features. A woman with the unmistakable sky-blue hair of a Velusyian, carrying two blades of Velusyian make; and the man with raven-black, purple-tinted hair, whose young face and dark eyes seemed overly cocky. The third, while striking in his own right, was not mentioned in the dispatch she had received. As for the two that concerned her, while their clothing did not match that of the description she had received, there was a foreign air to them that was unmistakable.

Slowly, her welcoming smile began to fade. By the time the trio came to a halt before the dais, she was positive the two matched the descriptions she had received, and her face had become a cold mask that elicited looks of concern from the newcomers.

"Doma Merandith," Allanian started to say, unaware of Marie's icy mood, "may I present to you Karalisa Yokonagi. . . ." His words trailed off as his vision switched to Marie. "Doma?" he asked, his words heavy with concern. "Is something amiss?"

Marie did not respond immediately. According to Allanian,

these three people, whose gazes were growing more worried with her lingering silence, were friends of his and Mathis. Try as she might, she could find nothing to cast doubt on the missive she'd received from Kale, and that broke her heart.

"Doma?" Allanian prompted again, naked alarm consuming his face.

Finally, she steeled herself and met his prying eyes with a stern gaze that nearly made him flinch. "Captain-Commander Allanian Raoitae – Arrest these two!" she ordered, pointing at Kara and Mat.

"Doma?!" Allanian asked, stunned.

As surprised as her friends, Kara looked from Marie to Allanian, seeking some sort of explanation for the sudden order. "Doma–" Kara started to say, her tone soft and respectful, as she prevented her brother from stepping before her.

"You have your orders, Captain!" Marie interrupted, her tone and posture brokering no argument.

Taken aback, Allanian nearly gawked at Marie before, despite her tone and bearing, he asked, "But, Doma – why?"

Looking at Allanian, she locked eyes with him, and what he saw in her gaze squeezed his heart with fear.

"Arrest them, Captain, for the kidnapping and suspected murder of Mathis Sormantale and Shi'doms Amroth Merandith!"

*

"Well, isn't this just great!" Mat bemoaned as he turned about, examining the small but clean cell he found himself in.

Stalking to the steel-banded, ironwood door, he peeked through the small, barred panel in it and shouted at the trio of guards seated at a table in the lamp-lit guardroom adjacent to his cell, "This isn't the way you treat guests!"

A rattle of chainmail and a couple of cold glares from the guards greeted his protest.

"It won't do you any good," Kara chided in his mind as the guards turned their attention back to their game of Pentagris.

Mat snorted and made his way over to the threadbare cot and sat down hard, drawing a groan of protest from the aged wood. *"No, but it made me feel better."* He sighed in frustration through the link. *"I can't believe he actually arrested us!"*

"What would you have him do? Explain to her what really hap-

pened?"

"It would have been a start."

The dry chuckle he received from Kara made him scowl.

"Oh yes, that conversation would have been much better. 'Doma, if you'll let me explain, I can clear this all up. He wasn't kidnapped. He's just fine. You see, Mathis wasn't really Mathis; his real name is Damion Masumaite, and he's an ancient guardian of Kylir. Amroth has the ability to be one of these, so he's taken him to train.'"

Mat rolled his eyes. "Fine! I get your point!" he huffed. "Where are you?"

"Three cells down from you."

Mat grinned wryly. "Guess they didn't want us talking to each other."

"The joke's on them, I suppose," she replied with a wry chuckle.

"Right," he responded with mild amusement. "So," he began, his tone turning serious, "what do we do now? We have better things to do than lounge about in a cell . . . even if it's one of the cleanest I've ever seen."

"We wait," Kara responded matter-of-factly. "Breaking down the doors and vanishing would not only make it more difficult to do our job, but it would make Lan's position far more awkward than it likely is. Arresting us was his only choice. Be thankful that the doma was unsure of Ember's involvement — he could have just as easily ended up like us. More importantly, our crusaders are in Allanian's hands instead of locked away or — Corith forbid — a trophy for some unwitting fool."

"Right. . . . I guess that is a blessing," he replied, the presence of his crusader on the edge of his senses telling him the weapon resided far above him. Suddenly, he snorted in amusement. "You know," he said, looking about his small cell, "I'd love to see them try and put Ember in here. He'd barely fit!"

"True," Kara responded, mildly amused. "If it makes you feel any better," she added, her tone turning conciliatory, "I've already spoken with Lan. Until Doms Merandith returns, Ember's movements have been restricted, and he's to be under constant guard. Limited as he is, he can still be our eyes and ears for now."

"And what about the kid? All it would take is his return to clear this mess up."

"Lan is going to contact Damion when he gets a chance. The last thing I want to do is reach out across that kind of distance — Corith knows we don't need to let any of the Betrayers know where we are."

Recalling their violent arrival on Triclose, Mat nodded grimly. *"Yeah. . . . I don't want anything resembling a repeat of that horrid night. So, do you think your brother will bring him back?"*

Kara remained silent for a moment. *"To be honest — I don't know,"* she declared thoughtfully. *"As much as I hope he will put a quick end to this, we don't know the state of Amroth's training. He may deem it necessary for us to remain here for a while."*

"That's just wonderful," Mat stated derisively.

"Believe me, I don't like it either. But if he were to bring Amroth back too soon. . . . Well, let's just say that a believable cover story would be the least of his — or our — worries."

Mat grimaced. *"Right. So, we wait, then?"*

"We wait," Kara confirmed. *"We wait, and we pray Allanian can do his job without incident or. . . ."*

"Or what?"

She sighed across the link. *"There are Betrayers on Triclose, Mat. Not to mention blackhearts, or possibly more of those . . ."* Mat sensed a repulsive shudder through the link, *"those shadow drakuma. There are dark forces at work, and they are maneuvering toward an objective with an urgency that seems to be growing."*

"Corith be good," Mat breathed, feeling the weight of her words, *"I hadn't given much thought to it. So, are you still sure we should remain cooped up in here?"*

"Yes, Mat, we wait," she responded quickly. *"Now, if you don't mind, I think I will meditate for a bit."*

Cutting the connection swiftly, Kara pushed off from where she'd been leaning against her cell door and moved to the rickety bed along the rear wall. Taking a seat on it, she folded and crossed her legs before resting her arms on her knees. She then took a deep breath, closed her eyes, and let it out. It should have been a simple thing for her to find her center and relax. Unfortunately, the nagging sensation she'd felt since joining Allanian and the Ice Walkers on their trek to Merset kept clawing at her mind. Thankfully, she eventually managed to suppress the disturbing thought and find her center. However, as her mind drifted toward a state of peaceful, reflective solitude, a single thought flashed through her mind, *"We wait, Mat. . . . We wait and we pray."*

*

"I know I may be overstepping my bounds – but I must protest!" Allanian declared vehemently, his haunting voice thick with the barely contained fury that had grown within him since his friends' detainment. Pacing across the room between the sturdy, thick oak desk at the center of the modest study and the lone chair set before it, his fists were clenched at his sides as he fought to remain calm.

Seated in the plush, high-back chair behind the large desk, the faces of which were adorned with carvings of majestic creatures ranging from gryphons to proud dragons, Marie calmly watched Allanian's irate trek. Light from the blazing hearth in the right-hand wall, as well as the brass lanterns spread evenly along the walls, set eerie shadows dancing about the windowless room, which lent Allanian a terrifying air. It would have been a truly unsettling sight if Marie didn't know him better, but it still twisted her gut to see him in such a state. In fact, she couldn't recall ever seeing him like this.

"And just what would you have me do?" Marie asked, bringing Allanian to a halt before the single star carved on the front of the desk.

Leaning over, Allanian planted his hands firmly on the neatly organized desktop, causing the brass lamp on the front-right corner to shake. "The evidence you have is purely circumstantial!" he declared with conviction, every ounce of gentleness gone from his tone. "Put them under guard! Put them under house arrest! Just not the dungeon!"

Marie sighed and her visage softened at the mix of passion and hurt she saw in his ice-blue eyes and heard in his voice. She had no doubt that Allanian believed what he said to be true, and she even had her own concerns about the situation. However, the newcomers did match the descriptions she'd been provided, which left her very little choice. She couldn't let them have free roam of the keep, let alone Merset, no matter how much he protested or vouched for them, and he knew it.

Leaning against the bookshelves behind the desk, which were filled with large tomes ranging from war to philosophy, Katan saw the anger and hurt in his captain's eyes. It was a shocking sight to behold, and one he did not like. Seeking to assuage Allanian's concerns, he interjected, his tone conciliatory, "Sir, if I may?"

"What?" Allanian snapped while keeping his gaze locked with Marie's.

Flinching visibly at his captain's tone, Katan said, "Only the two mentioned in Doms Merandith's missive have been detained. The third is free to roam the keep – within reason – while under guard. I know that you feel your friends have been wronged, but Doma Merandith has done only what she could."

Marie smiled weakly. "Thank you, Katan. While you have the right of it, I can speak for myself."

Chastised, Katan said, "My apologies, Doma. I didn't mean to presume."

Glancing at Katan, Marie offered him a consoling smile. "Think nothing of it." Turning her attention back to Allanian, she affirmed, "Katan is right, Captain. Circumstantial as it may be, my husband —your doms – has declared Mathis and Amroth missing – and possibly dead! Those two were cited as the only ones to have had prolonged contact with them. Furthermore, the night our friends – our family – vanished, so did they! If there is anything you can offer that could prove their innocence, I will gladly listen and consider it! Otherwise, whether or not they are guilty is for Kale to decide!"

Frustration tore at Allanian's stomach. He knew the truth of the matter, but he was in no position to divulge such knowledge. Besides, he knew that the truth would be viewed, at best, as a desperate attempt to clear his friends' names, or at worst, see him demoted or dismissed for mental instability. Seeing that Marie was awaiting a response, a thought dawned on him, and he quickly offered, "If they all vanished on the same day, then how did they get here so quickly? More importantly, why come to the home of the very people they wronged?"

Conflicted emotions played across Marie's face, and for a moment, Allanian thought he had gotten through to her. That brief hope died when her visage hardened and she shook her head. "Unburdened, motivated, and without a care for how many horses one kills, one can travel very quickly. As for coming here, I'd say plausible deniability. They may have hoped to arrive here before any word reached us, thus exonerating themselves."

Searching Marie's eyes for any hint of weakness in her stance, Allanian found none. Standing up with a barely suppressed growl of irritation, he stalked around the two chairs and end table situated before the hearth and grabbed the mantle tightly. Glaring at the dancing flames for a time, did his best to calm himself before finally conceding, "I understand your position, Doma, and will not fight you further on it."

"Allanian," Marie replied, her tone softening, "I truly am sorry. As much as I would like to believe you, I have to respect Kale's orders. He will be home soon, and then we can sort this terrible mess out. As we discussed earlier, the one you called Ember will be free to go and do as he pleases within the keep and within reason. As for the other two . . . . I hope you do understand why I cannot allow you to personally oversee them. As it is, I have already bent protocol by al-

472

lowing you to retain their possessions."

"I do . . . and I am grateful for the courtesy you have extended me," Allanian replied coldly as his ears twitched slightly and his grip tightened on the mantle.

"I know this is rough for you," Marie stated, her tone sympathetic, "but Katan will be in charge of their well-being, and I promise you they will be fed well and want for nothing until Kale settles the matter."

"I promise, Captain – no harm will come to them, and they will be treated with respect," Katan avowed firmly.

Allanian wanted to roll his eyes. He knew they meant well and would do as they promised, but it did little to quell his sour feelings about the situation. Pushing away from the mantle, Allanian straightened his tabard before turning to face Marie. "Understood, Doma," he stated firmly and formally. "Will that be all?"

Marie frowned at his formal tone, but thought better of trying to console him further. "The evening is yours. Katan can escort me to dinner with our guests. Just do me one favor, if you would?"

"Yes, Doma?"

"Look in on Shalen, would you? She's spent most of the day with Lalandra, and I know she would be thrilled to see you."

"Of course, Doma," Allanian replied with a respectful bow before making a hasty exit.

Once the heavy ironwood door closed behind the angry captain, Marie let out a remorseful sigh.

"Is there a problem, Doma?" Katan asked, concerned, as he took a step toward her.

Marie waved him off. "I never like delivering bad news – especially to family."

Katan nodded. "You had no other choice, and he knows that. His anger with you and Doms Merandith will be fleeting."

Marie sighed again. "I know, but still. . . ." She shook her head, banishing the thoughts. "It will work itself out in time. For now, I have a dinner to attend. Fetch me one of my thick cloaks, Katan. These upper levels have gotten too damnably cold in recent days, and I sorely miss my husband's warmth."

"Anger does not become you, Captain. Is everything alright?"

So focused was he on his own inner turmoil, Allanian was startled by the seemingly sudden appearance of the woman on the landing of the winding staircase he was just about to set foot upon. Blinking rapidly at the blue-eyed young woman, he said, "My apologies, Doma! You startled me."

Doma Lalandra se'Galivantra Trivant's thin red lips parted in a disarming smile as she pushed a stray lock of her shoulder-length, wheat-blonde hair behind her ear, causing her dangling diamond earring to sparkle in the lamplight as it swayed gently. "No apologies needed, Captain," she replied, her throaty voice warm and welcoming. "You appeared distracted, and given the day's events, I am not surprised. I am deeply sorry about your friends. I do hope this whole mess will be cleared up soon."

Allanian found the sincerity of the sympathetic expression on Lalandra's slender, tanned face to be genuine, eliciting a thankful smile from him. "As do I, Doma. This is merely a matter of an ill-timed coincidence. My friends are innocent of the charges . . . but that is a small problem compared to the disappearance of Mathis and Shi'doms Merandith."

Lalandra folded her hands together before the jeweled red bodice she wore over the low-cut, green silk gown that clung to her figure. "Yes, that is horrible news," she replied, her modest bosom heaving with a deep sigh. "I pray to Deo that they simply had reason to leave Haltho quickly . . . and if not, that they will be found hale and whole soon."

Allanian ground his teeth together, fighting the urge to let it be known that all was well with Amroth and Mathis. "Thank you, Doma," he said instead, with a polite bow. "I'm sure they will. But enough of dour topics – I have it on good authority that Doms Trivant will be with Doms Merandith when he returns."

Lalandra's smile widened. "So I was told! I have missed him as much as Marie has missed Kale!"

"Will you seek to head home?"

"Not that my time with Marie has been anything but wonderful, but I do miss Haltho and the sea," she replied wistfully. "Alas, with the situation here, and the difficulty of winter travel, I believe it would be prudent – and right – of us to remain and lend what aid we can in House Merandith's time of need."

"I am thankful for the offer, Doma, and I have no doubt that Doms and Doma Merandith will be, too." He paused, then his eyes widened with sudden realization. "My apologies, Doma! I am likely keeping you from something important! I did not mean to take up your time!"

Lalandra dismissed his apology with a wave of a ringed hand. "Think nothing of it. I just came from looking in on Shalen for her mother, and was on my way to join Marie and the Vultors for a late dinner."

"Ah, I was just on my way to visit the shi'doma. Is she well?"

"Quite," Lalandra said with a warm, yet weary smile. Chuckling, she added, "She is quite the handful. Thankfully, she wore herself out after her lessons. It's been my pleasure to babysit her, but I don't see how any parent keeps up with a child! So much energy!"

Allanian let out a small laugh. "Indeed. It's commendable that Doma Merandith seeks to be a part of her children's lives instead of relying solely on a nanny."

"Quite. I'm not sure I could attempt what she's doing." She laughed. "Still, it would be an honor to give my husband a child."

"Mother willing, you will. I have no doubt you will make a fine mother."

Lalandra blushed at the praise. "My thanks, Captain," she replied softly. Clearing her throat, she banished the intimate thoughts the talk had summoned. "While the conversation has been pleasant, Captain, but I must be on my way lest Marie thinks I have abandoned her. It should be an interesting night; I've never met an Ice Walker."

"Indeed. It is an experience. If you'll excuse me, Doma," he finished with a bow.

Lalandra started to step around him. "Oh," she stated, coming to a halt, "Shalen is asleep, Captain. You're welcome to wake her, but I think a visit from you in the morning would be a welcome surprise for the shi'doma."

Allanian smiled. "Agreed, Doma. Good night."

"You as well, Captain," she responded before making her way toward the Merandiths' rooms.

Thoughtful, Allanian watched her vanish around the corner before he descended the stairs. Three floors later, he exited the winding staircase on one of the more demure floors in the soaring keep. Home to the House Guard, the floor shared little in the way of decor with the rest of the keep except for its arched roof, brass lanterns, and its function-over-luxury design. Where other floors were home to elegant tapestries, sculptures, and other fine works of art, this floor traded such signs of wealth and stature for suits of polished armor displayed in alcoves, trophy shields and weapons mounted on the walls, and a few tapestries and paintings depicting the martial exploits of House Merandith.

Keeping his frustration from his face, he made his way quickly through the maze of narrow corridors, acknowledging the handful of servants and House Guards he passed. Along the way, his sensitive ears picked up muffled conversations from some of the rooms, as well as bawdy laughter from others. Had it been a typical night, he might have taken the time to speak with some of them or even joined in on some of the activities, but the day's events and his duties as a Seeker were foremost in his mind, quashing other thoughts with extreme prejudice.

Eventually, he found himself in a corridor that was home to the rooms of the higher-ranking members of the House Guard. The six doors, three on each side, were spread evenly along the long, lamp-lit hall that came to a dead-end at a large, iron-banded door emblazoned with five red stars. Allanian's long toe-heel strides carried him toward the door quickly, where he pushed open the heavy portal with ease. The room beyond was dark except for the moonlight spilling through the narrow and arched leaded windows at the back of the room, which flanked a pair of full bookcases separated by a stout door. Before him, a beautifully molded and carved desk of oak that he'd brought with him from Solarson occupied the center of the room. A lone, plush chair sat behind the elegant desk, while off to his left, a serving table was host to an assortment of decanters containing a variety of drinks. To his right, a small hearth laid dormant beneath an ironwood mantle that supported a pair of oil lamps that flanked a modest wooden statue that had been carved to resemble a silk-clad maiden with her head tilted back, breast thrust forward, and arms extended in welcome.

Closing the door behind him, he noted the fresh paperwork occupying the center of the desk. Ignoring it, he easily crossed the room in the dim light to the stout door while retrieving a key from the pouch at his side. Unlocking it, he gave it a firm shove. Near-frozen hinges groaned in protest as the portal swung open, admitting a blast of icy air. Inhaling deeply, Allanian stepped out onto an arching bridge that connected the main body of the keep to a robust spire, and closed the door behind him.

With the ease and grace of his race, Allanian started across the span. Careful to avoid icy spots on the narrow walkway, he paused halfway across the bridge and approached the chest-high, crenellated edge. Peering out at the city in the distance and at some of the balconies and vestibules below, Allanian took a deep breath and let it out in an attempt to calm his mind. From here, the roar of the triple falls melded with the crash of the breakers far below and the whistle of the wind to create a soothing melody that lent an ethereal quality to the flickering lights of the keep and city. Many a night he found serenity of mind gazing beyond the crenellations of the span, but on this night, peace was slippery prey. Eventually, he realized that the calm he sought would remain elusive until he completed his task. Closing his eyes, he took one more deep breath and let it out slowly before pushing away from the wall and continuing on to the heavy door at the spire-end of the archway.

Despite having visited his quarters earlier in the day to deposit his belongings, ice had already built up on the portal just like his office door. Unlocking the door, Allanian gave it a forceful shove and, with a groan of protest and a gentle shower of shattered ice, the door swung open. Stepping inside, Allanian shut the door, enshrouding him in a darkness that the moonlight spilling in from the high-set, arched windows struggled to pierce. For a moment, he considered leaving the lack of illumination as is, but he eventually decided light would help his mood. Taking a deep, calming breath, he focused inward for a moment as his breath escaped his thick lips in a puff of white. Suddenly, in a burst of warmth and light, the wood in the wrought iron, open-air hearth at the center of the room burst into flames just as the half-dozen lamps scattered about the room joined their light to that of the blaze.

Long ago, the upper levels of the spire had served as a prison for political and high-ranking prisoners. That practice, however, died out many years before Kale's father took the throne, and the spire had remained unused until Allanian rose to his current position. Many had thought him mad for seeking to use the spire for his quarters, but Kale's father had agreed to it in the end. Eventually, as a reward for his impeccable service, the spire underwent a robust renovation that left Allanian in possession of spacious quarters that were the envy of many.

Circular in shape, the room was centered on the open-air hearth and the iron chimney that pulled smoke from the room, while natural light was provided by a dozen small, arched windows set high on the curved wall. Directly in front of him, a pair of curved sofas made of polished oak flanked the hearth, and beyond that, a wrought-iron spiral staircase led to his bedroom on the next floor. Looking to his right, where an oak table, chairs and cupboard sat beneath a painting of the Mother, he eyed the dark, narrow opening next to the artwork and briefly considered making something to eat before he got started. He quickly decided against it, and turned to his left, where a quartet of full bookcases lined the wall behind a comfortable chair and the twin of his office desk, against which his bow and quiver, as well as Kara and Mat's weapons, rested. As he approached the desk, his footfalls cushioned by the vibrant forest-green rugs that covered the majority of the floor, he ignored the other items and instead focused on the precious coffers sitting atop his desk.

Situated between his writing kit and a stack of neatly organized blank parchment, the coffers were a thing of beauty despite their lack of adornments. Made of opalescent bone bound with iron-wood, the light played along their surface in a mesmerizing display of color that Velusyian firestars would struggle to match. Thankfully, Doma Merandith had allowed him to retain his friends' belongings as a gesture of good will and trust. If the weapons or coffers had ended up locked way, or Mother-forbid, as someone's prize, an already annoying situation could have gotten much more complicated very quickly. Looking at the coffers now, the thought of his friends nearly distracted him. Chiding himself, he cleared his mind once more before picking up the coffers with reverence and carrying them to the center of the room. Once there, he sat before the fire, legs crossed, and placed the coffers on his lap.

"It's been a long day full of bad news. If it be your will, Mother, what say we end this day on a good note?" he entreated.

Calming his mind, he released the latches on the coffers and opened the lids. Brilliant, pulsing red and blue light spilled forth, bathing his astonished face as he gazed at the two fist-sized crystals residing in their cushioned beds. He had expected the beating light within the crystals to be strong; after all, his initial Search had informed him their eventual owners resided in Merset, or at the very least, the surrounding area. However, it did not take a Seeker to understand what the energetic, rhythmic pulses meant.

Their owners were close.

"Mother, their owners are very, very close!" he said aloud, stunned by the revelation. Suddenly, he grunted. "I guess I shouldn't be surprised. Still, you've got some questions to answer, Damion."

Shaking his head vehemently, he banished the unneeded speculation. His questions could be answered later. For now, he had a job to do.

With reverence, he removed the crystals from their beds and held them before him. *Let's find you a home, shall we?* he thought as he took a deep breath. Letting it out, he closed his eyes and focused on the fir'gan within himself. Finding it quickly, he channeled a sliver of his power into the crystals, joining his consciousness and heartbeat to their rhythmic pulsing.

Suddenly, his mind was off, speeding along the currents like a hunter closing in on its prey. To his surprise, the blue crystal's trail ended suddenly and harshly near the keep, scattering like leaves in a violent storm. *"Odd,"* Allanian thought. In all the years he'd been a Seeker, he'd never experienced such an effect. Confused, he pulled back on the red crystal's trail, and focused on the blue trail. To his chagrin, the result repeated itself again and again.

Frustrated, and seeing no end to the puzzling result, he turned his attention to the red crystal. Like the blue crystal before, this trail headed toward the keep. To his profound relief, he found this trail free of oddities. However, as he reached the ghostly imprint on the currents at the other end of the connection, he gasped, and his relief melted into unbridled shock. His ice-blue eyes flying open, he dropped the crystals from his shaking hands, severing the connection.

"Oh, Mother! Please! Not this! Anyone but her!"

Gathering himself, he calmed his breathing before taking up the red crystal and joining with it again. With all his soul, he pleaded for the first Search to be wrong. To his horror, it ended at the same place, as did the next attempt, and his heart sank. In all the long years he had been a Seeker, and amongst all the Wardens he had found, no result had been as disappointing – as heartbreaking – as this one.

Forlorn, and with tears coursing down his cheeks, Allanian returned the crystals to their coffers. With effort, he closed the lids before sitting back hard against the couch. For a time, he sat there, staring blankly at the fire. Eventually, he managed to push past the shock and sorrow, and roused himself from his stupor. Sitting up, he let out a deep sigh full of grief before closing his eyes. With difficulty, he pushed through the turmoil that yearned to envelop him and cast his consciousness upon the currents of fir'gan. It took longer than he would have liked to find Damion on the sea of power, but when he finally did, he latched on to the Velusyian's presence forcefully, leaving him no room to ignore his call.

"I've got bad news and worse news," Allanian stated violently, unable to keep his anguish from showing in his words. *"Which do you want first?"*

*

Patience.

It was something he'd acquired over the years, and it had served him well at times; it had led him to greater power, and it had seen his greatest adversary and his lofty goals destroyed. But for every good, there is an evil, and his luck was no different. For when his ambitious, impatient nature became dominant, ill fortune followed. Favor lost. Control lost. Plans forced into the shadows. Instead of leading those loyal to the Darkness to greater power, he now found himself a subordinate to a fool.

Behind his wailing mask of bronze, a sneer tore at Garith's pale, scar-covered face.

A fool whose goals he viewed as small. Ruling a darkness-bound Kylir as the puppet of the Darkness was something he had once embraced with the same fervor as his current master now did. He couldn't recall when his view and desire had shifted. Maybe it was before the Exodus, or maybe after. In the end, however, it was irrelevant. His ambitions grew too much and too fast – and the Darkness took notice. Stripped of his position as leader of the Wardens of Shadow, he was forced into a subservient role that ate at his soul. However, from his fall, he once more learned the power of patience, and did what any man with his ambitions would do – he consolidated his power, kept close those loyal to him, and he waited. He waited for those who had taken power from him to show weakness; and he waited for the strength and knowledge that would elevate him to an unassailable position. For nearly two hundred years, that knowledge, that power, taunted him. It was always there, just out of his reach. It was maddening at times, but he had remained patient.

Garith suddenly smirked.

Oh yes, patience was the key. His enemies were still cautious around him, their gathering had reminded him of that, but they were still ignorant of his position and goals. Thanks to the knowledge Rae-falzyn had bequeathed to the Darkness, he and the other Wardens of Shadow, unbeknownst to the fools that still followed the Light, were once more armed with crusaders. It was a wonderful thing for the beast to have its teeth back, but even so, it would still be difficult to eliminate their foes. To that end, his master had given birth to a new army of shadowspawn that would soon be ready to cast its shadow across Kylir.

His grin widened.

Through guile and patience, he had used his master's gifts not only to grow his own army in secret, but to create weapons that would put an end to the Wardens of Light and the fool of a master he served. But what was a weapon without someone to wield it?

In the end, it would be he, and he alone, who ruled above gods and men, but until then, he would need the help of others. There were those amongst their ranks that were still loyal to him, but he had learned from a very old – and very dead – friend the value of being prepared for all possibilities. To that end, he had begun to seek out would-be Wardens that he could personally mold into weapons loyal to him. Many had been found, but found wanting. For their weakness, he had obliterated them; for if they could not serve his purpose, then they would serve no other.

Candidate after candidate had gone to death's cold embrace, either by his hand or by another. Such should have been the case for the Merandith boy if not for fool's luck. Two potential Wardens were a powerful gift, but to claim two was to risk drawing unwanted attention. The Merandith boy should have died that morning, a victim of bloody vengeance. But, where failure thrived, he adapted. Although it wasn't vital to his plans, he used the boy's bloodlines to foster chaos within the Merandith's ranks, further weakening his long-dead friend's pet project and leaving it vulnerable to outside incursions. More importantly, he had given the other man the nudge he needed. Would the clansman eventually find his way to him in search of the power his soul desperately yearned for? He had no idea. However fate decided to handle it, he wasn't concerned. For chance had just handed him an ideal candidate.

The darkness that enshrouded the room would have been absolute if not for the moonlight slipping through the shuttered window, and the weak glow of lamplight barely peaking beneath the door to an adjoining room. The feeble illumination played gently along his bronze mask as he gazed upon the sleeping child bundled beneath warm blankets on a luxurious canopy bed. Suddenly, his grin widened and hunger began to blaze in his dark eyes.

Oh yes, this was a tremendous boon! For what better way to mold a weapon loyal to him and no other than to do so with a child?

Delicious possibilities danced through his head faster than he could retain them as he gently pushed a finger through the child's mulberry-red locks and began to repeatedly trace something on her scalp. The child whimpered softly as her flesh burned where the icy finger touched, but she remained asleep. Once he was done, he stood up and grinned devilishly. There were complications to overcome, to be sure. The timing would have to be perfect, and more importantly, like the clansman, a crystal would be needed should either or both prove to be worthy of serving him.

"Oh Luthur, are you watching from whatever hell your soul was cast into? Does it twist your gut like a hot knife to watch your pet project destroy itself? Does it tear at your soul to know that whatever your plans may have been, I am using those you wished to protect to further my ambitions? Does it shatter your heart to know that, in the end, I will be a god above all?"

A sudden tingle along the edge of his senses pulled him from his reflections. He was prepared to deal with Allanian; hiding from him – despite the darlion's prodigious talents – wasn't too difficult of a challenge. However, the arrival of the two Wardens was unforeseen. Could he do the same with them? For a time and with difficulty, yes, but close scrutiny would eventually reveal him to them. He knew they already sensed something was amiss, and it was a credit to his skill that they had – for now – brushed aside the ripples he made in the currents. However, he knew that as long as he remained close, it was only a matter of time before they figured it out.

Garith's grin grew malicious. *"Oh yes, eventually you'll realize I've been right beneath your nose the whole time! But by then, it will be too late. The damage will be done, and Triclose will be plunged into the chaos that will give me the key I need to breach Luthur's tomb and claim the knowledge and power I need to regain the Darkness' favor and bring Kylir under my rule!"* he thought with dark, joyful glee as he stepped into the shadows and vanished.

Chapter Twenty-One

"*D*amn,*"* Damion thought, cutting the connection before returning his attention to the late morning activity in the courtyard.

Since their arrival at Gray Sky, things had gone rather well. Not only did Greatjon and Alsa defer to him without any real issues, but they also surprised him with another virgin Gifted in need of training. Going by the cyrian moniker T'sar, the young man was a Blackstone refugee and a newcomer to the Bestyne's ranks. Believing it would benefit all three young Gifted, Damion saw to it that T'sar participated in many of the training exercises. As he had hoped, combining portions of their instruction proved a boon for them all. Granted, it was immediately clear that T'sar and Aseria's martial prowess far surpassed Amroth's, but pitting them against each other, as they were doing this morning, put them on far more equal footing than facing off with their instructors.

Watching from his perch atop the ruins of once-proud battlements, Damion's visage soured as Aseria and T'sar pursued Amroth mercilessly around the training grounds. Though they only wielded practice weapons and wore leather armor of the Bestyne fashion over head-to-toe black attire, each combatant already sported a few welts and bruises. There was no objective to the drill other than improvement, but if the contest was to see who received the most damage, then young Amroth was winning handily. Unfortunately for him, that wasn't the case. Under orders from Damion, Aseria and T'sar had teamed up against Amroth more often than not during these exercises. As such, the end results of each session were hardly surprising given the gap in their skills – a beaten and battered Amroth as a consequence of situations like the one playing out below.

At the moment, Aseria, her mass of yellow-blonde hair secured in a ponytail by a pair of thick temple braids, had Amroth's undivided attention. The fluidity and quickness granted to her by her slender frame and whipcord build gave her a marked advantage over the corded bulk of Amroth, which meant he had no choice but to focus on her as she pressed her attack, which was steadily pushing him back. Damion frowned as he quickly discerned her intent. Free to do as he wanted, T'sar was slowly positioning himself behind Amroth, his amber eyes focused keenly on his target from beneath a black sweat rag that did little to hide his missing ear and the horrible scarring on the right side of his face. Suddenly, Aseria disengaged and leapt away from Amroth, startling him. An instant later, the air reverberated with the blow T'sar landed on Amroth's back, which sent the young Merandith stumbling forward. Damion flinched as Aseria stepped forward and planted her knee firmly in Amroth's stomach before slamming the flat of her wooden blade into his back, driving him to the ground.

"Not doing too well, is he?" Alsa commented from next to Damion, her lilting voice critical.

Grunting, Damion folded his arms across his chest. Bereft of his black longcoat, a gentle breeze washed across him and gently disturbed the loose white linen shirt he wore tucked into his black breeches. "That's a matter of perspective," Damion replied as Greatjon, his horsetail of rust-orange hair bouncing angrily behind him, stalked onto the field and brought a halt to the session. "Compared to the others, he's worse than an amateur. But," he added as Amroth climbed to his feet, determination radiating from his posture, "he is coming along, and he is stubborn."

The emerald-encrusted rings on her fingers, as well as the silver chains connecting them to the gold bracelets on her wrists, clattered gently as she folded her hands before her waist. A wisp of auburn hair slipped from her bun and drifted across her vision as her green eyes studied Amroth. "Stubborn is one way to put it, I suppose," she mused as Greatjon's lecture became more aggressive and Amroth began to bark back. The wind ruffled the split skirt of the green, high-neck dress she wore over a supple pair of brown boots and breeches as she added, "He's a tad willful, and has a bit of a temper when pushed. Case in point," she finished with a nod toward the courtyard.

Angered by Greatjon's admonishments, Amroth lashed out at him. With ease, Greatjon sidestepped the clumsy cut, and baited Amroth on with a sneer.

"Should we do something before he gets hurt?" Alsa inquired as Amroth franticly pursued Greatjon about the courtyard, his anger-fueled attacks failing time and again to reach their target.

Damion briefly considered her suggestion, but eventually shook his white-haired head, his horsetail swaying gently in the wind. "No. He needs to learn to better control his frustration in situations like this. This will be good for him," he stated, the tone of his deep voice adamant.

Alsa eyed him curiously. Given the cold nature of his coal-black gaze, she couldn't tell if he felt any pity for the boy. However, it was clear the elder Warden certainly found no pleasure in what he was putting his charge through.

A sickening thud sounded just before the wall beneath them shuddered. Switching her attention back to the courtyard, she saw Greatjon straightening as if he had just delivered a punch. A moment later, Amroth, his black hair having fully broken free from his horse-tail, stumbled into view from beneath the battlements. Somehow, he'd managed to maintain his grip on his practice swords, and as his legs buckled, he caught himself with the wooden weapons before his face could unceremoniously meet with the courtyard. Chest heaving and head bowed, it appeared to Alsa that Amroth was nearing the end of his endurance. Peering closely at him, she noticed a couple of growing dark spots on his dusty and torn red-trimmed gray leather armor.

"He's bleeding badly," she stated, a tremor of concern in her voice.

"Indeed. Thankfully, he'll heal quickly."

"That maybe, but I think he's had enough for now," Alsa stated firmly.

"Agreed," Damion said with a grunt before dropping nimbly to the courtyard.

Landing lightly on his black-booted feet, he approached Amroth as he declared to the others, "That's enough for now!"

"The boy has a temper, Damion," Greatjon stated as he moved toward the Warden. Garbed in a loose red shirt, black breeches and boots, his imposing stature was relaxed despite the brief melee. Suddenly, he smirked and his brown eyes lit up. Rubbing the knuckles of his right hand with his left, both of which extended from his brown bracers like meaty paws, he quipped, "And he has a strong jaw. Thought I might have broken something."

"Those of clan blood are a different breed, and many are tougher than steel," Damion informed him. Placing a comforting hand on Amroth's shoulder, he added, "His hard head has saved him on more than one occasion. Isn't that right, Amroth?"

With his breathing now steady, Amroth nodded weakly before slowly standing. "Seems that way," he muttered as the others joined them. "Although, I'm really tired of testing that theory," he finished, his deep voice and dark eyes icy as he glared at Greatjon.

A smirk spread across Greatjon's well-defined face in response. "If that's the case, then it would be to your advantage to rein in your temper and pay attention to your lessons."

"Right. . . . I think I've heard something similar before," Amroth replied sarcastically, a scowl marring his clean-shaven, normally somber, handsome face.

With a knowing look at Damion, Greatjon said as Alsa moved beside him, "Sound advice, then."

Seeing a flash of anger in Amroth's black eyes, Alsa hastily stepped between the two men. "Enough of the jabs and bruised egos, please!"

Amroth's anger quickly wilted beneath Alsa's stony stare. Closing his eyes, he took a deep, steadying breath and let it out. Opening his eyes, he said, "You're right. I'm sorry. I know better than to let my frustrations and anger get the better of me. I'm normally not like this, and I know I can do better."

Sensing his sincerity, and that there would be no more harsh words or blows, Alsa nodded. "Good. Then if it is agreeable to your teachers, I think it is time for a break."

Both Greatjon and Damion nodded their approval.

"Very well, then." Turning to Aseria, she ordered, "I expect you for our lesson at sunset."

"Yes, Lady Alsa," Aseria responded.

Turning to Amroth, Alsa added, "And you an hour later, child. You need far more guidance than either of these two, so I believe extra sessions with someone less inclined to use force to drive their instruction into your thick head is in order."

Embarrassed, Amroth averted his eyes and nodded.

"Good. Then, I do believe it's time for some lunch," Alsa declared firmly.

"Alsa and Greatjon, a moment, please?" Damion asked before they could disperse. "You three, go on ahead."

As T'sar joined Aseria, the darlion asked of Amroth, her almond-shaped blue-lavender eyes and musical voice filled with concern, "Are you okay, Amroth? Do you need any help?"

Shaking his head, he responded, "I'll be fine. Sadly, I'm used to this."

For a moment, she considered offering her help again but thought better of it. Turning toward the keep, she and T'sar moved off with a slow-moving Amroth in tow.

Once the trio was out of earshot, Greatjon asked of Damion,

"Something wrong?"

"Other than Amroth's thick-headed nature, possibly."

"It's what had you distracted, isn't it?" Alsa asked knowingly.

"Indeed – though I don't believe it is worth becoming too alarmed."

Greatjon grunted. "Spit it out," he prodded.

"I've been in contact with Allanian."

"He's found the crystals' owners?" Alsa asked hopefully.

"That depends on your perspective," Damion declared, his words heavy with concern. "The Osterias crystal has led him to . . . a child," he finished with a grimace.

Shocked expressions greeted his declaration.

"Corith, be good," Alsa breathed, her hand darting up to cover her mouth.

Greatjon, his face suddenly grim, asked, "Is he sure?"

"Painfully," Damion replied.

"Damn," Greatjon muttered. "So, we're short a Warden for a few years, then?"

"Unless you want to condemn someone to an eternity trapped in a child's body," he stated rhetorically, "we are, indeed."

Oppressive silence followed as the repercussions of Allanian's discovery settled in. Eventually, Alsa cleared her throat and stated, "Well, there's nothing to be done other than to protect the child until they are of age. Besides, this might work to our advantage."

"Our advantage?" Greatjon asked incredulously. "How in the hells does it work to our advantage? We're short on manpower as it is, and now we know that shortage will have to continue for a while in a key position!"

"I admit the situation is far from ideal," she conceded, "but we have a chance to do something that's not been done in millennia – raise *and* train a Gifted."

Greatjon scoffed. "That's just wonderful. I just hope the Betrayers decide to grace us with that kind of time!" he stated derisively, before exclaiming, "Be reasonable, Alsa! No matter how you look at this – this is not a good thing!"

Ignoring Greatjon's argument, Alsa looked at Damion and asked calmly, "How old is the child, and who is it? Furthermore, what about the other crystal?"

Damion shook his head. "Too young, and he doesn't know the child's name; he'll let me know when he has more details. As for the other crystal, I don't believe he's Searched yet," he lied smoothly.

Alsa's inquisitive gaze studied his face for any indication that he was holding back on them. When she was satisfied with what she saw, she nodded. "Very well, then. What of Kara and Mat?"

Damion cringed. "That's the . . . shall we say . . . funny part."

"Funny?" Greatjon asked, curious.

A small smirk pulled at Damion's lips. "They have been imprisoned for the disappearance and possible murder of Amroth Merandith."

Alsa blinked rapidly at the news even as Greatjon barked a full-throated laugh. "You're right – that is funny!" Greatjon eventually declared with a grin.

"I don't think they think so," Damion replied casually, "but they've no choice but to play along. Allanian says they will be treated well, and I have no reason to doubt it."

"Will you tell Amroth?" Alsa inquired.

"No," Damion stated firmly. "Eventually, I will, but for now, his attention needs to remain on his training. I know he already yearns to return home, and if he catches wind of the situation, then we may find ourselves having to physically prevent him from leaving."

Alsa planted her hands on her hips and sighed. "A terrible thing to do to him, keeping him in the dark, but a wise course. As it appears that we can do nothing about the situation on Solarson at the moment, I suggest we focus on the here and now. Let us get something to eat and discuss how we might better proceed with the fledgling Wardens."

"I'm telling you, he's dangerous," T'sar reiterated around a mouthful of juicy roast.

Smirking at him from across the small table they shared in the perpetually dour dining hall, Aseria asked, "And just how is he dangerous? He spends more time on the ground or sprouting new bruises than engaging either of us. Besides, I think we team up on him a little too much. It's hardly fair."

"It's what Damion asked of us. Besides, life is hardly fair," T'sar responded, his grim tone weighting down his young voice as he gestured to his scarred face.

Aseria frowned and took a sip from her mug of diluted wine. The black sweat rag T'sar wore on his shaved head did little to conceal that he was bereft of his right ear, nor could it hide the jagged scar that cut a horrific swath from the missing ear to the bridge of his nose. While the inflammation around the horrible disfigurement had relented some, it had done little to assuage T'sar's bitterness toward the terrible reminder of Blackstone's fall.

"You know that's not what I meant," she offered as she returned the mug to the table, the heartache she felt for her friend's situation displayed nakedly in her words and expression.

T'sar cringed inwardly. Despite her stained armor and the sweat-soaked fur that ruined the illusion that she had snow-white skin, she somehow managed to remain the most beautiful creature he'd ever seen. But the sadness lent to her expression by the way her frown pulled at the yellow accent stripes on her skin-tight fur, tore at his heart. He hated seeing her beautiful, slender face marred in such a way, so he quickly conceded, "I know, I know."

Aseria's blue-lavender eyes twinkled as she smiled and placed a comforting hand on his free hand. Glancing down at her hand as he grew flush with warmth, he again found himself amazed at the softness of her touch despite the calluses she'd developed from the heavy sword work of late. The first time he'd felt her touch, it had been a hug. Expecting to feel fur, he was surprised to find that, despite a silky sensation, it felt like touching any other human. Even now, he had a hard time believing her pallor was the result of fur.

"I understand your concern, T'sar," she stated, still somewhat uncomfortable with the name bequeathed to him by the Bestynes, which he'd fully embraced. "Yes, he's raw, and yes, he's got a bit of temper —which reminds me of someone," she added playfully, causing T'sar to look away in embarrassment. Squeezing his hand, she continued, "He's also clumsy . . . which doesn't seem all that unusual."

"How so?" T'sar asked, confused.

"Well," she started to say as she withdrew her hand and plucked a snow grape from her plate of winter fruits, bread, and a couple of slices of roast, "compared to me or even a cyrian, all humans appear clumsy," she finished, popping the grape in her mouth.

T'sar rolled his eyes as she merrily chewed on the juicy morsel. "Thanks for the compliment," he muttered as he grabbed his mug.

"You're welcome," Aseria responded playfully as he took a

long draw from his mug of watered-down wine. "Kidding aside, he does have his issues, but we all do — especially given our circumstances. Besides, I think he's growing on us both. Don't you?"

T'sar grunted as he put his mug down. "I guess so," he said, even as his mind bemoaned the clandestine glances the two Wardens-in-training stole from time to time. "There's a fighter's heart buried in there beneath layers of shyness, confusion, and his lack of confidence," he conceded grudgingly.

"Why, T'sar," Aseria declared as she sat back, looking at him in surprise, "you are far more astute and thoughtful than you let on."

Rolling his amber eyes, he stabbed at another piece of meat on his plate filled with a meal similar to Aseria's, and crammed it in his mouth even as his cheeks grew slightly flush.

Laughing at her friend's discomfort with her compliment, she suddenly sat up straight and waved. "Amroth! Come join us!" she called out, her voice turning vibrant.

Cursing silently, T'sar turned around and forced a smile as Amroth weaved his way from the direction of the kitchen over to them through the moderately full hall. As much as he would have preferred to spend the meal alone with Aseria, he knew protesting her choice of tables — located near the central hearths and in clear view of the kitchen — would raise questions he didn't want to answer at the moment. Besides that, he knew Amroth wasn't a bad person; in fact, he found him to be quite pleasant and, given that they were the same age, he tried to think of him as a friend. However, much to his chagrin, the joy Aseria projected when Amroth was around had grown by the day. That unabashed, undeniable escalation tore at T'sar's heart, scarring it as blatantly as the one on his face, allowing jealousy to take firm root. He continually tried to deny that resentment and give himself over to the friendship that could be, but he knew it was for naught so long as Aseria gazed at Amroth the way she did now.

"Yes, join us," T'sar said when Amroth drew close, his tone bereft of any emotion other than friendship.

Hair hanging loosely about his face and shoulders, he looked like a proper mess in his battered and stained armor as he paused at their table and asked, "Are you sure? I don't want to impose."

"Not at all," Aseria said with a warm smile. "In fact, we should probably apologize for beating you up," she finished with a friendly chuckle.

Offering her a dry smile as he sat beside T'sar, he declared, "None need. I earned every bruise."

Peering at Amroth as the tired Merandith tore a chunk of bread from the half loaf on his plate full of meat, a few snow grapes, and a selection of overcooked vegetables, T'sar commented, "For someone that just took a pounding, you sure don't look it. Lucky you," he finished, his words heavy with jealousy.

Swallowing, Amroth stabbed at some of the beef with his fork. "Yeah.... I don't feel that lucky. I may heal fast naturally, and even faster of late, but that doesn't make it any easier to keep taking the punishment." Cramming the beef in his mouth, he chewed on it silently.

Sipping on her watered wine, Aseria shot T'sar an admonishing glare over the lip of her mug.

"What?" he asked, shocked at the look he was receiving. "He *is* lucky. His Corith-given ability to heal is a blessing. At least he doesn't have to worry about something like this happening to him," he finished, gesturing to his scar.

Swallowing, Amroth took a sip from his mug of water. "He's right," he stated politely as he put his mug down, "I don't. Granted, I can't grow back a limb or an ear, but I've broken bones, burned myself at the forge, been cut and beaten bloody, and I've never once been left with a scar." Suddenly, he grinned slyly. "But it doesn't mean I shouldn't learn to duck. If our session had been a real fight, you two would have killed me ten times over," he quipped.

Aseria smiled sheepishly and T'sar let out a smug chuckle as Amroth's self-deprecating words and light tone put an end to the momentary tension.

"Don't be so hard on yourself," Aseria offered as she turned her attention back to her meal. "T'sar has much more training than you, and I more than him. I wouldn't expect someone of no—" she caught herself before she could say what she was thinking.

Amroth looked at her wide-eyed, apologetic expression and smiled knowingly. "You were going to say noble birth, right?"

"I didn't mean anything by it!" she blurted apologetically.

Amroth flashed her a congenial smile, and she felt herself blush in embarrassment even as he said, "Don't apologize. I've known a few nobles who wouldn't know the pointy end of a sword from its hilt."

T'sar snickered around a mouthful of food as Aseria let out a nervous chuckle of her own.

"To be honest, I almost wish I could claim to be one of those," Amroth mused.

"That's a bit harsh. You're not that incompetent," T'sar quipped.

Amroth smiled weakly and grabbed his mug, intent on taking a drink. Instead, he said, "True. But I am of noble blood, though not of the Merandith line." His statement drew looks of curiosity from the others, but he continued on, ignorant of it. "My home has been torn by war for a very long time. To lack martial skills – or even worse, to live a pacifistic life in spite of the conflict – is probably more shameful." He grimaced and lowered his gaze to the contents of his mug. "I chose that route . . ." he stated, his tone reflective. "In hindsight, it was a foolish notion; thankfully, the only person that ever had to suffer any consequences because of it was me."

"A peaceful existence is something to be admired, not something to be ashamed of," Aseria said gently, seeing the hurt in Amroth's eyes.

Staring at the clear liquid in his mug, Amroth replied stoically, "I know, but if you can't defend yourself or those you care about, then aspiring to a peaceful existence is nothing but a silly dream." Looking up, he flashed a pained, conceding smile at Aseria.

T'sar grunted. Lifting his mug, he declared, "That's something I think we can all drink to." Draining his drink as the others drank deeply of theirs, T'sar then planted his mug firmly on the table before standing abruptly. "You do have talent, you know," he admitted, his sudden motion and admission drawing surprised looks from Aseria and Amroth. "Using two swords is difficult, to say the least, and I know I never could do that. But if you need some help, I'll be happy to spar with you any time."

Before either could respond, he stalked off, wondering why he had just offered to help the person who was unwittingly stealing Aseria from him.

"Well, that was just . . ." Aseria started to say before trailing off with an astonished shake of her head.

"I'm shocked, too. I didn't expect such an offer from him," Amroth stated with a dry chuckle. "Well, from either of you, to be honest."

Aseria cocked her head. "Why not? Our situations aren't that dissimilar."

Amroth shrugged. "I don't know. I've met a few of the Wardens already, and while some have been nicer than others, it doesn't seem like getting along is one of their better traits."

Aseria flashed him a coy smile. "So, what you're saying is

that since T'sar and I have spent more time with the Wardens, you think we might view you more as a rival than a friend? Is that right?"

Amroth smirked, embarrassed. "Well . . . yeah," he replied with a shrug of his shoulders.

Aseria let out a musical laugh. "I don't know what your encounters with other Wardens have been like, but aside from Damion's cold demeanor and the cruel behavior of another," she suppressed a shudder as memories of her encounter with Darkon tried to resurface, "the Wardens I've met are some of the most caring, selfless people I've ever met. As for T'sar and I, we want to see you succeed as much as we want to succeed. We're not afraid to help, and you shouldn't be afraid to ask."

Stunned, Amroth stared at her for a moment before chuckling and shaking his head in amazement. "Good to know."

"Still don't believe me?" she asked with a wide grin.

"No, it's not that," Amroth blurted apologetically, her grin suddenly making him feel like he was on the defensive.

"No, I understand. Some people just need things proven to them," she declared playfully. "That settles it! There are some falls southeast of here, know of it?"

Puzzled, Amroth said, "The triple falls? I've heard people mention it."

"That's it. Meet me there after your lesson with Lady Alsa."

"Why?" Amroth asked, baffled.

Smiling brightly, Aseria stood up. "Why, help, of course!" Walking off before Amroth could respond, her stomach aflutter with nervous excitement, she said over her shoulder, "Don't be late!"

Alsa let out a huff of frustration and passed a hand over her eyes as another vase crashed to the ground.

"Sorry," Aseria offered, cringing.

Seated with her legs crossed at the center of the room, she had long since discarded her sweat-soaked shirt, leaving her in only her breeches and the soaked black linen bandage that served as her brassiere. Thirteen vases hovered in the air about the room in what was proving to be her most trying control test yet. She was awash with glistening sweat from the strain, the salty liquid not only dripping from her nose and chin, but also into her eyes, setting them ablaze with irritation. Blinking rapidly in a vain attempt to provide relief,

Aseria fought to regain control of the multiple strands of fir'gan she was using to keep the vases aloft.

Alsa nodded in approval as order returned to the wobbling pottery. "That's better, but still. . . . I may be pushing you a bit beyond your current skill at the moment, but sixteen vases should not be *this* much trouble."

"I'm sorry, Lady Alsa," Aseria said through clenched teeth as she fought to steady several vases that had begun to teeter. "I'm not as focused as I should be."

"*Humph*. . . . That much is obvious, child," she quipped, the patronizing tone of her soft voice drawing a heated look from Aseria. Meeting her gaze, Alsa studied Aseria with keen intent even as more of the vases began to wobble. Suddenly, it dawned on her what had her charge so distracted, and she smirked. "I see," she mused, her voice softening. "It's the Merandith boy, isn't it? You're infatuated with him, aren't you?"

Eyes wide above her warm cheeks, Aseria sputtered, even as her control over the vases failed, "I don't know what you–"

In rapid succession, the vases hit the floor with a resounding crash, causing both women to cringe.

Looking around the room at the shattered pottery, Alsa planted her fists on her hips and shook her head.

"I'm so sorry!" Aseria pleaded as she scrambled to her feet.

"You are a handful at times, child!" Alsa stated sternly. "Yet you are as prone to the same wants, desires, and frivolities as the rest of us, I suppose," she finished, her soft voice warm as she looked up at her charge.

Stunned at the sudden shift in her teacher's tone, Aseria struggled to find something to say. Finally, she managed, "I don't know what you mean?"

Smirking, Alsa folded her hands at her waist. "You are infatuated with Amroth. Am I right?"

Eyes wide with desperation, Aseria struggled to find some viable way to deny Alsa's assertion. However, beneath her knowing gaze, Aseria quickly realized it was useless to deny it. Sighing, she averted her eyes. "Yes, Lady Alsa. . . . I . . . I do like him."

Admitting it aloud left her feeling odd and a bit giddy. It was as if she had just breathed life into an idea that only existed in her head. That heady moment was fleeting, however, as a sudden realization dawned on her. Suddenly scared, her gaze snapped back to Alsa, and she blurted defensively, "I know we have rules that clearly state Wardens should not engage in romantic relationships, especially within the Orders, but—"

Smiling broadly, Alsa held up a hand, bringing a halt to Aseria's hurried plea. "That's enough, child! I know what the rules state. To be perfectly honest, the intent of the rules is quite valid – romantic and familial ties are a potential – and dangerous – weakness for a Warden. Yet, there are those of us that believe that while the spirit of the law should be respected, it should not be blindly followed."

Aseria studied her teacher's face for any clue as to her point. "I don't understand," she stated, confusion prevalent in her melodic voice. "How can you respect a law and not follow it?"

Taking a deep breath, Alsa let it out slowly. "Child," she started, her tone heavy with sorrow, "while I'm not privy to the exact reason for the rules, I do know that before many of us entered the ranks of the Wardens, we had families and loved ones. The Darkness' servants realized this and took advantage of it at the onset of this damnable conflict. Families were slaughtered, loved ones were made to serve the Darkness, and some were even torn apart before their very eyes. It was a . . . powerful and effective message, from what I understand. Many a noble soul bent knee to the Darkness or simply gave up the fight in order to save those close to them."

"Corith be good!" Aseria breathed, horrified.

Alsa nodded. "Agreed. Unfortunately, such danger is still a potential nightmare to this day."

"How so?"

Gauging her pupil for a moment, Alsa simply stated, "Damion is a good example."

"Damion?" Aseria asked, her brow furrowing in confusion.

Alsa began to pace about the room. "Damion has family within the Warden's ranks – specifically, his brother and sister."

"I. . . . I don't know what to say. . . . Can he not protect them?" Aseria asked, stunned by the revelation

"If they were merely soldiers? Possibly. But that is not the case. You see, when a Warden is chosen, it is done so by the crystal that empowers them, and it does so regardless of one's race, background, status, or connections. As such, Damion's sister, Karalisa Masumaite, was chosen as the Warden of the Kydan'fir Order, and she, in turn, chose their brother as her Knight."

Wide-eyed, the implications of Alsa's discloser hammered into her. Finally, she shook her head vigorously and said, "I see now. That settles it – I'll drop this childish thought immediately."

Sighing, Alsa stopped and approached Aseria. "Let me finish before you make a rash decision." Placing her hands gently on Aseria's shoulders, she continued, her voice suddenly gentle, "The letter of the law demands that we abstain from relationships that could make us vulnerable, but many of us believe the spirit of the law simply urges caution. For if we shun one of the greatest gifts Corith has ever blessed us with, then what are we fighting for?"

Confused, Aseria asked, "What are you saying? I should pursue this?"

Alsa shook her head. "I cannot answer that question for you. But what I can tell you is this," she stated as tears threatened to well up in her eyes, "if this infatuation is nothing more than that, it will do you no harm. However, if it is more than that. . . . If it might someday blossom into something as powerful as love," Alsa felt her throat constricting with emotion, "then the both of you will be in possession of something that could be a terrible weakness or a powerful weapon."

Listening to Alsa's impassioned statement, Aseria felt her heart break. She had no doubt that Alsa's concern was genuine, but the depth of the naked emotions in her words stunned Aseria for a moment. Then it struck her. "You lost someone, didn't you?"

"I–" Alsa started to deny it, then thought better of it. "I did."

"Who?" Aseria probed gently.

Releasing her grip on Aseria's shoulders, Alsa wiped away the few tears that had escaped her eyes. "It doesn't matter," she stated hastily. "What matters, is the choice is yours. Just know that should you seek out the end result of this infatuation, there are people like myself, Damion, and Greatjon who have chosen to embrace a life with love. And should anyone decide to persecute you for it, we will defend your right to such a life."

Amazed and a bit bewildered by all she'd just learned, Aseria barely managed to utter, "I don't know what to say. . . ."

Alsa smiled and laughed weakly. "Don't say anything – just be true to yourself and walk in the Light. That is all I can ever ask for you." Before Aseria could respond, Alsa clapped her hands sharply and stated, "Now, run along. I have to clean up this mess before putting your sweetheart through a grueling session that won't leave him a moment to think about you."

Blushing profusely, Aseria said, "I don't think he knows about . . ." she shrugged and laughed. "Corith! The man is dense! I'm not even sure he realizes I like him!"

Watching her charge blush even further at the verbal admission of her feelings, Alsa grinned. "Then make sure he knows, and leave no doubt! We may possess great power and live for a long time, but that doesn't mean death isn't lurking in the shadows. Embrace life, child – that is the best advice I can ever give you."

Giddy with excitement and nervous energy, Aseria nodded, retrieved her black shirt and pulled it on before moving toward the door. Gripping the handle, a sudden thought cut clean and crisp through her swirling emotions. Turning, Aseria asked, "Lady Alsa, what did you mean when you said Greatjon embraced a life with love?"

"Why," she stated, her happy tone tinted with jealousy, "he is married and soon to be a father."

Crouched atop a merlon high above the training grounds in the darkness, Aseria watched the sparring session below, her mind adrift on waves of conflicting thoughts and emotions. When she'd left Alsa, her mind was firmly set on pursuing Amroth. Their talk had brought a clarity of thought to her regarding him that initially left her overjoyed. To her chagrin, the conversation had also firmly imprinted the potential consequences, and as she traversed the keep, her fears about it began to overshadow her joy. So, instead of joining the others on the training grounds so she could cheer Amroth on, she retreated to the battlements, alone, beset by doubt.

Shifting her balance as a strong wind cut across her, ripping at her shirt and dusting her with snow, she sighed. "You never would have considered a human more than a friend before all this," she muttered.

"Before what?"

Startled, she nearly lost her balance as she spun toward the speaker. Catching herself with her hands, she righted herself with a curse. "Da'liq!" she spit the Tykani curse. "Don't sneak up on me like that!"

Offering her an amused smirk, Greatjon approached her, his black-booted steps purposefully heavy. "Like what? Even without fir'gan, your senses are far sharper than mine. I don't see how you missed me."

Rolling her eyes, Aseria crouched back down and turned back

to the courtyard. "Right," she muttered. "I seem to recall a similar situation at Blackstone."

Leaning against the adjacent merlon, his red shirt dancing in the breeze, Greatjon peered down at the training grounds. Below, Damion and several of the Bestyne troops looked on as Amroth and T'sar, both girded in their leather armor, franticly sparred. Time and again, T'sar pressed Amroth, scoring hit after hit to the accompaniment of his fellow soldiers' cheers. Occasionally, Damion stopped the two to chat or offer suggestions as they fought, but the cold Velusyian appeared content to let Amroth suffer.

"I see you're getting the hang of shielding yourself from the elements. That's good. It was but a few days ago that you were still trudging around in a cloak."

Aseria nodded. "It's still difficult, but I'm getting there," she answered with a dismissive shrug.

Puzzled by her distracted tone, he asked, "Something wrong? Alsa didn't work you too hard, I trust? Ever since Amroth's arrival, the training has intensified to the point that I'm a bit concerned about your wellbeing."

Aseria smirked slightly. "Says the man that tried to beat me into the ground," she quipped half-heartedly.

Greatjon chuckled. "That's fair," he conceded.

"Seriously, though, I'm fine. Don't worry," Aseria added dismissively.

"Are you sure? We can be more . . . aggressive with Amroth, but until you join with your cryst–"

"Alsa told me you are married," she suddenly interjected. "Is that true?"

Taken aback by the statement, he struggled to find something to say. Finally, he chuckled and leaned back against the wall, his brown eyes filled with amusement. "She said that, did she? Well, I guess my little secret is safe with you. Yes, I am married; and yes, we are expecting a child." Aseria nodded slowly, but said nothing, prompting Greatjon to ask, "Why do you ask?"

Aseria remained silent for a moment as she watched T'sar parry one clumsy attack and sidestep another before delivering a spinning backhand slice to Amroth's back, which landed with a loud crack, drawing a howl of anger and pain from the overmatch Merandith.

"Tell me," she finally said once Amroth had recovered and

charged back into the fray, "has anyone ever been punished for breaking that rule?"

Greatjon's brow furrowed, and he focused his gaze intently on her. "The rule prohibiting families and romantic relationships?" he asked, even though he already knew the answer, as the clatter of wooden weapons rang out.

Aseria nodded.

Taking a deep breath, he ran a hand over his rust-orange hair and tugged on his horsetail. "Why do you ask?" he asked again, suspicious.

She smiled weakly. "Humor me."

Puzzled, he offered, "Well, that really depends on your point of view. Assuming Alsa told you about Kara and Ember, then Damion has been suffering an eternal punishment."

"That makes sense," she stated softly. "I only grasp a small amount of the history of our conflict, let alone the lives of our allies, but it doesn't take a war like ours to understand the torment Damion must experience. Anything that might endanger a loved one is scary, but such events are normally over in a relatively short period of time. For him to have had to live with such worry – such a burden – for as long as he has. . . ." She trailed off with a shake of her head. "Any others?"

Turning his attention back to the sparing pair, Greatjon remained thoughtful for a moment. "There have been others, though thankfully, most of those relationships were ended before any dire consequence could come about."

"Most?" Aseria prompted as Amroth hit the ground hard.

Greatjon glanced at her briefly just as Amroth swept T'sar's legs out from under him, which bought Amroth enough time to scramble away and climb to his feet. "There was one," he started slowly. "Her name was Valisiana, and she was in love with Darius."

Shocked by the statement, Aseria's gaze flashed to Greatjon. "The Bestyne Preceptor? She and Darius were in love?"

Greatjon nodded slowly. "It was never a secret. Their relationship started long before the Exodus, and there are even a few of us that believe they were also married . . . though only they knew for sure."

"That seems to spit in the very face of the rule," Aseria stated incredulously. "Why were they never punished?"

"It's an odd rule, that one," Greatjon stated with an ominous chuckle. "I know it had to do with Damion, and I know that Luthur never chose to enforce it. Did he discourage such entanglements? That he did. But as to why he never did more than that, I haven't a clue." Greatjon sighed deep and dark, drawing a concerned look from Aseria. "Still, it doesn't mean they didn't pay a price."

"How so?"

"I have no proof, nor can I believe this was the case since there was evidence that there were other reasons, but—"

"I'm confused. What are you trying to say?"

Picking his words carefully, Greatjon said, "Years ago, not long after Luthur's fall and Darkon assumed leadership of the Wardens, our Order became infected by the Darkness."

"Corith!" Aseria gasped.

"Indeed. It's not easy to spot," he responded, his gaze still fixed on the sparring pair. "There's a thinner line than you would think between serving the Light and succumbing to the Darkness. There's power to be had in the shadows, and mortals, while susceptible to its wiles, seem to have an uncanny resilience to it that makes it particularly difficult to spot and root out. It starts innocently enough – a wish to do good turns into a desire for power; that power twists into greed, and before you know it, your heart has blackened and the Darkness has a new servant."

"That's just awful! How, in Corith's name, do you avoid that, or even spot it?" Aseria asked, aghast.

"Avoiding it is one of the reasons why we meditate. It not only deepens our connection to the currents, but it helps us reflect and focus. We are not immune to our emotions and desires, and to deny them would be to deny some of Corith's greatest gifts to us. But we must be wary of the lurking dangers should we give in too deeply, else we are washed away into the darkness." Greatjon frowned. "As for spotting it, that is initially very hard. When such darkness is buried deep in someone's heart, it's difficult to spot without overt action on their part. Eventually, a servant of the Darkness, even one that has unwittingly stepped into its maw, corrupts the currents to a degree."

"So that's what was found here?"

Greatjon nodded, his brown eyes seeing events long past. "It was subtle at first; a few soldiers here, a couple of Gifted there. All were relatively new to the Order, which called into question Valisiana's judgment. The resulting inquisition was the damming of our Order. Darkon has always been fervent, if not a bit unstable, when it

500

comes to rooting out the Darkness, and it showed with how he handled the inquest. By his word, our Order was sentenced to be purged, and it was by his hand that the majority of our order was slaughtered."

"That's just . . ." Aseria tried to say before trailing off with a shake of her head.

"Horrible," Greatjon stated with a growl. "For the longest time, I believe that was the case. How could I think else wise? The evidence was there, and more importantly, Valisiana vanished." Greatjon frowned darkly. "No one knows where she is or even if she's still alive. It was even assumed that her betrayal was an extension of Damion's." He paused thoughtfully. "Until Blackstone fell, I believed the story . . . but after its demise and Darkon's aggression toward you, not to mention his unbridled dislike of Gray Sky, I find myself believing something else."

"What would that be?" Aseria prodded, unsure she wanted to hear the answer.

"It was no secret that Darkon once loved Valisiana, and we believed that when she chose Darius over him, he eventually let go of his jealousy. But now. . . ." He shook his head. "I have no evidence, but there are those that suspect the extend of the purge – if not the whole damn mess – was an act of bitter jealously by a man now in a position to do so with little or no resistance from the others."

Aseria looked at Greatjon in horrified silence, barely aware of the duel raging in the courtyard. Finally, she mustered the courage to say, "I don't know what to say. . . . That just seems like the act of somcone that might be–"

"A servant of the Darkness?" Greatjon finished for her.

She nodded.

"Don't think that thought hasn't crossed the minds of those that share concerns about Darkon's leadership. But other than some questionable results from sound decisions, there's no evidence that what befell the Bestynes was anything more than proper protocol. Besides, you've been up close to him – did the currents in the Grove react oddly to him?"

Aseria remained thoughtful for a moment. "Other than the discord the threat of violence caused, I don't think so. Then again, I couldn't see the currents then, let alone interpret them."

"Trust me when I say that had a servant of the Darkness set foot in the Grove, you would have noticed it." He shook his head, then looked at her, his expression serious. "Enough of these dark thoughts. Why did you ask this in the first place?"

Meeting Greatjon's gaze for a moment, she shifted her focus back to the training grounds where, for the first time that evening, Amroth had T'sar on the defensive. Once more, instead of answering him, she responded with a question. "Aren't you afraid that Darkon might decide your choice of marriage and a family should be punished?"

Repressing an annoyed chuckle at her evasiveness, he replied, "The rule states that should a member of any of the Orders become involved in a relationship that threatens the security of the Orders, he or she is to be excommunicated and have their memories wiped. Should the offender be a Warden or Knight," he took a deep breath, "they are to be severed from their crystal and put to death."

Greatjon fell silent for a moment before continuing. "That damn rule weighed on me heavily for a long time until I decided that a world where we had to sacrifice Corith's greatest gift was a world not worth defending. If Darkon ever finds out, and if he is foolish enough to try to enforce it this time, I'll fight him till I have nothing left. And this time, I imagine I'll have others standing at my side to greet him." Looking at Aseria, he asked, his tone brokering no quarter this time, "Now tell me – why do you ask?"

"Because," she started to say when a cheer went up as Amroth disarmed T'sar and brought his crossed blades to rest over T'sar's neck, "I want to know if I'm doing the right thing."

Puzzled, Greatjon asked, "The right thing? What do you–" Greatjon's eyebrows shot up with realization. "Well, now that's something. . . . The cat has a thing for a human."

Blushing furiously, Aseria stood up and hopped down to the battlements. "This isn't funny!" she stated defensively, glaring at him. "Yes, I know my culture frowns heavily upon such relationships, but it's my life and my hea–"

"Aseria, I didn't mean anything by it!" Greatjon interrupted with a grin. "In fact, I approve of it."

"You approve?" she asked hesitantly.

"I do," he responded with a nod. "You both are new to our cause. Maybe this will give you something . . . more familiar to fight for and defend. If not," he shrugged, "there's nothing wrong with a little distraction to relieve some stress."

Greatjon's meaning sank in quickly, and she found herself turning away abruptly, her cheeks growing as warm as a roaring fire. Suddenly, her eyes landed on Damion and she found herself asking,

"What about Damion?"

"That ice-cold bastard?" he asked rhetorically with a grunt. "Don't worry about him. Believe it or not, beneath that callous exterior, he does have a heart. I imagine that as long as he sees it as a good thing for Amroth, he won't stand in your way." Hesitating, he added, "The choice is yours and yours alone, but if you still have doubts, come to the estate at the center of the village and meet my wife. She's been anxious to meet the girl that's been taking up all my time." Grinning, he added playfully, "Honestly, I think she might be a bit jealous."

Aseria laughed, rich and vibrant, and turned back to face him. "I needed that laugh. Thank you," she stated as the crowd dispersed and Amroth limped toward the keep and his lesson with Alsa.

"You're welcome. But if you don't mind a friendly bit of advice."

Aseria chuckled. "I have a feeling you'll give it whether I want it or not."

Greatjon smirked briefly before putting a comforting hand on her shoulder and stating, "Our lives potentially will last forever, but we can still die. Don't wait too long, or he may be gone from your life forever."

She smirked. "Someone else gave me similar advice," she responded softly with a warm smile. "Don't worry, I won't."

Giving her shoulder a squeeze, Greatjon saw the blossoming love in Aseria's eyes, and he felt his thoughts turn longingly toward his family. Offering her one last smile, he dropped down to the ground and took off at a trot, leaving Aseria to her thoughts.

Chapter Twenty-Two

"You're improving by the day, T'sar. This I am glad to see," Lieutenant Salina stated, her feral golden eyes and the soft tones of her coarse voice filled with pride as she led her quartet of soldiers from the dining hall.

Walking gingerly alongside his lieutenant, who was dressed in the same sectional red-trimmed gray leather armor and wolf-head adorned black tabard as the rest of them, T'sar smiled in appreciation. "Thank you, Lieutenant. I'm beginning to feel like I belong here more and more," he said with a hint of appreciation in his youthful voice. Tugging down on the black bandana, which he wore in a vain attempt to hide some of the jagged scar that ran from his missing right ear to the bridge of his nose, he added, "Still, I have a lot of catching up to do." He chuckled deprecatingly. "I feel like a child next to the lot of you."

"Well, T'sar, you're hardly that amongst the mundanes," quipped one of the others, a stout man with a shaved umber head and sharp yellow eyes set in a round face with black accent stripes that nearly blended with his goatee.

"True, Berson. But, the youngest Gifted among you has what? Fifty years on me?"

"More like twenty, T'sar," Salina answered. Shaking her dark brown, red-accent striped head, which set her waist-length braid of black hair swaying, she added, "But that's hardly the point. You're learning quickly, not to mention you're holding your own against soon-to-be Wardens. That's pretty damn impressive!"

"Thanks. I appreciate it," T'sar replied with a genuine, but weak, smile. "But it won't be long before their strength will make my skill look pathetic."

His lieutenant clapped him on the shoulder with a four-fingered hand and flashed a feral grin at him as they approached the main doors, which the two guards flanking it opened. "That'll happen eventually, but for now, you are kicking that Amroth boy's arse around the courtyard – enjoy it! Not many of us could say the same or ever have that pleasure."

Stepping out into the cold night, T'sar shuddered. The

Gifted in his squad immediately embraced the currents and shielded themselves from the cold, sparking a pang of jealousy in him. He still had not grasped that skill, and while his teachers assured him he would reach that point eventually, he found himself yearning for that strength and more.

Making for the barracks, they were just about to turn the corner of the ruined keep when he thought he heard footsteps behind him. Glancing back, he saw Amroth jogging away from the ruinous main building. Beset by sudden curiosity, T'sar said, "Go on without me. I think I'll take a walk and clear my head. I think it's still ringing a bit from earlier."

His squad paused and looked back. "Are you sure? There's a warm fire and some passable ale waiting for us," Salina stated.

"I'm sure," T'sar replied with a smile.

"Very well, then. Don't while away the hours. You've got an early morning."

"Yes, sir," T'sar replied.

Once his lieutenant acknowledged him and turned back toward the barracks, T'sar turned and sprinted in the direction Amroth went. He didn't know why he was suddenly curious about Amroth's activities, but he couldn't think of a good reason someone as important as Amroth would be allowed to venture outside the keep grounds without an escort. It was possible that he might simply be running an errand for one of his instructors, but when T'sar picked up Amroth's trail, it was quickly apparent that wasn't the case. He was giving the village a wide birth, heading east toward the forest.

"What the hells is he up to?" T'sar thought as he followed well back of his quarry. He was thankful for the sporadic and sparse snowfall, as well as the clear sky that night. Because of the fortuitous weather, Amroth's footprints would last long enough for him to pursue without fear of losing the trail or being spotted.

The enigma of Amroth's late-night sojourn grew as the tracks led T'sar to the edge of the woodland beyond the village. Coming to a halt, he eyed the forest, completely baffled by the situation. There was no reason he could fathom that would bring Amroth out here, and he considered returning to the keep to report this oddity. After a brief moment of reflection, however, he decided against it. If it was merely a personal jaunt, then he wasn't going to cause a ruckus over it.

"Hells," he mused, *"if Amroth is running away, I'm more than happy to give him a long head start . . . but on the off chance it something else. . . ."*

Resuming his pursuit, he was glad that, despite the deeper darkness beneath the canopy of pines, enough moonlight still reached the ground and reflected off the snow for him to see where he was going. Furthermore, from what he could tell, Amroth's tracks appeared to be taking a much more direct, southerly route.

"This doesn't make any sense," he muttered, giving voice to his curious concerns. "What in the hells could bring him all the way out here?" he asked of no one, baffled.

He couldn't decide exactly why, but at that moment, his uncertainty about the situation suddenly turned to unease. Almost instinctively, he scanned his surrounds and loosened his sword in his scabbard. He couldn't find anything to explain the abrupt transition, but that did nothing to quell his disquiet. Taking a deep breath to calm his nerves, he stated softly, "Guess the only way to settle this is to see where he's headed."

Continuing at a cautious trot, T'sar followed Amroth's footprints for what seemed like an eternity to him. The tracks never veered, except to bypass an obstacle, and gradually shifted firmly to the southeast. Eventually, after what seemed like hours of cautious pursuit, the dull roar of a waterfall could be heard in the distance, bringing T'sar to a stop. In the dark, T'sar had failed to recognize the terrain and where the tracks were leading. The sound of the waterfall, however, hit him like a battering ram.

"The Triple Falls?" he thought, jealousy and anguish abruptly twisting his stomach into knots violently, obliterating any other possibility for Amroth's clandestine venture. *"That's Aseria's favorite meditation spot. . . . Corith, no — please! Not this wet-behind-the-ears pup! She'll love me, I just know it! Corith give me the time to prove I'm right for her!"*

Confident of Amroth's destination, anger and jealousy washed away caution and fueled his strides as he sprinted off, veering to the northeast. Soon, the terrain began to drop, and T'sar found himself scrambling between snow-covered boulders and scattered evergreens until the wintery land leveled off and eventually deposited him on the rocky shore of a wide, fast-flowing river. Following the river back to the south, T'sar kept up a quick pace until the roar of the falls began to dominate his hearing. Slowing his pace, he moved to the riverbank and began picking his way across the jagged terrain toward a spot overlooking the falls from which he could observe.

Much to his chagrin, the slippery and lose footing slowed him further. However, he managed to push down his irritation at the delay and press forward. Eventually, to his foreboding relief, the crests of the falls finally presented themselves. Despite his inner turmoil, caution managed to return to the forefront, and he dropped to a crouch as he crept away from the riverbank toward a cluster of large stones blanketed with snow and ice at the edge of the falls. To his dismay, upon reaching the stones, the sound of two voices drifted up to him. While it was nearly impossible to make out the words, the voices were all too familiar, and his heart sank. Dropping to his knees unceremoniously, T'sar peeked between two of the larger stone specimens, and he nearly screamed in anguish. As he feared, there they were – Aseria and Amroth – standing on the bank of the waterfall basin, chatting as if they hadn't a care in the world.

A terrifying and confusing mix of emotions threatened to drown T'sar at that moment. Part of him wanted to scream. Part of him wanted to run far away, while another part of him wanted to charge in there and strangle Amroth. T'sar, however, did nothing of the sort. Paralyzed by the overwhelming emotions, he merely knelt there, straining to hear, and watched his world crumble about him once more.

Hands on her black-clad, cocked hips, and with a warm smile on the full lips of her slender face, Aseria quipped with a twitch of her ears, her musical voice playful, "Took you long enough! It isn't proper to keep a lady waiting."

Embarrassed, Amroth let out a nervous laugh as he approached Aseria. Standing on the shore of the icy pool, which was kept flowing by the three falls that roared in defiance of the cold that sought to halt its flow, Aseria's blue-lavender eyes were fixed on him from astride her slender, flat nose with a tenderness and joy that made Amroth's cheeks feel warm.

"Deo, she is so beautiful; not to mention kind for offering to tutor me. Though I have to wonder . . ." he thought as he watched her standing there, moonlight playing off her skin-tight white fur, blonde accent stripes and hair like she was made of gilded ivory. "Sorry," he replied sheepishly as he came to a halt a few feet from her. "T'sar beat me up pretty good, then Alsa got her claws in me."

"A rough night then?" she asked as she let her hands drop to her sides and approached him.

Amroth shrugged. "No worse than most so far. The bruises are healed, and I only broke seven vases this time."

"Seven? That's an improvement," Aseria stated as she came to a stop, gazing at him in admiration.

Finding himself suddenly nervous beneath her beautiful eyes, he thought, *"The way she's looking at me right now. I've seen that same look before, but there's something more there.*" He scoffed mentally. "*Right, Amroth. . . . Overlooking that she's an entirely different species, no one that beautiful would ever be interested in you. Still. . . .*" Tossing that train of thought aside, Amroth replied a bit awkwardly, "You're messing with me, right?"

Aseria laughed, its warmth and brevity making Amroth blush. "No – absolutely not. When you got here, you couldn't even lift one. Now, in just a few short weeks, you're able to lift three at a time."

"Yeah, but I can't maintain it."

Reaching out, Aseria gave his shoulder a reassuring squeeze. "You will, I know it. If it makes you feel any better, I dropped a few tonight."

Feeling a giddy mix of nervousness and excitement at her touch, Amroth barely managed to keep his deep voice under control as he asked, "Really? That's a shock."

Releasing his shoulder, she shrugged. "I was distracted. Still, I wonder where she's getting all the pottery?"

Amroth barked a laugh, deep and rich, and Aseria followed suit. "That's a good question!" he stated, suddenly at ease.

Aseria grinned. "We should ask her tomorrow, if for nothing more than to irritate her a bit."

A grin that made her heart leap flashed across Amroth's solemn, but handsome face as he said, "Should be good for a laugh."

"Quite," Aseria echoed. "So, shall we get down to business?"

"Sounds good. What did you have in mind?"

"You're having trouble accessing your fir'gan and harnessing it, right?"

Amroth winced. "That obvious, huh?"

"Well, I could lie to you and say no, but I'd be doing you a disservice."

Amroth shook his head and chuckled. "The lie would have at least made me feel a bit better, but I see your point. So you think you can help me with this?"

Aseria nodded. "I hope so. I thought that I might offer you a different approach."

"I'm definitely open to a new approach," he stated in optimistic agreement. "But why did we have to come here?" he added, curious. "Couldn't we have done this at the keep?"

Aseria's stomach twisted nervously, and she fought the urge to bite her lower lip. "I. . . ." She hesitated.

Puzzled by her hesitation, Amroth prodded, "Is something wrong?"

"Yes, you beautiful fool! Can't you see how nervous I am around you? Can't you see that I have feelings for you?" she thought anxiously. Flashing a disarming smile, she told him, "No. . . . Nothing is wrong. I was just thinking." Even as the words left her lips, she found herself silently begging, *"Please give me some sign you feel something for me similar to what I feel for you!"*

Before Amroth could question her further, she quickly added. "As for why we're out here, I thought a change of scenery might help. Some place away from everyone else; a place where . . . there would be no distractions."

Still a bit confused by Aseria's hesitations, Amroth looked around nervously and nodded. "This a good place. Kind of reminds me of home."

"There's a place like this where you live?"

Amroth nodded again. "Larger by far," he stated wistfully, "but this place is no less beautiful," he finished, returning his gaze to her. Aseria fought to stay upright as she felt her knees melt beneath the warmth of his dark eyes as he said softly, "The keep I call home is built upon a cliffside over a trio of falls that spill out from an underground river. Much of the year, they provide fresh water to Merset, and a beautiful song by which to sleep. In the winter, most of the falls freeze in a fashion that one can only be viewed as Corith's beauty on display."

Aseria blinked rapidly, trying to clear the tears that had weld up at his heartfelt description of his home. "It sounds beautiful," she stated.

"It is," he replied with a smile full of longing. "I hope to go home sooner than later; my family needs me. If it wasn't for the strength I can gain here, I would have never left."

Aseria smiled weakly and fought off the sudden urge to hug him. "You know that they won't let you do that? It goes against the Wardens' tenants to openly interfere."

Amroth shrugged, and she noted a hint of hard determination in his eyes. "I know, but I won't let my family suffer anymore. If I can find a subtle way to do it, then so be it. If not. . . ." He shook his head. "Well, I'll cross that river when I come to it," he finished with a small, forced smile. "So, why don't we get started?

It's cold out here, and I haven't even come close to mastering that trick to keep me warm – lucky you."

Aseria laughed. "I hardly have it mastered, but you'll get it, trust me. As for what I have in mind, I think I know what may be your problem."

Raising a curious eyebrow, Amroth asked, "And what would that be?"

"Your motivation," she stated confidently.

"My motivation?" Amroth asked, dubious of her statement.

She nodded. "Yes. I don't mean that you aren't motivated – it's clear that you are. But I think that motivation is clouded, or at the very least overshadowed by. . . ." She hesitated once more.

"By what?" Amroth prodded.

"Anger."

"Anger?" Amroth asked, taken aback by the statement slightly. "Of course I'm angry!" he declared, his brow furrowing and his voice rising slightly. "I've had my whole life ripped apart and turned upside down, as I'm sure you have! Should I not be?"

Aseria winced, hurt. She had not intended to sting him so, and knew his frustration was not directed at her. However, from what she'd seen, and the bits of conversation she'd overheard between their instructors, she knew in her heart it was true.

"I don't say that to hurt you – Corith knows I don't ever want to do that!" she avowed passionately and apologetically. "You have every right to be angry, and even I feel that at times! Anger can be a potent weapon, but it can also shackle you! I think if you can get past your anger and learn to channel it, a lot of your problems controlling and harnessing fir'gan will wash away!"

Skeptical, and feeling a tad admonished, Amroth fell silent, causing Aseria's stomach to twist with fear. Had she already driven a wedge between them before she could find out if he had feelings for her by calling to light his problem? The mere thought of it chewed at her gut with a ferocity that made her want to vomit.

"Please don't look at me like that," she nervously thought as she watched his injured pride battle with what he knew to be true across his face. *"I just want to help! Please let me do that! Let me in, Amroth!"*

Those thoughts wailed in her mind for what seemed like an eternity until, finally, Amroth's expression softened.

"You're right," he conceded gently. "I think Damion has

tried to beat that into me – or out of me, depending on your point of view – and the others have tried to get me to see that, too." Meeting her eyes, he suddenly flashed her an apologetic and appreciative smile, causing her heart to leap. "I guess I've been too damn stubborn to see what's right before me. I'm sorry, Aseria . . . and thank you."

Fighting the urge to cry at his words and what she saw in his gaze, Aseria shook her head, thinking, *"Thank you for letting me in, Amroth."* Aloud, she said with a hint of a wry smile, "Don't thank me yet."

He nodded. "Okay. . . . Well then, what do you want me to do?"

Turning away from him, Aseria walked toward the water. To Amroth's surprise, he watched her purple aura gently flare to life as she gathered the currents just over the water, forming a narrow path of hardened air out to the middle of the pool. Stepping up on it, she walked out to the center and turned to face him. Letting the currents fade until there was only the small section bathed in the light of her aura holding her aloft, she raised her voice and told him, "Your task is to reach me."

Stunned by the enormity of the assignment, Amroth approached the edge of the pool. "Are you kidding me?! I thought we were going to work on some basics! This task is far beyond me! Hells, I can't even believe you can do it!"

"You're right about that," she thought as she offered him a wide smile to hide the strain it was causing her to maintain her platform. "So far, they've only taught you with a focus on combat. This gives you something different to strive for . . . something that doesn't involve destruction. Beyond that, this exercise has consequences that affect someone other than yourself. It's clear to all of us you have a kind, caring heart; and I believe the thought of letting harm come to others is something you'd much rather avoid than broken pottery or physical injury to yourself."

Amroth blanched a bit at her observation, and she knew she'd hit the target with her assumption about him.

"You will need to focus on your objective," she continued. Clear your mind of distractions, and focus solely on reaching me before I lose control and drop into the water." She started to shiver. "And if I might add – this is taking all my focus right now, and that water is *very* cold!"

Wide-eyed, and his mind reeling a bit from both the task and her observations of him, Amroth merely blinked at her.

Seeing his hesitation, she said through clenched teeth, "Well, what are you waiting for, hero? Save the damsel in distress!"

The imagery her analogy conjured managed to cut through Amroth's mental paralysis, and he let out a loud, full-throated laugh. "Thanks, I needed that!" he told her with a grin.

"Good! Then get on with it! I'm freezing my ass off out here!"

Smiling once more, Amroth nodded, then let his grin fade as he focused inward. The inner light that was his fir'gan had become much easier to find, but when he tried to grab hold of it, it slipped through his fingers. Again and again, he attempted to take control of his power, but like so many times before, it felt like he was trying to catch a greased pig. Frustrated, he scowled and sighed. "I don't think I can do it this quickly!" he called out.

Smiling despite the strain of maintaining her platform, she told him, her tone gentle but loud enough to be heard over the falls, "Yes, you can! You're probably trying to take hold of it like a weapon – don't do that! This isn't a fight! Take hold of it with the same gentleness you would use on an injured bird, or with the affection you would hold a loved one's hand."

Slowly, Amroth's face softened with comprehension and he nodded. Once more, he focused on the light at the core of his being. As he reached out to it, he tried to picture himself doing as Aseria recommended. Gently, he made contact with the light, and for a moment, he thought the soft touch had succeeded. To his chagrin, when he tightened his grip, it slipped through his grasp. Scowling, he shook his head and looked out at Aseria for help. Meeting her gaze, he suddenly found himself at a loss for words. Hopeful and confident, those were things he'd come to expect and admire in her, but there was something else in her eyes now. At first, he thought it was the same warmth he'd witnessed before, but then it dawned on him that this tenderness was something new . . . something loving –and it was focused solely on him.

Standing at the heart of the pool, her legs beginning to tremble from the exertion, Aseria felt her heart leap as she watched realization spread across Amroth's face. At that moment, as their gazes locked with affection for one another, she felt happier than she'd ever been. Then she watched as he took a deep breath and tried again. In an instant, Amroth took hold of his fir'gan with an ease he'd never displayed. A joyful smile spread across her face, lighting up her eyes as his emerald aura burst to life, gentle and serene, and he began picking air from the currents to build his own bridge. It was clumsy and sloppy, and she found herself thinking that a blind weaver with no hands could do a better job, but to see him stretch well beyond his current capabilities made her heart soar with pride.

Eventually, his suspect bridge reached her and Amroth set a cautious foot on it. Once he was satisfied it would support him, he stepped up on it and began to inch his way out to her. Despite the cold, Aseria felt sweat beginning to bead up on her brow as she watched his progress. She knew she could hold on for a while longer, but Amroth's pinched features showed that he was already feeling the strain; what's more, his bridge was beginning to unravel.

"Just a bit further! You can do it!" she urged.

Smiling weakly, Amroth focused on her and pushed forward.

Nervous, her breathing quickened as the distance slowly closed. Twenty feet . . . ten feet . . . five feet. . . . Then suddenly, he was there. Granted, he was exhausted, breathing heavily, and his aura was sputtering, but by some miracle, he'd reached her, and the smile of pride filling his face was all she needed to know it was worth the effort.

Flashing him a broad grin of her own, she stated, excited and proud, "You did it! See! You've got more skill than you give yourself credit for!"

"Thanks," he replied, embarrassed a bit by the praise. "But you deserve the credit," he added as his aura faded out of normal visibility.

She shook her head. "No, you would have gotten there eventually. I just gave you a different kind of motivation."

Amroth smiled warmly, and tenderly said, "That you did. . . . It's a good kind of motivation. Thank you."

Standing there, gazing down into his warm eyes, she saw what she felt for him looking back at her. For a moment, the world seemed to drop away from them as they started to inch closer to one another. Giddiness bounced about her stomach as Amroth tilted his head slightly and leaned in further. Her breath coming shallow and rapid, she leaned down slightly and parted her lips. Just as she closed her eyes in anticipation of his warm lips on hers, she felt the currents of Amroth's bridge buckle and scatter. Her eyes flew open just in time to see Amroth's shocked expression in the brief instant before his emerald aura vanished and the bridge collapsed, plunging him into the icy water with a splash.

The frigid liquid quickly brought him back to reality, and with desperate strength, Amroth clawed his way to the surface to find Aseria, despite the concern in her eyes, laughing.

"It's not funny!" he bellowed as he struggled to stay afloat.

"I'm sorry!" she apologized. "But the look on your face was priceless!"

"Right . . ." he muttered. "Just get me out of here before I drown!"

Crouching down on shaky legs, she extended her black-gloved hand. Latching onto it with a gloved hand of his own, Amroth suddenly grinned mischievously. Eyes wide, Aseria started to say, "Don't you dare, Am–!"

With a yank, Amroth sent Aseria head-first into the icy water. The frigid liquid was a shock to her system, and she had to fight off the urge to gasp. With haste, she oriented herself and hurriedly made for the surface. Breaching it, Aseria quickly looked around to see Amroth swimming urgently toward the shore.

"That's not funny!" She shouted in mock anger before following his lead with haste.

Climbing out of the water, Amroth began to shiver as he stood up and turned to watch her approach. Once she reached the edge of the basin and hauled herself out without Amroth's help, she stood up to find him watching her with a chattering smile.

"W-w-what?" she asked through the clatter of her own teeth as she began to rub her shivering torso with shaking hands.

"I-t-t w-w-was fun-n-ny!" he said with a shaky grin. "B-b-besi-si-sides-s-s, we'r-r-re e-e-even no-o-ow — we'r-r-re bo-o-oth w-w-wet!"

Rolling her eyes, Aseria smiled and said, "Th-th-that ma-ma-may be-e-e, bu-bu-but at-t-t l-l-least I ca-ca-can wa-wa-wa-warm mys-s-self-f-f up!" To emphasize her point, she once more took hold of her inner fir'gan and did just that, causing steam to rise from her soaked garments, before shielding herself against the elements.

"S-s-show of-f-f," Amroth muttered when she smiled at him.

"Come on, let's get you warm. There's an old cabin down-stream a bit. It has some dry wood and a serviceable hearth. It should do until you get dry. Can you make it?"

Shivering, Amroth nodded. "Le-e-ead on, a-a-and l-let's-s-s be q-q-quick ab-b-bout it! I ma-ma-may h-h-heal q-q-quickly, b-b-but I'd-d-d l-l-like to av-v-void d-dealing w-w-with fr-fr-frostb-b-bite."

Nodding, Aseria put a loving arm around him and led him away.

T'sar ran. To where? He didn't know, nor did he care. Anywhere was better than having to bear witness to what he'd just seen any longer. It was as horrifyingly clear as the scar on his face that Aseria's heart belonged to Amroth and his to her, and the sight of it sickened him.

"No!" his thoughts railed. *"It can't be! I was her friend at Blackstone! I walked that hell with her! It was I that was her shoulder to lean on at Sentinel Keep! And it was I who came to her rescue when that damn darlion attacked her! I should be the one she loves, not that boy!"*

A rock hidden in the snow caught his foot, sending him tumbling forward. With a muffled cry, he hit the ground hard, the ice and stone hidden beneath the white powder biting into him with disorienting force. Whimpering, he ever so slowly rolled over, his black bandana slipping from his head, and stared at the dancing sky with tears of anger streaming down his cheeks.

"It's a mistake," he eventually told himself when he could think straight once again. *"It has to be. This is nothing more than a fleeting infatuation.... Yes! That's it! I've seen this before; soldiers living and training together sometimes form bonds that they mistake for love! A few nights rutting and they'll eventually part ways when they realize it's nothing more than that! That has to be it!"*

His momentary satisfaction was quickly washed away in a new wave of heated anger at the thought of Amroth touching Aseria in such a way. Repulsed and incised, T'sar began to pound the ground with his fists, oblivious to the pain lancing through his hands as the stone bit into his flesh despite his gloves. Driven by building rage and raw jealousy, his wailing came to a sudden halt and he scrambled to his feet. Looking about for something to lash out at, he saw several large stones jutting from the snow in the distance. Stalking toward them with clenched fists, T'sar reached for the inner light that was his wellspring of fir'gan and latched onto it with violent ease.

"See, Aseria! See how easily I can do this!" he growled as his green aura angrily burst to life. "I am better than him in every way! Why can't you see that!" he bellowed and lashed out with the currents, blasting a chunk from one of the stones. "Is it the scar?!" he howled. "Can you not see past it! I love you more than that boy ever can!" he cried as he approached one of the marred chunks of stone. "Why can't you see that!" he screamed as he gathered the currents before his fist and slammed it into the stone, shattering it, and showering the area with snow and stone shrapnel.

"WHY! WHY! WHY!" he raged, each time lashing out at

another of the stones, cleaving them apart and shattering them until his fury was spent. Collapsing to his knees, his aura winked out and he buried his face in his hands as he rocked back and forth, weeping.

"Why?" he moaned through his tears.

"Why? 'Tis such a broad question," stated a voice that sounded like a warm wind on a spring day.

Startled by the voice, T'sar scrambled to his feet. "Who's there?!" he cried as he spun about, looking for the speaker.

"Why doth the sun rise?" the speaker replied, ignoring T'sar's demand. "Why is the sky blue? Why doeth we live? Why doeth we die?" The speaker chuckled. "Thou must see that the question of why 'tis what a mind without focus asks. 'Tis better for one to ask how. How dost one discover why the sun rises? How dost one discover why the sky is blue? How dost one live? How dost one die? What's more, in thine case – how doeth thee impress upon her thou art the better man?"

Still searching for the speaker, and a bit irritated by the bizarre speech pattern, T'sar growled, "Who are you, and what in the hells do you want?"

"Thine friends appeareth strong and quite talented; this cannot be ignored. Yet, thou hardly must stand within their shadow, for thou appears to possess the potential to be their equal, at the very least."

T'sar snorted. "I know I've got potential. Even my instructors have admitted as much."

"Ah, but I doth believe they art inept or hath refused to teach thee properly. Either way, 'twould seem their . . . shalt we say, lack of faith in thee 'tis holding thee back. 'Tis clear a part of thee understands this, and yet it erodes thine soul, doest it not? Thou believes that if thou were stronger, thou could prove thine worth not only unto thine comrades, but unto the woman thou so desperately desires. Am I wrong?"

T'sar's brow furrowed in deep thought. "You are not wrong," he finally admitted grudgingly, "and by the way you've hidden yourself, it's clear you are a Gifted of some power, which means you know what you are talking about. But why should I listen to someone that I don't know and who won't show themselves? Even better, why not come back to Gray Sky and present yourself and your case to the others?"

The speaker laughed, drawing a deep scowl from T'sar. "Astute. Which means an idiot thou art not – 'tis good. Fools should never be entrusted with power. 'Tis a shame that so many of those thou currently serves bear such a burden." The speaker sighed. "Alas, I doth believe 'tis a flaw so many carry. Ignorance is bliss, or so I hath heard. Mayhap I am too hard on them.... However, if one never admits to a fault, it will never be corrected. Alas, I stray off course. Thou hath made valid points that art worthy of answers."

A sensation of movement from behind T'sar made him spin about, his hand straying to his sword hilt. Before him, a figure swathed in black stood motionless. It was clear that the man was tall and slender beneath the black cloak and cowl, but try as he might, T'sar couldn't see anything in the shadows of the hood.

"Who are you?" T'sar asked, his grip tightening on his hilt. "I'd guess you're a darlion, given the way your hood sits, but I've never seen a darlion whose ears jut out to their shoulders."

The man let out a patronizing laugh that made T'sar scowl. "Oh, I doth not intend offense. I can understand why one might mistake me for one of their ilk – they art our cousins, after all. However, no, I am not. Mine name is Raefalzyn De'lovania," he declared as he reached for his hood with slender, black-gloved hands, "and I am of the Second Race, the children of Dracus; I am an elvannue."

Pulling back his hood, the moonlight fell upon a fair-skinned, lean face with high cheekbones accented by a silver strip running along the bottom edge of each to a tapered point just shy of his slender nose. Elongated, upturned eyes the color of a stormy sea peered at T'sar from behind bangs of sliver-streaked, black hair that hung at eye level like a maw of jagged teeth. Long, nearly shoulder-width ears pierced his mass of moderately long hair before tapering down to slender points. Engraved with a sweeping pattern reminiscent of a leafy vine, silver ear cuffs protected the tops of those ears from their tips to his face, the base of which protected his earlobe and served as the origin for both the strips beneath his cheekbones, and the matching strips that traced his jawline halfway to his chin.

T'sar found himself at a loss for words as he stared at Raefalzyn in stunned amazement. The man was right; there was a passing similarity to a darlion in the cut of his features and the length of his ears and limbs, but that was where it ended. Granted, his exposure to darlions was severely limited, but there was an arrogant, dangerous beauty to the elvannue's features that sent a chill up his spine that was far more terrifying than anything his encounter with Darkon had elicited. Here was a man that was not only wealthy and powerful, but also remarkably dangerous. And that sensation of danger was all too familiar. He'd felt it in the presence of Darius. He'd seen it in action at Blackstone and in every violent encounter with Wardens and

Knights alike. This man was a dangerously powerful Gifted; this man was. . . .

"You're a Warden, aren't you?"

The man smiled, and bowed deeply with a flourish, permitting T'sar a fleeting glance at the dark, foreign attire he wore beneath his cloak. "Thou hath guess rightly, though," he added as he righted himself, "I doubt thou needeth go far to draw such a conclusion. I am the Preceptor of the Des'moloyor Order of the Light."

"Des'moloyor?" T'sar asked, puzzled. "I don't think I've heard of that one."

Raefalzyn smirked knowingly. "No, I suppose thou might not. I'm afraid mine Order 'tis but a small one whose tasks keep us isolated from the others more often than not."

"I see," T'sar said, dubious of the man's statement. "If that's the case, what brings you here?"

"A valid question. Alas, 'tis one I cannot answer. If it allays thine fears, I am only passing through; however, Darkon thought I might look in on the youngling's training ere I move on."

T'sar relaxed his grip on his sword. "Darkon, eh? And why should I believe that?"

Raeflzyn shrugged. "Believe it or do not, it matters little to me. If thou dost not believe me, thou could ask Greatjon to commune with Darkon. . . . Though, such an action mayhap be unwise. The tension betwixt the two 'tis already great, and mine presence mayhap exacerbate their relations."

Letting go of his sword, T'sar folded his arms before his chest with a grunt. "That might be putting it mildly. But if that is the case, why reveal yourself to me? Seems damn stupid if you don't want to make the situation worse between Greatjon and Darkon."

"I heard a pained soul crying out for succor, and I thought it wise to investigate. Grateful am I for doing so, for thou art clearly such a soul."

T'sar scoffed. "So, what do you plan to do? Can you do anything about this?" he gestured violently at his scars.

Shaking his head, Raefalzyn said sadly, "Alas, without the blessing of a crystal, thou will bear such a mark of pride for the remainder of thine life."

T'sar barked a sarcastic laugh. "Mark of pride? You think this horrific mess is something to be happy about? That idea is about as bizarre as your appearance and the way you talk!" he finished with a derisive sneer.

Ignoring T'sar's barbed words, Raefalzyn cast an appraising gaze on the tortured man. "Aye, pride. What delivered that unto thee should hath killed thee, yet thou survived. To endure such a horror 'tis a reflection of thine heart and spirit. To revile it as thou doeth is to cast aside the strength within thee. That 'tis thine flaw, but 'tis not the issue I wish to address."

Rolling his eyes, T'sar tossed his hands in the air. "That's just great! If you can't fix this, then what can you do? It's ruined my life, and it's cost me her!"

Raefalzyn frowned deeply, and T'sar couldn't tell if it was out of pity or disgust. "Such a pessimistic view. Still, I can work around such. If thou love her as strongly as though doth profess, and believe she can feel the same for thee, then this attitude thou embraces must be vanquished. Alas, I also fear the strength thou seeks is tepid within thee."

T'sar growled. "Damn right I love her!" he spit in anger. "And I know I'm not as strong as I should be! My teachers tell me I have talent, but they refuse to teach me the way they should! I'm clearly more talented than him, yet they toss me bread crumbs while everyone focuses their attention on that cowardly fool!"

"Ah, I see . . ." Raefalzyn murmured, tapping his chin. "This fool thou speaketh of, who is he? Darkon made no mention of another trainee."

"His name is Amroth," T'sar practically hissed. "That cold bastard Damion brought him here. Suppose to be special in some way, but hells if I can see it!"

"Damion 'tis here?" Raefalzyn asked with a raised eyebrow. "'Tis an interesting development," he muttered. "Still, of little consequence," he stated with a dismissive shake of his head. "I would say thine teachers art truly doing thee a disservice." He paused thoughtfully. "What if I were to teach thee? 'Twould be difficult – possibly harder than what thine fellow students currently endure – but I can promise thou shalt become more powerful than thou can imagine."

T'sar scoffed. "Not that I don't find your offer tempting, but no matter what you teach me, both of them are to be Wardens. I'll never match that."

Approaching T'sar, the man gripped his shoulders with surprising strength as he gazed intently down at him. "Mine dear fool, not every Warden 'tis as powerful as they doth appear, and they hath weaknesses that can be exploited. If thou will allow me to train thee,

I can show thee how a Gifted can defeat a Warden. What's more, thou shalt gain the strength and confidence to prove unto the girl thou profess love for that thou art the only man worthy of her affection. There is even a chance, mayhap, that one day thou could possess a crystal of thine own. Wardens doth die, after all." He paused for a moment and watched as his words sank in with T'sar. Finally, he asked, "Doth we hath an accord?"

Staring hard into Raefalzyn's eyes, T'sar felt his doubts about the man wash away in a wave of blazing hope. "I accept," he stated adamantly.

Squeezing T'sar shoulders again, Raefalzyn smiled and released him. "Good. I can delay mine journey for a week, mayhap two. Meet me here about this time every night and we shalt endeavor to accomplish all that we can in such time. If thou doeth indeed prove worthy of further attention, I shalt make thee mine student for the foreseeable future."

T'sar nodded. "What if I'm discovered? What should I tell them?"

Raefalzyn shrugged. "Whatever thou wants. Just remember – mine presence may be disruptive, and I dost not believe Darkon nor the others would take kindly to anything that 'twould interfere with their instruction."

T'sar nodded slowly, his brow furrowed in thought. "You're right. Your presence is safe with me."

Raefalzyn smiled, broad and warm. "Good. Then I shalt bid thee farewell until the morrow."

"Wait!" T'sar shouted as Raefalzyn turned and started to pull up his hood.

"Aye?"

"Can't we start tonight?"

Turning back to T'sar, Raefalzyn stated, "We could, but I doth believe thou hath more pressing matters to attend to."

Confused, T'sar asked, "Excuse me?"

"I must remain apart from mine fellow Wardens for now, mine task demands no less, else I would intervene."

"Intervene?" T'sar asked, his confusion growing.

"Mine dear, T'sar – the enemy 'tis encroaching upon the fool and thine love as we speak," he stated ominously, gesturing south. "Can thou not feel it?"

Horrified, T'sar spun and did his best to seek out his friends on the currents. It was a strain on him, and he could barely discern anything from the flow of fir'gan, but there was a sickening disruption that made his heart clench with dread.

"Thou should make haste. Mayhap they can protect themselves, but why take such an undue chance?"

Turning to Raefalzyn, T'sar set his jaw and nodded. "Thank you."

"Think nothing of it. However, dost endeavor to remain alive. 'Twould hate to lose one such as thee."

Nodding again, T'sar turned and retrieved his bandana. Settling it on his head, he did his best to harness the currents as he sprinted away, desperation fueling his strides.

Staring at T'sar's quickly vanishing back with a gaze full of revulsion, Raefalzyn turned away and pulled his hood up. "Humans," he said with a sad, disgusted sigh, "what a waste. 'Tis a shame mine brothers and sisters refused to see how unworthy Corith was of our veneration when the bastard bestowed those violent, short-lived fools upon Kylir."

Looking up at the night sky, he smiled. "Still," he added as the surrounding darkness began to envelope him, "even the foolish and unworthy hath their uses. Through the Light's greatest mistake and its greatest weapon against thee, I shalt purge Kylir of the mortal blight, and bring unto the land the pristine perfection that the Light burnt away in its arrogance! Isn't that so, Father Night?" he finished as he vanished into the darkness.

*

"You're looking better," Aseria quipped as she tossed another log on the fire.

Rubbing his torso with his hands beneath the threadbare blanket Aseria had found for him, Amroth smiled at her. "I've been through worse. But I'll admit, the fire is quite welcome." Looking about, he added for the second time since their arrival, "Glad you knew about this place, and that it's still standing."

Most of the modest cabin had collapsed long ago, but the main room and the hearth were still usable despite multiple holes in the roof and the dusting of snow that had collected since Aseria cleared the area.

"Any idea who lived here?" Amroth asked.

"Possibly a small family," Aseria replied as she checked on

the dryness of Amroth's dark garments and red-trimmed gray leather armor, which were arranged before the fire burning brightly in the remains of a small stone hearth, "but with as isolated as it is, it's more likely that this was a hunter or woodsman's home."

"Makes sense," Amroth replied as she flipped his shirt and pants over. "I'm just glad it and this blanket was still useable," he finished with a wry smile as Aseria sat down next to him.

"Agreed. Still," she snuggled close to him and leaned her head on his shoulder, "I'm sorry you fell in. I didn't intend for that to happen."

His cheeks growing flush with warmth at her touch, Amroth chuckled. "Sure you didn't. . . . I'm beginning to think this was your plan all along," he teased.

Laughing, Aseria closed her eyes. With a smile, she said, "Hardly, but I won't argue with the results. Will you?" she finished, glancing up at him.

Meeting her warm gaze, he smiled. "Not in the least," he replied before he adjusted his arm so that he could drape it and the blanket around her.

Smiling broadly, she tucked herself close to him and placed a hand on his chest over his heart as his arm and the blanket settled about her shoulders. "Your heart is beating strong and fast," she murmured softly even as she realized her own pulse had quickened.

"*Um-hum*," Amroth uttered as he squeezed her lovingly and placed his own hand on hers.

Reveling in his warmth, Aseria's eyes closed and she smiled with a sense of contentment she'd never felt before. She didn't know how long they sat there basking in each other's presence before Amroth shifted gently and she felt a hesitant, but tender, kiss atop her head. Smiling softly, she pulled back enough to look him in the eyes. What she saw gazing back at her made her heart leap with joy and excitement. Hesitating only a moment, she moved in.

Amazed at himself for mustering the courage to kiss the top of her head, he was both pleased and surprised when she pulled back and returned his gaze with a heartfelt one of her own. A momentary flash of concern cut through his mind when she appeared to briefly contemplate something, but that moment vanished in an instant when she moved her head toward his. Cocking his head slightly, he closed his eyes just before their lips met. Soft and silky, her kiss was gentle at first, sending waves of pleasing warmth through them both. Then, with a shudder of pleasure and desire, their lips parted and the kiss turned deep and urgent. Shifting, Amroth pulled her into a tight embrace as she snaked a hand behind his head and pulled him deeper into the kiss.

Lost as she was in the passion of the moment, with his firm lips upon hers as they exchanged gentle caresses, it dawned on the part of her mind that was still vaguely connected to reality that the man holding her close was bereft of clothing save the blanket and his smallclothes, stoking the desire that now burned within her. Blissfully lost to the moment, she moaned softly as her hand strayed over his forge-toned chest and abdomen. Their breathing quickened as her long fingers strayed lower. Just as they touched the damp under garment, to her surprise, she felt his hand clasp about hers tenderly.

"I'm sorry, but no," he said gently as he pulled away from their kiss a bit. "I really do like you, but this is all new, and . . . well . . . I'm not like that. As much as I deeply want to have you right now, it wouldn't be right this soon."

A bit surprised, she leaned back and could see just how much he wanted to give in to the desire that threatened to overtake them fully. Her people had long viewed humans as extremely sexually promiscuous and eager; and while her time amongst humans had proven that to be an exaggeration, she still found human restraint in that area to be highly commendable.

However, her increasing respect for Amroth only served to enflame her desire more even as she breathed, "Not even if I want it?"

Amroth shook his head gently. "Not even then, despite how tempting it is," he replied with a smile, his voice thick with desire. "Believe me – you are very beautiful, and I do have feelings for you. Let's just take our time and see where it goes, okay?"

Looking into his eyes, she had no doubt that what he said was true. Although a bit disappointed, Alestra nodded and smiled as she said, "Okay." Letting out a warm chuckle, she added, "You're full of surprises, you know that?"

Laughing, Amroth replied, "Hopefully, good ones where you're concerned."

Leaning in, she kissed him again, deep and long. Pulling away, she stated softly, her tone pleased, "Very good ones." Shifting, she tucked herself close to him, returned her hand to his chest, and leaned her head on his shoulder. "I'm sorry if I was too forward," she offered as an apology as he draped his arm around her shoulders. "I got lost in the moment."

Smiling, Amroth squeezed her. "There's nothing to be sorry for."

Tapping his chest gently, she replied playfully, "Good, because I don't regret it."

Amroth laughed. "Deo, you are amazing! I've only known you a short while, and already I am grateful for having met you."

Smiling broadly, she looked up at him and started to reply, "That's good. And I y–"

Suddenly, her ears perked up and she sat upright, her posture rigid and alert as she sniffed the air.

"What's wrong?" Amroth asked, any thoughts of their potential romantic encounter washed away by a mix of confusion and worry.

Darting to her feet, she did her best to probe the currents as she'd been taught. While what she could glean was sporadic and jumbled, she didn't need the currents' confirmation to understand what her other senses had alerted her to. Cold dread settling in her stomach, she looked at Amroth and declared, "We've got company! Get dressed now! We need to get out of here!"

Aseria's urgency was palpable, and Amroth had seen it far too many times amongst the Army of Five Stars to further question what had her so on edge. Scrambling to his feet, he hastily pulled on his clothing as Aseria moved to what used to be a window in the front wall.

"What's out there?" he asked as he secured his belt and stomped his feet into his boots.

"Something we don't want to face if we don't have to," she stated, doing her best to quell the fear tearing at her gut.

Pulling his sectional leather-armor top on, he started working on the ties and buckles as he asked, his own concern growing at the tightness of her words, "And that would be?"

Hustling over to him, her deft hands went to work on securing the different sections of his armor as she stated gravely, "We were damn fools for coming out here unarmed! Corith, I hope we don't have to put your skills to the test tonight!"

It felt like it took an eternity to finish securing all the buckles, but when it was done, she nodded gravely at Amroth and gave his pauldrons a firm pat before she bolted to the door, threw it open and sprinted off with him in tow.

"What in the hells are we running from?!" he demanded as

she angled them to the northwest and he pulled alongside her.

Grinding her teeth together, she barked, "Blackhearts!"

Stunned by the admission, Amroth nearly stumbled. "Are you sure?" he asked as they weaved through the trees.

"Too damn sure! Now stop asking questions, and run!" she barked, the panic in her voice nearly overwhelming her melodic tones.

Try as he might, Amroth was having difficulty keeping pace with Aseria's long strides, and he soon fell back of her a bit; furthermore, he couldn't find any indication that they were in actual danger.

Nearing the river, Amroth asked again, "Are you sure we're being pursued? I don't see or sense anything!"

Aseria nodded, her ears pinned back and her eyes wide with fear as the stench on the winds was growing stronger to her sensitive nose. "They're close! Keep moving if you want to—"

With a sharp intake of breath, Aseria came to a hard stop and threw herself at Amroth just as he came alongside her, driving him to the frozen ground violently just as an arrow whistled above them.

Dazed, Amroth could only stare at Aseria as she snarled and pushed to her feet. Rolling over, his senses tingled as the currents gathered around Aseria and her purple aura flared to life.

"Stay down!" she barked just before he felt a wave of warmth shoot past him.

Looking in the direction of her attack, he was startled to see a trio of figures in dark leather armor burst into flames, their screeching screams tearing through the air as they fell to the ground. For a moment, he lay there, both impressed by Aseria's display and horrified by their assailants. Suddenly, he felt Aseria tugging him to his feet.

"On your feet, lover boy!" she yelled just as Amroth spotted several more figures moving through the darkness beyond the now smoldering corpses.

Scampering to his feet, they sprinted away just as a flurry of arrows bit into the ground and trees around their previous position.

Fueled by a new sense of urgency, they weaved through the forest in a desperate attempt to keep their pursuers from gaining a clear line of sight. To their amazement, it worked, and they reached the river without being struck. That boon was short-lived, however.

Coming to a halt at the river's edge, Aseria cursed. "Da'liq! It's too damn deep to wade across! Can you build a bridge fast enough?" she asked desperately.

Swallowing hard, Amroth shook his head. "No," he whispered, distraught.

"Damn!" she snarled.

Turning to face the trees in the distance, it became clear to her that even if he could have woven a bridge with haste, there wouldn't be enough time. Their pursuit knew they had them cornered and were fanning out to pin them in.

"Go on without me," Amroth stated, his tone somber.

"What?" She asked incredulously, taking her eyes off the closing trap to glare daggers at Amroth.

Amroth ignored her fierce glower as he turned to face the oncoming threat, but said nothing as he noticed just how close the blackhearts were and his heart sank. There were a dozen of them visible already, their silhouettes marked by long ears and elongated proportions, and there was movement in the distance that suggested more were on the way. Setting his jaw, he told Aseria, "You can make a bridge much quicker than me and get across. I'll buy you what time I can. Who knows, maybe their poison won't work on me."

"Like hells I'm leaving you!" she growled before embracing the currents as deeply as she dared, causing her purple aura to flash violently. "You attack; I'll defend."

"Are you sure you can do that?" Amroth asked, his emerald aura flashing into existence as he took hold of the currents with as much skill as he could muster.

"I hope so," she muttered as her aura flared and she began to weave a defensive barrier.

Just as she saw the blackhearts before them set arrows to their twisted bows and take aim, Amroth managed to rip air from the currents and press it into a sloppy blade. Unfortunately, he was all too aware that he had very little time to act, and he lashed out before the blade was ready. To the young Gifteds' horror, the feeble attack struck home with minimal impact, and with only a few blackhearts knocked off balance, the dreadful creatures let fly.

"What do I do? Oh, Corith – there's so many of them!"

Crouched low behind a boulder, T'sar peered downriver at the blackhearts advancing on Aseria and Amroth. He figured there were close to two dozen, but that mattered little; one was dangerous enough, and he had no idea how he could help them.

"Run!" his mind screamed at them, but as he watched Aseria

526

and Amroth turn and steel themselves, he knew that wouldn't be the case.

"Help them, damn it!" he railed at himself, but his limbs refused to move.

Closer the blackhearts marched, tightening the noose; and as he watched the shadowspawn advance on the woman he loved and the man that had stolen her from him, he found memories of Blackstone's fall rising up to claim him. In a haze of terror, he screamed as visions of the horribly mutilated and corrupted bodies of his comrades reached for him, begging him to join them. Screaming again, he stumbled forward and collapsed just as a few of the blackhearts stumbled and let fly, but by then, his mind was already gone.

"Damn it!" Aseria thought as the haphazard arrows cut toward her. Throwing herself to the side, two of the arrows bounced off her hastily constructed shield, and a third whizzed overhead just as a cry of anguish echoed through the air.

Looking up, she saw that the scream had monetarily drawn everyone's attention. Bolting to her feet, she let the shield go as she screamed at Amroth, "Light them up!"

Startled by the horrifying shriek, and confused by Aseria's order, Amroth blinked at her just as she lashed out at the trees around the blackhearts, cutting them clean through. With a groan, dozens of trees crashed to earth, knocking some of the blackhearts from their feet and crushing others.

"Amroth!" she cried even as she shattered rocks around those climbing to their feet to buy more time.

Driven by desperation, Amroth finally realized what she meant, and took a tenuous grasp of the currents. Plucking fire from it, he shamefully mixed it with air and lashed out at the trees. To his horror, only a few small blazes took.

Shaking his head, he cried, "I'm sorry! The currents just keep slipping away!"

Sweating profusely, Aseria pleaded, "You can do it! Focus! Our lives depend on it!"

"I know, but— Lookout!" he screamed and dove toward her.

Twisting, Aseria turned in time to see a blackheart let fly. As the arrow streaked toward her, she knew she didn't have enough time to deflect or dodge it.

Then he was there.

Arms wide, Amroth was before her, his eyes growing large as the arrow thudded into his upper back.

Aseria's eyes bulged and her ears went rigid in horror as she screamed, shrill and heartbroken, "*AMROTH!*"

Almost immediately, Amroth felt a tiny pinprick of fire where the arrow struck. The sensation started to spread quickly, and sweat began to pour down his face. Smiling weakly, and his vision swimming, his aura winked out as he slumped forward.

"No, no, no!" she pleaded as she released her hold on the currents and caught him. "You fool! Don't be dead! Corith, no!" she wailed, tears streaming down her cheeks, as his dead weight dragged her to the ground. "Please, Amroth! Don't do—" she started to beg, when an ear-rattling bang tore through the air as the fallen trees suddenly exploded in a mass of flames.

Stunned, the blast knocked her on her back just as a massive furred form leapt over her.

"Stay back!" A rough voice barked as a large man surrounded by a raging green aura ran by.

Sitting up to the violent melody of snarls, and howls of pain filling the air, Aseria disentangled herself from Amroth and crouched down beside him. Eyes wide and lips trembling with fear, Aseria reached out and grabbed the dark arrow lodged in Amroth's back near its fletching. To her surprise, the arrow refused to budge. Snarling, she gripped it with both hands and pulled with all her might. Initially, it refused to move, but then, without warning, it tore loose, causing her to fall to her rear. Tossing the poison-coated, obsidian-tipped arrow away, she scrambled to Amroth's side and prided open the rent in his armor.

Expecting to see a quickly festering wound, she started to plead, "Don't you die on me . . ." but her words trailed off in surprise. "What in the world?" she breathed as she watched what looked like a spot of plate armor fade to off-colored, fever flesh.

Before she could begin to question what she just saw, the fever faded from the impact area, leaving unmarred skin behind. Instinctively, Aseria quickly reached for his neck, seeking his pulse. Elation flooded her when she found it strong and hale. Breathing a profound sigh of relief, she looked up to see a macabre horror playing out.

Deralina, her black- and gray-splotched fur drenched in blood, and a few arrows jutting from her hide, danced a bloody show with Greatjon as they weaved amongst the foul creatures. Fangs, claymore and scythes of fir'gan were a blur as they severed limbs and rent bodies asunder with a dreadful lack of concern for themselves. To Aseria's horror, the blackhearts fought with similar disregard, landing blow after blow upon the Bestyne Knight. Yet, instead of slowing the deadly pair, the wounds seemed to fuel their rage, spurring them to greater violence.

Positioning herself defensively above Amroth, the suddenly icy snow crunching beneath her feet, she looked about and saw more of the shadow-spawned creatures pouring from the night. "Corith, how many of them are there?" she growled in frustration, her breath coming out in puffs of white.

"Too damn many for my liking," a cold voice stated from behind.

Startled, she spun and stared.

Standing behind her, arms folded across his chest, was Damion.

"Corith be good! Damion?" she asked, alarmed by what she saw.

From just above his eyebrows to his jawline, red-trimmed black fangs framed a pair of silver-flecked white eyes that glared at the macabre scene as if death itself was judging the merit of the battle.

Letting his hands drop to his sides, he stepped past her without an answer, his icy-blue-tinted silver aura bursting to life for all to see. The air around her turned painfully cold as he passed by, ripping a hiss of pain from her as she quickstepped away from him.

"What the hells?" she asked in confusion.

Ignoring her, Damion barked as his aura writhed about him angrily, "Clear out, now!"

On cue, the direwolf and her master disengaged and, in a flash, were standing defensively before Amroth and Aseria at a safe distance.

Before she could question what was happening, the burning fires hissed out just as the blackhearts, living and dead alike, erupted in chilling, cold-blue flames, bathing the area in a haunting light. Peering at Damion, she felt a chill run down her spine as she watched the malice with which he wielded the currents to the accompaniment of the burning blackhearts' shrill screams.

How long the devastation lasted, she did not know, but the frigid flames continued to grow, even after the last scream faded, until the area was engulfed by the blaze. Desperate to find something else to look at, Aseria looked down at Amroth and was shocked to see a thin dusting of ice crystals on him. Crouching, she cleaned his face and rechecked his pulse.

"Is he alright?"

Looking up, she nearly jumped upon seeing Greatjon, drenched in dark blood and his eyes still burning with bloodlust, leaning heavily on his equally gory claymore as he gazed down at them. Nodding slowly, she said, "I think so. . . . But I don't know how. He took an arrow in the back." She shook her head, perplexed. Looking at Damion, she asked cautiously, her stomach twisting with unease as she watched the icy light from the raging inferno of cold dance about him, "What is he doing, and what is he?"

Frowning, Greatjon told her, "What is he? He is cursed. He is a man upon which a heavy toll was placed for his folly. He is *the* Death Bringer."

Aghast, she glanced back at Greatjon, and in his scarred visage, she saw fearful respect that made her shiver. Switching her gaze once more to Damion, she heard Greatjon grunt before shouting, "And he's being a bit overzealous! Regular fire would work just fine!"

Damion smirked darkly. "Just being thorough – and sending a message."

"*Humph!* And just who are you sending the message to? That kind of display would catch the attention of a Gifted clear across Triclose!"

"Don't be ridiculous," Damion replied as he smothered the blaze in an instant. "Maybe as far as Blackstone, I'll give you that," he added as he turned toward them and his aura winked out. "But even you have to admit," he stated as the markings on his face began to fade, and his eyes faded to their natural black, "this was no roving band of blackhearts. There's a Warden out there."

"Right," Greatjon agreed grimly as he stood upright.

Approaching them, Damion asked, "Are you and Deralina alright?"

"We'll need rest, and these clothes will need to be burned, but we're fine. Which reminds me. . . ." Turning, he tossed his sword aside, and as it hit the ground, the blade erupted in viciously hot fire. Greatjon let the blade burn for a moment before smothering the flames and retrieving his sword. Sheathing it along his back, he returned to them. "All better. But to be safe, don't get close, Aseria. I'd hate for something so asinine as blood on my clothes to do you in."

530

Nodding slowly, she asked, "And Deralina?"

Greatjon gave her a reassuring smile. "She'll just need rest. You see, our direwolves are not . . . natural. See?" he finished, pointing to the large wolf.

Wide-eyed, Aseria watched as the viscous, foul-smelling blood on the panting direwolf seemed to be evaporating. "Dear Corith. . . ."

"The workings of the Bestyne wolves can wait," Damion interrupted. "Greatjon, see to it that your wolves are out patrolling. Let's make sure we don't have any more uninvited guests."

Greatjon nodded, and his eyes suddenly went out of focus.

Turning back to Aseria, he walked over to her and asked as he crouched beside her, "How is he – and just what in the hells were you two doing out here alone and unarmed?!"

Flinching at his tone, Aseria offered meekly, "I didn't think it would be dangerous! I've been out here plenty of times . . ." she trailed off with a shake of her head. "I wanted to help him," she declared, her tone suddenly turning aggressive, "and I thought a change of approach would help . . . instead of hammering at him like an unyielding piece of metal!"

Greatjon's attention returned to the present just in time to hear Aseria's barbed finish, which drew a smirk from him and a grunt from Damion.

"Stupid and foolish," Damion muttered. "But I can't fault your purpose. Still, you should have informed us."

"I know, but. . . ." she trailed off again as tears welled up in her eyes at the thought of harm coming to Amroth through her actions.

Damion gave her shoulder a comforting squeeze. "Don't beat yourself up. Other than unconscious, he appears to be fine."

"I don't understand how, though." Pointing to the arrow, she declared, "That was lodged in his back. There's no way he should have lived."

Looking at the toxic arrow, Damion incinerated it with a quick burst of flame. "Show me where it hit him," he asked, his tone thoughtful and curious.

Nodding, Aseria pried open the hole in his armor. "There. It was stuck like . . . like it was lodged in a rib. But when I pulled it out, it looked like. . . ." She shook her head in denial.

"Looked like what?" Damion prodded.

She hesitated a moment, thinking that they might find her explanation silly. Finally, she offered, "This is going to sound stupid, but his skin looked gray and hard for a moment before it vanished. Then, just for an instant, his skin looked infected and feverish. But that disappeared just as quickly."

Looking up at Greatjon, Damion found him gazing back with eyes filled with knowing concern.

"It's not stupid, Aseria," Damion informed her as he switched his attention back to her. "For now, don't worry about it. He's alive . . . and appears to be suffering from nothing more than exhaustion. If he'd really been poisoned, we all know he'd be dead. For now, let's get him back to the keep so he can rest. We can worry about everything else later." Carefully, Damion rolled Amroth over before scooping him up and draping the young Merandith over his shoulder. "Greatjon, you and Deralina take the lead. Oh, and do me a favor? Get rid of that tainted clothing before we go."

Scowling, Greatjon responded, "Can't that wait?"

"Yes, but I don't want either of us accidentally stepping in any blood, and I also don't want to risk any of that accursed fluid getting back to Blackstone. I'd hate to have to cleanse the place."

Muttering to himself, Greatjon quickly disrobed. "This is just great. I get to run bare-arse naked back to the keep, and then I'm gonna have to break in a new harness and boots! What in the hells did I do to deserve this?" he complained as he removed his sword from the baldric.

Embarrassed, Aseria busied herself with checking on Amroth.

"Small price to pay," Damion quipped as Greatjon tossed the baldric onto his pile of useless clothing.

"Right," Greatjon muttered as he ignited the garments. Once his clothes were incinerated and the ground cleansed, he rested his sword across his broad, muscular shoulders, and shot a scowl at Damion as he said, "Let's get going. And no jokes about this!"

Smiling, Damion quipped as Greatjon and Deralina took off at a trot, "Of course not."

*

Slipping onto the keep grounds, T'sar wasn't surprised to see it in an uproar. Wolves and soldiers alike were gathering before their commanders before being sent off in a hurry. Still reeling from the night's events, he did his best to look as if he was on his way to the Keep on orders. To his chagrin, he wasn't so lucky.

"T'sar! Where in the hells have you been?!" a rough but soft voice called out in vexation.

Cringing, T'sar came to a halt and turned to see Lieutenant Salina stalking toward him from the direction of the barracks as she secured the last of the buckles on her sectional leather armor. With the way her braid of long black hair swayed violently behind her and her feral golden eyes stared daggers at him, it was immediately clear she was very angry with him.

Standing to attention, he saluted, fist to heart. "Down at the village, sir!" he declared, fully expecting her to verbally trounce him.

Scowling at him, which was made violently fierce by her red-accent strips, she replied, dubious of his excuse, "The village, eh? Whatever! I don't have time to rip you a new arsehole right now! We're on alert! Blackhearts have been spotted, and I need everyone out searching! So if it's not an inconvenience, get your arse to your squad and get out there!"

T'sar was momentarily surprised at the fairly tame chastisement, but his anger and heartbreak quickly reasserted himself, and for a moment, he thought about telling her what sunless body part she could shove her orders. However, he thought better of it. Instead, he barked, "Yes, sir!" before sprinting toward the barracks with his lieutenant on his heels.

Standing before the keep's open main entrance, relief and a bit of confused amusement flooded through Alsa when Greatjon and the others emerged from the darkness. Granted, she'd been in contact with Damion and already knew the situation, but seeing them put her fully at ease. As for the sight of a completely naked Greatjon trotting her way through the scrambling Bestynes, it was all she could do not to stare, and to keep the jokes that popped into her head from her lips.

"Don't say anything," Greatjon growled as he stalked past her and into the keep.

"I wouldn't dream of it," she stated with a smirk, which quickly vanished as Damion and Aseria stopped before her. "Is he alright?" she asked, motioning to Amroth with her chin.

Damion nodded. "Nothing that rest won't cure. I'm going to get him to bed." Walking past her, he linked with her and told her, *"Once things die down, we all need to talk."*

"Quite," she responded as she smiled softly at Aseria's worried expression.

"I'm so sorry, Lady Alsa!" Aseria cried, her ears drooping slightly. "I didn't mean for any of this to happen!"

"Child, none of us could have foreseen this. What's important is that you two are unharmed."

"I know, but I let my emotions cloud my judgment."

Alsa smiled sympathetically, even as her heart cinched with a knowing ache. "That you did. And for it, you have a better understanding of the risks of love between Wardens."

Aseria nodded as tears ran down her cheeks.

Wiping the tears away, Alsa cupped her charge's cheek and gazed up into her eyes compassionately. "I know you feel responsible for tonight, and though you could not have known blackhearts were around, it is a credit to you that you have accepted your role in this. I will not reprimand you; the pain you are feeling is a more potent lesson than any punishment I could devise."

Aseria flashed a weak, crestfallen smiled. "Thank you, Lady Alsa."

"Think nothing of it. However, what I want to know is this – will you let the horrors of this night dissuade you, or will you dare to pursue Amroth and discover what you can be for one another?"

Aseria stayed silent for a moment, considering Alsa's words. Then, her ears perking up, she stepped forward, startling Alsa as she embraced her teacher fiercely. For a moment, Alsa didn't know how to respond, but eventually, she smiled and returned the embrace. "Silly girl," she murmured. "To be young again."

Pulling away, Aseria smiled softly. "Thank you, Lady Alsa."

"You need not say anything," Alsa replied with a smile as she read Aseria's intent in her blue-lavender eyes. "Go on and see about your love."

Nodding, Aseria stepped around Alsa and took off at a trot, leaving Alsa to stare at the stars, her heart aching with longing, and her mind filled with dreadful thoughts.

*

He moaned.

Moaning again, as if the mere act was painful, Amroth opened his eyes and groaned as light stabbed at them.

"You're awake! Thank Corith!"

Blinking to clear his vision, Amroth looked toward the speaker and saw Aseria sitting by his bed in a simple chair, her face an exhausted mask of concern that was quickly fading to relief.

"What the hells happened, and how did I get here?" he asked groggily as he looked around the lamp-lit room. Right away, he recognized the simple desk covered in books as the one that occupied his small room. To his surprise, the light slipping in through the lone window set above a wash basin on the far wall was showing early signs of dawn's approach.

Smiling, Aseria grabbed his hand and kissed it. "You stupid fool!" she said. "You stupid, stupid, fool!"

"Hey now," Amroth muttered. "What did I do to deserve that?"

Aseria laughed, releasing the tension that had been building in her. "You stepped in front of a blackheart arrow!"

Blinking at her, Amroth ran a hand through his dark hair and tried to sit up. "I did what?" he asked as he finally managed it, causing the coverlet to slip down. Glancing down, he realized he was naked save for his small clothes. Falling back down with a grunt, he eyed her suspiciously before inquiring sheepishly, "You didn't undress me, did you?"

"No, this was Damion's doing, this time." Grinning mischievously, she teased, "I tried to volunteer, though."

Amroth blushed furiously.

Laughing at his discomfort, she added, "Don't worry, you were this way when I got here. As for your first question – Yes. Yes, you did."

Puzzled, Amroth asked, "Then how am I alive?"

Aseria shrugged. "Your guess is as good as mine. Something stopped the arrow from doing more than pricking your skin. You might want to thank whoever made your armor, by the way. As for the poison, if any of it entered you, then we're guessing it wasn't enough to overcome your accelerated healing."

"Uh-huh," Amroth replied, unsure of her explanation.

Guilt gnawed at her stomach. Damion had made it clear that she was not to tell Amroth what she'd seen, but seeing him doubt her words nearly made her tell him all. Suddenly, she stood up, startling Amroth, and climbed into bed next to him. Stunned, he offered no resistance as she tucked herself close to him and leaned her head against his chest.

Unsure of what to do or say, he found himself asking, "You haven't been here all night, have you?"

Aseria smirked slightly and gently slapped his chest. " You stupid, stupid, stupid man," she stated softly.

Amroth accepted the tender admonishment with a slight grin, but that was washed away as he felt warm tears fall onto his chest. His face softening with understanding, Amroth wrapped his arms about her, then kissed the top of her head. "There's no need to cry. It's okay – I'm okay."

Sniffing, she laughed softly. "I know. I'm just happy."

"About what?"

Looking up at him, she smiled before reaching up and kissing him full and gently. She let the kiss linger for a moment, basking in its warmth. Finally, she pulled away and smiled once more upon seeing her affections – albeit, a bit confused – reflected in his gaze.

Settling her head against his chest, she listened to his heartbeat. "Let me stay here for a little while, Mo'sali," she asked softly as she closed her tired, heavy eyes.

For a moment, Amroth couldn't find the words to respond. While he had no understanding of Tykani, he didn't need to know the language to comprehend what she called him.

Smiling, he gently settled himself back down and wrapped his arms around her already sleeping form. Kissing her head, he said, his tone gentle and warm, "As you wish."

Chapter Twenty-Three

Craigan was brooding, his mood as dark as the rest of the room and the nightshirt he wore.

Seated on the foot of his bed before the blazing hearth, his blue eyes absently focused on the dancing flames, he no more felt the heat it emitted than he tasted the wine he idly sipped upon. On the morrow, he would once again lead his army back into the fray, putting an early end to the rest he had hoped the winter would provide. Would it result in an actual campaign, or would it be no more than a short, focused siege to reclaim the fort? He had no idea. He hoped it would be nothing more than a quick task to retake the fort, but his gut suggested otherwise.

Taking a sip of his wine, he ran his free hand through his white-flecked, brown locks.

It had been two weeks since Private Ursa Delontis had arrived, broken and near death, with news of the Chalin border fort's fall. In that time, he had spoken with her a handful of times while awaiting word from his scouts. His first attempt the night of her arrival was as fruitless as Doms General Corandit had promised. Between her mental state and the poppy milk she'd ingested for pain and rest, her words were scattered and disjointed. Once he realized that pushing her would be useless, Craigan elected to check in each day until he could get something coherent from her. As such, it took four days for her to recover enough to deliver a report that made sense, and even then, Craigan wasn't sure he believed it all. An attack in the dead of night, spearheaded by archers firing from not only incredible range with unimaginable power, but shooting arrows that sounded like they were the spawn of nightmares. This rain of terror was followed up by a disorienting cloud of miasma, which crippled the defenders, that was delivered by infiltrators.

Craigan scowled.

To make matters worse, the fort's commander, Doms Captain Sagan Torvan, had thrown open the gates in a starlight dust-fueled, horror-stricken attempt to flee the miasma and rain of death. That, of course, was the proverbial killing blow. Merandith infantry was there to meet the fleeing defenders and serve as the anvil for Hagan's Hammer. In the end, the fort fell in short order, it's defenders all slaughtered save for Ursa, making it one of the most brutal losses House Suldamik had suffered. More importantly, it left only Chalin's nigh-impenetrable walls as the only significant barrier between House Merandith and Craigan's seat of power.

The scowl on Craigan's chiseled and scarred face deepened.

He wanted to believe that some of her tale was the result of a traumatized mind, but he couldn't outright dismiss the more outlandish parts of the tale. As far as the miasma was concerned, he knew there were concoctions that could be made that could choke a person or rob one of their faculties, so that situation wasn't a stretch to believe. As for the rest. . . . That someone could scale the walls unnoticed was inexcusable. The arrows, on the other hand, were something he was having a hard time swallowing. To fire such a projectile would take an archer of fantastical strength, and a bow with the power to rival a siege weapon. It was practically unfathomable. Yet, it wasn't the first time such terror had supposedly been unleashed. Rumor had it that such arrows had torn his troops asunder at Hagan Pass, though he'd never seen proof. Furthermore, there were the stories of the cyrian's fabled bows, and the slaughter that had followed any attempt to take Caith'tol before the Contested Territories existed. Once more, no physical proof existed of such weapons beyond the wounds on the recovered bodies.

Craigan sipped from his goblet once more, the warm liquid quieting his rising ire somewhat.

While he could ignore those stories and simply attribute the arrows to an unknown siege weapon, his mind kept returning to one example that gave him pause. The leader of House Merandith's House Guard. The Ghost of the Snows. Allanian Raoitae.

Craigan had heard many stories about the darlion, and had the unfortunate pleasure of witnessing his deadliness in battle on a handful of occasions. Be it at range, or in melee combat, the man was death incarnate. It was his bow, however, that left a profoundly scarring impression on many. He fired it with haunting accuracy and at a rate no human could hope to match. What's more, the arrows he used were far larger than normal. While he had never seen or heard of Allanian using his bow against fortifications, it wasn't too much of a stretch for him to believe the effect could be similar to what Ursa had described. If that was truly the case, it not only would help justify some of Kale's more surprising victories, but it meant the cyrians had broken from their neutrality years ago, and House Merandith had a potent weapon for which Craigan had no counter.

The sheets behind him rustled with movement, and a moment later, an arm clad in sheer white silk slipped around his shoul-

538

ders as Alestra pressed herself against his back and leaned her chin on his shoulder.

"You are too tense, my love," she purred as her white hair spilled down his chest, and her amber eyes peered deeply into the flames. "One would think House Merandith has you worried," she added, her throaty voice lending a seductive air to her words that was at odds with the statement.

Craigan grunted and took a sip from his wine.

Pulling back from him, she traced her fingers along his broad shoulders. Reaching his neck, she gently fingered the leather thong hanging from it before taking hold of his neck and massaging it gently. Working her way back out toward his shoulders, she heard a soft groan of relief, and almost immediately felt some of the tension flee his muscles. Expertly, she made her way all over his back, working the muscles gently where needed, and firmly when called for. Soon, Craigan was nearly bent over his knees, allowing Alestra greater access to his back.

As she continued to work, a playful smile split her full lips. "Careful, or you'll fall over," she quipped.

Suddenly, Craigan stood up, causing Alestra to fall back on the bed.

"Deo be good, Alestra! You are frustrating!" he barked with bemused irritation as he turned to face her. The sight of her sprawled on the bed, raised up on her elbows brought him up short. While her gown left nothing to the imagination, the way the firelight and shadows danced along her bronze skin, athletic figure, and full breasts was hypnotic in a way that muddled his brain.

Shaking his head to clear it even as she smirked at him, Craigan then downed his wine, padded over to the bedside table and placed the goblet atop it. Turning back to Alestra, he found her amber eyes fixed on him, her cunning and seductive allure glowing brightly in her gaze. Enraptured, his eyes began to wander down her body, as did his mind.

Realizing where his thoughts were turning, he shook his head again before seating himself on the bed, his back to her.

"Your right," he stated. "Kale has me frustrated. I had thought winter would provide a reprieve in which to recover. Now. . . ." He ran a hand through his hair as his visage turned sour. "Now, an army sits practically on our door step! Disaster is looming if we mess up now!"

The sheets rustled as Alestra moved behind him and once

more pressed against his back, her arms snaking around his torso to embrace him. "It is understandable, and," she purred as she placed her mouth next to his ear. "I won't try to make light of it. However, do not forget that it is not his main army, and all they did was take a border fort with an inept commander."

Craigan grunted in disgust.

"Furthermore," she added as her hands caressed his chest, "Haltho is the closest major source of supplies; if we can locate their supply train, we can severely cripple them. And last but not least, whatever they do, they cannot touch you here. They have nothing that can breach these walls." She kissed his cheek. "Then, of course, you have me," she purred in his ear.

Craigan shifted, and glanced at her, his doubt clear in his expression. "Forgive me, but while money is all well and good, your troops have contributed so little so far that it nearly amounts to nothing."

Alestra smiled broadly as she suddenly shifted around him to sit on his lap. The smile, however, held a hint of danger to it that raised Craigan's hackles.

"I cannot refute that," she declared off-handedly as she ran her hands through his hair. "However, once my elite forces arrive, you will forget all your troubles. They are unlike anything the North has seen."

Craigan fought off a scowl as he looked up at her. "I'll believe it when I see it, my dear," he stated, his doubt nakedly on display.

Caressing Craigan's face, Alestra smirked and met his intense gaze with one of her own, ignoring his distrust. Holding his head between her hands, she purred, "Oh, I do so like it when you call me that."

Suddenly, her head darted forward, and she pressed her lips against his in a fierce kiss that he returned just as strongly. As their kissing grew more frantic, Craigan stood up, and Alestra locked her legs around his torso even as his hands moved to the laces at her shoulders holding her gown up. The knots gave way with little resistance, and the near-useless gown fell down her torso as he turned and practically body-slammed her on the bed.

Alestra let out a throaty laugh of pure elation as he stood up, pulled the gown from her, and then removed his night shirt. Staring at his muscled figure in the dancing firelight, her eyes drifted to the simple silver amulet hanging from his neck by a leather thong. *"All too easy,"* she thought even as she beckoned him to her embrace.

Later that night, well after sleep had claimed Craigan, Alestra stood naked alongside the bed, watching his prone, blanketed form with a satisfied, but dark smile. Men were far too easy to manipulate; even those as strong and smart as Craigan. Maneuvering him to expend his frustrated energy in a night of rough passion had been child's play for her. Now, she could get on with the night's business.

With ease, she took hold of the currents and surrounded the bedroom and study with a barrier to mute all sound within. She then made sure it was self-sustaining before she dropped a similar barrier over Craigan, cutting him off from any noise outside of it. Once that was in place, she padded over to the wardrobe and opened it. Inside, she quickly located the handbag she'd brought with her hanging next to the red and white layered-silk dress she'd worn that day.

Opening the bag, she reached in an removed and amulet that was the spitting image of the one hanging from Craigan's neck. Turning it over in her hand, she examined the singular rune engraved on it one last time for any hint of a flaw. Once she was satisfied with the craftsmanship, she returned to Craigan's bedside and used the currents to gently lift his body a few inches off the bed. She then compressed the currents into a fine blade of air before shifting tendrils of the ethereal blue power to lift the amulet he wore off his chest. Using the blade of air to slice through the thong, she moved the amulet free of Craigan and into her waiting hand.

Letting the blade of air dissipate, she used the tendrils she still had under her control to transport her replica amulet to Craigan, where she ever so carefully slipped it over his neck. Once it was in place, resting on his chest, she lowered him back to the bed. Letting the currents under her control return to normal, aside from those supporting the barriers, she ran a finger along the lone rune occupying the amulet.

"My, my," she thought. *"there's more power in this than I imagined. . . . This is a key to be sure, but I do believe Garith is right. The power in it feels . . . incomplete. It's clearly meant to unlock more than a door, but what that is. . . ."*

Alestra shrugged. They would know more soon enough.

Pivoting on her heel, she padded into the study and approached the table they had installed the secret drawer in, the currents lighting her way as easily as the sun did daily. Reaching the provocative piece of furniture, she proceeded to press on the nipples of meticulously carved nude women that served as the table's legs in the proper order. Once she heard the hidden box release, she moved to the associated table face and removed it. Opening it, she placed the amulet on the green pillow inside before returning the box to its hiding spot. Once it clicked into place, she went back to the bedroom, a grin of immense satisfaction on her face.

Sliding into bed next to Craigan, she snuggled up close to him even as she let both barriers dissolve. A moment later, she let her mind drift free along the currents, seeking out her herald. Finding her quickly, she connected to her thoughts and told her, *"The amulet is in place. Let our plaything know it is time to earn her keep."*

"Yes, Mistress," her herald responded, emotionless.

"Oh, and do remember to gather the knowledge we seek. I'd hate for you to disappoint me . . . or Garith."

Cutting the connection before her herald could respond, she left the threat hanging in the air like a looming axe.

Smiling broadly, she thought as she let sleep claim her, *"It won't be long now, Garith. I do hope you are ready."*

*

Two weeks. Two long, irritating and disturbing weeks since her haunting encounter with Flute, and Mal still got chills when she reflected on it. Yet, despite her reservations about what Doma Ithikia's true endgame might be, she made ready for her task as soon as she received word that Doms Suldamik and his entourage had departed at the head of a sizable army. Unfortunately, the date chosen for her gambit meant two more arduous days of waiting, time during which Mal's concerns did their best to gnaw at her. While she couldn't ignore it completely, Mal did manage to keep her mind off her anxiety by focusing on the menial tasks Silvana assigned to her during that span.

Now that the appointed time had arrived, however, she focused on clearing her mind as she stripped down in the secret corridors near the hidden entrance to Craigan's quarters. With only the bandages that secured her breasts, and her loincloth for attire, she began to shiver as the cold air washed over her. Quickly, Mal undid the knot of her purported bag of laundry and promptly pulled out attire more appropriate for the night's venture.

"Can't wait to wash this horrible red out," she thought idly as she caught a glimpse of her red-dyed hair while sorting through her change of clothes.

A dark-gray sleeveless tunic went on first, concealing the bulk of the knotwork tattoos that ran from her navel, up between her breasts before spreading across her chest to flow down her arms. Settling the tunic's mask beneath her chin, she then donned supple black breeches, followed by a pair of soft, knee-length black boots. Pulling on a matching vest, she secured its ties, then settled the vest's hood about her shoulders before sliding on mesh arm sleeves that did little more than obscure the tattoos adorning her arms. Mal then put on her dark-gray fingerless gloves before securing a black belt low on her hips that was home to her tool pouches. Finally, she donned a dark leather harness, which she positioned so that the pair of fine long-knives it held were seated under each arm just below her breasts, before securing a pair of protective bracers about her forearms.

"Much, much better," she thought, content, as she stuffed her servant's attire in the bag.

Tossing the sack to the side, Mal then made her way to the hidden door that joined the corridor to Craigan's bedroom. Reaching the ascending stairs, she pressed on the third stone beneath the right wall sconce before climbing them. Pausing at the door, Mal pulled her gray mask up over her nose and her black hood over her head. *"Ere we go,"* she thought as she took a deep breath. Finding the knot that would release the door lock, she pressed on it. After hearing the confirming click, she cautiously opened the hidden door.

To her relief, the room was as dark and empty as she expected it to be. Having memorized the layout of the chamber during her numerous visits since her encounter with Flute, she could have traversed it in the dark. However, a small amount of moonlight graced the room with a veil of gentle illumination, negating her need to rely solely on her preparation. Giving her eyes a moment to adjust to the low lighting, she then quickly and silently crossed the room to the lone door baring her way to the adjoining study. Crouching, she peeked through the keyhole and saw that while the study beyond was darker than the bedroom, it appeared to be just as resident-free. Gently and quietly, Mal turned the door handle and pulled the door open as quietly as possible. Immediately, her eyes settled on the table situated beneath a chandelier in the center of the room, and she felt a surge of excitement rush through her veins.

"Careful now, lass. Don't be foolish. Stay cautious, and take this one step at a time," she reminded herself.

Taking a deep breath, she let it out low and slow as she examined the large, eight-sided study. Once she was sure no one besides her was lurking in the shadows that cloaked most of the room, she silently padded across the lush red carpet over to the provocative piece of furniture, which was surrounded by six plush chairs. It took Mal only a brief moment to recall the sequence that would reveal the cleverly hidden box, and she ran the progression through her mind as she quietly moved the chairs that were in her way before padding over to the table leg Flute had shown her on their initial encounter. Carved to resemble a nude woman, Mal pressed the carving's nipples in the proper order, resulting in the tell-tale click of a latch releasing, which sounded far too loud in the dark room. Mal then circled to her left, repeating the process at each leg. When she pressed the last nipple and finally heard the hidden box separate from the face of the table, she relaxed a little and let out a soft sigh of relief.

Moving around the table to it, Mal could just barely make out where the box had popped slightly out from the table face. Grasping it, she gently removed it, careful to keep any noise to a minimum. Her chest began to heave with anticipation as the box slid free and she noticed that it seemed much heavier than before. Placing it on the tabletop, Mal opened the lid and her breath instantly caught in her throat. It wasn't that the amulet was overwhelmingly beautiful, for she had stolen jewelry that was far more lovely; nor was her awe a result of the amulet's make. No, what caused Mal to stare in open awe and admiration was the power that the simple silver medallion seemed to radiate. Lifting it from its cushioned pillow of green velvet by the leather thong threaded through the ring on its top edge, Mal cradled it gently in her palm as she examined it.

Made of solid silver, the amulet showed no signs of wear. Its top face had a series of precise cuts engraved flawlessly into its surface, which worked together to form a lone rune. Mal had seen many runes during her time in the Sur'dathan Highlands, but there was nothing familiar about the rune on the amulet.

"So simple, but so valued," she thought as she examined the amulet for any indication of whom might have crafted such an object. *"Is this really a key. . . . No, not just any key — will this really open tha Utherian Valley gates?"*

Suddenly, Mal looked up, startled. Muffled and weak, what sounded like male voices conversing reached Mal's sensitive ears. Cursing herself for dallying, Mal quickly tucked the medallion into one of the empty padded pouches on her belt before quietly closing the box and returning it to its hiding place. Once she was sure all was as it had been before her arrival, Mal swiftly padded over to the bedroom and quietly closed the door behind her.

"No, Chamberlain, I can assure you that there are no rats on these levels," Mal heard Tythis' passive voice declare from just outside Craigan's bedroom, causing her heart to leap into her throat.

"It is not that I do not trust you, Magister, but I would be remiss if I did not inspect Doms Suldamik's chambers personally," she heard the chamberlain reply as the voices moved past the bedroom. "I doubt you are no more interested in being the target of Doms Suldamik's ill will than I."

"Of course not, Chamberlain," Tythis replied as their voices grew slightly muffled again.

Cursing herself for lingering, Mal quickstepped over to the gapping secret passage and closed it behind her just as warm light crept beneath the door separating the bedroom and study. Leaning her back against the sealed passage door, Mal let out a deep sigh of relief just as the chamberlain's barely audible, aged voice reached her ears again. "I'll examine the bedroom, Magister. If you wish to expedite this inspection, please start examining the study."

"Deo, that's too damn close, lass! Yer better than that!" she chided herself before pushing away from the door and padding down the stairs. Retrieving her discarded disguise, she took off on quick, silent feet.

"Now fer tha hard part, Mal," she reminded herself as she trotted through the maze of corridors. *"And ye better be ready fer this, 'cause if ye succeed, yer name will be spoken alongside tha likes of Ravenhand and tha Lithe Spider!"* She chuckled darkly to herself. *"Of course, ye have to survive whatever surprises hide in tha Valley . . . not to mention whatever ill designs that bitch Alestra and her cold handmaiden might be havin' in store fer ye."*

Turning a corner, she stepped onto a tight, spiral staircase and shrugged as she started down it. *"To tha Hells with them all! What will be, will be. What do ye say, lass? Let's make some history!"*

*

"Are you sure you want to do this, Mal? They're . . . we're just about asking the impossible of you. You know there are only two ways into the Valley."

"I know, Gathris — city entrance and tha private entrance. Tha city entrance is just way too damn public — and let's face it, it would be hard to miss those giant doors swingin' open — so, I guess I'll be goin' in tha back."

"I know you're good, but tell me something — just how are you going to sneak past all those soldiers and open the private entrance without anyone seeing you?"

That discussion had played out in Mal's head more than a few times over the last couple of weeks and kept creeping to the forefront of her thoughts on this night. To her chagrin, now that the moment was upon her, she still didn't have a plan that she was entirely confident in. Before recent conversations, she felt it would be manageable, but with an acceptably high risk of failure. Unfortunately, that was no longer the case. Then, there was her companion on this venture. She was a wild celum Mal couldn't account for on top of what she now knew about the fort. Trying to push the troubling thoughts aside, she focused on the task before her.

Crouched in the shadows created by the leafless trees that occupied the mountainous hills that surrounded the Utherian Valley, Mal shook her head and grimaced. Despite the glow of the silvery-blue moonlight that graced the night, there was still ample darkness to hide their approach, but that would only be of help until they had to deal with the fort. "This might be easier if we were to wait fer a new moon," she stated, her concern evident in her husky voice.

"Indeed," Flute replied from her position crouched next to Mal, her normally soft, melodic voice bordering on cold detachment. "But it would be wise to make good use of Doms Suldamik's absence. If it is discovered that the Valley has been so blatantly breached, or if Doms Suldamik discovers that the amulet he has is a fake, it is likely that you and those in the Resistance will be hunted with vigor, and if caught, executed. I would think you and your compatriots would want as much time as possible to make use of whatever we find in there . . . and to vanish if necessary."

Mal's scowl deepened, and she adjusted the pack on her back as she eyed Flute suspiciously. *"Deo, there's far more to this than I know."*

Adorned in black, most of Flute's outfit was familiar to Mal. The tunic and snuggly laced vest were of a recognizable cut, as were her lose black breeches. It was her hood, boots, and gloves, however, that had drawn Mal's curiosity upon meeting her at their rendezvous at the base of a Valley hill nearly half a mile outside the northern wall. Out of professional curiosity and concern that the delicate girl she had seen in florid attire two weeks ago was hardly suited to thievery, Mal had questioned Flute's attire. Politely, and with a small, knowing smirk, Flute had informed her that her gloves, which were secured around her middle fingers by a thong, were called tekko. As for her boots, which seemed flimsy and appeared to separate her big toe from the rest of her toes, Flute assured her that they provided excellent purchase and were extremely silent. When Mal asked about the black hood concealing her mass of ice-blue hair, Flute had just laughed softly and assured her that the cut was simply different.

What doubts Mal still had about Flute's attire and fitness for the job ahead of them were alleviated somewhat during their clandestine journey through the hills. The peculiar Velusyian moved with silence, grace, and confidence that was not only impressive and worthy of the finest thieves, but also of the most skilled of assassins. Mal had to suppress a shudder as Flute's movements and her sad smile rattled through her mind once more to combine with that terrifying revelation.

"Stay sharp, Mal. Ye could end up on tha wrong side of a knife when this is all done . . . assumin' this lass' demeanor isn't just givin' ye tha heebie-jeebies," Mal thought as she tore her gaze from Flute's dispassionate expression. Shifting as if she was checking her footing, Mal double-checked that her long-knives were easily accessible as she asked casually, "What about ye and yer mistress? What makes ye think they won't track this back to either of ye?"

The small, sad smile that had so haunted Mal since her first encounter with the girl crept onto Flute's face. "My mistress is . . . skilled at covering her tracks."

The implied threat wasn't lost on Mal. Turning her gaze back to the fort, which was gently illuminated by the crescent moon, Mal pressed her lips together firmly. *"Damn it all to tha Hells – it may be necessary to vanish completely after this. Thank Deo, this job is payin' enough to retire ten-times over. I just hope tha others are good at disappearin', 'cause there's no doubtin' this girl and her bitch of a mistress are not to be crossed,"* she mused before shoving the dark worries aside.

Flickering tantalizingly in the darkness, the fires that the Night Watch used to warm themselves gave Mal a very general impression of the fort's layout. On numerous occasions, Mal had scouted both the city entrance and the fort protecting the private entrance to the Valley to sate her curiosity, committing the guards' patterns and the surrounding terrain to memory. It had been difficult to accurately scout the fort over the years since it had been under construction for most of that time. This, regrettably, led to an incomplete picture of the interior of the fort. While she knew the general number of buildings and their position, she had no idea what they were for. As for the exterior of the fort, she knew what anyone with a functioning set of eyes knew. There were crenellated towers stationed at each corner of the three thick, thirty-foot tall stone walls, and two others flanked the lone gate. Serving as a rear wall was the granite rock face – and by extension, the Utherian Valley – jutting from the hillside, making the fort unassailable from behind. Furthermore, there was a deep, spike-filled moat surrounding it all to contend with.

At the time, her incomplete picture of the fortification had done nothing to dissuade countless wonderful and adventurous daydreams of breaking into the Valley. However, now that the moment was upon her, the thrill of it all was tainted by what she now knew about the fort, and more importantly, her fearful curiosity about her companion. Even worse, she was very concerned about how she was going to cross the spike-filled moat and sneak by a small army of soldiers unseen, not to mention finding and opening a gate whose location within the fort was unknown to her. Such reservations had driven her to protest against acting so soon. While in her mind it was nothing to sneak by the guards and pick a complex lock, or to merely scale a wall like a circus acrobat, the reality of the task was far more brutal.

By day, there were at least twenty guards stationed on the crenellated battlements of the walls and towers, all heavily armed and with standing orders to kill anyone who ventured too close. To her chagrin, nightfall never saw the number of soldiers on watch drop below ten. What she found even more frustrating was that, despite their relative isolation from the city, she had never seen any evidence that the guards were critically lax in their duties, nor had she ever witnessed any of the night guards asleep at their post. While this didn't mean such lapses never occurred, she was unwilling to trust her freedom and survival to luck.

Once more, with her gaze fixed on the fort, Mal asked quietly, "Are ye sure 'bout this? I've never been able to cook up a plan that didn't have an acceptable – but high – chance of failure, and that is by myself. I know I stand a good chance of scalin' tha wall unnoticed if I can get over tha moat, and I could probably incapacitate a few of 'um, but if what ye told me is true, there's a damn portcullis to get by! If it's closed, there's no way yer gonna open it without alertin' tha whole damn fort! Do ye really think we can get in there and open tha gate without bringin' death down on our heads?"

"I do," Flute replied coldly.

"And just how's that?" Mal asked for the third time since Flute had insisted upon accompanying her. "Not to be rude, but ye haven't given me a lot to go on, and I'm pretty damn sure yer music won't cut it no matter how enchantin' it may be!"

The sad smile pulled at Flute's lips. "We will make it to the gate safely, Malia – that is my purpose here. Now, wait here."

Before Mal could question the cryptic absurdity of Flute's declaration, Flute stood up and began walking down the hill. "What tha hells are ye doing?!" Mal hissed as loudly as she dared. "Do ye have a death wish or somethin'? Ye can't just walk up to them!"

Looking back briefly, Flute flashed her a knowing smile that seemed almost resigned to Mal. Cursing under her breath, Mal stood up and cautiously made her way toward the bottom of the hill, careful to keep Flute in sight while keeping her distance. *No way in hells I'm gonna let her get me caught!* Mal snorted mentally. *Hells, given who she serves, maybe she's intendin' to strip down to distract tha guards so I can sneak by. Wouldn't be my choice of distractions since there's no way in tha hells it'd work, but I don't know many men whose wits wouldn't be addled momentarily at tha sight of a pretty lass sauntering about naked. Of course, there could be women down there. . . ."* Mal shook her head as Flute reached the base of the hill. *"Focus, lass. Even if her mistress uses sex effectively to addle men's brains, it don't mean this Flute does. Besides, this isn't some tawdry tale where tha sight of naked breasts distracts the guards while tha hero saves tha day. I'm sure she's got a plan that works in real life. . . ."*

Reaching the treeline near the base of the hill, Mal crouched down and watched as Flute moved toward the fort with a determined purpose and a clear disregard for if she was seen. *"Damn,"* Mal thought and swallowed hard as Flute reached the midway point, and her stride changed into a provocative saunter. *"Then again, maybe she's a few kyrams short of a flock!"* Unease began to swim in Mal's stomach, and she frowned deeply as she struggled to keep track of Flute in the darkness. *"I dunna know what tha lass is plannin', but she's got no way to stun them unless she does get naked, and she sure as hells doesn't have a weapon on her! Well, 'ere's hopin' whoever is on duty is dumb as tha fools in some asinine story!"*

Mal battled her concern as she tried to keep up with Flute's progression. It was tempting to abandon her to whatever fate awaited the girl, but Mal knew with all her heart that if she did so, and Flute was harmed, Doma Ithikia would likely pursue her without end in search of vengeance.

Upon seeing that Flute had nearly reached the wall, Mal cursed herself and the fates that had led her to this place, then double-checked that her hood and mask were securely in place before moving along the tree line toward the fort with haste. Keeping to the shadows, Mal got as close as she was comfortable with before crouching down in the shadow of a pine and carefully peeking around it. To her chagrin, Flute showed no sign of halting her advance. Withdrawing her head just as Flute drew close enough to the fort that it would be impossible to miss her, Mal banged it gently against the tree trunk in frustration, drawing a muffled curse from her.

"Eh! Halt! Who goes there at this ungodly hour?!" A suspicious male voice shouted.

Cursing under her breath, Mal quickly returned her gaze to her troubling companion, who had come to a halt uncomfortably close to the moat.

"Well, this is a pretty one, eh? What have we done to discover such a fine reward?" another male voice asked, his tone pleased as he joined the first guard with another torch.

"Oh shut it, you damn fool!" shouted an aged, authoritative male voice as a man in an officer's tabard strode from the north tower. Reaching the two soldiers as others began to make their way toward the commotion, the man shouted at Flute, "Ma'am, you can't be here!" Receiving no response, and seeing no indication that Flute intended to withdraw, the man grasped the hilt of his sword and declared, "We have orders to shoot anyone who approaches! Be thankful we haven't done so already, and leave now!"

Mal's stomach twisted as she saw a few of the guards raise crossbows and train them on Flute. Glancing at her partner-in-crime this night, Mal swallowed hard. It appeared that Flute had no intention of heeding the soldier's advice, or doing anything at all for that matter. *"What in tha hells is she thinkin'?"* Mal thought as panic gripped her.

"Last warning, girl!" the officer shouted, his tone turning grim.

Whether it was the officer's tone or the weapons aimed at her, Flute's posture changed. Spreading her feet, her hands at her sides, Flute looked up at the soldiers on the wall. Watching her deliberate movements, Mal suddenly went cold. While she couldn't see Flute's face, there was an air of violence to her posture that was frightening. *"Deo, what is she plannin'? She can't possibly be thinkin' of rushin' them . . . can she?"*

"Right, then!" the officer stated grimly. "Archers! Fi–"

A concussive thud rocked the air, knocking Mal on her rump, stunning her. Head swimming and ears ringing, the world started to silently tumble around Mal. It seemed to her that an eternity passed as she rolled down the hillside before, and without warning, she came to a jarring halt, her breath knocked out of her. Struggling to regain her senses and breath, she watched the stars spin overhead for a moment when, suddenly, a flock of Flutes appeared over her, their sad visages floating about like leaves on the wind. Their sky-blue eyes seemed concerned, and it appeared that they were saying something, but the ringing in Mal's ears drowned out the words.

"What?" Mal managed to ask, unsure of the volume of her own voice. The Flutes seemed to ask her a question, to which Mal managed to shake her head. "I . . . I can't understand what yer sayin'!" Mal admitted.

A moment later, Mal's swimming vision began to settle down, reducing the flock of Flutes to just a pair of faces. They appeared to once more say something, but to no avail. Frustrated that she still couldn't hear, Mal squeezed her eyes shut and focused on clearing her head.

Mercifully, it wasn't long before the ringing in her ears began to lessen, and she finally heard Flute ask, her gentle voice filled with genuine concern, "Are you okay?"

"Deo, no!" Mal barked through clenched teeth. "What in tha hells just happened?!" Opening her eyes, Mal was relieved to find just one Flute watching her now. Seeing that her accomplice appeared unaffected by the mysterious blast, Mal added, "And why do ye look as if nothin' happened?!"

Flute flashed Mal a small, apologetic smile. "A special trick I picked up a long time ago. It's similar to Velusyian firestars, only without the light show. As to why I wasn't affected . . . lots of prac-tice." Offering Mal a hand, she asked, "Can I help you up?"

Flute's explanation rang hollow to Mal, and she eyed both the extended hand and the girl suspiciously; there was no way she could have concealed on her person anything resembling a firestar that was large enough to produce such a blast. Still, she'd done something to clear the battlements, and she didn't appear worried that there was any chance of discovery, so. . . .

"Right," Mal muttered as she accepted Flute's proffered hand.

With surprising ease, Flute pulled Mal to her feet. Imme-diately, Mal's vision went to the top of the wall. Seeing no one, she looked at Flute with a growing mix of suspicion and fear. "Where are they?"

"I suggest we make haste, Malia. We don't have all night," Flute replied coldly, ignoring Mal's question.

Scowling, Mal decided that she was right; they needed to move quickly before whatever she had done wore off. Trotting to the edge of the moat, she took off her pack and removed a substantial length of rope that was attached to a grappling hook. Unfurling the line, Mal looked up at the battlements. "Alright, let's get this done, but ye got a lot of questions to answer, and yer answers better be good. Ye got that?" Mal asked as she gauged the distance.

"No, I don't," Flute answered, her tone frigid and grim.

Shooting Flute a quick scowl, she muttered, "Bitch," as she began to twirl the grappling hook.

Looking back to the battlements, Mal got the hook up to the speed and let fly. Soaring high and fast, the grapple reached its apex before diving over the top of the wall. Collecting the rope, Mal pulled on it until she felt the hook catch. Giving it a couple of test tugs, she then retrieved her pack and secured it on her back before she looked at Flute and asked rhetorically as she gathered up the slack and backed up, "Ye don't mind if I go up first, do ye?"

Flute smirked slightly as she watched Mal continue to back up until the rope was taunt. Then, after a deep breath, Mal sprinted forward, and as she reached the edge of the moat, she lept. In a flash, she swung across the spike-filled gap, her feet absorbing the impact as she nimbly landed against the wall. Mal then dropped to the ground and gathered up the rope before lobbing it back across to Flute.

The Velusyian caught the line deftly and, like Mal, she moved back while gathering up the slack. Suddenly, and without pause, Flute sprinted forward and lept, swinging across with a grace and easy that made Mal's attempt seem clumsy. Then, as if to add insult to injury, Flute let go of the rope short of the wall, landing and sliding silently to a halt.

"Deo be good!" Mal thought as she practically gawked at Flute. *"Who in tha bloody hells is she?"*

Noticing that Mal had not moved, Flute motioned to the wall and said, "I believe you wanted to go first?"

Fighting the urge to curse, Mal set her blue eyes on the wall and stalked over to the rope. Giving it a tug to make sure it was still secure, she then planted her foot on the wall and began to climb. Nimbly, she quickly scaled the wall, but when she reached the top and started to haul herself between two merlons, she nearly froze in shock. All of the guards on the battlements were sprawled on the walkway as if they'd been dropped like sacks of grain. Regaining her composure, she pulled herself fully onto the wall before hopping down to the wide walkway. Looking around, she felt a knot of cold fear twist her stomach as everywhere she looked, she saw soldiers lying on the ground.

Frozen by the eerie sight, Mal barely noticed Flute's arrival on the battlements, but when she finally did, she asked as softly as her husky voice would allow, "Are they dead?"

"Unlikely," Flute replied with confidence as she joined Mal and looked out over the courtyard. "They are merely unconscious."

"Even those inside tha buildings?" Mal asked as her gaze shifted from the command building and barracks that flanked the gatehouse against the rock face of the hill to the smithy below them against the eastern wall. When her gaze moved to the stable along the western wall, she found herself adding, "Even tha horses?"

"Yes, everyone . . . *everything* is out cold," Flute reaffirmed as she returned to the rope and began to pull it up with speed.

Shaking her head in disbelief, Mal regained her composure before crouching down to inspect the guards laid out around her. To her relief, they all appeared to be just as Flute said – unconscious. Looking up at her accomplice, who, with the rope now piled at her feet, was gazing toward the gatehouse, Mal grudgingly said, "I dunna know what to say, but thank ye. I wasn't sure how exactly I was gonna pull this off. I'd even considered tryin' to scale tha interior Valley wall."

"Indeed," Flute replied absently. Prying her gaze from the gatehouse, Flute offered Mal a fleeting smile. "Though, from what I've heard, scaling the Valley walls is a fool's errand." She shook her head slightly before motioning to the courtyard and asking, "Now, shall we be about our business?" Without waiting for an answer, Flute made her way to the nearest staircase and descended to the courtyard.

Despite Flute's assurance that everyone in the fort was incapacitated, Mal kept her footsteps light and silent as she followed the confident girl. At the bottom of the stairs, Mal noticed that one of the fallen guards appeared to be staring at her blankly with blood trickling from his nose, and she cringed. *"I guess not every guard on tha wall was lucky,"* Mal thought before shaking her head sadly. Padding away quickly to catch up with Flute's determined pace, Mal found herself wondering once again just who the enigmatic girl was. *"Silent as a skilled thief, but demure as a chastised child most of tha time. Who in tha hells would'a thought tha behavior I've seen was in her?"*

Glancing at the illuminated windows in the barracks and command building as she moved between the two structures, Mal fought to suppress a shudder. The fact that soldiers had not come pouring from either building was clear evidence that whatever Flute had done had incapacitated the entire fort, just as she had stated. Chastising herself for her inability to stay focused, Mal turned her attention back to Flute, who was standing on the right side of the gatehouse, a hand on her cocked hip.

"You seem distracted," Flute stated.

There was no hint of concern or impatience in her voice, but for some reason, Mal still found a chill running up her spine. "It's nothin'," Mal responded as confidently as she could as she pulled her mask down while trotting up to Flute. "Is there something wrong?" she added as she reached the young woman.

"I thought you might like to handle this," Flute quipped, motioning to the closed gatehouse door.

Eyeing the sturdy oak panel, Mal asked, sarcasm blanketing her tone, "Dunna know what ye need me for? If ye can knock out a whole damn fort, I don't see how a door could stand in yer way."

Flute smiled gently, which felt all too patronizing to Mal. "It would be excessive to destroy the door. Besides, leaving such evidence of our presence would not be in our interest."

Mal scoffed as she retrieved her lockpick kit from one of her pouches. "And a fort full of unconscious soldiers isn't evidenced that somethin' happened 'ere?" Mal asked sarcastically.

"They won't remember that it even happened," Flute replied confidently as Mal selected the proper tools from her kit, crouched down and began working on the lock.

Snorting in disbelief, Mal muttered. "Right. And what about tha dead guard? I'd imagine that'll raise a few eyebrows."

"A tragic accident," Flute answered.

Stunned by her solemn tone, Mal paused and looked up at her. There was an apologetic sadness in Flute's eyes that was a match for her tone of voice, which baffled Mal. *'How can someone be casual about incapacitatin' a whole damn fort, then seem so bloody regretful about one of them dyin'? This lass gets more confusin' and frightenin' by tha moment,"* Mal mused. Aloud, she scoffed and turned her attention back to the sturdy lock. "Right," Mal muttered as she reinserted her tools.

With deft, practiced skill, Mal maneuvered her tools until, one by one, she felt the tumblers slide into place. Grinning as the lock clicked open, Mal then returned her tools to her pouch and stood up. Looking at Flute, she commented rhetorically, "A damn easy lock on such an important door. Ye'd think a soldier would take all possibilities into account."

"I don't think it ever crossed their minds that anything less than a small army would dare assault this place," Flute responded dryly.

"Aye, I know," Mal muttered. "Well, lass – who's gonna open tha gate?"

Gesturing to the door, Flute said, "Be my guest. After all, this is your job. I'm just here for support."

Glowering at Flute for a moment, Mal then vanished into the gatehouse. As soon as she was gone, Flute let out a sad sigh before walking back to the closed portcullis. Sparing a regretful glance at the rest of the fort, Flute shook her head before turning to face the gate. She didn't have to wait long before she heard a groan of protest from the steel grid, and it began to creep upward. As soon as it was high enough for a person to walk under without crouching, Flute heard it lock into place as Mal secured it. Staring into the inky blackness that filled the space beyond the gate, Flute shuddered. With the portcullis raised, the open gate reminded her of a giant, toothy maw that was intent on swallowing her whole. Though her impression of the gate would be enough to make many feel uneasy, it was something deep in the darkness that was responsible for the disquiet creeping up her spine. She, like her mistress and those her mistress consorted with, understood that danger awaited any of their ilk should they dare to breach the Valley. What that danger was, no one knew for sure. However, she knew with cold certainty that anything that could make her mistress and her allies take pause was something to treat with fear and healthy respect.

"Are ye alright, lass?"

Startled, Flute quickly glanced at who had spoken. Mal, her face a clear mask of concern, was walking toward her with a pair of lit torches in hand. "Of course," Flute replied after regaining her composure. "Why do you ask?"

"'Cause ye look like ye done glanced into tha Hells and found 'um starin' back," Mal responded as she reached Flute, her focus on the Velusyian's somewhat pale complexion.

Flute shook her head. "I am quite alright, Malia. There are many rumors surrounding the Valley and this gate. . . . I'm afraid I let my imagination get the better of me, that is all."

Mal snorted. "Right, lass," she quipped, clearly unconvinced. Presenting Flute with one of the torches, Mal said, "'Ere, that should help fend off tha dark and creepy thoughts that be lurkin' in there."

Ignoring the jab, Flute nodded her thanks as she took the torch.

"Well, shall I be leadin' tha way, or do ye want tha honors?"

Swallowing hard, Flute stared hard at the dark entrance. "No," she declared, doing her best to keep her concern from her melodic voice. "This is your shining moment. You should have the honor."

Eyeing Flute skeptically, Mal nodded slowly before holding her torch aloft and approaching the gate with measured, cautious steps.

As Mal crossed the gate's threshold, and her torch illuminated the gate's interior and a portion of the tunnel beyond, Flute closed her eyes in an attempt to calm herself, praying, *"Corith, I know that it is unlikely that my prayers reach you, or that you would hear the supplica-*

tion of a fallen such as me, but please hear my plea this night. I know not what fate awaits me, but know that I do not seek clemency for my soul; it is bound for the Nine Hells no matter what I do, tainted as it is. But should the worst happen this night, please find some way to let Father know that I did not perish that night so long ago. And. . . . And let him know that I tried to walk in the Light . . . and that no matter what she did to me, no matter what heinous acts she forced upon me, and no matter how vehemently they tried to bend what is left of my soul to the Darkness – I never lost faith in him or the Light."

Opening her eyes, a tear escaped her left eye and crystallized before sliding down her cheek, leaving a streak the color of blue ice in its wake. Reaching her chin, the tear fell free, shattering on the ground as she walked willingly toward an unknown fate.

From the moment Mal set foot in the tunnel, she felt more anxious than she had all night. This sudden surge of anxiety irritated her because she knew there was no valid reason to feel that way. Granted, she didn't trust the enigmatic Velusyian, nor did she completely accept the explanation for how she managed to incapacitate an entire fort, but at least it was somewhat believable. Moreover, they were in the fort and on the way to the private Valley entrance without so much as a hitch. Yet, here she was, her nerves feeling frayed and her stomach trying to tie itself in knots. Moving at a cautious pace down the rough-hewn tunnel, she tried to distract herself by examining the deep shadows that danced about her thanks to the torchlight.

The effort was doomed to failure from the start since, from the moment her torch gave life to the eerie shadows, it seemed as if they were reaching out to her in anger and desperation. She had no idea why it felt that way, but a part of her wanted to blame it on the constant breeze that brought with it the damp and oppressive air that now clung to her like a terrified child. It would have been an easy explanation to believe . . . except the breeze came from within the tunnel, not from the open gate they had left behind.

Shuddering, she tore her gaze from the shadows and glanced at the floor before her. For a moment, she thought she could see spots that were stained a ruddy hue . . . as if blood had once tainted the stone. Coming to a sudden halt, Mal closed her eyes and took a deep breath in an attempt to compose herself. *"Steady, lass. Ye've heard one too many tall tales 'bout this place, and yer nerves are on edge. This hole in tha ground isn't anythin' more than just that. There's no such thing as vengeful spirits."*

"Are you alright?"

Startled, Mal spun and dropped into a crouch as she reached

for her long-knife with her free left hand. Seeing that it was only Flute, Mal barked, the deep tones of her voice tight, "Hells' bloody balls, Flute! Don't sneak up on someone like that, else yer likely to end up gutted like a bramhen being readied fer a feast!"

Releasing her nerve-fueled, tight grip on her long-knife, Mal stood up as Flute smiled apologetically and said, "My apologies. I did not mean to startle you, but you were standing statue-still . . . and I was concerned."

Mal snorted and straightened her vest. "Right," she uttered doubtfully.

Flute's smile widened slightly with a hint of amusement. Gesturing down the tunnel, Flute suggested, "Shall we continue? The night is wasting away, and I would imagine we still have much to do."

Starting back along the gently descending tunnel with a slightly quicker pace thanks to the improved lighting provided by Flute's added torch, Mal asked, "Will whatever ye did to tha soldiers last long enough fer us to get back out?"

"Indeed it will," Flute responded confidently as she moved alongside Mal.

Glancing at Flute out of the corner of her vision, Mal saw that while the snow-blue-haired girl's face appeared impassive, the concern she'd heard in Flute's voice just before entering the tunnel seemed to be pulling at the corners of her mouth. *"Somethin' is bothe-rin' her 'bout all this. . . . Deo, what could unnerve a person capable of doin' what she did to tha soldiers? Hells, what does that mean fer me, then?"*

Without warning, after what felt like an eternity, the winding tunnel emptied into a chamber consumed by darkness.

"Damn! How big is this bloody thing?" Mal asked, her words echoing a bit in the chamber as she looked around in an attempt to discern the size of the space.

"Large, I would think," Flute replied with a hint of tightness in her melodic voice as she took a step back.

Peering at Flute with concern as the girl began moving to the right while examining the wall, Mal chuckled dryly in an attempt to lighten the mood. "That much would be obvious to a blind man, lass."

Mal couldn't tell whether Flute chose to ignore her joke or was simply too tense to find any measure of humor in her words as the enigmatic girl came to a halt and declared, "Ah, this should help."

Before Mal could question her, Flute moved her torch toward something on the wall, and an instant later, a new blaze sprung to life. Though only a measure better, the added light began to add definition to the chamber.

Chuckling, Mal said, "Wall torches. Good find, lass."

Moving back to the tunnel exit, Mal found the other side of the opening and began moving along the left-hand wall. It didn't take long for her to find an ensconced torch in a similar position as the one Flute had lit. Oddly enough, the brand appeared fresh to her as she moved to light it. "These look new," Mal stated, a bit surprised by the torch's state.

"Quite," Flute responded. "I would imagine Craigan visits fairly often."

"Huh? And why do ye think that?" Mal asked as she moved along the wall, lighting the wall torches she found at steady intervals.

"My mistress made mention that he seemed to like to 'waste' time in here," Flute responded absently. "Ah, that should do it."

Having only made it halfway along her wall, a portion of the vast oval chamber near Mal was still home to shadows that were only a few shades brighter than the darkness hiding the ceiling from sight. Mal, however, was oblivious to both the size of the room and the remaining darkness, as Flute's declaration had captured her attention. Turning around, Mal's breath caught in her throat as she laid eyes on one of the most – if not the most – bizarre things she'd ever seen.

Arranged in a larger circle at the center of the room, brightly burning torches mounted on iron stands surrounded a large marble disk embedded in the ground. Pristine and unmarred by time or dirt, the disk bore no marks or decoration except for a lone, bright blue jewel that surmounted the very center of it. Approaching slowly, Mal could not believe what she was seeing.

"What in tha hells. . . ." she breathed as she came to a halt at the edge of the disk. "I've never seen anythin' like it. . . . Hells, I didna know ye could find a crystal that large! It's practically tha size of a bloody wagon wheel!"

Enraptured by the odd disk, Mal was oblivious to the clatter of a dropped torch and the silence that greeted her statement. A moment later, it finally dawned on her that Flute had remained mute. "Did ye hear me?" Mal asked as she looked up. "What in Deo's name is th– Flute? What's tha matter, lass?" she finished, her husky voice filled with concern when she saw the Velusyian girl.

Standing motionless at the head of the circle, her back to the chamber entrance and her empty hands at her side, Flute stared straight ahead, her eyes wide with fearful surprise.

"Deo be good, lass! What's wrong?" Mal asked again. Receiving only ominous silence as an answer, Mal followed Flute's line of sight and immediately froze. "Deo be good . . ." she managed to utter.

Standing nearly as tall as five average men balanced on each other's shoulders, forged-steel doors were recessed within a relief-carved marble arch along the far wall. Torchlight shimmered over the perfectly polished doors and danced along the arch's relief carvings, painting both in fiery hues. Mal's gaze followed the doors up to the peak of the archway, which displayed the roaring dragon sigil of House Gravit'nas. Looming over the room with grandeur from its place of honor, the awe-inspiring badge served as the origination point for the finely carved, and amazingly detailed, dragons that twisted and turned about the length of the archway. Some of the beasts appeared to be playing, others flying, while still more appeared to be locked in mortal combat.

Mal had no idea how long she stood there trying to commit every detail of the magnificent doorway to memory, but eventually, she decided that she needed a closer look. Willing her legs to move, she walked around the marble disk until she was aligned with the doors and suddenly froze.

"What in tha Nine Hells . . .?" she thought in shock. Aloud, she asked, her tone full of disbelief, "Uh . . . Am I seein' things, or did those beasties' eyes follow my movements?"

"No," Flute started to respond, her voice tight with either fear or awe, though Mal could not tell which. Clearing her throat, Flute tried again. "No," she stated firmly as she moved around the disk to join Mal. "The eyes aren't moving; though I can see why you would think so. It's an artist trick that is normally seen in paintings."

Mal shook her head in disbelief. "Ye could've fooled me, lass. Still, I dunna think I've seen anythin' close to these doors – ever! I can't even fathom what it would take to make 'um."

"I would imagine the world would be lucky to see such a craftsman once in a generation," Flute answered. "Still, we are not here to admire art, Malia. Let us focus on our task, shall we?"

Oblivious to the anxiety in Flute's voice, Mal nodded slowly and said, "Right, lass."

With effort, Mal forced her attention back to her task and advanced on the doors. Right away, she saw that they were decorated at roughly eye level. Though she had never been able to get a close look at the similar adornments on the doors within the city, her clients had described them to her in detail.

"*Now, this is important, Mal,*" Logan had informed her before she had infiltrated the keep's staff. "*Assuming you manage to retrieve the amulet and reach the gates, you will find a lock the likes of which you've never seen.*"

"*And just how did ye come 'bout this info?*" she'd asked, extremely doubtful of how accurate his information could be at that time.

"*Long, tedious research, and the lives of a few of our compatriots,*" he'd responded tersely. "*Now listen — when you reach the doors, you will find that inscribed somewhere on their surface is a pair of concentric rings surrounding a central carving. The outer ring is likely irrelevant to our purpose, and the carving is meaningless as far as we know. But the inner ring — that's what's important. There are fourteen circular recessions, representing each of the original Houses of Triclose.*"

Reaching the door, Mal found herself distracted by the carving at the center of the concentric circles. Exquisite in its detail, it depicted two dragons circling each other with their gazes focused out upon the world. Oddly, it seemed to Mal that the way their taloned feet grasped at each other was almost combative. Shaking her head, she brought her focus back to Logan's instructions.

"*Each of the circles has a sister amulet, and that amulet is a key. Find the one that matches Craigan's amulet, and then insert it.*"

"*And that'll unlock tha doors?*" Mal had asked skeptically.

"*As we understand it, yes.*"

"*Right. . . . Never heard of a lock that works like that; fourteen keys, and any one of them can open it all by its lonesome? Seems like a daft design if ye ask me.*"

"*Possibly, but do you really want to question the design, especially if it is foolishly easy to open?*"

"*Nope. I'll take any help I can get. But doors this easy to open tend to have traps. So is there anything I should be alert fer?*"

"*None that I'm aware of. We can only assume that the proper key would disarm any traps that there might be.*"

"*Well, this is a dandy task ye've set me on. But tell me one thing, lad — what if one had all fourteen of these amulets? What would happen if ye used them all at once?*"

That question had baffled Logan, and as Mal looked over each of the circles, she found herself once more curious about it. "*That's not for now, lass,*" she thought. "*Maybe if ye come out of this with yer skin intact, ye can look into liftin' tha amulets from each of the other Houses fer amusement. But fer now, ye just focus on yer job."*

Examining the door carefully for traps, it became clear that there were none to be found. To Mal's chagrin, instead of making her feel confident about proceeding, it made her feel ill at ease. This was not an ordinary door, and she found it hard to believe it would be protected by ordinary, easy-to-spot defenses. Still, the doors and arch appeared clear of traps, and that meant she needed to proceed with her task.

Opening her pouch, Mal removed the silver amulet. Holding it in her hand, Mal flipped it over and examined the precise cuts that worked together to form the lone rune at the center of the amulet. "Still havin' a hard time believin' this is a key," she muttered before looking back at the circles.

Evenly spaced around the inner circle, each of the recessions was about half-a-finger deep. Looking closely at each one, Mal noted that there was an imprint at the back of each recession that resembled the medallion Mal held. Upon closer examination, she saw that the imprint actually varied slightly. "So, just got to find tha one that matches, eh?" she muttered. "Easy enough." Quickly, she scanned the imprints again, this time seeking one that bore the proper matching rune. "There ye are," she quietly asserted as her gaze landed on the top-right circle.

Looking back over her shoulder, she was surprised to see that Flute had not moved. In fact, she was visibly apprehensive. *"Bloody hells! I don't know what's got her wound so tight, but she better not turn tail and run now!"* Keeping her voice as calm as possible, Mal said, "Alright, lass, I've found tha lock. Ye ready for this? I don't know what's gonna happen, so stay sharp."

Eyes focused intently on the doors, Flute swallowed and nodded.

Scowling, Mal turned back to the doors and slowly placed the amulet within its parent receptacle. As soon as she felt it lock into place, she tried to turn it one way and then the other, but the amulet refused to budge. Cursing under her breath, Mal tried pushing on it. Once again, it refused to budge, and for the briefest of moments, she began to think that it was either broken or she'd set off some alarm in a hidden area that would soon have soldiers breathing down their necks. With cold dread running down her spine, Mal started to turn to order Flute to leave, when the amulet began to glow with a glorious golden halo.

"Corith be merciful!" Mal thought she heard Flute breathe as the glow appeared around the amulet.

Flute's odd appeal for mercy fled Mal's mind as shock flooded her at the sight of the glowing amulet. Yet, before she could fully register her amazement, the glow winked out. To Mal's horror, the amulet appeared to have merged with the door. "Damn it all to tha deepest of tha Hells!" she cursed, angry and shocked. "Just how in tha—"

Her words fell off as the thin sliver that delineated one door panel from the other began to radiate a dim white light at its midway point. Slowly, the light filled the tiny gap between the mammoth panels before spilling across their surfaces like water on a well-oiled table. As the glow progressed, it grew in intensity, illuminating the surrounding area as if the light of a mid-day sun had found its way into the room. Finally, the light reached the top and bottom of the delineating line, and without even the slightest creak or groan of protest, the ancient doors swung inward, permitting a blinding light to spill forth.

"Bloody hells!" Mal hissed as her eyes snapped shut and she turned away from the intense light.

A moment later, the glow that was trying to pierce her tightly shut eyelids seemed to dissipate, and she heard Flute say, her soft voice heavy with what sounded like sorrow, "It's alright, Malia. You may look now."

Slowly, Mal opened her eyes and turned to the open doors. Like the vast majority of Chalin's residents, she'd heard stories of what the interior of the Valley looked like. She always believed those tales to be nothing more than fanciful flights of imagination worthy of a child's bedtime fable. Now, as she tried to process what she saw beyond the open portal, she realized those stories fell far short of the truth.

Against a distant backdrop of leaf-filled trees was a small glade in which vibrant-green grass swayed beneath the influence of a gentle breeze that seemed unable to cross the threshold into the chamber. Though she couldn't see the entirety of the sky, it was disturbingly obvious that it was not the same night sky outside the Valley. Pristine blue-silver light from a full moon gently graced the glade along with the light from stars that glittered like diamonds in what appeared to be a clear sky. The atmosphere of it was serene and ethereal . . . almost otherworldly.

"What in tha hells is goin' on 'ere?" Mal asked in amazement as she tried to digest what she was seeing. Creeping forward to get a better view, she noticed a pair of glowing orbs in the distance that seemed to be hovering in the air. Her husky voice pitching a bit high, she stated in denial of what was before her, "None of this is possible!"

"No, it isn't," Flute responded, her voice tight, though Mal could not discern if it was from awe or fear. As Mal reached the threshold, Flute's tone became adamant as she added, "This is as far as I am allowed to go, Malia."

Turning, Mal stared at Flute incredulously. "What? After all ye've done this night, yer just gonna quit now?"

Flute nodded slowly. "Indeed. I have my orders, and they preclude me from entering the Valley. You will have to make the rest of the journey on your own." Mal started to retort, but Flute held up a hand, forestalling whatever it was Mal was going to say. "Fear not, for the interior of the Valley holds no threat for you."

"Then why do ye look so damn scared of it?" Mal barked. When Flute didn't immediately respond, a slight smirk crept onto Mal's face. "That's right, I noticed ye seemed downright fearful of this place ever since we opened tha gate outside; and given what ye did to tha soldiers, I dunna see what could make ye so damn scared of this place!"

"Again, Malia, I have my orders," Flute responded, but there was a quiver in her voice that made it clear to Mal she'd struck a nerve. "The Valley is no place for one such as myself. However, I will remain here for a while longer to ensure that you have a safe route to leave by once you have finished your task."

Shooting Flute a scowl of frustration, Mal looked back at the Valley. Though she could see very little, she knew from ventures around the Valley exterior that it was a very large place. Mal's scowl deepened and she cursed before turning back to Flute. "And just how long will ye wait? I've only got a general idea of where I'm goin', and that would have been easier to do if there'd been a simple way to get in through tha city entrance! So, Deo only knows how long it's gonna take me to get to tha graveyard, let alone find tha right tomb!"

Flute remained silent for a moment, and Mal watched her emotions play out across her face. Finally, Flute said, her voice soft as if she were offering to do something she desperately did not want to do, "I will wait here until dawn, but that is all the extra assistance I can offer. Will that suffice, Malia?"

Mal muttered something unintelligible under her breath. "Fine!" she tossed at Flute as she stripped her pack off her back, dissatisfaction dripping from her words. Tossing it to Flute, who caught it deftly, Mal said, "Just be sure I've got a clear path of escape, and I guess that'll be enough."

Flute nodded. "Agreed. And. . . ."

"And what?"

"If I may add, I would start by following the path at the edge of the woods, which I believe those lights are flanking. And if direction is the same within the Valley as it is outside, then the Royal Graveyard will be on the south side of the valley."

Turning her back to Flute, Mal barked, "I know which bloody direction to go! Just be 'ere when I'm done!"

Without waiting for a response, Mal crossed the threshold and began trotting toward the pair of glowing orbs in the distance.

Chapter Twenty-Four

"This has got to be a dream,"* Mal thought for what must have been at least the hundredth time since she'd set foot in the Valley.

The otherworldly quality that seemed to permeate the Utherian Valley was the first of many extraordinary surprises. Everywhere she'd looked, spring seemed to be flourishing; flowers in full bloom, treetops full and lush, and grass more vibrant than any she'd ever seen. As for the occupants of the Valley, she had only seen a handful of animals so far, all of which seem oddly ignorant of her presence – especially since she figured it was likely they had very little contact with humans. That oddity, however, flew from her mind when the first wisps had appeared.

Silver and blue, the glowing balls of soft light had emerged from the night like ephemeral spirits. At first, Mal had been both startled and fearful of the odd lights, but when none of the balls came within what she felt was dangerous proximity, she had relaxed a little. Eventually, as the dancing lights followed her from above, she came to enjoy the spectacle they provided as she walked along the path, which was illuminated by its own amazing oddity – flanking orbs of light that inexplicably hovered in the air. However, those astonishing sights paled in comparison to what she was currently fixated on . . . a sight she never believed she would see.

Bluish-silver moonlight slid across the mirrored surface of a large, pristine lake whose far shore was hidden from sight by the cloak of night. Dancing above the gentle ripples of the lake, countless wisps darted to and fro in a mesmerizing display that threatened to enthrall Mal. Shaking her head, she tore her gaze from the hypnotic show and started forward, her focus on the elegant stone bridge that connected her side of the shore to an island at the center of the lake. Made of white stone that seemed to glow in the moonlight, the gentle arch of the bridge guided her eye unerringly to the island, where a glass coffin hovered a few feet off the ground.

Reaching the foot of the bridge, Mal paused. Though she couldn't discern intricate details from her position, it was already clear to her that the coffin was captivatingly unique. Inclined slightly so that it faced the bridge, the six-sided casket appeared to be framed with gold; furthermore, it suddenly dawned on her that the coffin was not made of glass like she initially thought. *"Deo, this thing is made of . . . crystal?"* she thought incredulously as she realized the light passing through the panels arrived on the ground in a cornucopia of color.

Every inquisitive fiber of her being demanded that she cross the span, and she was dearly tempted to submit to that insistent hunger. However, as she placed one foot on the bridge, her practical side cut through her curiosity. *"Ye've got better things to be doin', lass. Finish yer job, and maybe, just maybe, ye can sightsee if ye got time. Besides, ye got Flute waitin' on ye; and Deo knows that lass seemed damned scared of somethin' in this place."*

That thought nearly made her laugh. Nothing about the Valley seemed malicious in any fashion, but she couldn't deny the fear she'd sensed from the enigmatic girl. Removing her foot from the bridge, Mal looked around carefully. "Maybe tha lass is just a bit daft," she muttered when she saw nothing that would warrant even the slightest amount of anxiety. "Still," she thought aloud as she placed her hands on her hips in consternation and examined the area again, "There's been no sign of a path leadin' tha way I really need to go, and that dunna seem right."

She snorted. "Maybe those fools in tha Resistance dunna know what they're talkin' about, and tha only way to tha tombs is through tha city entrance." A scowl marred her face as she continued her inspection of the area. "Deo help me, if'n those buggers are that daft, I'm gonna—"

Suddenly, as her vision turned westward, a pair of lights flared to life in the distance. Blinking, Mal stared at the new lights as if they were nothing more than a figment of her imagination. Then to her amazement, more lights began to spring to life in the woods, carrying her gaze ever upward into the hills.

Mal grunted. "This place is just full o' surprises," she muttered as she began jogging along the lakeshore toward the lights.

As she drew closer, it became evident that the orbs, like those that had greeted her upon entering the valley, flanked a path that would take her back into the woods. Crossing the clearing with a measure of caution, Mal couldn't decide if she was worried or relieved that there was still no hint of danger. *"Never knew a place could be both so damn beautiful and so damn eerie at tha same bloody time,"* she thought as she reached the light orbs at the base of the hillside. *"Deo, it's too damn quiet, even with tha crickets singin'. . . . It's almost like somethin' is missin'."*

Shaking her head, Mal suddenly cursed. A few yards into the woods, she could clearly see the base of an impressively wide marble staircase. "Great, stairs. . . . And a ton of them, from tha looks of it," she groaned, irritated.

Muttering to herself, Mal approached the stairs. Even before she reached the base, it dawned on her that the lights she'd seen springing to life from afar likely flanked the staircase. Cursing, her gaze traced the stairs' ascent to a landing, which was nearly thirty feet above her. When she saw that the stairs turned left at the landing before vanishing from sight, she cursed again. "Deo, this is gonna be one bloody irritatin' climb," she complained aloud as she set foot on the staircase. "Oh well, nothin' worthwhile is ever easy," she conceded with a sigh before increasing her pace.

Nearly half-an-hour later, with her winded and her legs burning from exertion, Mal reached the top of the winding staircase. Bending over, she grabbed her knees and drew in a series of deep breaths. When she finally felt that she'd caught her breath, and that her heart was no longer eager to burst from her chest, she stood upright and looked back down the stairs.

"Who in tha bloody hells builds a staircase that damn long?!" she asked aloud, her husky voice thick with annoyance. "Tha fool that would enjoy buildin' that . . . that . . . *thing* is a sadist or crazy!" She scoffed. "Hells, he was probably both!" Shaking her head in exasperation, she turned to examine where the stairs had deposited her.

Lush trees in full bloom reached skyward just beyond the soft glow of the light orbs that flanked the cobblestone path she now stood before, which appeared to run arrow straight for a few hundred paces before branching north and south. Determined to recoup a bit more after the long climb, but unwilling to squander more time, Mal started along the path at a leisurely pace. This high into the hills, the song of the stream and lake were lost, leaving her blanketed in a silence that seemed oddly tranquil. She felt a measure of surprise at this realization. Ever since she'd set foot in the fort guarding the private entrance to the Valley, a sense of apprehension had pervaded her mind and body. Now, however, that sensation was gone. Whether it was a result of the peaceful bearing of the Valley, or the realization that if something ill was going to befall her, there'd already been more than enough time to do so, she did not know.

Shrugging as she reached the junction in the path, Mal cast the thought aside. Nothing bad had occurred, and now that she'd mercifully found a path leading south, she felt she was finally nearing her destination.

"Be happy 'bout that, lass. Ye didn't know what awaited ye in 'ere. Ye could be dead right now if this place had been trapped," she chided herself. Glancing at the northward path and its trajectory, she scoffed. *"I'm betin' that way might be leadin' back to where I came in. Might could of shaved*

some time if'n ye'd taken that northward fork near tha entrance, lass." She shrugged and turned south. *"Then again, ye don't know that fer sure,"* she added as she stared forward. *"Might be that path takes a nice and leisurely route. Besides, ye wouldn't have gotten to see tha Sky Tomb fer yerself."* Laughing aloud, she shook her head. *"Stay focused, lass,"* she reprimanded herself. *"There's still a tomb to find and break into. Ye can reflect on all this when tha job is done and yer safe and snug back home."*

To her chagrin, irritation and anxiousness returned in force when she began to feel that there was no end to the cobblestone path. Several times, as the path wound its way through the trees, she found herself peeking at the sky — which only made her more anxious. The moon never seemed to move. It had been difficult enough to accept that the interior of the Valley did not reflect the seasonal conditions outside of it, but the fact that the moon seemed stationary had muddled her sense of time so much that she wasn't sure just how long she'd been there. Granted, she knew without hesitation that she'd been in the majestic burial grounds for hours, but for all she knew, she'd already passed the night away.

"Deo be good! Fer all I know, it's dawn outside, and Flute's abandoned me to whatever fate awaits me when I try to leave!" Scoffing at the morose thoughts, she chided aloud, *"That's right, lass, focus on what ye can't control; that'll do ye a whole hells of a lot of good. Keep goin' like this, an—"*

Rounding a bend in the path, Mal's conversation with herself came to an abrupt end as she came to a halt. Before her was a white stone bridge, similar to the one at the Sky Tomb, that spanned a modest — and unusually quiet — stream. On the far bank, the land was occupied for as far as she could see by a graveyard whose grandeur was a clear sign that royalty was entombed on the grounds. Forcing herself to move, Mal found her steps suddenly guided by a sense of respect. While she generally found the overtly wealthy to be wholeheartedly selfish and their shortsighted actions to be repugnant, she also believed the dead — aside from those whose lives represented tyranny and evil in its worse forms — to be worthy of respect.

As she crossed the bridge, she spared the stream a glance. To her surprise, it seemed to be moving sluggishly and appeared to have jumped its banks by a few feet. *"Odd,"* she thought. *"Everythin' 'bout this place has seemed so damn perfect. I canna imagine that it'd be possible fer somethin' to stop a stream like that."* She smirked dryly as she reached the far bank. *"Then again, I'm kinda glad to see that this place has a flaw. Nothin' should be so bloody perfect."*

Before her, an archway provided egress through the eight-foot-tall wall of white marble that, as far as Mal could tell from her position, seemed to encompass the graveyard. Stepping through the arch, Mal immediately noticed two things – first, there were no head-stones in sight, only tombs; second, every tomb she could see was opulent. As she proceeded along the raised path that bisected the graveyard, she couldn't keep her eyes from wandering. To her surprise, every crypt was set well below the path. Some of them were made of marble, others of stone, and she even saw a few that were gilded with gold in places. Despite differences in materials and design, the crypts did share a few similar characteristics. Each tomb was separated from the others by an eight-foot-tall wall, each sported matching marble stairs descending to them from the path, and each tomb also bore a House sigil at a prominent place. Many of the sigils she saw near the graveyard entrance were familiar to Mal, but as she proceeded deeper, more and more of the sigils were unknown to her, and part of her believed that even scholars would have a hard time identifying them.

"So many Houses," she thought incredulously. *"Has tha struggle fer Triclose's throne been that devistatin' over tha last. . . . Deo, I'm no scholar, but hasn't it been 'round two-hundred bloody years since House Gravit'nas fell? Deo be good! How could this many Houses have risen and fallen in that time? There's at least twenty crypts 'ere, and there doesn't appear to be an end to 'um."*

She shook her head in amazement as more crypts appeared along the gentle bend in the path. Suddenly she smirked, as for the first time, she saw a sigil she'd seen earlier. "Ah! That might explain tha ludicrous number of these tombs!" she declared aloud. "Some of tha House have more than one! Guess that makes some sense; after all, ye gotta run out of space in one of these places eventually."

Nearing what Mal figured was the apex of the sweeping path, Mal's breath caught in her throat as the endless line of crypts gave way to a familiar, yet unexpected, scene. Once more, Mal found herself confronted with a bridge reminiscent of the one at the Sky Tomb. This time, however, the bridge led to a large island in the middle of an impressively wide river, the water level of which seemed a bit too high. Once again, the oddity of the high water level was supplanted by something else. This time, it was an island, nearly identical to what Logan had described, occupied by several marble crypts that appeared to be set slightly below ground level. Without counting, Mal knew how many of the structures there were.

"Fourteen crypts, arranged in a circle, in which tha dead of tha original Houses of Triclose rest eternally," she thought with a measure of awe and anxiety. *"Deo be good. . . . Maybe tha sods in tha Resistance do know what they're talkin' about."*

Fending off her anxious curiosity, Mal approached the bridge and crossed its impressive span. Wisps danced over the sluggish river and in the air above her, adding their ethereal light to the moon's bluish-silver illumination. Once on the island, Mal passed between two of the impressive crypts to find herself at the heart of the isle.

Coming to a halt, Mal's breath caught in her throat at the sight before her. "Deo – what in tha bloody hells is goin' on with this place?" she asked, perplexed as she stared at the center of the courtyard.

Embedded in the center of the courtyard, and cast in silver, was the same crest that she'd seen on the Valley gate – fourteen sigils arranged in a circle around two dragons circling one another, their paws clasped together as if in combat. The moonlight gently played along the silver lines of the seal, infusing it with a gentle glow that made Mal feel welcomed and at peace. With her wide blue eyes taking in every exquisite detail, she started forward and, although she had no idea why, approached the seal with reverence. While its smaller twin on the Valley door had been impressive in its own right, she found herself in true awe of what she gazed upon now. She had no idea how such a breathtaking thing could be fashioned, but there was no doubt in her mind that whoever was responsible for the seal was deserving of unending praise.

With gentle steps, Mal made her way to the center of the seal and came to a halt in the space between the dragons' powerful limbs. Turning to face the top of the circle, she pried her gaze from the seal and examined the crypts. From what she could see, at least five of the structures were home to fluted marble colonnades that surrounded small atriums, another five of the crypts reminded her of domed churches, while a variety of angular roofing surmounted the others. Despite the difference in architectural tastes, every building was decorated in some manner. There was gilding of gold, bronze, and silver, doors made from materials far more exquisite than simple wood, as well as magnificent relief sculptures that left very few barren surfaces to be found.

Mal chuckled dryly. *"Expensive materials, bloated design and decoration. . . . I guess even in death a noble's got to flaunt their wealth. But I'll give 'um this – they at least don't appear to be gaudy enough to bejewel their final resting spot,"* she thought with sarcastic amusement. "So, which of ye lovelies gets my attention tonight, eh?" she mused aloud.

Mal's brow furrowed in consternation as she examined each crypt for any indication as to which House they belonged. Unlike the crypts on the other side of the river, these were free of House sigils. So, with nothing obvious to go on, Mal eventually chose one of the crypts to her right, a massive and flamboyant gray stone structure with a vaulted roof of black tiles supported by fluted marble columns, and padded over to it. Mal trailed a hand idly on the wrought iron railing as she descended a set of polished stone stairs and examined the facade of the crypt. To her chagrin, as she stepped off the stairs, she saw nothing on the front of the crypt that would indicate the House entombed within. Chewing on her lower lip, Mal began to make her way around the exterior of the expansive crypt, examining it as closely as she would a lock she suspected was trapped. Unfortunately, she finished one pass with no luck, and frustration took root in her belly. Another pass followed, and then another before she conceded that there was nothing to be found on the crypt's exterior.

Returning to the bronze double doors that sealed the tomb, Mal muttered as she looked for any sign of a lock, "Right then – if there's nothin' to be found on tha outside, guess I'll be takin' a peek inside." Seeing no indication of a lock of any fashion, Mal took hold of the bronze ring handles. "Of course there's no lock," she muttered sarcastically. "Why would there be in this crazy place."

Tugging on the handles, she was a bit surprised when the door refused to budge. Cursing under her breath, Mal adjusted her grip and pulled with all her might. Again, the door refused to move. Tossing her hands in the air in annoyance, Mal let out an angry growl. Fists planted on her hips, she returned to the plaza. Muttering under her breath, she set her sights on another crypt and stalked over to it. Once more, she examined the exterior and tried the doors, only to be met with the same exasperating results. Another crypt quickly followed, and then another, but each one refused to yield its secrets.

Stalking back to the plaza to the accompaniment of a string of curses, Mal began to pace around the seal. "Now what did that bloody bugger say about this place?" she asked aloud, her brow furrowed in frustrated concentration. "Fourteen crypts on an island in tha middle of tha river; each one servin' as tha final restin' place fer nobles of tha original Houses of Triclose." She looked up at the crypts. "Well, there's no doubtin' this is tha place. So, tha one I want belongs to House Suldamik. But that doesn't do me any bloody good if I don't know which is which!" Tossing her head back she yelled at the star-filled sky, "Leon, ye bloody bugger! Ye didn't mention they weren't labeled!" Dropping her gaze back to the seal, she growled, "How am I suppose to know which is which, much less get in. . . ."

Coming to a halt at the top of the circle, Mal's angry words trailed off as her eyes alighted on the outer ring of sigils. "Well, I'll be a kyram's ruttin' buddy . . ." she breathed as she approached the upper-right seal. "I must be denser than a kyram head. . . . Could it really be that obvious?"

Reaching the seal, she crouched down and examined it.

There was no mistaking it – the seal bore the same rune as the sigil on both the Valley's gate and the amulet. Looking up, she saw a domed crypt whose entrance aligned perfectly with the sigil. "Well, that solves that problem, ye dumbass . . ." she stated, a bit embarrassed that she hadn't noticed the sigil early. "But if this works like tha gate, then where do I get an amulet that bloody big?"

Tapping her forefinger against her chin thoughtfully, Mal stood up and turned back toward the bridge. "Guess I could call this a miserable failure and report that tha thing is sealed all magic-like?" She scoffed and shook her head. Planting her fists on her hips, she chided, "Right, lass. Like ye'd get another shot at gettin' in here." Shaking her head, she added as she took a step back forcefully, "No, ye've got to—"

The ground beneath her foot gave way a little. Retracting her foot quickly, Mal turned and examined the sigil again. "Deo be good," she breathed in surprise when she saw that the sigil had sunk ever so slightly.

Every nerve in her body suddenly rang with apprehension. Licking her lips, Mal looked around carefully. She had not seen even a hint of a trap, but then again, she had missed what she presumed to be a very cunning lock. Shrugging, she declared, "Well, didn't come all this way fer nothin'," before stepping forward and putting all her weight on the sigil.

Mal's eyes widened in amazement as the sigil sank further into the ground without the slightest groan of protest. An instant later, she heard what sounded like a steel latch releasing from the crypt aligned with the sigil; and with that familiar sound, nervous excitement began to twist her stomach. Licking her thin lips once more, Mal approached the crypt cautiously and descended the stairs.

Reminiscent of a basilica, the tomb's dome was ribbed with gold, and was made of marble shot through with veins of gray and black. Gray stone comprised its walls, many of which were home to relief carvings of warring soldiers or scenes of jubilation, and the facade of the atrium's gable featured a carving of a richly dressed man kneeling before another man seated on an impressive throne.

Mal's gaze lingered on the kneeling man for a brief moment. *"I wonder if that's tha first Suldamik in their cursed line?"* she thought absently before she stepped beneath the vaulted atrium.

Wide enough for three abreast, the atrium was lined with columns of grey-streaked marble that supported its roof. However, Mal was only partially aware of her surroundings as her attention was fixed on the soft glow emanating from the crack between two partially ajar, large stone doors. Caution guided her steps as she approached the doors, and when she reached them, she took a deep breath before peeking through the crack. Opened slightly toward her, the space between the heavy stone panels was only wide enough for her to make out what seemed to be a vast, unoccupied space. When she was satisfied that the room was safe, Mal took hold of the iron-ring door handles and pulled. To her amazement, the doors swung open with an ease that shouldn't have been possible for such sturdy panels.

"Nothin' 'bout this place is right," she mused. Letting out an exasperated sigh, she did her best to shake it off as she had done so many times on this venture. *"This is just one more bloody oddity in a place that seems full of weird things. Just ignore it fer now and get on with yer job. Yer almost done, and then ye can be gone from this place,"* she encouraged herself. Taking a deep breath, Mal did her best to clear her mind of unwanted thoughts, then stepped into the crypt.

The rotunda was spacious, just as she figured, but to her surprise, it was free of burial sites. Instead, the marble-sheathed walls were home to a haunting procession of relief carvings that appeared to represent nobility. Mal's gaze followed the procession from its origination point at the crypt's entrance to its end at the archway on the opposite side of the room. To her surprise, the descending passage beyond the arch was bathed in the glow of small light orbs hovering near the curved ceiling. With caution, Mal made her way across the rotunda, testing her footing as she went for pressure traps while her gaze darted about warily.

Passing through the archway, Mal made her way down the short passage, which was adorned with even more reliefs of what she figured were either prominent members of House Suldamik, or important scenes from their past. Once at the other end of the hall, she was greeted with a stone switchback staircase with iron railings, all of which appeared to be in good condition. Peaking over the railing, Mal felt a wry grin tug at her lips. As far down as she could see, the stairwell appeared to be fully illuminated.

"I really shouldn't be surprised at this point," she thought as she started down the stairs.

With the guarded pace she adopted, it took Mal longer than she would have liked to make her way down. Her pace was slowed even further when she discovered the first landing was home to a vault. Peaking inside the vault, which was lit by more of the floating orbs, she found it empty save for at least fifty coffin-less stone platforms. Descending to the second landing, she discovered it was home to a vault as well. It's interior also revealed an identical scene to the first, which elicited a curious raise of an eyebrow from her.

Upon reaching the third landing, she was beginning to believe each floor contained its own vault. Unable to curb her curiosity, Mal once again spared a moment to peak within. Seeing that it, too, was barren, a slightly amused laugh slipped out. "Guess they're figurin' on buryin' a few more generations 'ere," she mused as her laughter echoed about eerily. Cringing, she muttered, "And if there's anyone actually in 'ere – dead or alive – then that bloody well let 'um know they've got visitors."

Cursing herself under her breath for her carelessness, Mal returned to the stairs and continued downward.

Two more empty vaults followed before she finally saw the first coffins in the sixth vault. Pausing on the landing, Mal peeked over the railing. It appeared there were only two more floors below her, and it was likely the tomb she sought was down there, but this was the first floor that was in use, and the urge to take a peak was undeniable.

"What's one more small delay at this point?" she mused as she stepped into the vault. "Been in 'ere long enough that it's not gonna surprise me if I'm stuck 'ere. Dunna think I'd be blamin' Flute if tha lass done scampered off at this point," she added as she looked around.

Similar to the vaults above, most of the spaces were empty. However, this one had four spots in use. A pair of impressive sealed stone coffins occupied two of the spots at the very center of the room, while the third was topless, and the fourth appeared to have been shattered. Curious, Mal crept closer and saw that the relief-carved lids of the sealed coffins resembled a man and a woman. Upon closer inspection, she saw plaques at the foot of each sculpture that identified the interred as Doms Calvin Murandi Suldamik and Doma Jilifine se'Tavina Suldamik.

Moving alongside Doms Suldamik's sarcophagus, she saw that he was depicted in formal armor with his hands clasping a sword that ran the length of his body. A strong-featured face with a neatly trimmed beard was displayed with his eyes closed beneath a full head of hair upon which a simple crown rested. Looking over at Doma Suldamik's final resting place, she saw that the doma was presented as a woman close to half the man's age and was clothed in a modest gown. Locks of curly hair framed a serene and narrow face, while a smaller matching crown adorned her head. Hands folded at her waist, an impressive hinged ring adorned her left ring finger, which seemed to match the wedding torque around her neck.

Imaging how magnificent those pieces of jewelry must have been in real life, Malt thought with envious awe, "*What a prize that would be.”*

Taking a step back, she started to turn for the vault's entrance when a clatter echoed through the vault as she accidentally kicked a small piece of loose stone. Looking down at the shattered platform, Mal caught a glimpse of something metallic amongst the dust and rubble. Crouching down, she sifted through the mess and removed a small bronze placard. Holding it up to the light, it appeared to Mal that someone had attempted to scratch out the name engraved on it; however, she was still able to read it.

“Shi'doms Zalan Tavina Suldamik,” she read aloud. “Humph! Logan said ye might be buried down 'ere, and if so, what I'm lookin' fer might be on ye. But,” she said with a sigh as she tossed the plate on the rubble, “I'm guessin' that since ye died a traitor's death, ye got a traitor's burial. Poor bugger. . . . And all ye wanted was peace.” Shaking her head sadly, Mal left the vault and continued her descent.

Two floors later, she reached the bottom and let out a sigh of relief. Whether the Resistance's information was correct or not, her venture in the Valley would soon be over. Stepping through the vault's arched entry, Mal was surprised to see that not only was the vault small, but it lacked coffin platforms. Instead, the light orbs illuminated the only thing in the room – the relief-carved stone walls. Cursing her luck, she pressed her lips together tightly, and moved to the center of the vault with determined steps. Once there, she turned in place as she examined the walls.

Both flanking walls depicted soldiers in the throes of battle. There were armored soldiers on horseback that seemed to take far too much pleasure in cutting down their opponents from on high, while footsoldiers in an amalgam of armor tore at each other with an assortment of weapons, and in several spots, with fists and teeth. The dead and dying were depicted in twisted positions, crying out desperately to deaf gods. As Mal's gaze followed the macabre scene, her stomach turned at the naked violence and emotions on display.

“Deo be good – glorified or not, I'd say tha bastard buried 'ere deserves whichever hell he's burnin' in now! Hells, this might explain a lot 'bout this Deo-be-damned war, and tha Suldamiks in particular.” She snorted. “Hells,” she said aloud as she continued her turn, “It makes me think tha Suldamiks can't stand tha smell o' peace; and if that be tha real reason they'd kill one of their own, then tha Hells take tha lot of them!” she finished as her gaze settled on the far wall. This time, she paid more attention to it than when she'd entered the vault, and she snorted in disgust. “Arrogant bastard,” she muttered and then spit.

Occupying the entirety of the far wall was a simpler scene

than the rest of the vault, though no less glorified. Centered on the wall, and the focus of what seemed like countless prostrating soldiers, was a lone man sitting proudly atop an imposing destrider that was protected from hoof-to-head in full plate armor. Mal snorted in disgust at the armor. Horses and warfare were hardly her interests, but she felt that even a fool would find the destrider's barding excessive and overly gaudy. Each plate of the destrider's barding was heavily engraved with florid patterns that Mal suspected would have been gold-plated in life. In contrast, dangerous spikes adorned the destrider's shaffron, as well as its peytral and flanchard; even the crinet flowing down the beast's neck bore smaller but no less dangerous spikes. Where there were gaps in the barding, flowing chainmail provided protection.

"Deo, this bugger really is an arrogant bastard," she muttered derisively as she eyed the rider.

Encased in full plate that was a match in excessiveness to the mount's ensemble, the rider sat tall in his saddle against a shining, magnificent sun. A jeweled circlet rested atop a head that was home to a chiseled, broad face that was held in the lofty, pompous manner that Mal would have expected from such a man. A well-manicured goatee accented a slender-lipped mouth that held a slight hint of righteous self-satisfaction beneath a narrow nose. That same arrogance was reflected in the man's eyes, which gazed down upon the prostrating masses from beneath a cowl of wavy hair as if it was perfectly natural – and right – for all to bow before him.

Mal scowled and spit at the base of the wall. "Think I'm gonna enjoy stealin' from this bastard and his blood even more now. That kinda self-righteousness is what ends up hurtin' a lot of people." Approaching the wall, Mal grinned devilishly and said, "Now, why don't ye be a good little bastard, and show me where ye've hidden what I'm 'ere fer, okay?"

As she moved along the wall, examining it with both her hands and eyes for any sign of a hidden compartment, switch or lock, she muttered, "It's easy to read a man like ye, ye know that? Yer too conceited to hide it anywhere but on ye or near ye, but yer not so full of yerself to display it in tha open. So," she continued as she crouched down and examined where the wall met the floor, "tha question is, just how smart are ye?"

Moving to her right along the wall, Mal suddenly stopped and moved back a couple of steps. Holding her hand near where the floor met the wall, Mal concentrated on her hand. It took her a moment to be sure, but it was there, a slight stirring of the air. Grinning slightly, Mal slowly moved to the left, seeking an end to the subtle airflow.

When she found it, she stood up with a satisfied smile and stepped back from the wall. Nearly three-fourths of the wall was a door of some sort. "Now," she mused aloud, "where's tha lock?"

For a time, Mal stood there and examined the hidden door, looking for any imperfections or oddities in the relief sculpture. One of Mal's eyebrows shot up in surprise, and she took a few steps back for a wider view of the scene. A number of the bowed soldiers where holding standards, all of which were pointed toward the rider. "It can't be that easy," she muttered before returning to the wall and pressing on each of the standards.

When none of them budged, she tried different orders and even tried pressing on different areas of the standards. When she once again met with failure, she attempted to slide the standards in all directions. When that yielded no results, Mal focused on the rider as she mumbled to herself. Nothing seemed out of the ordinary to her other than the focus of the standards, and even then, that could have simply been a compositional choice. Mal shook her head. No, the man in the sculpture was too proud to be that deceptive. The key to opening the door had to be on him. However, the question that kept rattling in her skull was, what was the key?

Then it hit her.

At first, she thought it was too obvious, but there was nothing that stood out on the rider more than the talon surrounded by spikes on the center of the armored plate protecting the destrider's chest. Pressing on it, Mal felt it shift. The motion would have been imperceptible for most people, but Mal's sensitive hands felt the minuscule movement. Pushing harder, in case the button was simply stuck, Mal was disappointed, but not surprised, when it refused to budge any more than before. Grumbling to herself, Mal ran her hand over the surrounding area. There was a release for the lock somewhere, and now that she had a better idea of what she was looking for, she knew it was only a matter of time before she found it.

To her surprise, she found the release quickly. "Hidin' in plain sight, eh? Ye really were an arrogant – and dumb – bastard," Mal quipped as she eyed the spikes surrounding the talon. Arranged in a fashion that reminded Mal vaguely of a star, a series of eight spikes framed the lone talon like it was a family crest.

A chill ran down Mal's spine. *"Deo, could that tale Leon told me actually hold a hint of tha truth?"* Mal thought as her hand hovered over the top spike.

Taking a deep breath to steady herself, Mal then pressed on it. Unsurprisingly, it sank into the wall and she heard a click. Moving left around the pattern, Mal carefully pressed on each spike and listened for the click, as well as any hint of a trap. When all the spikes were depressed without ill effect, Mal reached for the talon and paused. *"Ye don't have to do this, ye know?"* she told herself, suddenly hesitant. *"If ye do find what they want in 'ere, Deo only knows what tha repercussion will be. Ye could just be makin' things worse. Hells, fer all ye know, tha war will sort itself out."* She snorted derisively at her hesitation. *"Right — that's about as likely as Deo himself steppin' in to end tha damned conflict. No. Ye got to finish tha job. Once ye've done that, take yer money and leave. Let tha bloody fools in tha Resistance deal with it and whatever bloody consequence follow."*

Licking her lips, Mal clenched her hand and, before she could have any more misgivings, pressed the talon. To her chagrin — though she wasn't entirely surprised — the spikes snapped back into place, and the door remained sealed. Grunting, she muttered, "Well, ye rarely get a pattern lock right on tha first go," before she repeated the simple pattern, but moving right this time.

As before, the spikes returned to their starting point when she pressed on the talon. She made three more failed attempts with different patterns before taking a step back and, with a deep, calming breath, examined the spikes again. The idea that the spikes formed and an eight-point star suddenly jumped to the forefront of her mind, causing her to tilt her head to the side thoughtfully.

"Well," she said after a moment of contemplation, "ye got nothin' to lose. . . . Might as well give it a go."

Stepping back up to the wall, she pressed the spikes as if she were drawing a star. As before, the spikes reset, but she tried again without hesitation. Flipping the order in which she pressed them, she once more pushed on the talon. This time, there was mild resistance as it sank into the wall, and as it settled into place, there was a loud clank followed by a series of groans that had Mal stepping away from the wall, excited. Suddenly, there was one final loud clank and groan that sent a shudder through the wall. Then, with a moan of protest and a cloud of dust and stale air, the wall moved.

Mal's heart began to race with nervous anticipation as she watched the large panel slowly rise into the air. Whatever was responsible for the wall's controlled ascent groaned like a beast in pain. *"Deo,"* Mal thought as a particularly loud moan made her cringe, *"when was tha last time this bloody thing moved?"* she mused.

Time seemed to lose all meaning for Mal as she waited for the wall to finish its anguished climb. When it finally did, two light orbs sputtered to life in the newly revealed chamber, setting the ancient dust that had been awakened aglow in a surreal fashion. Coughing slightly, Mal did her best to clear the air in front of her face. To her chagrin, it took a moment for the dust to settle enough that she could see and breathe well enough to proceed. When it finally did, she managed only a single step before her breath caught in her throat and a cold chill shot up her spine. Swallowing hard, she forced her legs to move and she stepped forward.

Small in size, Mal felt the weight of the new chamber as she moved within and stopped. Before her, a stone coffin, the lid of which resembled the man on the wall in repose, rested ominously at the center of the room. There was no placard on the coffin to identify the entombed, but Mal saw there was no need for it – for what was on the rear wall identified the dead man with chilling clarity.

"Deo – what have I gotten myself into?" she asked of the emptiness.

Carved upon the wall was a large, bold sigil that made Mal's knees tremble with weakness. Covered in scales, the taloned paw reminded her of those of the great dragon guarding the Valley's city entrance. However, what was hovering over the paw as if the appendage was holding it aloft was what made Mal tremble – five, four-pointed stars.

"It's not possible!" she breathed as she stared at the haunting sigil in astonishment.

Somehow, she managed to tear her eyes from it, but what her gaze landed on banished all doubt from her mind. Below the sigil, on a bronze placard that seemed hauntingly new, there was a medallion with a matching seal set beneath an inscription that Mal found herself reading again and again in disbelief.

'Betrayed by Blood and Cast Out, May the Souls of Those That Betrayed Him Quake in Fear, For Here Lies Duratain Suldam Merandith, the Last and One True Doms of the Glorious House Merandith.'

*

The silence should have been comforting.

Arms wrapped about her knees, sky-blue hair hanging freely about her shoulders, and her cheeks streaked with blue, Flute stared at the open gate with eyes red from crying as she struggled to calm her troubled mind and aching heart. For so long, no matter where her imprisonment took her, silence had been one of the few things she'd been allowed to indulge in. Had it always been a haven for her? She knew wholeheartedly that it had not always been so.

When her endless imprisonment first began, isolation and the silence it brought with it had been used against her with ruthless efficiency. Young and just beginning to grasp what her second chance at life meant, she had fallen prey to the vindictive machinations of a woman hells-bent on revenge. Days filled with physical demands and punishments were often followed by cold, isolated nights that chipped away at her young and vulnerable fortitude with remorseless vigor. In the end, her young mind nearly broke beneath her mistress' gleeful tortures, and suicide became a glowing harbinger of blessed relief.

"Suicide."

The thought lanced through her mind like a white-hot barb as she held her wrists before her and peered thoughtfully at where she had once sliced her arms open nearly to her elbow. Flute shook her head vigorously to banish the thought. Although the inclination to end her life had once held an alluring appeal, it had long lost its luster. Furthermore, it was no longer possible. Her hand drifted to her chest, where it alighted on the medallion set there. When her mistress had discovered her bleeding out on the floor of the lavish estate they occupied at the time, she had immediately embedded a sliver of her own crystal in Flute's heart. Blissful death had been stolen from her, and to add further insult, the foul device that adorned her chest had been implanted, rendering her newly amplified powers useless unless her mistress wished it.

Another crystallized tear slipped down her cheek. For her mission this night, Alestra had relaxed the restriction on Flute's powers just enough to serve her designs. Flute had desperately hoped she would be allowed enough fir'gan to reach out along the currents to the friendly presence she had sensed weeks ago. To her dismay, her numerous attempts since Mal entered the Valley had been for naught. She could reach four, maybe five, thousand paces in any direction, but there was nothing to sense other than the unconscious soldiers in the fort, and the life in the Valley.

Thinking of the Valley, she fixed her gaze on it. Although her orders regarding Mal depended mainly on the results of the woman's foray into the ethereal graveyard, her orders concerning the Valley itself were explicit.

"Using me as a test subject, again," she thought remorsefully. *"It should not surprise me, but it does. I have managed to find peace about a great many things, but despite your tortures, your cruelty, and your attempts to lure me to the Darkness, I somehow keep hoping a part of you still loves me . . . even though the Darkness has consumed your mind, heart, and soul. Alas, maybe I should accept Father's assessment of you so long ago — you belong to the Darkness, and nothing can redeem you. Yet, I know I cannot give hope up entirely; after all, if redemption can find him and I, why not you?"*

As fresh crystallized tears began to pour from her sky-blue

eyes, a sad voice asked in her mind, *"Child of aether, why do you cry?"*

Startled, Flute scrambled to her feet and looked about. "Who's there?" she asked, her muscles and soft voice tense. Not once had she sensed anyone in the vicinity, and upon searching the currents again, she confirmed that she was alone.

"Do you not recognize me, child? I certainly know you despite the millennia that have passed."

Slowly, Flute moved toward the center of the room, her senses franticly searching for the speaker. Given her limited strength, and if the man was a skilled Gifted, it would certainly be easy enough for him to conceal himself from her, but she didn't believe that was the case. Furthermore, something about the speaker's voice tickled a memory that refused to yield its knowledge.

"I . . ." she started to reply as she stopped short of the crystal-topped marble circle. "You sound familiar, yet I cannot place you, nor can I see you," she said hesitantly.

The voice chuckled, though she sensed no mirth in it. Instead, she felt that the laugh seemed . . . sad. *"Time has little meaning for me, child, and I have had so few visitors of worth in the centuries since the Valley's birth that I sometimes forget my state. You once knew me as Mathis Hyren, brother to Lord Dragon Luthur Hyren, may his soul forever rest in Corith's gentle embrace."*

Stunned, Flute stared at the Valley entrance, her mind racing to comprehend what the voice had just uttered. "Mathis? How? That's not—" she started to say.

"Possible? Though my memory is clouded by the centuries, I believe you were old enough to absorb the wonders of our Age of birth, were you not? Cities — be they elvannue, human or darlion — fueled by fir'gan, environments frozen in time for the enjoyment of all, bountiful crops, wonders to make life easier. . . . Ah, 'twas a time to be alive!" the voice finished, its tone wistful.

"I remember it . . . to a degree. But I also remember the poverty, slavery, and violence that existed. I do not think it was the utopia you recall."

"Perhaps, child. . . . Perhaps. Time does not hold the same meaning for me as it does for you. But is it wrong to recall the good that brought joy to so many? Mayhap you recall the bad too vividly? Those of your blood have seen the horrors of life to an extreme, and have paid a heavy price. Might that cloud your view of the past?"

Flute wiped fresh tears from her cheeks. "Cloud my view of the past?" she reiterated with a dark, sarcastic laugh. "Those wonders you speak of were but the veil that Kylir's scars hid behind. We warred with each other, starved the poor, sold others into slavery, and that was probably the least of our sins!" she cried as the emotions boiling within her summoned more tears. "For all the good the elvannue claimed to serve, they viewed the other races with contempt, and seemed satisfied to distance themselves from us until it was too late! And even then, they left us to the horrors my . . . my. . .!" The words caught in her throat, and Flute let out a scream of frustration. "Corith! Even the dragons watched on with indifference until their very existence was threatened!

"No! The world was not the shiny utopia you recall! It was a festering boil that was ready to explode one way or another, and it's never really gotten any better! What Luthur and the others fought so long and hard for did little more than staunch the flow! The Darkness is patient, ever patient! I have seen this firsthand, and know better than anyone that it will win in the end!"

Deafening silence greeted her morose outburst, and for a moment, she thought she had scared off the voice that claimed to be Mathis. But when it finally spoke again, she felt a sensation of relief. She'd had too few people to speak with, let alone this freely, and she knew it was folly to scare off a friendly voice, even if it had no corporeal form.

"Those are the words of a servant of the Darkness," the voice stated, its hard tone blunted by an edge of sadness. *"Yet I do not sense its touch on you or your heart . . . though I do sense something else. It hums in my mind and threatens to disrupt my thoughts."*

Flute's hand darted to her chest, and she clutched at the bone amulet. "Dragon bone," she whispered, her tone pained.

"Aye, child. Its presence does not go unnoticed. Alas, its usage is most foul and perverse," the voice responded, its words filled with concern.

Flute squeezed the amulet and felt the pressure pull on the skin that was fused with it. "Foul, indeed!" she spit. "My . . . *mistress* gave unto me a piece of her crystal to prevent me from taking my own life."

"I see," the voice responded sorrowfully. *"To be pushed to such lengths. . . . None of us knew of your fate, else we would have sought you out."*

Flute laughed darkly. "That was her plan . . . her revenge on Father. Keep me from him and bend me to the Darkness' will, then unleash me upon him. She wants nothing more than to see his beloved daughter, the daughter he gave all to save, drive a crusader through his heart the way Garith did with your brother!"

"So that was how he died," the voice replied to her outburst, its

words unnervingly passive. *"Would that Damion could know his suspicions were true. 'Tis a shame you did not visit with this knowledge earlier. I could have imparted it unto him upon his last visit."*

Flute's breath caught in her throat. "He.... That was him, wasn't it?" she asked, her melodic voice suddenly hopeful. "That night a few weeks ago.... That outpouring of power.... That was him, wasn't it?"

"Indeed, child, 'twas he."

Thousands of thoughts sprung to life and faded into oblivion too fast for her mind to latch onto firmly. "Why?" she finally managed to ask.

The voice remained silent.

Flute's momentary joy turned to ash at the voice's refusal to answer, and she laughed sarcastically. "Fine, don't answer! But I would imagine his business with the Valley has to do with the weakening of the fir'gan that fuels it, doesn't it?"

"So, that is why you are here. I knew it would be noticed, and I told him so."

"And what did he say?"

"Tell me, were you sent here to test the Valley's defenses?" Mathis asked instead.

Flute's jaw muscles clenched in consternation at Mathis' deflection. "Aye, she did."

"And what have you discovered?"

"That they have weakened, though by how much, I cannot accurately say."

"Do you wish to test me for your mistress' sake? Be warned, that while my strength is diminished, it is more than enough to end your life should I choose to do so."

"Chose to do so?" Flute asked curiously.

"You are a Gifted, child, and my defenses are keyed to those bearing the gift. If it had been my will, you would not have survived entering this chamber."

"Then why did you not do so? You know whom I serve and – if Luthur's body really is interred within – what they are after. If I report to them what they suspect is true, they will seek to breach your defenses."

"You live because the Darkness does not control you," Mathis replied solemnly. *"More importantly, my master would be heartbroken should he discover you are truly dead. As for your masters,"* he finished ominously, *"let*

Flute barely heard the end of Mathis' statement because of the ache that had taken root in her heart. "He. . . . He doesn't believe me dead?" she asked, ignoring his ominous boast.

"Indeed he does not," Mathis replied, his tone gentle. *"There was never any proof of your eternal demise. Thus, he never gave up hope, and neither should you, dear Inkeri."*

Flute's knees buckled, and crystallized tears began streaming down her cheeks as her emotional barriers fully ruptured at the mention of her true name. Collapsing to her knees, Flute wrapped her arms about herself and squeezed, cracking bone as years of pain burst forth. For what seemed like an eternity to her, she cried as raw, long pent-up emotions raged from the hidden depths of her soul, only to tear from her throat as agonizing wails. The heart-crushing, gut-wrenching cries reverberated throughout the chamber, drowning out the sound of her crystallized tears dancing on the marble dais.

Slowly but surely, the cries eventually grew silent, the heaving stopped, and the tears slowed to a trickle. For a time, she sat in a deafening silence that was occasionally broken by a sniff or a soft sob. Eventually, though, Flute managed to gather herself, and with slow, deliberate motions, she wiped her eyes with a trembling hand.

"My mistress stripped me of my name," she finally said softly, her voice raw with emotion. "I have not heard it spoken for a very long time."

"It is your name, Inkeri, gifted to you by your father — and it is something no one can ever truly take from you."

Flute tried to smile, but felt her emotions threatening to overwhelm her again. When she managed to fight off the onslaught, she slowly stood up and said, "You are right . . . Mathis, and as wise as I remember," she declared with a weak smile. "I am Inkeri Masumaite, and no one — no matter how much they try — can take that away from me. Thank you for reminding me of that."

"No thanks are needed, child. You are your father's daughter, and possess his strength of will — how else could you have lived so long beneath the Darkness' roof without succumbing to it?"

Inkeri shook her head. "Perhaps, but I had given in to hopelessness. Maybe I needed a reminder of who I was . . . or maybe I simply needed to hear my name spoken aloud by someone who cares. Either way, your kind words provided the catalyst needed to leech away some of the shadow that had fallen over my soul." She smiled weakly. "It is only a start, though. I can feel it even now trying to smother the spark you ignited."

"Will you let it do so?"

Inkeri shook her head with resolve. "No – never again. In the last few weeks, I have been shown kindness that I have not known in what seems like lifetimes by a man who has no reason to do so. And you . . . you have given me both my name and hope – two things I had thought long lost."

"Your thanks are not necessary; however, I must ask – what do you intend to tell your mistress?"

A deep scowl pulled at Inkeri's lips. "I cannot avoid telling her of what I've learned – she will use the amulet to make sure of that. But, I think I can . . . manipulate what I tell her." She eyed the Valley suspiciously. "You have more power stored in there than we realize, haven't you?"

"Alas, I believe our conversation is coming to an end," Mathis responded instead, drawing a sarcastic laugh from Inkeri. *"You're friend will return anon. And I believe she found what she sought, for there is a joy about her that her amazement cannot hide."*

"Fine, you don't need to answer," Inkeri said with a shake of her head. "I will make sure to conceal just how much power I believe actually resides within. Maybe you can put an end to whoever comes for the prize you guard."

"Perhaps," Mathis replied stoically.

"Indeed," Inkeri said. "And what about my friend? Do you care about what she was sent in to find?"

"No. It is a piece of history, nothing more. . . . Though I must wonder what impact it will have on people whose understanding of history is . . . different."

"Indeed," she said again, and then laughed softly. "Corith, I do sound a bit like him when I say that, don't I?"

"Indeed you do, Inkeri. Indeed you do."

Chapter Twenty-Five

*I*t was a particularly damp night as fat droplets of driving rain pounded the ramshackle town known as Forsaken, turning its rocky dirt streets to mud. The deluge, however, did little to keep people indoors. In fact, the streets of Forsaken were as busy as they would have been on a good night. Composed predominantly of laborers and miners, the denizens of Forsaken were generally as hard and callous as the unforgiving land they occupied, and they weren't about to let rain, no matter how intense, impede them in the slightest. As such, the resilient residents of this far-flung town trudged across the sloppy terrain in dilapidated and mud-stained attire as if it were just a regular night. Normal, however, meant something different here than it did elsewhere on Solarson. In Forsaken, normal also meant living and working in the presence of the eerie green, ever-burning fires of the Burning Grounds, which loomed over everyone from just outside the southern edge of town.

With those very same uncanny green flames at her back, the tall, hooded woman weaved her way through the crowded streets with far less grace than she was used to while fighting the urge to vomit. The foul stench of the sulfuric flames on top of the smell of mud and rancid humanity was nearly overwhelming to her heightened senses, but blending in was paramount to her. While she couldn't conceal her height completely, procuring appropriately tattered attire from the discarded clothes around the Burning Grounds had been a simple task. The heavily patched woolen garments were too large for her, but the loose fit helped to conceal her slight build, and the decrepit black cloak's hood hid her face in deep shadows.

Despite the hood, however, she kept her head bowed. She was already drawing more inquisitive looks than she would have liked because of her height, and the last thing she wanted was for someone to get a good look at her face and realize that not only was she an apparently unarmed woman, but that she wasn't even human. Had her destination been located in a more civilized city, or one familiar with darlions, she would have been far less concerned about her safety or drawing attention to herself. Granted, she could easily defend herself without a weapon, but she had little desire to draw needless attention to herself so deep in enemy territory and so very far from home. Regrettably, her brief time in Forsaken had already made it clear that it might be difficult to complete her mission without having to defend herself at some point. Almost as if some malign deity knew her thoughts and wished to reinforce her concerns, numerous brawls caught her attention as she made her way along the ill-planed streets. Whether it was just two combatants or a throng of muddy and bloodied fighters, the town's would-be law enforcement seemed content to ignore most of the violence.

Garbed in studded leather armor and armed predominantly with cudgels, the men and women known as the Skullcrackers were easy to spot due to their better-maintained attire, and their reprehensible lack of concern for the citizenry. In fact, she noticed quite a few of them standing idly by in their watch stations, while others sat beneath shelter of some sort playing dice or celum games instead of doing their job. Indignant anger twisted her stomach at not only their casual disregard of the open street violence, but at their clear indifference to the horrifying sounds of rape her keen hearing picked out from some of the dark alleys. As if the Hells thought such heartless behavior wasn't enough, on the rare occasion that the Skullcrackers did get involved, it was with such bloodthirst that she was dearly tempted to intervene.

With the almost gleeful way they indiscriminately swung their cudgels or lashed out with fist and foot, it was nigh impossible to tell whether the guards' intent was to break up the fights or to simply kill the combatants. On more than one occasion, she saw people go down with damage that was either as mundane as profuse bleeding or broken appendages, or as dangerous as a collapsed face or skull; even more ghastly, there were quite a few people who fell victim to a combination of the injuries. Vile as it was, she found the way the crowd turned a blind eye to such violent displays nearly as appalling. Granted, such casual disregard for life wasn't uncommon for humans, but seeing it in such volume, and in such a short amount of time, was a cold reminder of what the short-lived species was capable of.

"Alas," she thought as she caught sight of a pile of bodies nestled in the mouth of an ally running between two of the many taverns that occupied the city, *"blood-letting in the streets must seem droll to a people who hath permit bodies to pile in the streets like detritus for cultists to collect and burn."* She shook her head slightly, her disgust filling her almost to breaking. *"Corith hath mercy upon their souls — the Darkness lies heavy upon this land. What hast occurred in our absence? Hath those long sworn to protect this world cast aside all hope?"* She shook her head again as she pressed her full lips together firmly. *"Nay. I cannot believe such! There must exist a valid explanation for such decadence and decay. Yet . . . why hath we only sensed one of our allies? Mayhap the Darkness hast already triumphed, and we art too late? If that be so, then our mission 'tis already a failure, and we*

Coming to a halt before a rickety tavern that was declared the Bountiful Trio's Tavern by its poorly painted sign, which displayed three bare-breasted women grinning broadly as they held aloft over-flowing tankards, the woman scoffed.

"Humans," she thought with disgust before moving toward the dark alley to the right of the establishment.

As she did so, the misshapen door to the tavern slammed open, spilling forth a nauseating plethora of smells and rowdy noise. A large, clearly inebriated man and a half-dressed woman stumbled out, laughing merrily at what seemed to be nothing in particular. Reaching the stairs, they took one step, slipped and crashed to the muddy earth where they lay cackling.

Pausing momentarily to glance at the couple, she tugged her hood close. *"Humans,"* she thought again, derisively, as she stepped into the dark alley.

Almost immediately, she encountered a large pile of bodies. Some appeared dead, while most of them – at least for the moment – were simply unconscious. Scowling as she noticed a few more piles lining the alley, she leaned against the tavern wall and glanced back at the opening. Once she was satisfied that she couldn't be seen from the street, she sighed deeply and closed her eyes. There could be no doubt that her target resided within the tavern. Ideally, she would have preferred to contact their ally without going near the town, but she was well aware that their enemies were far too close to risk contact over a significant distance, so proximity was necessary. Unfortunately, she also felt it unnecessarily risky to enter the tavern. In such a cramped space, her stature would assuredly draw far too much attention, even in this town of vagabonds, misfits, and criminals. And should they see her face. . . .

She shrugged off the anxiety that suddenly twisted her stomach.

She wasn't against going in there and dragging out the person she sought if it became necessary, but she hoped that wouldn't be the case. Instead, she took another deep breath and focused on the chaotic currents of fir'gan. *"Every morsel of information we hath gleaned from the currents and the compass declares thou art here. Now, let us see if that 'tis true,"* she thought hopefully.

Taking hold of a thin tendril, she compressed it and narrowed its focus so that she could avoid disturbing the natural flow as little as possible before letting her consciousness creep along the strand and into the tavern.

Hazy with smoke from a multitude of pipes, not to mention the fire burning in a large hearth that was in desperate need of repair, the air of the cramped, sordid tavern was strikingly harsh. Heavy with the smell of sour alcohol, the sickly-sweet scent of deathweed, the heady aroma of the local strand of maujin, and no small amount of urine and sweat, a civilized person most likely would have fainted or vomited from the stench. Mercifully, no one of a gentle or civilized nature dared venture so deep into the Wildlands; as for vomit, plenty of it soaked the heads of patrons who had drunk and smoked their way into oblivion. Such inebriation left those lost souls at the mercy of the tavern staff. If they were lucky, one of the scantily clad, over-painted waitresses would turn the poor sods heads before they suffocated. That, however, was the extent of the tavern's generosity. If a fierce slap or splash of booze didn't eventually wake them, then the brawny bouncers would drag them from the establishment and unceremoniously dump them on one of the piles of bodies that littered the ally running beside the establishment. Once left with the dead and unconscious, it was up to fate if they were fortunate enough to awaken before the Burned Souls made their rounds to collect the bodies for sacrifice to the ever-burning flames of the Burning Grounds.

At the rear of the tavern, situated before a wall crammed full of shelves filled with clay tankards and mugs, was a bar made from several old, broken doors supported by drink-filled kegs. Patrons seated on an amalgam of stools packed the bar as they drank and bantered with other customers or the barkeeps. The proprietor of the tavern, a large, middle-aged woman in a ragged, beer-stained green dress that exposed far too much of her buxom bosom, worked franticly with two younger women to keep the drinks flowing for the seemingly endless thirst that possessed the night's customers. At one point in her life, she had been considered homely, but after years of breaking up drunken brawls, the features of her round, shaved-headed face were battered, and her dark eyes held a violent edge that even her best gapped-tooth smile or laugh couldn't soften.

Even as she served and chatted with customers seated at the bar, she did her best to keep an eye on the group seated around a wobbly table beneath a sizable section of the recently patched left-hand wall. On more than one occasion, the table's occupants had her fingering the often-used cudgel hanging from a hook on her broad leather belt. Trouble and fights were a natural part of life in Forsaken, and even more so during the long rainy nights of winter, but trouble seemed to be a constant companion for the lone woman at the table. The tavern owner had lost track of just how many brawls she'd broken up that were started because of, or by, the odd woman.

Most customers of such a bothersome nature would have been, at best, banished from her establishment long ago, or at worst, bludgeoned to death and left for the Burned Souls. However, the woman was a constant and extremely reliable source of coin – which was a rarity in Forsaken.

In no small way, the woman's wealth played a large part in keeping The Bountiful Trio's Tavern in business and in a better state of repair than many other establishments. It not only had allowed her to hire the extra muscle watching over the rowdy crowd from their positions near the door and along the walls, but it had on more than one occasion covered the outrageous 'protection' fees any sane proprietor paid to the gang of thugs that Forsaken considered its Thieves' Guild. So, as far as the tavern owner was concerned, as long as the coin kept flowing, the unusual woman was welcome no matter how much of a headache she could be.

Closing the spout on one of the kegs supporting the bar top, the tavern owner stood up, two full tankards in hand, and glanced over at the peculiar woman, which nearly made her roll her eyes. For the last three hours, the woman and three other regulars had been playing Death's Deceit while emptying six pitchers of some of the cheapest beer the tavern had to offer. It was clear they were all drunk to varying degrees, but there was a growing sense of tension and anger at the table, and that worried her. It had already been a long day and night, and the last thing she wanted to do was to break up another scrap because of that woman.

Passing the tankards to the waiting patrons, she eyed the table again and her hand slid to the handle of her cudgel. When it came to that woman, she'd learned to smell the fight before it ever started; and while she always hoped the tension would pass, she couldn't remember that ever happening. So, with a repressed sigh, she tapped the young girl working next to her on the shoulder to get her attention.

"Tess," the tavern owner said firmly in her scratchy voice, prompting the spindly young blonde to turn and face her with a smile.

At one time, Tess had been a beautiful young woman with bright gray eyes and a vibrant smile, but like so many people born and raised in Forsaken, life had treated her harshly. Her looks had always drawn the lustful attention of many a man, and like many other women in the town, those attentions were mostly unwanted and violent. It was amazing that her eyes still remained bright and hope still lingered in her despite all the emotional scars she hid behind her smile. As for the physical scars, one violent night had left her with a missing left ear, which her long locks hid, and a vivid scar ran up her left cheek from where part of her upper lip had been removed. Those scars alone would have crushed the spirit of many, but another scar – and arguably her most horrific one – was buried beneath her silence. The same assailant that marred her face had also removed part of her tongue as punishment for screaming for help.

"Lass, go tell Bould to be checking on her table. Things look to be getting tense a wee bit early tonight," the tavern owner stated forebodingly.

Peeking around the tavern owner, Tess needed only a momentary glance to confirm the situation. Pivoting quickly, the dark brown skirt of her revealing threadbare dress flourishing, she left the bar and expertly weaved her way through the crowd toward the large man leaning against the side of the blazing hearth. Tess could see that the man's small but sharp hazel eyes were focused intently on the packed room from beneath the mass of curly brown locks capping his round, glowering face. While she knew he had to project an intimidating presence, she much preferred it when he smiled. As such, her heart lept a bit when he saw her approach, and his glower quickly turned into a broad, toothy grin.

Straightening his cushioned muscled bulk, Bould absentmindedly adjusted his stained black tunic before wiping his hands on his brown pants. "What can I be doing for you, Miss Tess?" he asked as the petite girl stopped before him, the excitement in his strong voice muted a bit by the knot of nervous shyness he felt in his gut when he was near her.

Tess flashed him a quick, bright smile before her look turned serious.

"Trouble?" he rumbled upon seeing the change.

Nodding, Tess pointed to her eyes and then motioned to the woman's table. Following her gesture, Bould's gaze immediately fixed on the table, where voices were beginning to rise in anger. It was impossible to hear what they were saying, but the posturing and gesturing of the table's occupants made it clear the situation was quickly deteriorating.

"Hell's bloody balls," Bould muttered in exasperation. Looking back at Tess, he smiled gently. "Go back ta the boss, Miss Tess. I'll see what I can do."

Smiling appreciatively, she grabbed his forearm and squeezed it as if to say be careful before heading back to the bar. Bould watched her for a moment before his smile vanished and he turned his vision to the two large, dark-skinned men dressed like himself flanking the tavern's door. Catching the attention of the bearded man on the left side of the door, Bould motioned to the other bouncer, then cocked his head in the direction of the woman's table. The bouncer grimaced slightly before acknowledging Bould.

Once his compatriots started toward the back of the tavern, Bould began moving with an inward sigh, his black-booted feet thumping heavily on the floor. *"Here we go again. Corith help us all."*

"Sheo is aghast at how much coin you fine gents have parted with," she drawled around her pipe in her deceptively soft voice as she began stacking the most recent pot neatly with the rest of her winnings. Maujin smoke drifting lazily from the dull green bowl of the pipe secured between her unusually white and straight teeth, while her large, hooded yellow eyes gazed perceptively at the four other men sharing the table with her.

"Parted with, my arse!" grumbled the man to her right before he drained his tankard quickly, sloshing dark beer all over his thick, unruly brown beard and his threadbare red tunic. Glaring at her with his angry green eyes, he slammed the tankard down, splashing his dirt-stained, sun-darkened hand with even more of the alcohol. "I've played ye more than my fair share, and I ain't seen a soul with the luck ye have! It's the Hells' luck, I'm tellin' ye, or I'm a kyram's pile of shite!"

The other men at the table voiced their agreement as Sheo cocked her long, sharp-featured head curiously and pursed her large, full lips around her pipe. "Sheo's luck is only practiced skill, my dear Tilben," she chided, drawing a sneer from him. Removing her pipe, she blew out a long trail of smoke before adding, "What's more, that is such an ineloquent way to address a woman, Tilben. Sheo would be offended normally, but she has chosen to attribute such language to gratuitous inebriation, and to a lesser degree, you're failings at Death's Deceit. Sheo knows it stings a man's pride when he loses to a woman . . . even if she is his better in talent."

"Woman, my arse!" Tilben said with a snort and a shake of his head of oily brown hair. "Ye may have good birthin' hips, and big ol' tits tryin' ta jump out of yer tunic and distract us, but that don't be meanin' yer a woman or skilled!" He gestured to her and added, "Whatcha think, boy'os? Ever seen a woman worth a shite with the side of 'er head shaved like a barbarian, and 'er hair hangin' down tha other side as if she's hidin' a scar like littl' ol' Tess?"

"Not me, Tilben," agreed the short, dark-skinned man in a dilapidated gray tunic and brown leggings seated next to Tilben. Fixing his angry bloodshot brown eyes on Sheo, he jabbed a stubby finger at her. "Ye've got more earrings lining yer ears than most women could ever own, and ye've got arms larger than many a man, and are covered in tattoos o' bird wings and thorns! And I bet me mum's soul ye've got a way o' riggin' the game, or ye've made a demon's deal – no one wins as much as you do!" He turned his shaved head and spit on the floor for emphasis.

The third of their group, a man of generous girth draped in ragged leathers that might have once been dyed blue, grinned at Sheo as he pushed aside a pair of red-pipped bone dice and began collecting the five-sided celums scattered about the table. Bald, his horridly lined and battered pale face already had the look of someone who'd fought a bramhen bull and lost, but the crooked yellowed teeth that showed when his thin lips parted made him look like a reanimated corpse. "And don't be forgettin' those hams she calls hands! I've seen bears with smaller paws," he growled as he began violently shuffling the deck, the backs of which were painted with an unapologetically nude and gratuitously endowed woman. "If not fer them tits, and black hair cleaner than any man's, there's nothin' that could convince me she ain't hidin' a prick in those nice trousers of hers!"

Sheo listened to the insults patiently, but her ire was rising. She'd heard far worse over the years, and there was no denying there was a masculinity to her that her breasts and hips were incapable of hiding. Her tribal heritage meant she'd been raised to fight and survive. Amongst her people, the shaved side of her head, and the intertwined thorn and raven-wing tattoos adorning her deeply bronzed skin were signs of tribal pride and the marks of a warrior. No one at the table could have known that, however. All they saw was a powerfully built woman in a sleeveless white tunic with a wine-red vest over it that matched her leather pants and boots; it was attire that was, at least in Forsaken, more befitting of a man than a woman. Then there was the large, broad-bladed longsword hanging at her left hip from an equally hefty black leather belt. No woman, even in Forsaken, would have worn such a belt, much less been able to lift the sword.

"Gentlemen," Sheo responded with a hint of sarcasm that only served to rile the men more as she placed her pipe on the table, "Sheo believes you have misunderstood the game, and are merely angry at your losses. Sheo is purely skilled, that is all," she finished with a shrug, causing Tilben to spit on the floor in anger. "But let it not be said that Sheo is not fair. She is happy to give you fine gents ample opportunity to win your coin back." She glanced slyly at the battered, robust man. "You most of all, Guralt. Sheo believes you have fallen on the wrong side of lady luck tonight, no?"

Snarling, Guralt slammed the deck on the table and glared

menacingly at Sheo. "Ye can't hide yer insults behind yer pretty words, bitch!" he barked, his dark eyes flashing. "And ye bet yer arse yer gonna give us a chance to win back our coin, or we'll have no choice but to label ye a cheat and liar!"

The growing tension at the table and Guralt's outburst quickly drew the attention of some of the other patrons, and rumblings of a fight began to ripple through the tavern. Returning Guralt's glare, Sheo thought seriously about defusing the situation for the moment. Bould and two other bouncers were already approaching the table, and she wasn't quite ready to brawl. What's more, the thought of dodging the Skullcrackers and returning home early held little appeal. However, before she could say anything to soothe the situation, what felt like a gentle breeze touched her mind.

In an instant, all other notions were washed away by more serious, and conflicting, feelings. Typically, she would have ignored such contact until they gave up or, at worst, she was forced to acknowledge the person. Her former friends and compatriots knew she'd done her best to remain withdrawn from events as much as possible in recent decades. She'd long ago lost her taste for the endless conflict, and there were very few people she felt were worthy of her service – and Darkon definitely didn't qualify. Watch and report – that's all she'd agreed to, and even that she approached with a nonchalant attitude that bordered on complete disregard. However, this contact – this nearly forgotten presence – was a mind-numbing shock that stirred a sense of baffled curiosity in her that she found impossible to ignore.

Guralt's scowl deepened when the normally quick-tongued Sheo didn't immediately retort. Instead, she looked straight ahead, either ignoring him or oblivious to his threat. "Well, bitch? What'll it be? Gonna give us our shot, or are ye gonna sit on yer arse pissin' yer britches?" he goaded.

Once more, she appeared to ignore his barbed words, pushing Guralt to his breaking point. Snarling, he shot to his feet, his fists curled. "Ye pig ruttin', she-beast of a–!"

The sudden weight of a heavy, meaty hand on his shoulder cut him off.

"Is there a problem 'ere?" Bould asked, his tone threatening.

The other two men at the table pushed back their chairs, but didn't stand up, as Guralt looked over his shoulder. Cheeks flush with drink and anger, Guralt stared daggers at Bould, and spit, "Damn right there is! This whore be cheatin' again!"

The loud declaration cast a heavy silence over the tavern as patrons turned their attention to the brewing situation. Bould noted

594

the change in the atmosphere even as he fought the urge to roll his eyes. He'd heard this complaint many times before. Everyone who frequented The Bountiful Trio's Tavern knew Sheo was skilled at Death's Deceit, and not once had anyone been able to remotely prove she cheated. However, that didn't stop those whose pouches were lighter after playing against her from crying foul, especially when drunk.

Squeezing Guralt's shoulder as a warning, Bould said, "You know as well as everyone Sheo don't cheat."

"Quite so, dear Bould," Sheo quipped in agreement, breaking her silence.

Guralt's angry gaze swung to Sheo even as Bould shot her a reproachful glare and added, "So why don't you sit back down, enjoy your drink and play all peaceful like? If that's not ta your liking, you can head on home."

For a moment, with the way Guralt's jaw muscles clenched and his dark eyes darted back and forth, Bould thought he would do something rash. However, much to his immediate relief, Guralt did nothing of the sort. Instead, he spit on the ground and pointed an accusatory finger at Sheo.

"Mark me words, ye cheatin' bitch! Yer ways keep makin' enemies around here, and yer gonna eventually make the wrong people mad! Ye better grow eyes in the back of yer head, ye hear me!?"

"Right – That's enough, Guralt!" Bould stated firmly as he placed his other hand on Guralt's other shoulder. "Time ta head home," he added as he started to steer him toward the door.

Scowling, Guralt shrugged him off. Turning, he glared at Bould and barked, "I know the damn way, whoreson!" Ignoring Bould's disapproving scowl, Guralt then noted the crowds' eyes were on him, and he yelled, "What in the hells are ye all lookin' at?!"

When no one responded, Guralt grunted and muttered, "Thought so," before straightening his leather tunic and heading toward the door with an air of indignant rage about him. Not wanting to risk his seething wrath, patrons quickly made way for him, allowing Guralt a speedy and direct route to the exit. Yanking the door open, he stepped into the night, slamming the door behind him. As if the door's closure was their cue, the tavern sprang back to life, conversation once more filling the air as if the whole incident had never happened.

With Guralt's departure, Bould turned his attention to those remaining at the table. "Anyone else have a problem?" he asked, his tone making it clear he was in no mood to humor them.

The remaining men glanced at one another as if they were sharing a silent conversation before they grabbed their drinks and beat a hasty retreat to the bar.

"Alas," Sheo quipped after the two men had departed, drawing Bould's attention, "such are the woes of the talented and skilled! Their lessers are always envious of what they cannot attain. Don't you think so, dear Bould?"

Waving his fellow bouncers back to their posts, Bould looked at Sheo, who was idly collecting her winnings in a fattening coin purse. "Hells' bloody balls, Sheo!" he declared with a resigned shake of his head. "Would it hurt ta just lose a bit more often? We all like a good fight, but tha hell you stir up with just a damn deck of celums is a royal pain in my arse!"

Sheo pushed a sizable stack of mostly silver coins mixed with a few gold ones from her winnings toward Bould, saying with a smile, "For the tavern's woes. Let it not be said that Sheo does not compensate this fine establishment for her troubles."

Bould couldn't decide if he should reprimand her further or smile. Instead, he rolled his eyes before grabbing one of the empty tankards on the table and quickly sweeping the coins into it. He then sat down and watched as Sheo deftly collected the celums and dice from the table. "He's right, you know? One day you're going ta piss off the wrong person ta much. We all know you are damn good in a fight, but Corith forbid you get ta far on the Guild's bad side. We'd hate ta lose your patronage."

She smirked as she returned the dice and deck of celums to their leather case. Putting the case in one of her belt pouches, she then collected her pipe as she said, her voice full of mock humility, "Sheo is touched to her heart by your words, sweet Bould. But Sheo thinks such tenderness should be saved for the charming Tess."

Bould fidgeted in his seat. Blushing slightly, he cleared his throat, then said, "Yes . . . well. . . . I think I need ta get back to work." Standing, he offered, "If you don't mind some friendly advice – you might want ta call it a night, Sheo."

In response, Sheo flashed him an appreciative grin and planted the stem of her pipe between her teeth. "Sheo believes such a course to be wise this night as well." Standing she tugged on her vest and added with a nod, "Be well, dear Bould."

Nodding his gratitude, Bould remained there as he watched

Sheo weave her way to the door. Once the door closed behind her, he shook his head at the enigma that was Sheo before he moved to the bar to give her gift to the tavern keep.

Stepping into the cool night, Sheo sighed. One of the few joys she still had in life was the frustration her skill at Death's Deceit delivered unto her opponents and the ensuing fights. She had sought out such a riotous evening to get her mind off of the more troubling than normal news and events of the last few days. To have her plans spoiled – even if it was by such a surprising guest – was nearly unacceptable. Yet here she was, fightless and about to meet with her second guest in as many weeks.

Descending to the muddy street, the night's downpour immediately soaked her as she emptied the bowl of her pipe into the churned grown. Easily ignoring the urge to shield herself from the elements, she shoved her pipe into a pouch before turning right and starting toward the south side of town, the eternal flames of the Burning Grounds squarely in her sights. Almost immediately, she noted that she was being shadowed by at least two people. It wasn't an unfamiliar situation. Agents of the Thieves' Guild – and by extension, the Toranis' – kept tabs on anyone they deemed of interest or a threat. In Sheo's case, she meet both criteria the day the Toranis discovered her. Normally, she would have simply ignored whoever was stalking her this night, but given the nature of her guest, she felt a bit of caution was in order.

Reaching out along the currents as she casually strolled down Forsaken's main thoroughfare, Sheo sorted through the chaos on the currents caused by the mass of humanity in the area. It took a moment to cut through the noise, but when she did, she quickly pinpointed her stalkers. There were three of them: her guest was shadowing her through the alleyways on her right, a second person was keeping tabs on her from the opposite side of the street, while a third was tailing her closely, using a body-filled wagon destined for the Burning Grounds as cover. Aware of who two of them were, Sheo focused on the third for a moment. While she couldn't identify the person, she had a pretty good idea who it was.

"Alas, that damn fool must be quiet drunk, or more of a fool than Sheo thought. . . . Most likely both. Well, if Guralt seeks a fight, Sheo will be more than willing to oblige," she thought with a measure of excitement.

Sheo continued to monitor all three as she moved toward the edge of town. As she got closer, the people on the streets quickly dwindled, which made it easier to keep tabs on her pursuers. None of her three shadows ever moved closer to her, but neither did they drop off.   However, as she drew within about a hundred yards of the town's edge, and the buildings thinned out, the person she assumed was Guralt broke off his pursuit. Sheo was a bit surprised when his signal moved to the side of the road and caught up with the spy from the Thieves' Guild.

"Curious," Sheo thought. *"Sheo would dearly like to investigate such an odd meeting, but those claiming friendship must be addressed first."* She suddenly grinned broadly. *"Perhaps they will call upon associates for some late-night entertainment for dear Sheo?"*

She monitored the two signals for a bit longer as her steps continued to guide her toward the Burning Grounds. Once she was sure they'd given up the chase, She turned her attention fully to her guest. Free of the citizenry's impact on the currents, Sheo could clearly make out her visitor as well as a few other people in the vicinity. While the Burning Grounds were open to any who wished to visit, very few people cared to spend time at what would likely be their final resting place. As such, Sheo figured the majority of people she sensed were probably Burned Souls. Still, she had no idea what eyes might be on her even here, so she proceeded with a measure of caution.

As she began trudging up the gentle incline to the Burning Grounds, the muddy terrain grew increasingly rocky, and she passed two monks wrapped in haphazard layers of shredded black cloth who were hauling an empty cart back to town. The mute monks of the Burned Souls made note of her passing with a gesture of warding; pressing the tips of their fore and index finger to their forehead, then to the chin before swiping them in front of their eyes. The gesture was said to ward off evil visions and protect the mind from devilish spirits. The notion almost made Sheo laugh as she returned the gesture. Like so many of the superstitions she'd witnessed through the millennia, it was utterly pointless; furthermore, its purpose felt empty in the face of the darkness festering in Forsaken. Yet, like so many cults before them, their offering of salvation through the purifying flames of the Burning Grounds attracted the desperate and destitute like moths to a flame. As such, a cult that initially sought to purify souls as a means to placate the supposed angry deity responsible for the eternal flames blossomed into a religion that fed on the misery and desperation that permeated Forsaken and much of the Wildlands.

"Ah, it truly is sad," Sheo thought as she passed one last wagon headed to town. *"Those that are so lost that they grasp at the tiniest, most fragile strands of hope are truly worthy of profound pity. Sheo does wonder what those lost souls would think of their 'salvation' if they knew the truth about their mute saviors,"* she mused as she stepped off the road and turned west, moving toward her guest, whose presence on the currents came

to a halt with her change of direction.

After she was sure no one could see her, Sheo shielded herself from the elements and warmed herself up. In a matter of moments, with the rain bouncing off her protective, skin-tight shield, Sheo was warm and dry. Unencumbered by the rain, and with her fir'gan assuring her footing, Sheo nimbly picked her way across the treacherous terrain. It took her a bit to make her way through the maze of boulders and rocky outcroppings, but she eventually reached a stone overhang that was nearly bereft of the green glow of the flames from above. With the aid of the currents, however, Sheo could easily see the cloaked figure lurking in the shadows beneath the overhang, and she knew they could see her as well.

"Well, this is a surprise to Sheo. Guests do come and go on the rare occasion, but never one so . . . singular. Sheo does not know if she should be humbled, concerned . . . or if she should care," she stated, her soft voice reflecting the mixed emotions this meeting stirred in her.

There was no immediate response. Instead, Sheo watched the figure study her like a predator stalking prey. It was unnerving, to say the least, and Sheo resisted the urge to fidget under the perceptive gaze. When the silence dragged on, Sheo finally shrugged her shoulders and said, "Well, if you do not wish to speak with Sheo as you indicated, then Sheo wishes to get out of this dreary weather."

Just as she started to turn back toward town, her visitor finally spoke. "Present thine seal, Rivinia Darkclaw, Preceptor of the Velsan'lyr Order of Light, so I might take mine measure of thee," declared a rich, warm female voice that was heavy with caution.

Turning back to the speaker, Sheo said with a raised eyebrow, "An odd request in this age, Sheo must say . . . but if it will speed things along. . . ."

Holding her hand toward her visitor, palm skyward, it took Sheo a moment to recall the old procedure. Then, with a bit of exertion, a cold, bright, blue-white flame manifested above her palm. Twisting and turning, the flame morphed into a circular seal depicting two dragons circling each other while gazing out upon the world with their paws clasped in what appeared to be combat.

"Does this suit your needs, Lady Rynthalia?" Sheo asked even as frost spread over her hand.

Rynthalia peered intently at the seal as if seeking something. After a moment, she nodded and extended her hand as if to return the gesture.

Closing her hand, Sheo snuffed out the seal with a puff of frost, and she shook her head. "There is no need for that," she stated as she dropped her hand to her side. "As Sheo stated, it is an odd request in this age. None have used that greeting for some time. . . though it occurs to Sheo you would not be aware of it. Those that serve the Darkness long ago learned to suppress their taint upon the seal."

Rynthalia cocked her head as she dropped her arm to her side. *"'Tis not good,"* she thought, suddenly apprehensive. *"If the seals art worthy of trust no longer, then the situation 'tis most dire."* Aloud, she responded, "'Tis an unfortunate development, Rivinia. So, I must query – art thou still worthy of the Light's trust?"

Sheo, mildly insulted by the question, planted her hands on her hips. "Alas, Sheo cannot speak for Rivinia, as that one perished long ago. As for Sheo, that is up to the Light, as she has abstained from that conflict for quiet sometime."

Rynthalia stared at Sheo, her expression incredulous. *"Corith, what ails her? The succor of her crystal would deny injury most heinous. Yet, 'tis clear her mind suffers,"* she thought, baffled by the woman's behavior. *"Nay, 'tis a problem for another time."*

"Very well, Rav. . . Sheo. I shan't pry further, nor shall I impose upon thee much longer. Please, join me if thou would, so we might converse free of prying eyes?"

Sheo shrugged. "Though there is no one in the vicinity, Sheo cannot fault your prudence. There are eyes everywhere in Forsaken, and most are of the unfriendly sort," she stated as she moved beneath the overhang.

There wasn't much room beneath the shelter, but it was better than standing in the downpour. Letting her shield drop, Sheo was suddenly struck by her guest's height. It was rare that she had to look up at someone – especially with women – but her visitor was a head taller than she. Suddenly, she wrinkled her nose as she caught wind of a stench emanating from the Rynthalia.

"Sheo can only imagine what an irritant that smell must be for her. Death is a ghastly scent in its own right, but whomever once wore those garments left behind a stench far fouler!" Sheo thought as she eyed the Rynthalia's tattered attire.

"That cannot be pleasant, even if we were not so close to the fires," she stated, unsure of what to say otherwise.

Rynthalia shrugged. "'Tis a necessary inconvenience," she replied as she reached for her cowl. "An elvannue 'twould attract much attention in these lands," she added as she lowered the hood.

Immediately, Sheo's attention was drawn to Rynthalia's bright, piercing violet eyes, whose slight upward tilt lent an exotic intensity to her welcoming gaze, which was further heightened by the smile splitting her full lips beneath her slender nose. Sheo then noticed that the elvannue's violet hair, which was a match in color to her arched eyebrows, was secured away from her graceful, alabaster visage by a tattered brown headband that was also pinning her long ears behind her head.

"Sheo believes that cannot be comfortable in the slightest," she said after seeing how the woman's ears were secured.

Rynthalia shrugged. "As I did say, 'tis a minor inconvenience, but necessary." She paused for a moment, letting a heavy silence take hold as she studied Sheo.

Sheo knew her guest was trying to decide if she was trustworthy, so instead of waiting for her to take the lead, Sheo said, "Sheo understands your predicament. You are out of touch with the situation beyond the Storm Sea, and you are trying to decide just how much you can trust Sheo, am I correct?"

"Perceptive."

Sheo shrugged off the compliment. "It was an easy assumption for Sheo to reach. So let her offer this advice – use discretion. Sheo knows she is stating the obvious, but you and your people have long been removed from the war, and to have knowledge of your existence would embolden the Darkness' servants."

Rynthalia nodded slightly. "Thine words art wise, though they carry little weight now. 'Tis why I hath journeyed so far. We fear the Darkness may now possess knowledge most dire, and I was sent to inform the Lord Dragon of the situation."

Sheo's already closed expression grew solemn at the title, and Rynthalia did not miss it.

"Pray tell, Sheo, where is the Lord Dragon? I hath sought him upon the currents with nary a sign of him."

Sheo shook her head sadly. "Sheo is sad that she must inform you that Luthur has been dead for quite a while. Nearly two-hundred years if memory serves her."

Sheo expected to see shock overtake Rynthalia. Instead, the elvannue woman seemed to absorb the news as if she had expected to hear it. After a brief moment more of contemplation, Rynthalia finally said, her tone reverent, "'Tis unfortunate to hear. May Corith watch over his soul."

"Sheo agrees," She stated with a nod.

Rynthalia's violet gaze met Sheo's hooded yellow eyes as she asked, "Pray tell, whom now leads? Preceptor Damion, I would presume?"

Sheo shook her head, and this time, genuine surprise broke through Rynthalia's serene facade. "Not so, Sheo is afraid to say. Darkon has held the title since Luthur's death and Damion's disappearance."

Rynthalia's eyes widened with shock. "Darkon. . . . And Preceptor Damion 'tis missing?"

Sheo nodded. "Quite so. While Sheo is not privy to all news, she is also aware that Darius and Catharina have fallen recently."

"Troubling," Rynthalia stated, her brow furrowing with concern. "'Tis a grave situation upon which I must reflect ere I proceed." Looking at Sheo, Rynthalia suddenly smiled and reached for her hood. "Mine thanks, Sheo. This meeting hast been . . . informative," she stated as she pulled her hood back up. Stepping out into the rain, which fell just short of touching her, she offered, "May the Light illuminate thine path, Preceptor Sheo."

"Wait!" Sheo declared before Rynthalia could leave.

Turning back to face Sheo, Rynthalia asked, "What may I do for thee, pray tell?"

Arms folded beneath her breasts, Sheo asked, "You mentioned the Darkness may know something vital; care to share with Sheo? She would be able to pass it along to Darkon for you if you wish it."

A slight smirk pulled at Rynthalia's lips. "Nay. Though thine offer 'tis most kind. Light illuminate thine path," she replied before, with a mild surge of fir'gan, she took a step and vanished into the night.

Sheo's thoughts were as heavy as her soaked clothing as she made the trek back to Forsaken. Ever since she had removed herself from the war and settled in Forsaken, her life had remained relatively peaceful. In fact, it wasn't until nearly a century after Luthur's death that her measure of serenity was disturbed. That was when the Torani brothers made their return. Initially, she kept a low profile, unwilling to move if she didn't have to. However, it was far more difficult to hide from Wardens than to take on a new persona every few decades. Thus it came as no surprise that soon after their arrival, she

602

began to notice more eyes on her than normal. She quickly realized that moving would be the only way to maintain the peace she had obtained. Unfortunately, it wasn't meant to be as her plans were ruined by an unexpected source.

Shortly before she was going to leave, Darkon showed up. She was shocked that he'd managed to find her, and devastated when she learned of Luthur's death and Darkon's ascension to leadership. When he put forth what he wanted of her, she tried her best to convince him to leave her alone. For her efforts, Darkon threatened to expel her and take her crystal. While death held no fear for her, the thought of possibly rotting away as a mortal did. So with Darkon's refusal to kill her outright, she relented and offered to be his eyes on the Torani brothers in exchange for asking nothing more of her, to which he agreed. Since then, he or his representative would visit from time to time to make sure she was holding up her end of the bargain.

As for the Torani brothers, Darkon's visit did not go unnoticed.

"Sheo sought out peace, and found madness of another kind," she thought regretfully. *"Maybe she should have forced murderous hands. If so, she would not feel the noose tightening around her neck like a slow death."*

"Well, well. . . . What a stroke of luck," a smug voice declared from the darkness to her right.

Sheo came to a stop, jolted from her morose thoughts. She was still a few minutes from town, and given the night's revelations, she'd forgotten about Guralt. What's more, she was mad that she hadn't noticed his approach.

"I don't be knowin' why ye be out in this damn weather," he added as Sheo turned to face him, "but I'm not gonna be wastin' this opportunity!"

Sheo shook her head with a resigned sigh as the robust man in faded blue leathers brandished a sword. She had already scouted the currents, and they confirmed what her fir'gan-enhanced vision had already noted. Guralt wasn't alone. "Guralt, Sheo does truly believe you to be a fool. If she had known losing would drive you to such ridiculous lengths, she might have let you win a few more hands."

Her barbed words caused Guralt's lined, pale face to grow flush with anger. "Ye cheating, mud-crow ruttin', bitch!" he barked, his dark eyes flashing as he pointing his sword at her. "No one cheats the Guild, ye hear me! No one! We're gonna gut ye and hang yer corpse in the square as a reminder to all! Hold her down, boys!"

The five people who'd been lurking in the darkness behind Guralt advanced, their figures draped in an a variety of dark garments that were worn and threadbare. If Sheo had passed them on the streets, they would have seemed like nothing more than an average denizen of Forsaken or, at worse, nothing more than a street thug. Clearly that wasn't the case, and the pristine, deadly sharp daggers and swords they drew forth made it quite clear who they were.

"Guild Enforcers," she thought, both annoyed and impressed. *"Sheo is quiet surprised at Guralt's pull. She thought him merely a low-level scoundrel. Not that it matters. They should know better. . . . If ignorance is their choice, however, then who is Sheo to deny the beating they seek?"*

Pivoting so she presented a slim profile, Sheo flexed her fingers and rolled her head as a show of willingness to fight, but made no move for her own blade. "Let us be about it then, shall we?" she declared as the group advanced on her cautiously despite their numbers advantage.

Residents of Forsaken knew everyone was a danger, and if one took an opponent lightly, it could lead to a lost fight or even death. As such, given the poor lighting and treacherous terrain, Guralt and the Guild Enforcers picked their footing carefully as they advanced and spread out to encircle her. More importantly, they never took their eyes off Rynthalia, which garnered them a bit of respect from her.

"Credit is due — the Enforcers do take their work seriously even when they have the perceived advantage," Sheo thought with a small, appreciative mental chuckle.

Suddenly, one of the Enforcers to Guralt's left pulled up and peered at Sheo closely. "Hell's bloody balls, Guralt!" the Enforcer declared, his deep voice a mix of surprise and anger. The others came to a stop, their attention now on the speaker.

Enraged by the interruption, Guralt turned on the speaker and screamed, "What, ye piss-soaked coward?!"

Pointing one of his two daggers at Sheo, he barked in reply, "What bloody mess have you dragged us into? You said nothing about the person who cheated you being the damn Night Raven! Even a virgin pickpocket knows we aren't suppose to touch her unless she commits a grave offense, or the boss orders it!"

Guralt spit on the ground, then snarled at the man. "If cheatin' a member of his money ain't a grave offense, then what is?"

Smirking, Sheo quipped, "Possibly killing one of you might justify your ill-conceived plan, dear Guralt. Would you like Sheo to test it?"

Scowling at Guralt, the Enforcer sheathed his daggers, and angrily told him, "We're done here! The boss' wrath isn't worth your bruised ego!" Before Guralt could utter a protest, the man said to Sheo, "As for you, Night Raven, I apologize on behalf of the Guild for this arse's behavior. However, if you two still wish to fight, we'll turn a blind eye to the results."

Sheo inclined her head. "Sheo thanks you for the courtesy." To Guralt, she added, "Well, Guralt? Still wish to make an example of Sheo? You heard the man – you and she are free to do as they wish. Sheo will be happy to humor you."

Guralt, his face red with drink and indignant rage, glared at the Enforcers, all of which had sheathed their weapons. "Damn ye all! Cowards, the lot of ye!" he snapped at them. To Sheo, he spit, "As for ye, bitch! I'll have me pound of flesh!"

With that declaration, the Enforcers took a few steps back, giving the pair plenty of room.

With rain pummeling the gathering, Sheo remained stationary, her attention solely on her opponent. Guralt, on the other hand, began to circle her, muttering to himself. Sheo's advantage was evident to everyone except her opposition, and that advantage grew in proportion to his irritation. So she merely turned to keep Guralt in front of her, leaving it to him to make the first move. As she watched Guralt closely, it became clear that he was nearing his breaking point. With that in mind, she suddenly smirked at him and winked.

Taken aback by her action, Guralt came to a halt and stared at her, momentarily perplexed. It didn't last long, however, as his snarl returned with a vengeance. Letting out a growl of rage, Guralt charged hard, slashing wildly and violently once he was within reach. As she expected, each slash and thrust was a bit wilder than the last, so she gave ground, easily dodging the wild cuts without the aid of fir'gan. Again and again, Guralt came at her like a man possessed, only to find empty air with his sword.

"Come now, Guralt," she goaded as she skipped back from a violent slash aimed at her stomach, "you will have to do better than that!"

Snarling, Guralt responded by charging forward as best as he could, feigning a thrust at her chest. Sheo wasted no time sidestepping the sloppy attack, but was caught off guard as he quickly altered the thrust into an upward backhand slash. Driving herself back, the surprise attack nicked her chin.

Grinning at his luck, Guralt declared with a sneer as he gathered himself and readied his sword, "Next one won't miss, ye bitch!"

Wiping the blood away, Sheo glanced at the red liquid on her thumb and her mood suddenly changed. The sudden stillness that encompassed her was palatable to some of the onlookers. It was a primal, cold stillness that any true-blooded killer would recognize.

Guralt, however, was oblivious to it as he advanced on Sheo.

"Well, well," she said softly. "It has been a long time since Sheo has seen her own blood," she declared as she looked up at Guralt, a sudden, seething fire burning in her hooded yellow eyes.

Taken aback by the sudden violence in Sheo's gaze, Guralt came to a sudden halt.

"Sheo has given you every chance to abandon this foolishness, but she now sees this was a fool's errand. So, if you really wish to find your death here, then who is Sheo to deny you?" she finished, her soft voice deathly calm.

With a sudden burst of speed, Sheo charged in hard. Ducking beneath a wild, defensive swing, she latched onto Guralt's wrist as she rose up. Twisting his sword arm as she spun behind him, she leveraged her hip into him, flipping him over her shoulder. With a spray of water and mud, Guralt crashed into the ground violently, his breath driven from him. Before he could even hope to recover, Sheo was on top of him, driving her knee into his chest with bone-crushing force. Stunned and his sternum shattered, Guralt could do nothing as Sheo slammed her palm into the forearm of the wrist she still clutched, snapping the bone like a twig and driving the shattered ends through the skin.

Guralt's sword fell from his limp grasp as he started to howl in agonizing pain, but the scream was cut short by Sheo's fist hammering into his face. Blood spurted from his nose as the blow crushed it flat against his face. The next punch hit with just as much force, shattering his right eye socket. Another blow followed, then another, and another, driving Guralt to the brink of unconsciousness. By the time Sheo relented some, his face was a bloody mess of shattered bones and massive bruises. The reprieve was brief, however.

Standing up, Sheo hauled Guralt to his feet. His head flopping on his neck like a dead goose, Guralt could barely register what was going on. He was unable to speak through his split and swollen lips, and his vision was blurry and nearly blocked by swollen eyes. Suddenly, his legs buckled and he would have fallen if not for Sheo holding him up by a fist full of hair. For a brief moment, he managed to focus on Sheo, and he found three of her dancing in his vision, snarling like demons. With as tenuous as his grasp on consciousness was, it was hard for him to fully comprehend what was happening. Still, he was distantly aware that the fists he saw cocked before him were meant to finish him off.

Just before Sheo could unleash the fatal blow, a woman's voice, heavy with authority, rang out. *"Night Raven – halt!"*

For a moment, it seemed like Sheo would ignore the order. Luckily for Guralt, She decided to acquiesce.

"Well, dear Guralt, it seems luck favors you this night. Do try to remember this the next time you seek to challenge Sheo," she finished with a patronizing pat on his cheek. Then, with a small surge of fir'gan, she turned and hurled him the twenty paces between her and the speaker.

Guralt landed at the speaker's feet without so much as a groan of protest. The dark-cloaked and hooded speaker peered down at his limp form for a moment before looking at the Enforcer nearest her and ordering, "Take him to the Burned Souls for cleansing and sacrifice."

Sheo hid her surprise at the order, but she said nothing as two of the Enforcers scooped up Guralt before the group headed toward the fires. As they departed, Sheo and the newcomer stood quietly, watching each other until the others were out of earshot.

"Sheo believes it odd that you would spare Guralt only to send him to the flames."

The other woman gave an almost imperceptible shrug. "What we do with these people, or how we punish our members, is none of your concern. Or have you forgotten our agreement?" the woman responded, her airy voice tinged with an edge of dark violence.

Sheo inclined her head. "Sheo has not forgotten. She was merely curious, just as she is curious what brings you out here, Yevesa?"

"You've had another visitor . . . and so soon after the last. My Master found that most curious."

Sheo shrugged indifferently. "It was nothing of importance. Merely a visit to let Sheo know that Darkon would be indisposed for a time, which he had forgotten to mention last he was here. Sheo was going to inform Warden Torani, but as you may have already noted, she got distracted," she lied smoothly.

"Be that as it may," Yevesa replied, her head cocked slightly, "my Master insists on speaking with you."

Sheo didn't need to hear the warning in Yevesa's tone to know it wasn't a friendly request. "Very well," Sheo replied, her tone conciliatory, "Sheo would be glad to assuage his concerns. Lead on, dear Yevesa."

Turning, Yevesa vanished into the night.

Sheo, with a surge of fir'gan, followed suit, thinking, *What fickle times, dear Sheo.*

A few minutes later, the pair came to a halt at the end of a mountainous ravine nearly four miles east of Forsaken. The terrain here was far more rocky and rugged than near the Burning Grounds, and to make matters worse, the rainfall had turned into a deluge by that time, making the stone terrain perilously slick while also turning the soil into a mud bog. The torrential downpour had even begun to form a shallow river on the ravine floor. While none of this truly mattered to the two Gifted, the demanding landscape served as a deterrent to most people in the best of weather, and was nearly impassible in the current monsoon-like conditions. As such, it was an ideal location to establish a base of operations.

Peering up through the rain at the cliff face, Sheo was unable to see any sort of clear indication that someone resided here. Granted, the way the currents flowed hinted at the presence of cracks and crevasses, but there was nothing unusual about the flow. In fact, when she probed further, she could find nothing to even hint at anyone else's presence other than Yevesa.

"It seems to Sheo that your Master's domicile is quieter than normal. Perhaps one or both of them are out for a stroll on this fine night?" Sheo offered glibly.

Yevesa tossed back her hood and glared at Sheo with striking red eyes astride a broad nose. Tilting her angular, ebony head to the side in annoyance, her topknot of dark hair standing atop her shaved head like a rigid mane, a menacing sneer parted her thin lips as she replied, "You might want to reign that tongue of yours in, Night Raven. Your antics have already caused enough trouble tonight. It would be a *great* shame if I had to remove it."

Sheo met her gaze and offered her a smirk that was just as malicious as her sneer. "Why, my dear Yevesa, Sheo's heart is filled with joy that you would care so much for one such as she!"

Yevesa's sneer turned into a deep, dark scowl. "Let's get this over with. He's waiting for us above."

Without waiting, Yevesa gathered the currents to her and lept. Soaring upward, she quickly vanished over the lip of an outcropping nearly three-fourths of the way to the top.

Sheo waited a moment, impressed by the Torani's ability to mask his presence. *It is impressive how well he does that . . . and frightening. Sheo wonders if all the Wardens of Shadow have become so skilled,* she mused, not for the first time, with a mix of admiration and fear.

Shrugging away the thought, Sheo gathered the currents as Yevesa did before her, and lept skyward. Arching over the edge of the ledge, Sheo landed nimbly on the stone surface even as Yevesa approached the dark fissure before them in the cliffside.

Halting short of the opening, Yevesa said, "She is here, Master."

"You're dismissed, Yevesa," a malevolently deep, but soft voice responded from the darkness within the fissure.

Bowing slightly, Yevesa then vanished in a surge of fir'gan.

At the same time, a tall, lean man emerged from the darkness on long, smooth strides. From his knee-boots to the bracers on his toned and bare pale arms, he was adorned in all black. Yellow eyes peered intently at her from dark sockets astride a hawkish nose on a broad face whose narrow lips were drawn, and shoulder-length blonde hair was unkempt. Halting a few paces from Sheo, he hooked his thumbs behind the tarnished buckle of his belt even as a strong breeze whipped at his shirt and vest, sending his hair dancing about his face.

"You've been busy of late, Sheo," he declared over the cry of the pouring rain.

Sheo pushed a wind-blown lock of her dark hair out of her vision. "Sheo does not consider taking the coin of stupid or amateur players being busy. But if you insist on labeling it so, Ivanus, then who is Sheo to argue?" she finished with a shrug.

A smile, which appeared strained, pulled at the man's lips. "Cute," he stated, irritated, with a wag of his finger. "But you know that is not what we meant, nor do I mean the talented thief your escapades cost us this night." He shook his head. "No, dear Sheo, you had a Gifted visitor tonight. . . . A visit far too soon after Darkon last graced us with his presence."

Graced is hardly the word Sheo would use, she thought with disdain. "Oh, you mean that," she responded aloud with a bit of mock surprise. "Sheo admits a bit of shock that you noticed such a trivial thing," she stated, even though she was well aware that very little in

Shadowtown escaped the Toranis' notice.

Ivanus chucked, dark and malign, then flashed her a toothy grin that dripped with malice. "Your attempts at humor are unwelcome. But do keep it up. I wouldn't mind an excuse to end a Warden . . . much less one as trivial as you."

Sheo placed a hand over her heart, feigning shock. "My, my, those words do wound Sheo's heart deep! She thinks your humor could use some help."

Sneering, Ivanus looked like he had a cutting retort at the ready, but the words seemed to die in his throat. Scowling, he said, "Enough of this! We grow weary of this prattle, and my brother requires my assistance! Tell us who the visitor was, and what they wanted!"

Sheo arched an eyebrow in curiosity. "Sheo knew something was amiss. Where is dear Sevene? You two are rarely without the other."

"Sheo . . ." Ivanus warned.

Waving a dismissive hand, Sheo rolled her eyes. "Fine. Fine. Sheo doesn't want to be here any more than you want her here." Fixing her gaze on him, she continued, "You may be at ease. The visitor this night was a messenger from Darkon. Nothing more."

"A messenger?" Ivanus asked, skeptical.

"Quiet so," Sheo replied with a nod. "Darkon, in his haste, had forgotten to inform me he would be indisposed for some time," she lied smoothly.

Ivanus peered at her intently, trying to decide if he believed her or not.

Sheo could tell he wasn't entirely convinced, so she offered, "Sheo knows it seems unusual that Darkon would send a messenger, for Sheo felt it unusual as well. Maybe there were ulterior motives, but nothing was revealed to Sheo." With a look of concern, she added, "If you think Sheo's answer is unsatisfactory, the messenger headed west. It would not take one such as you long to find them."

For a moment, Ivanus looked like he was considering it, and a knot of fear gripped her stomach. To her relief, he shook his head.

"No, we think not. It is irrelevant as far as we are concerned. We simply wanted to look you in the eyes when we asked."

"Sheo understands. Then may she take her leave?"

Ivanus nodded. However, as she turned to leap to the ravine

floor, Ivanus said, "Oh, and Sheo?"

Turning back to face the Torani, Sheo responded, "Yes, dear Ivanus?"

Ivanus' gaze hardened further, and Sheo saw barely contained violence in his eyes as he said, "Remember – if we find you are lying to us, or hiding something from us, our accord will end with your death. Is that clear to your broken mind?"

Sheo nodded, and forced a receptive smile. "As crystal, dear Ivanus," she stated before turning and leaping to the ground.

As she ran off into the distance, Ivanus snorted derisively. "Remind me again why we tolerate her?" he asked.

"Because she has been a fairly reliable source of information," Sevene responded as he emerged from the fissure in the cliffside.

Ivanus' mirror image in every aspect, Sevene wore attire that matched his brother's. Stopping next to his twin, he continued, "We know she is hardly a threat as well."

Ivanus scowled. "She lied to us this time," he stated firmly.

Sevene nodded as he followed her trail of power back to Forsaken. "Of course she did, and we know she has done so before. It changes nothing."

Ivanus glanced at his brother, his gaze reflecting a hint of uncertainty. "Are we sure about that, Brother? Whoever it was, was far more skilled than a simple messenger. It was luck that we even noticed their presence."

Sevene shrugged and turned to face Ivanus. Patting him on the shoulder, he declared, "Even if Luthur himself rose from the dead, it would not be enough to stop us." Giving his brother's shoulder a reassuring squeeze, he added, "Now come, Brother. Time is growing short, and we have much to prepare."

*

Fueled by fir'gan, Rynthalia's smooth strides carried her to the north and east with speed. Every morsel of information they'd gathered since making landfall pointed to one conclusion – the situation beyond the Storm Sea was dire. Granted, they had expected there to be issues given the head start Raefalzyn had, but to learn that so many Wardens had either perished or gone into seclusion was well beyond expectations. More importantly, if what Sheo told her was true. . . .

"Hark unto me, Corith – doeth not permit her words to be true. If

such hast befallen thine Wardens, then I fear what darkness may hath taken root here." She shook her head in admonishment. *"Nay, Rynthalia. . . . Let not thine thoughts wander such malign paths. The Light doth provide succor and a way forward when our need is most dire. We but needeth the fortitude to tread the path when 'tis made clear."*

Her attempt to reassure herself was mildly successful. While her faith in Corith and the Light was steady and strong, it couldn't prevent apprehension and dread from taking root. While their preliminary findings made it clear they had arrived in a terrible situation, it remained to be seen just how bad things actually were. More information was needed, not to mention it needed to be reliable. For that, they would need to speak with someone whose mind wasn't lost to madness, and more importantly, someone trustworthy.

As her route took her to the cliffside overlooking the rocky coastline, Rynthalia tried to make sense of what she knew to no avail. As such, she switched her focus to who they should contact next.

"Darkon 'tis the obvious choice," she mused. *"Yet I am wont to do so. Sheo's testimony dost cast a dower light upon him, and I ever hath been wary of trusting one with such haughty views of one's self. Nay, we shan't seek him out, for now. With Darius' fall — Corith grant his soul eternal rest in the Light — the Masumaite siblings art the logical choice. I can but hope mine sister hath fared better than I with her task."*

A short while later, Rynthalia stopped at the cliff edge. Behind her, the sun was beginning to burn away night's veil, and below her, the surf pounded the rocky shoreline relentlessly. Taking a moment to gather herself, she took in a lung full of the salty sea air and let it out slowly. She then checked her immediate surroundings on the currents for prying eyes. Once she was sure she was alone, Rynthalia stepped off the cliff without hesitation. Falling quickly for the first half of the towering drop, she then used the currents to slow her descent before landing on the rock-littered, sandy shore as softly as a cloud's caress.

The roar of the sea was nearly deafening here, and sea spray fell about her like a torrential rainfall. If not for her skin-tight shield of fir'gan, she would have been drenched the moment she landed. Picking her way nimbly to the north, she traversed the next five-hundred or so yards with grace and agility that shouldn't have been possible on such turbulent terrain. About a hundred yards from her destination, she felt a number of gazes focus on her from the lookouts her sister had stationed on the cliff face and amongst the larger rocks. It wouldn't serve as much of a warning against a Warden or strong Gifted, but it would be enough to discourage any mundanes that got too close to their clandestine port. What's more, it could also grant them enough time to destroy evidence of their presence if an enemy approached.

Just ahead of her, the sea waters were much calmer as they split the shore and flowed into a massive breach in the coastal cliffs. Approaching the breach, she stepped inside and found herself in a cavernous grotto. Deeper and taller than she could naturally see, most of the grotto was consumed by darkness at this early hour. Some of the darkness could have been alleviated if they'd chosen to light the way to their ship with torches or light orbs, but they had decided against it. Granted, it was a mute effort if an intruder was a Gifted, but it could at least prevent a curious mundane from seeing the ship if they somehow got this far. As for Rynthalia, she let her vision shift so that she could see the currents, which bathed the area in ethereal blue light, allowing her to quickly make her way forward. As she moved deeper into the grotto, the sea waters grew calmer and eventually still enough, nearly three-hundred yards in, for their sleek, white ship to be safely anchored.

Picking her way along the narrow sliver of rocky ground that the high tide left exposed, Rynthalia saw some of the crew in their wide assortment of sparse attire waving at her from the deck, welcoming her back. Her sister was also there, waiting calmly at the head of the gangplank that connected the deck to shore.

With her deep-red hair hanging loosely about her shoulders and slender face, Alyxaria watched her sister approach with large, almond-shaped green eyes full of hope that shone brightly against her warm ivory skin. A slight wind swept through the grotto, swirling about, causing her hair and simple white dress to flutter about, and her golden kasleu earrings to gently rock beneath her nearly shoulder-length, pointed ears. Offering Rynthalia a welcoming smile as she reached the gangplank, she asked, her lilting voice hopeful, "Pray, dear Sister, what news dost thou bring?"

Shaking her head slightly, Rynthalia met her sister's gaze as she ascended the plank and stated, keeping her concern from showing too much warm voice, "Let us speak in private."

The weight of Rynthalia's words was not lost on Alyxaria, and her smile vanished like dust on the wind. "Very well," she replied as Rynthalia reached the deck.

Turning, Alyxaria led the way past the retracted masts toward their cabin door in the aftcastle. On the way, she glanced at Captain Valmon, who was watching them from the wheel on the second tier of the aftcastle. "Dear Captain, pray let no one disturb us."

Valmon nodded, his array of long white braids, and his

bronze kasleu earrings swaying in the breeze. Despite the cold weather, he wore only his tool belt and baggy red pants on his lean, sun-darkened figure. "Aye, m'lady," he replied, both his deep voice and his green eyes filled with curious concern.

Once the sisters were in their cabin, and the door was sealed behind them, Alyxaria dropped a shield over the room to ward against prying ears while her sister lit the light orbs. As the orbs' soft glow grew, illuminating the room and its roof of white-wood latticework, Alyxaria walked over to the two goblets and the half-full decanter sitting on the elegant table of flowing white wood in the center of the cabin. "If thou would, Sister, dispose of those rags ere the stench infects this room." Picking up the decanter, she added as she filled the two goblets, "I cannot fathom how thou hath tolerated such a miasma, nor why thou would doest so."

Rynthalia winced. "'Twas necessary," she responded as she used the currents to slice the rags off, her disgust with the clothing obvious. "Anyone of moderate cleanliness in such a town would hath been like a beacon in the night," she added as the rags fell to the ground, leaving her in a dark tunic and leggings. "Therefore, an el-vannue bereft of a disguise 'twould seem as a god amongst those humans," she finished as her sister approached, goblets in hand.

Stopping before her sister, Alyxaria sniffed the air. "Thine attire will require purging as well," she stated, wrinkling her nose. "What's more, pray change and see to it thine disguise is incinerated anon," she finished, gesturing to Rynthalia's remaining attire.

"Quite so," Rynthalia agreed.

Removing her ankle boots, Rynthalia placed them against her artful desk on the left-hand wall, which was the twin of the one on the opposite side of the room, before disrobing and placing the garments atop the boots. Naked to the world, orb light played along her toned, supple muscles, languid curves, and flawless alabaster skin as she padded over to the wardrobe between their well-kept beds at the rear of the cabin. Opening it, she retrieved a gown similar to her sister's before pulling it on. Turning as it settled in place, she then returned to Alyxaria and took the goblet she was offered. The sisters then seated themselves in the matching high-back, red-velvet cushioned chairs that flanked the table.

Taking a sip from her cup, Rynthalia reveled in the warm, giddy sensation that washed over her as the rosy liquid slipped down her throat. "Much better," she said with a weak smile before placing the goblet on the table.

Alyxaria nodded in agreement after sipping from her drink.

"Aye. 'Tis nothing quite like a reminder of home and better times when ill tidings lurk upon the horizon," she said with a hint of trepidation.

Rynthalia grimaced slightly. "Aye, Sister, 'tis such tidings that I doth bear."

"Out with it, then," Alyxaria prodded.

Taking a deep breath, Rynthalia then said, "I did meet with Warden Rivinia. Alas, 'twould appear her mind mayhap is broken, for she speaks of herself as another person."

Perplexed, Alyxaria said, "That should not be possible. . . . Her crystal should hath warded against such maladies."

Rynthalia shrugged, then sipped on her drink again before responding, "'Twould seem impossible, I agree with thee. Yet, I cannot deny what mine eyes and ears hath witnessed. Regretfully, 'tis not the worst of the tidings I bear. Pray, doth not accept what I say for the infallible truth as it comes from one I doth question the sanity of. . . ." Taking a deep breath, she stated, "Rivinia hath spoken of the deaths of many a Warden."

Cold dread settled in the pit of Alyxaria's stomach. "Pray tell, how many?" she asked, fighting to keep her voice under control.

Rynthalia took another deep breath to steel herself. "While I doth not know how many hath fallen, we art bereft of several Wardens of import." Shock began to claw at Alyxaria's face, which tore at Rynthalia's heart as she knew what she had to say next would hurt far more. "Of more import," she continued, her voice growing thick with emotion, "be the absence of Preceptor Damion Masumaite, and the deaths of Preceptors Darius Fultain, Catharina Durasala, and. . . ." Her voice broke, and she had to steady herself before adding, "And the passing of Lord Dragon, Luthur Hyren."

Gasping with horror and heartbreak, Alyxaria's free hand shot to her mouth as if trying to keep her shock from spilling forth. "Corith be good," she intoned after a moment, distraught, as she lowered her hands. "Art thou sure her words ring true?"

Rynthalia shrugged, her expression crestfallen, then she downed the rest of her drink. "As I alluded, Rivinia's mind doth appear fractured," she reminded her sister as she stood. Grabbing the decanter, she refilled her goblet. Turning, she leaned against the right side of the table and took a sip as she looked at the object occupying her sister's desktop. As the warmth spread through her body, she continued. "Woefully, I shan't doubt her words hold some measure of truth. How truthful 'tis the mystery we must unravel. Ere we let emotions lead us down a path of woe, let us seeketh the truth of the matter."

Looking at her sister, Rynthalia met her gaze and could see the heartache and dread dancing in their green depths. It was clear Alyxaria was struggling with the news and its implications, but to Rynthalia's relief, her sister eventually regained control of her emotions.

Sipping on her wine to buy her a moment more to recover, Alyxaria then declared firmly, "Agreed, dear Sister."

"Good," Rynthalia responded. "Pray tell, hast thine efforts yielded anything more while I was away?"

Placing her goblet on the table, Alyxaria stood and moved to her desk, atop which sat a sizable, convex silver disk surmounted by an array of smaller blue crystals inset in concentric circles around a large central crystal. "I fear mine efforts hath born little fruit, though less dire," she stated as she fed a tendril of fir'gan into the device.

With the infusion of power, the crystals began to glow, illuminating from the outer ring to the central crystal before fir'gan poured forth, twisting and turning as the currents were quickly molded into a three-dimensional map of the coastline and the surrounding area.

"As before, 'tis nary a sign of Wardens or their subordinates in the immediate area aside from Rivinia and the Torani brothers," Alyxaria reiterated as her sister approached the map.

"Nay, I did not pursue the Toranis' presence," Rynthalia interjected, anticipating her sister's question. "I thought it prudent to keep mine visit brief and as inconspicuous as possible."

"Prudent, indeed," Alyxaria agreed as she manipulated the device, taping on the clear crystals embedded at the base of it. "As for mine search, I decided to risk a deeper search inland," she said as the terrain on the map seemed to speed by, appearing at one end of the projection and vanishing at the other end.

"Pray tell, was anything of import yielded?"

"Little, dear Sister," she responded as the map slowed and came to a halt. "I did discover this . . . anomaly," she said, gesturing to the map.

What appeared to be a sprawling plain was displayed before the sisters. On it were a series of dots ranging in color from bright white to violent blue. While the dots were scattered somewhat, it was clear they progressed south and east.

"Who doth thee perceive it to be?" Rynthalia asked. "I cannot determine the source with the signal so weak. Yet, 'tis a passing familiarity to it that I cannot place."

"I concur. Yet, we can infer the source from these traces," Alyxaria declared as the map moved further to the north and west, where it stopped on a massive, ghostly spot in a wooded area.

"'Tis very little to work with, Sister," Rynthalia stated after examining it for a moment. "Yet, I must agree. The traces art weak, yet 'tis enough from which the impact can be discerned. Coldfire was used."

Alyxaria smirked. "Thine eyes art keen as ever, Rynthalia, as is thine mind. I must confess, it tooketh me significantly longer to unravel the puzzle."

"We each hath our own talents. Be proud, sister. Thine ability to read the currents in such detail is far greater than thou doth believe. Determining a source from such a feeble trace 'tis no small feat, no matter the time it cost thee."

With a nod, Alyxaria accepted the praise. "Mine thanks, dear Sister," she stated humbly.

Peering closer at the ghostly signal, Rynthalia stated, "Wielders of coldfire art few. While I would be remiss to trust anything truly at this moment, 'twould be foolish to ignore this. We must hope none beyond the Death Bringers hath gained such power."

A visible shudder ran through Alyxaria at that thought. "Agreed," she stated. "Ergo, I did follow the signal's path and found this. . . ."

The map sped southeast before coming to a halt at an expansive forest.

"Corith be good," Rynthalia breathed as she instantly recognized what she was seeing.

"A Desolate Zone," Alyxaria confirmed, her voice and eyes grim.

Rynthalia shook her head at the destruction. "'Tis old, to be sure. 'Twill be centuries ere it heals, if at all. Yet. . . ." She shook her head. "'Tis a matter to mourn at another time, however." Pointing at the small, nearly invisible white dot, Rynthalia said, "'Tis very weak, yet recent. Last night . . . mayhap the night before."

"My thoughts as well. Had it been anywhere else, 'twould be indistinguishable from the currents. What's more – and correct me if I ere – 'twould need to be a strong surge to maketh such impact in a Desolate Zone."

"Aye," Rynthalia stated, eyeing the dot thoughtfully.

After a moment of silent contemplation, Rynthalia looked at her sister and stated, "I shalt investigate."

Taken aback by the declaration, Alyxaria said, "Pray, pardon me, Sister. Did thou say what I believe I hath heard?"

"Aye," Rynthalia replied adamantly.

Folding her arms beneath her breast, Alyxaria matched her sister's determination as she stated, "Pray tell, why? Such an area speaks of danger. As thou declared earlier, we hath our particular talents. Mine surpass thee where combat 'tis involved.

Rynthalia conceded the point. "'Twould be foolish to dispute this fact, Sister. Were I to believe 'tis simply combat at risk, I would not hesitate to agree."

Puzzled, Alyxaria asked. "What doth thou see?"

Staring at the dead area for a moment longer to assure herself that she was indeed seeing what she believed she saw, Rynthalia then met her sister's gaze before stating, "While I cannot accurately gauge when the Desolate Zone came into being, I can, with dreadful certainly tell thee this – the land should hath healed more than this. Woefully, we both art aware of what this mayhap mean."

Eyes wide, Alyxaria said, an edge of panic to her voice, "Surely 'tis not so! The cleansing mayhap been powerful beyond the norm! Mayhap even–"

"Alyxaria," Rynthalia interrupted. "While such an option would be preferred, we know 'tis unlikely. The Darkness hast found succor there."

Suddenly angry at the implications, Alyxaria declared forcefully, "All the more reason I should–"

"I will not broker debate on this!" Rynthalia barked, her own ire sparked.

Stunned at the sudden, and rare, outburst, Alyxaria backed down. "Mine apologies, Sister," she intoned softly.

Taking a breath to steady herself, Rynthalia replied, her voice soft and apologetic. "Nay, I should not hath spoken so harshly. Thine intent was pure, and thine heart in the right place." Smiling warmly at her sister, she continued, "Yet, if 'tis as I fear. . . ."

"No more need be said, Sister," Alyxaria stated, waving away her sister's apology. "'Tis I that hath erred. We all art acutely aware of what such a mission means to those of the Academy. I merely sought to spare thee the heartache such a task will entail. Yet, I must ask what thou hopes to accomplish? We hath not the means to provide succor to the land."

"Well met, and aye, we doeth not," Rynthalia agreed with a nod. "Yet, I doth believe some of the weapons we brought mayhap serve to cleanse should the situation be as I suspect."

Alyxaria nodded. "Very well. So shall it be. While thou attend to those matters, I believe I shalt investigate this. . . ."

With a few taps on the crystals, Alyxaria sent the map speeding north and west, where it came to rest on a valley nestled in a towering mountain range. In the valley, a lone red signal shone brightly.

"What 'tis this?" Rynthalia asked, curious. "I thought thou had limited thine search?"

"I did. 'Twas mere curiosity that provoked me to begin examining areas at random."

"Prudent. Gifted which mayhap felt the search 'twould likely dismiss it as a mere anomaly. Perchance, doth the signal seem familiar?" Rynthalia inquired, even though she recognized it.

Alyxaria's grim expression presented her answer before she spoke. "Aye. Long hast it been since we last saw him, but 'tis no mistaking it. Warrick is there."

"Dost thou intent to engage him? Surely, thou art not *that* foolish?" Rynthalia asked dryly.

Chuckling, Alyxaria replied, "Nay. Thine mind may rest at ease. 'Twould be unthinkable at this moment if not for the . . . suggestion that Darius is lost to us."

"Ah," Rynthalia said as it dawned on her. "Thou intends to see if the seal is in place?"

"Aye, sister. I would prefer thou to do so, but I understand in full what expunging a nest means to thee." Alyxaria flashed her sister a warm, understanding smile, which Rynthalia returned appreciatively. "Be that as it may," Alyxaria continued as her smile faded, "we art still blind to the extent of the knowledge Raefalzyn did absconded with when he vanished. If even a sliver of what Luthur carried unto this land hast been bequeathed unto the Darkness. . . ."

The weight of her words settled on the room like a heavy, suffocating miasma. They were risking their mission by pursuing this course, but neither sister could see another path forward. Rivinia was useless to them, and they had no idea where the other Wardens were. All they could do now was trust in the path before them and adjust as the situation dictated.

"Very well," Rynthalia finally declared. "Let us pursueth this course with all the strength and courage Corith hast granted us. If thou will be so kind as to fetch us something with which to break our fast, I shalt ready our equipment?"

Nodding, Alyxaria said, "Agreed. I shalt ensure breakfast is a hearty one."

Moving to the door, Alyxaria removed the shield around the room. "Oh, and lest either of us forgets," she suddenly said.

An instant later, the rags Rynthalia had been wearing were incinerated, leaving no trace behind. Alyxaria then dispersed the smoke before exiting the cabin.

Alone, Rynthalia shook her head in amusement before moving to the wardrobe again. Opening it, she dug out two long, thin cases. She then returned to the table and placed them on it even as she used the currents to retrieve the chests at the ends of their beds. As the chests came to rest at her feet, she placed her hands on the cases and closed her eyes in prayer.

"Corith," she thought, *"bless these blades and guide our hands. We venture forth in thine name to confront the Darkness in this land. Let thine light illuminate our path and direct our feet. Guide us unto victory if 'tis thine will. Should we find death, lift unto thine bosom our souls so that we may rest eternally in thine grace."*

Nearly two hours later, as dawn's light finally began to creep deep into the grotto, the sisters emerged from their cabin. Dressed in near matching attired, one could almost mistake them for twins. Dark gray bodysuits of elvannue make, which were light and flexible, covered them from neck to feet. Over it, they each sported an armor harness to which was attached convex breastplates of white enameled bluesteel, which provided ample protection while still allowing full freedom of movement. Matching sabatons protected their lower legs and knees over supple black boots, while elvannue scaled tekko girded their arms. Each sister clasped a white-enameled, winged faceguard in their fingerless-gloved hands, and each also wore a silver armlet on their off-hand forearm upon which an array of small blue crystals were arranged around a larger, elongated crystal. While neither sister sported the flamboyant gilding typical of elvannue armor, there were still some flowing embellishments reminiscent of a leafy vine that added an elegant flare to their attire.

As for differences between the sisters' garb, Rynthalia sported matching pauldrons that flowed eerily with her shoulders, while Alyxaria elected for an open-face gorget along with banded steel on her shoulders and upper arms. Furthermore, a long, slender-bladed sword similar to a katana hung from Rynthalia's left hip on a sturdy swordbelt that was home to numerous pouches and a winged belt buckle. Alyxaria, on the other hand, wore a similar belt, but her weapons of choice, two short, leaf-blade swords were stowed on her back, their filigreed pommels and dark-red leather hilts jutting over her left shoulder.

The crew of the *Sy'ladrial* took note of the sisters immediately and quickly gathered around them just outside their cabin. It had been years since the sisters were girded for battle, and the sight was enough to leave them in awe.

"Maketh way!" Captain Valmon bellowed as he pushed his way past his crew. "What spell hath enchanted thee? All hath seen the ladies robed thusly!" he chided as he reached the sisters and turned about, glaring at his crew. "Back to thine posts! We art within enemy territory – do not forget this!" he finished, glaring sternly at the crew.

It took the crew a moment to react, but they eventually dispersed.

Turning to the sisters, the captain smiled. "'Tis been long since thou hath adorned thineselves thusly. Shalt I prepare the crew for battle?" he asked, his pleasure at seeing the sisters in their gear squashed by concern.

Rynthalia shook her head, her now braided dark-violet hair swinging gently along her back. "Nay. 'Tis no immediate threat. Mine sister and I must depart, for the situation requires us to venture inland, and we must be prepared."

"Very well," he responded with a nod. "Mine orders?"

Alyxaria, her deep-red hair pulled back in a braided foxtail, said, "Maketh for the deep sea after we hath departed. Remain there until we return. If it be Corith's will, we shan't be long."

"Very well, m'ladies."

"One last thing, Captain," Rynthalia interjected before he could set about preparing to sail.

"Aye?"

Glancing at Alyxaria, she met her gaze and saw reassurance there. "Should we not return within a fortnight, maketh for home," Rynthalia declared.

"M'ladies!" Valmon exclaimed, shocked.

"We shalt broker no argument, Captain," she responded resolutely. "Furthermore, should servants of the Darkness discover thee, see all technology destroyed, and scuttle the ship."

The weight of the order was like a punch to the gut for the captain. Eyes wide with shock, he started to protest, but Alyxaria prevented it with a raised hand.

"Please, Captain, thou art aware of what 'tis at stake," she remarked, her tone sympathetic, but just as resolute as her sister's. "The Darkness cannot be allowed to acquire passage home. All of us knew the risk, and mayhap our lives be sacrificed. Honor our mission, and protest no more."

Seeing the determination in the sisters' eyes, Valmon swallowed his objection. Saluting fist to heart, he bowed slightly. "Aye, mine Ladies, it shalt be done. Corith illuminate thine path," he stated before turning and making his way up to the wheel while bellowing orders.

Shouldering their packs, the sisters made their way over to the gangplank and down it before proceeding to the grotto entrance, both of them lost in thought. Elvannue preferred to approach problems methodically, gathering as much knowledge as possible before committing to a course of action. Regrettably, this entire mission had flown in the face of that approach from the very beginning, and that was never more evident than it was now. With so little to go on, it was just as likely that they were walking into a dragon's den as it was that they would find one of their allies, and that weighed heavily on their minds.

Just outside the grotto, they stopped and turned to face each other, their expressions solemn. A pair of sailors soon sprinted past them, offering brief nods of acknowledgment on their way to retrieve the lookouts stationed outside. The sisters, however, ignored them as their attention was focused solely on one another.

After a moment of this somber reflection, an amused smile cracked Alyxaria's face and she suddenly laughed. "Thou would believe we were about to march unto our deaths!"

Cracking a smile of her own, Rynthalia chuckled in response. "Aye. . . . 'Tis not the case, though, is it not?"

"Agreed, sister. So let us part ways knowing that we shalt see one another ere long."

"Aye," Rynthalia stated in agreement. Placing her free hand on her sister's upper arm, she gave it a warm, reassuring squeeze.

"May Corith guide thee, and the Light illuminate thine path."

Alyxaria returned the gesture. "Thou as well, Sister."

Releasing Rynthalia's arm, Alyxaria secured her faceguard on her head and watched as her sister did the same. Sparing each other one last glance, they offered parting smiles to one another before they separated under their own power, Alyxaria to the north and Rynthalia to the south. They followed each other's presence on the currents until they were each well away from the grotto. Then, with a surge of fir'gan, the sisters turned inland toward the unknown.

Chapter Twenty-Six

"**O**n your left!" Cid cried as he glanced back to check on Caldain.

With a snarl pulling at his hawkish face, Caldain kicked the foul-smelling blackheart free of his longsword before spinning to see two of the abominations in dark leather armor charging toward him, their jagged, obsidian-esque swords poised to strike. Ducking beneath a clumsy swing, Caldain drove up and away from the greasy-haired blackheart, dragging his longsword across its chest before kicking the creature into its companion. Knocked off balance, the second blackheart dropped its poison-coated sword and fell backward, only to have its boil-littered head cleaved from its shoulders as Kay's broadsword licked through its dark-skinned neck as she darted by. Immediately, Caldain ignited the pair of corpses, adding another blaze to the fires trailing their frantic push southeast.

Racing to Cid, they dispatched the three blackhearts harassing him. Caldain cringed as he felt an arrow bounce off the hardened air shielding his back, causing a nauseating ripple in the currents. "Keep moving!" he barked, his gray eyes flashing, and his strong voice ringing with authority. "There's more coming, and there's at least one archer with them!"

Setting the corpses ablaze, the siblings fell in behind Caldain as he moved forward, his long braided horsetail of dark hair whipping behind him. Taking a moment to quickly check his white shirt, black pants, bracers and knee boots for blood, he was relieved when he saw none. He then shouted as he increased the pace, "Everyone unharmed?"

"Just fine!" Cid replied after a cursory check of his black leathers, the brash tones of his voice strained. "Not a speck of blood on my clothes.... Although...." A sudden flare of fire illuminated the area for a moment. "There! Now I'm good."

"Kay?" Caldain inquired.

Muttered curses met his question, followed by cloth tearing.

"I'm fine!" she shouted, an edge of aggravated disappointment in her husky voice.

Looking back at her, Caldain smirked. While her brown pants, calf-boots, and black fingerless gloves appeared intact, the sleeves of her white shirt were now missing, exposing her strong arms and broad shoulders to the silvery blue moonlight. Her hooded brown eyes flashed with anger from astride the slender nose on her defined face as she glared at him.

"Sorry about the shirt," he quipped.

Kay rolled her eyes and shook her head of short-cropped, auburn hair. "Keep moving!" she barked as she used fire to cleanse her sword and long-knife.

Grinning, he asked, "How about a little more speed? No need to hide our presence, now! All this fighting and that trail of burning corpses will have alerted any Gifted in the area!"

Nodding their agreement, the siblings followed Caldain's example. In an instant, the world became a blur as their fir'gan-fueled pace pushed them beyond the limits of ordinary humans.

Pulling alongside Caldain, Cid peered at him with eyes that were a match for his sister's while a look of concern marred his youthful features. "Where in the hells are they coming from?!"

"Don't know! And I'm not inclined to find out!" Caldain replied as he finally cleansed his longsword with a quick blaze of purifying fire.

"Ahead of us!" Kay suddenly cried, drawing their attention forward.

While the ethereal blue currents illuminated the night for their fir'gan-sensitive eyes, it was the dead areas on the currents that made it easy to spot another dozen blackhearts moving from behind a series of rocky outcroppings in the distance. Scowling as a trio of the creatures raised bows and began to let loose, Caldain slowed the pace as he shifted his shield of air to the front and quickly expanded it.

"Any time now!" Caldain growled as the distance closed and obsidian-tipped arrow after arrow ricocheted off the shield.

"So impatient," Kay quipped as she lashed out with the currents with violent accuracy, cutting down half the blackheart ranks, including the archers, just before her brother ignited the bodies.

Unable to break free of the incinerating mess, the remaining blackhearts caught fire as their burning compatriots flailed about in agony.

Altering their course to avoid passing close to the shadows-pawned creatures still clinging to life, Caldain altered his shield, focusing it and molding it into a tight mass. As soon as they were past the burning corpses, he tossed the seething mass of power into the middle of the blackhearts. With a resounding thud, it exploded, showering the immediate area with flaming bits of bone, flesh and stone.

Looking back, Cid let out a low, impressed whistle as he shook his shaved head slightly. "Damn, Old Hawk! That was unnecessary!"

Caldain smirked. "True, but it felt good!"

Rolling her eyes at the two men, Kay said, "Stay focused, will you? That's the third group this night!"

Amusement fled the two men's faces at her chastisement.

"You're right," Caldain replied with a nod. "Bad enough they've been chasing us, but now we've got them coming from two directions." Sneering with disgust and frustration, Caldain asked, "Anyone sense more of them?"

"Nope," Cid stated as he returned his broad-blade shortsword to its scabbard on his right hip.

"Same here," Kay confirmed as she slid her long-knife into its sheath on the right side of her broad hips.

Nodding, Caldain slowed them to a natural run and let his sense expand on the currents for a moment. Once he felt sure that the only corruption on the ethereal ribbons of power was the quickly dwindling presence of their pursuers, he began searching for shelter as he sheathed his longsword at his left hip. To his chagrin, the rolling, grassy terrain that denoted the start of the Wildlands provided very little protection. There were a few recessions in the ground, as well as several crude natural shelters formed by the stones jutting from the earth all about the open terrain, but none of it was ideal or defensible.

"The old watchtower," Kay suddenly said as if she knew what he was pondering.

Looking at her as she stowed her medalion-pommel broadsword over her right shoulder, he offered his thanks with a nod. "I'd nearly forgotten about it. Is it still habitable?"

Kay shrugged. "Your guess is as good as mine. It's been ages since I last saw it, and that was at a distance. Nature may have finally reclaimed it, or – Corith forbid – someone might be living there. If it's still standing, it'll give us a good view of the land and we could easily defend it from an army of blackhearts."

Caldain considered her suggestion for a brief moment. It was heartening to see her so confident after that night of terror. Kay had spent the days afterward doting on her brother while he recovered, which took him a week. During that time, Caldain did his best to nurse them through their first encounter with blackhearts; unfortunately, there was only so much he could do. It had been centuries since either of the Kaskia siblings, and Caldain for that matter, had truly been forced to confront death. As such, when it came to that topic, he knew he could do little more than offer his support while they wrestled with the realization that there was now a very real threat to their lives that wasn't a Warden's crusader. However, when it came to combating blackhearts, he could do much more than act as a supportive shoulder to lean on. So, once the siblings had improved enough to truly be combat-ready, Caldain took a couple of hours each day before they rested to work on techniques that were effective against blackhearts. During those sessions, he could see both the fear and the rage birthed by the encounter threaten to overwhelm them. To the siblings' credit, it never went past that point. As a result, by the time the blackhearts began harassing them once more, they were confident enough in their ability to fend off the creatures that they no longer ran the risk of freezing.

"Alright," he finally said with a nod. "Let's give it a look," he added before turning south and accelerating once more.

They maintained their increased pace for another hour before the terrain began to change. The rocky outcroppings became larger and more numerous, and grass gave way to dirt and gravel. A few miles later, scattered trees soon made an appearance. Twisting their way skyward, the barren trees sat atop massive chunks of stone jutting from the hard ground. Slowing their pace so no one would trip on the large, gnarled roots exposed to the air, Caldain picked his way toward a tower rising above a forest of the haunting vegetation that ran east and west for as far as he could see.

"Damn," Cid muttered as their slower pace allowed him to properly take in their surroundings, "The Sea of Petals. . . . I've never made it down here, but I've heard the stories."

"What happened here was a travesty," Caldain told him, his tone morose. Studying the sluggish, almost sick way the currents were already moving over the dead land as they drew closer to the forest, Caldain added, "The lands beyond this place escaped the brunt of the battle, and have thankfully long since recovered. But this place. . . ." He shook his head as a chill ran up his spine. "Ten thousand blackhearts died that day. One day – maybe – the land will truly heal, but until then. . . ." He trailed off with a sigh.

Silence traveled with them until they reached the forest edge, where they came to a stop. Sadness and regret filled the trio as they silently offered prayers to Corith and their condolences to the forest.

"There's nothing in there," Kay stated, sorrowful. "No animals, no birds . . . not even insects. It's just death and decay for miles."

Caldain's jaw clenched as he recalled the thriving forest it had once been. Food, shade, and water aplenty, the forest had once provided its bounty to the green-haired forest dwellers that called it home. Millennia ago, Velusyians disenfranchised with the less palatable aspects of their culture left Velusyia and settled in this forest. Calling themselves Valkolians, they lived in harmony with the trees that provided shelter and the animals that provided substance. Such a balanced nature allowed them to thrive until the day one of their own betrayed them.

"You were here, weren't you?" Kay asked, seeing a mix of anger and regret play across his gray eyes.

Caldain nodded, the trio of scars running from his brow to jawline over his right eye adding an air of ferocity to the emotions battling on his face. "Let's get going," he responded tersely before starting forward.

Moving at a trot, it took them longer than they would have liked to reach the stone rise. Along the way, they saw the scattered remnants of a civilization long dead; a few cobbles underfoot left by roads long gone, the remains of a chimney, partial buildings that nature had yet to tear down, and even a crude well. All of this was made even more dismal by the combination of the skeletal branches overhead casting their shadows over everything, and the smell of decay that permeated the air.

Once at the base of the rise, they found what looked to be the remains of a fort. Piles of aged stone and rotten timber were scattered within the confines of a broken wall that was no taller than any of their waists. Picking their way through the ruins in search of a way up, they soon found a gate in the rock face that was sealed with a portcullis that surprisingly still stood despite being rusted through. Grabbing the bars, Caldain shook his head in sadness as they started to crumble.

With a grimace, Caldain stood back and encased the ancient barrier in air. Giving the malign currents a gentle squeeze, he crushed the ruined iron into dust. Stepping over the pile of powder, Caldain led the siblings up a stone staircase chipped and worn by the years. As they climbed, the heavy and damp atmosphere made breathing annoying, forcing them to expend a bit of power to purify the air. Given the state of the currents, that simple task required far more focus and effort than normal, which slowed their pace. To make matters worse, they had no choice but to stop and manually clear large chunks of rubble a few times.

Eventually, they reached another rusted gate at the top of the stairs, which Caldain disposed of quickly. Stepping out into the night, they were pleased to find the air was much cleaner, and they were able to release the power they'd been using to purify it. Looking around as they breathed in the fresh air, it was immediately clear that the majority of the rise was occupied by the tower before them, which had once soared skyward. Now broken, the bulk of the structure was a crumbled mess, littering the rise with busted stone, shattered tiles whose color had long since faded, and splintered, rotted wood.

"Well, I've made camp in worse places," Cid quipped sadly as he started forward.

"We all have," Caldain agreed. "Still, the memory of what once was haunts this place." He frowned deeply. "Let's see if we can scrounge up some wood for a fire. It might help to have some warmth."

They all knew this wasn't true since they had no need of a fire for warmth. What's more, it risked exposing their position to unwanted guests. However, that was hardly a concern as the siblings nodded in agreement before they started sifting through the rubble. What drove the decision was the atmosphere of sadness and anguish hanging about the ruins like a heavy fog. Granted, a fire couldn't actually dispel the aura created by a land deeply wounded, but it would provide a small, familiar comfort in the midst of the depressing landscape.

Eventually, they found enough useable wood, and made an impromptu fire pit out of bits of stone in the shadow of the broken structure. Though the fire was small, and they did their best to use the tower to shield it, it would be hard to miss if anyone was in the vicinity. Caldain disregarded such worries as they double-checked one another for any blood. It was nearly a pointless exercise since they'd already be violently ill or dead if they'd been exposed, but it was worth it to make sure no one was accidentally exposure to any poison that might have been overlooked. Once they were sure everyone were clean, they broke out their provisions and settled about the fire. With a brooding silence hanging about them, Cid removed his fingerless gloves before he proceeded to fill a small pot with a measured amount of water from their supplies. He then used Kay's long-knife to dice up a small potato before tossing it into the pot along with a handful of dried beef, and a mix of spices. Stirring it a bit with the long-knife, he settled in to wait for it to boil.

Looking about, Kay decided to break the uneasy silence. "This was Juliana's doing, wasn't it?" she asked, her husky voice somber.

Staring into the fire, Caldain slowly nodded. "That it was." He paused before adding, "She played us all for fools. We didn't know she'd built nests below her countrymen's feet until it was too late. When she betrayed him . . . betrayed *us,* it was a scramble to discover the depths of her deceit." He grimaced. "We didn't learn of the nests here till the later stages of the war. We'd already lost a large portion of the Bestyne and Kydan'fir Orders in our attempt to destroy all the nests around Kylir, but it was here the losses were most grievous. Yasuin, a third of the Bestynes, nearly all that remained of Kydan'fir, as well as a host of good people. . . . All gone in the span of two days."

"When we were brought into the fold by Vann after he replaced Yasuin," Cid said softly, "we were told the nests here were deep, and the city all but destroyed by the time Luthur sent Damion in."

Caldain nodded slowly as the memories played out in his mind. "It was the last resort. There weren't enough healthy Bestynes and Kydan'fir for a standard purge, and it was taking all we had left to safely contain the remaining blackhearts within their nests, not to mention keeping the Betrayers' attention elsewhere. We couldn't retreat nor could we advance, so we went with our last resort. We'd only done it once early in the war, and the results led to altering the Bestynes into their current state. Here though. . . ." Cal shook his head and his voice grew soft.

"With the elvannue long gone, we did not have their . . . affinity for the currents, nor their technology, so we didn't fully realize the damage that had already been done to the land. The land and the currents were already ravaged to near collapse by the flood of miasma, but the unleashing of coldfire on such a large scale was what sealed the area's fate. When Damion was done, everything was dead, and the land was razed of its life-giving properties. It was catastrophic, to say the least, and short-sighted of us, but the sacrifices made here were what hamstrung the Betrayers. Bereft of their most potent weapon against us, we eventually hunted down the Betrayers and disarmed them all before exiling them," he finished with a small, disgusted sneer.

"Still," he continued, redirecting the conversation back to the original subject, his voice growing a bit more optimistic as he looked about, "it appears that fir'gan has begun to return to the area – albeit minimally. . . . So, there is hope that one day this place might return to a shadow of its former self."

"I hope that's more than wishful thinking," Kay stated, trying her best to ignore the anguish in Caldain's eyes. "And maybe you're right about it being short-sighted, but it was what you had to do to cripple the Betrayers."

Caldain nodded with a slight dry smirk.

Seeking to lighten the mood a bit, Kay said, "I seem to recall reading that it was a favorite pastime of the elvannue to chastise us humans for our short-sighted, rash behavior." She smirked. "I imagine they hoped the humans that were chosen as Wardens, as well as their followers, would grow out of such flaws."

Caldain chuckled slightly, and Cid did as well, though with more amusement.

"I imagine they'd be displeased with us, Sis," Cid offered as he moved to the pot and stirred it with the long-knife. "We may be more patient than we would be if we were still mortal, but we're still rash and quick to violence. This place is a testament to that."

"Possibly," Kay conceded. "But I'm not convinced of that."

Oh really?" Cid quipped, his expression curious, as he tasted the soup on the long-knife.

Kay nodded as her brother grimaced with displeasure. "Think about it. If we were as rash and destructive as the elvannue believed, then I think this place would be completely dead, not to mention all of Kylir." She shook her head as Cid added a pinch of seasoning to the soup. "None of us knows what Luthur and Damion were thinking, but I'd like to not only believe the force they used was necessary at the time, but that they understood that with enough time, the land would recover."

Tasting the soup once more, Cid nodded with satisfaction before returning the knife to his sister, who quickly stowed it. "It's a nice thought, and I hope you're right," he said as he retrieved a trio of small bowls from their supplies. Dipping each container into the pot, he filled each one before handing them to his companions.

"It is that," Caldain agreed. Sniffing his meal, he then took a slow sip. Looking up with a hint of surprise, he smiled slyly and joked, "Not bad. Better than the slop you served me in Solac."

"You're an ass at times, Caldain. You know that?" Cid stated playfully.

"And you could have learned to cook over the centuries," Caldain retorted with a sly grin.

Laughing at the exchange, Kay said with a grin pulling at her full lips, "He's right, Brother."

Placing a hand over his heart in mock pain, Cid cried, "You break my heart, little Kay! That you would take his side is insulting!"

Sipping on her hot meal, she kept her grin fixed on Cid. "It shouldn't surprise you," she stated as she lowered her bowl. "And you really should be used to it by now. Besides, taking your side would only condone your lazy, bachelor lifestyle. I can't keep cooking for you, and you know it."

"And there is the dagger!" Cid declared, feigning insult. "I live a fine life free of the smothering shackles women seem to be hells bent on slapping on every man!" Peering at Caldain, he teased, "Watch out, Old Hawk. She's been alone for a long time – she may try to trap you again."

"Cid! Please!" Kay blurted, suddenly embarrassed as emotional pain squeezed her heart.

"What?" he asked innocently as he turned his wide eyes on her.

"Yes, well," Caldain muttered, clearing his throat. "I think I'll take the first watch." Downing the remains of his soup, Caldain tossed the bowl at Cid's feet. "You two get some rest," he stated before walking off.

Following him with sad eyes for a moment, Kay then turned her attention to Cid. Glowering at him, she leaned over and punched his shoulder. "You really are an ass!"

Rubbing his sore shoulder, Cid whined, "You didn't have to hit me so hard!"

"Yes, I did – and it should have been harder! You know very well that Caldain took our breakup very hard! To use it in jest is just rude!"

Sighing, Cid conceded, "Alright, alright! I get it! I'm sorry! Still," he added softly, "you both still love each other. It's as obvious as the sickness that covers this land."

Averting her eyes, Kay struggled to calm emotions she'd long sought to keep buried too deep to ever see the light again. "It was the right choice, Cid. Lasting, dedicated relationships are too dangerous for any member of the Orders." Pausing for a moment, she composed herself before looking at her brother. Smiling, she added, "Keeping it simple by staying friends is for the best. Makes it easier to fight, and easier to deal with if. . . ." She trailed off.

Concerned, Cid watched his sister put her bowl aside and stand up. "Where are you going?"

"For a walk," she replied, her husky voice soft but curt, before walking off.

Sighing, Cid leaned his shaved head against the broken wall behind him and peered at the sky. *"You deserve better than this,"* he thought with regret. *"You and Cal, both. I may not be a Warden, but I promise, Sis — one day soon, this damnable conflict will be over, and you can have the life you've always wanted."*

For hours, she walked.

For most of their journey, it had been easy to keep her feelings for Caldain contained where she'd buried them long ago. Despite the hurt she'd caused him, Caldain had been the perfect gentleman, never once speaking of, or ill of, their relationship or the breakup. While Kay appreciated his discretion, he couldn't keep the love he felt for her from his eyes when he looked at her, and that tore at her defenses. Those same defenses were pushed to the brink after Caldain saved them that first dreadful night against the blackhearts. Emotions long caged had threatened to rise up and consume her, but her will had proven stronger, and she'd managed to fight off the onslaught. However, as the days turned into weeks, she'd slowly felt her guard wearing away. There'd been a few times over the last week where she'd been tempted to broach the subject with him if only to ease her own conscience. The constant string of blackheart attacks never gave her that chance, however. Much to her chagrin, and despite the danger, she found that a part of her was glad for it. Combat and their flight kept them focused on survival, which left very little time for personal feelings or contemplation.

As she wandered the dead city, feeling the weight of the suffering and destruction that lingered, she wondered if the aura of hopelessness was more responsible for breaking down her barriers than her brother's careless words. Maybe it didn't matter? The feelings were real and undeniable, and it was clear they needed to be addressed. In her mind, it was becoming obvious there would never be an ideal time to deal with them. So, maybe now would be as good a time as any to bring clarity to the situation?

Reaching what had once been a square, she came to a halt as a soft breeze blew loose debris across the shattered cobbles and the remains of what she believed had once been a beautiful fountain at the center of the square. Watching the mournful display, she felt tears welling up in her eyes as her short-cropped auburn hair danced across her vision in the wind. She did her best to quell the emotions and thoughts the sight summoned forth, but in the end, the tears won. As they slipped free of her hooded brown eyes and slid down her cheeks, she let out a sad laugh and shook her head.

Placing her fingerless-gloved hands on the upper curve of her broad hips, she let out a rueful sigh. "Corith," she whispered to the wind as she looked skyward. "I just had to say yes to this, didn't I? I thought because I said no to him once, I could handle this, but I don't know anymore. . . . Maybe it's this place. . . . A lingering reminder of betrayals and our failures. We all feel the hurt, but what I see in his eyes. . . ." She squeezed her eyes shut.

For a time, she stood with her eyes closed and head tilted skyward, listening to the sorrowful breeze as it echoed the emotions tormenting her heart. Unable to resolve her inner conflict, she opened her eyes, dropped her hands to her sides, and glanced toward the rise. She couldn't sense her brother or Caldain thanks to the decrepit currents, which meant anyone seeking them through the flow of fir'gan would find it very difficult, if not impossible to do so. The glow of the fire, however, was impossible to miss.

"Stupid idea," she muttered with a slight laugh and a shake of her head. "This place must be conjuring terrible memories for you," she said softly as she looked upon the glow and tears once more formed in her eyes, "and while you made it seem like the fire was more for you, I know you better. This place," she shivered slightly, "isn't the worst you've seen, but for Cid and I, it is."

Suddenly, she laughed, the sound short and thick with emotion. Wiping a tear away, she shook her head as she folded her bare arms beneath her modest breasts and smiled weakly. "Corith, you're just too damn easy for me to love, Cal. . . . And the longer I'm around you, the more I'm afraid I haven't the strength to deny you again." Her smile turned into a self-deprecating smirk. "I never should have tried. Seeing you again, fighting by your side, has reminded me that I'm better with you in my life, and you with me in yours." Taking a deep breath, she let it out slowly. "I guess this means you and I need to have a long talk," she stated as confidently as she could, even as she felt her newfound determination waver at the thought of breaching the subject with Caldain.

Grasping the hilt of her dagger firmly, she took a few deep breaths to quell the nervous storm raging in her gut. At first, her efforts seemed in vain. It'd been so long since they'd spoken of it – so long since she'd said no to him – that her fears that he'd reject her, or punish her by sending her away, nearly made her toss aside the notion of rekindling what they once had. Then she heard a voice in her head.

"I'm sorry if I touched a nerve, Sis," the weak words echoed apologetically in her mind. *"But I know you, Sis, and you've never been the same since you turned down his proposal. You avoided any type of relationship, and trained like a woman possessed. Hells, I'm pretty sure the rumors about why the Bestynes were purged added to your determination to keep Cal at a distance, but it was the wrong thing to do. And after seeing the two of you together over the last few weeks, I'm more sure of it than ever. Talk to him, Sis."*

The love and certainty in her brother's words quickly settled the storm in her gut, and a wave of peace washed over her. Smiling softly, she used her brother's touch to follow it back to him, albeit with no small amount of effort, and responded, *"I'd come to a similar conclusion, but was wavering. Thank you, Brother — I needed to hear it from someone else."*

A pleased, echoing chuckle crept across the link. Thanks to the weak connection, it sounded creepy, but she knew her brother well enough to know what it really sounded like and that it came from the heart. *"I do what I can for you, Sis. I might be a little crazy, but I do see things, and I do care."*

Kay smirked. *"Only a little crazy?"* she teased.

"Smart-ass. If this is what I get for trying to help, I may have to rethink things." He chuckled again, eliciting a heartfelt, pleased laugh from Kay. *"Still, get back here and talk to him. He's trying to hide it, but I swear, you'd think the world was ending the way he's sitting there, moping. If you don't talk to him soon, I may throw him from the cliff just to put an end to my misery!"*

"Okay, okay," she replied with a laugh through the link. *"I get it. I'm on my way back."*

"Thank merciful Corith," he responded with mock relief before cutting the connection to prevent her from retorting.

Smirking, Kay shook her head and started back as a weak breeze made a futile attempt to stir the air. She'd only gone a few steps before a sensation of cold dread washed over her, bringing her to a halt and banishing her smile. Slow and deliberate, she turned and scanned the area. Had the currents been healthy, it would have been a simple matter to examine her surroundings for the source of the sickly, unfamiliar sensation, but as it was, they were nearly useless. Still, as she peered at her surroundings, which were poorly illuminated by the weak moonlight and the ailing strands of power, she took hold of the sluggish energy as best she could. Instantly, even as the currents seemed to be trying to slip from her grasp, the immediate area came into sharper focus. To her chagrin, there was nothing to see but the ruins. At that moment, a less experienced soldier or Gifted might have simply dismissed the notion that something dangerous was lurking about. However, like many of those amongst the Wardens' ranks, she'd learned to trust her instincts even when the currents couldn't provide confirmation. There was something out there. Whether it was something wrong with the city that went beyond the destruction wrought so long ago, or something as simple as more blackhearts, it couldn't be ignored.

Using her brother's contact as a guide, she reached out along the currents toward the rise but struggled to find either man's imprint. Knowing she just couldn't stand there all day trying to reach them, she pushed as hard as she dared, and when she felt a brief, tenuous connection, she said, *"If either of you can hear me, I think we've got a problem."*

When she didn't receive a quick response, she cursed under her breath and drew her bastard sword, the medallion pommel of its leather-wrapped grip glinting dully in the moonlight. *"Damn this place,"* she thought, annoyed, as she advanced slowly in the direction she believed the disturbance was emanating from. *"The currents are muddled to hells, and I can't spare more energy to get through to them if I want to see and have some semblance of a defense ready."*

Pushing her irritation aside, she continued to reach out to her brother and Caldain as she proceeded deeper into the city's remains, hoping that one of them would eventually take note of her probes. Caution governed her pace as she followed the shattered streets between the skeletal remains of structures the sick forest was trying to reclaim. An occasional listless, cold breeze moaned in a feeble attempt to stir the tension-filled air as it passed through the rotting remains of the city. Time and again, as the minutes of the tense trek dragged on, Kay caught herself nervously adjusting her grip on her sword.

As she edged toward what appeared to be the remains of a plaza, where it seemed like the currents were pooling, she told herself, *"Easy, girl."* Her hand tightened on her sword hilt. *"You've been in far worse situations than this. Besides, it's probably nothing more than the dark history of this place playing with your nerves."* She scoffed softly, and settled her blade protectively in front of her as the plaza drew closer. Eyes narrowing in concentration, she thought admonishingly, *"Right. . . . You've been through way too much to believe that. Something is definitely out there. The question is — what? It's close, that's for damn sure, and I have no doubt it's not friendly."*

Peering intently into the inky blackness beyond the tepid light provided by the ailing currents, she scowled. *"Corith damn this place!*

This is no place for a Gifted, much less any living creature!"

Suddenly, she came to a halt and blinked, perplexed. Lowering her sword to her side, she cocked her head and stared at the dark plaza. *"Odd,"* she thought. *"I've seen my fair share of cities, but I can't recall ever seeing a plaza this big. I can't even see the other side of tha—"*

A sudden breeze came up, and a loud clatter from behind echoed through the tense night, shattering her thoughts. Startled, Kay spun and dropped into a crouch, her eyes wide and her sword held ready to strike.

"Corith damn it all!" she muttered in exasperated relief when she saw a piece of rusted metal rocking to a halt atop a bed of rotten wood.

Standing up, Kay let out a frustrated sigh. Rolling her eyes, she turned around, gathered herself, and started forward.

"Of all the things that could scare me right now," she muttered as she stalked forward, "it had to be nothing more than the stupid win— OH, CRA—" she started to bellow as the ground beneath her feet gave way, dropping her into a dark abyss.

With fir'gan-fueled strength and speed, Kay spun around and drove her sword into the earth racing by, bringing her to a sudden, jarring halt. Shocked and breathing hard, Kay clenched tightly onto her sword hilt as a small amount of debris fell about her, plummeting into the gaping darkness below. Dangling by one arm, Kay cautiously twisted about as she gathered her wits and quickly assessed her situation. Half the length of her sword was lodged firmly in the dark earth, providing her a stable anchor, though her sore right shoulder made it clear she couldn't rely on it for very long. What's more, she could see nothing more than yawning, harrowing darkness in every direction but up.

Cursing the luck that had put her in her current situation, she turned her attention to extracting herself. With as much speed as she could muster with the lethargic currents, Kay gathered what she could about her free hand before swinging herself toward the earthen wall and driving her hand into it. With ease, her hand sank into the earth, providing her with another anchor and relieving the stress on her sore shoulder. Repeating the process with her feet, Kay released her grip on her sword and drove that hand into the wall. Grimacing slightly at the pain shooting through her sword arm, she started to climb.

Initially, she moved slowly so that her shoulder had time to heal before she reached the top. Something was causing the disturbance that had drawn her deep into the dead city, and the last thing she wanted was to reach the top in a weakened state only to find that the ruckus caused by her fall had drawn unwanted attention. To her overwhelming relief, not only was her shoulder hale by the time she pulled herself onto solid ground, but she also could neither see nor sense a living thing as she lay on her belly and looked about. Once she was satisfied that there was no immediate danger, she pushed herself to her feet and turned to retrieve her sword, only to come to a sudden, gawking halt.

"Dear Corith . . ." she breathed as she stared in shock at what was before her.

It wasn't the plaza that stretched into the darkness beyond her limited vision, for it terminated just in front of her. Instead, it was a seemingly endless yawning chasm.

Edging toward the rim cautiously, she strained to see the other side, but the darkness was absolute. Irritated, Kay stopped at the edge and tried to use the currents to amplify her vision, but that effort quickly met with disappointment. Perplexed, and growing more anxious by the moment, she studied the currents closely in an attempt to discern why exactly her efforts were failing. In the end, she couldn't decide if it was the result of the weak light provided by the anemic currents, the weakened state of fir'gan in the ruins, or if it was simply a matter of the chasm being far larger than she believed it could be.

Frustrated, the movement of the currents suddenly caught her attention, and her eyes narrowed with cautious curiosity.

"They're flowing . . . down?" she whispered, shocked, as a foreboding chill ran through her.

Subtle and sparse, it was easy for her to understand why she'd missed the flow during her panic to climb out of the pit. However, now that she was aware of the oddity, cold dread gripped her gut. Had the area been healthy, the currents would have been so thick that the sinking motion would have simply been an illusion created by the terrain. This, however. . . . This was unnatural. Chasm or not, with as anemic as the currents were, they should not have been sinking unless. . . .

"Unless something is drawing them down," Kay whispered, her eyes growing wide as the realization caused her stomach to churn with nauseating dread. Immediately, she knew it would be best to report back to the others quickly, but first, she needed more information.

Ill at ease, she peered down into the dark maw and saw her sword jutting from the wall, but little else. Taking a deep breath to relax her nerves some, Kay gave herself over to the currents, letting her mind travel along their downward course. As thin as the strands of power were, it came as no surprise when it quickly became a struggle to push onward. With effort, she slowly made progress, but she felt like she was trying to force her way through water on the verge of freezing. Sweat soon began to bead up on her brow from the focused exertion, and her breathing became shallow as if the air was being sucked away from her.

Gritting her teeth after a few minutes, her knees began to shake from exhaustion, and the color began to drain from her face as she thought, *"Corith, how big is this . . . this thing? It's like I'm trying to plumb the depths of a never-ending abyss! What's worse, the currents are nearly nonexistent! I'm going to have to pull back before I pass out or lose myself!"* Scowling in defiance of her quickly deteriorating state and the growing resistance to her downward advance, she shook her head weakly. *"Come on, Kay! You're stronger than this!"* she chided herself. *"You need answers! There's definitely something down there, and you need to know what before you go running back to the others. So send the danger to the Hells and push through, damn it!"*

Growling, Kay gathered herself for a final push. It was a risky gamble at best. Given the decrepit state of the currents, she knew that if they faded completely, she would be lucky if the worst that happened was the exertion caused her to pass out. However, she'd heard the stories of Gifted's attempts to span or enter dead zones, and the results were terrifying. On rare occasions, their consciousnesses were suddenly returned home, rendering them comatose for a few hours at best or weeks at worst while their mind healed. Unfortunately, in the majority of the cases, their minds were scattered to oblivion, killing them or condemning their bodies to live on as nothing more than soulless vessels. None of the likely repercussions sat well with her, but she felt it was worth the risk to find out just what was happening with the dead city.

Sucking in a final deep breath through clenched teeth, she drew deeply on her internal fir'gan, braced her mind for the pain she knew was coming, and poured the power into the area beyond her consciousness before plunging her mind forward with all her might. With the influx of fir'gan into the area, her mind instantly careened along the surge of power as it plummeted toward whatever was attracting the currents.

Kay's stomach lurched and she staggered as the chaotic descent tore at her senses. Futilely, she tried to regain control, but it was all she could do to stay focused enough to remain conscious and not lose herself in the chaos. Suddenly, her mind began to slip on the speeding currents as the downward pull grew stronger and began to shred the fir'gan.

"Oh Corith . . ." she managed to think in dread before her raft of fir'gan was torn asunder, dumping her mind into an abyssal darkness that was nearly bereft of fir'gan.

Pain lanced through her mind with staggering ferocity, tearing a cry of agony out of her as she collapsed to all fours. Jagged pieces of stone tore at her hands and knees as she hit the ground, and she screamed as the emptiness her consciousness floundered in ripped at her psyche. Somehow, she remained conscious. How she managed it, she didn't know, nor did she care, as every survival instinct she possessed fought for her continued existence with panic-driven intensity. Muscles clenched and tore under the strain, and blood vessels burst, causing ghastly bruises to form all over her body. As blood began to trickle from her eyes, nose and ears, what was left of her mind suddenly noticed something gleaming in the writhing dark depths. She wasn't sure if she was hallucinating or not, but the part of her mind that still understood what her mission was latched onto it with strength born of desperation.

Kay's arms began to shake as blood began to pool beneath her sagging head, but she somehow found the strength to fight off the urge to withdraw her mind. *"Just a little further!"* she begged of herself.

The phrase echoed through her mind like a mantra as her consciousness clawed along what remained of the currents toward the shimmer in the darkness. How long she struggled onward, she did not know, but the skin over many of her bruises had split, and her short auburn hair was soon touching the quickly growing pool of blood.

"Just a little further! Just a little further!" she continued to chant as she drew closer to the gleaming object, and a hum began to fill the air. *"Just a little. . . ."* Suddenly, the object and the surrounding area came into focus, and she trailed off in shock.

Made of what appeared to be glass, the multi-faceted orb seemed to be floating on a sea of dark water as the remnants of the currents flowed into a recessed steel bowl set atop it like a funnel. Gilded in gold and lined with glowing blue rings, the bowl was beautiful, and completely unfamiliar, but something about it screamed wrong to her. Much to her chagrin, it took her failing mind a moment to pinpoint just what disturbed her about the scene.

"Oh, Corith. . . . The darkness. . . . It's miasma!"

Gritting her teeth as her arms began to give out and her nose touched the bloody pool beneath her face, Kay's consciousness desperately latched onto one of the remaining thin tendrils of fir'gan and scrambled back toward her body. She knew she only had to get back to where the currents were thick enough for her to cut the connection safely, but between their feebleness and her weakened state, it was a slow, floundering venture.

"Don't give up!" she screamed in her mind as she clawed franticly upward. *"They need to know what's down there!"* she urged herself as darkness began to eat at the edges of her vision. *"They need to know the nest is—"*

Eyes rolling back in her head, darkness claimed her mind, and she collapsed in a pool of her own blood.

"You look like a man expecting a fight," Cid observed as he sat down next to Caldain just a few paces away from the fire and offered him a tin cup of steaming liquid.

Crouched along the edge of the rise with his longsword resting against his chest, and his face pinched with concern, Caldain pried his gaze away from the city and peered at the proffered cup curiously.

Smirking, Cid said, "It's tea."

"Tea?" Caldain asked in surprise. "I thought we ran out of that a few days ago," he stated as he took the cup and sniffed at the liquid contained within.

Cid chuckled and sipped from his own cup. Letting out a sigh of satisfaction, he said, "I saved a little for a night like this. I thought it might help relax our nerves. I know none of this is new to you, but the last few days have been unlike anything I've experienced."

Looking back at the city, Caldain took a swig from his cup. The honey-sweetened liquid hit his tongue with welcomed warmth that soothed his tense muscles as it slid down his throat. "That is good," he said absently. "Nice thinking."

"I aim to please," Cid quipped, drawing a slight smirk from Caldain. The brief moment of mirth on Caldain's face was gone as quickly as it appeared before being replaced with a dour expression that Cid studied with concern for a moment before he asked, "What's bothering you? We've fended off numerous blackheart attacks, and it looks like we've shaken them for now. Seems to me we should be quite happy."

Caldain nodded slowly. "That we have . . . but. . . ." He suddenly looked skyward. "It's been a harsh reminder of how lax we've grown."

Cid nodded and scanned the ruins below as he sipped on his

tea. "Understandable, Old Hawk. Just one blackheart is enough to make you question our vigilance. But with what happened at Blackstone, and now this...." He shook his shaved head. "It's clear we've been in the dark for a very long time – and that's damn disturbing!"

"Agreed," Caldain replied with a nod. "But what's bugging the hells out of me is how they've managed to stay on our trail. While blackhearts affect the currents, their very nature prevents them from being Gifted, which means they shouldn't be able to track us." He scowled. "Then there's the issue of their origin.... Just where in the hells are they coming from?"

Cid shrugged and chuckled darkly. "You tell me. You're the expert here," he replied as he continued to study the city intently. "Could it just be that this is nothing more than one of the Betrayers' pet projects?"

Caldain shook his head adamantly and finished off his tea. "There's no chance of that," he responded, his strong voice firm, as he placed his cup on the ground. "Blackstone's fall aside, if we'd only encountered a dozen or so of them, I might be inclined to agree with you – and even that is a stretch." He grimaced. "The numbers we're talking about, however, indicate the existence of at least one large nest, but there's no evidence that such a thing exists."

"Is there a way to hide a nest?"

"Not really, no," Caldain responded, his face grim. "You can try to mask it – make it look like a large population of people – but the corruption a nest inflicts on the currents can't be missed."

Cid nodded slowly. "Is that what was tried here?"

"Indeed," Caldain responded gravely. "The only reason we didn't notice it sooner was because we trusted Juliana, not to mention the war was a huge distraction. Now, however, it'd be impossible to miss." He scowled. "Besides, there's more to creating blackhearts. It's not like all you need to do is keep a male and female alive and let them mate."

Cid shuddered as his vision focused on the heart of the city. "Thanks for the revolting image," he drawled.

Caldain smirked slightly. "You are quite welcome. Seriously, though, what's needed to create blackhearts simply does not exist anymore."

"Sorry, Old Hawk, but you'll have to refresh my memory. Blackheart creation isn't exactly required study to be a Seeker or Knight."

"Besides a large source of fir'gan? You'd need elvannue, and the war wiped them out."

Cid let out a low whistle even as his brow furrowed in concentration. "That is a huge hurdle. Wouldn't darlion's work?"

"I honestly don't think so," Caldain responded with a shrug. "Granted, they are loosely related to the elvannue, but I think that'd be like using strawberries to make apple pie. Besides, they'd need elvannue machinery." He grunted. "Assuming that was even possible, they'd still need dra—"

Cid suddenly shot to his feet like a black-leather-clad lightning bolt, dropping his cup, startling Caldain.

"Cid?" Caldain inquired, standing up.

"Have you heard from Kay?" Cid asked, his normally brash voice tight.

"No," Caldain replied, concerned. "She's been gone for a few hours now, but there shouldn't be anything around that could harm her." Noticing the growing worry and fear in Cid's hooded brown eyes, Caldain added, "Cid – what's wrong?"

"I can't be sure. I thought it was just the sick, sluggish currents, but. . . ." He scowled.

"Cid?" Caldain prodded ominously.

Cid turned and looked at Caldain, and the fear in his eyes made Caldain's stomach lurch. "I thought she tried to reach me earlier, and I've been trying every since to contact her. But now, I sense. . . sense something ominous down there," Cid stated, his voice breaking with dread. "And. . . . I can't sense her at all, Cal. . . . Corith have mercy – I can't sense her!"

Panic clenched at Caldain's heart as he quickly turned his attention to the city and reached out with his senses. Instantly, the anemic currents resisted his anxiety-fueled probes. Grimacing with effort, Caldain pushed onward in hopes that his less skilled and experienced friend had simply overlooked Kay. However, try as he might, he could not find her. Pushing harder, he added his own fir'gan to his search. To his relief, the surge of power helped, and his consciousness plowed onward. A moment later, he found her collapsed on the ground at the edge of a yawning abyss. His mind flipped between relief and concern upon finding her and seeing her state, but it lasted only a fleeting moment as something dark caught his attention.

"Oh Corith, we have to find her, Cal!" Cid begged, his eyes filled with dread, and his thin lips quivering with fear. When Caldain didn't respond, Cid grabbed his friend's arm with fir'gan-fueled strength. "Do you hear me, Cal?!" he practically screamed. "We have to—"

Caldain suddenly glared at Cid, his gray eyes flashing with ferocity, and his face a mask of icy dread and determination. "She's alive . . . barely," he stated coldly. "Now let go of me, Cid. We have more to worry about than your sister."

A mix of relief and horror twisted Cid's face as he let go of Caldain and stepped back. "How can you say that? For Corith's sake – you love her! What could be more important than helping her?"

Making his way quickly to their belongings with an incredulous Cid in tow, Caldain told him, "I do love her, but that's irrelevant right now."

"Irrelevant!" Cid cried as Caldain grabbed his large pack and practically tore it open. "How can you say that?!" he demanded.

"Because," Caldain stated darkly as he began removing the pieces that composed his armor harness from the pack, "we've been damn fools! There are blackhearts here, Cid! There's a Corith-damned nest!"

Cid gawked at Caldain in disbelief. "That's a load of bram-hen shite, and you know it! We'd have sensed them if there were that many! You said so yourself!"

Pulling the leather harness on, Caldain paused and looked at Cid. The certainty and dread Cid saw in his friend's eyes told him everything he needed to know before Caldain even opened his mouth.

"The ailing currents made it impossible to notice their presence unless you were damn near on top of them, and that's where Kay is right now! I never would have discovered it if I weren't looking for her," Caldain stated, his words soft with dread. "The nest is deep, Cid. Very deep. Corith watch over us – we're standing atop an army of the damned!"

About the Author

Born and raised in the Southeastern United States, J.M. Williamson has always been an avid fan of fantasy in its many forms. He developed a love for writing, myths and fantasy lore at an early age; as a result, he wrote and fleshed out many stories to hone his skills throughout the years. His training mainly came from observation of other authors and entertainment media, as well as formal training in the development of video games and their plotlines. The Dracus Saga combines Williamson's love of fantasy and history with some of the more outlandish features of comics and manga to create a style of writing and fantasy storytelling unique to him.

Follow on social media:

Instagram: @Senshi_Imagineworks

TikTok: @CreativeGeek7